# THE WISDOM OF CROWDS

By Joe Abercrombie

THE AGE OF MADNESS
*A Little Hatred*
*The Trouble with Peace*
*The Wisdom of Crowds*

THE FIRST LAW TRILOGY
*The Blade Itself*
*Before They Are Hanged*
*Last Argument of Kings*

*Best Served Cold*
*The Heroes*
*Red Country*
*Sharp Ends: Stories from the World of the First Law*

THE SHATTERED SEA TRILOGY
*Half a King*
*Half the World*
*Half a War*

For Lou,

With grim, dark

hugs

Copyright © 2021 by Joe Abercrombie

Cover design by Lauren Panepinto
Cover art by Sam Weber
Cover copyright © 2021 by Hachette Book Group, Inc.

Orbit
Hachette Book Group
1290 Avenue of the Americas
New York, NY 10104
orbitbooks.net

First Edition: September 2021
Simultaneously published in Great Britain by Gollancz

Orbit is an imprint of Hachette Book Group.
The Orbit name and logo are trademarks of Little, Brown Book Group Limited.

The publisher is not responsible for websites (or their content) that are not owned by the publisher.

The Hachette Speakers Bureau provides a wide range of authors for speaking events. To find out more, go to www.hachettespeakersbureau.com or call (866) 376-6591.

Library of Congress Control Number: 2021938174

ISBNs: 9780316187244 (hardcover), 9780316379359 (signed edition), 9780316379250 (BarnesAndNoble.com signed edition), 9780316379151 (Barnes & Noble Black Friday signed edition), 9780316341912 (ebook)

Printed in the United States of America

LSC-C

Printing 1, 2021

# THE WISDOM OF CROWDS

Book Three of The Age of Madness

## JOE ABERCROMBIE

orbitbooks.net

# PART VII

"The great are only great
because we are on our knees.
Let us rise up!"

Elysée Loustallot

# Like a King

"You know something, Tunny?"

The corporal's lightly bloodshot eyes slid towards Orso. "Your Majesty?"

"I must confess to feeling rather pleased with myself."

The Steadfast Standard rippled on the breeze, its white horse rampant and its golden sun aglitter, the name of Stoffenbeck already stitched among the famous victories it had witnessed. How many High Kings had ridden triumphant beneath that gleaming scrap of cloth? And now—despite being outnumbered, derided and widely written off—Orso had joined their ranks. The man the pamphlets once dubbed the Prince of Prostitutes had emerged, like a splendid butterfly from a putrid chrysalis, as the new Casamir! Life takes strange turns, all right. The lives of kings especially.

"You damn well should feel pleased with yourself, Your Majesty," frothed Lord Marshal Rucksted, and few men knew more about feeling pleased with themselves than he. "You out-thought your enemies off the battle-field, out-fought 'em on it and took the worst traitor of the lot prisoner!" And he stole a self-satisfied glance over his shoulder.

Leo dan Brock, that hero who a few days ago had seemed too big a man for the world to hold, was now contained in a miserable wagon with barred windows, bumping along in Orso's wake. But then there was less of him to contain than there used to be. His ruined leg had been buried on the battlefield alongside his ruined reputation.

"You won, Your Majesty," piped up Bremer dan Gorst, then snapped his mouth shut, frowning off towards the approaching towers and chimneys of Adua.

"I did, didn't I." An unforced smile was creeping across Orso's face, all by itself. He could hardly remember the last time that happened. "The Young Lion, beaten bloody by the Young Lamb." His clothes just seemed to *fit* him better than they had before the battle. He rubbed at his jaw, left unshaven for a few days in all the excitement. "Should I grow a beard?"

Hildi pushed back her oversized cap to doubtfully assess his stubble. "*Can* you grow a beard?"

"It's true I've often failed in the past. But one could say that about a great many things, Hildi. The future looks a different sort of place!"

For perhaps the first time in his life he was eager to find out what the future might hold—even to grapple with the bastard and force it into the shapes *he* desired—so he had left Lord Marshal Forest bellowing the battle-mauled Crown Prince's Division back into order and ridden ahead for Adua with a hundred mounted men. He needed to get to the capital and set the ship of state on *course*. With the rebels crushed, he could finally embark on his grand tour of the Union and greet his subjects as a royal winner. He could find out what he could *do* for them, how he could make things *better*. He wondered fondly what name the adoring crowds would roar at him. Orso the Steadfast? Orso the Resolute? Orso the Dauntless, the Stone Wall of Stoffenbeck?

He sat back, rocked gently by the saddle, and took a deep breath of the crisp autumn air. Since a northerly breeze was carrying the vapours of Adua out to sea, he didn't even need to cough afterwards.

"I finally understand what people mean when they say they feel like a king."

"Oh, I wouldn't worry," said Tunny. "I'm sure you'll feel baffled and helpless again before you know it."

"Doubtless." Orso could not help glancing towards the rear of the column yet again. The wounded Lord Governor of Angland was not their only significant captive. Behind the Young Lion's prison wagon rattled the heavily guarded carriage containing his heavily pregnant wife. Was that Savine's pale hand gripping the windowsill? The mere thought of her name made Orso wince. When the only woman he had ever loved married another man, then betrayed him, he had fondly imagined he could feel no worse. Then he learned she was his half-sister.

The smell of the haphazard slums outside the walls of Adua hardly reduced his sudden nausea. He had pictured smiling commoners, little Union flags waved by freckled children, showers of perfumed petals from beauties on the balconies. He had always turned his nose up at such patriotic guff when it was directed at other victors, but he had been rather looking forward to its being directed at him. Instead, ragged figures frowned from the shadows. A harlot chewing a chicken leg laughed from a misshapen window. One ill-favoured beggar very noticeably spat into the road as Orso trotted past.

"There will always be malcontents, Your Majesty," murmured Yoru Sulfur. "Only ask my master. No one ever thanks him for his pains."

"Mmmm." Though as far as Orso could recall, Bayaz was always treated with the heights of servile respect. "What's his solution?"

"To ignore them." Sulfur considered the slum-dwellers without emotion. "Like ants."

"Right. Don't let them spoil the mood." But it was a little late for that. The wind seemed to have turned chilly, and Orso was developing that familiar worried prickling at the back of his neck.


The wagon grew even gloomier. Its clattering wheels began to echo. Beyond the barred window Leo saw cut stone rush past, knew they must be riding through one of Adua's gates. He'd dreamed of entering the capital at the head of a triumphant parade. Instead he came locked in a prison wagon stinking of stale straw, wounds and shame.

The floor jolted, sent a throb of agony through the stump of his leg, squeezed tears from his raw eyes. What a fucking fool he'd been. The advantages he'd tossed away. The chances he'd let slip past. The traps he'd blundered into.

He should've told that treacherous coward Isher to fuck himself the moment his prattle tilted towards rebellion. Or better yet, gone straight to Savine's father and spilled the whole story to Old Sticks. Then he'd still have been the Union's most celebrated hero. The champion who beat the Great Wolf! Not the dunce who lost to the Young Lamb.

He should've swallowed his pride with King Jappo. Flattered and flirted and played the diplomat, offered Westport with a giggle, swapped that worthless offcut of Union territory for all the rest and landed in Midderland with Styrian troops behind him.

He should've brought his mother. The thought of her begging on the docks made him want to rip his hair out. She'd have pressed that shambles on the beach into order, taken one calm glance at the maps and set the men flowing southwards, got to Stoffenbeck first and forced the enemy into a losing battle.

He should've sent his reply to Orso's dinner invitation on the end of a lance, attacked with every man before sunset and swept the lying bastard from the high ground, torn up his reinforcements as they arrived.

Even as Leo's left wing misfired and his right wing crumbled, he could've called off that final charge. At least he'd still have Antaup and

Jin. At least he'd still have his leg and his arm. Perhaps Savine could've teased out some deal. She was the king's ex-lover, after all. From what Leo had seen at his own execution, likely his current one, too. He couldn't even blame her. She'd saved his life, hadn't she? Whatever his life was worth now.

He was a prisoner. A traitor. A cripple.

The wagon had slowed to a juddering crawl. He heard voices up ahead, chanting, ranting. King Orso's loyal subjects, come out to cheer his victory? But it sounded nothing like a celebration.

The training circle had been Leo's dance floor. Now it was an ordeal just to straighten the leg he still had, so he could grasp the bars of the window with his good hand and drag himself up. By the time he felt the chill breeze on his face and squinted out into a street murky with foundry smoke, the wagon had shuddered to a halt.

Strange details jumped at him. Shop shutters smashed, broken doors hanging from hinges, rubbish scattered across the road. He thought a heap of rags in a doorway might be a sleeping tramp. Then, with a creeping worry that made him forget his own pain for a moment, he started to think it might be a corpse.

"By the dead," he whispered. A warehouse had been burned out, its charred rafters like the ribs of a picked-over carcass. A slogan was daubed across its blackened front in letters three strides high.

*The Time is Now.*

He pressed his face to the bars, straining to see further up the street. Beyond the officers, retainers and Knights of the Body on their nervous horses, figures were crowded outside a spike-topped wall, banners bobbing over the mob like standards over a regiment. *Fair pay for fair work* and *Down with the Closed Council* and *Rise up!* They were already drifting towards the king's column, droning with sullen anger, booing and jeering. Were these...Breakers?

"By the dead," he whispered again. He saw people down a side street, too. Men with labourer's clothes and clenched fists. Running figures, chasing someone. Falling on them, kicking and punching.

A bellow came from up ahead. Rucksted, maybe. "Clear the way, in the name of His Majesty!"

"*You* clear the fucking way!" snarled a man with a thick beard and no neck at all. People were filtering in from the alleys, creating a troubling sense of the column being surrounded.

"It's the Young Lion!" someone barked, and Leo heard half-hearted cheers. His good leg, which a few days ago had been his bad leg, was on fire, but he clung to the bars as people crowded towards the wagon, hands reaching for him.

"The Young Lion!"

Savine watched from the carriage window, utterly helpless, one hand clutching her bloated mass of belly, the other gripping Zuri's, while ruffians crowded around Leo's prison wagon like pigs around a trough. She hardly knew whether they were trying to rescue or murder him. Probably they had no idea, either.

She realised she could not remember how it felt, not to be scared.

It had probably begun as a strike. Savine knew every manufactory in Adua, and this was Foss dan Harber's paper mill, a concern she had twice declined to invest in. The profits were tempting, but Harber's reputation stank. He was the kind of brutal, exploitative owner who made it hard for everyone else to properly exploit their workers. It had probably begun as a strike then turned, as strikes quickly can, into something altogether uglier.

"Get back!" snapped a young officer, lashing at the crowd with his riding crop. A mounted guard dragged one man away by the shoulder, then clubbed another across the scalp with his shield. Blood showed bright as he fell.

"Oh," said Savine, her eyes going wide.

Someone hit the officer with a stick and rocked him in his saddle.

"Wait!" She thought it might have been Orso's voice. "Wait!" But it made no difference. The High King of the Union was suddenly as powerless as she was. People pressed in on every side, a sea of furious faces, shaken placards and clenched fists. The clamour made her think of Valbeck, of the uprising, but the terrible present was bad enough without reaching for the terrible past.

More soldiers rode in. A cry cut off as someone was trampled.

"Bastards!"

A faint ring as a blade was drawn.

"Protect the king!" came Gorst's shriek.

A soldier struck out with the pommel of his sword, then with the flat, knocking a man's cap off and sending him tumbling to the cobbles. One of the other Knights of the Body was less forbearing. A flicker of steel, a high-pitched scream. This time, Savine saw the sword fall and open a yawning wound in a man's shoulder. Something smashed against the side of the carriage and she flinched.

"God help us," muttered Zuri.

Savine stared at her. "Does He ever?"

"I keep hoping." Zuri slid a protective arm around Savine's shoulders. "Come away from the window—"

"And go where?" whispered Savine, shrinking back against her.

Beyond the glass it was utter chaos. A mounted soldier and a red-faced woman wrestled over one end of a banner that read *All Equal*, the other tangled up in a mass of arms and faces. A Knight of the Body was dragged from his horse, lost in the crowd like a sailor in a stormy sea. They were everywhere, forcing their way between the horses, shoving, clutching, screeching.

A crash as the window shattered and Savine jerked back, broken glass showering in.

"Traitor!" someone screamed. At her? At Leo? An arm hooked through, a dirty hand fishing for the catch. Savine smashed at it clumsily with the side of her fist, not sure whether it would be worse to be dragged from the carriage by the mob or dragged to the House of Questions by the Inquisition.

Zuri was just getting up when there was a flicker outside. Something pattered Savine's cheek. Red spots on her dress. The arm slithered away. Fire bloomed suddenly beyond the window and she hunched over, both arms around her belly as pain stabbed through her guts.

"God help us," she mouthed. Would she give birth there, on the glass-littered floor of a carriage in the middle of a riot?

"You fuckers!" A big man in an apron had caught the reins of that blonde girl Orso kept as a servant, the one who used to carry messages between him and Savine, a thousand years ago. He clutched at her leg while she kicked back, spitting and snarling. Savine saw Orso wrench his horse around and start punching the man about his balding scalp. He grabbed at Orso, trying to pull him down from his saddle. "You—"

His skull burst open, spraying red. Savine stared. She could have sworn that man Sulfur had slapped him with an open hand and torn his head half-off.

Gorst spurred past, teeth bared as he hacked savagely on one side then the other, bodies dropping. "The king!" he squealed. "The king!"

"The Agriont!" someone bellowed. "Stop for nothing!"

The carriage lurched forwards. Savine would have been thrown from her seat had Zuri not shot out an arm. She clung desperately to the empty window frame, bit her lip at another flash of pain in her swollen stomach.

She saw people scatter. Heard shrieks of terror. A body was knocked reeling by the corner of the carriage, clattered against the door and went down under the milling hooves of a knight herald. There were strands of blonde hair caught in the broken window.

Wheels bounced over a trampled sign, whirred over pamphlets stuck flapping to the damp road. The prison wagon clattered ahead, striking sparks from the cobbles, maddened horses all around, whipping manes and flapping harness. Something clonked against the other side of the carriage, then they were past, leaving Harber's mill and its rioting workers behind.

Cold wind rushed through the broken window, Savine's heart hammering, her hand frozen on the sill but her face burning as if she'd been slapped. How could Zuri be so calm beside her? Her face fixed, her arm so firm around Savine. The baby squirmed as the carriage rocked and jolted. It was alive, at least. It was alive.

Outside the window she saw Lord Chamberlain Hoff clinging to his reins, chain of office tangled tight around his red throat. She saw the king's old, grey-haired standard-bearer gripping his flagstaff, the sun of the Union streaming overhead, an oily smear across the cloth of gold.

Streets whipped by, so familiar, so unfamiliar. This city had been hers. No one more admired. No one more envied. No one more hated, which she had always taken as the only honest compliment. Buildings flashed past. Buildings she knew. Buildings she owned, even. Or had owned.

It would all be forfeit now.

She squeezed her eyes shut. She could not remember how it felt, not to be scared.

She remembered taking Leo's ring, with the Agriont and all its little people spread out beneath them. The future had been theirs. How could they have so totally destroyed themselves? His recklessness or her ambition alone could not have done it. But like two chemicals which, apart, are merely mildly poisonous, combined they had produced an unstable explosive which had blown both their lives and thousands of others to hell.

The cut beneath the bandages on her shaved head itched endlessly. Perhaps it would have been kinder if the chunk of metal that scarred her had flown just a little lower and split her skull instead of just her scalp.

"Slow!" Gorst's squealing voice. "Slow!" They were crossing one of the bridges into the Agriont, the great walls looming ahead. Once they had made her feel safe as a parent's embrace. Now they looked like prison walls. Now they *were* prison walls. Her neck was not out of the noose yet, and nor was Leo's.

After they brought him down from the gallows, she had changed the dressing on his leg. It seemed the sort of thing a wife should do for her wounded husband. Especially when his wounds were in large part her doing. She had thought she could be strong. She was notorious for cool ruthlessness, after all. But as she unwound the bandages in an obscene striptease they had gone from spotted brown, to pink, to black. The stump revealed. The dressmaker's nightmare of clumsy stitching. The weeping purple-redness of the jagged seams. The terrible, bizarre, fake-looking absence of the limb. The cheap spirits and butcher-shop stench of it. She had covered her mouth. Not a word said, but she had looked into his face and seen her own horror reflected, then the guards had come to take her away, and she had been grateful. The memory made her sick. Sick with guilt. Sick with disgust. Sick with guilt at her disgust.

She realised she was shivering, and Zuri squeezed her hand. "It will be all right," she said.

Savine stared into her dark eyes and whispered, "How?"

The carriage juddered to a halt. When an officer opened the door, glass tinkled from the broken window. It took a moment to make her fingers unclench. She had to peel them away, like the death grip of a corpse. She wobbled down in a daze, thinking she would piss herself with every movement. Had she pissed herself already?

The Square of Marshals. She had wheeled her father across this expanse of flagstones once a month, laughing at the misfortunes of others. She had attended Open Council at the Lords' Round, sifting the blather for opportunities. She had discussed business with associates, who to raise up, who to grind down, who to pay off and who would pay the price. She knew the landmarks above the soot-streaked rooftops—the slender finger of the Tower of Chains, the looming outline of the House of the Maker. But they belonged to a different world. A different life. All around her men goggled in disbelief. Men with faces grazed, fine uniforms torn, drawn swords stained red.

"Your hand," said Zuri.

It was smeared with blood. Savine turned it stupidly over and saw a shard of glass stuck into her palm, where she had been gripping the window frame. She hardly even felt it.

She glanced up, and her eyes met Orso's. He looked pale and rattled, his golden circlet skewed, his mouth slightly open as if to speak, hers slightly open as if to reply. But for a while they said nothing.

"Find Lady Savine and her husband some quarters," he croaked, eventually. "In the House of Questions."

Savine swallowed as she watched him walk away.

She could not remember how it felt, not to be terrified.

Orso strode across the Square of Marshals in the rough direction of the palace, fists clenched. The sight of her still somehow took his breath away. But there were more pressing concerns than the smouldering ruins of his love life.

That his homecoming triumph had degenerated from anticlimax into bloodbath, for instance.

"They hate me," he muttered. He was used to being despised, of course. Scurrilous pamphlets, slanderous rumours, sneers in the Open Council. But for a king to be politely loathed behind his back was the normal state of society. For a king to be physically manhandled by a crowd was a short step from outright revolt. The second in a month. Adua—the centre of the world, the zenith of civilisation, that beacon of progress and prosperity—was plunged into lawless chaos.

It was quite the shocking disappointment. Like popping some delightful sweetmeat into one's mouth and, upon chewing, discovering it was actually a piece of shit. But that was the experience of being a monarch. One shocking mouthful of shit after another.

Lord Hoff was wheezing away as he struggled to keep up. "There are always . . . complaints—"

"They fucking *hate* me! Did you hear them cheering for the Young Lion? When did that entitled bastard become some man of the people?" Before Orso's victory, everyone had considered him a contemptible coward and Brock a magnificent hero. By rights, surely, their positions should have been reversed. Yet now he was considered a contemptible tyrant, while they cheered the Young Lion as a pitiable underdog. If Brock had wanked in the street it would have been to thunderous approval from the public.

"Bloody traitors!" snarled Rucksted, grinding gloved fist into gloved palm. "We should hang the bloody lot of them!"

"You can't hang everyone," said Orso.

"With your permission, I'll head back into the city and make a damn good start at it."

"I fear our mistake has been too many hangings rather than too few—"

"Your Majesty!" A knight herald of horrifying height was waiting on the Kingsway beneath the statue of Harod the Great, winged helmet under one arm. "Your Closed Council has *urgently* requested your attendance in the White Chamber." He fell in step beside Orso, having to shorten his stride considerably. "Might I congratulate you on your famous victory at Stoffenbeck?"

"That feels a very long time ago," said Orso, stalking on. He was concerned that if he did not keep moving, he might collapse like a child's tower of bricks. "I have already received the congratulations of a considerable crowd of rioters on the Kingsway." And he frowned up at the looming statue of Casamir the Steadfast, wondering whether he had ever been obliged to flee from his own people through the streets of his own capital. The history books made no mention of it.

"Things have been...*unsettled* in your absence, Your Majesty." Orso did not care for the way he said *unsettled*. It felt like a euphemism for something much worse. "There was a *disturbance* shortly after you left. Over the rising price of bread. With the rebellion, and the poor weather, not enough flour has been getting into the city. A crowd of women forced their way into some bakers' shops. They beat the owners. One they declared a speculator, and...murdered."

"This is troubling," said Sulfur, with towering understatement. Orso noticed he was carefully wiping blood from the side of his hand with a handkerchief. Of the slight smirk he had managed to maintain through the execution of two hundred people outside Valbeck, there was no sign at all.

"The next day there was a strike at the Hill Street Foundry. The day after there were three more. Some guardsmen refused to patrol. Others clashed with the rioters." The knight herald worked his mouth unhappily. "Several deaths."

Orso's father was last in the procession of immortalised monarchs, gazing out over the deserted park with an expression of decisive command he had never worn in life. Opposite him, on a slightly less monumental scale, loomed that famous war hero Lord Marshal West, that noted torturer Arch Lector Glokta, and the First of the Magi himself, glaring down with wrinkled lip as though all men were complaining ants to him indeed. Orso had often wondered which retainers would end up opposite his own statue, in future years. This was the first time he had ever wondered if he would get a statue at all.

"There'll be order now!" Hoff struggled to lift the funereal mood. "You'll see!"

"I hope so, Your Grace," said the knight herald. "Groups of Breakers have taken over some of the manufactories. They march openly in the Three Farms, calling for...well, the *resignation* of His Majesty's Closed

Council." Orso did not care for the way he said *resignation*. It felt like a euphemism for something considerably more final. "People are stirred up, Your Majesty. People want blood."

"*My* blood?" muttered Orso, trying and failing to loosen his collar.

"Well..." The knight herald gave a rather limp parting salute. "Blood, anyway. I'm not sure they care whose."

It was a sadly reduced Closed Council that struggled to its aged feet as Orso clattered into the White Chamber. Lord Marshal Forest had been left behind in Stoffenbeck with the shattered remnants of the army. Arch Lector Pike was terrifying the ever-restless denizens of Valbeck into renewed submission. A replacement had yet to be found for High Justice Bruckel after his head was split in half during a previous attempt on Orso's life. Bayaz's chair at the foot of the table was—as it had been for the great majority of the last few centuries—empty. And the surveyor general, one could only assume, was once again out with his bladder.

Lord Chancellor Gorodets' voice was rather shrill. "Might I congratulate Your Majesty on your famous victory at Stoffenbeck—"

"Put it out of your mind." Orso flung himself into his uncomfortable chair. "I have."

"We were set upon!" Rucksted stormed to his seat with spurs jingling. "The royal party!"

"Rioters in the bloody streets of Adua!" wheezed Hoff as he sagged down and began to dab his sweat-beaded forehead with the sleeve of his robe.

"Bloody streets indeed," murmured Orso, wiping his cheek with his fingertips and seeing them come away lightly smeared with red. Gorst's handiwork had left him speckled all over. "Any news from Arch Lector Pike?"

"You haven't heard?" Gorodets had graduated from his usual habit of fluffing and combing his long beard to wringing it between clawing fingers. "Valbeck has fallen to an uprising!"

The *glug* of Orso swallowing echoed audibly from the stark white walls. "Fallen?"

"*Again?*" squealed Hoff.

"No word from His Eminence," said Gorodets. "We fear he may be a captive of the Breakers."

"Captive?" muttered Orso. The room was feeling even more intolerably cramped than usual.

"News of turmoil pours in from all across Midderland!" blurted the high consul, warbling on the edge of panic. "We have lost contact with the authorities in Keln. Troubling news from Holsthorm. Robbings. Lynchings. *Purges.*"

"Purges?" breathed Orso. It appeared he was doomed to endlessly repeat single words in a tone of horrified upset.

"There are rumours of bands of Breakers ravaging the countryside!"

"*Huge* bands," said Lord Admiral Krepskin. "Converging on the capital! Bastards have taken to calling 'emselves the *People's Army.*"

"A bloody *plague* of treason," breathed Hoff, eyes fixed on the empty chair at the bottom of the table. "Can we get a message to Lord Bayaz?"

Orso dumbly shook his head. "Not soon enough to make a difference." He imagined the First of the Magi would choose to keep a discreet distance in any case, while calculating how he could profit from the aftermath.

"We have done all we can to keep the news from becoming public—"

"To prevent panic, you understand, Your Majesty, but—"

"They may be at our gates within days!"

There was a long silence. The sense of triumph as Orso approached the city was a dimly remembered dream.

If there was a polar opposite to feeling like a king, he had discovered it.

# Change

"You must confess," said Pike. "It's impressive."

"I must," said Vick. And she wasn't easily impressed.

The People's Army might have lacked discipline, equipment and supplies, but there was no arguing with its scale. It stretched off, clogging the road in the valley bottom and straggling up the soggy slopes on both sides, until it was lost in the drizzly distance.

There might've been ten thousand when they set out from Valbeck. A couple of regiments of ex-soldiers had formed the bright spearhead, gleaming with new-forged gifts from Savine dan Brock's foundries. But order soon gave way to ragged chaos. Mill workers and foundry workers, dye-women and laundry-women, cobblers and cutlers, butchers and butlers, dancing more than marching to old work songs and drums made from cookpots. A largely good-natured riot.

Vick had half-expected, half-hoped that they'd melt away as they slogged across the muddy country in worsening weather, but their numbers had quickly swelled. In came labourers, smallholders and farmers with scythes and pitchforks—which caused some concern—and with flour and hams—which caused some celebration. In came gangs of beggars and gangs of orphans. In came soldiers, deserted from who knew what lost battalions. In came dealers, whores and demagogues, dishing up husk, fucks and political theory in tents by roadways trampled into bogs.

There was no arguing with its enthusiasm, either. At night, the fires went on for miles, folk drawing dew-dusted blankets tight against the autumn chill, blurting out their smoking dreams and desires, talking bright-eyed of change. The Great Change, come at last.

Vick had no idea how far back that sodden column went now. No idea how many Breakers and Burners were part of it. Miles of men, women and children, slogging through the mud towards Adua. Towards a better tomorrow. Vick had her doubts, of course. But all that *hope*. A flood of the damn stuff. No matter how jaded you were, you couldn't help but be moved by it. Or maybe she wasn't quite so jaded as she'd always told herself.

Vick had learned in the camps that you stand with the winners. It had been her golden rule ever since. But in the camps, and in all the years since she left them, she'd never doubted who the winners were. The men in charge. The Inquisition, the Closed Council, the Arch Lector. Looking down on that unruly mass of humanity, fixed on changing the world, she wasn't so sure who the winners would be. She wasn't sure what the sides were, even. If Leo dan Brock had beaten Orso, there might have been a new king, new faces in the Closed Council, new arses in the big chairs, but things would've stayed much the same. If this lot beat Orso, who knew what came next? All the old certainties were crumbling, and she was left wondering whether they'd ever been certainties at all, or just fools' assumptions.

In Starikland, during the rebellion, Vick had felt an earthquake. The ground had trembled, books had dropped from shelves, a chimney had fallen into the street outside. Not for long, but for long enough, she'd felt the terror of knowing all she'd counted on as solid could in a moment shake itself apart.

Now she had that feeling again, but she knew the quake had only just begun. How long would the world shiver? What would still be standing when it stopped?

"I notice you are still with us, Sister Victarine." Pike clicked his tongue and nudged his mount down the slope, towards the head of the bedraggled column.

Vick had a strong instinct not to follow. But she did. "I'm still with you."

"So you are a convert to our cause?"

There was a hopeful piece of her that wanted to believe this could be Sibalt's dreams of a better world coming true and was desperate to see it happen. There was a nervous piece of her that smelled blood coming and wanted to cut out that night and run for the Far Country. There was a calculating piece that reckoned the only way to control a mad horse is from the saddle, and the danger of keeping your grip might be less than the danger of letting go.

She looked sideways at Pike. In truth, she was still trying to work out what their cause really was. In truth, she reckoned there was a different cause for every one of those little dots in the People's Army. But this was no time for the truth. When is? "I'd be a fool to say I'm not at all convinced."

"And if you said you were entirely convinced, I would be a fool to believe you."

"Since neither of us is a fool...let's just say maybe."

"Oh, we are all fools. But I enjoy a good maybe." Pike showed no sign of enjoyment or of anything else. "Absolutes are never to be trusted."

Vick doubted the two leaders of the Great Change riding towards them across the grassy slope would have agreed.

"Brother Pike!" called Risinau, with a cheery wave of one plump hand. "Sister Victarine!"

Risinau worried Vick. The one-time Superior of Valbeck was considered a deep thinker, but far as she could tell he was an idiot's notion of a genius, his ideas a maze with nothing at the centre, heavy on the righteous society to come but light as air on the route they'd take to get there. The pockets of his jacket bulged with papers. Scrawled theories, manifestos, proclamations. Speeches he whined out to eager throngs whenever the People's Army halted. Vick didn't like the way the crowd greeted his flowery appeals for reason with shaken weapons and howls of approving fury. She never saw more damage done than by folk acting on high principle.

But Judge worried Vick a lot more. She wore a rusty old breastplate rattling with stolen chains over a ball gown crusted with chips of cracked crystal, but she sat her saddle astride not aside so the flounce of tattered petticoats was gathered up around her thighs, her muddy bare feet shoved into battered cavalry stirrups. Her face was like a bag of daggers, lean jaw angrily clenched, black eyes angrily narrowed, her usually flaming crest of hair turned brown by the rain and plastered wetly down one side of her skull. Principles only interested her as an excuse for mayhem. When her Burners had taken the courthouse in Valbeck, her jury had found no one innocent and the one sentence she'd given was death.

If Risinau was forever gazing up, no thought for the wreckage he was stepping through, Judge was glaring down, trying to trample everything she could. And Pike? There were no clues on the ex-Arch Lector's burned mask of a face. Who could say what Brother Pike was after?

Vick nodded towards grime-streaked Adua, its pall of smoke inching irresistibly closer. "What happens when we get there?"

"Change," said Risinau, smug as a rooster. "The *Great* Change."

"From what, to what?"

"I am not blessed with the Long Eye, Sister Victarine." Risinau giggled at the thought. "From the pupa alone it is hard to know what kind of butterfly might emerge to greet the dawn. But *change*." He wagged a thick finger at her. "Of that you can be sure! A new Union, built from high ideals!"

"The world doesn't need changing," grunted Judge, black eyes fixed on the capital. "It needs burning."

Vick wouldn't have trusted either one of them to herd pigs, let alone to herd the dreams of millions into a new future. She kept her face blank, of course, but Pike must have caught some hint of her feelings. "You appear to have doubts."

"I've never seen the world change quickly," said Vick. "If I've seen it change at all."

"I begin to think Sibalt liked you so because you were his opposite." Risinau laid a playful hand on her shoulder. "You are *such* a cynic, Sister!"

Vick shrugged him off. "I think I've earned it."

"After a childhood stolen in the camps," said Pike, "and a career of making friends to betray for Arch Lector Glokta, how could you be otherwise? But one can be *too* cynical. You will see."

Vick had to admit she'd been expecting the Great Change to collapse long before now. For Judge and Risinau to move past bickering to tearing each other apart, for the fragile coalition of Breakers and Burners, moderates and extremists, to shred into factions, for the resolve of the People's Army to dissolve in the wet weather. Or, for that matter, for Lord Marshal Rucksted's cavalry to crest every hill she saw and carve the ragged multitude to pieces.

But Risinau and Judge continued to tolerate each other and the King's Own made no appearance. Even now, as the rain slacked off and they marched into the ill-planned, ill-drained, ill-smelling maze of shacks outside the walls of the capital, water spattering from the broken gutters and into the muddy lanes below. Maybe Orso's forces had been fought out against Leo dan Brock. Maybe there were other uprisings to deal with. Maybe these strange times had stretched their loyalties in so many directions they hardly knew who to fight for any more. Vick knew how they felt as the sun showed through, and she caught her first glimpse of the gates of Adua.

For a moment, she wondered whether Tallow was in the city. Fretted that he might be in danger. Then she realised how foolish it was to worry over one person in the midst of all this. What could she do for him, anyway? What could anyone do for anyone?

Risinau nervously eyed the damp-streaked battlements. "It might be wise to take a cautious approach. Deploy our cannon and, er—"

Judge gave a great snort of disgust, dug her bare heels into her horse's flanks and rode forwards.

"One cannot fault her courage," said Pike.

"Just her sanity." Vick was rather hoping for a shower of arrows, but it never came. Judge trotted on towards the walls, chin scornfully raised, in eerie silence.

"You inside!" she screamed, reining in before the gate. "Soldiers of the Union! Men of Adua!" She stood in her stirrups, pointing back at the horde crawling up the soggy road towards the capital. "This is the People's Army, and it's come to set the people free! We only need to know one thing from you lot!" She held high one clawing finger. "Are you with the people... or against 'em?"

Her horse shied, and she ripped at the reins and dragged it around in a tight circle, that finger still extended, while the thunder of thousands upon thousands of tramping feet grew steadily louder.

Vick flinched at an echoing clatter from behind the gates, then a slit of light showed between the two doors and, with a creaking of hinges in need of oil, they swung slowly open.

A soldier leaned from the parapet, grinning madly and waving his hat. "We're with 'em!" he bellowed. "The Great Change!"

Judge tossed her head, and dragged her horse from the road, and with an impatient flick of her arm beckoned the People's Army forwards.

"Fuck the king!" screeched that lone soldier, to a wave of laughter from the oncoming Breakers, and he took his life in his hands by shinning up the wet flagpole to tear down the standard above the gatehouse.

The High King's banner, which had flown over the walls of Adua for centuries. The golden sun of the Union, given to Harod the Great as his emblem by Bayaz himself. The flag folk had knelt to, prayed to, sworn their loyalty to... came fluttering down to lie in the puddle-pocked road before the gate.

"The world can change, Sister Victarine." Pike raised one hairless brow at Vick. "Just watch." And he clicked his tongue and rode on towards the open gates.

So it was with almost over-heavy symbolism that the People's Army marched into Adua, trampling the flag of the past into the mud.

# The Little People

"They're here!" Jakib was so choked with excitement his voice cracked and went all warbly. "The Breakers are bloody *here!*" All the days and weeks and months waiting and now he stared wildly around their little parlour with his hands opening and closing, hardly knowing what to do first.

Petree didn't look excited. She looked worried. Sour, even. The lads had warned him he was marrying a sour woman, but he hadn't seen it then. He'd always been a hoper. "You're a hoper," they'd said. Now every day she seemed more sour. But this was hardly the time to be fretting about his marriage. "They're bloody here!"

When he grabbed his coat he sent pamphlets scattering off the table. Wasn't as if he'd read them. Wasn't as if he could read, really. But having 'em felt like a fine step towards freedom. And who needed pamphlets, when the Breakers were come in person?

He went to fetch his grandfather's sword from the hook above the fire. Hissed a curse that Petree had made him hang it out of reach. Had to go up on tiptoes to get the damn thing down and near dropped it on his head.

He felt bad when he saw her face. Maybe she wasn't sour so much as scared. That's what the bastards wanted, the Inquisition and the Closed Council. Everyone scared. He caught her by the shoulder. Tried to shake some of his hope into her. "Price o' bread'll go down now," he said, "you'll see. Bread for everyone!"

"You think so?"

"I *know* so."

She put her fingertips on the battered scabbard. "Don't take the sword. Having it might make you try to use it. You don't know how."

"I know how," he snapped, though they both knew he didn't, not really, and he wrenched it from her hand, twisted it the wrong way up and the rust-spotted blade slithered halfway out of the scabbard before he caught it and slapped it back in. "A man should be armed, on the day of the Great Change! Enough of us have 'em, we won't need to use 'em." And before she could voice any more doubts he dashed out, letting the door clatter against the frame.

The streets were bright outside, everything glossy and gleaming and seeming new-made after the rain just fallen. People everywhere, somewhere between a riot and a carnival. People running, people shouting. Some faces he knew. Most were strangers. A woman grabbed him around the neck, kissed him on the cheek. A whore stood on some railings, clinging to the side of a building with one hand, pulling her dress up with the other to give the crowd an eyeful. "Half price all day!" she screeched.

He'd been ready to fight. Ready to charge ranks of royalist spears, freedom and equality as his armour. Petree had not cared for that idea, and honestly, he'd been having some doubts of his own as the day grew closer. But he only saw a few soldiers, and they had smiles on their faces and jackets hanging open, cheering and jumping and celebrating like everyone else.

Someone was singing. Someone was crying. Someone was dancing in puddles, spraying everyone. Someone lay in a doorway. Drunk, maybe, then Jakib saw blood on their face. Maybe he should help? But he was swept along by people running. Couldn't tell why. Couldn't tell anything.

Out onto the Sparway that cut wide through the mills of the Three Farms towards the centre of the city. He saw armed men there—polished armour, brand new and glittering. He froze at the corner, heart in his mouth, sword half-hidden behind his back, thinking they must be King's Own. Then he saw their bearded faces, and their swaggering gait, and the banners they carried, roughly stitched with broken chains, and he knew this was the People's Army, marching to freedom.

Workers were pouring from the manufactories to join the throng and he pushed through them, laughing and shouting himself hoarse. He clambered around a cannon. A bloody cannon wheeled along by grinning dye-women, their forearms stained strange colours. Folk sang, and embraced, and wept, and Jakib wasn't a shoemaker any more but a fighter for justice, a proud brother of the Breakers, struggling in the great endeavour of the age.

He saw a woman at the head of the crowd, on a white horse, wearing a soldier's breastplate. Judge! Had to be Judge. More beautiful and furious and righteous through the blurring tears in his eyes than he'd dared to hope. A spirit, she was, an idea made into flesh. A goddess, leading the people to their destiny.

"Brothers! Sisters! To the Agriont!" And she pointed up the road towards freedom. "I've a fancy to greet His August fucking Majesty!"

And there was another raucous wave of laughter and delight, and down an alley Jakib thought he saw some men kicking someone on the ground, over and over, and he drew his grandfather's rusty sword, and lifted it high in the air, and joined in with the singing.

"They're here," whispered Grey.

Captain Leeb drew his sword. Felt like the right thing to do. "I am aware, Corporal." He tried to project an air of confidence. Confidence defines an officer. He remembered his brother telling him so. "I can hear them."

Judging by the noise, there was a considerable number of them. A *considerable* number, and steadily approaching. It put Leeb in mind of the crowd's clamour at the Contest. Hundreds of voices raised in delighted excitement. Thousands of voices. But there was a definite edge of madness to it. A touch of fury. An occasional punctuation of shattering glass, splintering wood.

Leeb would have very much liked to run away. He didn't want anyone's blood on his hands, especially not his own. And he wasn't without sympathy for their cause, up to a point. Freedom and justice and so on, who doesn't like that stuff, in principle? But he had sworn an oath to the king. Not to the king directly, of course, but, you know, he'd sworn it even so. He'd been happy to swear it when things were going well and supposed he couldn't just unswear it the moment things turned dicey. What kind of an oath would it be then?

His colonel had assured him help was coming. From the King's Own. Then from Westport. Then from Starikland. From ever less likely directions. But no help appeared to have arrived at all.

Leeb glanced at his men, spread out across the width of the Sparway. What a flimsy little red line they looked. Perhaps forty flatbowmen, eighty spearmen. Half of his company hadn't come out. Somewhat looser in their oaths than he was. He'd always thought there was no more admirable quality than being a man of your word. Loyalty defines an officer. His father had often told him so. But it was starting to look as if a certain elasticity could be a useful thing.

"They're here," whispered Grey again.

"I am aware, Corporal." Leeb's mouth turned very dry as the murk from the foundry down the street was thinned out by the breeze. "I can see them."

More of them, indeed, and more. Many looked like ordinary citizens, women and children among them, brandishing chair-legs and hammers and knives and spears made from mops. Others looked like professionals, armour and bright weapons glinting as the sun peeped through. Leeb's jaw slowly dropped as he began to appreciate the sheer number of them.

Plainly the Closed Council's increasingly shrill proclamations, curfews, threats, examples had not achieved the desired effect. Quite the reverse.

"By the Fates," someone muttered.

"Steady," said Leeb, but it came out a squeak that couldn't have steadied anyone. It might have unsteadied those already steady, indeed. It was painfully obvious that his brittle little line had no chance of stopping that boiling tide. No chance at all.

When they saw Leeb and his soldiers they wobbled to a halt, bunching up uncertainly, chants and cheers dying on their lips. There was an intensely awkward silence, and an inappropriate memory floated up from the depths of Leeb's mind. The intensely awkward silence after he, drunk, had tried to kiss his cousin Sithrin at that dance and she jerked away in horror so he ended up sort of kissing her ear. This silence was like that one. But a great deal more terrifying.

What to do? By the Fates, what to do? Let them through? Join them? Fight them? Run and never stop? There were no good ideas. Leeb's lower lip twitched stupidly, but no sound emerged. Even a least-bad idea was beyond him. Decisiveness defines an officer, but he hadn't been trained for this. They don't train you for the world suddenly coming unravelled.

And now a rider pushed through to the front of the throng. A woman, with a tangle of damp red hair and a furious sneer. It was as if her rage was an infection, spreading instantly through the crowd. Faces twisted, weapons lifted, screams and cries and taunts burst forth, and suddenly Leeb had no choice at all.

"Raise bows!" he spluttered. Almost as if, running out of time to think of a better idea, he was left only with this self-evidently terrible one. His men glanced at each other, stirred uncomfortably.

"Raise bows!" roared Corporal Grey, veins bulging from his thick neck. At the same time, he looked at Leeb with a vaguely desperate expression. The pilot of a foundering vessel, perhaps, looking to his captain, silently asking if they really did intend to go down with the ship. Perhaps that's why captains do go down with their ships. No better ideas.

"Shoot!" squeaked Leeb, chopping downwards with his sword.

He wasn't sure how many actually shot. Less than half. Afraid to shoot at so many? Unwilling to shoot at men who might have been their fathers, brothers, sons? Women who might have been their mothers, sisters, daughters? A couple shot high, on purpose or in haste. There was a scream. Did two or three fall in the front rank of that seething mob? It made not the slightest difference. How could it?

The terrifying she-devil at the front stabbed towards Leeb with a clawing finger.

"Kill those fuckers!"

And they charged in their hundreds.

Leeb was a reasonably brave man, a reasonably honourable man, a reasonable monarchist who took his oath to his king very seriously. But Leeb was not a fool. He turned and ran with his men. It was not a company any more, but a squealing, jostling, whimpering herd of pigs.

Someone shoved him and he fell, rolled. He thought it might've been Corporal Grey, damn him. They all were scattering now, tossing their weapons, and he scrambled towards an alleyway, barging past a surprised-looking beggar and nearly falling again. How could one man keep his oath when everyone else was breaking theirs, after all? An army very much relied on unity of purpose.

Run for the Agriont, that was all he could think of. He plunged through the crooked backstreets, his neck prickling with fear, his breath sawing at his chest. Damn weak lungs, he'd been cursed with them all his life. *Can you name a lord marshal with weak lungs?* his brother used to ask. *Lungs define an officer!* Adua's foul vapours hardly helped. He sagged into a doorway, trying to suppress his cough. He'd dropped his sword somewhere. Or had he thrown it away?

"Bloody hell." He stared down at his officer's jacket. Bright red. How could it be redder? The whole purpose was to make him stand out. Like a bullseye on a target.

He stumbled from the doorway, struggling with the brass buttons, and almost straight into a group of heavyset men. Workers, maybe, from one of the foundries in the neighbourhood. But there was a wildness in their eyes, whites showing stark in their grease-smeared faces.

They stared at him, and he at them.

"Now listen," he said, raising one weak hand. "I was just doing—"

They were not interested. Not in his duty, or his oath, or his sympathy for their cause, or his reasonable monarchism. It was not a day for the reasonable, let alone for whatever defines an officer. One of them put his head down and charged. Leeb managed to throw a single punch as he came. A harmless one, which missed the mark and bounced off the man's forehead.

His brother had once told him how to punch, but he hadn't really been listening. He wished he'd listened now. But then his brother hadn't really known anything about punching, either.

The man caught Leeb in the side with his shoulder, knocked his wind out, lifted him bodily and brought him down on the wet cobbles with a stunning crash.

Then they were all on him, kicking, swearing. Slavering madmen. Furious animals. Leeb curled up as best he could, whimpering at each blow. Something hit him so hard in the back he was sick. To his horror, he saw one of them take out a knife.

It was a shock when Cal pulled the blade. Maybe it shouldn't have been. Doors knew he carried one. He stopped kicking the officer to stare at it. Thought about shouting at him not to do it. But by then Cal was stabbing.

"Shit," whispered Doors. Hadn't planned on killing anyone when he left his spot in the mill and ran out to join the Breakers flooding down the Sparway. Not sure what he had been planning. Setting things right, maybe. Getting a fair deal for once. Not this, anyway. They all looked shocked. Cal most of all.

"Had to be done," he said, staring down at the poor bastard wheezing and spitting blood and leaking red all over the street. "Had to be done."

Doors didn't see why. Wasn't like this fool had set their wages. They could've given him a kicking. Taught him a lesson. Left it at that. But whether it had to be done or not, it was done now. No undoing it.

"Come on." Doors turned. Left the dying officer behind. Started hurrying back towards the Sparway. Towards the Agriont. Didn't know what'd happen when they got there, just like they hadn't known what'd happen when they started kicking that officer.

Regrets were for tomorrow.

"They're here." Shawley watched a set run down the alley below, footsteps clapping from the fronts of the narrow buildings, and he tossed back the last of his wine and swung his legs from the window seat.

"Who's here?" slurred Rill, her eyes all unfocused from the husk.

"The Breakers, you fucking dunce," and he planted his hand on her face and shoved her back onto the bed. She caught her head on the headboard

25

as she fell, and put fingers to her scalp, and the tips came away bloody, and Shawley had to burst out laughing. He'd always been quite the joker.

He took his hatchet from the table and slid the haft up his sleeve. "Good time to settle some scores, I reckon." And he perched his hat on his head at just the right angle, straightened his collar in the mirror, took one last pinch of pearl dust, then trotted jauntily down the stairs and out into the street.

There was an explosive feel to the air. A feel of things ripped up so they could be put back together a new way. A woman ran past him, screaming, or maybe laughing, and Shawley tipped his hat to her. He was known for his good manners. Then he stood out of the way so some men could dash by, gripping his axe all the while. Just in case, you understand. He wasn't the only one with scores to settle, and Shawley had a lot of enemies. Always had a talent for making 'em.

He passed a ragged old couple stripping a dead officer lying in a slick of blood and swaggered on, keeping his head down, sticking to the back streets and the shortcuts. Always had a knack for finding his way. He'd been worried that getting through Arnault's Wall might be a problem. Been thinking about slipping through the sewers, though it would've ruined the nice boots he'd stolen off that merchant. But the Sable Gate stood wide open. Must've been a fight there, a crowd dragging the bloody corpses of some King's Own up onto the walls. The guts were hanging out of one. The head was off another. Shawley had no clue where it might've ended up. Seemed impolite to ask. He tipped his hat to a hideous woman with no more than four teeth in her head and slipped through the gate.

He could hear the violence, further on. The mad noise, spreading through the richer districts inside Arnault's Wall. They might call it the People's Army, and there might be a few high principles tossed about, but if you wanted his opinion, there were plenty of thugs with pretty excuses mixed in, and no small number who weren't even bothering with the excuses, just turning a quick profit from the chaos. Evidence of their handiwork all over. Shawley stopped to filch a nice ring off a corpse that someone had left begging. Always been blessed with sharp eyes.

He saw the house. How often had he stood outside, in the shadows, planning his revenge? Now, thanks to happy circumstances, it dropped in his lap and he just had to catch it. The gate was locked but he slipped off his coat and tossed it over the railings on top of the wall while no one was looking. He took a run up and jumped over, slipped through the wet garden where the bushes were clipped to look like birds or some

26

such. Bloody waste of money if you wanted his opinion. Money that should've been his.

The dining-room window still didn't lock properly and Shawley eased it open, slipped over the sill and dropped down silent in the darkened room on the other side. Always had a knack for treading softly. Place hadn't changed much. Dark table and chairs, dark dresser with the silver plate gleaming. Silver plate that should've been his.

He heard laughter, talking, more laughter. A woman's voice, he thought, a young woman, an older man. They'd no idea what was happening in the city yet, by the sound of it. Strange, that fifty strides from the madness it could be just an ordinary day. He padded down the corridor and peered around a door frame.

It was an odd scene given the carnage in the streets. A girl of twenty with a mass of blonde hair stood admiring herself in a mirror of Visserine glass which must've cost more'n Shawley's house. She wore a half-made dress of shining fabric, two seamstresses attending to her—a young one with a mouthful of pins and an old one on her knees busy stitching at a hem. Furnevelt sat in a corner, wine glass in his hand. He had his back to Shawley, but you could see him smiling in the mirror as he watched it all done.

And Shawley realised the girl must be Furnevelt's daughter. That was how long he'd been waiting. Should've just killed the old bastard where he sat, but Shawley wanted him to know. So he stepped around the door frame and tipped his hat.

"Ladies," he said, smirking into the mirror, and they turned to look, puzzled. Not scared yet. That'd come. Shawley couldn't remember her name, Furnevelt's daughter, but she'd turned out so pretty. That's what happens when you grow up with all these advantages. These advantages that should've been his.

"Shawley?" Furnevelt jumped from his chair, a delicious shock across his face. "I thought I told you never to come back here!"

"You told me a lot of things." Shawley let the axe slide from his sleeve so he was gripping the haft. "You self-righteous old shit." And he hit him on the side of the head.

Furnevelt got his hand up and knocked it wide, but the blade still caught his scalp, blood flying across the room.

He made a funny little gasp, stumbled, dropped his wine glass and it broke across the floor.

One of the dressmakers screamed, pins falling from her open mouth. Furnevelt's daughter stared, the tendons starting from her pale bare feet.

Second time, Shawley caught Furnevelt right between the eyes, axe sinking into his skull with a bang.

The dressmaker screamed again. Bloody irritating scream she had.

Furnevelt's daughter sprinted out, fast as a ferret given she had all that half-stitched cloth about her. "Damn it!" Shawley had to get her, too, to make it fair, but the axe was stuck fast in Furnevelt's skull and however he tugged it wouldn't come free. "Get back here, bitch!"

Lilott ran. There was no thought involved. She fled in terror down the hall, spurred on by the shrieks of her dressmakers. She fumbled with the locks, plunged across the gardens, crashed through the gate. She ran, clutching up the gauzy skirts of her unfinished wedding dress, her bare feet slapping at the wet cobbles.

She burst into the square. People everywhere. People shocked, joyous, curious, furious. Strange people with strange intensities of emotion twisting their pale faces into animal masks. Where had they come from?

A man stood on a packing crate, screaming something about votes. Leering labourers bellowed back at him. A woman with wild hair bounced on a big man's shoulders, shaking a sword and swearing at the sky. Lilott had been about to scream for help, but some instinct made her bite her lip and shrink against the wall, trying to catch her breath. She hardly knew what had happened. The Breakers, she supposed. It must be the Breakers.

She once listened to one of them give a speech. Hidden at the back of a meeting in a shawl she borrowed from her maid. She had thought it such a daring thing to do, had been expecting fire and fury and, well... *danger*. But it had all sounded so reasonable. Fair pay. Equitable hours. Decent treatment. She had hardly been able to understand why everyone was so afraid of them. Later, flushed and eager, she had repeated all the arguments to her father. He had told her she had no notion of the complexities of managing a labour market, that what seemed to her eminent good sense might sound to some ears like treason, and that this was not the kind of thing the lady of taste he was raising her to be would ever need to worry about.

In that much, at least, he had been horribly mistaken.

She limped down a crowded street. The sun had gone in and a chilly gust brought a new sprinkle of rain. Someone was playing a fiddle far too fast and they danced, and whooped, and clapped, like guests at a particularly wild party, and not far away a well-dressed corpse was draped over a railing, blood dripping from its broken skull and trickling in the gutter. Was her father dead? She gave a kind of moan, had to bite her knuckle to keep from screaming.

There had been warning signs. The price of bread and meat, she heard from the cook, kept going up. Loyalty in the army, she heard from Harbin, kept going down. There had been that uprising in Valbeck. Vague worries that there might be more when the rebels landed in Midderland. News of the king's victory had brought relief. But then came the rumours of Breakers approaching Adua. Then came the curfew, then the arrests by the Inquisition, then the hangings by the Closed Council.

She had suggested they postpone the wedding, but her father was as deaf to that as he had been to the Breakers' arguments. He refused to put off his only child's happiness on account of a crowd of ruffians. Harbin laughed at the notion that the capital could fall to an army of peasants, so Lilott forced out laughter, too, since agreeing with your husband-to-be was expected of a young lady. At least before the marriage. They had convinced themselves it would not happen.

They had been horribly mistaken on that score, too.

She hardly recognised the streets she had grown up in, flooded with crazed humanity, surging on invisible currents of joy and fury. She was so cold. Not exactly crying but her eyes and her nose constantly leaking, her bare shoulders clammy from the drizzle and her bare feet bruised from the unforgiving cobblestones. Her breath came in terrified whoops, her skin crawling under her half-finished, pearl-stitched bodice.

Only that morning it had felt so important that all the right guests should accept their invitations. That the words of their vows be perfect. That the hem of her dress was stitched just so. Now the hem of her dress was black with road-filth and, Fates help her, speckled brown with her father's blood, and all the world was turned upside down and inside out.

She hobbled on. Not knowing where she was or where she was heading. Some unsewn flap of her dress caught on a broken fence as she ran past and nearly jerked her off her bare feet. Someone laughed at her. Another clapped. On any other day, a desperate, barefooted girl in a blood-spattered wedding dress would have excited some attention. Today it was nothing to remark upon. The whole city had gone mad. The whole world.

Over the roofs she glimpsed the parapet of the Tower of Chains, the tallest tower of the Agriont, and she gave a moan of relief. But when she burst gasping onto the paving stones beside the moat it became a groan of horror.

She had wandered lazily across this bridge on happy summer days, among the wealthy revellers, on her way to the Agriont's park to see and be seen, to applaud the fencers at the Summer Contest. She remembered smiling at floating ducklings following their mother in dignified single file, remembered counting the green and red and purple lily pads with Harbin, on the day he proposed. So picturesque.

The gates were sealed now. People were crushed against them, waving frantically, wailing at the towering gatehouse to be let in. An old woman in a very fine dress was scratching at the wood with her fingernails. Lilott added her voice to the rest as she staggered across the bridge. She hardly knew what else to do. "Help!" she screeched. "Help!"

She saw a pale man with a red scarf staring past her and spun about to follow his eyes. A crowd was coming up the wide Middleway, banners bobbing over it, steel of pikes and armour glinting.

"Oh no," she whispered. She could not run any more. There was nowhere left to run to. A house was on fire, smoke rolling from the upstairs windows into the spitting sky.

People began to scatter, knocking each other down, trampling each other in their mindless haste. Lilott took an elbow in the face and tottered back, tasting blood. Her foot caught in her torn dress, the parapet hit her in the knees and, with a despairing gasp, she tumbled over.

It was not that far to the moat, but even so the water hit her hard, knocked out her breath and sucked her down in a rush of bubbles. The floating glory of her dress became an instant dead weight, fabric clutching at her, dragging her down. She was beyond exhaustion. Beyond terror. Part of her wanted just to sink, but another would not let go, made her thrash, kick, struggle.

She came up coughing dirty water, wriggled through the clutching, slapping lily pads, far less picturesque at close quarters, and into the darkness under the bridge. She pressed herself to the slimy stones, hair plastered across her face, her head full of the smell of vegetable rot.

Not far away a corpse floated, face down. A hint of sodden cloth, of tangled hair. She watched it turn slowly, bump against the moss-covered wall of the moat, drift away. She wondered who it had been. She wondered who she was now. She wondered if she would live out the hour. Everything was changed.

The People's Army was coming. Wasn't she the people, too? When had she become their enemy? She squeezed her eyes shut, shivering in the icy water, and gave up trying to smother her own sobs. No one could have heard them over the deafening noise of the mob above. Tramping boots, clashing metal, breaking glass, rumbling wagon wheels. A demon with many voices.

"Bread! Give us bread!"

"Send out the Closed Council!"

"The Great Change is come!"

"Let us in, you fuckers."

"Let us in or we break in!"

And, louder than all, a sawing, maddened shriek. "Bring out His fucking Majesty!"

"Bring him out!" screamed Mother Mostly, shoving forward.

They'd made it to the Agriont. Ready to seize their own justice for once, rather'n be crushed by the king's. But now folk held up. From some shred of respect for their old masters, or fear of 'em, at least. They loitered at the head of the bridge.

"There's men up there!" someone said. "King's men, with bows!"

Mother Mostly's eyesight weren't near good enough to see any king's men that far off. The whole gatehouse was a looming blur over the heads of the folk packed in front. The king's men couldn't kill this whole crowd, but no doubt they could kill a few, and no one was eager to be first.

But Mother Mostly wouldn't be fucking bullied. Her father had tried it, when she was a girl, and she'd stabbed him with a knitting needle and run away from home. Her first husband had tried it, and she'd stabbed him with a butcher's knife and rolled his body into the canal. The Styrians had tried it, when they came to put their boot across the Arches. They'd come asking for money and she'd told 'em to go back where they fucking came from. They'd beaten her, but she healed. They'd cut two of her fingers off, and she got her hands back in the soap the same day. They'd smashed her doors, smashed her shutters, smashed her tubs, but she got new ones. In the end their boss turned up, and she was sure he'd kill her, but he gave her a nod of respect instead. She needn't pay, he'd said. She alone.

It was just a fact. Everyone in the Arches knew it. Mother Mostly won't be fucking bullied. Not by Styrians. Not by king's men. Not by anyone.

So she shouldered through the crowd, skirts gathered up and tucked into her belt the way she did when there was work to do. She jostled her way to the front, which one way or another she'd been doing all her life, using her elbows and her fixed jaw and her great loud voice. "Out o' my way!" Forced a path through the big men, the armed men, the armoured men, still loitering. They might be hard on the outside, but they were soft where it counted. Mother Mostly hadn't been born with much softness in her, and a life in the laundries had pared away what there was and left her as yielding as a length of wire.

She shoved onto the empty bridge, giving the towering gatehouse, and its notched battlements, and its slitted windows the kind of baleful frown she gave to folk owed her money.

"I'm a woman of the Union!" she roared. "Fifty years, and I've worked every one of 'em! I won't be bullied, you hear?"

Cheers and jeers behind her, whoops and hoots, like folk watching freaks dance at a sideshow.

"Bring out that Styrian cunt!" she screamed at the battlements, shaking her knife. "The king's mother!"

"She ain't there!" someone called from behind. "Scurried back to Styria months ago!"

Mother Mostly glowered up at the gatehouse, still a blur, more or less, but she knew there must be men up there, and she wasn't about to be bullied by the bastards.

She took another step forward. "Then bring out her cunt of a son, the king!"

Rithinghorm pressed his mouth to the arrow-loop and bellowed at the very top of his voice. "Halt! In the name of His Majesty!"

He leaned back to survey the results. Those words had always worked magic before, conjuring obedience from thin air. But now, suddenly, the spell had no effect. "I order you to bloody *halt*!" He doubted the crowd could even hear him over their own clamour. He could hardly hear himself over his own thudding heart.

Earlier that week, Lord Marshal Rucksted had addressed their regiment. Told them they were the last line of defence. Told them failure was unthinkable, retreat impossible. Rithinghorm had always admired Rucksted. Excellent beard. Lot of dash. The very style of officer he wanted to be. But the man had looked positively dishevelled. Beard in disarray. Now Rithinghorm knew why.

People continued to flood from the buildings on the other side of the moat and into an ever-thicker press at the end of the bridge. Breakers! Traitors! *Here*, at the very gates of the Agriont! And so *many*. He could scarcely credit it. They were starting to move out onto the bridge itself. One in particular, leading the way, some dirty bloody peasant woman with her skirt tucked into her belt so her pale, sinewy legs showed, waving a knife, screeching words he could scarcely hear. Something about someone's son.

"Incon*ceiv*able," whispered Rithinghorm. If he had read it in one of his sister's storybooks he would have dismissed it as a fantasy.

They had to be kept away from the gate. They had to be cleared from the bridge. They had to be taught a damn *lesson*.

He pointed towards that shrieking woman.

"Shoot her!"


"Sir?" said Parry, blinking. Damn, his mouth was dry. Kept having to lick his lips.

Captain Rithinghorm came close to point through the arrow-loop. Close enough that Parry could hear his breath echoing in the narrow chain room. Close enough that he could smell him. He must wear some kind of perfume. Hint of lavender. He pointed down, white with anger. Down towards that laundry-woman.

"I said *shoot her!*"

Parry licked his lips again. Bow was ready. He'd made sure of that. Or his hands had done it for him, following the old routine. He sighted up, nice and careful. Strangest thing. She reminded Parry of his mother. She used to tuck her skirts in like that, when she was mopping floors.

"Shoot, then!"

Parry wanted to follow orders. Always followed 'em before. But his hand wouldn't let go the string. The woman was coming closer, screeching away. That reminded him of his mother, too. Folk were starting to follow her example, edging out onto the bridge, towards the gate.

He licked his lips. Again. Just didn't seem right, to shoot that woman.

Slowly, Parry lowered his bow.

"What are you *doing*?"

Parry took the arrow from the string and, not sure what to do with it, put it behind his back. "Doesn't seem right," he said.

Rithinghorm seized him by the jacket. "I gave you an *order!*"

"I know." Everyone was looking at them now. "I'm very sorry, sir."

Rithinghorm started to shake him. "Are you a damn *traitor*?"

Parry could only swallow, and blink, and grip that arrow tight behind his back, and shake his head. "I...don't think so." He honestly wasn't sure. "Just...doesn't seem right."

Rithinghorm threw him back against the wall, jaw muscles squirming on the sides of his taut face. "Sergeant Hope!"

"Sir?" said the sergeant.

Rithinghorm pointed a stabbing finger at Parry. "*Kill* this man!"

33

Sergeant Hope stared down at his drawn short-sword, a long slit of light from one of the arrow-loops making the broad blade glint in the shadows. He'd have followed his old captain into hell. He had done, out in Styria. But not this little fucker. This little bastard with his fine accent and his pale face and his thin fingers and his bloody perfume, ordering good men killed. Ordering the citizens of Adua shot at. It came to him that he had more in common with those Breakers chanting outside on the bridge than he did with Rithinghorm. They were just people. People who wanted to be heard. People who wanted enough to get by, while others had so much more'n they could ever need.

Twenty years, he'd been doing as he was told. Never seen another way. But just like that, sharp as fingers snapped under his nose, he decided to stop.

"No," he said.

Rithinghorm gave a strange sort of hoot, mouth and eyes wide with surprise, when the short-sword slid into his well-pressed uniform jacket. Hope dragged the blade back and Rithinghorm plucked weakly at his shoulder, cheeks puffed right out. Hope shoved him away, lifted the sword and hacked it into Rithinghorm's skull. Blood spattered. It's always a surprise, how much a man holds.

He blinked at his captain's corpse for a moment. He felt light-headed. He felt light all over. As if a fully laden pack had been snatched from his shoulders.

Through the slitted windows he could see the bridge was a solid press of people. He could hear the gates creaking below under the pressure.

He turned to the men. They were staring at him. Parry and all the rest. So young, they were. Good lads. Could he ever have looked that young, when he first joined? They didn't know what to say. What to do. Hope didn't know, either, but they had to do something.

He pointed towards the stair. "Guess we'd better open the gates."

Smiler heard the clonk of the bar, the rattle of bolts, then the gates gave under the pressure and people surged forwards like a river in spate through a burst dam. Folk pressed against him so tight, he struggled not to prick 'em by accident with the spike on the back of his war hammer.

There was a maid there, bonnet skewed across her face. There was a man might've been a wheelwright, or a cooper. There was a fellow looked no better'n a beggar. Citizens of Adua picked up that day, citizens of the Union picked up in their march across Midderland, all mixed in with the First Breakers' Regiment, men like Smiler who'd fought in the wars in Styria, then in the bread riots in Keln, then struggled in the mills in Valbeck, then been armed with Angland steel and marched to free 'emselves from tyranny. Now all that sacrifice and struggle were finally bearing fruit—the Great Change, come at last.

They tumbled eagerly up the tunnel into the rotten heart of the old order. Into the Agriont, grand buildings rising up on every side. Into the Square of Marshals where once, as a boy, Smiler came to watch the Summer Contest, and screamed his lungs raw as Jezal dan Luthar beat Bremer dan Gorst in the final.

There were swords here today as well. A double line of soldiers strung across the square, crooked and hastily gathered, shields and weapons at all angles, an officer shouting in a broken voice.

The Breakers charged. Didn't need an order. They couldn't have stopped even if they'd wanted to, there was so much shoving from behind. The whole People's Army at their backs. Every ground-down worker in the Union. But Smiler didn't want to stop. He wanted to smash this whole corrupt place. These grasping bastards who'd sent his friends to die in Styria, to die in the mills, to die in the cellars. He wanted to burn away the rot and make a country for its people.

Smiler picked out a man to charge at, peeking over the top of his shield with desperate eyes. He let go a roar of hate, of joy, of triumph, the flagstones flying under his feet, the brothers surging to freedom all around him.

Their shields crashed together. They struggled and strained, and Smiler got a glimpse of the man's bared teeth and his wide eyes then suddenly the pressure was gone and he was stumbling forwards, and he saw Roys had swung his halberd and staved the man's helmet in.

It was a slaughter, really. The royalists were already breaking, and they scurried away towards the great statues at the far end of the square, and men charged after them, whooping and screaming, leaving Smiler to stare down at the dead soldier with the dented helmet.

Came to him then how easily he could've been in that line, if things had worked out just a little different. If he'd stayed in the army when they came back from Styria, instead of walking away in disgust. There was only a coin-toss between him and these corpses.

"You're a hero!" And a woman with a strong chin and her hair bound in a red scarf craned up to plant a great soft kiss on his jaw. "You're all bloody heroes!"

*

35

The soldier blinked down at her, his helmet skewed, surprised, she thought, but not disappointed. So long since Adnes last kissed a man she didn't know how to tell. But it wasn't a romantic thing so much as joy at having hope again. Or maybe it was a romantic thing, 'cause he grabbed her around the back of the head and kissed her on the mouth, and she clung on to him, which was uncomfortable on account of the hardness of his breastplate, and there was a great warmth right through her and she was sucking greedily at his tongue which tasted of onions, and a fine taste it was, too.

She never would've dreamed she might kiss a stranger like that, but it was a new day and the king's men were beaten and all the old rules were gone, and the sun showed through again and made the soldiers' armour glitter, made the little puddles on the flagstones sparkle. Was this freedom?

They were dragged apart by the flood of cheering people then shoved back together, carried across the Square of Marshals and up the grand steps of the Lords' Round, through the inlaid doors. Adnes stared up to the dome, high, high above, and around her, in the vast and heavy silence, hundreds of people who never thought in their lives to pass through those doors did the same.

She looked at the gilding, and the different-coloured marbles, and the rare woods, and the suns stitched into the cushions on the benches, and the stained-glass windows that showed scenes she didn't understand. A bald man holding out a crown. A bearded man with a sword standing over two others. A young man lit by a ray of sun as he stood up alone from a crowd. The spotless grandeur of the place. Nothing could be further from the farm she'd left when the People's Army came through, where they'd slept on straw on the floor of a shack, and worn their hands to the meat, and been treated by the local lordling like they were less than dirt.

Well, they were the masters now.

They carried Risinau in on a gilded chair they must've torn from some chamber, some office, some hall. Adnes grabbed at a leg of it, one in a forest of hands, helping it pass, and Risinau laughed, and they laughed, and the joyous crowd cheered as they carried him bobbing down the aisle between the curved benches, and set him on the great table.

Folk had got up to the public gallery and were singing and clapping, the echoes of their joy bouncing about the great space and bringing it alive like it couldn't have been since that dome was raised. There was a flower girl up there and she had a sack of petals and was throwing handfuls down, fluttering like butterflies through the shafts of coloured light to carpet the tiles below, and Adnes had never seen so beautiful a thing.

Made her think of her husband's grave, and her sons' graves, down in the wood where the wildflowers grew, and that brought a blur of tears to her eyes. So much joy and so much pain together she thought her chest would split with it.

"You have brought the dream to life, my friends!" roared Risinau, and there was a cheer so loud it made Adnes's teeth rattle and her ears ring and her heart throb.

"Risinau!" people squealed. "Risinau!" And Adnes made a great sobbing, meaningless wail, reaching out towards him.

"Equality, my brothers! Unity, my sisters! A new beginning! A country governed by all, in the interests of all. You will say on your deathbeds, with a smile, that you were here! The day the Lords' Round was made the Commons' Round! The day of the Great Change!"

She was crying, and all about her men and women were crying and laughing, all at once.

It was the day their dreams came true. The day their new Union was born.

The soldier caught her hand, and there were tears on his face, too, but he was smiling. He'd a fine smile, she thought. "I don't know your name."

"Who cares a shit?" And she dragged his helmet off so she could push her fingers through his sweaty hair, and started kissing him again.

Ettenbeck slipped from a side door of the Lords' Round and into a narrow street behind the building. He had thought he would be safe in there. Where could be safer than the very heart of the Union? But now the Breakers were inside. He could hear them cheering. He could hear them crashing through the buildings all about him!

Perhaps this was how it had been when the Gurkish invaded, and the Eaters broke into the Agriont. He remembered his uncle telling him the story, his watery eyes fixed on the far distance, as though at horrors beyond imagining. But these were not cannibal sorcerers, not inhuman and unknowable demons, not the wielders of forbidden powers. Just ordinary people.

A window shattered in the Commission for Land and Agriculture and a desk came flying through, crashing to the ground not far away. Ettenbeck could feel the sweat running down his scalp. Leaking out of him as if he was a squeezed sponge. It took every vestige of self-control he had not to break into a desperate sprint. The walls of the palace compound might still hold firm. Perhaps if he could make it there—

"There's one!" He heard footsteps clapping from the buildings. "Stop him!" Now he ran, but not far. Someone caught him under the arm and threw him down. A flash of a bearded face, armour that looked new-forged. He was dragged up again by the elbow. A strange gang. Like the people you might see at one of the cheap markets. Only furious.

And Ettenbeck realised that ordinary people can be utterly terrifying.

"Where you going, fucker?" growled a man with a scar on his chin.

"There's no escaping the people's justice!" squealed a woman and slapped him across the face.

"We're in charge now!"

He could hardly understand their grinding accents. He did not know what they wanted. Did not know what he could possibly give them. "My name is Ettenbeck," he said, for no reason that made any sense. They shoved him onwards. His cheek was burning.

There were other prisoners caught up in the crowd. Administrators. Bureaucrats. Clerks. A couple of soldiers. Herded like animals. Prodded along with spears. A grinning coachman was flicking at them with his carriage whip, making them howl and whimper. Ettenbeck knew one man's bloody face, but his name had gone. All their names had gone.

"Profiteers!" someone was screaming in a broken voice. "Speculators!"

A dark-skinned fellow was being kicked along the street, and he would stumble up, and be kicked down again, up, and down. Ettenbeck thought he was an ambassador from somewhere. Kadir, maybe? A charming, cultured man. Ettenbeck had heard him speak very movingly to the Solar Society about closer cooperation across the Circle Sea. Now they had knocked his hat off and were spitting on him.

"Bastard!" snarled a man in soldier's clothes who had stripped his jacket off, his shirt spotted with blood. "Bastard!" And he stamped on the ambassador's head.

Something hit Ettenbeck on the side of his face and he fell. The ground cracked him hard. He wobbled up to his hands and knees. His jaw was throbbing. "Oh," he muttered, blood pattering on the cobbles. "Oh dear." A tooth fell out of his numb mouth.

He was caught by the elbow again, dragged up again, pain shooting through his armpit, and sent stumbling on.

"Profiteers!" a woman shrieked, spit spraying, eyes bulging, pointing at him with a rolling pin. "Speculators!"

"He's one o' those Closed Council bastards!"

"I'm just a clerk!" Ettenbeck's voice was a desperate squeal. It was a lie. He was one of the senior under-secretaries for Agricultural Taxation. How proudly he had murmured the title to himself when he received the

38

promotion. His sister would *finally* have to take him seriously. How he wished now he had never even come to Adua, let alone to the Agriont. But you'll buy nothing with wishes, as his mother always loved to say.

He kicked and twisted as they dragged him across the little square in front of the Land Registry Building towards the fountain. An ugly thing, a wide, waist-high stone bowl of water with a twisting mass of spouting stone fish rising from the centre. It was by no means improved by a corpse draped over the rim, arse in the air and the pointed toes of fashionable shoes scraping the flagstones.

Ettenbeck realised they were dragging him up next to the body. "Wait!" he squealed, and he caught the stone basin, spray splashing in his face, thrashing desperately, but there were hands all around him, one of his legs was lifted, the other shoe falling off as it scuffed on the ground. Someone caught the back of his head.

"One last drink at the people's expense, Councillor!"

And they shoved his face into the water. Through the gurgle of the fountain he heard shouting. Singing. Laughing. He fought his way up, just for a moment, gasped in a breath, saw the mad crowd surging on towards the House of Questions. They shook swords and spears in the air. One had a severed head spiked on it, bobbing obscenely over the mob. Absurd. Like a cheap prop in a badly produced play. Except it was real.

He was shoved down again, into the fountain, bubbles rushing.

# No More Trouble

Broad did what he'd been doing ever since they locked him in this cell. He paced back and forth, back and forth, back and forth. It was only five steps from one side to the other and those were small ones, but he paced anyway, and while he paced he chewed over and over all the stupid things he'd done to land himself here. Sometimes he kicked the wall, or dug his aching fist into his sore hand, or slapped himself hard enough to hurt. Seemed he couldn't help hurting people. With no one else to hand, he hurt himself.

He'd promised no more trouble, then let himself get sucked in yet again. High Treason would be the charge, he was guilty as hell and there was only one punishment. Savine wouldn't be saving him this time. She was locked up, too, somewhere in this buried warren of a place. She couldn't even save herself.

He made a promise, then. If, by some undeserved twist of fate, he wriggled free of this, he'd live for Liddy and May. "No more trouble," he whispered, and he ground his forehead against the rough stone wall. "*No more.*" He swore it. One more time.

Then he heard footsteps beyond the heavy door. They were coming. To ask their questions? Or just drag him straight to the scaffold? He clenched his fists, but he knew fighting would do no good. It was fighting landed him here in the first place. The key scraped in the lock, his breath coming fast through his clenched teeth as he watched the door creak open.

A face showed at the gap. Not the black-masked Practical he'd expected. A small woman, cheeks full of broken veins. She looked nervous, like she hadn't known what to expect, then when she saw him standing there, she broke into a beaming smile. "Brother! You're free!"

Broad couldn't do much but stare. "I'm what?"

"Free!" She shook a ring of keys at him. "We all are!" And she vanished, leaving the door wide open.

He heard laughter out there now. Cheering and singing. Was that a high little flute playing somewhere? Like a rowdy market day in the village when he was a boy. He nudged his lenses up his nose, scraped his courage together and went to the door.

"Brother!" A man wearing bright new armour spotted with blood hauled Broad out into the mould-stained corridor, but the way you'd greet a long-lost comrade rather than the way you'd drag a convict to their death. "You're free!"

They were unlocking the cells, and with each door flung open they'd give a cheer, and at each prisoner pulled out they'd give another. Armoured men hugged a woman must've spent months in the darkness, pale and shrivelled, squinting at the light like it hurt her. "What's your name, Sister?"

She just sat against the wall, floppy as a rag doll. "Is it… Grise?" she whispered. Broad saw one of her hands was all smashed, crooked fingers bloated like sausages.

Someone clutched at his shirt. "Have you seen my son?" An old man with wild, weepy eyes. "Do you know where my son is?"

Broad brushed him off. "I don't know anything."

Someone threw their arms around him from behind and he had to smother an instinct to lash out with an elbow. "Ain't it wonderful?" A girl no older than sixteen with a patchy shawl about her shoulders, crying and smiling at once. "Ain't it wonderful?" And she grabbed someone else, and they danced a floppy jig together and barged over an old woman who'd been brandishing a mop with a knife tied to the end. She nearly stabbed Broad with it as she fell.

Maybe he should've felt a caper coming on himself at his unexpected taste of freedom, but Broad had seen this mix of mad joy and mad anger before, during the uprising in Valbeck. Knowing how that turned out didn't make him want to dance. Made him want to slip back to his cell and lock himself in.

There were Breakers among the crowd. Veterans with shiny new gear Broad well recognised. The arms and armour he'd brought from Ostenhorm on Savine's orders and handed over to Judge in return for the Breakers' support. Looked like they'd risen up after all. Just on their own timetable.

Broad had to push against a joyful current of people to get up the steps, into a wider, brighter hallway. A man in a leather apron ran past laughing, a wedge of documents clutched to his chest, papers slipping out and flapping to the floor. Another man bashed at a lock with a heavy ale flagon. This was where the music was coming from, a woman sitting cross-legged with some clerk's tall hat jammed down to her eyebrows, eyes closed as she tooted jauntily on her flute.

And shuffling through the madness, freed as unexpectedly as Broad himself, came his old employers, the Lord and Lady Governor of Angland. Even with his lenses on, it took him a moment to recognise them. The Young Lion had his right arm around his wife's shoulders, his gaunt face scattered with scabs and twisted with pain, moving in lurching hops with his left arm uselessly dangling and one trouser leg rolled up to the stump. Savine had one arm around her husband, the other under her swollen belly, struggling along with back bent and teeth bared, tufts of dark hair sticking from the bandages around her head.

They'd owned the world, these two. Now look.

"Broad!" Savine clung to his arm painfully tight, a sheen of sweat on her blotchy face. "Thank the Fates you're here!" The warble in her voice made him think of that terrified waif who'd begged for his help on the barricades of Valbeck.

Brock was clinging to the wall with his fingernails to stay upright. "What the hell's happening?"

"Not sure. But their gear..." Broad nodded at one of the armed men, lowering his voice. "It's from your armoury in Ostenhorm."

Savine worked out in a blink what Broad had been slowly putting together. "The Breakers have stormed the Agriont?" she whispered.

"They've *what?*" squeaked her husband.

"We'd best get out while we can," said Broad. "Find a safe place."

Savine's eyes were huge and scared and bloodshot in the shadows. "*Is* there a safe place?"

Broad had no answer. He held out his other hand to Brock. The one with the tattoo on the back. You could see how much it hurt him, to need the help. But this was no time for pride. Wasn't easy, steering a pregnant woman and a one-legged man through that jostling crowd of rescuers and looters. Beyond a set of broken double doors men smashed and laughed, turned over furniture, flinging armfuls of fluttering papers in the air.

"That was my father's office," whispered Savine as they hobbled past. Inside that room, the all-powerful Arch Lector Glokta had ordered life and death with a flick of his pen. Times had changed, all right.

"Lord Marshal Brint!" called Brock. "You're alive."

"Just barely." A grey-haired man was pressed against one wall. He'd a trace of military bearing, if you squinted, underneath a filthy officer's jacket with all markings of rank ripped off. Brock reached out to shake his hand. Not the easiest thing to do, since Brint had only one and Brock only one that worked. "They took me prisoner before you landed. Lord bloody Heugen spilled his guts the moment we were caught."

Brock shook his head. "What a crowd of useless bastards the Open Council turned out to be."

"Who . . ." Savine forced through clenched teeth, "could have guessed?"

They struggled out blinking into bright daylight, down the steps at the front of the House of Questions, the wind chill on Broad's face. Should've been a relief, but the crowds outside were madder than ever, cheering and chanting, brandishing lit torches and swords and broken furniture.

Papers scattered everywhere. Drifts like snow, ankle deep. Folk were flinging heaps of 'em from the windows, blowing about on the wind, yesterday's secrets suddenly worthless. Place stank of smoke. A laughing man had blood all over his hands. Broad felt cold as he realised a smug-looking bastard not far away had a head spiked on his spear. Its back was to Broad so he couldn't see the face. Put him in mind of Musselia. A bag of foul memories he tried never to open.

"It's the Young Lion!" someone called, and suddenly folk were crowding around them, reaching out for Leo. "Look, it's Leo dan Brock!"

"Can't be him!"

"I saw him at his triumph!"

"Where's his leg?"

"Lost it in the cause o' freedom."

"The Young Lion!"

"Please." Leo struggled to hold them back with his one good arm. "Let me—"

"He's a bloody hero!" A big man dropped down behind Brock, and before anyone could do a thing about it he'd stood, hoisting the Young Lion high into the air on his shoulders.

Someone struck up a martial tune on an old violin. One that Broad had marched to out in Styria. Folk danced, and saluted, and patted the stump of the Young Lion's leg like he was some bloody mascot. Whether it made any real sense or not, seemed they'd got their own successful rebellion and Brock's failed one mixed up into one thing.

"Still bowing to the nobles?" A fellow with heavy brows that met in the middle had come up with quite the scowl. "Where's your *fucking* dignity?" he snarled at the man who had Brock on his shoulders. "Carried these bastards on our backs all our lives, haven't we? Ain't we all equal now?"

Broad could feel the mood shifting. There were doubting looks pointed his way, and Savine's way, too. If they realised she was the daughter of the man who'd tortured thousands in the building right behind...

"Hold these." Broad handed his lenses to Brint. Then he realised the ex-lord marshal couldn't hold Savine and the lenses at once, so he tucked 'em in Brint's jacket pocket and turned back to the crowd, which had become a mass of smeared colour.

"I was at Stoffenbeck!" the fellow with the brows was snarling. "And he didn't fight for the fucking people, all he did—"

Broad's fist smashed into his blurred face. Before he fell Broad caught his collar and punched him again.

"I was there, too, and I say you're a liar." And Broad punched him one more time. "The Young Lion's a fucking *hero!*" It'd been a while since he believed in heroes, but plainly some folk still liked the notion. "Gave his leg and his arm for the people!" Broad flung the man against the wall of the House of Questions so he bounced off and rolled on the cobbles, hands clasped to his broken face.

"A cheer for the Young Lion!" bellowed Brint, stepping forwards with his one fist raised.

Like that, the mood was changed back and they were cheering again, Leo dan Brock jolting about on that dancing man's shoulders with his stump in the air and his limp arm flopping.

"Wish I could get him down," said Broad.

Savine shook her head. "I've a feeling it will be safer for us all if he stays up there."

"That was...quick and decisive action," murmured Brint, pressing the lenses back into Broad's aching hand. "You were a Ladderman?"

Broad frowned down at his tattoo. He realised there was a little piece of tooth stuck between two of his scarred knuckles.

"I was," he said, wincing as he picked it out and flicked it away.

Brint watched the crowd cheer as they bounced Brock on their shoulders. "The Union will need men like you in the days to come. Someone will have to restore order."

"My family needs me. That's what matters."

"Of course," said Brint. "But...you may serve them best by serving here."

Broad slowly hooked his lenses over his ears, carefully settled them into that familiar groove on the bridge of his nose and gave a heavy sigh. He'd sworn to keep away from trouble, but here was the problem.

Trouble wouldn't keep away from him.

# Bring Out the King

Orso stared down from the palace gatehouse, hardly able to believe the evidence of his own senses.

What could only be described as a horde of people had boiled from the Kingsway and into the park, past the commanding statues of his father, of the First of the Magi, and of a still-unfinished Arch Lector Glokta, surging towards the palace gates in an apparently endless flood.

"Where did they come from?" he muttered. A fool's question to which he already knew the answer. They came from Valbeck, from Keln, from Adua, from every corner of Midderland. They were the Union's citizens. They were his subjects. Or they had been, at any rate. It appeared his grand tour of the country was no longer necessary.

It had come to him.

He watched in stunned horror as Union flags were torn down, vandals dancing in triumph on the roofs. A few buildings remained in loyal hands, but they were islands in a stormy sea, hopelessly besieged. Here and there, bloody little dramas unfolded. Tiny figures chased down a street. Tiny figures tumbling from a window. Tiny figures hanged from trees.

The palace was its own well-guarded fortress within the fortress of the Agriont, but the Breakers were crowding in against its gates, swarming more thickly with Orso's every faintly wheezing breath.

"Master Sulfur, would it be possible...?" He was sure the magus had been right beside him, but when Orso turned, Sulfur was nowhere to be seen. It appeared there would be no spectacular magical rescue today. Saving the king from a dozen Breakers was one thing. From countless thousands was clearly quite another. There comes a time, Orso supposed, when even such mighty creditors as the Banking House of Valint and Balk must cut their losses.

"Bring out the king!" someone screeched, their voice somehow rising above the sullen murmur. There was a surge through the crowd, a shriek as someone fell in the midst, crushed underfoot. Did he hear the heavy gates creak under the pressure? Something shattered against the parapet, not far away, and Orso ducked back on an instinct.

"Your Majesty?" asked one of the officers. His face looked very pale above his crimson collar. "Should we shoot?"

"No!" Orso struggled to put some authority into his voice. "No one shoots! I won't kill my own people. No more...of my own people," he added lamely, memories of the mass graves at Stoffenbeck floating up unbidden.

Lord Chancellor Gorodets drew himself up to his full height. Not a very impressive height, but Orso appreciated the effort. "Every man here would die for you, Your Majesty."

Certainly there were plenty of square jaws firmly set on the palace battlements. Knights of the Body and Knights Herald, the elite of the elite. But one could discern a stiffening undercurrent of doubt behind the heroic façade. Laying down one's life for one's king sounds very fine in principle, but when it comes to actually doing it, and one realises one has just the single life to give, enthusiasm understandably wanes.

"I'd rather they didn't have to," said Orso. "Besides, there are plenty of ladies about the palace, too." He glanced at Hildi, doing her very best to look fearless, and forced out a grin. "It would be most ungallant to ask them to sacrifice themselves. Further violence will achieve nothing anyway." He thought again of the charming stretch of countryside he had transformed into a mass grave and shook himself. "I'm not sure it ever does."

"You must not despair, Your Majesty!" Lord Hoff wrung his hands. "Thirty years ago, when your father was newly crowned, the city fell to the Gurkish."

"A far more fearsome enemy than this rabble!" croaked Lord Marshal Rucksted, whose appearance had degraded far past artfully rugged and into the realm of total disarray.

"*Eaters*, Your Majesty! Inside the Agriont. Inside the very *palace*."

"I remember my father telling me the story," said Orso. He remembered his mother looking enormously bored during it, too.

"He never gave up!" Rucksted slapped fist into palm. "The Gurkish were driven out! The Eaters vanquished! We can still—"

"The Gurkish were driven out by my grandfather, Grand Duke Orso, and by Lord Marshal West and his loyal troops, freshly embarked from Angland." Orso raised one brow. "My grandfather was killed long ago by the Serpent of Talins, the Anglanders have rebelled against us already,

46

and Lord Marshal Forest is retreating eastwards, hard-pressed, with the few loyal troops that remain. We beat the Gurkish, but..." Orso waved a helpless hand towards the crowds beyond the wall. "How can the Union beat itself?"

Hoff stared about, mouth open, as if searching for a counterargument. Orso patted his fur-trimmed arm. He had never really liked the man, but he felt sorry for him now. He, after all, loved the monarchy more than anything. Orso had never much cared for it.

"As for the Eaters," he went on, "it was the First of the Magi who dealt with them, and he destroyed half the Agriont doing it. Bayaz is noticeable by his absence today. Even Master Sulfur appears to have pressing business elsewhere." Orso looked towards the House of the Maker, rising stark and black and decidedly unhelpful beyond the Agriont's walls. "I fear the age of wizards is truly over. And one does wonder, after all, whether their price was ever really worth paying."

"Then..." Lord Chancellor Gorodets hesitantly licked his lips. "What?"

*Then what* had been the question ever since Orso re-entered his capital and learned that the Breakers were converging upon it in countless multitudes.

*Then what* indeed.

He wormed a finger into his collar. Tried to loosen it without actually undoing the hook at his neck. It didn't work, of course. That's what the bloody hook's there for.

He would have liked to ask Tunny for his opinion. No one had better instincts for self-preservation, after all. But Tunny had, of course, followed those very instincts and slipped away as the riots worsened. No tearful goodbyes, he had simply not been there one morning. King who? Never heard of him. Orso had to smother an inappropriate snort of laughter at the thought. The corporal had never pretended that his first loyalty was to anyone other than himself.

And the truth was, Orso knew very well what he had to do. It would just have been nice to hear someone try to talk him out of it.

"Bring out the king!" floating belligerently from below was the wisest counsel on offer.

Orso sighed. "Lord Hoff, I fear I must surrender myself to the Breakers."

"Your Majesty..." The lord chamberlain looked as pale as his own particularly horrified ghost. "You cannot be serious—"

"I can, and for once I am." He glanced at the mayhem beyond the walls. "The time has come for someone to nobly sacrifice themselves. In the absence of anyone better qualified...it will have to be me."

The remaining worthies of the Closed Council shuffled down the steps after him. Seven old men bent under the weight of their over-heavy robes, chains, responsibilities. They suddenly looked like a set of senile retirees being taken for a brief walk by their nurse.

"Bring out the king!" A shrill shriek, then a bass growl. "Bring out the king!"

"I'm bloody coming," muttered Orso.

The palace gardens were crowded with memories. He had played hide and seek among those statues with his sisters. Playful little Carlot and serious little Cathil. Over there his father had taught him how to grip a steel. Over there his mother had taught him how to express intense displeasure while still smiling. They had never been the happiest of families but, by the Fates, he missed them now he was the only one left.

"Hildi," he said, leaning towards her, "when the gates open, I need you to vanish."

That sharp look of hers was exactly the same as when he first met her, ten years old and tough as nails. "Thought you said the age of wizards was over?"

He smiled. Good to see she still wasn't letting him get away with a thing. "I mean smear some dirt on those freckles, pull that cap down to your eyes and melt into the crowd. You used to clean floors in a whorehouse, you can fit in with this lot."

"I'm not leaving you."

"Of course not! You're making a tactical withdrawal. If I come through this, I'll be a prisoner. I'm going to need someone loyal to help me escape. Bake lockpicks into a cake or something."

"I'm not much of a baker."

"But I bet you know how to find one."

"I guess." And she wiped her cheek on the back of her hand. He wondered whether she knew he was lying. Probably. Only the most committed optimist could imagine he would live out the hour, and neither of them qualified. "You still owe me money," she grunted.

"I'll have to pay you back later," said Orso, giving her shoulder a parting pat. "Left my purse inside."

If he lingered any longer he might think better of the whole thing, and right now they all needed to see some kingly composure. This would likely be his last chance to show any, after all. It would be a shame to waste it. So he straightened his jacket and crunched on across the gravel paths, so perfectly raked you would think no one had ever stepped on them before. Nice to see that standards were still being maintained. He felt strangely calm, now. As he had in Stoffenbeck, when the cannon-stones were raining down around him.

The shouts outside the gate had resolved into a kind of chant. "Bring… out…the king! Bring…out…the king!" The rhythm was marked with crashes of metal, with screams and laughter, with a stomping of boots, so many and so hard they seemed to make the ground shake. "Bring… out…the king!"

He wondered if there had been some choice he made, or didn't. Some way to avoid this. If there had, it had passed without his even noticing. Probably he had been worrying about his mother, or the hook at his collar, or what people thought of him. He wished he had been a touch more purposeful. But people are what they are.

He puffed out his cheeks. "Open the gates, please, Colonel Gorst."

Gorst only stared.

"I understand," said Orso gently. "And I release you from any and all oaths. You are no longer my First Guard."

Gorst's eyes had a strangely lost expression. "What am I, then?"

"I suppose…that's up to you." In the last few moments before they were torn to pieces by the mob, anyway. "It's time."

Gorst swallowed, then turned and screeched, "Open the gates!" However often you heard that voice, you never quite got used to it.

The bars were lifted, the bolts were pulled and a slit of light showed between the great doors. The chanting fell silent as they swung open to reveal a row of staring faces. People stumbled, off balance, at the pressure from those behind. Orso faced them alone, head held high. King's circlet on his brow. Jewelled sword at his side. Cloak stitched with the golden sun of the Union about his shoulders. A vision of majesty.

The rioters' weapons drooped as he strode towards them. A couple went so far as to slip them behind their backs, as though vaguely embarrassed by their presence. In eerie silence Orso walked forward, his heart thudding but his face kept carefully nonchalant, until he stood in the very archway. Close enough that if he, and they, had reached out, their fingers might have touched.

"Well?" he said, firmly and plainly. A little sternly, even. The voice of a disappointed father. A tone his own father had often been called on to use. "Here I am." His eyes came to rest on an elderly woman in a patched dress and stained apron, sleeves rolled up even in the cold to show heavy pink forearms. "Might I ask your business, madam?"

She snapped her open mouth shut and eased back, saying nothing.

Orso raised one brow at a balding man with a faceful of broken veins and an old hatchet. "Might I enquire as to your purpose, sir?"

He glanced left and right, and his lower lip wobbled, and perhaps the faintest croak emerged from his grizzled throat, but no more.

Orso took a step forwards and the crowd shuffled away. Once, at a meeting of the Solar Society Savine had persuaded him to attend, he had seen iron filings moved by magnetic repulsion. The effect was similar.

That tension in his throat was only getting worse. He worked his shoulders, suddenly annoyed at, of all things, the delay. "Come, come, let's get to it!"

But rather than falling on him like hungry wolves, the silent mob parted, revealing a man in a simple, dark suit of clothes. A hairless man, his face hideously burned, and at his side a hard-looking woman with a hard-looking frown.

Orso could only stare in amazement. "Arch Lector Pike?" he whispered.

"I think we should consider this my formal resignation, Your Majesty. Though you see that, in truth, I have never been your servant."

Pike was no captive of the crowd. By the way they treated him, he had their respect. Their obedience, even. By the Fates, he was their *leader*. The realisation was almost a comfort. It seemed plain now that there was nothing he could have done. There had been a traitor beside him all along.

"You're the Weaver?" whispered Orso.

"I have used the name at times."

"I never had an inkling." Orso raised a brow at Teufel. "Did you have an inkling? You always struck me as the woman with all the inklings, if there's ever been one."

Teufel's eyes slid to Pike. "No," she said, simply. Her feelings on the whole business were, as ever, impossible to judge.

"Well. I surrender the palace, I suppose. I ask that you show mercy to my guards and retainers. They have only tried to serve me."

"There has been enough bloodshed," said Pike, but added rather ominously, "for today."

There was a pause. Faint cheering was still coming from the direction of the Square of Marshals. Angrier noises from the direction of the House of Questions. But no one appeared to be hacking him to pieces on the spot.

"So…" Orso rather awkwardly cleared his throat. "What happens now?"

"The people will decide," said Pike.

Orso glanced about him. At the people. "Really?" He gave a puzzled smile. "Are they equipped for that?"

# All the Cards

A wind blew through the tall windows of Skarling's Hall, chilly with mist from the river. It shook the trees across the valley, made the hanging over the great fireplace, stitched with the design of the Long Eye, flap and rustle. Rikke drew her cloak tight around her, and huddled into her hood, and watched the grey water churning, far below, and thought about what had to be done.

You have to be hard to sit in Skarling's Chair. Have to be. Whether you want to be or not.

"Thinking o' jumping?" asked Isern.

"It's where the Bloody-Nine fell. Or so I hear."

"So what's the lesson? Folk who scramble to power up a hill of corpses will always take the long drop down?"

Rikke peered down that long drop, then took a cautious step away from the window. "Not sure I like that lesson."

Isern grinned, tongue wedged into the hole in her teeth. "If you only listen to lessons you like you'll learn nothing. Nice fur you got there."

"Ain't it?" And Rikke rubbed her hand against it, fine and white and so very soft, stitched onto that red cloth Savine dan Brock gave her, to make a cloak fit for a queen of legend. "A gift from the people of Carleon."

"Warming to you, are they?"

"I've always been very lovable."

"Specially with a few hundred armed men at your command."

"I find the better armed they are the more lovable I get. Reckon the townsfolk are grateful I haven't burned the city yet. Seems mercy can work after all."

"No doubt it has its season," said Isern. "And no doubt folk have a yen for it, after Stour's dark moods and mean spirit. But don't get cocky, girl. Gratitude is like spring blooms, fine-smelling but short-lived. I'd keep a

51

torch burning, d'you see, somewhere it brings to mind cities aflame. Make sure they stay grateful."

"Maybe they'll get you a fur, too."

"I've no use for one." Isern gave a haughty sniff and whipped a shred of her ragged shawl over one shoulder. "Perfection cannot be improved upon."

One of the great doors clattered open and Corleth burst in, got the haft of the axe at her belt tangled with her knees and near fell over, took a couple more slapping steps then stood, hands on her thighs, panting for breath.

"Interesting." Isern pointed a tattooed finger at her. "This woman is usually quite calm in her manner."

Corleth waved towards the door. "They're coming!"

"Who's coming?" asked Isern.

"All of 'em."

Rikke could hear the commotion now. A crowd of gabbling voices, happy and angry at once. The warrior's favourite mood. She shoved her hood back and scrubbed some life into her flattened hair with her fingernails, heart suddenly pounding. "They've got him?"

Corleth nodded. "They've got him."

Someone sent the other door shuddering open with a kick and a pack of warriors tramped into Skarling's Hall, laughing and jostling and glowing with triumph. Shivers led the way, with a bottle of spirits that'd seen some action, and Jonas Clover, with a shifty lad and a blank-faced woman at his back. The Nail and some big bearded bastard were dragging a filthy, half-naked prisoner by his arms, head hanging and legs trailing limp behind him.

"By the dead," muttered Rikke. The last time she'd seen the King of the Northmen outside of her dreams of vengeance had been at her father's funeral, sleek as a snake and every bit as vicious. "Time has not been kind to him."

"Time's kind to no one," said Shivers, pressing the bottle into her limp hand.

They flung him down in front of the dais Skarling's Chair was set on. So Rikke stood over him. Stood in judgement, where he'd stood over so many others, the stones he lay on stained with the blood he'd ordered spilled.

"Welcome back to your throne room, Great Wolf," she said, and took a long pull at the bottle, and winced as it burned right down her gullet, while her warriors strove manfully to out-gloat each other.

Stour tried to push himself up, arms trembling, making a blubbing whimper all the way. Then Hardbread stepped up and kicked him in the guts, and knocked him flat again.

"Grovel, you fucker!" he spat. Harsher than Rikke was used to from her father's old white-haired War Chief, but men's mercy often runs out the very moment they're called upon to use it.

"What's wrong with his legs?" she asked.

"Didn't want him running off." Shivers shrugged. "Slit the tendons behind his knees."

Isern stuck her bottom lip out approvingly. "That'll do it. Here's where cocky gets you." And she gave Rikke a meaningful glance from under her brows.

Stour managed to get as far as his knees this time but looking like he might fall any moment. Rikke hardly knew him, his nose was so broke and his mouth so bloated and his cheeks so scabbed and swollen. Kept licking at his bloody top lip with this little slurp. He stared about like he didn't recognise the place, one of his eyes near swollen shut and the other with a great red stain on the white. Rikke found she was rubbing gently at her own blind eye and had to force her hand away from it.

"You took Carleon," croaked Stour. Even his voice sounded broken.

Gloating felt like something of an effort, but folk were expecting it. "Aye, well," said Rikke, "Leo's little jaunt to the Union seemed like more of a boy's trip. Thought I'd invite King Orso to join you while I stayed here. Make better use o' my time. Got me a new chair out of it." Her warriors laughed, but Stour was in no state to appreciate a joke.

"My father alive?" he whispered.

"For now," said Isern. "Hiding away in the High Valleys."

Stour hung his head. "He'd give anything... to get me back." Something dripped on the floor. Bastard was crying. To suffer bravely takes practice, and he'd never had any. "I'm the future o' the North," he mumbled, like even he could hardly believe it might ever have been true. No matter how much pride a man has, it don't take much, in the end, to beat it all out of him. To make him want nothing but for the beating to stop. "Please."

Rikke had a real bruiser of a speech all worked out, about the wrongs he'd done the North and the price he'd have to pay and how we all build our own gallows and he was about to hang from his and blah, blah, fucking blah. She'd been polishing it up for days like a champion might his feast-day helmet. But she felt no joy in crowing over such a broken thing as this. She took another pull on the bottle and nearly gagged on it.

"Please." Stour's scabbed fingers crept across the floor and plucked at the gold-embroidered hem of her new cloak. "Please."

By the dead, he stank. When he fought Leo in the Circle she'd felt her hatred for him had no bottom. Now the well ran suddenly dry and all she had left was disgust for the whole business. But she knew what the lads wanted to see. You have to make of your heart a stone, if you want to sit in Skarling's Chair.

"You dare *touch* me?" she barked and kicked him in the face. Since he was on his knees she caught him right under the jaw, snapped his head up and sent him sprawling over backwards.

"I'm sorry," he whispered, curling up on his side, broken hand trembling over his bloody face. "Don't hurt me."

This hadn't been the plan. In the plan he'd stood up, for one thing, and sneered and spat insults, and she'd burned bright with righteous fury and cut him down with the cleverest stuff you ever heard. But how can you cut down what already can't stand?

She curled her lip and looked over at the Nail. "You want to put him in the cage?"

"The one he put my father in?"

"Have I got another?"

He grinned, and a fine grin he had. She was quite pleased to have it aimed at her. Then he caught Stour by the hair and dragged him whimpering over towards the cage, his ruined legs flopping after.

"Not killing him?" asked Clover, the slightest frown about his grey-flecked brows. "He comes through this alive, I doubt he'll forgive."

"Not really the forgiving sort," said Isern, pulling out a lump of chagga and starting to cut a little piece off.

"Black Calder even less so." Clover watched the Nail manhandling Stour across the floor. "Just can't see any future where this bastard breathing is a good thing for us."

"Don't worry about seeing the future." Rikke nodded towards the sign of the Long Eye and tapped at the runes that matched it on her own face. "That's my business." And she plucked the chagga out of Isern's fingers 'fore it got to her mouth and stuck it behind her own lip. "I can trust you, can't I, Clover? My father once said that if he ever needed a dependable man...it wouldn't be you."

"Your father was a straight edge and a fine judge of character." Clover gave a little shrug. "In my humble opinion, it'd be a mistake to trust anyone too much."

"Specially someone already betrayed one master," said Isern, cutting another little piece of chagga from the lump and rolling it into a pellet.

"Don't be too generous to me, Isern-i-Phail, I've betrayed about five

54

o' the bastards." And Clover nabbed the pellet from Isern's fingers with surprising dexterity and squinted to the rafters as he stuck it behind his lip, as though bringing to mind the full catalogue of his faithlessness was quite the challenge. "There was Bethod, and Glama Golden, and Cairm Ironhead, and I reckon I betrayed Black Calder at the same time as I betrayed his son. Wouldn't be surprised if there's one or two I've forgotten about besides." And he patted thoughtfully at his belly. "I don't think I flatter myself to say I've betrayed some o' the greatest names in the North. But the thing they had in common?"

"Do tell," said Rikke, offering him the bottle.

"They made it stupid for me not to betray 'em. I'm hoping you'll be craftier." And he slid something from an inside pocket. A golden chain of weighty links, its dangling diamond sparkling in the light from the tall windows. The one she'd seen Scale Ironhand wear at the duel. The one she'd seen Stour Nightfall wear at her father's funeral. The chain Bethod had forged, before she was born, when he forced the North together with fire and sword. "Guess this should come to you now."

"You keep it," said Rikke.

Clover's brows shot up. "Me?"

Isern's shot up, too. "Him?"

"Bethod wore it, and Scale, and Stour. Look how things turned out for them. Look how they turned out for the North. Don't think it'll suit me." Rikke hooked a thumb into her necklace of green stones and dragged them gently around her neck. "Reckon we've had enough kings for now."

Clover held up the chain, frowning at the dangling diamond. "It'll suit me even worse."

"Melt it down for coins, then. Set the stone in your eating knife. Consider it a fair price for bringing me its owner."

"Then I will." Clover tucked the chain back into his pocket. "You are as wise as you are generous, Chief."

"I wouldn't count too much on either one," she said, narrowing her eyes. "What happened over in the Union?"

"I didn't hang around for the outcome." Clover took a swig from the bottle, daintily wiped the neck, then handed it to Isern. "There was quite the battle going on and I do my best to avoid 'em. From what I could tell, Orso won."

Rikke found she was rather pleased about that. And not only 'cause she'd betrayed the other side and victory for the Young Lion could've put her in quite the awkward spot. Never took much to make her thoughts wander back to the palace in Adua, morning sun streaming through the windows. Time had softened the smashing headache she'd been nursing. She remembered Orso coming through the door, grin on his face, tray in his hand. *I brought you an egg.* He hadn't struck her as a winner of battles, it had to be said. But then neither had she, and here she was with Skarling's Hall for her living room.

There was a clang as the Nail flung the cage door shut on Stour and left him huddled, filthy back pressed against the bars and one hand dangling between them. "Looks like we hold all the cards."

"You've still got to play 'em right," said Clover, frowning over at the remnants of the Great Wolf.

"Carleon's ours," said Shivers.

"And half the North besides," crowed Hardbread, "and Nightfall's men are trickling back wounded and ruined and Black Calder hasn't much left to fight with, I reckon."

"We should hit him now," said the Nail. "Hit him hard."

"Calder's weak!" growled the big man with all the beard.

"Calder's canny," said Isern. "No doubt he'll have spies here."

Stour was one kind of enemy. He'd come right at you. Black Calder was another. "Doubt he's halfway as weak as he seems," said Rikke. "He's still got friends, and he'll already be gathering 'em."

"And the year's getting late," said Shivers, nodding towards the white sky outside the windows.

"We need to bring him to us." Rikke dropped into Skarling's Chair and slung her leg over one of the arms, trying to look right at home, though the dead knew there was no getting comfortable in that bloody thing. "Fight him on the ground we choose at the time we choose."

"How you figuring to do that?" asked Hardbread.

"I already know how." Rikke put a fingertip to her tattooed cheek and gave Shivers a big wink with her Long Eye. "I've seen it."

No one laughed at that these days. No one mocked and no one disagreed. There was a respectful murmur at it, in fact. Fearful glances and nervous shiftings from one foot to another. These Named Men, killers all, standing in awe of Skinny Rikke and her Long Eye. A year ago she'd hidden from Stour Nightfall in a freezing stream. Now she had him locked in his own cage. She who used to have fits and shit herself in the streets of Uffrith had stolen half the North. Was enough to make her burst out laughing, almost. But that would've spoiled the mood.

"Patience," she said, softly, tapping at the peeled paint on the arm of Skarling's Chair with her fingernail. "We need to chew what we've bit before we bite off more. While you boys were having fun on the way from Uffrith there's been work to do up here."

"I'm always ready to work," said Shivers.

"We've been laying in food for the winter, and I've a sense folk in the next valley are holding out on us. Might be..." She glanced sideways at Isern. "I've been too soft-hearted with 'em. Need you to take some stonier hearts up there."

The curved reflection of the tall windows gleamed in Shivers' metal eye. "A warning or a wounding?"

She wanted to say warning. But they all were watching. Watching and judging. And before this set of bastards she couldn't afford to look too forgiving. "You be the judge. And take Hardbread with you, since he's in such a bloodthirsty mood."

"Right y'are." And Shivers beckoned Hardbread and a few others after him as he headed for the door.

"Clover?"

"Rikke?"

"Take your people up to the Redwater Valley. Calder's boys've been busy over there. Burned a few farms. Make it clear this side of the river's mine."

"Right back into the cold." Clover aimed a wistful sigh at the fire. "We'd be honoured, wouldn't we, Sholla?"

The blank-faced girl looked blank as ever. "Inexpressibly."

Rikke beckoned Corleth over as Clover and his people tramped out. "Get some water boiled and clean that bastard in the cage, eh?"

"Kindness?" she asked.

"On my nose. He fucking stinks."

"I still reckon the moon would smile upon him face down in the mud." Isern prodded at the bars with one blue finger, making the cage turn gently, the Great Wolf limp as a heap of filthy rags inside. "Remember when he chased us through the woods, all cold and hungry and gnat-nibbled? Remember how bitter your feelings then?"

"I'm not forgetting," said Rikke.

"He said he'd send your guts to your father in a box. Break what they love, he said."

"I'm not forgetting. But we might yet find a use for him."

"I'll admit he makes a fine adornment. Caged in the very cage he had forged, d'you see. Brought to naught in the very room where his hero the Bloody-Nine was brought to naught." She gave a little chuckle. "My da would've laughed long at that one." And she patted Rikke on her fur-clad shoulder as she passed and pushed the near-empty bottle into her hand.

"You're always saying your da was an arsehole."

"Most yawning arsehole in the whole Circle of the World." She wagged that blue finger. "But he saw to the chilly heart o' things, more often than not." And she swaggered to the doorway, gave a great showy stretch and spat into the hall. "Don't get cocky, now." She pulled the doors shut and the latch dropped with an echoing clatter, leaving Rikke alone with the ex-King of the Northmen and the Nail, his pale eyes on her.

"Still say we should hit Black Calder while the hitting's good," he said.

"You would. You like hitting things."

"You don't?"

"Not for its own sake. I want to hit once, and that so hard I never have to hit again."

"Thought your father swore to see Black Calder back to the mud?"

"So they say, but my father didn't think much o' vengeance, and since he's dead into the bargain I feel sure he can wait a spell."

The Nail gave a little grin, tip of his tongue stuck between his teeth. "You're a clever one, ain't you?"

"I do my humble best." And Rikke realised she was threading her chain of emeralds through her fingers, feeling the cool stones tickle at the webs between them.

She gave the Nail a considering look. You could not have called him pretty, slouched long and loose against the wall with his thumbs in his belt and his elbows stuck out and his chin stuck forward. But then Rikke doubted pretty was the first word anyone would've picked for her these days. And there was something about him. All calm, and confident, and in no hurry. Like he was happy in his own skin, the very thing she'd never been. We're always drawn to our opposites. Drawn to them and scared by them at once. And where's the fun in someone who don't scare you just a touch?

She got up and walked over, taking one more swallow from the bottle. Tasted worse than ever, mixed with chagga bitterness, but it wasn't burning any more. Just glowing nicely, like the embers in the great fireplace.

"What do your friends call you?" asked Rikke, handing him the bottle.

He frowned at the little dribble in the bottom, more spit than spirits. "The Nail."

"Aye, but folk who are close."

He took a swig of his own, watching her all the way. "Don't have anyone that close. Not now my da's dead."

"What did he call you?"

A pause. "The Nail."

"Can I borrow that cloak o' yours?"

He raised those pale blond brows, and undid the buckle, and tossed it over to her. She wandered to the corner of the hall, taking her time. Felt tense in there, like there was something about to happen, and she enjoyed it. She reckoned she'd earned just a streak of cockiness, whatever Isern said. She went up on her tiptoes to hang the cloak over Stour's cage.

"Don't really want him looking." And she bent down and pulled one of her boots off, left it lying. Kicked the other off into the corner, and it bounced from the wall and fell on its side.

The Nail frowned over at it. "Why you taking your boots off?"

She undid her belt buckle. "'Cause I can't get my trousers off over 'em."

That was when she realised, skirts have many downsides but you can step right out of the bastards. Or pull 'em up in a pinch. But there's no slick way out of trousers. She got 'em down past her knees all right, then nearly fell over pulling her right foot free, and had to hop along dragging the other leg off.

Not quite the sultry swagger she'd planned. Maybe she'd got too cocky after all. But there was nothing for it now but to see it through. She wriggled into Skarling's Chair, trying to arrange her fine new cloak in a manner that preserved the delicate balance between too much mystery and not enough.

The Nail considered this performance, then Stour's covered cage, then scratched the back of his head. "Fair to say the afternoon has took an unexpected turn."

A brief silence. Outside, the river thundered. Bad idea, this. One of her worst. She wondered where her trousers ended up, and how far the shameful shuffle would be to squirm back into 'em so she could pretend it never happened. "Not planning on turning me down, are you? 'Cause that'd be quite an embarrassment."

"Fuck, no." And he cracked out a grin. "Just thought I'd fix the scene in my mind, while I've got the chance." He tapped the side of his head with the bottle. "It's a good one." Then he sucked the last drops from it and walked over, undoing his sword-belt on the way and kicking it off. Which was a hell of a relief, 'cause apart from anything else the chill breeze through the window was spreading gooseflesh up her thighs.

"It don't bother you?" He planted one big boot between her bare feet, then glanced over towards the cage in the corner, creaking slightly, with his cloak over it. "Knowing he's under there?"

"It's half the point. He once said he'd see me fucked by dogs."

The Nail planted his other boot beside the first. "That was rude."

"Now he'll learn I decide who gets fucked and how."

"So...you're using me to teach him a lesson?"

She turned her head and spat out the chagga pellet. "I guess."

He gave a little giggle. "Grand." And he tossed the empty bottle out of the window, leaned down over the chair, a hand on each arm, and kissed her on the mouth. A delicate, polite little kiss, it was, catching her top lip between both of his, and then her bottom lip. So delicate and polite she almost laughed.

Kissing's a simple thing in a way, but everyone's got their own style at it, like talking, like walking, like fighting, like writing. He kept on kissing her, one lip, then the other, and she had to stretch up to kiss him back, to make the kisses a little deeper, to get the point of her tongue involved, and now she didn't feel like laughing any more, not at all. She slid her hands along the scarred arms of Skarling's Chair till they slid onto his, till she was gripping his wrists, till his knees were rubbing against the insides of her bare thighs, just gently, like there was nothing much in it, but to her mind there was quite a lot in it, actually.

He had his eyes open all the time, looking at her, and she had hers open all the time, looking at him—well, the one that worked—and that felt dangerous, somehow, like each little kiss was a risk. She craned up to kiss him harder but he moved his face away so she couldn't quite get there, and she found she'd made an excited little gasp and he'd made a satisfied little grunt and the breath between them was hot and smelled of spirits. Good idea, this. One of her best.

She'd got his belt undone with one hand, rather pleased about her nimble fingers, and now she slipped them inside and dug around till she brought his cock out, halfway hard and definitely going in the right direction. She wouldn't say she was drunk but she was on the road there, rubbing at him with one hand, fingers of the other around the back of his neck, scratching at his red-blond beard with her thumbnail.

"I'm going to need your help with something," she whispered.

"Not sure...how I can show more willing—"

"Not that. Well, yes, that. But something else, too. Doubt you'll like it."

"You pick a hell—ah—of a time to ask for—ah—a favour," he whispered, nudging at her lips with his.

"They say you should always bargain from a position of strength."

"That so?"

Her turn to gasp as he pushed his hands under her arse, knelt down and pulled her towards him so her head slid down the chair back and her back slid down the chair seat and she was left lying half on it and half off it, her bare toes on the cold stone and her knees spread around his head and her hips pushed up towards him, the warmth of the fire on the side of her bare leg and the cold breeze from the window tickling her bare belly. She squirmed this way and that, couldn't find anything close to comfortable among the unforgiving angles. You have to be hard, after all, to sit in Skarling's Chair. Goes double for fucking in it.

He grinned up at her over her bush and she grinned back.

"Still need to get me a cushion," she muttered.

# Questions

"Can you hear me in there?" bellowed Vick, at the top of her lungs. Felt like all she'd done since the People's Army arrived in Adua was shout. Her throat was raw from it. In the new Union, you got nothing done talking quietly.

A faint voice echoed from beyond the monstrous, studded doors in the towering, spike-topped wall of that fortress of a bank. "I can hear you."

"I'm Inquisitor—" She ground her teeth. "I'm Chief Inspector Teufel! I have a warrant signed by Commissioner Pike to search any and all branches of the Banking House of Valint and Balk." She held the document high, though how the hell anyone was supposed to tell whether it was genuine or not, she'd no idea. Everything had to be printed now, but they'd smashed all the good presses the day the Agriont fell so the warrant was all smudged, the seal was a blob and the signature a blur. "It'd be a lot easier to have this conversation if you opened the *door*!" And her voice died away entirely on the last word.

"I don't have the authority to open the door, Inspector."

A curious crowd was gathering in front of the bank. These days, crowds built up at the slightest provocation. Risinau insisted they be allowed to. They had to promote the national conversation, he said. They had to politicise the masses, he said. Risinau said a lot, but as far as Vick could tell none of it ever *meant* anything. The masses were far too politicised for her taste already.

"Who does have the authority?" she barked. A question people were often asking, in the new Union.

She had to strain to hear the reply. "The manager."

"So where's he?"

A pause. "Not here."

Vick was out of patience. She'd a lot less patience than she used to, one way or another. "Get the cannon," she snapped.

There was an excited murmur from the onlookers as the Practicals gathered around the wagon. They were calling them Constables now, but you could still see the tan lines on their faces where their masks used to sit. Vick planted her hands on her hips and tapped one finger impatiently as she watched them strain at the spokes of its wheels, spit flying from their clenched teeth as it ground ever so slowly over the cobbles. When she wasn't shouting, she was tapping her finger impatiently.

Tallow watched the whole business while blowing into his cupped hands with his usual air of hangdog resignation. "So...we're not the Inquisition any more?"

She was damn glad he was alive but she didn't let a trace of it show. Only growled back as impatiently as ever. "Commissioner Pike felt the name gave the wrong signals."

"Six centuries of torture, exile and hangings, you mean?"

"I daresay. But someone still needs to keep folk in line." One of the Constables slipped and fell, the wagon rocking back alarmingly. "Even if the line's turned blurry as hell."

"Who better'n the folk who used to do it, I guess?"

"You can't say we don't have the relevant experience."

"So...the same people, doing the same job, but called something else?"

"You may have hit closer to the essence of the Great Change than Chairman Risinau has in a hundred hours of speeches. Welcome to the new Union and its People's Inspectorate, headquarters at the House of Truth. It's the big building in the Agriont with the little windows, in case you were wondering."

"They're not asking questions there any more?"

"Oh, they're asking questions."

"Just...nicely?"

"I doubt it."

"But truth is more important than it used to be?"

"Time will tell." Though Vick had her doubts about that, too.

"I hear the People's Army let out all the prisoners."

"Some of whom I worked hard to put in there. Most of whom weren't even Breakers. Thieves, smugglers, more than one murderer and an idiot who liked to set fires. Not to mention the Young Lion and his co-conspirators. You're all free, Brothers! Did they let your sister out?"

"They did."

"Good." She regretted saying it right away. New Union or old, letting a feeling show was like pointing out a chink in your armour. An invitation to stick the knife in. She frowned sideways at Tallow. With his sister

63

released, he'd no real reason to work with her. Still less to be loyal to her. "You're still here, though, I notice."

"I'm standing with the winners." He gave her a weak grin. "And where else would I go?"

"Fair point." What with all the folk who'd flooded into Adua with the People's Armies, and the mills and manufactories that were shut up or broken down, and the shambles on the roads, canals and docks, work was hard to come by and prices were higher than ever. And who knew where anyone's loyalties sat these days? Old friends were set at odds and old enemies made allies. In the new Union, everything was ripped up and spun around, and who was to say it wouldn't be ripped up fresh tomorrow?

"You got a uniform, at least," said Tallow.

Vick frowned down at herself. Bloody thing was too tight under the armpits and the boots pinched. "Seems black never goes out of fashion."

"Looks good on you. Very fearsome."

"I guess this has all been worthwhile, then." It was hard to point out much else the Great Change had achieved so far. No doubt some folk had gained and some folk lost, but that better world she'd let herself hope was coming felt as far away as ever.

The Constables had finally heaved the wagon into position, maw of the cannon pointing at the bank's doors. She leaned towards their leader, a big-shouldered bastard so acne-scarred he'd probably looked less frightening when they still wore masks. "This bloody thing loaded?"

"I've got shot," he said, "but there's no powder to be had."

All shot and no powder summed it right up. She'd just have to blow the door down with lies, like usual. "Get the match-cord lit at least, make it look like *we* think the damn thing works." She cleared her sore throat and turned back to the bank. "Can you hear me in there?"

"I can hear you."

"Can you see me?"

A pause. A tiny slot slid open in one of the doors. "I can see you," came considerably louder from the opening.

Vick ground her teeth again. They were going to be down to the gums by the time this door was open. "Then why didn't you open the bloody slot before?"

No answer.

"You see we've got a cannon pointed at you."

No answer.

"I'll take that as a yes." There was a puff of sparks as one of the

64

Constables finally got the match-cord to splutter into life, and some of their growing audience took nervous steps away. "I'm going to count down from ten. If this door isn't open when I get to nothing, I'm going to open it the hard way."

No answer, but she thought she saw a pair of eyes behind the slot blink.

"Anything within twenty strides of that door'll get opened the hard way, too."

"What do you mean?"

"*You*," said Vick. "You'll be open. You'll all be wide fucking open."

"Perhaps we could—"

"Ten."

There was a clattering of keys, a rattling of bolts, one half of the double doors opened and a balding head stuck around it into the chill autumn air. "We surrender," it said.

Vick looked over at the lead Constable. Something she would rather have done as little as possible. "Well, then?"

"Oh. Right." And he pulled out his stick and stomped forwards, beckoning the others after him.

"Why's the Commissioner so interested in banks, anyway?" muttered Tallow. "Why not, I don't know, the armouries, or the barracks, or the granaries?"

"Daresay we'll get to those."

"But why banks *first?*"

When Arch Lector Glokta was in charge, Vick had found it helped not to waste too much thought on the whys. She guessed the same applied to Commissioner Pike. Probably it applied double. So she just shrugged.

"Better raiding bankers than Breakers, I guess," said Tallow.

"Is it?"

"On the right side of history, maybe."

Vick snorted. "The thing about history is you don't know what the right side is till long afterwards, and by then it hardly matters."

"That's the sort o' thing you hear from folk who know they're on the wrong side."

Vick conceded the point with a weary grunt. "I daresay."

"Safe!" bellowed the Constable from inside and, with care, Vick stepped through the open front doors of the Adua headquarters of the Banking House of Valint and Balk.

The knot of employees inside hardly looked like a threat to the new Union. They looked like a set of very scared clerks with a cannon pointing at them. Vick picked out the best dressed. A balding man trying to hide behind the others.

"You're in charge?" she asked.

"Well..." He glanced about nervously, but no one fell over themselves to take responsibility. "I suppose I am the longest serving member of staff on site. I am Ario Matterno, senior over-clerk for loans—"

"Styrian?"

"Is that..." he swallowed. "A problem?"

"Not for me." Vick was keenly aware that most of the considerable harm done to her in her life had been by her own countrymen, but foreigners were not popular with the mobs. A few days before, a dozen Gurkish immigrants had been burned as spies in the Three Farms. Being too dark or too fair or too rich or too poor or too mad or too sane was a bad idea in the new Union. Freedom did not seem to have made anyone any less angry. But then the price of bread kept going up, and Chairman Risinau's oratory wasn't edible.

"The vault's this way?" Vick started walking. Matterno managed to keep pace with her while hurrying along sideways, rubbing his hands. "Inquisitor—"

"Inspector," corrected Tallow.

"Sorry, yes, so many changes to keep track of...are you really *sure* you want to do this?"

"It's not a question of what I *want* to do." Vick wasn't sure it had ever in her life been a question of that. "Commissioner Pike has ordered every branch of Valint and Balk shut down. At once."

The man looked baffled. As though Commissioner Pike had ordered water to flow upwards. "But...it's Valint and Balk. You can't do that."

"You didn't see the cannon?"

He tried to explain it again. "The Banking House is owed money everywhere. *Everywhere.* So many, *many* friends, here in the Union and abroad. It would be very unwise...it would be utter *madness*—"

"Have you been outside lately? Wisdom is not at a premium, madness is the fashion, the balance sheets are all torn up and the friends that were assets have become liabilities." Vick kept walking. "Threats for tomorrow don't cut very deep when today is so damn threatening. You might want to keep 'em to yourself."

It felt cold in the banking hall. Colder than outside, almost. Vick had to resist the urge to put her feet down softly on account of the volley of echoes produced by every step. The place was high as a Gurkish temple, carved from dark marble and dark wood, gilt glittering in shafts of dusty

66

light from the high windows. There were little islands of expensive chairs where supplicants would wait to receive the bank's blessing, or to hear their schemes ripped to tatters, but no business was being done today. The only merchants in attendance were marble busts of history's richest men, frowning greedily at them from the past.

"Now *that* is a door," said Tallow.

It was the door to end all doors, taking up most of the far wall and towering over the room, an expanse of black iron with the weighty names *Valint and Balk* etched in gold in the centre. Down near the bottom was a brass wheel like the wheel of a ship, a tiny-looking lock to either side.

Tallow gazed up at it, open-mouthed. "I'm guessing that's the vault?"

"It'd be a fancy door for the kitchen." Vick waved some of the Constables out into the room and they began to drag drawers from desks, root through papers, throw things around in that slightly disinterested way they had.

"Shouldn't it be hidden?" asked Tallow. "Underground or something?"

"The whole point is that no one who comes in can miss it. They all have to imagine how much money sits behind a door as big as that. How much power." She nodded Matterno towards the brass wheel. "Open it."

The senior over-clerk for loans spoke in a very small voice. "I don't have the authority, Inspector."

Vick planted her hands on her hips again. "Don't make me wheel that bloody cannon in here."

"It's a two-foot thickness of Angland steel. You'll barely scratch it with a cannon."

Vick looked him right in the eye. "It's you I was going to point it at."

Matterno swallowed, and slipped a key from his pocket, and offered it out. A very long, thin, delicate key for such an immensity of door, wards so complex they looked like a tiny maze. "I only have one. You need the other."

"Don't tell me. The manager has it."

Ever so slowly, Matterno spread his palms. "I... think?"

"Arrest him," said Vick. "And the others. Seal this place up."

"But... Inspector!" Two Constables caught the disbelieving senior over-clerk for loans under the armpits and started manhandling him away. "It's Valint and Balk!"

"You can explain it to Commissioner Pike!" Vick called after him. "Get them all to the House of Questions."

"House of Truth," corrected Tallow.

67

"Whatever." She winced as she rubbed at her stiff hip. Damn thing always started niggling as the weather turned colder. "Lots of empty cells up there these days."

"Aye." Tallow gave a faraway sigh. "I suppose it's high time we filled 'em up again."

# Citizens

"The *deeper* question..." Risinau sank back, the ornate chair that was once Orso's creaking under his bulk, to consider the gilded dome above. "Is what *are* we now?"

Orso considered that one of the best questions of recent times. A few tiles were cracked, a few benches broken, and one of the glorious stained-glass windows had been smashed and badly boarded up so a chilly draft occasionally swept through the hall, but otherwise the Lords' Round was much as it had been. They called it the Commons' Round now, though. They'd turned the cushions over so the embroidered suns of the Union didn't show, and the unruly gathering who sat upon them was no longer the Open Council, but the Assembly of Representatives.

There had been votes in the districts of Adua, apparently. Votes from every Midderland-born man, no matter how mean and ignorant, resulting in a body of representatives, as far as Orso could tell, every bit as mean and ignorant as they were. Votes. He could only imagine his mother's reaction to that. The tyranny of the majority. Representatives would be elected in other cities of the Union in due course, but those benches were still empty while the Assembly argued over the rules. They argued even more than the Open Council had, if that was possible. They argued every point. They argued the order of the points. They argued the method of argument.

"What *are* we?" one of Risinau's cronies pronounced, with great emphasis. "Or... *what should we be?*" Everything was said with great emphasis. The most banal observations became profound revelations, tear-tracked protestations, chest-thumping declarations.

"A republic?"

"How?" Someone frowned towards Orso. He looked vaguely familiar. Impressive whiskers. "We still have a *king*."

"A regrettable state of affairs." Orso could not tell who had said that.

69

Probably everyone thought it. He had long been thinking it himself, after all. He was not at all sure why the Breakers had not done away with him on the day of the Great Change. Perhaps they could not quite shrug off some vestige of deference to the monarch. Perhaps they thought his presence might lend proceedings a patina of legitimacy. Perhaps they preferred him as a contemptible prop than a martyr to be avenged. More likely they feared to smash the past all in one go, and were holding him back for a spectacular finale.

Whatever the reasons, they had built an absurd little enclosure to contain the royal person, halfway between a theatre box and a dock for the accused, splattered in cheap gilt, already peeling. He felt like the ridiculous peacock some Southern ambassador had once given his mother. She had kept it in a silver cage as a curio for visitors. It had looked deeply unhappy, produced an astonishing quantity of dung and not lived very long.

It would have helped at least a little if all the old denizens of the Open Council had lost their places in the Great Change, but a smattering of Orso's worst enemies had managed to cling to their seats. Lord Isher had slithered from hiding, Lord Heugen had slipped out of prison and the Young Lion sat in the front row along with several other surviving aristocratic rebels. Those few noblemen who had stayed loyal to the Crown were languishing in cells beneath the House of Truth. The world was turned upside down, indeed. Traitors were patriots, turncoats were loyalists, corruption was purity and the truth a lie.

Aside from the reduced Lord Brock there were no delegates from Angland. Lady Finree was back in charge there, carefully considering her options. Starikland was not represented, either. Lord Governor Skald had denounced the Great Change and, if Orso knew his brother-in-law at all, would even now be wondering how he could twist it to his advantage. The only representatives from beyond the shores of Midderland were a few alarmed Aldermen of Westport, no doubt regretting their decision to remain inside the Union more with every passing day. Orso wondered absently if he might get a message via them to his mother and sister in Sipani. Just to let them know he was well. Reassuring lies had always been the glue that held his family together, after all.

"The Union *is* and has *always* been a monarchy," came Risinau's endlessly overemphasising voice. Chairman Risinau, he was calling himself. Appropriate, for a man forever sitting down. "We *must* acknowledge the past even as we shape the future. But we are a new *variety* of monarchy and must devise new terminology!" Nothing pleased him more than to tinker with terminology. The man was a positive manufactory of verbiage. "You might call it a *representative*, or perhaps a *constitutional* monarchy…"

Among the newly elected there were labourers, merchants, printers, lens-makers, clock-makers, candle-makers, even a couple of maids and a belligerent laundress, but also a disproportionate number of artists, poets and that most nebulous of designations: *intellectuals*. Risinau clearly considered himself to be artist, poet and intellectual combined, though in his labyrinthine speeches Orso perceived little artistry, only the cheapest kind of poetry and no intellect whatsoever.

"I have been considering a written constitution!" Whiskers, again, leaning over the parchments on the High Table, pen in inky hand. It finally came to Orso who he was: Spillion Sworbreck, that bloody writer in whose office he used to meet Savine. In spite of everything, the memory brought a rare smile to his face. "I was thinking something along the lines of…we consider these facts to be self-evident—"

There was instant opposition from among the great thinkers. "What? Nothing is self-evident!"

"Pretentious! Presumptuous!"

"Asking for trouble."

"Terrible first line."

There was the scrape of a nib crossing out. "Thorny, isn't it, once you start drafting? Not at all like fiction."

Judge delivered one of her explosive snorts of scorn. She was draped over a chair with one bare foot up on the High Table, its dirty sole directed at the Chairman, her lip permanently twisted and her eyes forever narrowed. Her followers, the Burners, had taken to dyeing parts of their clothes red. You could see a few of them on the benches. Red hats. Red sleeves. Red trouser legs. As if they had been dipped in blood. Perhaps they had.

"Let us skip over the first line for now."

"The first line? And already we're skipping over?"

"Don't writers always say you should write the first line last?"

"Just the sort of bloody rubbish writers would say…"

This was the way of it. Business was steered by Risinau's whims, or whoever could shout loudest. Halfway through discussing one thing they'd be dragged onto another. It was the most dispiriting display of mismanagement Orso had witnessed, indeed, since the last time he sat in this room, before the Great Change. He leaned sideways, holding out his goblet. "Don't suppose you could fill me up again, Hildi?"

The day the Agriont fell she had melted into the crowd as ordered, then melted straight back when he was not immediately torn to pieces. He had admonished her sternly for her disobedience, but in truth was pathetically grateful for this one undeserved shred of loyalty. They had confiscated her old cap—leading to a flood of swearing which had still not quite dried up—but otherwise allowed her to stay in post, wearing an absurd livery. This was typical of the new regime. Some things they furiously tore down. Others they let stand, even tearfully celebrated. All without apparent pattern or purpose.

"You sure?" she muttered through tight lips.

"Worried they'll take a dislike to my drinking? They took enough of a dislike to me already to overthrow the monarchy. They've given me wine. Bad wine, but still. Might as well make use of it."

His eyes met Corporal Tunny's for a moment, slumped upon a bench towards the back. It hurt Orso more than it should have, to see his old standard-bearer seated among his enemies. But one can hardly expect paid hangers-on to keep hanging on after the pay dries up, and it could not be denied that no one better represented the faithlessness, degradation and low character of the commons than Corporal Tunny.

Sworbreck droned on. "If we accept, just for the time being, temporarily and reversibly, that we *do* consider these facts to be self-evident..." There was an expectant pause. "Which facts should they be?"

"Ah." Risinau placed a finger on his lips and considered the dome once again. "Well, *that* would be the *deeper* question."

Orso sank into his chair with a groan, letting his gaze wander lazily along the front row. Only one man there met his eye. The Young Lion looked neither young nor particularly leonine any more, his face hollowed out and lined with pain, beard scattered with still-healing scars on the left side, one of them dragging his mouth into a permanent half-frown.

Orso raised his goblet in a silent toast. Why waste energy on hatred, after all? The world in which they had been rivals had dropped into oblivion beneath them like a sunken ship. They all were treading water to survive.

Leo sat there, in agony.

The cold throb through his ruined arm and into his shoulder. The salty sting where his teeth were missing. The endless ache in the foot he no longer had. The tormenting itch in the butchered stump.

"By the dead," he mouthed, squirming in his seat.

He wanted to rip open his sewn-shut trouser leg and tear at the red wounds with his nails. Gnaw at the stitches like a wolf might at a leg caught in a trap. He squeezed his eyes shut, trying to breathe, trying to listen, but he could hardly follow a word. The crowd bellowed and warbled along with the blood rushing in his ears, no more meaning in it than in a stormy sea.

He was a crippled shell. A tortured ghost. He'd never be himself again.

"You all right?" asked Heugen.

Leo got as near a smile as he could. A skull's rictus. "Fine." He'd never been much of a liar, but this must've been one of his very worst.

"If I was in your position," drawled Isher, "I'd be straight out of this madhouse and back to Angland as fast as my legs could carry me." He realised his dire choice of words. "On the next tide, I mean to say."

"Savine's due any day," grunted Leo. "Be a while till she can make the voyage." Even speaking was painful. "But Commissioner Pike's invited us to stay. Meaning we're still prisoners. I think he's got people watching us."

"He has people watching everyone with a 'dan' in their name," murmured Isher.

"He has us watching each other." Heugen glanced suspiciously about the surrounding benches. "Better value for money."

"Gentlemen, if I may?" someone shouted.

"Citizens!" someone roared back.

"Citizens, of course, my profuse apologies!" The man looked terrified. There was a feeling that little mistakes were being noted down and would soon enough be counted against you. "I wished to speak of the walls! The city walls, the walls of the Agriont. They are, practically speaking, an impediment to the growth of the city. They are, symbolically, a reminder of *monarchist oppression*."

Isher sprang up. The man could move fast, when he wanted to. Scurrying from the Battle of Stoffenbeck, for instance. Or scurrying back, once he saw something to gain.

"They're damn useful for the defence of the city, though!" Leo thought he might be roughing up the clipped accent of the Midderland nobleman to sound more like a commoner. "There'll be foreign enemies, jealous of our freedoms. There'll be enemies in the provinces, keen to take us back into the past." Isher pointed across at Orso, watching this performance with weary scorn. "There'll be enemies among us, wanting to raise a king above our heads again."

Those who've snatched power always fear it'll be snatched away. There were murmurs of agreement, nods rippling through the benches. The public gallery was less enthusiastic, though. Not so much the message, Leo reckoned, as the messenger.

"Aristocrats!" someone bellowed from above. "Clinging to aristocratic symbols!" Insults were thrown down, and scraps of food, and crumpled pamphlets, and the king acknowledged them by raising his goblet and taking a lazy swallow.

"What does the Young Lion say?"

"Let's hear from Brock!"

Risinau banged on the table for order and Leo flinched. The sound made him think of the cannon blast in Stoffenbeck. The shattered Guildhall. His horse falling across him. Antaup with bloody hands in his lap. Jin riddled with flatbow bolts.

He tried to wipe his face, greasy with cold sweat.

"You should say something," muttered Isher, frowning up towards the jeering gallery.

The thought of standing terrified him, but there must still have been some stubborn remnant of the Young Lion, hidden deep inside. *Better to do it, than live with the fear of it*, the Dogman used to say. Leo might have lost a leg and an arm, but he'd show these bastards he still had his heart.

Heugen hauled him up while Isher wedged his crutch under his arm. Then they sat back, applauding his pluck. Not the man he was—he'll never be the man he was—but the crippled curiosity can still raise a cheer or two.

Leg trembling, stump burning, Leo drew himself up, raised his chin, bellowed at the echoing hall they way he'd once bellowed at the cavalry of Angland, working them up to a charge.

"Citizens! We've changed the world! A Great Change!" For the massively worse, in his case. But he heard applause. Or he hoped it was applause, and not just the blood rushing in his splitting head. "But there's still so much to do!"

Sweat tickled his scalp, trickled down his forehead. He paused to catch his breath, to think through the pain. All his life he'd been fixed on what he wanted to say. Never given a thought to what they wanted to hear before.

"Walls...won't protect us now, only unity!" By the dead, the hall was swimming. "Those who've enjoyed great privileges must make great sacrifices." They needed some noble gesture. He bared his teeth. "So I give up the 'dan' in my name! I renounce it! I cut it out! We must all...be equal."

No doubt it was clapping now, and lots of it. Folk were standing. Someone was shouting, "The Young Lion!" over and over. It took Leo an age to turn around, good leg quivering, aching hand sticky with sweat on his crutch. Isher, Heugen and the rest of the lords looked more than a bit queasy.

"I'm sure my comrades…who once sat on the Open Council…will all happily do the same. I for one…" He gathered himself for a final effort, roared it at the dome in a broken voice. "Cannot think of a title that makes me prouder than *Citizen*!"

Furious applause, and the thudding of boots from the public gallery seemed to merge with his thudding heartbeat, the pulsing pain in the stump of his leg. He could hardly make out Risinau's words.

"The Assembly no doubt wishes to thank the Young Lion for his sacrifices on behalf of the Great Change! It is an inspiration to us all, that he has so soon overcome his wounds and returned to the service of the nation! Let the walls of the Agriont be demolished! There is no need for we in power to separate ourselves from the people." Risinau thumped the table with his chubby fist. "We *are* the people!"

More cheering. One more hopping, lurching step and Leo collapsed onto the front bench. Isher caught him under the arm, clapped him on the back, waving to the public gallery.

Through his fixed smile he hissed furiously, "We did not agree to this!"

"You will." Leo didn't care a shit about that coward's discomfort. He'd too much of his own to deal with. "When you've lost an arm and a leg," he snarled, gripping at his throbbing stump, "a piece of your name doesn't seem such a sacrifice."

Broad stood there, where he swore he'd never be again—in uniform.

They called him Captain Broad now, if you could bloody believe it. He wondered what Liddy would've made of that. Asked him what the hell he thought he was doing, most likely. He wished he'd got an answer. He hadn't asked for it. Hadn't even agreed to it. But he hadn't stopped it, either.

"Symbols have *power*!" It was that bloody writer, Sworbreck, near foaming at the mouth with passion. "And the statues on the Kingsway are the most powerful symbols of *all*! Must the Representatives of the people pass every day below the very feet of such oppressors as Harod the Great or the Magus Bayaz? Why, I would sooner lay down my *life*! Lay it down on the gallows where so many martyrs were slain by the Inquisition, than see it continue for another day!"

"Citizen Sworbreck wants to set the people free," murmured Brint, who by some magic had gone, within weeks, from lord marshal in the old regime, to imprisoned traitor, to general in the People's Army. Those kinds of wild falls and rises were everywhere in Adua these days.

Broad thought of Valbeck. The streets strewn with rubbish. The mobs and the fires. Wallpaper being boiled for soup. "Folk want bread," he said. "Then safety. Then shelter. Freedom's far down the list, and principles far behind that."

"Perhaps you should be a Representative."

Broad raised his brows at the benches. There were some good folk on them. Honest folk with good ideas and good intentions. Shame they could hardly get a word in. The first day the Assembly sat there'd been this moment, when they all swore an oath to serve the people, then applauded loud enough to shake the dome and threw their hats in the air. Some bastard's cap was still snagged on a bit of carving, just below the gallery. Broad had been sure then that things would get better. Better for everyone. But before the end of the session things were turning sour. Even when they could agree on what the people wanted, they couldn't agree on how to get there. Ever since, they'd been mired like a wagon with a horse at each corner.

Broad folded his arms over the breastplate they'd given him. "I've a shitty enough job as it is, General, thanks all the same."

"Good men must stick together," said Brint. "Try to contain this madness."

If that was the aim, it looked to Broad like they'd already failed. "Can't make you any promises."

"Best you don't. No one's keeping the damn things anyway."

"We should dismantle the House of the Maker!" a man with a huge beard was squawking out, shaking a great sheaf of papers. His plans for the future, maybe. There was no shortage of those. "It's a regressive symbol!"

"The House o' the Maker ain't our problem," roared a great big fellow with an anchor tattooed on his cheek, "or the statues, or the bloody walls." He took a great breath, nostrils flaring. "It's the fucking *foreigners!*"

Broad winced. Everyone was furious all the time. Everyone looking for someone to blame. Everything teetering on the brink of violence. He felt like he had in Styria, in the war. A clenched fist, itching to strike. And the worst thing about it—he wasn't sure he didn't like the feeling.

"Citizens, please, we must stand together!" A bony fellow with a shock of wild white hair had jumped up, something desperate in his voice that made everyone fall silent. "I have been administering charity in the Three Farms for these past twelve years, and I swear to you things have never been worse. Never."

Some nods from the more ragged members of the commons. Some rolled eyes among the noblemen.

"We have wrested the reins of power from the Closed Council. I applaud it! They dragged our nation towards the abyss. But the granaries are emptier than they have ever been. Coal is in scarce supply. The injustices that led to this upheaval—the want, the scarcity, the degradation, the disease—they will not simply vanish because we remodel some statues. All the signs point to a harsh winter on the way. We must prepare, Citizens, we *must* be ready!"

Broad found he was nodding along, but the noise in the hall was mounting again. Jeers and cheers together. The old man's voice was failing, and Sworbreck sprang up to thunder over him.

"Prepare, of course, but we must not indulge in *defeatism*. We must not encourage a *dangerous nostalgia* for happier times that never were! I would rather lay down my *life* than see this proud assembly cavil, nag and nay-say. We *must* not talk the nation down!"

"Before we can feed the people's bellies," agreed Risinau, "we must feed the people's *minds*. Only with a government founded on sound principles of fairness and justice can they prosper!"

As the old man dropped spent into his seat, the rest of the Representatives were rising to applaud their Chairman. They did that a lot. Broad clenched his fists tighter and glanced towards Judge, flopped loose in her chair with her head resting on the back, scratching gently at her stretched-out throat. With something stuck between horror and excitement, he realised she was looking right back at him.

He remembered being chained to a chair with her in his lap, crotch grinding against his, and he felt that guilty tickle, deep inside. He remembered her grinning face spotted with blood when he split that banker's skull, and he felt that tickle even worse. Even better.

A little smile quivered at the corner of her mouth. As if she guessed everything he was thinking. *Some men can't help 'emselves . . .*

"I have a point to raise!" As the Representatives sat back down, one man was left standing in the aisle. Ordinary-looking, in travel-stained clothes, a walking staff in one hand.

Risinau peered up at him. "I do not recognise you, Citizen. What district do you represent?"

"Oh, this is Master Sulfur!" The king tried to swig from his goblet, frowned, upended it and shook a couple of drips into his lap. Then he turned his lazy eyes towards the benches. "He represents the First of the Magi."

That got a murmur from the Assembly, and from the gallery, too. Broad raised a brow at Brint. The general could only shrug. Not much would've surprised any of them now. If a dragon had risen from the benches, it would likely have been calmly dismissed on a point of order.

"My master, Bayaz, is gravely concerned by recent events!" called Sulfur. "In the Union he founded. In the city he built." He gestured towards Orso, who was sitting back and holding out his goblet for a refill. "To the king he crowned."

"Do thank your master for his concern," replied Risinau, "but tell him he should keep it for himself!" Laughter at that, and an approving banging of fists on benches. "The free people of the Union have no further need of his meddling!"

Sulfur's eyes narrowed. "How soon you all forget. It was within your lifetimes that he saved Adua from the terrors of the Eaters!"

"By destroying half the city and causing the deaths of thousands!" called Risinau. "Bayaz saved us from the Eaters, perhaps, but one wonders... who will save us from Bayaz?" More laughter, and more anger, and Risinau flashed that prim little smile. "General Brint, could you see our visitor out? The age of wizards is over, Master Sulfur. An age of reason has dawned!"

"Reason?" Sulfur glanced about the benches and gave a hiss of disgust. "I'd like to see it." And he stalked off up the aisle, staff tapping against the steps.

Before he'd even reached the doors, someone else was bellowing to be heard. "I demand we reopen the question of whether we should be called the *Assembly* of Representatives. I would like to propose *Colloquium*—"

A chorus of groans. "Again?"

# Miracles

Savine's throat was raw from screaming.

Dark outside. No chink of light between the shutters. It had been hours, then. It felt like for ever. That same question chased itself around and around her mind.

How many women had she known who died giving birth?

"My lady—" began the surgeon.

"Don't fucking... *call me that*," she snarled over her shoulder between whooping breaths, nearly swallowing her own tongue with fury. "No one... calls *anyone* that... any more."

"Of course not, I apologise. The times take some adjusting to." He spoke in the blandest of drones. As if they were discussing the weather and he by no means had his fingers in her quim. "You can push if you feel the need—"

"Oh, fucking *can I?*" she screamed at him. The idea that she might be able to stop herself was absurd. The one thing she wanted in the world was to push.

The ridiculous shift they'd given her was tangled around her neck, choking her, and she dragged it up, got it stuck, tore at it, spitting, stitches popping, finally ripped it off and it dropped on the bed around her wrists. It was spotted red. Zuri's hand slipped in and whisked it away, folding it so the blood did not show.

How many women had she known who died giving birth?

She grunted, and the pain tightened in her belly, and the grunt became a groan, and the groan a moan, and the moan a wail, and the wail a howl, and the howl a grinding scream. She clutched up fistfuls of the sheets, tried to climb the headboard, but that was worse, and she flopped back, and that was worse, and she twisted desperately this way and that on her hands and knees, but it was all worse.

"Fuck," she gasped. "Shit. Cunt." She wished she knew worse words.

Wished Zuri had taught her Kantic. They had some savage-sounding curses in the South. The room was so bloody hot. Sweat tickled her scalp. But her arms were so locked and trembling she couldn't lift a hand to scratch.

People came and went. Barged in with water, with cloths, with muttered messages. Naked on her hands and knees with her arse in the air, honking like a sow, she barely even cared. If anything she was grateful for the waft of breeze when the door opened.

"I do apologise," murmured the surgeon, "for all the coming and going."

"You can let the whole *fucking* city in," she snarled, "as long as you get the fucking baby *out*." The spasms were coming so quickly now it was one continuous agony, and she clenched her teeth again, ground them so hard she thought they might crumble.

They all say, *It's the most painful thing there is*, of course. In a slightly gloating way, with a knowing raised brow as they look down at your massive belly. They all say it, but you persuade yourself they are being overdramatic. Savine's mother had held the pain of childbirth over her like a debt that could never possibly be paid, but then Savine's mother was one of the most overdramatic people in the world. Now it seemed she had been understating the case all along. By the Fates, Savine wished her mother was there. No doubt she would have been at least half-drunk, but she always kept her head in a crisis.

Savine felt Zuri's hand firm on her shoulder, rubbing at her aching back, and was pathetically grateful for it. She wanted to cry, but she was crying already.

"It might be easier if you were to lie on your back—" murmured the surgeon.

"Easier for *fucking who*?"

"That's the spirit."

She gave another ripping growl, panted and shuddered and twisted desperately but there was no wriggling free of it. She had wanted so many things. Beating everyone, and winning everything, and having it all, and being seen to have it all. Now all she cared about was getting this over.

How many women had she known who died giving birth?

She wondered if dying might be preferable to much more of this.

"One more push should do the trick—"

"*Fuck* yourself!"

"Good, good."

She screamed again. She screamed her face off. She screamed her guts out. She screamed as if she was being murdered. She felt as if she was being murdered. A stinging, burning, ripping to add to all the rest and she ran out of breath, her scream dying off into a wheezing groan as she felt something slither out.

Zuri cradled her head. "Done," she whispered. "Done."

The best words Savine ever heard. She slumped onto her face, breath coming in shivering gasps.

Someone helped her to roll. Someone was wiping her thighs. Someone pulled a sheet over her. Cool linen, up to her chin.

The bed was wet. Wet and sticky and she didn't care. She lay, eyes closed, breathing. The agony had faded. Just a dull after-ache in her back.

She was floating. Drifting on a cloud. Someone was dabbing her face with a flannel. She doubted it would help much but if it made them happy she let them get on with it.

She could hear singing in the distance. One of the Breakers' marches, out on the Middleway. So long kept prisoner, they loved to march. So long kept silent, they loved to sing. To blurt their opinions from every street corner. Food and fuel might be in short supply, but of opinion there was a glut.

She could hear crying. High and wild and desperate. Like a wounded cat. Very loud. Was it in the room? Was it her? There were a lot of people crying lately. Making an exhibition of your emotions was in fashion. Ranting them at a crowd, even more so. But she supposed people had a lot to cry over. Some more than others.

There was the odd absence, of course, among her circle. Those with particularly bad relations with their workers, or those with particularly bad luck. She heard the most appalling stories. Such-and-such was found drowned in the canal, by the way. And what's-his-face knifed and stripped in a sewer, did you hear? She pretended they were nothing more than stories. She pretended she could not recall the faces of those people, laughing at some function before the Great Change.

There was chaos, of course, in the Agriont. The Closed Council suddenly snuffed out, the bureaucracy wobbling on like a chicken with its head cut off. The Breakers had ripped out most of the machinery of government; now Risinau and his stooges waggled the levers around, apparently never realising they were no longer connected to anything. She asked Leo how things were in the Assembly of Representatives. He said he had lost battles and never seen a mess like that.

But, at the same time, things carried on. Over in the Arches and across the Three Farms, the furnaces still burned. Most of them. The wheels still turned. Most of them. Goods were still made and prices still paid and business still done. In hushed tones, perhaps, with heads shaken over the state of things. Actors still strutted on the stages of Adua, though they had rushed out new pieces in praise of the common man, and asked for applause for Chairman Risinau when the curtain went up, rather than for His Majesty.

So Savine heard. She had not been out of doors recently herself. She was not sure how she would be received. With boos and jeers, like the villain in a street play? With the cheers her husband always enjoyed, for doing nothing more than whatever he pleased? Or with fists and sticks and nooses from a warehouse jib, like some of her more unpopular business partners during those bloody first days?

She had spent her life making an exhibition of herself. But there are times when it is only good sense to take a tasteful absence from the public stage.

"It is a boy," said Zuri.

Savine had been drifting on the edge of sleep. Lamplight sparkled in her wet eyes as she opened them. Zuri stood over her, offering something out. A clean white bundle, carefully wrapped, like a present. A white bundle with a tiny, squashed-in face.

Savine gave a kind of sob, right from her guts.

She reached for it. She hardly had the strength to lift her arms, but she wanted to hold it so badly. She hardly even knew why. She was blubbing, snot clicking in her nose and her sore mouth hopelessly twisted. She pressed the little bundle to her chest and made noises at it.

"I'm a mother," she muttered.

Zuri raised her black brows. "I can see no other conclusion."

She heard the sound of trickling water. The surgeon, washing his bloody hands in a basin.

"Well done," he said, a neat smile on his face. "Very well done. Tell Lord Brock he might meet his son."

Savine was vaguely tempted to swear at the surgeon again, but it would probably have been in bad taste now. And she was too busy staring at her baby's face and smiling. Smiling in a weepy, trembly, utterly unguarded way that was quite unlike her.

A person. A tiny, helpless person, that had emerged from her body.

Savine had always scorned babies even more than pets. When other women cooed over them she used to smile indulgently, and say the things she was meant to say, and think to herself what ugly, wrinkly, pointless things these little shrieking people were, that needed help for everything and shat themselves once an hour.

They all say, *Yours will seem beautiful*, of course. In a smugly knowing way, as if shitting out a child comes with secret knowledge, like joining the Order of Magi. They all say it, but you tell yourself the poor things are just trying to wring some shred of advantage from the curse of parenthood and let them have their self-delusion.

Now it appeared they had been understating the case all along. Her own baby was astonishingly, breathtakingly beautiful, its every twitch a miracle. What a cliché.

"A boy," whispered Savine. She vaguely remembered preferring a daughter. But now somehow a son was exactly the thing she had always wanted.

She could hear talking near the door. Men's voices. Warm words. Congratulations. As though they had done any of the work. She heard the uneven thumping of crutch on boards. She looked up through her swimming eyes to see Leo standing over the bed. He had this odd slant to his shoulders, these days. One dropped, where his useless arm was tucked into his jacket, one high, with the effort of leaning on his crutch.

"There's a lot of blood," he croaked, eyes wide.

"Entirely normal," said the surgeon. "No need to worry."

"It's a boy," said Savine, smiling and crying at once.

His brow furrowed as he stared down at the baby's tiny features. As though the whole business was coming as a total shock to him. "I have a son."

"*We* have a son— Ah!" She gritted her teeth at a sudden, stabbing pain through her stomach, down into her legs. "Ah!" And another, even worse, that made her jerk up.

"What is it?"

"Take him," she grunted, offering the baby out with trembling arms.

Leo tried to rest his crutch against the side of the bed, got his wrist tangled with it, was nearly knocked over as Zuri slipped around him. "Damn it!"

"Take him— Ah!" Savine arched her back. Another spasm of pain, much longer, much stronger, and she had to twist onto her side, kicking, whimpering, wriggling in her bloody sheets back onto her hands and knees, groaning for breath, shaking with weariness, trembling with fear.

How many women had she known who died giving birth?

"What's wrong?" stammered Leo, leaning against the wall beside the bed.

The surgeon was behind her now, frowning, his cold hand pressing at her belly. "Lord— I mean *Citizen* Brock, you might be happier waiting outside—"

83

"Who cares a *shit* whether he's happy!" hissed Savine through her gritted teeth. "What's wrong?"

"Nothing." The surgeon looked up at her over his glinting lenses. "But I fear you still have some work to do."

She felt a kind of cold horror, then, along with the pain. "What is it?"

Zuri had the baby in the crook of one arm, but she slid her free hand under one of Savine's and squeezed it. "Twins."

# A Little Public Hanging

As a child, Orso had delighted in the sound of distant crowds. Crowds meant spectacles, festivals, excitement: the thrill of the Summer Contest, the pomp of a parade. As a young man, he had begun to find that noise tiresome. Crowds meant functions, rituals, responsibilities: the disappointment of grand banquets, the tedium of state visits. Now the sound of a crowd filled him with horror. In the new Union, crowds meant riots, terror, random violence. The baying of the mob.

Lost in the anonymity of a crowd, people would commit horrors that would have sickened them alone. That no doubt sickened them afterwards. But their regret was scant consolation for the victims.

"What's going on, Hildi?" he murmured.

"Don't know." And Hildi bit her lip, as if steeling herself for bad news. She always looked that way, these days.

As soon as they stepped out into the Square of Marshals the nature of the occasion became clear.

"Oh, damn," said Orso, his shoulders slumping. "I bloody hate hangings."

It was a new kind of gallows. Progress, he supposed. Instead of a cross-beam with ropes, five tall spars stuck up at an angle behind the platform, like the fingers of a clawing hand. There were pulleys at the tips, a counterweight of iron plates behind each one. Instead of rope, steel cables had been looped into five nooses. Orso noticed, as he was herded by his guards towards an enclosure where, as usual, he could be made an exhibit for the curious, that there was a life-sized dummy hanging from one of them.

Chairman Risinau sat at the very front of the crowd, Judge on one side and Pike on the other. The leaders of the Great Change. That bloody writer, Sworbreck, was leaning towards them, waving up at the towering gallows. "The trouble with the previous system was that the bodies fell *beneath* the trapdoor. Justice was done, but justice was not *seen* to be done. Now, with a counterweight released . . ." He gave a showman's flourish. Nothing happened. "Go on, then!"

There was a clatter of machinery, weights dropped, cable whizzed and the dummy was jerked up by the neck to flop about in the wind some five strides above the platform. The crowd gasped, then began to applaud, to cheer, to hurl good-natured abuse. A carnival atmosphere. Orso winced and tried to loosen his collar with a finger.

"Ingenious." Risinau nodded sagely, as though at a demonstration of a machine to peel fruit. He might not have been much of an administrator, but he knew the power of a good show. "You should be *immensely* proud."

"A happy combination of my flare for theatre and Citizen Curnsbick's technical know-how." And Sworbreck put an arm around the Great Machinist and gave him a friendly squeeze. Curnsbick, who had abandoned his spectacular waistcoats and was now modelling the inconspicuous tones of mud, looked more than a little nauseous.

"Ain't it a bit bloodless?" said Judge, with her usual deadly sneer.

Risinau rolled his eyes. "I do declare, Citizeness Judge, you would see the condemned torn apart by wild dogs if you thought it could be managed."

She sat back, rubbing thoughtfully at her rashy throat, as if weighing up the benefits of public execution by canines. "Let's see how this works first. Bring out the prisoners!"

"Oh no," muttered Orso.

Lord Chamberlain Hoff came first. Orso remembered him ushering portraits of potential brides into his mother's salon in tedious procession. What happy times those seemed, now. Lord Chancellor Gorodets was next. Then High Consul Matstringer. Then the surveyor general—by the Fates, he'd been kept away from the Closed Council by his bladder so often that Orso couldn't remember the man's name. Lord Marshal Rucksted brought up the rear, walking with a pronounced limp. It looked as if half his moustache had been torn out. Chains clanked as they were led up onto the platform, into the shadows of those five tall beams. The great lords of the Closed Council. The men who had ruled the Union in Orso's name. They made a sorry sight now, in sackcloth rather than fur and braid, in fetters rather than chains of office, their grey hair and beards in greasy tangles.

"Fellow Citizens!" Risinau never missed a chance to address a crowd. "We are gathered to see five enemies of the people receive their just deserts. To see righteous retribution on behalf of the Union's oppressed. To wave farewell to the age of tyranny." He spread his arms wide. "And to welcome the age of equality with open arms!"

Cheers. Boos. Laughter. A few bits of rubbish flung at the scaffold as nooses were tightened around necks. The Great Change had made little difference to the behaviour of the mob at an execution. A rotten orange spattered against the side of Gorodets' head.

"We've danced for their benefit the last few centuries!" screeched Judge, twisting to face the crowd. "Now they can dance for ours!"

Orso had never harboured much affection for his Closed Council. He had thought of its members as a man thinks of his creditors, his landlords, his jailers. But seeing them like this, he had to hold back tears.

Hoff shuffled forwards as far as the cable would allow, which was not far. "Your Majesty!" he cried over the noise. "I'm sorry!"

"It's me who should be sorry!" Orso rounded on Judge, Risinau and Pike. "Please! What crime are they accused of?"

"Corruption, profiteering and exploitation," said Risinau.

"Treason against the People of the Union!" hissed Judge.

"Is there evidence?" asked Orso.

Judge glared back at him. "They sat on the Closed Council. What more evidence do you need?"

"Were they allowed a defence?"

"They sat on the Closed Council. What defence could there be?"

"We sat there, too, Your Majesty," said Pike softly. "You know each man of them was a willing cog in the monstrous machine, a callous accomplice in the purges and injustice. Can you truly pretend that these are better men than the ones they ordered hanged outside Valbeck?"

Orso swallowed. "The ones *you* ordered hanged."

"A better world comes with a bill to pay. We *all* must make sacrifices. And look around you." Pike calmly scanned the baying crowd. "The people have given their verdict."

"Get on and hang the bastards!" someone roared, and other voices joined him. Plainly, there was no appetite for clemency. When was there ever?

"Whatever they did, they did in my name," said Orso, his voice cracking. "At least put me up there with them."

"All in good time, Your Majesty," he heard Judge murmur.

Risinau held up a hand to quiet her, his hard little eyes fixed on Orso. "If the king cannot remain silent while the People's Justice is administered, he will have to be restrained. Captain Broad?"

A monster of a man stepped up to the royal enclosure. The royal pigpen. A neckless bull made to look even more savage by a pair of wire-framed eye-lenses perched on the flat bridge of his nose. He planted one great hand on the rail before Orso, a tattoo on the back. An axe and a bolt of lighting, with stars on the scarred knuckles. Hildi took a step towards him, bunching her fists, like a kitten raising its hackles at a bear. The big man just gave her a sad smile and took off those little lenses to show tired, weak eyes.

"It's a brave show, Your Majesty." No threat in his soft voice, just a weary pragmatism, and he breathed ever so gently on his lenses and gave them a wipe with his cuff. "But it'll do no good. You don't want to get hurt, and I damn sure don't want to hurt you." He perched them back in their place and raised his brows at Orso. "Things are bad enough. Why make 'em worse?"

He was right. Thousands of people had crammed into the Square of Marshals to see these men hang. Orso was powerless. More so than ever. He let Hildi drag him back into his chair and sat mute, hands limp in his lap.

Lord Hoff noisily cleared his throat. "If I might say . . . a few words before—"

"No." And Judge snapped her fingers.

A clank from beneath the platform. With a whirring of gears, the counterweight dropped and Hoff was snatched up, just like the dummy. He bounced wildly at the top, his head caught the beam and he flopped, swinging, blood bubbling down his face, his neck grotesquely stretched.

Orso clung to the rail of his enclosure, his white hands either side of Broad's.

Judge snapped her fingers again. Gorodets gave a whoop as he was whisked into the air. Pike watched his one-time colleagues dangle, emotionless, eyes glittering.

"Wait!" Matstringer left one shoe behind as he was plucked from the platform by the throat. The surveyor general squeezed his eyes shut, then his counterweight dropped and he was flung up, too.

Hoff swung, his distended neck turning black. The surveyor general did not appear to have been killed instantly. He was still kicking. Perhaps just some nervous impulse. Orso hoped so. Something ran from the leg of his sackcloth trousers and spattered to the platform below.

Curnsbick put his head in his hands.

Rucksted bared his teeth. "Fuck the lot of you."

Snap. The last counterweight dropped. Rucksted flew up, but something must have gone wrong with the mechanism. Instead of being left hanging high, the noose was jerked all the way into the pulley. His head flew off one way. His body dropped the other, crashing onto the platform, showering blood.

"Ha!" screeched Judge, leaping to her feet in delight.

The crowd gave an almighty roar of approval. A woman danced, pulling off her apron to wave it over her head like a flag.

"Oh," said Hildi, in a high little voice. Because she was so clever and so tough, Orso forgot, sometimes, how young she was. He wanted to put his hand over her eyes. He wanted to put his hand over his own. But it was far too late.

He had sat horrified through those meetings in the White Chamber where, beneath the blandly monstrous oversight of the First of the Magi, principles were squashed beneath profits, corruption was raised to an art form and justice was reduced to a jelly. He had known it was wrong, but he had thrown up his hands and told himself it was the way things were. The way things had to be. He had failed to protect his people from his councillors. Now he had failed to protect his councillors from his people.

"I have failed at everything," he whispered.

The four corpses hung limp. Gorodets dangled a little lower than the others, for some reason, twisting slowly one way, then the other. The crowd had turned quiet. Towards the back, people were already drifting away. There was a sense of disappointment. Perhaps they had discovered that when enemies fall, they leave a hole. No doubt they would find new ones to fill it with soon enough.

"Well." Risinau stood, hands on his paunch. "I for one am glad to have *that* behind us. Now we can focus on putting things right."

"Behind us?" Judge growled as she glared up at the dangling bodies. "We've barely begun."

Orso closed his eyes. He realised that, somewhere deep inside, he had been supposing this was all temporary. A passing fad. A nightmare from which they would all soon wake.

But perhaps this was simply how the world was, now.

Perhaps this was how it had always been.

# Nest of Vipers

"I can feel it in my liver," whispered Isern, "the little bitch is up to something."

Corleth strode through the crowd ahead, down the rain-slick cobbled streets that led from Skarling's Hall into the chilly city, a canvas bag over one shoulder.

"I see it," said Isern, "and the moon sees it, and the only one can't see it is you."

"Not the only one," said Rikke. "Aside from the moon and your liver, everyone likes her well enough."

"So you're saying there's a lot of fools about, a thing I well knew already. Did she tell you she was going?"

"She did not," said Rikke, "but why should she?"

"Did she ask leave to go?"

"She did not, but why should she?"

"What's she got in the bag?"

"Folk sometimes have bags, that's no proof of anything."

"Didn't I tell you not to get cocky?"

"Only a thousand times."

"If you'd listened to one of 'em I could hold my tongue now." Isern bared her teeth, showing that missing one, eyes still fixed on Corleth. "I'm telling you she smells wrong."

"You're a fine one to complain of odours."

"Sneaking out o' Skarling's Hall."

"You'd no objection to us sneaking into it."

"When we were sneaking around our enemies."

"We did somewhat leave the Brocks with their arses in the breeze, and we'd been welcoming them with a smile not long before."

"You had, but you smile far too easily." Isern slipped around a corner, pulling Rikke through a knot of people and behind a cart where they could watch Corleth walk on. "Bloody Brocks. They'd have stabbed you in the back if you hadn't stabbed 'em first. I see it, and the moon sees it, and the only one can't see it—"

"No, that one I saw pretty clearly, too." Rikke hooked a finger into the chain of emeralds Savine gave her and pulled them around a little. They weren't tight. They weren't heavy. But they seemed to chafe at her these days, since she started sitting in Skarling's Chair. "Guess we'll never know for sure now, will we..."

Isern shook her shaggy head in disgust. "We're not here to prod at the soft underbelly o' your guilt, which is a thing a leader needs to toss into the shit-pit along with her mercy, but to find out what your friend Corleth is doing creeping through Carleon, all flighty and furtive."

"She don't look all that furtive." Wasn't like she was padding on tiptoe, or sliding around corners, or checking behind her, the way Rikke would surely have done if she was about some shifty business. "She's just walking through town."

"Aye, but *where's* she walking?" Isern pressed herself to a wall and peered around its corner, and Rikke found herself doing the same. Corleth was ahead still, trotting up the steps towards a little house like a hundred others in the city, rain drip-dripping from the eaves of its mossy thatch. "She comes to this house every other day, d'you see. Regular as the moon."

Rikke frowned. That did sound a little troubling. "Maybe she's found a man to keep her warm in the winter." She blew into her cupped hands, thinking of the Nail, and what they'd got up to that morning, and had to grin. "They can be worth the effort."

"A lover would be nothing to hide."

Rikke shrugged. "A really ugly lover?"

"Shush." Isern swept Rikke into a doorway with the back of her arm. What with the clammy cold it reminded her of their times out in the woods, hiding from Stour Nightfall's men, and that brought back a stab of the fear she'd felt then, followed by a warm wash of satisfaction that she currently had the bastard hobbled in a cage.

The door opened. Corleth grinned, which seemed strange, as she wasn't much of a grinner. She went in and the door shut.

"Right," growled Isern, striding towards the house. "Now we'll plumb the bottom of her schemes."

"Who's cocky now?" hissed Rikke, hurrying after. "What if she *is* hiding something?" She pictured a room crammed with Black Calder's cut-throats, all turning as Isern kicked the door open. "We should get Shivers and a few of his lads..."

But Isern was already thumping at the rickety door hard enough to rattle it in the frame. It whipped open and Corleth frowned out, somewhat suspicious to see the two of them crowded onto the doorstep. "What are you two doing here?"

"What're *you* doing here?" roared Isern, triumphant, and she caught Corleth around the neck and shoved her into the house, pulling a dagger with the other hand.

"By the dead," squeaked Rikke, scrambling after, "don't knife her!"

It was a pretty ordinary sort of house, far as she could tell once she was into the gloomy inside. One room lit by one little window, a fine cook-smell wafting from a pot on the fire. The canvas sack lay open beside it, but instead of secrets it held carrots and a couple of bones. There was no gang of cut-throats. Just a bent old woman with weak eyes and a generous wart on her cheek, highly surprised by the blade-wielding hillwoman just burst into her house.

"What the fuck?" croaked Corleth, flattened against the wall with Isern's hand clamping off her windpipe.

The old woman snatched up a broom. "Let go o' my granddaughter!"

Rikke sighed, feeling more'n a little guilty over her part in this farce. "Reckon you can stow the dagger, Isern. Less you plan to chop carrots with it."

"My grandma lives here," muttered Corleth, rubbing at her pink neck as Isern let her go. "I come see her when I can. Make sure she's got wood for her fire. Bring her scraps for soup."

"Why didn't you tell me?" asked Rikke.

"Got enough weighing on your shoulders." By the dead, Rikke felt worse'n ever. "D'you think you could put the blade up now?"

With a level of sourness few indeed could match, Isern secreted the knife in the ragged depths of her clothing.

"You understand we've got to be watchful," said Rikke. "Black Calder's a crafty one. Could have spies anywhere."

"You thought my Corleth was *spying*?" The old woman lowered her broom, lip all a-wobble, poor thing. "All she talks about is how clever you are. How proud she is to be serving you. How you'll change the North. Folk come to me for advice and I'm always telling 'em what a good thing—"

"All right, Granny," said Corleth, waving her down. "We have to be watchful, it's true. Just a misunderstanding, is all."

"Aye," said Rikke, giving Isern a hard side-eye. "It's easy to stuff the blame in the wrong places."

92

"And it's true Black Calder's crafty." The old woman took a step towards Rikke, lowering her voice. "Between you and me, there's this old bitch lives two doors down I've never trusted. You should keep an eye on her."

"Might be we'll do that."

"Now." Corleth's granny stared sternly around. "Who's for soup?"

The cold rain was flitting down harder when they made it back into the street, and Rikke pulled her hood up again and twitched it tight against the cold. "Thank the dead we smoked out that nest o' vipers," she said.

Isern was not amused. "You can't let your guard down. Now, with your arse in Skarling's Chair, less than ever. You have to be hard. Have to make of your heart a—"

"Yes, yes. I'll have Corleth cut with the bloody cross for taking those kitchen scraps, soon as I get back." Rikke shook her head. "I like the girl. She has sturdy hips."

"Where do her hips come into it? Planning to sire children upon her?"

"No, I mean, she's solid. Steady. Not likely to suddenly catch fire." Rikke raised a brow at Isern. "Unlike some I could mention."

"My narrow hips did not offend when I saved your life out in the wasteland."

"Eh. They did a little."

"I'm telling you there's something off about that girl." Isern spat over her shoulder towards the house. "And her granny, too."

"Oh, aye, the granny especially. Never saw such a terrifying presence." Rikke puffed out her cheeks as she strolled back up the steep way towards Skarling's Hall. "Must be the Bloody-Nine in disguise."

# Lines of Communication

They spread out around the farm. Clover counted ten, but he kept sitting on his stump all the while so he wouldn't spook 'em, only moving to give the carcass over the fire a prod, and that very slowly. The sun was getting low beyond the hills and the valley full of shadows, so he couldn't really tell the faces, but there was one old-timer with a grey beard, one with a leather hood, one who wore a dented helmet, one young lad. Friends, enemies, the longer Clover lasted, the more they all looked the same. The more they bloody were the same.

Finally, one strolled up to the fire and held his palms out to it. Clover knew his face as it came into the light. Trapper. One of Black Calder's boys.

"Hey, Trapper," he said, friendly as he could. Always keep it friendly, if you can.

"Clover? That you?"

"I believe it is, though these days I'm sure o' nothing."

"Where the bloody hell have you been?"

"That there is quite a story." Trapper's men were poking around, but not too carefully. It was chilly, and they were drifting over to the warmth, and that homely smell of cooking meat. "Sailed to Midderland with the Great Wolf and the Young Lion, felt seasick on the way over, got caught in a storm, fought a battle, lost, felt seasick on the way back." They'd gathered about the other side of the fire, now, off guard. "Then Tricky Rikke sent me down here to have a word with you lot. Some doubts over where the border's at, apparently."

Took 'em a moment to catch up. Then the one with the grey beard hefted a big axe. "You're working for that witch?"

Clover scratched gently at his scar. "Honestly, the situation's a little… changeable. Trying to pick my way to solid ground, as usual. I was hoping to offer you lads some meat. A token of good intentions, you know." He pushed his knife into the carcass and the juice leaked bloody. "Don't think it's done yet, though. Unless you want to come back later?"

Trapper shifted one hand to sit on the pommel of his sword and slowly shook his head. "Don't think we can."

"Then I guess we'll have to do this hungry." Clover gave a sharp whistle and an arrow flitted from nowhere and stuck quivering into the carcass.

His hope had been they'd stay calm, realise they were surrounded, do the sensible thing. But thinking about it now, the sensible thing's a lot to ask once arrows start flying, even into things that are already dead.

"Fuck!" someone shouted. The old boy with the grey beard whirled about, axe all over the place. One of the others had to dodge it, nearly fell, stumbled back and kicked a shower of sparks from the fire. Trapper drew his sword. Another in a lambskin cloak took off running like a hare at a handclap. Total shambles.

"Whoa!" said Clover, holding his palms high. "Everyone, whoa!"

The one with the helmet took a step at him, raising his spear. An arrow stuck into his shoulder and he breathed in hard and gave a great squeal, spear dropping into the fire and sending up more sparks. He twisted around, reaching over his shoulder, then under, trying to get to the arrow, but his fingertips couldn't quite touch it.

"I'm shot!" he hissed between his gritted teeth. "They fucking shot me!"

"We see," said Clover, pointing around the farm. "I've got men in the barn there, and over there. And in those trees, and those. All around you, shafts nocked and strings drawn." There was only Sholla and a few others, really, but Clover had no problem with a lie that saved lives. Or any other kind, for that matter. "Unless you all want an arrow you can't reach, my strongly worded advice would be to stack your weapons neatly over there and come join me at the fire, so we can all have a little chat without the distraction of the Great Leveller breathing on our necks."

"How do we know you won't just kill us?" asked a scratty-haired young lad beside Trapper. His version of Flick, it appeared, both in age and sense, or lack thereof.

"'Cause if the purpose was to kill you, I'd have ordered 'em to shoot while you were still blundering up the road. Believe me—and Trapper'll confirm it—I'm not one for taking unnecessary risks with my person. All I want is a chat. No call for further bloodshed."

Now Downside came striding from the trees, dragging the one with the lambskin cloak along with one big hand, heavy axe gripped in the other.

"Chief," he grunted, and threw the man down next to the one with the arrow in his shoulder.

"I'm shot," whimpered the one with the arrow in his shoulder.

"I'm clobbered," groaned the one with the lambskin cloak, a bloody hand clapped to his bloody head.

"We see." Trapper lowered his sword and dug it point-first into the ground. With bad grace the others swung bows from backs, pulled out axes and knives, set down spears, till there was quite a little armoury heaped up in front of the farmhouse.

Clover gave a satisfied nod. "Don't that feel better?"

"Not really," said Trapper, frowning at Downside's axe.

"Well, it does for me, I can tell you that." Clover whistled again, and Sholla, Flick and a couple of others slipped from the hedgerows, from the barn, from their hiding places and padded over, arrows still nocked to their bows, while Trapper and his men dropped in a reluctant half-circle around the far side of the fire, like children about to listen to a story.

"Now then," said Clover. "Why don't we start with what Black Calder's about? What's his mood, what's his strength, what's his thinking, you know. And naught but the truth, if you please."

"Truth?" said one of Trapper's men, the one with the big grey beard. "Truth is there'll be a price to pay for this, Jonas Clover." And he curled his lip and spat in the fire, and might have caught the carcass, too, which was somewhat of an annoyance. "Man can't just flip sides whenever the wind changes."

Clover rubbed at the bridge of his nose. "There's always one."

"Black Calder's going to win back the North!" the old man growled. Quite the voice he had, rough as a throat full of gravel. "No fucking painted witch and no fucking Long Eye'll change it." He glanced up at Downside, standing over him. "When he does, the lot of you will—"

There was a sharp crack as Downside buried his axe in the man's head and dragged him over backwards. His leg kicked so hard he kicked his boot off and it went flying high in the air, onto the roof of the barn, and that was the last move he made.

Downside leaned over, working his axe free. "That boy had a big mouth," he grunted, by way of explanation.

"He did rather," Clover had to admit. He spread his hands at the men on the other side of the fire, all staring at their dead comrade's one bare foot. "But could we all work at making that the last corpse we leave here? Reckon we can all agree if there's one thing we got too much of in the North, it's corpses."

"You killed my uncle, you bastard!" hissed the scratty lad. "You better be looking over your shoulder, 'cause one o' these days I'll—" There was a crack as Downside split his skull and blood spattered right in Clover's face.

"Gah!" he squawked, flinching back and nearly falling off his stump, and the body pitched forwards, boots swinging up, then flopping down. A red pool quickly spread, hissing faintly as its edge touched the embers of the fire. Downside frowned at his stained axe-blade, started wiping it on the boy's back.

"Could you bloody *not*?" Clover shouted at him.

Downside shrugged. "Sorry, Chief. Had the feel of a feud brewing, and it's always best to settle a feud at the outset, rather'n let it fester."

Clover took a hard breath, still wiping spots of blood from his face. "I can see your point, I suppose."

"I'm shot," whimpered the one with the arrow.

"We see. Where was I?"

"Black Calder," said Flick.

"Right, yes. Black Calder. How's his mood?"

Sholla slipped her arm around Trapper's head and eased the point of her knife up his nose. "And like the man said, naught but the truth."

"Never seen him this angry," squeaked Trapper, staring cross-eyed at Sholla's knife. "But cold, too. Cold and careful."

"I was worried that might be the way of it," muttered Clover. "How many men does he have?"

Trapper winced as Sholla's knife tickled his nostril. "More coming in every day. Fresh men, and strays got back from the Union, and he's made a deal with this new bastard from beyond the Crinna. What do they call him?"

"Stand-i'-the-Barrows," said one of the others. "They say he sleeps in a nest of bones."

"That don't sound good," said Flick.

"Sounds bloody uncomfortable," said Sholla.

Sounded bloody uncomfortable for the whole North. When Black Dow brought Stranger-Come-Knocking and his savages over the Crinna to help him fight the Union, the trouble had lasted years. It was plain Calder was going to make a real fight of it. And that was a fight Clover didn't want to be on either side of.

When he turned on Stour, he'd had no doubt it was the right choice. For his own sake, for Wonderful's sake, for everyone's sake. But he'd been sure Rikke would kill the bastard. Then she hadn't, and he started to worry she might be too soft for the job. Siding with the winner is forever sensible, of course. The trouble starts when you're not sure who the winner might be. Quite the pickle.

"All right, Trapper, I'm letting you and your lads go." Clover winced at the dead old man's bare foot, dirt under the big toenail. "Well, the ones still capable o' going. Tell Black Calder you ran into us. Tell him I tried to be reasonable."

"This what you call reasonable?" squealed the one with the arrow in his shoulder.

"Reasonably reasonable, anyway. Tell him I'd like a word, in due course, explain how things stand. Information to our mutual advantage and so on."

Trapper slowly nodded. Didn't say what he thought of the idea. He knew better'n that. "Reckon we'll head off, then. Can we take our weapons?"

Clover cocked an eyebrow at that heap of ironware. "Can't say the notion delights me."

"Come on, Clover. Don't make me head back disarmed. It's fucking embarrassing."

"Aye, but if you're anything like me, you'd rather be embarrassed than dead. I really don't want you chasing after us."

The one with the leather hood looked quite put out. "I need my sword, though. Let me get my sword."

"I'm saying no," said Clover, firmly as he could without raising his voice. "It's not a negotiation. No exceptions. It's a no."

The one in the hood looked to be getting a bit upset about it.

"That was my father's sword, you—"

There was a crack and Clover blinked as blood spattered in his face again. Downside had split this bastard's head, too.

"What the—"

"Sounding a bit feudy to me, Chief," said Downside, wiping his axe.

"Me and you need to have a talk," growled Clover at him. "The rest o' you, get moving." And he waved Trapper and the others off into the night. The one with the lambskin cloak groaned as his friends helped him up, and they hurried off towards the darkening trees, leaving their three dead behind, the one with the arrow-stuck shoulder still whining that he was shot.

Clover prodded at the meat. "Well, this is no bloody good now." Spat on by that dead old-timer, bled on by a couple of others and not cooked anyway. "Feels like all I'm ever doing is trying to convince new masters I can be trusted."

"Maybe if you didn't betray the old ones..." muttered Sholla, poking through the weapons.

"You think we should've stuck to Stour?"

"I do not." She took a knife she liked from the pile and pushed it through her belt. "Just saying there are consequences."

"Don't much care for that word."

"Which one?" asked Flick.

"Consequences. Which one do you think? There?" Clover shook his head. "By the dead, boy, you are dense as a stump."

"If they've crossed the river..." Flick was still catching up with where they'd been when Trapper and the rest arrived. "Weren't we supposed to kill 'em?"

"You may not yet have realised this, but I prefer, in general, to kill as few people as possible." And Clover gave Downside a significant glance, which had all the impact of an arrow on a rockface. "If we kill 'em all, they can't take a message back to Calder, and it seems wise to keep the lines o' communication open."

"Lines o' what now?"

Clover sighed. "To keep talking. Downside, since you made the corpses, reckon it's only fair you bury 'em, too."

"Fuck," he grunted, sliding his axe away. "Tell you what, it's thankless work, killing folk."

"In a way you'd hope so, wouldn't you?" said Sholla.

Clover jerked his head at Flick. "You can help him."

"What did I do?" squeaked the lad.

"Naught but be young and clueless and the easiest to order around, now get to it."

He nodded sadly, seeing the evident justice. "Which side *are* we on, then?"

Clover scratched gently at his scar again. "That's one o' those questions you try not to answer till you have to."

# The Politician

"How does it feel?"

"Sore," growled Leo, through clenched teeth. "Sore as hell. But if I can stand on my own two feet in the Assembly, it'll be worth it." He frowned in the mirror at the steel rod sticking from his rolled-up trouser leg, the springs around the socket that served as an ankle, the curving metal plate that passed for a foot. "Stand on my own one foot, anyway."

"So...you mean to keep going there?"

"I won't just sit crying over lost glories. The future of the Union will be decided in the Assembly." He looked at Savine in the mirror, propped up on the chaise in a mass of pale skirts with one of the babies to her breast and the other asleep beside her. He still couldn't tell which of them was which.

"Are you sure it's wise..." She had a nervous tone he wasn't used to hearing. "To make an exhibition of yourself?"

"I never thought I'd live to hear you arguing against making an exhibition."

"You almost didn't live to hear it," she said, softly.

He frowned at that. "I don't need reminding. It was *my* neck in the noose. But I've been given a say, and I mean to use it." It'd be a different kind of fight than he was used to. Words instead of swords, ideas instead of armour, speeches instead of charges. He'd be standing alone, with no faithful brothers-in-arms to watch his back. But he was as hungry for victory as ever. More, maybe. Every twinge in his leg, every throb in his arm, every shocked glance at his stump or his scars was a spur in him.

*Pain is the price of doing the right thing*, Leo's father used to say. Strange. He felt he hadn't really understood that till now. Maybe he hadn't really understood anything till now. He grimaced as he tried out a step and his weight went through his aching stump.

"Curnsbick said he could make you one that looks more..."

"Like a leg?"

"Well, yes."

"This is better. I want them to see what I've sacrificed. I want to shove it in their faces. I suppose I could get a prettier one to wear around the house—"

"Not on my account. I married you, not your leg."

"Regretting it?"

"We made mistakes." He saw her swallow, and frown down at the floor. "We made terrible mistakes. But our marriage makes more sense than ever."

She didn't mention love. Leo wasn't sure when they'd last used the word. Before Stoffenbeck, certainly. He remembered what she told him, the day he proposed. Or the day their mothers did. Their marriage was a business arrangement. A political alliance. And that was what he needed now—partners and allies. Love was a luxury he couldn't afford.

Savine was gazing down at her sleeping baby. Their baby. There was love in her eyes then, he noticed. "Given all that's happened," she murmured, "we are lucky to be where we are."

Crossing a room was an ordeal, pissing hard labour and dressing himself near impossible, but it was true things could've been worse. They'd been confessed traitors, after all, rotting in the cells at King Orso's pleasure. Now Orso was a prisoner in his own palace and they were back in Savine's cavernous house just off the Middleway. Most of it was shut up for lack of servants, but even so.

"We know people living far worse," he said.

"We know people not living at all. We have to protect ourselves." She gently stroked the dark fuzz on her baby's head. Their baby's head. "Protect our family."

"The people still admire me. We can use that." Being bounced on the shoulders of that mob outside the House of Questions hadn't been pleasant. But a lot better than being torn to pieces by them. "That and my place on the Assembly." Leo tried to force his scarred mouth into the easy-going smile he used to have, the one he'd worn when King Jezal handed him that badly balanced commemorative sword, but that felt like a thousand years ago. There was still a trace of the Young Lion there, if he tried. "No recklessness this time. No vanity. No sentiment."

"No overambition," said Savine. "No gambles. We have to stay safe. Take care who we trust."

Leo snorted. "We could hardly have picked worse friends."

"Isher, Heugen and Barezin."

"Cowards and fools," grunted Leo. "Though they might still have their uses."

"That savage Stour Nightfall."

"I should've kept him on a tighter leash."

"That weasel Vick dan Teufel."

"Quite the liar." He'd have been outraged by that once. Now he almost admired it. Things he'd taken for failings looked like strengths these days, crowning virtues like fatal flaws.

"Your old friend Rikke."

Leo frowned. "She was held up by bad weather."

"Please." Savine curled her lip. "She sent a letter to King Orso, months in advance, warning him about the whole plan. He knew we were coming."

Leo's nails bit at his palm as he clenched his fist. "That fucking treacherous *bitch*," he snarled, dotting the mirror with spit. "I risked my *life* for her! Why the hell would she—"

"We cannot waste time on what is done," said Savine. "We have to learn the lessons and find better friends for the future."

"You're right." Leo took a long breath and pressed the anger down. He couldn't let himself be swept off by whatever emotion blew his way. "What about your man Broad? He's close with the Breakers. A captain in the People's Army."

Savine thoughtfully pursed her lips. "Too close with the Breakers, perhaps."

"Aren't his family still in Angland?"

"You're suggesting we squeeze them?" She looked surprised. Shocked, even. "You've changed."

"To regret the methods, you have to win." He couldn't stay on his feet any longer, and he grunted as he took one lurching step and the padded socket squeezed at his stump. "Once you've won...who cares about the methods?"

"Have you been taking lessons from my father?"

Not long ago he would've thought of Sand dan Glokta as his utter opposite. Now he hissed with pain as he dropped down on a chair facing her. "The man ruled the Union for thirty years. He's the aspiring cripple's hero. He must still know useful people. Useful things. Where is he?"

"Out of sight and staying there, would be my guess. As for Master Broad, I owe him and his family. They saved my life in Valbeck."

"Now who's changed?" He worked himself forwards to fumble with the buckles that held the iron leg on. "I thought you had no use for sentiment."

"I've always paid my debts. That's just good business." She frowned at him, the scar on her forehead puckering, and held her baby tight. Their baby. Whichever one it was. "Since we are being unsentimental, the Broads are not the only useful people left in Angland. What about your old friends Glaward and Jurand?"

Leo froze. That image of the two of them kneeling on a Sipanese carpet thrust itself into his mind, and not for the first time. Glaward gripping two fistfuls of the covers, eyes squeezed shut. Jurand pressed against his back, fingers tangled in his hair, biting at his ear. The blissful look on their faces—

"Think I need a nursemaid?" he snapped, forcing the thought away. "Someone to keep me out of trouble?"

"I think we need people around us we can trust," said Savine. "You never told me what happened between the three of you."

Leo curled his lip and carried on undoing the buckles. He pretended to be disgusted. He *was* disgusted. Of course he was.

"I caught them fucking," he said, trying to sound like he hardly cared, even if his heart was pounding. "In Sipani."

"Isn't that what one does in Sipani? Fucking who?"

He cleared his throat. "Each other."

"Ahhh." She closed her eyes for a moment then gave the slightest nod, as if at a puzzle she had just realised the obvious solution to. "That explains a great deal."

He frowned. Explained their falling out, or explained something... more? "You're not surprised?"

"In business one encounters every kind of person." She was busy trying to work her nipple back into the baby's mouth. "You have to separate their preferences from their value. Imagine how much poorer I'd be had I never gone into partnership with Curnsbick."

Leo looked up from the buckles. "The Great Machinist? The father of the new age? He..." Fucks men? The words lurked in Leo's dry mouth, but he couldn't quite seem to force them out.

Savine raised her brows. "Have you not seen those waistcoats of his?"

"I thought he was married."

"So was Queen Terez, and by all accounts she's been through more quims than her son. Jurand is clever. A great organiser. And Glaward is faithful and diligent. If they had been with us at Stoffenbeck—"

"We might have won?" snapped Leo.

She shrugged it off. "They have the kind of loyalty one cannot buy."

"I thought *you* could buy anything."

"I thought so, too, once." She frowned towards the floor again. "It turns out I was wrong."

"I never thought I'd live to hear you admit *that*. You *have* changed."

"I've had to." He caught a glimpse of the old iron as her eyes flicked up to his in the mirror. "Can you get past it?"

That memory bubbled to the surface again, but it was Leo's hair Jurand's long fingers were tangled in, and Leo's ear he was biting at, whispering at, and Leo's legs he was reaching down between...

"Leo?"

He turned his shoulder towards his wife, so she wouldn't see the blood had rushed to his face. And not only his face.

"I suppose...I'll just have to separate...their preferences from their value." Certainly it would feel good to have someone beside him he could rely on. Someone who could make him smile again, even. With a grunt of relief, he finally pulled open the last buckle and the iron leg clattered to the floor. "I'll write to Jurand."

"Good. You've changed, too." Savine lifted the baby from her breast, its tiny eyes flickering with ecstasy, and plumped it down next to the other. She was doing her dress back up when that one stirred, began to squeak. She gritted her teeth and started to unbutton again.

Leo winced, and looked away, and was able to sit up without embarrassing himself. Luckily, perhaps, there was nothing he found less arousing than his wife's swollen, veiny, leaking tits. "You should get a nurse," he said. Or at least she should do that somewhere he didn't have to see it.

"I want to do it myself."

"Well, you're in tune with the times." Leo rubbed ever so gently at his aching stump. "The Assembly never stops blathering about the proper responsibilities of a Citizeness. The sublime duty of motherhood, Risinau calls it."

Savine snorted. "Fuck that fool."


There was a green space outside the Agriont where they'd taken to dumping the old statues. Noseless, handless, legless lords and ladies who'd once presided over palaces now ruled over a stretch of patchy grass that smelled of the rotting water-weed in the bottom of the drained moat. Here or there some monstrous remnant from the famous statues on the Kingsway loomed over the rest. A towering hand. A mighty boot. Half a majestic sneer.

Leo had pushed himself too hard, as usual. He sat on the fist of Harod the Great, his iron leg stretched out in front of him. He was desperate to unbuckle the bloody instrument of torture but doubted he'd get it back on without help. He watched the workmen on their teetering scaffold chiselling away at the battlements of the Agriont—an endless, pointless, impossible task of demolition. The mornings were turning chilly and he huddled into his coat, blew smoke into his good hand. Even up in the North, he never used to feel the cold. Now it was in his bones all the time.

He heard footsteps crunching in the frost-stiff grass and caught hold of his cane to rise. "Chairman Risinau—"

"Don't get up, Citizen, don't get up!"

Leo sagged back with some relief. Getting up was no simple matter these days. He watched the Chairman's frowning guards take up their positions, still as the broken statues. "Thank you for seeing me."

"We are honoured to have a hero of your calibre among us!" Did a true word ever leave this bastard's fat mouth? He'd no respect for Leo at all, and their causes had never been a bit alike, but there were still people who'd cheer for the Young Lion, and Risinau wanted their support. His own was starting to crumble.

"I'm the one who's honoured," said Leo, matching lie for lie. "To be given a seat on the Assembly. A place in your great endeavour."

"I did not bring all this about simply to see oppressors and oppressed trade places. It is *equality* I want! *True* equality." And Risinau happily fingered the rich fur he wore. "*All* must be represented in the Assembly. Even those we might once have considered rivals. Even those we might once have considered *enemies*. Look around us, after all." And he pointed out the great bald head of Bayaz, on its side in the grass, an optimistic little growth of ivy already making its way up his stony top lip. "A graveyard of ideas. The lies of the past swept away, to make way for all our futures!"

"You have the nation's gratitude for that," said Leo. "I'm not what you'd call eloquent—"

"You do yourself a disservice!" Risinau wagged a fat finger at him. "I have been most impressed with your contributions in the Assembly thus far."

"I'm just a blunt soldier. Or...I was."

"And now?"

"And now..." Leo paused. Plainly he was no soldier. And bluntness, like love, was a luxury he couldn't afford. "I suppose...I'm a politician." Wasn't long ago he'd have taken that as an insult, but constant pain was quite a thing for changing your perspective. "And a father."

"Twins, I understand. A double blessing! You must congratulate your wife for me. There is no higher contribution a woman can make to the nation than the fruit of her womb, would you not agree?"

"She certainly would." Leo smiled as he imagined her kicking him in the face for his fucking cheek. "Fatherhood has made me think about the world I'll leave to my children. The truth is … I'm worried about Angland."

"I, too," said Risinau. "I, too."

"A gulf has opened between Midderland and the provinces. I blame myself, in part. But it goes back a long way. I don't want to see it widen. I hate to think the province of my birth might … break away from the Union."

"Unthinkable," said Risinau, the slightest dangerous gleam in his eye.

"You're so right. When I was Governor there …" Leo didn't think the word "Lord" would help his case. "I tried to move Angland forward." Or Savine had persuaded him to look like he was trying. "New labour laws, fairer taxes."

"I am aware and admire your efforts."

"Small steps beside all you've achieved. But I want to help bring them the rest of the way. To bury the past." He gestured towards Bayaz's fallen head, just the way Risinau had. "To lead them into the future you're building."

The Chairman put the tip of one finger to his thoughtfully pursed lips. "You think you can coax your erstwhile countrymen back into the fold?"

"I have to try. Let me write to my mother. Assure her of your good intentions. Assure her that I, and my wife, and her grandchildren, are here as willing believers in your cause." Leo winced as he leaned hard on his cane and stood, so he could speak as one friend to another. "Let me bring like-minded men to represent the province in the Assembly. Trustworthy men. Blunt men. Men who can see first-hand the merit of the changes you're making. The changes *we're* making. Men who can support us, and argue our case back home."

Quiet, while Risinau considered Leo with those small, black eyes. The chill wind fumbled between the broken statues. Chisels tapped in the background. Leo used to be always restless. Following an argument had been painful. Sitting still had been torture. Now he knew what torture really was, and he was happy to wait. When every movement hurts, you come to appreciate a little stillness.

Then Risinau smiled. "Young Lion, I feared you would be an obstacle to our Great Change. I knew we needed you, because of your popularity with the people *and* the nobles, because of your value to your mother, but I was sure I would have to drag you bodily with us into the future!" He seized Leo by the shoulders, sending a stab of pain through his leg. "Now

I see I have in you a kindred spirit!" And he dragged Leo close, into his smell of sweat and rose water, and kissed him on both cheeks.

It was the most Leo could do not to butt the bastard in his fat face. Instead he followed Savine's example and smiled his widest smile. "We're both fathers. I've brought two new children into the world, but you've brought a whole new nation."

"An apt metaphor, Young Lion! No birth happens without pain. Without blood. Without risk. They are joyous occasions even so!"

"But newborns are so fragile," said Leo. "They must be protected."

"Such insight." Risinau looked at him with something close to admiration. "*Such* insight! Write your letters, Citizen Brock! I will see them delivered. We will stride into the new future together!" He slapped Leo on the shoulder as he turned away and strode off with his guards following.

"We'll hop into it, at least," muttered Leo. Looking down, he saw his useless arm had dropped loose without him even noticing, the pale hand dangling. He had to lurch to Bayaz's head and lean awkwardly against the magus's nose, breathing hard, before he could stuff his hand back between the buttons of his coat.

# Anger

"If it isn't Inspector Teufel." Gunnar Broad hadn't got any smaller. And he still had the lenses and the Ladderman's tattoo. But he looked harder, somehow. Or maybe hard times had ground the softness off and revealed the man beneath.

"If it isn't Captain Broad."

He peered unhappily at the badges of rank on his sleeve. "No notion how that particular folly came about."

"You could say the same for most things these days." She planted her hands on her hips, pressed her thumb-tip into the stiff one and frowned out across the bridge. She couldn't see them yet, but she could hear them. That familiar sound of anger on its way. "Seems we keep meeting. And in shitty circumstances."

"They're the only kind I get." Broad wiped his lenses, then hooked them carefully back over his ears. "But no worse'n I deserve, I guess."

"Well, I'm glad you're not holding a grudge." Vick thought of the last time she saw him, with the Brocks, before the Battle of Stoffenbeck. Noblemen fighting against a king. Seemed a different world. "Last time we met, you called me a traitor."

"Aye, well, I've said a lot of shit in my time that didn't add up to much."

She could see the people now, tramping out of the murk on the other side of the bridge. Protest, strike or riot, it was hard to say. Harder than ever. They were armed, in a way. Tools and planks and bars. One had a pick with a string of sausages hanging from it. Not weapons of war, exactly, but tell that to someone who gets clubbed over the head with a shaping hammer. Looked like a lot of them were drunk, but then a lot of folk were these days. Drink was the one thing still cheap.

"Let's remember they're just people, eh?" Vick called over her shoulder. "Try not to kill anyone."

"You reckon they've had the same orders?" muttered Broad, sliding his shield onto his arm and gripping the handle. Vick doubted it. Lot of them wore red. Red hats, red sleeves, coats spattered with red paint. Burners, then. Or at any rate expressing preferences in the Burning direction. You saw more and more of it. People's patience was wearing thin. Who could blame them?

"There's a lot o' the bastards," muttered Tallow, peering around Vick's shoulder. He'd got a Constable's uniform and a Constable's stick, but it was hard to imagine him doing much good with either one as he gazed across the bridge with those big, sad eyes.

"Stay behind Captain Broad," she snapped at him. Honestly, behind Captain Broad was looking a pretty appealing place to her right then.

"They look bloody angry," squeaked Tallow.

Hard to say exactly what they were angry about. No doubt they all had their own recipe. Price of bread. Price of housing. Price of fuel as the weather got colder. Wages too low, hours too high, too many laws or too few. Pike had taught them a lesson—if enough people got angry enough, they could change things. Now anger was the answer to everything.

The Great Change had been a basket of dreams. A bouquet of promises. All things to all men. Which was grand until, against all expectations, the Breakers won. Then, all of a sudden, it wasn't enough just to have a change, it had to be a change *into* something. Trouble was, soon as you tried to actually deliver the bastard, to mould it into policies, with costs as well as benefits, and losers as well as winners, well, nine-tenths of folk found the Great Change wasn't the change they'd wanted after all and wouldn't fucking have it.

"I could tire of the wisdom of crowds," Vick whispered to herself. Tallow was right, there were a lot of them and they all looked angry. She felt an urge to glance over her shoulder and count Broad's men, but she fixed her eyes ahead, feet planted wide. She told herself this was her bridge.

"Hit 'em now?" she heard Broad grunt.

There was a big part of Vick that wanted to say yes, but she forced it down. Someone had to. "Let's try talking first."

"I've a feeling words won't solve this."

"They'll leave no one crippled, either," she murmured, then roared as loud as she could, spraying spit. "That's far enough!"

They gathered uncertainly at the far end of the bridge, frowning across the damp stones at her as the first drops of a chilly rain sprinkled the cobbles. There were all sorts mixed in there. A crook-back old man with no shoes. A scrawny boy with his hollow cheeks blotched from the cold. A pregnant girl wearing a damp newsbill as a bonnet.

"I'm Chief Inspector Teufel!" called Vick. "Commissioner Pike sent me. The Weaver himself, you hear?" Some muttering at that, but none of the scowls went away. Vick clenched her teeth and took a hard breath. "Look, I get it! You're disappointed! You're frustrated! Let's face it, you're fucking furious! Believe me, so am I."

A woman shouldered through the press ahead. Big pink fists clutching a wooden paddle. A laundress. Hard women, those. Vick reckoned if she spent all day with her hands in hot water she'd be angry, too. "We don't need talk!" she howled. "We need bread!"

There was an answering growl of approval from the crowd, and an old man shook a placard, and a little girl up on someone's shoulders screeched, "Fuck the Closed Council!" which somewhat missed the boat since all the ones they could catch had been hanged a few weeks before.

Vick showed one palm and let the noise die down, then she fixed that laundry-woman with her eye and searched hard for the right words. The ones Malmer might've picked. The ones Sibalt might've found.

"I understand," she said, and she did, for what that was worth. "You were promised a better world, and all you've got so far is the same old shit. You can't fill your belly with promises. You can't warm your house with hopes. You're tired of being told lies! Believe me, so am I." Or she was tired of telling lies, at least. So bloody tired of it. "But we've got a *chance* here!" Ridiculous, that it fell to her, who never let herself hope for anything, to try to kindle some hope in these bastards, but she gave it all she had, her voice cracking. "A chance to build something *better*. We just have to be patient. Have to—"

Something came spinning from the crowd, missed her by a stride and clonked from the shield of one of Broad's men. They almost charged then. She could feel their fury, harder to hold in than to release, like dogs straining at the leash, but Vick held up a trembling hand, giving it one last go, preaching patience while she fast ran out of it.

"Go home!" Her voice came out a warning growl, and she took one step forwards, soles of her boots grinding against the stones, while behind her back she slipped her fingers into her brass knuckles. "Because I tell you what—anyone tries to cross this bridge will regret it."

"Maybe you'll be the one with the regrets!" called a sly-looking bastard, wearing a tall hat with half the felt worn off and gripping an old piece of iron railing. "Thought o' that?"

"I'll file 'em with the others," snarled Vick.

Something else came flying at her. A bottle, maybe. She whipped out of the way, and it spun past and smashed somewhere behind, and that was the end of the attempts at reason. As if it had been a signal, the two sides charged screaming at each other, meeting in the middle of the bridge with a clattering and shattering, a thudding of sticks and chair-legs and workmen's tools.

That laundress came right at Vick, lifting her paddle high. "Fuck you!"

"Fuck *you*." Vick slipped around the paddle and punched the woman in the throat with her brass knuckles, left her clutching at her neck, eyes bulging. The safe thing would've been to go for her knee and bring her down, but when it came to anger, Vick was not immune.

When the mob broke into the Agriont, they'd ransacked her mean little set of rooms. They'd taken what there was to take, which wasn't much, smashed what there was to smash, which wasn't much more, and left that ridiculous book Sibalt used to love torn on the floor. It had made her oddly furious.

So Vick punched this bitch in the face, snapped her head back, punched her again, and she tripped over someone's outstretched leg and went down hard. She tried to get up, blood streaming from her nose, and Vick planted a boot on her chest and shoved her back down. "Stick to laundry," she said.

There might've been a lot of them, and they might've been angry, but on the bridge there was no way the rioters could make their numbers tell. Broad's men were all veterans and they formed an armoured line, shoving with shields, beating with sticks, trampling the fallen, making no distinction between perpetrators and bystanders, between rioters and demonstrators, trampling the lot just the same.

Vick heard cries further back, the Constables she'd sent around spilling from a side street and straight into the rioters' flank. They came apart like a flock of starlings, taunts turned to whimpers, tossing down weapons and pamphlets and stolen food, crushing each other in their panic, one man knocked over the parapet, shrieking as he splashed into the canal. Here was the wisdom of crowds, and the courage of crowds, too.

"All right!" bellowed Vick, hopping up on the parapet and waving her arms. "That's enough." One of the Constables had a look of glee plastered across his face as he kicked the snot out of a scrawny boy. "I said *enough*!" She dragged him clear, near got an elbow in the face for her pains.

The anger could whip up in no time. But it could leak away just as fast. Those who weren't running were a sorry sight now. All hanging heads and wobbly lips, like children caught talking after bedtime.

Vick grabbed Tallow by the shoulder. "Pick out some ringleaders. And someone fish that idiot out of the canal!"

He blinked at her. "How do I tell who the ringleaders are?"

"They'll be the ones you're pointing at."

Broad dragged the sly one up by his jacket, hat knocked off and blood running from a cut on his scalp. "You fucking *bitch*—" he snarled at Vick.

Broad dug a fist into his stomach and doubled him up. "Have some respect." And he shook him like a rag doll, toes of his boots scraping the cobbles.

"Thought we were meant to be free!" he whined, a string of drool dangling from his lip.

"Turns out liberty needs boundaries." Vick jerked her head towards the Agriont. If they were still calling it that. "Get this arsehole to the House of Truth."

Broad plucked a pamphlet from the man's pocket, then shoved him towards the Constables so they could clap the irons on him. "One o' Sworbreck's, I reckon."

"Don't tell me," said Vick as he peered at the ill-printed pages through his lenses. "The Great Change didn't solve every problem, so the answer must be more of it."

"That's about the gist," said Broad, crumpling the pamphlet in his big fist and tossing it away. "That was a nice speech you gave, by the way."

Vick worked the brass knuckles from her aching fingers and frowned around at the mess. "Didn't do much good."

"Did a little for me. You can't fill your belly with promises." Broad nudged his lenses up his nose, slowly nodding. "Reminded me o' Malmer."

Vick took a long breath. "Look where he ended up."

"It's chaos out there," snapped Vick. She still felt angry. Like she'd been tricked. Tricked into believing things could be different. When the truth was she'd only tricked herself.

Commissioner Pike looked calmly back at her from across his desk. The same bare, stark room from which Arch Lector Glokta had ruled the Union, some of its furniture still bearing the scars of the day the Agriont fell. Behind the mirrored halls, and the velvet curtains, and the gilt façades, the real decisions always seemed to be made in bare, stark rooms.

"I understand there have been some disturbances," he droned, with his usual flare for understatement.

"A mob hanged two coal merchants the other day. They were already selling as cheap as they could. Prices are higher than before the Great Change. Higher than they've ever been. Folk broke into a shop, paid what they thought was fair. Then someone said they were profiteers. So they hanged 'em. Then they marched up the street to the flour merchant."

"And committed outrages against his person?"

"Luckily for him, I got in the way."

"You, as far as I can tell, remain unhanged."

"Luckily for me, there were some Breakers there who knew how to break heads as well as chains."

"Then make sure you take some with you next time."

"That's your solution? Armed men on the streets? Wasn't that the problem with the old regime?"

"We cannot blame everything on the old regime. Some problems, and some solutions, are simply...the way people *are*. We can have no illusions, after what we have seen, you and I, about the way people *are*."

"Isn't the point of all this to make them better?"

"In time, Inspector. By degrees. We must not be distracted. There is still so much work to do. In the bureaucracy. In the banks."

"Really?"

"Corruption has eaten into every part of Union society. No one can be truly free until it is burned away. Replaced with...*pure* institutions."

"Is there any such thing?"

Pike gave that twitch of his mouth that passed for a smile. "So cynical, Inspector. It is what makes you such a fine investigator. But we are changing the world. There were bound to be...teething pains."

"We're talking about dead shopkeepers. Not teeth. There are parts of the city we don't go into at night. There are parts of the city we have to ask the Burners' permission to go into at all."

Pike let a breath sigh away, as though dead shopkeepers were an inconvenient by-product, like the slag from a foundry. "You never struck me as a worrier, Inspector Teufel."

"Then when I worry you should take me seriously."

"I would take your solutions more seriously still."

That gave Vick pause. In all those years she'd worked for Glokta, she'd never once been asked for a solution.

Pike stared back at her, eyes flinty hard. "You should feel free to speak your mind."

"Without consequences?"

"Without consequences, a solution is merely an opinion." He curled his lip in the direction of the Commons' Round. "Of those, we have a surfeit."

"Risinau has to *go*!" Vick blurted out, smashing Pike's desk with her sore hand. Breaking all her rules, maybe, but there was no going back now.

"He's got no *grip*. He blathers on about making people free like that's the answer to every problem. But all he's done is give them the chance to kill whoever they blame."

"Someone must lead, Inspector. Who would you put in the chair instead?"

She knew she couldn't say what she was starting to think—that the Great Change was in danger of becoming a change for the greatly worse and that King Orso was beginning to look a paragon of leadership. She settled for second best. Or for second least worst, maybe. "You're the Weaver. You started this."

"So I could give power to the people. Not so I could seize it for myself. I never wanted to be in charge."

"Can I ask what you did want?"

"The same as you. The same as all of us." He did not smile. He did not frown. "A better world."

# Opportunities

Savine used to flit from one engagement to the next. Every day had been a mosaic of neatly kept appointments, an intricate dance to the music of the book and the watch, an endless, pearl dust-fuelled social whirl. Home had merely been a place to sleep and dress for the next function, occupations on which she had spent roughly equal time. Now, she was not sure how long it had been since she last left the house. Before the birth, certainly.

She told herself it was because there was not a sniff of pearl dust to be found in the city. She had hunted through every box and drawer, rationed her dwindling supplies as best she could, but now she had run entirely dry, and without it she was twitchy and sluggish at once and had a constant headache.

She told herself it had nothing to do with fear. There was no tide of sick dread when she considered stepping over the threshold. No swallowing the memories of the uprising in Valbeck, or the battlefield at Stoffenbeck, or the fall of the Agriont.

She told herself she could leave whenever she pleased. But what for? She had everything she needed here.

She smiled down at Ardee, fast asleep in her cot. She could watch them sleep for hours. Sit holding them for hours. Kiss the dark fuzz on their heads, over and over, and be delighted by the feeling every time. The smell of them. The softness of them. The unformed innocence of—

The bell tinkled downstairs and she felt a stab of panic, whipping around, hand at her throat, mouth sour with terror. She hardly even knew what enemies to expect. She crept to the window, brushing back the curtain with a finger, peering towards the road that used to be the Middleway. She understood they were still arguing over its new name, in the Assembly.

It was better not to mention things unless you were sure of the right language. Every day brought new wrong words to avoid. New ideas at odds with the Great Change. Everyone was free to say what they wanted now, of course. You just had to be careful in case it got you hanged.

There was a heavy quiet, out there. Her hearing was constantly sharpened for that first hint of an angry crowd. That first warning of riot and violence. She had not been sleeping, that was all. The twins were so demanding. And not a sniff of pearl dust anywhere in the city. She let the curtain drop, then jerked around at Zuri's voice.

"I found two beggars wandering the streets," she said, with the trace of a playful smile, "and my scripture teacher always told me that charity is the first of virtues, so I thought I would show them in..."

Savine felt a flood of relief as Zuri pushed the door wide to reveal her two brothers. The Great Change did not appear to have changed them, at least. Haroon was as solid and serious, and Rabik as smooth-faced and smiling, as ever.

Her first instinct was to rush over and hug them. She even took a step to do it before she remembered herself. "No one could be more welcome," she said, and she meant it.

Haroon bowed his head. "We are glad to be back with you."

"And to see you so blessed." Rabik leaned over Harod's cot, making little kisses, then peered beaming into Ardee's. "So *doubly* blessed."

"I am sorry it took us so long to come. We tried to find you, after the battle—"

"I should be the one apologising," said Savine. "You came to the Union to escape the madness in the South, and now look." She had to dab at her eyes with her wrist. "We have made our own." When she was younger, she must have gone ten years without shedding a tear. Now she could hardly get through an hour without a weepy moment. "I can't tell you what it means...to have friends around me I can trust. To have—"

Downstairs the bell rang again and Savine felt that surge of panic. Nothing to worry about, of course, as Zuri slipped out to answer it, but Savine had to peel her hand away from her throat even so.

"They say God puts us all where we are meant to be," said Haroon, softly.

"And you believe that?" Her voice sounded needy. With no beliefs of her own, she wanted at least to believe in someone else's.

"I used to think my faith was unshakeable. When I was a soldier..." Haroon gave the slightest wince, as though at an unpleasant taste. "I did things in the name of God and never doubted. Things...I have come to very much regret."

"We all have regrets," murmured Savine. Haroon at least could blame God for his. She could only blame herself.

"Faith must be shaken from time to time, or it becomes rigid. An excuse for any outrage. I have come to believe that the righteous...should *always* have doubts."

Rabik took Savine's hand in both of his and smiled. Such an open, honest, beautiful smile. "We must have faith in each other," he said simply. It was enough to make her smile herself.

"Citizen Kort is here," said Zuri, from the door.

"Kort?" The name floated up from the distant past. As if a visit from great Juvens had been announced. Savine prodded ineffectually at her wig, trying to scrape together some shreds of her old self-assurance as Zuri's brothers left the room. "Show him in...I suppose."

"Lady Savine!" Kort had prospered, that was clear. His clothes were simply cut, of course, since simplicity was the fashion, but she knew expensive cloth when she saw it, and the broken-chain pin he wore to show allegiance with the common man was set with little diamonds.

"*Citizeness* Savine." She used to be able to calibrate her smile with all the accuracy of a gunner ranging his cannon. Now it felt clumsy on her face, like a once-favourite pair of boots that no longer quite fit.

His eyes flickered only briefly to the scar on her forehead, and his own smile did not slip at all. "Whichever it is, you are as beautiful as ever." Nimbly done, since she wore a shapeless bag of a nursing dress, was bleary from lack of sleep and not painted or powdered at all. Her old clothes fit her no better than her smile. She had tried to squeeze her mother's body into one of her looser dresses a few days before and could hardly believe how thin she must once have been.

Kort took her hand in his slightly damp paw and kissed her warmly on one cheek. One would never have guessed that he had once tried to cheat her, while she threatened him with rumour, ruin and finally actual violence. But the warmth of their greeting only showed what excellent people of business they both were. One simply must forgive, after all, when there are profits on the table.

"How is your husband?"

"He is..." Crippled, struggling to find a place for himself, ground down by pain and burning with anger. "Adjusting to his injuries."

"Yet I've never seen him absent from the Assembly, rain or shine. He proves to be a fine speaker." Kort smiled beneficently down. "And this is?"

"My daughter, Ardee." Savine felt absurdly proud of her children and delighted in showing them off, even to people whose opinions she could not have cared less about. "Named after my mother. And almost as demanding."

"I am an engineer, and don't always see the appeal in babies, but this…" And he poked one thick finger at her. "*This* is a well-favoured infant!"

Little Ardee had only just begun to focus her eyes, but she focused hers on Kort's ruddy face now with her mouth suspiciously pursed. Evidently an excellent judge of character already.

"And this is my son, Harod." Savine led Kort to the other cot. "Named for Leo's father."

"Not for the first King of the Union, then?"

"I doubt that would be in keeping with the times."

"Certainly our most recent monarch finds himself short of support. Aside from a few die-hards in the east of Midderland, no one even bows to him any more, let alone kneels."

"We are all equal now…" Though it had not been long ago that Savine had knelt before the king to beg for her husband's life, and not long before that she had knelt before him in Sworbreck's office for… other reasons.

"I hear they have him shut up in six rooms of the palace, under constant guard," Kort was crowing. "He has to ask permission to use the latrine. Imagine that!"

Savine did not care to. Orso had shown mercy to her and her husband, however little they deserved it. More mercy than she would have shown, in his place. She wondered what the future held for him, as the Breakers tightened their grip. As people forgot the past. As they needed him less and less as a reassuring figurehead. Her brother, Orso.

She winced, the way she always did when the thought occurred. She wondered what might happen if the secret somehow came out. If they learned her children were the grandchildren of King Jezal…

Kort flicked out the tails of his coat to sit. "It seems that motherhood very much agrees with you."

"Somewhat to my surprise."

"Not to mine. I heard one Citizeness we both know wonder aloud whether you might give birth to a set of razors. I told her she was an idiot if she thought you wouldn't excel at anything you put your mind to."

"There has been a Great Change." Savine frowned towards the window, sure she had heard something outside. She waited a moment, but there was nothing. "We must change, too."

"I could not agree more." Kort's bulk had subsided into his chair, but now he eased it earnestly towards her. "And the greater the change, the greater the *opportunities*. Commissioner Pike seems fixed on crushing the banks. Between the lack of credit, the price of bread, the interruption in coal supplies from Angland...through nothing but buying and selling shrewdly, fortunes can be made in a day! And for those who know the right people, see the right openings, those who can actually bring goods into Adua...Selest dan Heugen—"

"There are no 'dans' any more, remember?"

"Whatever her name is, she's adjusted to the new reality like lightning. She's dispensed with the wigs, it's all about honesty now, apparently, and she's not even a redhead, would you believe?"

"I am astonishment itself."

"But she wears a red sash! In sympathy with the bloody Burners, and talks as though she's been arguing for the Great Change for years while she's making an absolute fortune buying flour in the provinces. They say the weather will only get colder, and the royalists are about in the east, burning crops. Lord Marshal Forest and his men, refusing to lay down their arms. Everything will get scarcer. With our canal, we—"

"No."

"No? Motherhood *has* changed you."

"On the contrary, I have always been extremely careful about which opportunities I take, and which I turn down." She lowered her voice, glancing towards the window again. "When they have hanged all their enemies, do you think they will *stop*? Things will unravel and they will need people to blame. Do you read the pamphlets? They print more than ever! Attacking aristocrats, and foreign agents, and speculators and hoarders and profiteers. Attacking everyone!" She thought of the mob, the clawing arm slithering through her broken carriage window. "I will *not* be making myself conspicuous. I strongly advise you to do the same."

Kort stared at her, his mouth ajar. "I never supposed that you, of all people, would lack the nerve to seize what is right in front of you. Lady Savine—"

"*Citizeness* Savine."

"There are such *opportunities*—"

"Haroon will see you out."

Zuri's older brother had eased silently into the room. His head was respectfully bowed, his smile almost apologetic, but there was something in the set of his broad shoulders, in the way one strong hand clasped the other, that made it clear it was time to go. He was almost as good as his sister at saying it all without saying a word.

Kort blinked at him, then gave a sigh, and heaved himself to his feet. "I fear you will regret this."

"I have so many regrets, I doubt this one will figure much."

Harod had woken now and started to mew, and Savine bent over the cot to attend to him, so she hardly even noticed Kort leave. She frowned as she sank down, unbuttoning the flap of her dress so she could scoop out one sore, sticky breast.

"Damn it," she growled as he chewed at her. You would never imagine they had no teeth for the pain they could thoughtlessly inflict.

She had been the most envied woman in the Union. Now here she was, trapped in a few rooms like the prisoner-king, milking herself like a farmer milks a cow. For the benefit of these two thankless little monsters, she had made herself a supporting character in her own life. Had the room always been this hot? She felt suffocated.

There was a crash outside and she gasped, nearly jumped up, staring towards the window, half-straightened legs trembling. Voices out there. Shouts. Then laughter, dying away. Disturbed in his feeding, Harod had started to cry. She settled herself, put him back to her breast, his head fishing desperately for what was right in front of him.

Savine found herself wondering what her parents would have said, if they could have seen her now. Making no plans. Taking no steps. Exerting no *grip*. Kort was hardly the shrewdest social operator, but even he had seen it at once. She had lost her nerve. Inevitable, perhaps, given all she had been through. But headaches or not, pearl dust or not, fears or not, she could not afford to hide away here, smiling wanly at her sleeping babies. Fretting over what would happen to Orso. Living in a drowsy, deadened, milk-smelling fug while the world collapsed around her. Then wetting herself with fright at every noise.

That was not protecting herself. That was not protecting her children. That was not caution, it was cowardice. It was *surrender*.

Savine forced her shoulders down. Her chin up. The posture she used to have, when she ruled the Solar Society. Or as close as she could get to it. "Zuri?" she called, and her voice was harsh. Not the tone in which she cooed at her babies. The tone in which she once blackmailed her rivals.

It only took a moment for Zuri to appear, opening the book and sliding her pencil from behind her ear. "What can I do?"

"Could Rabik find out what dressmakers are still alive and in business? This…" and she looked down at the milk-stained flap of her dress, hanging open like torn sacking, "will not do. I need a proper face-maid, too. A clever one."

"One who can make the paint look like there is no paint." And Zuri turned towards the door, scribbling a note. Savine brought her up short.

"And I want you to talk to our agents. Those still in business. I want them to scour the marketplaces. Secure as much food as they can. Flour and livestock especially. Have Haroon see if we can buy some bakeries. I understand it is dangerous work these days. Lots of them selling up." She was standing now, pacing up and down, rocking Harod and feeding him and thinking all at once. "Then I will talk to Leo about coal. See if he can bridge his mother and the Assembly, open up the supply from Angland again."

There was that little silence Zuri left to register her concern, pencil hovering over paper. "Playing the markets would be quite the risk in the current climate. Hoarders are being lynched, and I understand the Assembly plans to outlaw speculation—"

"I am not going to sell it."

"Then—"

"My scripture teacher tells me that charity is the first of virtues."

Zuri's black brows were raised very high. "She sounds exceedingly wise."

"She is. And my very good friend Honrig Curnsbick always tells me I have a generous heart. So I have decided to give it away. I want to go out into the poorest districts, and...give it away."

Savine had always thought that people who were liked were simply not trying hard enough to be envied. But it had not been her money that saved them, when the People's Army stormed the Agriont. It had been Leo's popularity. It was high time she had some of her own. Perhaps she could even do some good, for whatever that was worth.

Zuri gently shook her head. "If you had told me a year ago we would be giving anything away..."

"There has been a Great Change, Zuri. We must change— Ah!" She gasped as Harod chewed at her nipple again, pulled him angrily away and he started to cry. That helpless, desperate cry that felt like nails hammered directly into her red-rimmed eyes.

"Fuck," she snapped, pushing her sore breast back inside her dress and fumbling with the buttons on the other side, "and for the Fates' sakes, find me a reliable nurse. I can't manage them both alone."

# An Exhibit

"Really?" asked Orso as the plate was flung violently down in front of him. A piece of rancorous matter he did not dare describe as meat, some carrots virtually raw and some peas boiled to mush, all thoroughly cooled on the labyrinthine voyage from the kitchens to the remote corner of the palace which had become his prison.

The cook leaned down over him, her jaw jutting. "Do I look like I'm joking?"

"Rarely if ever," squeaked Orso, shrinking back.

Of all the things he missed about *before*, it was his cook Bernille that gave him the sharpest pangs of loss. Those delicate soups. Those miniature pastries. The things she had done with shellfish! Positively *indecent*. He wondered what had become of her and her extensive staff. He remembered visiting the kitchens, a fragrant hive of good-humoured industry. Executed, or herded off to hard labour, or... most likely, now he thought about it, cooking for someone else. Orso frowned. Might they even be happier cooking for someone else? Might they have had no choice but to put on those sweaty smiles? Might that kitchen have been a prison to them?

"Enjoying your dinner, Your Majesty?"

Orso tried to ignore his audience entirely but, as usual, he couldn't help glancing up. A few days before, they had opened the palace to tours. The people had paid for the place, Risinau had told the Assembly, with their blood and tears, so it belonged to the people, and they should be allowed to enjoy it. Even the miserable set of attics in which Orso was now confined, with its split floorboards, peeling wallpaper and rich festoons of cobweb, restlessly stirring in the constant chill draft. The Assembly evidently believed that the monarch was public property, too, and had determined to make an exhibit of him. Now a constant queue filed in through one door, gawped at him from behind a railing and filed out through another.

They laughed, and pointed, and Orso acknowledged them with a weary smile. "One humiliation after another," he murmured, flicking open his napkin, tucking it ever so delicately into his collar, and letting Hildi nudge the little table towards him. She had to slip a dog-eared political pamphlet under a loose leg to stop it wobbling.

"Thank you, Hildi. Everyone else might have forgotten themselves, but there's really no need to let one's own standards slide."

"Couldn't agree more." Hildi leaned close to whisper, "Managed to get you some of the good bread today." And she slipped a slice onto his plate.

"Hildi, you absolute treasure."

"Don't flatter me too much, you owe me two marks for the loaf."

"Bloody hell!" Orso had rarely indeed been called upon to spare much thought for the price of things, but that struck even him as steep. "Our tab must be *soaring*."

"Everything's dear these days."

"Especially to kings," he murmured, forking over that slice of bread and starting to carve it up. Somehow it tasted better if he treated it with the same ceremony as one of Bernille's wonderful cuts of beef.

"He should fucking dance for us."

Orso couldn't help glancing up, yet again. A man with a tall hat perched at a ridiculous angle leaned on the railing to leer at him, an overpainted woman giggling as she clung to his elbow.

"Good one, Shawley!"

Orso gave that weary smile again. Or at any rate it was still clinging to his face from last time. "A *very* good one," he said. "But I only dance with countesses and above, I'm afraid."

"We don't have lords or ladies here no more," said Shawley.

"Then unless you're foreign nobility I fear you're out of luck." And Orso raised his glass to them. "Cheers."

Some of the onlookers chuckled. Shawley decidedly did not. "We'll see who's out of luck, I reckon, in the end."

"Step back from the railing," grunted one of the guards. A man called Halder, blessed with even less sense of humour than the cook. No one seemed to have much sense of humour these days. Or perhaps they were simply no longer obliged to be merry in his presence.

Shawley looked even more put out. "I'll move when I'm ready—"

"You'll move when I say," said Halder. One of the other guards pulled out his heavy stick. "Or we'll move you to the House o' Truth."

Shawley tipped his hat so far, the brim was virtually touching his sneer and slouched away with bad grace, the woman glaring balefully back over her shoulder.

"Thank you *so* much for visiting!" called Orso, waving his fork at them. "Watch you don't catch your cock in the door on your way out!"

Biting into his meat cured him of any sense of triumph. It was like biting into a boot sole. "I'm a bloody sideshow curiosity," he murmured as he struggled to chew and retain his teeth at once. "The heir to the throne of Harod the Great, with a clear bloodline from Arnault himself, made into a zoo animal."

Hildi was too busy frowning towards the door. "Don't look up," she said, which had precisely the opposite effect, of course.

"Oh, damn," muttered Orso around a mouthful of carrot with the consistency of firewood. Who should be leading the next batch of gawkers but that noted member of the Assembly of Representatives, Corporal Tunny?

"He looks prosperous," grumbled Hildi.

"Debauchery is profitable under any government," said Orso, trying and entirely failing to look as if he was relishing his vile meal.

"Well, well, Your Majesty!" Tunny flashed his yellowed teeth. "It is *always* a pleasure."

"You really didn't have to visit me at home. We see more than enough of each other in the Assembly."

"Must say your quarters look rather humble for a monarch." Tunny glanced up at a mouldy stain that spread out from one corner of the ceiling. "You should complain to Chairman Risinau."

"Ignore him," said Orso, but Hildi could never stop leaping to his defence. A singularly thankless task these days. She stalked towards the railing, bristling.

"Your entourage seems diminished." Tunny peered down at her. "Never could make up my mind whether she was one of your bastards or one of your whores."

"Whereas I was always sure you were a *cunt*!" Hildi went for him, tried to claw at his face, but Tunny caught her arm and they tussled over the barrier. Orso sprang up, making his plate rattle.

"Step back from the railing," grunted Halder.

Tunny shoved Hildi roughly away and she stumbled and fell, cracking her head.

"You *bastard*!" snarled Orso, knife and fork clenched as though they were long and short steels.

Tunny touched his fingers to a red scratch on his grizzled neck and grinned. "What'll you do? Fork me to death?"

"I'll give it a fucking try!"

"Step back from the railing," growled Halder. "The lot o' you. And lower the cutlery." The guards mostly treated Orso with the put-upon contempt of underpaid nannies supervising a spoiled child. If there had been a fight, he honestly could not have said on whose side they would have intervened.

"He's not worth it." Hildi scrambled up, guiding Orso back towards his chair. "I'm fine."

"I always knew he was a bastard, but that *bastard*." Orso glowered towards Tunny as he swanned out through the far door. "Betraying me is one thing, everyone's at it, but taunting you—that *bastard*. How could I ever have trusted him—"

Out of sight below the tablecloth, he felt her hand slide into his lap.

He blinked at her, shocked. "Hildi, I think of you more like a little sister— Oh."

There was something in her hand. A scrap of paper. Tunny must have slipped it to her in the scuffle. She gave him a significant glance from under her blonde lashes. "More wine, Your Majesty?"

"I think I will. And pour a little for yourself as well, eh? We've both had quite the shock."

As the vinegary vintage slopped into his glass, he hacked away at his chop, plate rattling, and peered down at the note on his leg, pencilled in a bold hand.

*Apologies for the scorn. Apologies for anything said in the Assembly. Apologies to Hildi for the shove. Sorry Hildi! They have to think I am against you.*

*I am in touch with Forest. Most of the Crown Prince's Division stayed loyal, along with the rugged country in the east of Midderland. I also had word from Princess Carlot. Her husband Chancellor Sotorius is ready to help. And Bremer dan Gorst has his steels handy.*

*You still have friends, Your Majesty. When the time is right, I will have your standard ready.*

*With best wishes,*

*(always) Your Friend and Servant, (always) Corporal Tunny*

"By the Fates." Orso wondered for a moment if it could be some elaborate ruse, but to what end? No. He knew the truth. The notoriously faithless Corporal Tunny was the one truly loyal man in Adua.

"How the hell could I ever have doubted him?" he whispered, tears brimming in his eyes. Halder was frowning over, and Orso took a long sniff and waved at his plate with his fork.

"It's these peas," he said, in a quavering voice. "They've been absolutely *murdered.*"

The man gave a snort. Orso would have liked to see him absolutely murdered. And thanks to Corporal Tunny, not to mention Lord Marshal Forest, his sister Carlot and Bremer dan Gorst, it seemed there was the glimmer of a chance that it might happen. Not today, perhaps, and not tomorrow, but the weather was turning cold. Soon enough, people would turn against Risinau. The man had simply promised too much and delivered too little.

As far as Orso could tell, he was incapable of delivering anything.

He laid down his cutlery, and carefully tore the note up into strips, and slipped them into his mouth, and chewed with relish. Without doubt, the most enjoyable part of the meal.

"Good news," murmured Hildi, under her breath.

"Very good news," said Orso, around his papery mouthful, and he chinked his glass against hers.

He was not rescued and the world was not set to rights. Not by any means. But he could see a path to it. He was not alone. He was not forgotten.

And he remembered how it felt, to have hope.

# Different This Time

Leo sat, fussing at a loose thread in the sleeve on his useless arm. A year ago, he would've been pacing up and down. But pacing was another thing that wasn't worth the pain these days.

"Are you sure about this house?" he grumbled. A fire crackled in the grate, and it was warm and welcoming, and Savine would never have permitted a detail that wasn't in the best taste, but you couldn't have called it a grand room.

"If I was not sure we would not be here. It sends the right message."

"That we're of no account?"

"That we are humble, responsible Citizens who have put the excess of the past behind us and accepted that we are all equal."

Leo snorted. "Have you seen that bloody palace Selest dan Heugen's having built? Or that town house of Isher's? There are plenty of people still living well."

"They may come to regret it," said Savine. "How things look used to be the difference between success and failure. In these times it might be the difference between life and death."

Leo frowned at that painting of his grandfather, Lord Marshal Kroy, cramped now under a far lower ceiling. "You always loved fine things." Meaning he'd realised now they were gone how much he'd liked them.

"I loved fine things when they said the right things about me. Fine things say the wrong thing now. And we are that much closer to the Agriont. It's a shorter trip to the Assembly."

He knew he should've been grateful. Instead, he felt faintly nettled. "I can walk."

"I know. But it hurts you. Why walk further than you have to?"

"To prove that I can," he grunted, gripping the handle of his crutch.

She floated over his annoyance, as usual, which, as usual, only annoyed him more. "In any case, the other house is filled."

"Tenants?"

"Children."

"What?"

"Have you seen how many of them are homeless in the city?" Honestly, he hadn't. He spent all his time out of doors focused on staying upright. "Gangs of them. Orphaned, abandoned, lacking the most basic necessities. Forced to prey upon each other, to thieve, to sell themselves. Children starving on our streets."

Leo frowned over at her. She'd shed her shapeless nursing clothes now and, despite a lack of jewels, looked mostly her sleek, sharp, ruthless old self. But then she'd serve up something like this. "So...the Darling of the Slums has opened an orphanage?"

Now she looked nettled. As if she hated thinking of herself as a philanthropist as much as he hated thinking of himself as a cripple. "They just need a chance. And we can give them one."

"Or at least appear to."

"Exactly."

"Well, I suppose you're right."

"I usually am," she said, which was where these conversations generally ended up.

The chair seemed to buzz under him and a moment later there was a throbbing boom, ornaments rattling on the mantle. They'd made pathetic progress at demolishing the Agriont's mighty walls with hammer and pick, so the Assembly had voted to move into the modern age and try blowing them up with Gurkish Fire. Gravel was routinely raining out of the sky for streets around as a result.

"Fucking idiots," he snarled at the window, grinding his crutch into the carpet.

He felt Savine's hand on his shoulder. That calming touch, just the fingertips. "All you need to do is apologise."

"I'm no bloody good at apologies," wanting to shake her hand off but somehow wanting it to stay both at once.

"Apologise badly, then."

"Why should I be the one saying sorry?" Though he knew exactly why.

"Because we need him." Which was exactly why. "And you were a fool to push him away in the first place. If it helps, tell yourself you're not apologising for what you did, but for being a fool."

"I'm not sure that does help."

"Be charming. You can be charming, when you want to be. You charmed me."

"Really? The way I remember it, you seduced me, fell pregnant, then talked me into a match."

A hint of an exasperated sigh, and Savine took her hand away. "Talk him into a match, then."

That felt like a dangerous choice of words somehow. Out in the hall, Leo heard an echoing knock on the door, felt an absurd surge of nerves. "Help me up."

Savine dragged him out of his chair, none too gently, and he winced as he put his weight on his iron leg. He was right, he could walk. And she was right, it hurt.

"I will be in the next room," said Savine. "If you get into difficulty."

"What can you do?"

"I'll think of something." And she shut the door behind her, leaving him alone.

Leo stood, stump throbbing, blood thumping in his head. He could hear voices in the hall.

He wondered what pose to strike, but when you've only one leg, and that's a poor one, and one arm, and that has to grip a crutch, you haven't many options. So when the door clattered open and Haroon showed in Leo's oldest friend, he was still standing lopsided in the middle of the carpet with a quivery smile on his face.

"Jurand!"

Leo hadn't been ready for the rush of feeling. He could hardly breathe for it. He'd been stuck for months among traitors, thugs and cowards, and the sight of that familiar, trustworthy face, as handsome as ever, was like a lamp in a pitch-black room. It felt as if a part of him that died at Stoffenbeck—the best part of him, even—came suddenly to life again.

What he wanted to do more than anything was lurch into Jurand's arms and never let go of him. He was poised to do it. Then he saw the shock on his friend's face. His wide eyes flickered over the scars, the useless arm, the iron leg, and it dropped on Leo with the weight of the Agriont's falling walls how ruined he was since the last time they saw each other. How broken and disfigured. How utterly crippled.

Leo turned away. Might've hidden his scarred face behind his left hand, if he could've pulled it from his jacket without help.

His words crept out in a nervous croak. "I can't tell you...how glad I am you're here—"

The shock had passed and Jurand's jaw was angrily set. "I'm here because Lady Finree ordered me to come. Not because you asked me."

That sank into the silence between them. Leo swallowed. Not long ago his pride would've made him stomp from the room. But his pride must've been in his leg, as it hardly seemed to bother him these days. "How is she?"

"Worried. Desperately worried, about you, but she doesn't let it show. She has to put Angland back together. I don't know what would have happened without her. She's a great leader."

Leo flinched. "Far better than her son."

"You'd have a hard time arguing otherwise."

He knew he couldn't deny it. Being in his mother's shadow used to feel unbearable. Now he saw how lucky he'd been to have her. He took a hard breath and drew himself up. "I'm sorry, Jurand. I'm...I'm very sorry. For the way it all turned out. If you'd been with me, at Stoffenbeck, things would've been...well." He frowned down at his leg. At his crutch. "I was a fool."

Jurand didn't break out the long-suffering smile he always used to find at Leo's latest recklessness. The only hint of warmth in his face were the spots of colour from the heat of the fire after the chill outside.

"You're right for once," he snapped. "You were a fool. A selfish fool, and one hell of a poor friend." Leo blinked. He'd known he needed to apologise. He'd never supposed Jurand might not accept it. "I always thought you knew, deep down. Honestly, I always thought..." He trailed off, hands opening and closing, frowning hard at the floor.

Leo's mouth was very dry. "Thought what?"

"Who cares what I thought. I'm as big a fool as you are, in my own way."

Leo took an awkward step towards him, his metal ankle squeaking. Wanted to reach out, comfort him, but he didn't have the limbs for it. "You're about the cleverest man I know—"

"At least my stupidity didn't get anyone killed." Now Jurand looked up again, and so bitterly Leo had to take that awkward step back. "Remember when there were seven of us?"

Leo was left frozen, his mouth slightly open. It was a long time since he'd thought of the happy brotherhood who'd gone to war with him. Risked their lives for him. Most of his energy went into finding ways to do what used to be easy, the rest into twisting the future into a shape he could live with.

"Ritter," said Jurand, "Barniva, Jin, Antaup, Glaward, me and you."

Each name was like a slap. Leo took another wobbling step back, and his stump twisted in the socket of his false leg, and the stab of pain made his knee buckle. His crutch clattered down, but he caught the arm of a chair, managed to sag into it.

"They chose to fight," he whispered.

"They chose to follow you, and you led them to their deaths."

"I miss them," said Leo. "I miss them like my leg and my arm." He missed them almost as much as he'd missed Jurand. Now that he thought about them. "But I can't bring them back...any more than you can take back what you did...in Sipani."

And that familiar image came up, of Jurand and Glaward, pressed against each other, half-naked on their knees, and Leo winced at the rush of painful excitement that always came with it, worse than ever with his old friend right in front of him.

He looked even angrier, now. "Who says I want to take it back?" he snarled. "You wouldn't understand! You've never had to hide a thing in your life. You've always said and done whatever you pleased. However hurtful. However ignorant. You've been celebrated for it! How blunt! How manly! Well, it's a new world now, I hear. We all have to live with things we don't like."

"Oh, there's been a Great Change, it's true." Leo felt his own anger bubbling up, never far from the surface, and he slapped at his aching stump. "I'm fucked, and the world's fucked, but there are still some things that—"

A rattle as the door opened and Savine swept in, smiling radiantly with a baby in the crook of each arm. "Jurand! Thank the Fates you're here. It's so good to see you again!"

"Lady Savine..."

"*Citizeness* Savine!" She leaned close, to speak out of the side of her mouth. "We are all equal, apparently." Jurand was staring at the two bundles. "Ah, yes. *These.* This is Harod, and this is Ardee. At least, I think that's the right way round." She laughed, just as if there was no icy tension in the room at all. "This is your father's dearest friend, Jurand," she cooed at the babies. "Yes it is, he's the brains of the business, and everything will be all right now, you'll see. Two of the little monsters, would you believe it?"

"I...wouldn't," said Jurand, still staring.

"And they're almost as unreasonable as their father. Shush, shush, come now." One of them had started to wriggle and squeak. Leo couldn't be sure, but he wondered if Savine might've pinched it. "Could you hold him, just for a moment?" Without waiting for an answer, she dumped the other in Jurand's arms.

"He's beautiful," whispered Jurand, and as he stared down at little Harod, a hint of that familiar smile touched his face.

"He takes after his mother in that regard," murmured Savine.

All she'd done was walk in with the children. *Put aside the past*, those little bundles of innocent potential seemed to say. *Look to the future.* As simply as that, the mood was changed.

Leo had sworn never to let another chance slip by. He dragged himself up, set himself as best he could, hesitantly reached out and laid his hand on Jurand's shoulder. He didn't shake it off.

"I'm sorry," said Leo. "I'm so sorry." And he was. For the mistakes he'd made. "I was a fool. I need you."

"*We* need you," murmured Savine, gripping Jurand's other shoulder. "The Union needs you. Risinau's position gets weaker and weaker."

"No one loves him, no one fears him, no one respects him."

"I read a newsbill more savage about him than they used to be about the king," said Leo.

"One of Sworbreck's, no doubt," said Savine. "Even he's turning on the Chairman."

"Things are coming apart. Riots every day. Someone has to step into the gap."

Jurand glanced at Leo's hand on his shoulder, then up into his face. "Or limp into it?"

The time was Leo might've punched him for that, but now he smiled. "I was actually hoping you might carry me into it."

Jurand looked back to Leo's son, sound asleep in his arms. "Things will have to be different this time."

"Of course," said Leo.

"No hotheaded folly."

"I'm with you there," said Savine.

"And I want something for myself."

Leo squeezed Jurand's shoulder. "You deserve it."

"One thing even my enemies will concede," said Savine, "I *always* pay my debts."

"We could begin with seats in the Assembly." Leo tickled his daughter under the chin and made her squirm. "For you, and for Glaward, then... our success will be your success."

The side of Jurand's face twitched as he set his jaw. "How do we begin?"

The ground trembled. A moment later came the echoing rumble of another explosion.

# Quarrels

She slapped him as hard as she could. It made her hand sing with pain, so she was pretty sure his face must've felt worse.

"You fucking arsehole!" she screamed.

"You mad bitch!" he roared back, spraying spit in her face. "That's it! I'm done!" And he kicked the door wide and stomped from the bedchamber which had once been Bethod's, once been Scale Ironhand's, once been Stour Nightfall's, and now was Sticky Rikke's.

Corleth, who'd been waiting outside, flattened herself against the wall as the Nail stormed past.

"You're mad as a bootful o' bees!" he snarled over his shoulder, trying to do his sword-belt up at the same time and making a mess of both.

Rikke's bare feet slapped at the steps as she chased after him. "Better bloody mad than bloody stupid, say I!"

"No need to pick! You've managed the pair!" He stalked out into grey daylight, raindrops prickling the chill puddles scattered about the yard, and she followed.

"Running away, are you?"

"Aye," he growled, "'fore I wring your twig of a neck."

Folk all about had perked up at the shouting. A girl with an armload of firewood was gawping at them from under a dripping oilcloth.

"Back to the West Valleys!" The Nail jerked his arm at his men and they fell in with him, tramping in a sullen crowd out of Bethod's fortress and into the city, dark stone turned darker with wet, dark roofs glistening with rain. "You can fight Black Calder on your own."

"I'll do that, and I'll bloody beat him, too!"

"You'll bloody lose and piss away all you took."

"My da always said the West Valleys were a fucking sty!" she shrieked at his back. "And you don't need the Long Eye to see they've birthed a litter of swine wi' you lot!"

"Long fucking Eye?" The Nail spun about, looming over her, face so twisted with rage she stumbled back and almost slipped on her arse. "Don't make me laugh!" And he stuck his great scarred forefinger in her face so hard it near went up her nostril. "You can't see what's right under your nose, you half-blind witch!"

"Well, at least one of us has something long." She started forwards and jabbed her little finger in his face. "Guess we know why they call you the Nail now!"

"My cock's...*decent-sized*!" He spat at her feet. "Used to shit yourself all over Uffrith, now you're shitting yourself all over Skarling's Chair!" And he gave a bark of fury that nearly made her slip over again, then stomped off faster'n ever, his dour-faced family crowding after him.

"Go on!" she screamed at their backs. "Back you go to your mummies, you batch o' cowards! Not one decent set o' bones in the lot of you! We're well rid o' you bloody chicken-fuckers! I never saw such a stack o' fishy cunts! You bloody...bloody..." She'd run out of insults. Even bad ones. And the Nail and his boys had already made it to the gate of Carleon and vanished down the entrance tunnel. She was shouting herself raw at the wet air.

She realised she'd wandered halfway through the city, bare feet cold on the damp cobbles, bare legs covered in gooseflesh under her cloak, damp hair plastered to her head by the chill rain. Reckoned she must have trod in something on the way, one foot was smeared brown down the side.

"By the dead," she muttered, hopping about while she tried to wipe it on a slippery doorstep. That was when she saw a curious crowd had built up. Townsfolk. Carls and Thralls. A couple of dirty children with a big, bedraggled dog.

"Haven't you shits got aught better to do?" she snapped, pulling that red cloth tight about her along with such shreds of dignity as she had left. She turned back towards Skarling's Hall with her chin in the air, doing her best to look like a screaming row half-naked in the pissing rain was just one more step in her grand plan.

Corleth, Isern and Shivers stood in the street behind her, and did not look convinced.

"I've heard it said a clever woman can turn enemies into allies with her quim," mused Isern, eyes thoughtfully narrowed. "Yours seems to work the other way around."

"Very funny." Rikke pushed past her and strode back up the hill. "The Nail had his mind set on going after Calder now. If you can call it a

134

mind. Bastard wouldn't be argued down. Now, mark you! With winter coming on!"

"I warned her about getting cocky," muttered Isern from the side of her mouth. "Maybe I should've warned her about getting cock."

"We'll make do fine without him!" Rikke roared it at the town in general. "A fucking carrot can do the same job!"

Shivers raised his one good brow. "Doubt we'll beat Black Calder with a carrot," he said.

"We will not beat him with vegetables of any kind," said Isern as they stepped back through the gate in Bethod's great wall. "For that we will need men, and my guess is the Nail will be taking his cousins and his uncles and his friends back to the West Valleys with him."

"We'll be short-handed if Calder comes knocking."

"*When* he comes knocking."

"All right, all right!" snapped Rikke, stumbling on the mud-heavy hem of her cloak and having to pull it up clumsily above her ankles. "Might be I got a little carried away. But we managed before he turned up, eh, Isern?"

Isern considered her, jaw muscles squirming as she chewed a chagga pellet. "When we were running for our lives through a freezing forest, d'you mean?"

"I was thinking of a bit after that."

"When we dragged you half-dead and all mad up into the hills to be paint-pricked by a witch with her head stitched together?"

"You're in one o' those moods," snapped Rikke.

"No," said Isern. "*You* are. Sitting in Skarling's Chair don't make you Skarling, and wearing Savine dan what's-her-face's necklace don't make you Savine dan what's-her-face. It ain't pouting or wrath that got you here, it's care and planning and a humble respect for your enemies and your allies. It's those things'll keep you here. Head on along this path, you'll end up taking the drop from the windows sooner'n I thought." She gave a long sigh and put her chin in the air. "And all my efforts wasted."

Rikke stood in the thickening rain, watching her swagger away. She badly wanted to take a parting shot but found the quiver was empty. She glanced up at Shivers, who was frowning back at her, his grey hair turned dark by the rain.

"Am I to take it you agree?"

Shivers' real eye gave away no more than his metal one. "Well, I don't disagree."

Rikke hissed in disgust as she ducked back inside, wet feet slapping on the flagstones.

"Here," said Corleth, handing her a chagga pellet.

"Nice to see *some* folk can yet be relied upon." And Rikke pushed the pellet up behind her lip and shoved open the doors to Skarling's Hall.

Stour was clean now, bruises mostly healed even if his legs never would be. He'd stopped begging. Stopped talking at all. Just sat there, one white hand up on the black bars, waiting. She felt his bright, wet eyes following her, and it made the hairs on her neck prickle.

Jonas Clover didn't look bothered by the Great Wolf, mind you. He was one o' those bastards could look pleased with himself sat on broken glass, warming his hands at the fire like some smug old tomcat, his wet cloak thrown over a bench to dry like this was his hall.

"Chief!" he said, glancing up. "My hearing ain't all it used to be, but I could swear I caught some manner of commotion."

"Only the Nail on his way out o' town."

"A short trip or a long?" Clover raised his brows at Corleth, but no further details were forthcoming. "Well, we went over to the Redwater Valley, like you told us."

"And Calder's boys were down there?" asked Rikke, dropping into Skarling's Chair. Either it was softening or her arse was hardening, it didn't feel so uncomfortable as it used to.

"Ran into a dozen, led by a fellow called Trapper."

"Put 'em back in the mud, did you?"

A brief pause, and Rikke got the feeling he was considering how to cast something in the best light. He did that a lot. "Some of 'em."

"The rest?"

"Sent 'em back to Black Calder with my cordial greetings and hopes for a mutually beneficial future."

"Kept your options open, in other words."

And from his cage, she heard Stour Nightfall give the faintest hiss of contempt.

"Kept the lines o' communication open, I'd say," said Clover. "Thought the time might come when that could be useful."

"Useful to me, or useful to you?"

"Our fates are wove together, Chief! I see no difference 'twixt the two."

"Huh." She shifted her chagga pellet from one side of her mouth to the other and leaned forwards, turning her left eye towards him. "I've seen your future, Clover."

He winced. "At least tell me I get to sit down."

"Not yet, anyway. You're going to go pay Black Calder a visit."

That wince became a full grimace. "That doesn't sound like something I'd do."

"Think better of where you're at and decide you'd rather be somewhere else? Sounds like the sort of thing you're famous for."

"Knew that'd land me in trouble sooner or later. So if Calder doesn't kill me for betraying him in the first place, what then?"

Rikke considered him a moment. Considered the position. Turned in the chair to consider Stour Nightfall, sitting calm in his cage, hungry eyes gleaming in the shadows. She weighed the words carefully. "Tell him I'm willing to deal. Peace in the North. In return for his son."

Clover glanced over at the cage. Rikke heard the chain creak as Stour shifted inside, pressing himself to the bars. Heard him make that hiss again.

"You sure?" asked Clover.

"I'm sure about asking the question."

"As you wish, then." He dragged his wet cloak from the bench and over his shoulder, slapping dew from the wolf-pelt collar. "If your answer is my head in a jar, don't say I didn't warn you."

"I'll weep a river. And Clover?"

"Aye?"

"Probably best you don't mention this business with the Nail. Wouldn't want Calder thinking we're weak."

"Goes without saying." And he gave a little bow, and walked out.

Corleth put one hand on the arm of Skarling's Chair and leaned down towards her. "Reckon we can trust him?"

"Anyone we can trust, Calder won't talk to. Sometimes you need a man no wind can shift." Rikke turned towards that patch of floor that was getting somewhat stained from her chagga spit and spat on it. "Sometimes you need one who bends with the breeze."

# Too Many Principles

"This is the Lords' Round?" asked Glaward, dumbfounded.

"It was," said Leo. The place his father had talked of as the cradle of noble ideals. Where the great lords of the Union had engaged in dignified debate. Where Arnault stood alone to challenge Morlic the Mad and changed the course of history. It was easy to forget. "They call it the Commons' Round now."

The stained-glass windows, with their scenes from centuries of the Union's proud history, had been declared symbols of repression and replaced with free, equal, ideologically sound clear glass from a new manufactory in the Three Farms. Harsh daylight wasn't kind to the place.

The public galleries had been the playground of Adua's highest society. Now, if they hadn't died or fled the country, the highest society were staying well out of sight. The lowest had crowded into their place, rowdier every day. Sometimes bands would strike up bawdy songs above the Assembly, the Union's government creaking to a halt like a mired cart till they could be clumsily evicted.

The days were getting shorter and the endless sessions dragged into the darkness, haggard faces lit by flickering candlelight. The place was chill as a tomb in the mornings, overhot by lunch, stinking of stale sweat and bad breath and chagga smoke. Representatives ate at their seats, remnants of meals rotting under the greasy benches. Gunnar Broad and his men regularly broke up fights. A week before, a drunk had fallen from the upper gallery during a scuffle and been smashed to pulp on the floor before the High Table. They'd paused long enough to scrape the corpse out, then carried on arguing while the mess was being mopped up.

"We need to be bloody *civil*!" Ramnard, an old tailor with a face pitted by some childhood sickness, was making one of his rude demands for politeness. "I *damn well insist* that Citizen Sworbreck reduce the number, not to mention the savagery, of his attacks upon members of this Assembly in his newsbills and pamphlets—"

Sworbreck leaped up as if he was mounted on a spring. "Nothing would delight me more than to do so! The very *instant* we reduce the number, not to mention the *corruption*, of the traitors, profiteers and simple incompetents *in* this Assembly!"

Laughter, applause. The public gallery were as hungry for pain, tears and passion as any audience at the theatre. Leo's clapping days were over, but he slapped the bench beside him one-handed in fake approval.

"Friends, please!" Risinau whined from his gilded chair. "We still have so much work to do on our *constitution*. The people are restless. So easily roused to anger." As if he hadn't ridden a wave of it to power. "Citizen Sworbreck, we merely ask for a little *moderation* in the frenzy of your denouncements."

"Moderation sells no pamphlets," muttered Leo.

Sworbreck was well aware of that. "Sully the high principles of this august body with *dishonesty*? I would rather *die*!" He tore his shirt open to expose a wedge of pale chest. "Plunge in your dagger *there*, Citizen! I will happily wash the benches of this Assembly with my heart's blood in the cause of the Great Change, I have said so often!"

"Washing them with something would be a step forward," Jurand muttered in Leo's ear. Sitting between him and Glaward was far from comfortable, given the history. What happened in Sipani. What might *still* be happening... But it felt better than letting them sit together.

In the clamour produced by Sworbreck's latest offer of martyrdom, Representatives shouted over each other to be heard. It was noisy as a battle, and Leo watched the back and forth with the care of a general feeling out his moment to advance. A white-haired old merchant had kidnapped the floor now, his bass voice so powerful the benches seemed to vibrate.

"If the attention of the Assembly might be steered to other matters?" Far too easily, if anything. "I move that Commissioner Pike presents himself to explain his recent actions!"

"Hear, hear!" blustered that heavyset oaf who used to be one of Savine's partners. Kort, was it? "The Commissioner's private war against the banks is bad for business. We're losing our advantage to the Styrians! It's a war out there in the markets!"

A foreman from the Three Farms shook a great fist. He was called, appropriately enough, Hefty, though Leo wasn't sure whether it was a nickname or a surname. "There's a *real* fucking war going on!" Whoops in the gallery. He turned red in the face. "Begging your pardon." Laughter in the gallery. He turned redder. "But there's royalist *rebels* to worry about in the east!"

"Treacherous bastards set on raising the king up above us again!"

"We couldn't possibly have *that*," drawled the king himself, whose gilded enclosure had become a wooden one, then a high dais, then a low dais, and finally a nursing chair with a rail around it.

The usual rage, meanwhile, from above. Crumpled pamphlets were flung down. An apple core bounced from the shoulder of an ex-lord a few seats away and Jurand flinched.

"Don't worry," said Leo. "They rarely throw anything hard."

"What's the People's Army doing?" someone howled.

"I have men, but no *leaders*." General Brint frowned from his chair beside Risinau's. "I beg you, Citizens, allow me to bring in officers from the old King's Own—"

"How can we trust men who served the old regime?"

"Who else were they supposed to serve? That was the only regime going!"

"You have staunch patriots!" Hefty stabbed a finger at Broad, who looked more worried than staunch. "Men of good common stock!"

"It's not a question of birth, but of experience!"

"Principle trumps pragmatism!" someone screeched.

"Not on the battlefield!" growled Brint. "But the moment I need a grocer's advice on running an army, yours will be the first address I call at!"

Leo winced. Brint was a good enough man, but he didn't understand the rules of this engagement.

"Is it like this all the time?" murmured Glaward.

"Most of it."

"How do they get anything done?"

"They don't." Leo sensed the slightest lull in the melee, and he settled his stump in the socket of his iron leg, his crutch in his aching armpit. "Could you help me up?"

"The Young Lion!" someone screeched as Glaward guided him to standing, and the hall fell silent. As close as it ever got, anyway.

"Citizens!" Leo limped a few steps onto the tiled floor so that he stood alone. "Friends! Good men and women of the Union!" He aimed that at the public galleries and got a reassuring murmur of support. He'd found if he could bring the scum up there onto his side, the scum down here wouldn't dare disagree. "We can't afford to bicker! We've got enemies everywhere, keen to divide us!"

Leo was careful not to name the enemies, of course. He let everyone fill in their own.

"Bastard Styrians!" someone snarled.

"Bloody Southerners!"

"Aristocrats!"

"We've won a great victory against tyranny," he called. "We've won the chance to forge a Union that's the envy of the world." And he set himself so he could strike his crutch on the tiles with an echoing bang. "But we have to build *bridges*. We have to bring good men *in*. Like my old friends from Angland. Discord won't help us. We need *equality*. We need *loyalty*. We need *unity*!"

He hobbled to his seat with the applause ringing in his ears and dropped down wincing, shaking his leg to loosen it on his sore stump.

Glaward looked more dumbfounded than ever. "You didn't...*say* anything." Perhaps he was faithful and diligent, like Savine said, but Leo had forgotten how slow he could be.

"Only an idiot stands in front of this rabble to *say* something," muttered Leo, wiping the fresh sheen of sweat from his forehead. "You shuffle a few of the right words together and make sure you look 'em in the eye." He flashed the humble smile he'd been working on. Waved away the congratulations as men leaned from the benches behind to slap him on the shoulder. "You're going for a *feeling*. Make them think you're one of them. Prove the mob's behind you. You want to get something done, you pick a few men to talk to behind closed doors."

Jurand looked almost admiring. A happy hint of the way he used to look at Leo before...all this. "I thought you were a blunt soldier?"

"I'm still a soldier." Leo shifted his useless arm in his jacket and saluted the gallery. "It's just a different battlefield."

"When did that fucker get eloquent?" grumbled Orso, slumping into his ridiculous little chair. He had half a mind to applaud himself. "Equality? He must be the most privileged bastard in here."

"Other than you," murmured Hildi.

"Other than me, yes, thanks for that, Hildi. His family's had a seat in this bloody chamber for centuries. His grandfather was almost elected king himself and betrayed the Union when he lost the vote. Like grandfather like grandson, eh?"

"You can't deny folk warm to him, though."

"Oh, yes. People have *always* loved the Young Lion." He still seemed to be the same honest Anglander, none of Sworbreck's flowery style, but these days he was playing the mob like his own personal orchestra and leading the nervous ex-lords wherever he pleased. Now he had a dozen virile young heroes of Angland on the front benches ready to nod along at his every utterance as though it fell from the mouth of Euz himself. Orso was starting to think he was far more dangerous now than he had been with all his limbs.

"An appeal for loyalty, can you imagine? A few months ago he was leading his own rebellion!"

The hypocrisy was breathtaking. But the public appetite for hypocrisy appeared insatiable. Isher, who not long ago had enriched himself beyond the dreams of avarice by evicting impoverished tenants from common land, had risen to preach thrift in the most conspicuously humble, dirt-coloured clothes one could imagine.

"Citizens, please!" Risinau was struggling vainly, as he had been for weeks, to impose order on this shambles. "Our *constitution!*"

And Orso started to laugh. A little snigger at first. He tried to hold it in, but it burst out again. An explosive giggle. Every face he noticed made it worse. The monstrously wealthy traitor Isher, hiding in an honest man's feast-day clothes. The turncoat loser Brock, cheered to the rafters for his patriotism and prowess. The cowardly fantasist Sworbreck, posing as the common man's fearless champion. The onslaught of overblown preaching, sentimental one-upmanship, angry stands on shifting principles, tearful declarations of shifting loyalty. The worst of mankind jammed into the sockets where the best should have been. A crown of turds.

"You all right?" muttered Hildi, looking worried.

Orso was shuddering with mirth now, laughter echoing about the chamber. No one else looked amused. The Chairman especially.

"Perhaps His Majesty might explain what he finds so amusing?"

"What *don't* I?" Orso's eyes swam with tears. "Your grand experiment? Your wondrous new system? Believe me, no one liked the old way of doing things less than I, but my forebears ran the Union for six centuries. You'll be lucky if you make it six months."

"Captain Broad! We cannot have this cavalier disrespect for our Assembly!"

Broad wearily nudged his lenses up his nose and began to trudge towards the royal enclosure.

Orso jumped up. "Are we not all equal here?" He addressed the public gallery in a wailing mockery of Sworbreck's overwrought delivery. "Does not every Citizen deserve an equal chance to speak? Even so base a creature as a king?"

"Let him talk!" someone shouted.

"Let him talk himself into a noose!"

"I begin to wish you'd follow through on your threats!" called Orso. Bravery had descended inexplicably upon him, as it had at Stoffenbeck. Bravery born of fear, boredom, frustration and at least a little drunkenness. Far from heroic ingredients, to be sure, but no one asks what went into the pie so long as the results taste well. "You've hanged a good many decent people already! I'd rather join them than suffer this chorus of flatterers, thugs and hypocrites."

"How *dare* you?" But Risinau's voice was more plaintive whine than outraged roar. "We are shaping the *future!*"

Orso almost sympathised. "Take it from a man who's been there, you're the figurehead on a ship of fools. I daresay there are good people here, and good intentions. You had a chance to make things better and, believe it or not, no one looked forward to seeing it more than I did. But you haven't achieved a damn thing. I know this is rich coming from me, but...you're simply *poor quality*. You're a worthless bag of bluster. A spent match."

"Never thought I'd agree with His fucking Majesty."

There was a rustling as the Representatives turned to stare towards the top of the aisle. One could make many criticisms of Judge, but never that she didn't make an entrance. She came stalking down the steps between the benches with all the swagger of a champion to the fencing circle, her stolen chains scraping her breastplate, her red hair greased into a flaming crest, the flinty point to a spearhead of grim-faced, hard-handed, red-clothed men. Her black eyes swept the benches with the kind of burning purpose the Assembly had been sorely lacking, but Orso felt far from relieved as her gaze fell upon him.

"Sit down, Citizen Orso," she said.

Orso sat.

Judge stopped before the High Table, hands on hips and her bare feet planted wide. "I have watched the fucking pantomime in this ill-behaved nursery with growing disgust," she said.

"Aye!" growled the Burners, in echoing unison.

"You were meant to put things *right*, but all you've done is spill a sea of *talk*. One might almost say," she leaned towards Risinau, planting her clenched fists on the tabletop, "that those who have allowed this state of affairs to develop," lips curling back from her teeth, "are, through intent or omission," spraying spit as she snarled the words, "guilty of *betraying the Great Change*."

"We *are* the Great Change!" Risinau pointed his chin at her, the wattle beneath his jowls wobbling. "We hear your carping, Citizeness, but no reason for your attendance!"

Judge grinned. A skull grin that got nowhere near her eyes. "Oh, I'm here to arrest the perpetrators."

One of the secretaries set down her pen to hurry around the High Table, one ink-stained finger wagging. "With respect, you have no warrant here—"

"You sure? Brother Sarlby, could you produce our credentials?"

"With pleasure." A rat-faced Burner with a red-spattered cap stepped forward, sliding his hand into his jacket pocket. He brought it out in front of the secretary. There was nothing there but his fist. He smashed it into her face and knocked her down, her head bouncing on the tiles. She was left gazing up in amazement with blood running from her broken nose.

There was a stunned silence in the Commons' Round. Orso had the sense that, in that moment, all the rules had changed. Again.

Then Judge burst out laughing. "You fools have got as coddled as His Majesty used to be. As useless as the Open Council used to be. What is it about some folk, that power makes 'em weak?"

Risinau had turned very pale. "I am still Chairman of this Assembly!" He gripped the gilded arms of his chair as though to prove it to himself, but the echoes of his voice had become scared squeaks in the high space of the dome above. "Captain Broad! See this woman removed forthwith!"

Broad frowned towards the doors. He'd been doing it ever since Judge strutted in. She hadn't been the last person through. Dozens of folk wearing red had slipped into the chamber. Red caps, red sleeves, red rags tied around their heads. Some with their hands behind their backs, or hidden by their sides, or wedged in their jackets. One grinning little girl carried a great dripping pot of paint, scattering red dots across the dirty marble.

Burners.

There were splashes of red everywhere. Broad lifted his head so he could peer through his lenses and saw red flatbows at the rail of the public gallery.

"Captain Broad?" Brint had an odd tone, suddenly. Less of an order than a wheedle.

"No, no, no," purred Judge, the ragged train of her dress hissing across the dirty tiles towards Broad, those black eyes fixed on him all the way, and she reached up, and touched his face with her fingertips. The gentlest touch, just under his ear, sliding down his jaw till she held his chin, and it made his flesh crawl and his heart pound both at once.

He could've shoved her away. Bony as she was, he could've backhanded her across the hall. But all he did was stand there, helpless. Helpless as he'd been tied to a chair in a Valbeck cellar with her sitting astride him. "Captain Broad and I understand each other," she said, softly.

And she was right, Fates help him. Judge was trouble made flesh. The monster off the leash. She was madness, and fire, and violence, and all the things he'd told himself he didn't want.

But here's the sorry truth—if you really don't want a thing, you don't have to keep telling yourself so.

The little girl held up the paint pot and Judge stuck her hand into it. Drops spattered the tiles as she smeared four streaks across Broad's breastplate with her red fingers. "You're one of us now." She went up on her tiptoes to whisper, "But we know you always were."

No one did a thing as the Burners brought out chains and started to shackle the men and women gathered around Risinau. Not the king, sitting meekly on his little chair. Not the Young Lion, watching warily from among his Anglanders. Not the artists and the thinkers Risinau had brought to the Assembly. Even the rowdies in the public galleries had swallowed their tongues.

And Broad was quietest of the lot. He knew a lost cause when he saw one.

"You can't do this!" Risinau clung to his chair as Sarlby caught him under the arm, dragging it squealing over the tiles. "I will go to the Weaver—"

Judge's red-rimmed eyes slid sideways to him. "Who d'you think gave me the keys to the chamber, you fat fool?"

Risinau gaped at her as he was finally bundled from his chair and Sarlby snapped manacles shut around his wrists. "But...we need a new *constitution*—"

"What we need is *purpose*," sneered Judge. "What we need is *purity*. What we need is a *fresh start*."

"Shall we hang 'em?" asked Sarlby.

"Hang 'em? No. Wouldn't send at all the right message." Judge dropped into Risinau's chair and swept some of his papers off onto the floor to clear a space. "The bright future's come at last." And she propped one bare foot up on the polished table and crossed the other one on top of it, their soles grey with dirt. "Don't want to usher it in with a hanging, do we?" Broad took a sharp breath. Only realised then that he'd been holding it the whole time. Mercy was the last thing he'd expected from Judge.

"We need to kill these bastards with more *guts*," she said. "We need something spectacular. Anyone got any ideas?"

Not mercy, then. Its very opposite. There was a brittle silence. The Representatives glanced at each other, at Risinau and his underlings being chained, at all the well-armed Burners, no one wanting to stand out from the crowd.

Then Ramnard cleared his throat. "I suppose...there's always beheading?"

And now those very same bastards who'd competed for Risinau's notice that morning competed to dream up the most savage way to kill him in the afternoon.

"I thought Curnsbick's hanging machine was a great improvement."

"Boring!" sang Judge.

"Hanged and emptied?"

"The methods of the old regime," sneered Judge.

"In the North I hear they sometimes crush miscreants with rocks."

"Meh," grunted Judge.

"Boiling alive?"

"Impalement?"

"Execution by cannon?"

"If I may?" Sworbreck had risen, eyes shining with barely contained excitement. "The situation calls for something *unforgettable*. Something that will serve as *lesson* and *deterrent*. Something *representative* of the crime."

Judge narrowed her eyes at him. "Yes."

"Might I suggest that those who have fallen short of the principles of the Great Change...should *themselves* fall! In full view of the Citizens they have failed. From the top of the Tower of Chains, perhaps?"

A murmur ran around the hall. Fear? Awe? Excitement? All three mixed up? "By the Fates," whispered Brint. A Burner had closed a cuff on the one wrist the general had but was scratching his head over what to do with the other one.

"Huh." Judge tipped her head back so she could gaze up towards the gilded dome, scratching gently at her rashy neck with the backs of her broken fingernails. Slowly, the smile spread across her face. "My thanks, Citizen Sworbreck, and the nation's thanks." She jerked her head towards the door. "Take 'em up the Tower of Chains. And push 'em off."

One of the arrested gave a little whimper. Another sagged against the High Table.

"No trial?" It was the king, and he wasn't laughing now. His throat shifted as he nervously swallowed.

Judge grinned back at him. "The trial can be on the way down. The ground can give the verdict. You go with 'em, Broad. Make sure they all take the drop. Sarlby?"

"Judge?"

"Make sure he makes sure."

Broad nudged his lenses down to rub at the sore bridge of his nose, then nudged them back into place and started rolling up his sleeves. Slowly. Carefully. Helps to have a routine, after all. Then he calmly set about it, like it was any other task. Or maybe his body set about it, without the need for him to be involved at all. They organised the dozen prisoners who'd been behind the table into a line, Brint near the front, Risinau near the back, Burners around 'em with weapons drawn. Then they shuffled across the tiled floor to the aisle, and up it, between the silent benches. Everyone watched. No one spoke.

"First things first," Judge was saying as Broad trudged dumbly from the Round behind the prisoners. "This ain't so much an Assembly now as a courtroom. And in it we will purge the Union of its enemies."

The doors clattered shut.

It was cold outside, but Broad's face felt hot. Across the Square of Marshals, Square of Equality, Square of Murder, whatever they were calling it now, curious eyes following them all the way. He narrowed his own eyes as a chilly gust swept up, brown leaves chasing each other across the flagstones.

"You cannot do this!" gurgled Risinau. "You cannot *do* this!"

"Shut up, fat man," said Sarlby.

"I will see you all punished—"

Sarlby slapped him, and again, and again. Slapped him till his face was pink. "Understand yet?"

Risinau blew a bloody bubble from his nose, breath coming fast and his eyes a little crossed. "Yes," he squeaked.

Broad stepped through an archway and the Tower of Chains reared up ahead, slim as a lady's finger, white stone streaked with sooty dirt. He'd heard it toppled the day Bayaz destroyed the Eaters, and he'd had it rebuilt even taller.

A woman near the front must've fainted when she saw it, suddenly collapsed, skirt billowing. Broad picked her up under the arm. Not rough, but firm. They could do this without being disrespectful. Guided her back into the queue.

Closer came the tower, and closer. It was like he stood outside himself. Couldn't change a thing. If he didn't do this, someone else would, and he'd take the drop with the rest and never go home to Liddy and May.

"Captain Broad," hissed Brint, from the side of his mouth. "You have to stop this now. You have a chance to stop this." Broad didn't speak. Wasn't sure he could speak.

One of the prisoners was crying. Another tried desperately to wedge himself in the doorway to the tower, pressing his face to the stone. "No! No! No—"

A Burner clubbed him across the skull and he fell senseless, blood from his cut head pattering across the threshold.

"Oh, that's just brilliant," said Sarlby, hands on hips.

The man looked a bit put out. "I couldn't just leave him there, could I?"

"Give him a kick, then! Now we'll have to carry the bastard. Or you will, anyway."

"Fuck," said the man, bending down to heave him over one shoulder.

Onto an endless stair of neatly cut stone, shoving the prisoners ahead. Echoing of footsteps. Echoing of breath, of cries, of whimpers, of words. The tone changed the higher they got. Bluster, at the bottom.

"How dare you!"

"I have friends, you know!"

"You'll pay for this!"

A glimpse of the rooftops outside the Agriont, through a narrow window. Then came the bartering.

"I can give you a thousand marks. Two thousand!"

"Only let me reach my pocket!"

"I have friends, rich friends!"

Scrape, scrape, scrape of boots on stone. Then came the begging.

"Please!"

"I have three children! They don't even know what's happened!"

"Please!"

"I tried to do the right thing. No one's more loyal to the Great Change than I am!"

"Please!"

All wasted breath. All herded on up the endless stairs.

"Be strong," someone was whispering, "be strong." Broad didn't know if they were talking to themselves or someone else. What difference could being strong make? Strong or weak, the fall was still the fall.

How many steps? Hundreds, it felt like. Risinau's wheezing getting worse and worse behind him. Not a man built for steps.

"Get up there, you fat bastard."

"Can't we just roll him out here?"

"Ain't a window big enough." Laughter.

Broad kept climbing. His legs burned. The breath cut at his chest. But he hardly felt it. Someone else's legs. Someone else's breath.

Out from the darkness and onto the roof and he blinked at a clear, crisp day. Adua spread out below them, the chimneys jutting, plumes of smoke carried off by the chill wind, tiny ships at tiny wharves in the bay. Toy people swarming in a toy city.

"Damn, that's high!" Sarlby took his red cap off to wipe his forehead, thin hair whipping around a smile full of yellow teeth. He'd found an empty crate somewhere, and he dragged it up next to the parapet. A little step to stand on.

The prisoners were dragged from the stair, breathing hard from the climb, whooping sobs, puffs of smoke on the chill air. The Burners watched in their red hats and their red sashes and their clothes dashed and spattered with red paint, their weapons drawn and their eyes bright and righteous.

Broad noticed a bird perched on the roof of the little turret above the stairwell. Watching the whole business, unblinking.

"Right, then."

Sarlby and one of the other Burners took the nearest prisoner under the arms and marched him across the rooftop. Tall fellow, he was, with a birthmark under his ear. He went meekly enough, till he got to the box, then he snarled and twisted, his shoes scraping on the stones.

"Help us out, Bull!"

Broad caught a fistful of the man's jacket from behind, kicked his foot away and helped shove him up onto the box. He stood there, breathing hard, staring down in disbelief at the city below, feet level with the embrasure in front of him.

Broad saw the lump on his neck bob as he swallowed. "Tell my wife that I— Oh!"

Sarlby shoved him off. He turned in the air, surprised. Then he was gone. Broad felt like he should flinch, look away, cover his face with his hands. But he just watched. Sweat from the climb tickled under his red-daubed breastplate. He scratched at his sticky armpit.

Sarlby peered eagerly over the battlements, like a boy who'd tossed something off a bridge into a river and was waiting for it to show up on the other side.

There was a sharp smack far below. Like a whip-crack. Sarlby straightened up, puffing out his cheeks. "Well, that's the end o' that, eh?"

Sarlby had been a good man. In Styria, and in Valbeck. One of the better ones. Better than Broad had been. A good man. What kind of good was this, though? What would Liddy have said to it? What would May? Broad felt like he should be crying. Should be screaming. But all he did was check his sleeves were rolled right, then guide another one over from the stairs. A clerk, he thought, used to sit at the far end of the table with a ledger. The man had rolled his eyes at Broad when Risinau was spouting off one time, and Broad had stopped himself smiling. Across the roof he went now, towards the box, stumbled on the way, but one of the Burners caught him before he fell, helped him back up. Wouldn't want him falling before time.

"Sorry," he muttered, trying to get his foot up on the box but it was trembling so bad he couldn't manage it. "So sorry."

"Here you go." Sarlby gave him a shove and he tumbled straight over, then beckoned for the next one.

"I'm just a sculptor! I'm just a sculptor!" She was saying it over and over, in a Styrian accent, which wasn't helping. No one liked a foreigner any more. "I'm just a sculptor!" Like a prayer. Higher and higher, faster and faster, more and more desperate. "I'm just a sculptor!" She'd pissed herself. A trail of spatters across the roof, hem of her dress dragging through it. "I'm just a sculptor!"

"You're a sculptor found guilty o' treason," said Sarlby, and he pricked her up onto the box with the point of his knife.

"No! I am only here to help carve new statues! I'm just a—"

And over she went. It was the way he didn't even let 'em finish a sentence. Like nothing they could say would matter. Like they were rubbish tossed in a ditch. And those behind just stared. Like it was nothing to do with them. Even as they were herded closer to the parapet. Even as Broad helped.

Brint was next. They never had found anything to put that other cuff around, on account of his one arm, so when one of the Burners caught hold of him he shook the man off, waved the others away, walked without a word towards the box. He took a breath, stepped up himself, and stepped off himself, and made no sound on the way down.

Broad blinked. Brint had been a good man. He was reasonably sure of that. He'd tried to do the right thing, when everything fell apart. But good or bad, right or wrong, the fall is still the fall.

Some went off flailing, like they were trying to find something to catch hold of. Some dropped, limp. Some made no sound. Some made strange ones as they were pushed. A shocked gasp. A surprised little hoot. A scared whimper. A lot of 'em screamed. Screamed all the way down. They were the worst. The scream, and the way the scream suddenly stopped. The sound at the bottom. A sharp smack. But with a kind of wetness to it. And then maybe a distant spatter. Like slops thrown from an upstairs window.

A crowd had gathered now. You could hear them whooping and cheering and gasping down there in the city, beyond the dry moat. You didn't see a thing like this every day.

Broad looked at the smear of red paint across his breastplate. Had he been forced to do this? Had he chosen to do it? Had he wanted to do it? Was he one of them, like Judge said? Had he always been? He took off his lenses, rubbed his eyes.

"You all right, Bull?" asked Sarlby.

Broad swallowed as he hooked his lenses back on, nudged them into that groove where they belonged. Helped to have a routine. "Aye," he lied. "Fine."

Risinau looked near dead already from the climb. Face pale and beaded with sweat and tears, mouth hanging open, gasping for breath. "I wish… to say—"

"You've fucking said enough," said Sarlby, and jabbed his knife into the Chairman's arse, herding him up onto the box.

Vick watched another little speck fall from the Tower of Chains. Took a long time. Seemed a lucky thing, that from where she stood she couldn't see them hit the ground. In the slimy bottom of the drained moat, most likely. But she heard it, she thought. The faint scream, carried on the wind, suddenly cut off. Felt like the last shreds of hope for Sibalt's better world were cut off with it.

Vick had borne witness to some horrors in her life. In the camps. In the mines. In the rebellion in Starikland, the uprising in Valbeck, the battle at Stoffenbeck. But she'd never seen anything like this.

"What have you done?" she whispered.

Pike raised one hairless brow at her. "What have *we* done, you mean? It was you who told me Risinau had to go. And you were right."

"Risinau had to go, but…" She wanted to be sick as she said the name. "*Judge?*"

"Too many principles did not work for us."

"So we'll try none at *all*?" Her voice had become a disbelieving shriek.

"The time for half-measures is past." Pike looked evenly back at her.

"Sometimes, the only way to improve something is to destroy it, so it can be rebuilt better." There was a time she'd thought that burned face was a perfect mask for his feelings. Now she wondered whether there were any underneath. "Sometimes, to change the world, we must first burn it down."

Another little speck tumbled from the top of the Tower of Chains. Beyond the ruined walls of the Agriont, the crowd applauded.

# PART VIII

"In crowds it is stupidity
and not mother wit
that is accumulated."

Gustave Le Bon

# A Sea of Terror

"Welcome, Citizens and Citizenesses, to this sixteenth biannual general meeting of Adua's Solar Society. Somewhat delayed, I regret to say, by... *events*."

Curnsbick, understated in a rough-spun waistcoat with a flavour of workman's apron, held up his broad hands for silence, though more from habit than necessity. The members used to raise the roof. Now they sat in anxious silence.

"With thanks to our distinguished patron, Citizeness Brock." Curnsbick gestured in the vague direction of the box where Savine sat. She forced an awkward smile and eased deeper into the shadows. She had spent half her life trying to stand out from the crowd, but only fools made themselves conspicuous these days.

"I come before you full of optimism!" called Curnsbick, with the sweaty demeanour of a pedlar who would never buy what he was being forced to sell. "The Great Change offers us brave new opportunities! Workers flock to the cities." Or were driven there by cold, hunger and war to freeze on the roads or starve in the doorways. "Regulations are relaxed." Because no one knew who was in charge or whether anything would be enforced. "Land long occupied becomes available." Chiefly through the mechanism of uncontrolled fire.

He neglected to mention the worsening shortages of food, coal and raw materials, the dangers of riot and summary arrest, or the never-ending trials for profiteering, speculation and usury. The many empty seats in the audience testified to them more eloquently than even the Great Machinist ever could.

"Our friends in Starikland, Angland and Westport are... a little wary." On the verge of declaring their secession from the Union, indeed. "Traditional markets may, for now, have been closed off. But a world of possibilities opens up for the enterprising innovator!" Those not rendered into pulp at the foot of the Tower of Chains. "There is a grand harvest to be reaped, not merely material but, far more importantly, moral, social and cultural." If one could overlook the Burners' slogans daubed on every mill and manufactory. "With liberty and equality added to our traditional virtues of imagination and endeavour, the Great Change will surely bring prosperity to *all* its children!" Those it did not eat alive. Curnsbick spread his arms wide as he built to a crescendo of insincerity. "No man can stop, nor would any man want to stop, *progress!*"

Nobody dared stand out by being first to clap, and so an agonising silence stretched, huge and heavy.

It struck Savine as profoundly strange that, out in the foyer, beneath the two great chandeliers and the broken plaster where the third had once hung, no one was screaming. No one wept, vomited or tore at their faces with their fingernails. Life simply went on. The knots of conversation, the babble of business, the offers, the promises, the investments of a lifetime.

"Where's old Hogbeck?" someone was asking. "Arrested?"

"Killed himself testing a flying balloon, the old fool. Hoped to swoop down and carry away young Citizenesses, presumably."

"No woman ever entered his basket and emerged with virtue intact. And Zillman?"

"Ruined. Bet everything he had on glazing, what with all the windows being smashed. Trouble is no one's bothering to replace the bastards in case they're smashed again tomorrow..."

Nothing was more changed by the Great Change than fashion. Rich men's costume had gained workmen's flourishes, while the ideal for women was the artless shepherdess. Cheeks were painted slapped-arse pink while fans had become a loathed aristocratic affectation. Some women had stopped wearing wigs altogether, proudly displaying their conspicuously lifeless actual hair as if it was a badge of revolutionary pride. Exotic curios had been all the rage; now anything foreign was scorned with a patriotic side-eye. Jewels had plunged in popularity, but fortunes were spent on dried flowers and woven grasses. It was a wonder no one had brought a herd of goats as an accessory. Nurturing bosoms were thrust up so high they presented a danger of suffocation to bystanders. The Great Change had brought freedom to all, of course, but the corsetry of the Citizeness was, if anything, even more constricting than that endured by a lady of King Jezal's reign.

"Equality never quite comes in equal shares," murmured Savine.

"I am from Gurkhul," said Zuri, checking the watch. "I am well aware."

"Nothing sells but coupling and pratfalls," the theatre's owner was lamenting to an acquaintance in a quavering bass. "Once great Juvens' exhortation to the senators echoed from the rafters! Now we watch a fat man trip over the night pot and pretty people pretend to fuck."

"Can we not admit that fucking has always been popular?"

"I suppose. These days I hardly know whether I'm hiring actors or whores."

"There's a difference?" Followed by stutters of forced laughter.

They all were skaters on thin ice, their smiles stretched tight over their terror, gliding on as the cracks shot out beneath them. People startled at every noise in the street, expecting Burners to burst into the theatre and drag away the membership of the Solar Society wholesale. The workmen of Adua had lived in constant fear of the people in this room. Now it was their turn. But life went on, even as the world simultaneously froze and burned around them. What was the alternative?

"Credit!" a man with immense side-whiskers frothed. "There's no bloody credit anywhere. All the banks are shuttered!"

"Most of the bankers are in the House of Truth. Sorry, House of Purity. The ones who haven't taken the long drop yet, anyway. Usury. Is that even a crime?"

"If it is, aren't we all guilty?"

"If Pike wanted to strangle business he's gone about it the right way..."

Savine had once felt nowhere more at home than here, flitting from one opportunity to another, hopes and dreams left wrecked in her wake. Now all she wanted was to slit the laces of her corset and sag down with her children, slap the stopper from the decanter and never put it back.

"By the Fates," she muttered. "I have become my mother."

"There are worse things one could become," said Zuri.

It had all been so much more fun with a ready supply of pearl dust and no ever-present threat of death. But there was no pearl dust to be had, and life had never been cheaper.

"I hear old Marnavent took the long drop," someone brayed carelessly.

"So who's running things at the patent office now?"

"You assume there *is* still a patent office. Last I heard they were keeping pigs in the place."

"Count yourself lucky if it's just your ideas that are stolen. Yoslund lost every stick of furniture in the uprising. They made off with his damn doors!"

"At least during King Jezal's reign one knew who to bloody bribe..."

"Citizeness Savine!"

"Citizeness Selest."

If simplicity was the fashion, Selest Heugen bucked the trend. Her look was bread-rioting grand duchess. Militant millionaire with a dash of top-end prostitute. Dark rubies spilled down her neck like blood from a slit throat and her black dress was artfully slashed to show Burner's scarlet. Most women had stopped wearing swords. Having Leo's wounds in her face had entirely killed Savine's appetite for tools of death. Selest had gone the other way, with a genuine horseman's axe dangling from her crimson sash.

"You look...wonderful." Savine had been aiming at earnest, but had not the history to pull it off, and Selest's bosom heaved with offence. Probably there was nothing Savine could have said that would not have caused offence, and certainly nothing that would have stopped that bosom heaving.

Selest gave Savine a sneering look up and down. "You look...*motherly.*"

That would once have been an insult punishable by a slow social death, meticulously engineered. Now it hardly drew a shrug.

"After the year I've had..." The aftermath of Valbeck, her marriage to Leo, their treason against the king, the mass violence of the battle at Stoffenbeck, the almost-hanging of her husband, the even greater violence of the Great Change, the birth of her children, the coming of Judge and the whole world slowly, painfully ripping apart. Savine realised she had put a hand to the well-powdered scar on her forehead and forced it back down. "I'm only surprised I look alive."

"I spend much of my time at the Court of the People these days. You really should see your husband address the Representatives. He still makes the ladies gasp, up in the balcony. *Quite* the man. Even if he is half a man now."

Savine smiled. "As tired as I am, half is more than I can manage."

"Fancy. And you used to have such an appetite." Selest spun away, that ridiculous axe bouncing against her leg.

"Haven't you heard?" Savine muttered wearily at her back. "Everything is changed."

"Citizeness Brock!" A young man she did not know, with cheap clothes and the light of ambition in his eyes. "Would you have a moment to hear about a new type of mirror? Tougher, clearer, cheaper. We'll put those swine in Visserine out of business—"

"I fear you must do it without me." She used to swoop on every hint of opportunity, hawk-eyed, eagle-taloned, every mark clawed up a point triumphantly scored against the world. Now the thought of profits made her sick. With a little guilt, when she thought of the bread queues, the homeless in the doorways, the dead in the frozen graveyards. With a lot of fear, when she thought of them rendered into accusations in the Court of the People, screamed from the benches, flung down from the public galleries.

It was coming. She knew it was coming. They all would have their moment in the dock. She pressed a smile down on top of her dread like the lid on a box of snakes.

"But, Citizeness—"

"I wish you every success, but I am not seeking to make money. I am looking for opportunities to give it away."

A flicker of incomprehension, and the man drifted on.

"All that effort to acquire it." Curnsbick stood, shaking his head. "And now you're simply giving it away. Do you really suppose charity will help, Savine?"

"We can hope," she said, pressing his hand.

"We can." He had lost weight. He looked a shadow of himself. "But, given where we are, it might be better if we didn't."

"It was a very…carefully judged address this year."

"It was all shit. But what should I say? The truth? I'm no keener on climbing the Tower of Chains than anyone else. Though no one will need to climb soon." He dabbed at his sweaty forehead with a handkerchief. "I've been commissioned to install a hoist."

"I'm sorry?"

"The Burners can't march the prisoners up the stairway fast enough. They cry, they faint, they beg for mercy. Judge wants me to build a steam-powered platform that can haul two dozen at a time."

Savine's skin prickled under her dress. "Oh." What else could be said to that?

"When I was a boy," muttered Curnsbick, "patriotism was kissing the flag and pretending to love the king. Now, suddenly, it's spitting on the king and having poor furniture. One must keep a close eye on the current definitions. To be unpatriotic would be terrible. To be patriotic in the wrong way could be fatal. I feel I can admit to you, as an old friend, that since the Great Change…I am constantly terrified." He gave a little laugh, but she could see tears on his cheeks. He removed his lenses and wiped them on the back of his sleeve.

Savine put a gentle hand on his arm. "I hardly think you are alone in that."

"I freely admit that I have never been a brave man. Once, out in the Far Country, I met a fellow called Lamb, who had travelled hundreds of miles, facing down Ghosts and mercenaries and Dragon People and every danger searching for his children. Whatever the odds, he simply...would not be cowed. I think about him often. I wish I was more like him, but every day out there, I was scared. I am—"

"You are an inventor." She took his hot, limp, sticky hand between hers. "You have done more good in the world than a thousand warriors. Show me someone who denies it and I'll spit in their eye."

He gave a brittle smile. "I believe you would."

"Citizeness Brock." The speaker had curly hair and was unremarkable apart from his different-coloured eyes. "I was hoping I might see you here."

"Citizen Sulfur...is that the right term of address for a magus?"

"I hardly know the right terms for anything these days. Even if I did, I fear they would be the wrong ones by tomorrow morning."

"What brings you back to the Solar Society?"

"I have a great deal of money to invest, in fact."

"Then you will not be short of friends here. Commissioner Pike's tireless crusade against the banks has made investment hard to come by."

"I understand you are providing bread and coal to the poor. Perhaps we might do some good together? Would you consider accepting a loan...?"

Savine felt a coldness on the back of her neck. She remembered her father's words. About magi. About Bayaz. About Valint and Balk. She made sure she kept smiling, but she made sure she was firm. "I am afraid I cannot help you."

"Ah, what a shame. I remember the last time we met, on the docks of Ostenhorm, before your rebellion against the Crown. You could not help me then, either. That proved a rather notable *mistake*."

Holding on to her smile took some effort. "Far from the only one I have made. Even so. You understand a woman must not put herself in too much debt."

"She must take care over the partners she chooses."

"Precisely."

"But even more over those she turns down." The softer he talked, the more worried she became. "A woman with secrets, especially."

She wished she had a fan now, so she could brush him off with it. "We all have secrets, Master Sulfur."

"We are not all bastard offspring of a king."

Her smile crumpled. Time seemed to slow. She felt cold and burning hot at once. The foyer was an overbright whirl of faces. Keen ears. Judging eyes.

"Perhaps...you might reconsider?" Sulfur had drifted very close. "The crown has become an awful weight to carry." The back of his hand brushed her arm. "And since King Orso has no heir, perhaps one of your children might inherit it?" His lips curled back to show sharp teeth. "Now tell me, which popped out first? The boy, or the—"

"I'll fucking *kill you!*" she snarled in his face, catching his jacket in her trembling fist. "Threaten my children? I'll see you *dead!*"

He looked far less surprised than she was. And only for a moment. Then he let his head drop on one side. "You really would have been my master's first choice. But in my experience, and yours, too, I daresay, one never has to go far to find someone who will take your money. Or your secrets. Citizeness Heugen!" He brushed off her limp hand and stepped away into the crowd. "A moment of your time!"

Savine saw Selest's eyes dart over, as keen for any trace of opportunity as her own had once been. She tried to smile, but the muscles in her face would not work the way they used to. She could not see Zuri. The blood was pulsing behind her eyes.

Her instinct was to run. To the docks. Then Angland. Styria. Distant Thond, for that matter. But she knew she was watched. She would not get far with two babies. And to run would be to admit her guilt. Of what, she hardly knew.

They would think of something.

# Conspiracies

"**A** conspiracy typical of those that *riddle* Adua!" thundered Sworbreck. "Just as maggots will riddle a harvest if left unchecked!"

Orso did not doubt it was typical. In that it was a total fantasy. Sworbreck stalked past the dock, pointing out the accused one by one, finger vibrating with righteous rage. "A banker... a miller... a baker... and a *Styrian agent!*"

It sounded like the start of a bad joke, but there had been little to laugh at since Judge had her predecessor tossed from the Tower of Chains. Risinau had swapped the old liars on the benches for new ones, ripped out the stained glass and turned the Lords' Round into the Commons' Round. Judge had installed clumsy boxes, docks, rails of rough-sawn wood, splattered the marble walls with slogans and turned it into the Court of the People. In the morning, Representatives wrestled over the details of government every bit as ineffectually as they had before. From the moment Judge flung herself into the chair where Risinau used to sit, her dirty feet propped on the High Table, court was in session and the people's enemies should tremble.

"The banker lent the money," bellowed Sworbreck, "so the miller could adulterate his flour, so the baker could sell bread at inflated prices, causing hunger and discord in the service of a Styrian plot to manipulate the markets and undermine the Great Change!"

Shrieks of horror from the overflowing public galleries. Grumbles of upset from the Representatives' benches. Orso wondered how the accused had been picked. What terrible roll of the dice had nudged them over the invisible line from *being* the people to being *enemies* of the people? Citizen Brock was carefully silent, Orso noted. He had developed a fine sense for when to speak and when not to. What to say and what not to. It was coming to something when one wished one could have the Young

Lion's good judgement, as well as his wife. Orso frowned. Had he really just thought that?

"I never met them!" the Styrian woman was wailing, wringing her hands. "I never even met them before now!"

Orso winced at her strong accent, which drew instant jeers from above. Any hint of difference aroused suspicion. *Be watchful!* screamed one slogan hacked into the wall in letters twice the height of a man. *Freedom means Punishment*, roared another in streaky red. *Conspiracies are everywhere!* Gurkish Eaters sent by the Prophet Khalul to debase the coinage. Imperial ruses to weaken the People's Army and annex the Near Country. Styrian plots to spread the rot through infected whores. Even Angland, Starikland and Westport were filthy with regression, royalism and treachery against the Great Change.

Orso had intimate personal experience of government and felt petty selfishness, incompetence and bad luck were far more likely explanations for its shortcomings than intricate webs of malice spanning the Circle of the World. But then they were far less satisfying explanations, too. He rather wished the wilder theories were true. Had there been half as many secret monarchists as people claimed he would never have been deposed. Then he might have been sitting in that gilded chair presiding over his own, more polite brand of rank injustice. The crowned puppet for Bayaz to dangle before the nation with one hand while he picked its pocket with the other. The grinning figurehead of a ship crewed by ruthless torturers like Old Sticks, self-serving embezzlers like Lord Isher, brutal users like Lord Wetterlant.

Orso winced and rubbed at the bridge of his nose.

Sworbreck was dealing with the baker first. He was a chubby man, which made him look guilty of eating well, and he was sweating profusely, which made him look guilty of being warm, both of them capital crimes in this lean winter of the Great Change.

"I been a baker twenty years," he was saying. "My father was a baker."

"Hoarders!" someone screamed.

"Take 'em to the Tower!"

"Take 'em all!"

The Styrian woman clutched her face with her hands as if she wanted to crush it between them. "Mercy!" she blubbed. "Mercy!"

The court was not without it. Judge was the voice of the mob. She was their bitter rage, their envy and their greed, but she was also their sentimental forgiveness. When the mood turned for some well-spoken old man, some innocent-looking young woman, first Judge's chin would crinkle, then her lower lip would tremble, then her black eyes would well with tears. Sometimes she would vault from behind the High Table, kiss the accused, clasp their head to her rusted breastplate. Then they would be embraced by weeping guards, applauded on their way out of the hall while songs were sung and slogans chanted, free Citizens and Citizenesses, enemies no more!

Perhaps Judge liked seeing the hope in the eyes of the accused, so she could see it crushed. Perhaps she truly believed she was doing the good work and rejoiced in those righteously acquitted as much as those rightfully convicted. Perhaps—surely the most terrible possibility of all—she *was* doing the good work, and somehow he could not see it.

The baker was trying to defend himself, but how to prove false what was self-evidently absurd? "I charged the lowest prices I could and still stay in business! But flour's gone up so high—"

"And so we come to *you!*" roared Sworbreck at the miller. He was bony and severe, with a habit of peering up shiftily from under his brows that did him no favours.

"There was a poor harvest!" he barked out. "Now the cold weather's frozen the canals, snarled up the roads. It's hard to get goods into the city."

"Ah, so the *government* is to blame?" Sworbreck spread his arms towards the benches behind the dock, where the Representatives gravely shook their heads at such a slander. "And since the government consists of those chosen by the people..." Sworbreck leaned back, raised his arms to the balconies. "The *people* are to blame?"

"It's not a question of blame!" shouted the miller, hardly heard over the insults pouring from above. "It's about facts!"

But it was not about facts at all and was very much a question of blame as far as the public galleries were concerned. Someone threw something. A coin? It missed the miller and hit the Styrian woman on the forehead. She gave a shriek, slumping in the dock.

"Who fucking threw that?" screamed Judge, veins bulging from her rashy neck. Captain Broad, who'd been lurking behind the High Table sipping from a hip flask, now burst forth, flinging a chair out of his way and sending it bouncing across the tiled floor, making everyone within twenty strides, including Orso, shrink back.

"Who *fucking* threw that?" he roared, the tendons starting from his great fists, made furious by Judge's fury as surely as a dog by its master's. In the guilty silence that followed, the banker's efforts at a defence could finally be heard.

"I merely *worked* for the Banking House of Valint and Balk, I never profited personally from any—"

"Usurer!" someone screeched. No doubt there were profiteers and speculators everywhere. Before the Great Change they had simply called that business, and the worst offenders had been celebrated as society's greatest successes.

The banker's cracked lenses flashed as he glanced nervously upwards. "As you see..." He balanced a heavy ledger on the rail so the densely written numbers were angled towards Sworbreck. "The loans I handled were mostly to mining interests, mineral exploration, some foundries."

Representatives craned forwards to squint at the figures. Judge wrinkled her nose. Evidence in general was of little interest to her, but paperwork she treated with particular disdain.

"This one typical, you see, six thousand marks—"

"The court has not the time to indulge in this trivia," grumbled Sworbreck, waving it away.

The man began to look alarmed. He had clearly considered this a cast-iron defence. "But...these ledgers prove my innocence—"

"Bastard!" someone shouted. "Liar!"

"Enough numbers," snarled Judge. "Get rid of the bloody books!"

The thin Burner, Sarlby, seized the ledger. He and the banker wrestled over it, paper ripping.

"But the numbers *prove*— Ah!"

Sarlby finally tore the book free and started to beat the banker over the head with it. His co-defendants stared in horror, but the public gallery was thoroughly entertained.

"Make him eat it!" Someone screeched with laughter. "Make him eat it!"

"Order in the fucking court!" roared Judge.

Sarlby flung the ledger away, pages flapping, and it spun across the tiled floor. The banker stood gasping, eye-lenses skewed, collar torn, blood running from a gash on his scalp. "The numbers..." he breathed, astonished, "prove..."

Orso put his hands over his face and watched from between his fingers. The poor man had it backwards. Whatever the question, the Great Change was the answer. That was a fact none dared challenge. So the scarcity, the failures, the defeats, must be caused by profiteering, betrayal and conspiracy. If you could only purge all the disloyal, all the unfaithful, all the foreign agents, then there would be victory. Then there would be plenty. That the prescription was killing the patient could only mean that not enough had been administered. It was not a rational argument. Facts were useless against it. It was an argument based on faith. It belonged in a temple, not a court. The irony, of course, was that the Burners had burned the temples. So they had turned the Lords' Round into a temple and called it a court.

And none are more fanatical in their faith than the convert. Sworbreck strutted across the tiled floor until he stood before the weeping Styrian. "And *you*!" he screeched. "*You* were the mastermind!"

The woman stared, her lip wobbling, her bloody hand clapped to the coin wound. Rarely had Orso seen anyone look less like the mastermind of anything. The pink point of her tongue darted over her pale lips, breath coming fast. Blind panic, and who could blame her? Orso felt his shoulders sag. Everyone in the court knew what came next.

"I denounce them!" she wailed, desperately. "I didn't know what they were doing! They're guilty! They're all guilty!"

"I *knew* it!" shouted Sworbreck, delighted.

"I never met her!" screeched the baker.

"Lies!" said the miller. "Lies."

The banker pulled off his lenses with a trembling hand and put the other over his eyes.

"Guilty!" shouted Judge, banging dents in the High Table with the smith's hammer she used as a gavel. "Guilty, guilty, fucking guilty!"

There was no need to pronounce a sentence. The only outcomes here were acquittal or the Tower of Chains. Hildi stared at Judge, and Broad, and Sarlby, and the red-smeared Burners jeering from the public gallery. "They're monsters," Orso heard her whisper.

"I almost wish they were," he muttered. "That would be easier. But they're just people."

"They're the worst people I ever saw."

"Of course they are. We hanged all the best ones. The ones who might have helped, might have compromised, might have built bridges, we left dangling over the road to Valbeck. Of course they are cruel, and greedy, and brutal. Those are the lessons we taught. That was the example we set."

"I never met them!" the Styrian woman burbled as the prisoners were manhandled up the aisle. "I'm innocent!" But it was far too late for that. It was too late the moment they were put in the dock. There was only one real conspiracy here. To find people to blame, and they were all complicit.

Judge tossed down her hammer and sat back, picking her teeth. "What's for lunch?" she asked.

# Worse Than Murder

"**D**amn," whispered Tallow, steam puffing about his face, "it's cold." And he wrapped his thin arms tight around his thin ribs, and worked his chin into his scarf.

Vick's brother used to do the selfsame thing, in the camps. Bundled up in every scrap of cloth they had, huddled together for warmth under a blanket she'd got a bloody nose stealing. Gave her a sudden urge to hug Tallow, rub his back, clamp her gloved hands over the red tips of his ears.

But Sibalt was the last man she hugged, and he ended up slitting his own throat. So she hawked up cold snot and sent it spinning into the frozen dirt beside the cart instead.

"Why do you never have enough clothes?"

"No one's got enough clothes now."

"Scarf on a Constable. Not exactly fearsome, is it?"

"More fearsome than froze to death, I daresay."

Vick conceded that with a smoky grunt. He'd hardly be the first one froze to death, they were finding them every morning. In alleyways. In doorways. In cellars. Frost in their eyebrows. Ground was frozen too hard to bury the poor bastards.

"Don't you ever get cold?" he asked.

Vick got cold. Her throat had been sore for days, her nostrils raw from the running and wiping, running and wiping. But she knew better than to let the pain show. Letting it show is the same as asking for more. "Got colder than this, in the camps. Look on the sunny side." And she snorted up more snot. "If it was warmer we'd have a plague."

"Sounds like you got the plague anyway," muttered Tallow.

"If you're concerned about infection you could always join the Burners." And she nodded down the street towards them.

They'd built a great bonfire. Images of royalty. Symbols of the past. Portraits of King Orso, King Jezal and the many crowned arseholes that had preceded them. Furniture carved with the blazing sun of the Union. Curtains embroidered with the devices of great families. Cutlery stamped with patriotic mottos. Flags. Uniforms. Wigs. Fans. Anything that could be considered aristocratic. A Burner stomped from a house and flung a full set of crockery splintering into the blaze. Folk gathered dangerously close, eager hands out to the flames, light playing on pinched-in faces.

Tallow huddled even deeper into his scarf. "I reckon I'll stay here."

"Lucky me," said Vick. Though if she was honest for once she was glad of the company. A sad indictment of the life she'd chosen. The one person she trusted was the one she'd blackmailed into betraying his friends.

Pike came striding from the cellar, pulling on his gloves. "Fine work, Chief Inspector Teufel," he rasped as he watched the Constables file up the steps to dump armloads of papers into the cart, the odd one floating free to stick in the half-frozen mud. "A bank hidden in a wine-merchant's cellars. We have driven them underground, like rats."

"A bank of a sort," said Vick. "They loaned money to pimps and fences here in the slums, ran pawn shops and jerry shops, invested in gambling houses, husk houses, doss-houses, whorehouses."

"A criminals' bank," muttered Tallow.

Pike narrowed his eyes. "All banks are criminal. The loans here may have been smaller, the interest higher, but the profits flowed into the same coffers. The same ledgers. The same bottomless well of greed. This cellar was a branch of the Banking House of Valint and Balk, as much as the grand building on the Four Corners." The one in which that vast vault door was still frustrating every effort of locksmiths, engineers and Gurkish Fire.

"The roots of these vile institutions have dug into every part of Union society." Pike's lip curled as he watched more paperwork flung into the cart. "A web of debts and corruption that stretches from the lowest to the highest. Their rot must be hacked away." Two Constables had dragged a squealing clerk into the street. "Without doubt." Sticks rose and fell, black against the fire. "Without hesitation." A limp body was hauled away, head hanging. "Without mercy."

Pike's war on the banks was starting to look fanatical, but there was no denying fanaticism was in fashion. "What about everything else?" asked Vick.

The Commissioner turned, his breath a smoking cloud about his high collar. "What about everything else?"

"No riots lately, I'll admit—"

"Too cold for it," Tallow whispered, trying to cup the warmth of his breath in his pale fingers.

"But robbery, burglary, violence, just as bad as when Risinau was Chairman."

"Worse," muttered Tallow, "if anything."

"Lot of homeless on the streets. Lot of desperate people. They're coming in from all over. Looking for work, when there's less work than ever. Mills closing. Manufactories shuttered. No coal. No food." Vick licked her sore lips as she watched the shackled employees of Valint and Balk hauled from their cellar. "No money."

"We must focus on the grand crimes. Let the Burners worry about the petty ones."

Vick winced down the street towards the bonfire. They weren't burning people on it, as far as she could tell, but only because Judge wanted the proper show of pushing them off the Tower of Chains later.

She should've kept her mouth shut. She always kept her mouth shut. But somehow it was getting harder and harder to keep her mouth shut. "With respect, Commissioner, the Burners are as likely to punish the innocent as the guilty."

Pike hardly seemed to hear her. "The banks remain our focus. Usury is the worst of crimes."

"Worse than murder?"

"Murder leaves one Citizen dead. The banks infect us all with greed." The flames down the street glimmered in the corners of Pike's eyes. "Are we any closer to finding the manager of the Adua headquarters of Valint and Balk? I would very much like to see the inside of their vault."

"We're closing in. Questioning the employees. But there are hundreds, and most only know their little splinter of the business. The bank owns property all across the city. No one would ever have believed how much."

"We will take it all back," said Pike, "and give it to the people."

Vick glanced towards the fire. "What'll they do with it?"

"Sometimes, to change the world we must first—"

"Burn it down," she finished, softly. But it was sounding more and more like something a madman says to justify all the fires he loves to start. "If the manager's in the city, we'll find him."

Pike gave her a stiff nod. "Keep me informed." And he strode away, a dozen Constables in tow, past someone standing in the shadows of a doorway on the far side of the street. A woman with a board propped against her hip, bright eyes darting over Pike and his retinue, towards the cellar and the cart, away to the firelit crowd.

"Make sure this all gets to the House of Truth," Vick grunted at Tallow.

"We call it the House of Purity now, remember?"

She was already walking over, slipping her hand into her pocket, finding the chilly angles of her brass knuckles. Best to approach everyone as if they were a threat, though this woman didn't look too formidable. Her lips had a bluish tinge, nostrils pink at the rims, an old quilt around her shoulders with a hole cut for her head to go through.

"Your name, Citizeness?"

"Groom, Inspector. Carmee Groom." She lowered the board. There was a sheet of paper clipped to it, a stub of charcoal in the blackened fingers of her other hand. "I'm an artist."

Vick relaxed a little. About as much as she ever did. "So I see."

"I am sketching. For a painting."

Vick frowned towards the bonfire, the ragged figures warming their hands, the Burners dragging people from the buildings, the Constables emptying out the cellar that had been a bank. "You want to paint this?"

"Future generations might never believe that it happened." She blew some yellow hair out of her face with a smoky breath and went back to sketching, charcoal hissing on paper. "Then it might happen again."

# Lessons

"There was a hell of a battle fought here," said Shivers, pausing on the side of the hill to frown across the snow-covered valley, all silent in that brittle way only winter countryside can be.

Isern gave a smoky snort. "You could say that of all the North. Is there a stride of sod, anywhere 'twixt the Crinna and the Whiteflow, hasn't been watered with blood at one time or another?"

"Not like it was here," said Shivers. "Greatest battle the North ever saw. Black Dow had his standard on this very hill." He pointed to the white fields below them on their right, slashed by black walls, studded with black trees. "Scale down there, still wi' both hands, and Brodd Tenways, and Cairm Ironhead, Glama Golden, Caul Reachey over on the left, in Osrung." As Rikke struggled up level with him he turned around and carried on climbing. "Every one of 'em back to the mud."

"Well," said Isern, using her spear like a walking stick, "being a War Chief is a business heaped high with both risks and rewards."

"Lord Marshal Kroy stood on the other side," said Shivers, "and thousands o' Union soldiers, and your father, too. Three red days we had of it. Men struggled here with all they had for each step of ground. Died and killed for every handful of soil." He frowned out at the crisp, quiet white, stretching away to the hazy fells all around, and shook his head like he couldn't make it fit. "Now you'd never know. Few years passed and... it's just fields."

"You've turned talkative," said Rikke. She couldn't remember the last time he'd said this much in one afternoon.

"Brings it all back, I guess, being here." Shivers stepped over the crest of the hill and onto its flat top, frowning towards the great ring of stones they called the Heroes, black against the white sky, like the prongs on a giant's crown. "The good and the bad."

"No trouble planting your flag here now." And Corleth stuck Rikke's rolled-up standard of the Long-Eye into the snow, her face all blotched pink from the cold.

One of the stones was broken halfway up, a couple more had toppled down the centuries, another sheared off and cloven by a crack, like it was dealt a blow with a mighty hammer. Rikke stepped over to the nearest and kicked the snow from her boots against its side. By the dead, it was a size. Four times a man's height or more, topped with snow, streaked with wet, spattered with lichen, crusted with moss.

"How did they get the bastard things up here?" Her face was pinched and her chest raw from the winter but her body all sticky-hot from the climb under her cloak, so she couldn't decide whether to draw it tight or fling it off. "Just getting myself up here was a struggle."

"This is where Black Dow fought Calder." Shivers was standing at the edge of the ring of stones, looking in at the snow-covered circle of tangled grass and thistle inside. "A duel to the death."

"Aye, and you cheated," said Isern, "and dinged Black Dow in the back of the head with that sword you're wearing, and so Calder became Black Calder, and stole the North, and gave Skarling's Chair to his brother to sit in, who gave it to his nephew to sit in." She stuck her bottom lip out and scratched at her throat. "Come to think of it, all this is your fault."

Shivers frowned down at the grey hilt of his sword, then over at Isern. "Calder seemed the better choice, then."

"And now?"

"And now," said Rikke, "there's no unpicking the warp and weft of all the things said and done since that day. It's not a right choice or a wrong, any more than wind blown or snow fallen." And gingerly, as if she was laying her hand on a sleeping dog, she put her palm to one of the stones. Maybe she'd hoped for her Long Eye to pop open and show her hidden truths, but if there'd been high magic here it was long faded, or at any rate she hadn't the key to unlock it. It was just a stone.

Corleth pulled out a flask, took a little nip and offered it around. "Seems your friend's not here yet."

"He's no friend," said Rikke, taking a nip of her own.

"Then we can trot off 'fore he arrives," said Isern. "You took Uffrith without his help, and you took Carleon without his help, and you've took half the North without his help, and *now* he slinks up, sniffing about like a badger at the henhouse. You don't need his help getting your hands on the other half."

"Might need his help keeping the half I've got, the way things are going."

"'Twas your own cockiness set things going that way, d'you see. Did I not say cockiness was the grave you'd trip into if you didn't mind your step?"

"Only about a thousand times. Can't hurt to hear the man out."

Isern turned her head, spat chagga juice and left a brown streak down her chin. "You'll be telling me next it can't hurt putting a crab down your trousers."

"Aye, well," grunted Rikke, handing the flask to Shivers, "my trousers, my choice to make."

"No doubt, 'tis only that the choice you're making is a very poor one, as most of your choices have been since your skinny arse touched Skarling's Chair."

Rikke ground her teeth. "I could tire of your slighting references to my arse."

"And I could tire of your way of managing the North."

"Oh, you've made that very clear. I think what first gave it away is how you keep saying it, straight to my face, in front of anyone who'll listen."

"A wise leader sups well upon the wisdom of their advisors."

"It's a shame my advisors don't have any, then, isn't it?"

"Oy," said Shivers, lowering the flask. "I've a lifetime o' defeats to draw on." Rikke ignored him.

"There was a time your lessons smacked of wisdom, Isern-i-Phail. Now they smack of mad witterings summoned on the spot. Or worse yet, the maddest bits picked out from your father's mad witterings, like a drunk squirrel picking nuts from a turd. I could do without the constant whittling down of my authority."

"One cannot much whittle what is hardly there," snapped Isern. "First you shat yourself with the Nail, now you think Jonas Clover's the jug to hold all our hopes?"

"There are some tasks trustworthy men aren't suited to," growled Rikke. "You catch rabbits with weasels, not with bulls."

"That's one weasel might end up down your trousers."

"What is this obsession with animals down my trousers?"

"I don't get it, either," muttered Corleth.

"You can shut your face, girl!" snarled Isern, rounding on her and shaking her spear in her face. "'Fore I give it a shutting from which it will not soon open."

"Don't carp at her!" Rikke stepped between the two of them. "You've had it in for her from the start and all she's tried to do is help. By the dead, your bloody *carping*! Have you ever heard of a woman with such a tongue for carping as this one, Corleth?"

Corleth blinked at Isern, then at Rikke, and swallowed. "Honestly, I'd rather not get stuck between the two o' you."

"There's wisdom," said Shivers, frowning at the worsening row.

Rikke talked over him. "You're too generous, Corleth! See how generous she is? You couldn't carp any more if you were a carp."

Isern's knuckles were white on the haft of her spear. "Saved you, didn't I? In the woods? In the winter? Not bad for a fish."

"You did save me, and my ears are sore from being reminded, and my throat's raw from thanking you for it. If I was planning to get lost in the woods again you'd be my first pick for a companion. But since I'm planning to sit in Skarling's Chair, I'm beginning to doubt you're fitted for the role." She waved her hand towards Corleth. "There are folk with leveller heads and sweeter tempers one could have at one's elbow."

Isern narrowed her eyes. "That a fact?"

"It is! And if it's a hard one to swallow, you can take yourself back into the hills whence you came and make houses out o' shit or whatever it is your lot do up there. You made a promise to my father, but my father's back to the mud and as far as I'm concerned your promise went with him, *d'you see*." And Rikke made a mocking imitation of Isern's hillwoman accent on the *d'you see* which she was rather pleased with.

Isern was less pleased. Indeed, she'd had a look of gathering fury during that last speech which was slightly troubling and made Rikke wonder whether she might've taken at least one step too far. "Well, have a *shit*, then, you little ingrate maggot!" she snarled, spraying chagga juice and making Rikke flinch back. "You little painted piss-smear! You fucking one-eyed wanker!"

"There's some very pleasant one-eyed folk," grunted Shivers.

"My arse to you!" hissed Isern in Rikke's face. "And the moon's curse to you and the dead drip on your Long Eye. You can roll your own chagga!" And she stalked off in high dudgeon, the very highest, indeed, shouldering Corleth aside, between the stones and away to the north the way they'd come.

"I've a fear..." said Shivers, his scarred brow furrowed in a frown. "That was a mistake."

"Wasn't my first," snapped Rikke, well aware of what she'd done, "and I doubt it'll be my last."

"Surely. But you might want to spread 'em out a bit."

"Daresay she'll be back," muttered Corleth, though she looked less than convinced and in fact slightly scared.

"Don't care a monthly bleed whether she is or isn't," snapped Rikke. "Away to fuck with you!" she roared after Isern, whose shaggy head was disappearing behind the frozen grass on the hilltop. She didn't answer.

"A bad time?" came a voice, from behind.

And there he stood. No arcane robes or golden wands. Just a worn old coat and a time-polished stick, the winter sun gleaming on his bald head. He wasn't breathing hard, though the dead knew there was no way to get to the Heroes without climbing the hill it stood on. It was as if he'd been there the whole time, but they'd only just now noticed him.

"Bayaz!" Rikke stowed her mood away and strolled towards him with a smile, boots crunching in that circle of fresh snow, the Heroes a ring of disapproving giants frowning on their meeting. "First of the Magi! First apprentice of great Juvens! Don't I feel special to get an audience?"

"Rikke of the Long Eye!" He walked towards her, not seeming quite so smart and smug as he had in the Hall of Mirrors in Adua. He had a hungry look now. Sunken around the eyes. Scratty about the beard. "Daughter of the Dogman, mistress of Uffrith, Carleon and half the North besides. You have grown a great deal since we last saw one another."

"That'll be the hood," said Rikke, "gives me an inch at least." And as they came together in the centre of the circle she pushed her hood back, and dragged her hair over to the side, and turned her left eye towards him.

For an instant, she saw the flicker of shock. "Grown not so much in stature," he breathed, eyes flickering over her face with keen curiosity, "as in power. Who tattooed the runes around your Long Eye?"

"A friend. Up in the hills."

"A friend of rare talent, in these latter days. Eleven wards, and eleven wards reversed. Truly a most potent enchantment! I feel more blessed than ever that you consented to a meeting."

Rikke wasn't above being pleased by flattery. But she was above letting it show. "Man o' your age, outdoors in such bitter weather, figured it must be important." And she grinned wide. *Your best shield is a smile*, her father used to say, and she'd a feeling she might need a shield or two in this conversation. "Besides, I was in the neighbourhood. Business in Osrung." And she waved towards the thin smoke rising from the town's chimneys, off down the river. "Been taking a little tour of the North. Or the bits I'm in charge of."

"And how have you found it?"

"Seems I'm more in charge of some bits than others," she said, casting a frown after Isern. "No easy business, keeping a crowd of Northmen all facing one way."

"I have been trying for centuries and it never seems to stick. When we met in Adua, I told you we should speak later."

"So later has arrived," said Rikke.

"It's got a habit of doing that," murmured Shivers, whose watchful presence a pace or two behind her she was rather grateful for.

"I thought we might discuss the future," said Bayaz.

"We might." And Rikke set off walking, slowly, pacing a circle around the old wizard. "But I'd have thought a man old as you would be more concerned with the past."

The magus smiled as he followed her with his eyes. "The past has never interested me. For better or worse it is done, and set, and littered with disappointments as a battlefield is littered with the dead. But the future is a ploughed field, full of potential. The future we can twist into wonderful shapes. With my help, the North could be yours. All of it, and not only for today. Imagine all the good we could do together."

"Who says I want to do good?"

"Isn't that what we all want?" Bayaz gave a sigh through his nose. "History is not the story of battles between right and wrong, but between one man's right and another's. Evil is not the opposite of good. It is what we call another man's notion of good when it differs from ours."

Rikke had her doubts on that score. "So you want to help me stamp my notions on the North?"

"Why not? We all need help, from time to time."

"Oh, we do. All I've got was got with help." She'd come a full circle now, and she patted Shivers fondly on the shoulder as she passed, then turned to Bayaz with a thoughtful frown, still walking, slowly, crunch, crunch, crunch. She'd never liked standing still. "Bethod had your help, if I heard the story right. How's he getting along?"

"I made him king. But he grew arrogant, and fell."

"The Bloody-Nine, I think, had your help next. How's he faring?"

"I made him king, too. But he grew wrathful, and fell."

"Then it was Black Calder who had your help. He must've prospered!"

"I made him the man who made kings," said Bayaz as she passed behind his back, then he turned his head and caught her from the corner of his eye. "But he grew lazy, and let you in the back door. My help is not the word of Euz. It cannot protect a man from his own faults."

"So if I have your help, who'll protect me from all *my* faults?"

Bayaz took an impatient breath, like the teacher of a pupil who can't get their sums straight. "I know things have not gone smoothly for you lately. I know some of your friends are friends no more. The Nail, and his people in the West Valleys. Even the hillwoman Isern-i-Phail loses patience. I know, on your little tour of the North, you are thought of as too soft, too wild, too strange. But then, as your list of names shows, sitting in Skarling's Chair is one thing. Staying there is another."

She'd finished another circle now, leaving him in the centre of a ring of her snowy footprints, and she looked him in the eye. "You know a lot."

"Knowledge is the root of power. I could share mine with you."

Rikke doubted Bayaz became Bayaz by sharing more than he had to. "I see things, too," she said, turning her left eye towards him and opening it very wide. "Who knows? Maybe even a thing or two you don't. I know things haven't gone smoothly for *you* lately. You left the North in Black Calder's care and he pissed his trousers. His brother's dead and his son's in a cage and now you have to listen to me flap my lips. And then there's your Union, where I saw you give such a fine address, the countless little people laid out before you like a carpet before an emperor. I doubt you'd be so welcome since their Great Change, eh? Not so many statues of you in the Agriont as there were. And who can blame 'em? Wasn't long ago you gave *them* your help, and it laid waste to their proud city and killed them by the cartload. Or did my father tell the story wrong?"

"Talking to you is *quite* the adventure." The weather might've been bitter, but the edge on Bayaz's voice was chillier yet. "You wander off in every direction."

"I'm a constant surprise even to myself!"

One more impatient puff of smoke, this time through gritted teeth, like a shepherd whose flock won't obey. "Do you see these stones, child?"

"I do." And she set off wandering again, over towards the cloven one. "They're hard to miss, old man."

"This is where Black Dow died. This very spot. He ruled the North, after the Bloody-Nine fell. A mighty warrior. A fearsome leader. He held off the Union here. But he thought he could manage without me." Bayaz narrowed his eyes towards the flat, white country spread out to the north. "He lies in a pit out there, unmarked and unconsidered."

"The Great Leveller catches us all," said Shivers, softly.

"And he has no favourites and makes no exceptions." Rikke reached up to run her fingertips down the great split in the stone, already a little smoothed, a little weathered in the years since the battle. "Where did the stones come from?" she asked.

The First of the Magi frowned. "The Heroes?"

"Aye. Who put them here? And how? And why?"

"None alive know that." Bayaz glared over at Corleth, and she swallowed, and blinked down at the ground. "They come from an age before the Old Time. They were ancient even when my master Juvens was born."

"So old as *that*? A good thing stones don't wrinkle, eh, or run to flab, or lose their hair, or have all their little schemes fall apart around 'em? I daresay they mostly look as fine as the day they were raised. Though how did this one get so bruised? Magus Art?"

Bayaz frowned harder. "No."

"A cannon," said Shivers.

"A cannon!" It was hard to walk back towards the magus. Like walking into a great wind. But Rikke made herself swan carefree across the snow, leaving a new track of footprints in the white. "Like the ones my good friend Savine dan Brock, who gave me these lovely emeralds, turns out by the dozen in her new foundry in Ostenhorm. So I know not whence the stones came, either, but I know what broke that one. In this matter, at least, it looks like I'm as wise as you. There was a time of stones before you. And there will be a time of cannons after. And the time before was, and the time after will be, so vasty and so deep that the age of your mastery will seem like the snapping of a child's fingers." And she snapped hers in Bayaz's face. *Click.*

His eye gave the slightest twitch of annoyance. "It appears that Tricky Rikke is a name well earned."

"And Sticky Rikke, too," she muttered from the side of her mouth, "I promise you."

"No doubt there will be a time after me." Bayaz's eyes were fixed on hers, hard and glittering green. "But that time is *not yet*. For a girl blessed with the Long Eye, you have made some short-sighted blunders."

She got as close to a carefree shrug as she could, no easy thing, with the weight of his displeasure on her shoulders. "You told me once that people must be allowed to make their own mistakes."

His eyes narrowed, and he closed the gap between them with one step. She felt Shivers shift behind her, the faint rattle as he gripped his sword, and she had just the presence of mind to raise one finger to still him.

"You are very brave," said the First of the Magi, and his voice was almost painful on her ear. "Or very *rash*. To cavil with a man who has called up storms and snatched down lightning. Who scattered the mighty Hundred Words like chaff on the wind." He leaned forwards, baring his teeth, and it was the most she could do to stop herself cringing, stumbling back, dropping to her knees. "Why, you must know, that with a thought I could make *ash* of you."

Now that was a hard moment. Worse than hiding in an icy stream while she heard her death plotted on the bank. Worse than when she watched the Young Lion losing to the Great Wolf. Worse than when she had to choose which eye to have pricked out. It took all she had to meet Bayaz's gaze. All she'd learned and all she'd lost. As if his anger was a crushing grip, squeezing the breath from her chest. But she did it. Then she pushed her lips out in a thoughtful pout, then she pressed her finger against them for a moment, then she shrugged.

"No," she said brightly. "I don't see it. If everyone knew *you* chose the kings, and *you* had all the power, they might get it in their heads to take it from you. I reckon you'd sooner stay behind the curtain, where it's safe, and have others do the burning."

There was a chilly silence, then, as the cold wind cut between the stones and across the snow-heavy grass. A hard and chilly silence, stretching long, while Rikke wondered if she might've made her last mistake. Then the first of the Magi gave a sigh, and stepped back, and the awful pressure was released.

"Then you have made your choice. Perhaps I will go to Currahome. Black Calder, I think, will be grateful for my support."

"I expect so," she said, trying to stop her voice quavering with relief. "He needs it. Perhaps, when I've settled with him, we should talk again. By that time, you might want to buy secrets from me! Fare you well, First of the Magi."

"I would say fare you well, Rikke of the Long Eye." He gave her the hint of a smile, even as he turned away. "But I fear you will fare badly." And he walked swiftly between the stones, and was soon gone down the side of the hill.

Corleth puffed out her cheeks and rubbed sweat from her forehead on the back of her hand. "Don't much care for that old bastard," she muttered.

"Nor I," murmured Rikke, folding her arms and hoping her thumping heart would soon settle.

Shivers was frowning towards the white fells on the south side of the valley. "He was here, after the battle."

"I guess there were a lot o' crows, picking at the leftovers."

"Him in particular. When Black Calder and the Union and your father struck a deal."

"And my father spat in Calder's hand and swore to kill him if he ever crossed the Cusk again."

"That's right. Bayaz was the one pulling all the strings."

"Well, he won't be plucking ours."

Shivers' good eye turned towards her. "Better to have 'em plucked than cut, maybe."

"Maybe." But her father fought all his life so they could be free. She gave a shiver, and pulled her fur collar tight and her hood low, and headed back the way they'd come. Northwards, leaving the Heroes behind. "Till then, we'll dance to our own tune."

# Far from Finished

Clover nudged some wet bushes out of the way and peered across the river. His eyes weren't all they once were, but he'd an unpleasant sense there were some familiar faces at the far end of the bridge.

"By the dead, my luck," he muttered, trying to catch any warmth his breath might hold in his cupped hands. "Is that Trapper and his boys?"

"Aye," said Sholla. "The ones Downside didn't kill, leastways."

"Better that than leave scores at your back," said Downside.

Sholla rolled her eyes. "And what about the score Trapper has against us 'cause you killed three of his people?"

Downside scratched his thick beard as he pondered that. "So you're saying...I should've killed the rest, too?"

Clover sighed. "Life surely has a way of bringing old offences back to haunt you."

"Was only a few weeks back," said Flick.

"New offences, then." Clover had arrived with small expectations of living out the day and his odds just took another tumble. "You lot better stay out here."

"I'd no idea you cared, Chief."

"I don't." He raised a brow at Flick. "But you're so dumb you'd make things worse." He pointed it at Sholla. "And you're far too skinny to hide behind." He pointed it at Downside. "And let's not even start on you."

"Sure you want to wear that?" asked Sholla. "For this?"

Clover frowned down at the fine wolfskin cloak Stour used to wear. She had a point. Turning up to talk to Black Calder in his stolen son's stolen finery would be less than wise. "Shit," he said, undoing the buckle with some reluctance, since it was by no means the weather for disrobing, and tossed it over to Sholla. "If my luck's a lot better'n usual, I'll see you back here soon."

"And if your luck's about like usual?" Sholla hissed after him, grinning as she pulled the cloak about her own bony shoulders.

"Then I reckon you got a good cloak out of it." And Clover stepped from the trees, wedged his hands under his armpits and trudged towards the bridge.

Trapper stood at the far end with his thumbs in his sword-belt and a wrinkle to his lip. "If it isn't Jonas fucking Clover."

"It's the longer version of my name," said Clover, already shivering, "but used often enough that I'm obliged to answer to it."

"Funny." It was the one with the lambskin coat, the one Downside coshed on the head last time they met. "I'd find the sight of your guts funnier yet."

"You don't seem to be killing me, mind you."

Trapper turned his head and sourly spat. "No."

"A better result than I'd expected, if I'm honest."

"Aye. Black Calder told us you'd be along."

"How did he know?"

"He's Black Calder, ain't he? Knowing things is what he's known for." He held out his hand and snapped his fingers.

"Right y'are." Clover unbuckled his sword-belt and handed it over. Could scarcely remember the last time he drew the damn thing except to oil it anyway. "You should know I regret what happened last time we met," he said, following Trapper up the muddy road. "Didn't want anyone dead, but bloody Downside, he's one o' those bastards leaves a trail o' wreckage with every stride."

"You choose to have a man like that in your crew, you could do a better job o' reining him in." Trapper shook his head in disgust. "You could hardly have done a worse."

"Not entirely fair," said Clover. "You're still casting a shadow."

No surprise that they walked the rest of the way in moody silence. There was snow on the sloping fields, and the low stone walls, and the bare trees on the valley side, and on the steep roofs of the houses scattered towards the top. There were tents about, too, and campfires, and fighting men huddled close around their warmth. Fewer than Clover had been expecting, though. Thralls and Carls, a few grizzled old faces he recognised. Not enough to pose any threat to Rikke, even now the Nail and his West Valley boys had cleared off.

Maybe Black Calder had lost his edge. Happens to everyone, in the end. Folk get comfortable. Get so stuck on thinking they're the best, the strongest, the most cunning, that when someone better, stronger, more cunning comes along they don't even realise they're yesterday's bread. Not till it's too late.

He was waiting, under the ice-fringed eaves of the hall at the top of the hill. The man who'd ruled the North for twenty years. A little greyer, maybe, than last time Clover saw him. A little more lined. But wasn't everyone? He looked relaxed, for a man whose dreams had all come crashing down.

"Jonas Clover!" He spread his arms like he was greeting an old friend, a gesture which Clover found anything but reassuring. "Welcome to Currahome. What d'you think of the place?"

"A charming winter scene," said Clover as he looked back down the valley, catching his breath and trying to rub the chill from his pink fingertips. "I'm climbing a lot more hills than I'd like to be at my time o' life, mind you."

Calder waved towards the smattering of men camped on the hillside. "You think mustering warriors was what I'd been planning for my dotage, you lazy bastard? I much preferred Carleon but my fool of a son lost it. Give him his sword back, Trapper, what are you doing?"

Trapper frowned sideways at Clover. "I thought, you know, he might try something."

"It's Jonas Clover, what would he try? Bad jokes? There's probably not even a blade in the scabbard. Just a spare sausage or something."

Clover felt a touch offended about that as he buckled his sword back on. Probably he shouldn't have. Offence did no one any good, after all, and Calder was right. Trying anything here was the style o' manly madness Jonas Steepfield might've contemplated. And look what happened to that idiot.

"Let's get in out of the cold." Calder turned towards the hall. "You're a connoisseur of sword-work, you'll enjoy this."

As the doors were opened, the unmistakable clanging of steel on steel rang out. Blade-music, as the skalds have it, making their living setting poetic terms to the world's horrors. Shadows danced among the carved rafters of the firelit hall, hot as a forge after the chill outside, bringing a prickle to Clover's frost-numbed extremities. Men sat on benches, drinking, eating, oohing and ahhing at the sight of two men fighting. Or maybe training. Or one big man and a stringy lad. Seemed quite the mismatch at first, but as Clover got closer he saw it wasn't going the way you'd expect.

During his long and undistinguished career teaching sword-work, he'd watched hundreds of boys practise with a blade, usually while wearing a look of pained disappointment. He'd seen no more'n a dozen with any high talent for the business. It wasn't so much bravery that it took, which was reasonably common, as a lack of fear. Lack of fear that you'd get hurt, which was rare. Lack of fear that you'd hurt someone else which, strange to say, was rarer yet.

Thick black hair was stuck to the lad's face with sweat, and every time he outfoxed the big man, or slipped around one of his efforts, or brought a gasp from the onlookers, he noticeably didn't smile, or shout, or throw his arms up in triumph. It was like his face was sculpted from pale clay and could make no expression at all. Wasn't so much a lack of fear as a hole where his fear should've been. There was a scar between his mouth and his nose. A cleft lip.

"I know this lad," said Clover, fumbling off his hat and scrubbing at the sweaty wisps stuck to his pate. "He was with you that day I offered you an apple."

"He was."

The boy darted around a lunge, flicked his sword out and nicked the big man's hand. He gasped through clenched teeth, blade dropping to the straw. The lad stepped in, sword raised.

"Stop!" called Calder. "I don't have so many warriors you can go carving 'em up for your amusement. You remember Jonas Clover? Used to be Steepfield? Won some duels?"

"And lost one," muttered Clover, under his breath.

"I remember," said the lad, watching from behind that curtain of black hair. Showed no sign of respect. Showed no sign of scorn. Just took it all in.

"Don't say much, does he?" said Clover.

"No, but he can make a sword sing." A thickset old bald bastard with a short grey beard had stepped up beside them. Clover didn't know his face, which was odd, since he thought he knew everyone in the North with a big enough name to start spilling his thoughts to Black Calder. "He reminds me of a young Skarling, in that regard."

"Really?" asked Clover, brows high, since Skarling Hoodless was back in the mud lifetimes ago.

"This is Bayaz." Calder had acquired the grin of a man keen to please, which by no means fit him well. "The First of the Magi."

Clover raised his brows even higher. That explained a few things. His being on intimate terms with long-dead heroes for one. The way Black Calder scraped around him for another. He hadn't the look of a legendary wizard, truth be told. Thicker in the neck and quicker to smile. But there was something in Bayaz's eyes as he took Clover's measure. Something that made him think this would be a bad enemy to have.

"Steepfield was the name?" he asked.

Clover had a policy of never setting magi right. "It was."

"Come to Currahome as I have, no doubt, to make sure the proper person sits in Skarling's Chair."

Since opinions might differ on the best arse to fill that uncomfortable piece of furniture, it was easy for Clover to give a hearty, "That's right."

"We cannot have our plans for the North wrecked by some over-clever girl with a magic eye."

Clover cleared his throat. "Without wishing offence, seems she's knocked 'em a bit crooked already."

Bayaz's eyes glittered in the light of the fire-pit. "Nothing that cannot be straightened out again, with the right knowledge and the right friends." All in good fun, it seemed, but there was a threat in there somewhere.

"You can never have too many friends," said Clover, while thinking that there were a few a man was better off without.

Calder was twisting one hand with the other, like a serving girl hoping some lord didn't take against the ale she'd poured him. "You know how grateful I've always been for your help."

"You lacked somewhat of manners when you first came to visit me, as I recall." Bayaz peered down his nose at Calder as if he was still a prideful pup. "But in all the years since the battle at the Heroes, my support for you has never wavered."

"Nor mine for you." Calder swallowed, a little queasily. "Manners should be answered with like manners, I've always felt."

"Well said. If only the younger generation had your hard-won wisdom." And Bayaz gave Clover a nod and made for the door, sparing a sideways smile at that black-haired lad, already making a fool of another grown warrior.

Clover frowned after him. "Haven't I heard you say the help of magi is never worth the cost?"

"He only shows up when he knows you've got no choice." Calder's face had snapped back into its frown like a bent willow switch snaps back into the shape it grew in. "But there comes a time you have to play every card, no matter the price." He led Clover past the fire-pit to the high chair at its end, leaving the clash of steel and the appreciation of the warriors behind. "This was my father's hall. Before he took Carleon. This was where his dream of a North united was born."

"Like most births," said Clover, "I hear there was a lot of blood."

"Couldn't get anything done without a lot of blood in those days."

"And now?"

Calder conceded the point with a little shrug of his shoulders and dropped into the chair Bethod must once have sat in. "You want some ale, Clover?"

"I've never yet said no to ale." He swung one leg over a bench, tossed his hat down as a cushion and perched himself by the fire-pit, watched a girl slosh ale into a cup for him. "Have to say I feared I might not get so warm a welcome."

"Always got along, haven't we?"

"We have." Clover glanced about at the hard faces. The hard hands near the hard weapons. He decided if Calder had wanted him dead he wouldn't have wasted poison, and took a sup. "But then I turned on you and your son." Might've seemed madness to bring it up, but he judged it better to face it now than find it stabbing him in the arse later.

Calder narrowed his eyes. "I'd assumed you must've come to tell me how sorry you are for that."

Lies would get him nowhere with Black Calder. The truth might not, either, but he liked the odds better. "For turning on you, I'm sorry. For turning on your son, I'm not."

"You're saying he deserved it?"

"I'm saying he fucking demanded it."

Calder sat back, tendons standing from the backs of his thin hands as he gripped the arms of his chair. "I heard Caul Shivers hobbled him."

Clover wiped sweat from his forehead and tried to flap some air in around his collar. By the dead, it was hot in here. He was doubly glad he'd left that cloak behind now. "He did. And the Nail beat the snot out of him and Tricky Rikke's keeping him in the cage he had forged for his own amusement. You can't say she don't have a sense of humour."

Fury wouldn't have surprised him, but all Calder did was stare into the glowing embers and slowly nod. "Might be he'll finally learn the lessons I could never bring myself to teach him. Love can be a weakness. I blame myself."

"I've done a bit of that, down the years." Clover took another swallow from his cup. "Didn't help."

"Huh." And Calder grinned at him, teeth shining in the light of the fire-pit. "I still like you, Clover. I never can bring myself to trust loyal men. Can't understand the bastards."

"I'm with you there."

"Man who'll be loyal to someone might one day up and decide he'd

186

rather be loyal to someone else." He wagged a finger at Clover. "But a man who's first loyalty is to himself? It always will be. You don't pretend to be what you're not. You're reliable."

"I am?"

"Let's say reliably unreliable. Which makes you an interesting choice of messenger."

"She didn't say so in so many words, but I've a feeling Rikke thought you might not listen to someone less flexible. Might send their head back in a bag, in fact."

"But I won't send yours?"

Clover scratched gently at his sweaty neck. "Honestly, I doubt she cares much on that score either way."

"Clever, isn't she?"

"She is."

"A little too clever for her own good, maybe."

"Maybe."

"So what's the message?"

Clover leaned forwards. Towards Calder. Towards the warmth of the fire-pit. "She sent me with an offer. Split the North. Leave it as it is now. She'll keep Uffrith and Carleon. You'll keep what you've got. And you get your son back."

Calder watched him, in silence calm as a mountain lake. There was some laughter and clapping down where the sword-work was happening. There was a crunch and a whirl of sparks as a glowing log shifted in the fire-pit. Clover glanced around. Still the hard faces, the hard weapons. Still the ever-present threat of a quick trip back to the mud.

He cleared his throat. "So…"

"Truth is I'm tired, Clover." Calder sagged back with a weary grunt. "Lots of folk gone back to the mud. My father, my wife, my brother. Friends beyond counting. I'm tired and I'm lonely and I can't remember when I last laughed. Maybe that's what she's counting on. Ruthlessness belongs to the young." And he frowned into the fire like it was full o' disappointments. "To those who don't know where it gets you."

"So…you'll make a deal?"

Black Calder's eyes slid across to Clover's. "Make a deal, with that scrag?"

"So…you won't make a deal?"

"I'm tired. I'm not dead." And he stood up. "Come with me."

Clover drained his cup, put his hat back on, and followed Black Calder out the back of the hall.

There was a valley behind the hill, too. That's how hills and valleys work, after all. Snow on the fields, and the low stone walls, and the gorse and sedge on the slopes, and the roofs of the huts and the hovels. This valley wasn't scattered with men, though. It was crawling with the bastards. Tents everywhere, dotted all the way down to the half-frozen stream in its bottom and up the far side again. Fires and torches like stars in a night sky. He heard laughter, and snatches of song, and the constant clang of hammers from the many smithies, smoke drifting up in thin streams from their chimneys and into the pink evening.

"By the fucking dead," whispered Clover, slapped in the face by the sight and the cold both at once.

"Were you thinking that dusting out front was all I could gather?" asked Calder. "My son's mean temper might've bruised some feelings but I've got a few friends yet. In the south, down near Ollensand. In the High Valleys, up towards Yaws. A fair few men still wandering back from that fucking disaster in Midderland." He pointed towards the top of the ridge ahead, where the fires were brightest, and as far as Clover could tell there were ragged standards poking up against the chilly dusk. "And, thanks to the First of the Magi, I've some friends out beyond the Crinna, too. You meet Stand-i'-the-Barrows yet?"

"No, but I've a sense the name gives some hint o' what to expect."

"You remember Stranger-Come-Knocking?"

"Wi' some reluctance."

"Stand-i'-the-Barrows makes him look quite the humorist."

"And bringing the likes of them into the North is a strong notion?"

"Wasn't my choice. You're worried over the mess they'll make, I'd take it up with your friend Rikke."

"I'll get the chance?"

"When we march on Carleon."

Clover gave a smoky sigh. "I was worried you'd say that."

"I was thinking my work was done. Time to put my feet up, leave the plotting to the next generation. But you know what? I find I'm rather pleased to be called on to save the North once more."

"Ah. So you're the hero here, are you?"

"As a man who's been cast as both hero and villain, you should know better'n anyone, Jonas Steepfield—the hero's whoever wins." And Calder smiled out at all those fires, the deep lines spreading around the corners of his eyes. "Reckon I've a trick or two to teach Tricky Rikke yet. No doubt she's crafty, but I heard she's making mistakes. Heard she had a little falling out with the Nail."

"Aye, well, he's one o' those bastards folk start falling out with the moment they meet him. You hear a lot."

"It's just a question of listening." Calder took a satisfied breath of the chill evening air, and let it sigh away. "This was where my father's dream was born. One North. One nation with one king. My idiot brother's folly couldn't stop that dream. My idiot son's folly won't, either. The Dogman couldn't stop it, even with the whole Union at his back. His daughter damn sure won't, Long Eye, Short Eye, or whatever bloody eye."

"I should bring my people into the warm," said Clover. "They're down in the woods at the—"

"They're rounded up and disarmed."

"Really?"

"Really."

"Huh." Clover scratched thoughtfully at his scar and resisted the urge to ask whether they'd live out the day. Calder knew what he was thinking anyway.

"Don't worry, I'm treating 'em as guests. I'm not my brother or my son. I don't break things I can use. There's only one question you need to worry about."

"Where I go to piss?"

"Which side you're on."

Clover puffed out his cheeks. In all the strutting and waste when Stour was in charge, he'd forgotten what a formidable bastard Black Calder could be. They're like that, thinkers. While your eyes are on the fighters, they creep up on you. This wasn't how he'd wanted it. But when was anything?

"Well, if I'm so damn reliable…" He looked out at the valley, and all those fires, right to the far hills. "You already know what side I'm on."

# The Only Explanation

"The only explanation for your defeat is *treason*!" screeched Sworbreck, bashing the rail with his fist.

Leo had lost a battle with the odds well in his favour, so he could think of plenty of others. Recklessness, arrogance, trickery, hesitation, bad weather, bad allies, bad luck. Or, for instance, that when money was finally found to send the army new boots, Risinau had ordered them supplied with a collection of his essays instead. Sworbreck had written the foreword. But treason was the only explanation the Court of the People wanted to hear.

"I did everything I could to win, sir!" bellowed General Bell. "I mean, Citizen. You won't find a more loyal man than me!"

"*Precisely* what a traitor would say!" screeched Sworbreck, while drunks in the gallery jeered like the crowd at a slum prizefight.

Leo had watched them turn Sergeant Bell into General Bell after Judge seized power, standing red-faced on the very spot where he now stood trial. Made commander of the People's Army without a day's experience as an officer. Brint's jacket had fitted him badly. Brint's responsibilities fitted him even worse. But the Representatives had filled the dome with sentimental applause even so. Slapped his back as they sent him up the aisle to fight Lord Marshal Forest and his royalists. Most of them must've guessed how it'd end. Leo certainly had. But since the Great Change, appearances were more important than realities. Savine would've said they always had been.

"From what I hear," muttered Leo, "that man was the best sergeant in the army."

Glaward nodded sadly. "Solid, careful, caring, not much imagination." He could've been describing himself.

"All the qualities that make a terrible general," murmured Jurand.

"I understand you served with the notorious royalist *Lord Marshal*

*Forest?*" Sworbreck sneered the name as if Forest was some monster no adult believed in. "At the Battle of Osrung, when he was a sergeant major? During the wars in Styria, when he rose by the king's favour through the commissioned ranks?"

Bell blinked about at the benches, but there was no sentimental applause now. "I did, but—"

"You knew him well?"

"Everyone in the army knew him."

"And respected him?"

"Of course, he was—" Bell saw the trap too late. His face turned even redder than it had at his promotion. "No one had a reason to disrespect him. No one had a bad word for the man!"

"Admiration!" shrieked Sworbreck. "For one of the most implacable and perfidious enemies of the Great Change! For a man who sheds Union blood on Union soil to put the *snake* Orso back above us!" And he pointed to the king with that always-trembling finger.

Risinau had put Orso on a smaller and smaller chair. Now Judge had gone a step further and locked him in a cage while the court was in session. All it had done was give him a kind of louche dignity. His knowing smile seemed to ask what kind of a coward someone would have to be to fear a coward like him.

Sworbreck thumped at the rough-sawn rail of the dock again. "An army of *honest patriots* could never be beaten fairly by Lord Marshal Forest's *royalist hirelings!*" He rubbed at his hand, having clearly picked up a splinter from the shitty carpentry. "You came to an *accommodation* with them, didn't you? You betrayed the Great Change!"

Gasps of disgust from every side. Leo expected the truth was simpler. Bell had been promoted far beyond his ability and thrown against a dedicated enemy on ground of their choosing. His army was ill-provisioned, ill-equipped and stuffed with Purity Officers who bastardised every military decision with politics. The surprise was that disaster hadn't struck sooner.

"There was no bloody accommodation with the enemy!" shouted Bell. "They caught us strung out on the roads, in the rain. My men were exhausted. The Purity Officers insisted we march double time!"

"Always someone else to blame! The Purity Officers now, Burners of unimpeachable pedigree, keen to get to grips with the hated enemy!"

"But the People's Army have been in the field for weeks. They've barely been paid. Now they're hardly being fed—"

"And whose responsibility is it that the army should be prepared, might I ask, if not the general in charge? Ours, I suppose?" The benches bristled.

Even Leo grunted denials. You couldn't give seeds of accusation the chance to take root. Before you knew it, suspicion would be sprouting everywhere. Disgust rained down on Bell from the public gallery.

"Poor bastard," muttered Glaward, with the sympathy of one big, lacklustre man for another.

"I've always been loyal." Bell had tears in his eyes. "Ask anyone I've served with."

The chamber fell silent as Judge shifted forwards from her chair, long fingers sliding across the table like a cat stretching out to sharpen its claws. Sworbreck might blather up a hurricane, but everyone knew it was Judge's few words that counted.

"It's true I hear some fine reports o' your conduct, Bell. It's how you got the job in the first place. Put yourself in danger to save wounded soldiers. Gave up meals so others could eat. Walked while sick men rode on your horse. Noble stuff. It'd make me weep in a storybook." Judge stretched further, her black eyes fixed on the accused. "But I weep very easily. You told us you did everything you could to win."

"I did, Citizeness Judge, please believe—"

"But you didn't win."

Bell blinked, mouth half-open.

"Can't say for sure you're a traitor," said Judge, "but I know for a fact you're a loser. And for a general that's just as bad. Dare I say it's fucking worse?" She lifted her hammer and smacked the battered table. "Guilty. Get him to the Tower o' Chains." Broad caught Bell under the arm and hauled him from the dock.

Leo dimly remembered a time—a few weeks ago—when there had been a middle ground. Room for compromises, on some things, some of the time. Now everyone was an extremist or a traitor to the cause and any trace of doubt was a betrayal.

"We need a new general!" someone roared from the back of the benches, while the old one was still being dragged to his doom.

"These damned royalists have to be stopped!"

Jurand leaned close. "Now?"

Leo had to smother a smile. Their thinking was more in step than ever. "Let's test the ground, at least," he murmured.

"Citizens!" Jurand sprang to his feet. "Representatives! Officers of the court! Thanks to foreign intrigues and royalist conspiracies, we have faced frequent defeat in the field." He'd always been one of the quickest thinkers Leo knew, and it had taken him no time at all to learn the language of the Great Change. He made a fine speaker, earnest and believable, with a little flush of passionate colour in his cheeks. "Lord Marshal Forest and his traitors should never have been allowed to get the better of the People's Army. But now our patriots are in disarray. Low on morale. Paralysed by corruption, conspiracy and criminal incompetence."

Leo glanced over at Kort and gave him the slightest nod. He rose to roar the piece they'd agreed on. "Only five days ago, a group of farmers on the coast near Keln, banding together against Gurkish invaders, were mistaken for Gurkish invaders themselves and attacked by a group of armed fishermen. Twelve men died!" It had actually been one, but nobody got excited over a single corpse any more.

"What we desperately need is *organisation*!" called that leader of fashion Lord Heugen, now the soberly dressed Citizen Heugen, right on cue. "What we *must* have is tried and tested leadership."

"Might I put forward a name known to us all?" asked Jurand, with a zealous shake of his fist. "A name already at the tip of many right-thinking men's tongues when it comes to the defence of the Union. A name synonymous with courage, loyalty and fighting spirit. None other than Citizen Brock, the Young Lion!"

Leo had expected a mixed reaction. The ex-lords and the Anglanders cheered, along with Kort and some other representatives Savine had bribed his way. There was scattered applause in the public gallery. He hadn't lost all his charm along with his leg. But there was a low murmur of suspicion, too. There were shaken heads and sullen glances.

And then there was Judge, considering Leo with the same narrowed eyes that had just considered the ill-fated Bell. Charm against her was like a match against the ever more merciless winter outside—unlikely to make much difference. "I'd have more faith in a man who'd won a battle rather'n lost one," she said.

"Stoffenbeck was a battle he knew he couldn't win!" lied Jurand smoothly, clapping Leo on the shoulder. "But one he chose to fight anyway, whatever it cost him. Against the odds. Against countless royalist forces. Every Citizen can see the sacrifices he made on their behalf!"

The king's snort of scorn could've been heard in the upper gallery. No doubt he remembered Stoffenbeck differently, and no doubt he wasn't alone, but if these trials were teaching Leo anything, it's that what really happened doesn't matter half so much as what people want to hear. He caught Glaward's shoulder and dragged himself to his feet, took his cane from Jurand and lurched out onto the tiles as the hall fell silent.

"Citizens!" he called. "Citizenesses! I gave up the 'dan' in my name. Gave it up happily, right on this spot. I gave up my Lord Governorship, my birthright, because I *believe* in what we're doing here. Because I *believe* in the Great Change!"

He waved down shouts of support from those Representatives he'd persuaded to shout support. "Still! It's true I was a nobleman. And the Army of the People should be led by a man of the people." Just as Sergeant Bell had been, when they buttoned him into General Brint's ill-fitting uniform and sent him off, armed with essays, to lose to the royalists. "I regret I cannot take up this honour."

King Orso gave another great snort, but it was soon lost in the applause at his selflessness and sacrifice. Perhaps he'd convinced some of the doubters to cheer. Even Judge gave him a cool nod as he dropped back onto the benches.

"You turn it down?" whispered Glaward.

"Better to turn it down before they refuse to offer it," murmured Jurand, lips carefully pursed as he gauged the feeling in the galleries. "Then we can take it up later."

"We need a patriot!" someone was shouting.

"Enough bloody *generals*! Enough bloody *experts*!"

"We need someone who truly *believes*!"

Leo adjusted his useless arm in his jacket. Belief won't stop a cannon-stone. He could've told them that.

# Charity

Snow fell weighty on the slums. Wisps and flutters, dirty from the smoke of the furnaces, drifting grey into the corners of the windows, the doorways, the alleys.

The Burners' slogans were everywhere, daubed in red paint across the houses. *All Equal* and *Death to the Royalists* and *Sacrifice Everything*. The fury of Sworbreck and his ilk at the world and everything in it had spread like a sickness from books, to newsbills, to pamphlets, until the poorly printed tantrums were pasted everywhere directly onto the sooty walls, today's rant against those who would drag the Union back into the past splattered on top of yesterday's, torn paper fluttering.

A snatch of song floated across the frozen street. A man staggered by, sucking at a bottle. Someone screamed with laughter from an upstairs window and Savine flinched. Laughing in Adua these days felt as grimly inappropriate as laughing at a funeral. At an execution.

"I hope you are well, Citizen Vallimir."

"I am alive, Citizeness Brock, and my wife is alive, which, after the events we endured in Valbeck, I consider to be remarkable good fortune."

"Your fortunes otherwise?" She could see those at a glance. Vallimir had always been lean, but he looked positively skeletal now, frayed clothes carefully darned. "I still fondly remember that jelly you served at your house in Valbeck."

Vallimir snorted. "There have been no jellies lately. I was employed as a foreman in a textile mill for a while, but following the Great Change… the price of coal… the place shut down. My wife takes in laundry. I have been carving toys. Soldiers are always popular." He leaned close to murmur, "Providing they sport no royalist symbols."

"These are difficult times for everyone."

There were hawkers everywhere, struggling to turn a few bits from matches, ribbons, apples, shoestrings. Beggars, too, offering up their wounds, their diseases, their misery for inspection, knowing that despite the poverty, people here were more generous than in the richer parts of town. People here understood what it was to have nothing. Most of them were only one payday away from it.

Prostitutes stood shivering on a corner in the same tall shoes and slit skirts they had worn when King Jezal was on the throne. The Great Change had not changed much for them. It took a brave woman now to show a bare leg to the freezing winter, but they tried their best, pale gooseflesh and pinched faces chapped pink from the cold, breath smoking as they whined hopeless come-ons to the uncaring chill. Then there were the footpads and tricksters, circling anyone who looked as if they might have a coin. There had been a time when Savine counted on her father's name to keep her safe on these streets. Now she never stepped out of doors without Haroon and a few well-armed men.

"You know I have the highest regard for you as a woman of business." Vallimir cleared his throat. His voice had an ill crackle to it. "But prominent connections are not the safest thing these days. Might I ask why you sent for me?"

"In Valbeck you helped me make money. Now...I want you to help me give it away."

They had reached the back of the queue. Dozens of lumpen figures crowded along one side of the street, bound up into shapeless bundles of torn clothes, blankets, rags. They stamped at the snow to keep warm, hugged themselves, hugged each other. Further on, someone sawed at a violin while a woman danced. Danced well. Children pelted each other with snowballs. Caught bystanders. There was laughter. Clapping. A cheerful feeling all too rare in the city now.

"What are they queueing for?"

Savine sighed. She still was faintly embarrassed to utter the words. "My charity, Citizen Vallimir." She gestured towards a tin chimney peering over the roofline, dark smoke billowing up as the pale specks swirled down. "I own six bakeries now in the borough and have agents scouring Midderland for flour. Soup is made from whatever we can find. Thread is brought from Valbeck and the blankets woven just up the street. Coal comes in from my mines in Angland through an agreement with Lady Governor Finree. I was using the canal I own with Dietam Kort to move goods, until it froze."

Everything in the city had frozen. The water in the fountains. The river around the boats. Festoons of ice hung from broken gutters. In some of the cheaper taverns, she understood, the wine was known to freeze in the cups.

"When I first tried to give bread away it turned into a riot. One of the wagons was upended. People wrestled in the mud for crumbs. People who got away with what I had given them were robbed in the next street. I observed the whole sorry business pressed into a doorway while my companion's brothers shielded me with their bodies."

"It is not like you to show too much faith in people's good nature."

Who knew generosity could be more dangerous than greed? "A mistake I will not make again. Ever since then I have been applying the same rigour to giving my money away as I did to making it." They crunched through the boot-mashed snow to the front of the queue, where it passed through the iron gates into the warehouse. "Real estate in these parts has *plummeted*. I bought this place for a price you would not believe." She had bought half the decaying buildings in the neighbourhood, in fact, and slashed the rents. "I saw the roof mended and invested in guards and gates. I hired locals to drive wagons, handle goods, stoke ovens, knead dough. I distributed some carefully judged bribes among the local Burners, secured some help from an old contact in the criminal fraternity and made sure she kept order on the streets."

She waved towards one of the braziers, a matching pair of Majir's frowning thugs in attendance. "The people queue, hopefully without freezing. They receive a bag of coal, two loaves of bread, a blanket. There might be meat or milk for children, on a good day. Names and addresses are taken, marks and signatures given to discourage fraud. But sometimes examples have to be made even so."

Vallimir raised a brow at her, and she shrugged. "It is not like me to show too much faith in people's good nature. These days we have fewer disruptions."

"Charity on an industrial scale," murmured Vallimir. "You were never one for half-measures."

"No. I mean to set up a similar operation across the river and need to leave the management of this one in capable hands."

"Mine?"

"Unless they are fully occupied carving toys? I have no doubt I could make use of your wife's talents as well. My parents' house is currently filled with orphaned children. The work has no end…" She trailed off into awkward silence.

Vallimir was studying her with a healthy degree of suspicion. "I read that pamphlet, you know."

The pamphlets that circulated under the old regime had been bad enough. Some of the ones that circulated now went far beyond slander into the realm of sordid fantasy.

"I hardly dare to ask which one," said Savine, already feeling pinched by the cold.

Vallimir took out a paper, creased and faded. *The Darling of the Slums.* And there was that etching of a radiantly smiling Savine dan Brock dispensing coins to the starving while orphans clutched at her skirts. The sight of it made Savine feel faintly nauseous.

"What did you think?"

"I could not avoid the conclusion that you were a damned liar."

Savine gave a brittle smile. "I would not dream of denying it."

"So I am forced to ask...what is the angle?" Understandable, of course, given he had known her before Stoffenbeck. Before Valbeck. Hard to believe it was only a year and a half ago. Savine dan Glokta seemed a faint acquaintance, dimly remembered, and not with much affection. "Is there some profit hidden in all this?"

Savine thought of Zuri shaking her head over the numbers in the book. "Not of the financial kind, certainly."

"Goodwill, then? Popularity?"

"We could all use a little goodwill in these troubled times, but I daresay I could polish my image for a fraction of what I am spending here."

"So why..." Vallimir waved towards a woman waddling from the warehouse gates with a bag of coal, the bulge of pregnancy showing even through her mass of clothes, three children of decreasing height waddling after her like ducklings after their mother, the one at the back with a loaf in his pink hand and two glistening streaks of snot down his face. "All *this*?"

Why indeed? Savine took a deep breath, the cold of it almost painful, and gazed into the flames in the brazier. "It is, as you have no doubt guessed, entirely selfish. The truth is...the past seems to be a scab I cannot stop picking. I often think about Valbeck. About the uprising, and what I did there...and what I did before. About the children we used in our mill. The children...I made you use." The fire, the queue, the snowy street, it had all become a sparkling blur, her eyes focused beyond. "I think about the battlefield at Stoffenbeck, too. The graves there. You would hardly believe...the *size* of the graves. The truth is...I wonder if the Great Change has really made things worse, or if it simply made them worse for me. Are there more beggars now, or do I simply see them for the first time? Was I any better than Judge, when I held the power?

Was I worse? The truth is... I jerk awake, in the night, sure the Burners have come for me at last, and I know... that I deserve it."

Savine cleared her throat and wiped her stinging lower eyelids carefully with one gloved fingertip. "I have started thinking it might be a fine thing... if the world was a better place for my existence." Curnsbick had always told her she had a generous heart, and she had thought him a sentimental fool. Perhaps it had simply been hidden under all the pearl dust and ambition. Hidden even from her. "I find... I feel a little lighter for every mark I give away. *That*... is the angle."

She tore her eyes from the queue and found her one-time business partner staring at her, pamphlet still in his hand, almost as surprised by that unguarded moment as she was.

"By all means you can give me the lecture now," she snapped. "You will tell me nothing I have not told myself. That this is a feeble sponge to soak up the rivers of misery I spilled for my own profit. That this is the pinnacle of soppy hypocrisy. A woman who made slaves of children, handing out a few lumps of coal as though it makes her a heroine."

Vallimir paused, mouth slightly open, perhaps trapped between denying it out of politeness or agreeing with the obvious truth. Then he turned to the queue, tucking *The Darling of the Slums* back in his coat pocket, and blew out a smoky sigh. "I suppose... it's better to give it away than to keep it."

And they stood together as the snow came down, and watched the loaves being given away.

"They tossed General Bell from the Tower of Chains," called Leo. A moment later, Savine heard the clonk of his leg tossed onto the floor as he dropped back against his pillows.

She winced. Not just at the thought of the execution, but at the offhand way he spoke of it. "I heard."

"Jurand told the court they should give me his position."

She stepped into the bedroom, staring over at him, sprawled on the bed in the light of one candle. "You want it?"

"Not yet. When the time's right." He looked surprised that she was surprised, even though they had been throwing generals off the Tower of Chains almost as fast as they had bankers. "Command of the People's Army, Savine. I could sway them my way. They're in a wretched state, though, I hear. No food, no equipment, no morale."

"We could send them blankets. Winter coats for the officers. Bread, maybe." She still was not used to the shape his body made, under the covers. The one leg, the strange absence of the other. Like some fairground trick. It was a struggle not to stare. "Make sure they know it all comes from the Young Lion. To one set of heroes from another."

The gap in Leo's teeth showed as he grinned. "You always know the right gloss to put on things."

If only. She looked at the floor, wondering how she could possibly put any gloss on what she had to say. "There is something... I need to share with you. Something I found out shortly before we were married."

He narrowed his eyes slightly. "Why didn't you tell me then?" He had changed. Before Stoffenbeck it would never have occurred to him to ask.

"I should have. But I never thought you would find out. I never thought anyone would."

He narrowed his eyes further. The look of a wary customer who suspects he is being palmed off with inferior goods. "But someone has?"

"It seems so. And they might make it known to others." She swallowed. Every word felt like a weight to lift. "Secrets, in my experience, rarely stay buried."

"So you judged it was better to tell me now than risk me finding out for myself. Excellent strategy. I'd expect nothing less."

"Please, Leo."

"What kind of secret worries you?"

The disgusting and potentially lethal kind. She clenched her fists. Forced out the words. "King Orso... and I..."

Leo waved her away. "Selest dan bloody Heugen told me you were lovers, remember?"

"Not that." Well, yes, that, but so much more than that. It still shocked her to say it. Still repelled her to think it. She squeezed her eyes shut, her ears full of the sound of blood surging, and blurted it in a rush. "We have the same father!"

Silence. When she opened her eyes, Leo was frowning at her. Puzzled. As though he must have misheard. "Wait..."

"King Jezal and my mother were lovers! Long ago. Before he was king, even. And I was the result."

"Orso's your brother?" whispered Leo.

She grimaced. "Yes."

"That's why he didn't hang me."

"Maybe. Part of it."

Leo sat back, frowning at the ceiling. "So... my wife..."

She closed her eyes again, face burning. "Yes."

"Is King Jezal's oldest child?"

"What?" That she had enthusiastically practised incest did not seem to have occurred to him. Or, if it did, there were aspects of the case that interested him far more.

"Our children...are King Jezal's grandchildren. By the dead, Savine, our children might be next in line to the throne!"

It was not fear in his voice, or disgust. It was excitement. Somehow that worried her even more.

"But, don't you see..." She sat on the bed, nervously clutching up a handful of the quilt. "The danger this puts us in, puts *them* in—"

"Of course." He clasped her hand, eyes gleaming in the candlelight. "But danger and opportunity often walk hand in hand."

Savine stared. "My father used to say that."

"Which one? Old Sticks?" He leaned from the bed and fished up his iron leg again. "I can't say we got on." He jammed his stump into the padded socket and started to fasten the buckles. "But no one ever denied he was a clever bastard. Can't be lying around, Savine. I've got work to do!" And he grasped his cane and stood.

She sat in silence as he limped out, teeth gritted. Click, tap, grunt. Click, tap, grunt. That mixture of cunning, ruthlessness, burning ambition and constant pain was far from unfamiliar.

She had heard it said that every woman ends up marrying her father. Until that moment, she had always imagined herself the exception.

# The Good Work

The setting sun was a great fiery smear around the Tower of Chains, through the wintry haze and the furnace smoke, over the broken teeth of the Agriont's part-ruined walls. They'd given up on taking 'em down, more or less. Another job left quarter-done, like most things since the Great Change. Most things but murder, anyway.

The Square of Marshals had become the Square of Martyrs—the sea of flagstones chiselled with the names of Breakers and Burners killed in twenty years of Old Sticks' purges. Hammers tap, tap, tapped away all day as they added more. Hundreds of them. Thousands.

There were fewer folk come out to watch the executions than when Judge first took charge. Maybe they were tiring of the blood. No doubt they were tiring of the cold. Bitter chill out here. Clouds of smoky breath as the angriest ones screeched insults at the accused.

Broad could hardly see the point of screaming at folk already good as dead. But he was what you'd have to call blind drunk. Spent most of his waking hours blind drunk, now. Like he had in Styria. The only way he could see to get through it.

It was society in miniature, in the Square of Martyrs. Every type of person and every type who preyed on 'em. You'd have thought the aristocrats and the bureaucrats would've stayed well away, but they were here, too, with red ribbons in the ex-ladies' hair and red stains on the ex-lords' clothes, howling their hate at the convicted louder'n anyone, as if that might save them from being next.

They'd brought carts into the Agriont and opened 'em up to make improvised souvenir shops, jerry tents, food stalls. Some enterprising bastard had turned a guardhouse into a pawn shop, so you could sell your watch for a quarter of what it was worth and go straight upstairs to where they'd turned some administrator's office into a brothel, the bookcases pushed over to make bawdy stages, the desks made into beds, the easy chairs into husk-dens. Enterprise always finds a way.

Broad gave the closest prisoner a little nudge in the back, just to keep him moving. Didn't say anything. Saying something encouraged them to say something, and the last thing you want is a conversation. Reminds you that it's not just stuff you're pushing off a tower, but people. He took another nip from his flask. Had to keep drinking. Nice and regular. Always put a bottle by his bed when he went to sleep now, so he could start drinking soon as he fought free of his nightmares. Helps to have a routine.

Kept wondering how many he'd herded across the Square of Marshals. Kept counting 'em up. It'd been one at a time when the trials began. Now it was pairs, threes, fours. *Here's a triple!* Sarlby would say. He was leading the way, flatbow under his arm. Jaunty, almost, how he strutted across the square, across those dead men's names. Used to be a good man, Sarlby. There was a piece of him missing, these days. He had no doubts.

Sometimes felt like all Broad had was doubts. But they changed nothing. He took another nip. The more he drank, the harder it was to keep count. The more he drank, the less he cared about innocence or guilt. The more he drank, the less their crying bothered him. Their arguing. Their endless fucking reasoning. A cuff across the head would shut 'em up, when it got too much. It'd been the same with the prisoners in Styria. No food to spare for the enemy, so...get Gunnar Broad. He'll do what needs doing.

And he did. The families gathered here, in the cold shadow of the Tower of Chains, to say their last goodbyes. To hope for some nick-of-time reprieve that would never come. There was a woman bundled up in a blanket, her face all pink and raw from cold, eyes shining with tears. She blundered out and caught the prisoner closest to Broad.

They clasped each other. Whispered something to each other, foreheads pressed together. Broad wondered what he'd have done, if that was him and Liddy. Him and May. Maybe he'd find out, one day soon. If there was any justice.

He drank again, spirits burning his sore gullet. It was like taking the lenses off his mind. Made everything a blur. So he didn't have to see Liddy's face, or May's. Didn't have to think of what they'd say. Didn't have to put 'em next to what he was now. Didn't have to fear what he might do to 'em. Made it easier, being drunk. Or did it make it easier to have something to blame? I was drunk, so I wasn't thinking straight. I was drunk, so I couldn't help myself. I was drunk, so it wasn't really me, even though, when he was drunk, it was really him even more than when he was sober. It was never really him *until* he was drunk.

Truth be told, he was a man who broke everything. He'd been running from it ever since Styria, and all he'd done was run straight into it again. Told himself it was the safest thing for Liddy and May to stay in Angland, and for him to stay here. Told himself he was doing it for their sakes. Better'n the alternative. That he was doing it for his own.

They clung to each other with desperate strength, these two, trying somehow to put off that final parting. Broad had the pain of sentimental tears at the back of his nose as he prised them apart, hands numb from the cold, numb from the drink. But he still did it.

"I love you!" the woman called as one of the other Burners pulled her away and Broad pushed her man on towards the Tower of Chains. I love you. Like her love might be a cushion he could bounce on when he hit the frozen ground.

Over the anger of the crowd, faint from beyond the Agriont's broken walls, he could hear the dogs. A different kind of bloodthirsty. There were packs of 'em in the streets now. Turned almost as feral as the people. Wolves and foxes, too, drawn out of the cold countryside and into the city by some glimpse of fire, some whiff of blood. They slipped through the crowds outside the Agriont, darted up to lap at the half-frozen spatter at the base of the tower.

Broad pulled his lenses off to rub at the bridge of his nose with a shaky hand, but even without them he could smell it. Even in the cold you could smell it from streets away now, the place of execution. The place where the fall passed its final judgement.

Didn't even shock him any more. Part of his workday, like scrubbing out the tubs at the brewery in Valbeck. The unspeakable made commonplace.

They handed the prisoners over to the Burners at the foot of the tower. Herded them onto Curnsbick's new lift. A wonder of the modern age. The signal was given, the machinery clattered into life and the platform lurched upwards. The climb had almost been kinder.

The families sobbed and wailed, blew kisses and streamed with tears, a forest of reaching hands. Wives and husbands, parents and children. The condemned tried to stay strong. The same wearying pattern as ever.

Broad turned his back on it. Trudged across the frosty stones towards the Court of the People. Sarlby was whistling a tune. All the faces they passed were tilted up now, the light of torches flickering on their expectant grins, the sunset glimmering in their eager eyes as they waited for the little specks to start falling and knew, for certain, the joy of being the ones still alive.

He took another nip. Easier when you were drunk, so he kept drinking. Helps to have a routine. Innocence and guilt had made no difference in Styria and they made none here. No one was guiltier'n him, were they? But he wasn't the one falling, he was the one doing the pushing.

All that mattered was what Judge said. That was all the folk on the benches cared about, the folk in the galleries cared about. Guilty, guilty, guilty. How could Broad say different? He wasn't special. Since the Great Change, being special was not a good idea.

Told himself he didn't want to do it, but he was scared. A coward. That was better'n the alternative. That he did want to do it, 'cause there was a pit of rage in him there was never any filling. He'd rather tell himself he hated Judge than admit he was just like her.

He looked up the trash-scattered steps to the Court of the People. "I'll give Judge the report," he said.

"Oh, aye, you wouldn't want to miss that." Sparks was grinning at him. The man liked to taunt him. Maybe 'cause of the beating Broad had given him in Valbeck that time. Some men never learn their lesson.

"Meaning?" he asked.

"Meaning she's got quite an itch for you, and what Judge likes she tends to get."

"Leave it be," grunted Sarlby. "Broad's a good family man."

"Perfect!" Sparks's grin had become a leer, and he did a few thrusts of his hips in case anyone was still struggling to find the point. "While one family's up in Angland you can start another here—"

Broad caught Sparks by the collar and smashed his fist into his face. Then he hauled him over a plinth some statue had been broken off from, so his neck was over the edge of the block, stuck the heel of his hand on the side of his jaw and started to push.

Sparks plucked helplessly at Broad's wrists, clawed at his red-smeared breastplate with his fingernails, made this hissing, squealing groan, eyes bulging as his skull was twisted further and further around.

"I should pop your fucking head off," said Broad. Not some wild, hissing threat. Just a dull observation. Bored, almost.

"Come on, Bull," said Sarlby. "He's a fucking idiot, aye, but if that's a crime we'll all be for the drop, eh?"

Broad let go, and Sparks tumbled off the plinth and knelt, blowing bloody bubbles from his nose, clutching at his neck.

"We are all for the drop," said Broad, and he stomped up the steps of the court. Told himself he'd lost control a moment. Stopped himself before he did something he'd regret. That was better'n the alternative. That he'd loved every moment of it and would've regretted nothing if he'd snapped Sparks's neck apart.

Court was over, the galleries emptied, the last few Representatives making their way through the foyer, where the marble walls were smeared with streaked slogans, red paint turned black by candlelight. Broad shouldered through 'em, glaring. He was in a fighting mood. He always was.

Bannerman was standing guard in the anteroom, sneer on his face and red paint all up his sleeves. Wasn't long ago he'd been beating labourers for Savine dan Brock. Now he'd joined the Burners and was beating aristocrats for Judge and taking equal pleasure in his work. Chances are that men who'll hurt folk for one master won't flinch at hurting folk for another. It's a job. A potter doesn't need a grand cause to shape his clay for, does he? Why hold a thug to a higher standard?

Broad thought about punching him in the face. But then he thought about that with everyone now, more or less. They didn't speak to each other. Didn't acknowledge each other. What was there to say?

"Bastard," Broad muttered to himself, then nearly tripped over his own feet. Damn, he was drunk, but damn, he wasn't drunk enough. It was sixty-five since dawn. In case anyone was asking. They'd done twenty just after sunup who'd been convicted last night, in the dark. He pulled his lenses off, squeezed at the bridge of his nose. Squeezed it so hard it hurt. At least in Styria there'd been an enemy. Now the enemy was all around. The enemy was everyone. The enemy was yourself.

"Hard day." Judge sat in her chair, the chair Risinau once sat in, the chair the king once sat in, the chair she gave the judgements from, passed the sentences from, one bare foot up on the hammer-battered table. She'd a husk-pipe in her hand, and she took a long pull from it and blew out a great plume of sweet-smelling smoke that tickled at the back of Broad's throat, made him want to cough, made him want to puke, made him want to rip at his face with his nails. She let her head drop back, long, thin throat stretched out, and he could swear he saw the thick veins pulsing.

"You're hurting," she said, looking at him sidelong.

"I'm all right." Had he said that? Didn't sound like something he'd say. He was about as far from all right as could be. Even further from it than he'd been in Styria. He'd promised no more trouble. But if life had taught him one thing, it was that he was shit at keeping promises.

"Sixty-five today," his mouth burbled out.

"We'll do better tomorrow."

When she said better, did she mean they'd kill fewer? He'd a horrible feeling she meant they'd kill more.

He had the pipe. Hardly remembered taking it, but he had it. Sucked on it hard as he could, deep as he could, till it filled his lungs and his head, and when he blew out, everything turned numb.

"It's not easy." said Judge. "Believe me, I know it's not easy." She was across the table. Had she slid under it like a snake? Or had he climbed over it? "But if the good work was easy, it would've been done long ago." Seemed like her black eyes saw right through him. Saw his guilt and his horror and his black memories. No doubt in her eyes. Just the fire. Just the certainty, brighter'n ever. Or was that him, reflected back?

"You know why they call me Judge?" she asked, and her fists were clenched, and her teeth were bared, like each word hurt her. "'Cause if the world's going to change, someone has to give the verdict. Someone has to bury their feelings and sentence the past to death." He felt her hand, pressed light against his breastplate. "And someone has to carry out the sentence. Not 'cause we want to. But 'cause it *has* to be done, and we're fitted for the task…"

They were alone in that vast space, alone with the empty benches, and the empty galleries, and the empty slogans, echoes of their whispers whispering back at them from the darkness.

"We won't be thanked. We won't be forgiven. Not by anyone. Least of all ourselves…"

He could kill her now. Catch her thin, rash-speckled throat and choke the life from it. Smash her head against the table, spray her blood across the tiles, easy as crushing a beetle. He could put an end to this madness.

But all he did was stand there. He told himself he was a coward. That was better'n the alternative. That there was something in her he couldn't resist. Something he wanted like a drunk wants the bottle, knowing it's bad for him, bad for everyone, but knowing he can't stop himself.

"We have to bear the weight of it," she whispered. "For those whose names are carved in the stone outside. For those who gave everything they had. For those who'll come after us…"

She narrowed her eyes, and reached up for him, and he stood there dumb and drunk as she pulled the lenses off his nose, so the Court of the People became nothing but dots of haloed light in a great blurred, husk-smelling darkness.

"Can't see a fucking thing," he muttered.

"Maybe it's better that way," she whispered, breath hot on his face and smelling like spirits. "Maybe it's time to let go."

She grabbed him. Or did he grab her? They were kissing, anyway, if you could even call it kissing. Too hard, too violent, too painful for that. Growling and biting. Like they were eating each other.

He tried to fling her away. Or did he pull her closer? Clutching at her. Tearing at her already-torn clothes, his fists tangled in the tatters of her ruined old dress and his nose full of the sour smoke smell of her. Wanted her more than he'd ever wanted anyone. Hated her more than he'd ever hated anyone. Except himself, maybe.

He had her by the dozen chains around her neck, and she had him by his belt with one hand, dragging it open, the other clawing at his face, hard, at his jaw, merciless, her thumb was inside his cheek, pulling his head down towards her, pulling him down on top of her. He wanted her to hurt him. Her bare feet around the back of his bare arse, stuck tight to him, and he ripped her torn skirts up over the tattooed treatise on her thigh, dragging his face close to hers, close enough that he could see the fire reflected in her eyes.

"You're mine," she hissed in his face. "You're mine," and they snapped and snarled at each other like coupling cats.

He'd promised no more trouble, and now here he was fucking it, or letting it fuck him, maybe, on the floor of the Lords' Round. Or whatever they were calling it now.

He was crying while he did it, maybe. At least to begin with.

But that doesn't mean you're not doing it.

# The World a Camp

T he procession wended from the gloom of falling snow. The Burners walked ten abreast in their paint-spattered clothes, their red-speckled armour, each of them holding high a torch, light falling hard on their hollow faces. Everyone else had to scrape out of their way, press themselves to the buildings and the doorways. Even Vick and her Constables and their prisoners.

Now came the coffin, borne on the shoulders of eight women looking mighty cold in white dresses slush-stained around the hems. There was an antique feel to it all, as if the funeral procession of great Juvens had marched from the pages of the storybooks for this one moment.

"Who's in the casket?" grunted Vick.

"Some Burner. Led the revolt in Keln, I heard." Tallow glanced about, then leaned close to whisper, "They say he was killed by royalists, but he was a moderate."

"Meaning what?" Extreme last week was moderate now. By next week it would have become collaboration.

"The rumour is Judge done away with him. They say she's drunk on blood. Gone mad with it."

"To go mad you have to be sane to begin with." Vick watched the shuffling column fade into the snow, off towards the Mausoleum of the Great Change, not even half-built beside the Four Corners, where the heroes of the Breakers and Burners were being laid to rest. "Let's move!" she called, trudging on through the slush and the crowds and the frosty cold, past a great heap of burning books, pages occasionally floating on fire into the night, and down the echoing entrance tunnel of the Agriont.

On the street that was once the Kingsway the statues had been replaced. Or, at least, their faces, their hands, their clothes had. Clumsy alterations had turned them from centuries of kings and their advisors into miners, builders, farmers, nursing mothers. Heroes of the common folk. Risinau's plans, cheaply realised, awkwardly posed, something pained and accusatory in their clumsily carved expressions.

"Bloody hell it's cold." Tallow hugged himself, blathering steam into the early darkness. "My sister's got ice on the inside of her window. She spends half her time queueing. For coal, for bread, for meat. When she gets to the end, often as not they've run out. There was some lunatic on the corner screeching *long live the king* all night, preaching that Harod would rise from his grave and bring order, and Bayaz himself was flying to the city on a great eagle to appoint a new Closed Council."

"Wish there was a great eagle coming," muttered Vick. "We could eat it."

They tramped past the Court of the People, light burning from its windows. They were trying groups of a dozen now, till dusk and beyond, those with evidence against them and those with none mixed together as if their cases were all connected, so the guilt of one would splatter the rest and they all could be dragged down, like swimmers chained together. The only folk who got acquitted these days were those who denounced freely. Those who denounced anyone and everyone. Denounced their lovers, their parents, their children.

The House of Purity was overflowing with bankers and clerks. Traitors against the Great Change, suspected of aristocratic plots, foreign conspiracies, royalist schemes, arrested by the Burners and awaiting trial, had to be squeezed in elsewhere. They'd made the Fortress of the Knights Herald into a prison, then the walled treasury buildings. Families traipsed the courtyards, begging to know where their loved ones were being held, gathered in the snow outside the windows with children on their shoulders for a glimpse of daddy.

"I hear they're setting up new courts," said Tallow.

"I guess Judge can't pronounce the death sentences fast enough on her own."

"Aiming at one in each district of Adua."

"In each district?"

"And each town in Midderland. Three in Keln. Two in Valbeck. They say they'll have to set up more when Forest and his royalists are finally brought to justice. They're appointing new magistrates to hear all the cases. I hear they're paid by the conviction."

"Fuck," whispered Vick.

"New places of execution, too."

"I guess they'll need them."

"They tried to use the bell tower on the old Spicers' guildhall, but, well, it wasn't high enough."

Vick winced. "Fuck."

"They didn't all die right off. Had to have a Burner at the bottom with a pickaxe to finish the poor bastards—"

"All right, Tallow, I get the picture." It was coming to something when a child of the prison camps was finding life in the capital too dark for comfort.

Her mind wandered back there. To the camps. To her own father, coughing blood in that cold winter. She'd tried to trade for a blanket, work for an empty sack, steal a little knuckle of coal, but it was never enough. Her mother, wasted away to nothing. So thin at the end you could see her bones. Her sister's screams behind her in the mine as the floodwater rushed into the tunnel.

Vick came to a stop in the snow, watching the Constables herding her latest batch of prisoners across the Square of Martyrs.

"I'd hoped it might get better," she muttered. "But it's getting worse."

Tallow hopped from one foot to the other for warmth. "You could've said that any time since I met you."

"That's your comfort? We're not at the bottom yet? Judge is more powerful now than the king ever was. Even Harod the Great answered to Bayaz. Judge answers to no one but the fire. She won't be happy till she's burned it all to the ground."

"Not even then, I daresay." Tallow glanced towards another sorry set of the accused being driven hunched through the snow. "But you might want to keep your voice down."

"This was meant to set us all free. Instead we've turned the whole Agriont into a prison." Vick frowned at the names cut into the stones under her feet, half-seen through the slush. She wondered if Sibalt's was there, somewhere. She remembered lying in his narrow bed, talking about how they'd change the world. She'd known they were dreams. But they'd been pretty dreams, at least. Was this the better world he'd died for? "We've made the whole city into a camp. The whole Union."

"You always say we should stand with the winners..."

One of the prisoners broke from the line, chains on her ankles clanking, rag-wrapped hands clutching. Vick was ready to punch her. Almost did it. But all she wanted was to push something into Vick's hands. A folded paper.

"You've a kind face! Take this to my daughter, please."

"Come here," grunted one of the Burners, grabbing her under the arm without malice, without gentleness. The way a shepherd grabs a sheep. "Sorry 'bout that, Inspector."

"Please!" the woman blubbed as he dragged her away.

Vick knew she had nothing close to a kind face. A bag of chisels was how she'd always thought of what she saw in the mirror. She'd been given the letter, not Tallow or someone softer, because she looked like someone who got things done. She unfolded it, fingers cold and sluggish even in her gloves.

"What does it say?" asked Tallow.

There was no poetry to it. Scrawled on a scrap of candle-wrapper with a stub of charcoal from a dead fire. Just love, and best wishes, and keep going, and don't forget me. She realised she'd no idea who to take it to. No idea who the woman had been. Could've been anyone. Could almost have been Vick herself. Except she had no one to write a letter to.

"It says goodbye." She crumpled the paper in her fist. "Get the prisoners where they're going." And she turned and strode off, back the way they'd come, boots crunching in her own footprints, already turning dirty white with new snow.

Seemed the Great Change had been almost as tough on Styrian spies as on everyone else. The warren of gloomy cellars under the sign of the fish-woman reminded Vick more of the mines of Angland than ever. Not only was it underground but freezing, too, puddles of icy meltwater from the streets above gathered in the corners.

There was no music. No dancers. Few patrons of any kind. The barman stood where he had on her last visit, the same magnificent array of glass-ware behind him, but a lot of the bottles were down to dribbles. Seemed a fine metaphor for where the Great Change had taken them, all in all. Same bottles. But empty.

"Victarine dan Teufel graces my establishment for a second time," said the barman, raising one orange brow at her.

"No 'dans' any more, remember? Where's your monkey?"

"Off sick."

"Shame. Of the two of you, he was my favourite."

The barman grinned. "Most of my clientele would concur."

"Have you got any of that piss you poured me last time? What did you call it?"

"Sworfene, and sadly no. Supply of late, what with the weather, and the politics, is something of a nightmare. If you can get stale bread from the end of the road you're doing well. To get liquor in from Jacra requires a magician." His hand skimmed across the bottles, then plucked one out.

"Why don't you..." And he slipped a glass in front of her and poured a shot. "Try this instead?"

She grimaced as she tasted it. "Damn, that's sweet."

"Sometimes we need challenge. Sometimes we need comfort."

"Do I look that bad?"

"You look far better than most in Adua."

She drank again. "That bad. I don't suppose our mutual friend in Talins, the woman with all the whispers, might be tempted to intercede in affairs on this side of the Circle Sea? Help put an end to this...chaos? Get the liquor flowing again?"

The barman gave a sad smile. "I wouldn't demean us both by making such a suggestion to our mutual friend. Her mistress, lest we forget, is far from the most open-handed of rulers at the best of times, and positively delights in chaos on this side of the Circle Sea. I hear the news makes her giggle daily over breakfast."

"Didn't have the Serpent of Talins down as a giggler."

"No one did till now."

Vick pushed her empty glass at him. Like most drinks, it got better with time. "A little optimistic of me, I'll admit. If not to say desperate."

He poured her another. "There is no place for either optimism or desperation in our business."

Vick raised her glass. "To pessimism and hard heads."

"I can drink to that." And he slipped another glass onto the bar. "The Union, I fear, is beyond help. This Great Change is a fever that has to burn itself out. But you always struck me as a woman who'd save herself." She stopped sipping to watch him over the rim of her glass. "If you decided Adua no longer held any charms..." He glanced up and down the vaulted cellar. "Which would be *thoroughly* understandable...I expect our mutual friend would still welcome you with open arms."

"Spring in Talins, eh?"

"The weather alone would be worth the trip. The time comes..." And he swallowed his shot in one and slapped the empty glass down on the bar. "You have to get out."

She slowly nodded. Wouldn't be the first time she'd got out. Saved herself in the camps, hadn't she? And in Rostod, during the rebellion. And in Valbeck, during the uprising. Saved herself, even if she saved no one else.

Truth was, she wouldn't be missed. She'd made sure of it. Never stay in a place you can't walk straight out of without a backward glance. Never own a thing you can't leave behind. Never make a friend you can't turn your back on. A life that leaves no marks. She thought about that, as if for the first time. The people she'd tricked, betrayed, left behind, and she wondered—is a life that leaves no marks a life at all?

She hadn't come for a way out. Not really. She'd come to try one on and see how it fit.

"Can't say I'm not tempted." She thought about that last look on her brother's face, before they dragged him away. The last words Sibalt said, before he cut his own throat. "But the time comes…" She drained her glass and set it down. "You have to stand up."

"Where are you going?"

She set a coin spinning on the counter and left without looking back. "To stand with the losers."

# Better Than Carnage

Orso woke to the clanging of Corporal Halder's truncheon on the bars of his cellar. He much preferred the word "cellar" to "dungeon." The place was designed for wine, after all, even if the purpose it was being put to now was, one had to admit, more than a bit dungeony.

"Wake up, Your Majesty," grunted Halder.

Orso sighed, then flung back the rags he preferred to call blankets and swung his feet to the clammy floor.

Bloody hell, it was cold down here. But then it was cold everywhere. He took perverse pleasure in tolerating the same conditions his least fortunate subjects must be enduring. He used to have such privilege and such guilt. He felt far lighter, carrying neither one.

Hildi had been busy scrubbing his other shirt. In cold water, of course, since that was all that could be had. Now she was pegging it up to dry near the bars. The washing had frozen there a couple of times, cloth turned stiff as chilly card.

"Get back from the door, girl," said Halder, keys in his hand.

Orso distracted him by ostentatiously stretching. "You know my mother searched for years to find a bride who'd meet my standards, but we never could light upon quite the right balance of outstanding beauty, impeccable breeding, piercing intellect, ethereal grace, subtle diplomacy and boundless patience." He pressed one hand to his chest. "If only you'd presented yourself at the time, Corporal Halder, perhaps there'd be a royal heir or two already..."

Halder stared at him with those heavy-lidded eyes. "You reckon you're quite the funny fucker, don't you?"

"Laughter is a tonic in hard times. I have your welfare in mind."

"No one laughs where you're going."

"What does that mean?" asked Hildi, frowning at him.

"His Majesty has been sent for." And Halder pulled the barred door open.

"Oh, damn." Orso draped himself as nonchalantly as he could against the damp pillar in the middle of the cellar. "Must I really leave my suite?"

"'Fraid so."

"Have the chef prepare my morning repast for my return, Hildi." And he flounced from the cell. He knew how much his attendants hated it when he did that. He much preferred the word "attendants" to "jailers."

He hadn't realised how warm it was beneath the palace until he stepped into the open air.

"It's like winter's tits out here!" he gasped. The gardens were all frozen, every branch on every tree picked out with a line of snow, the drain-pipes dangling with glinting icicles, the heaps of fallen leaves from the creeper that covered the palace walls glittering with frost. It might've been beautiful had he been better dressed, but even wearing every stitch he still possessed the air had a bitter bite. He was not sure whether to blow on his hands or wedge them under his armpits. He settled for blowing on the left one while wedging the right and swapping them every few strides. "Where are we going, anyway?"

"Oh, you'll love it," said Halder, with a glance over his shoulder that implied he wouldn't. Not that Orso had liked anything for some weeks now. Before the Great Change, he'd often joked that being High King of the Union was the worst job in the world. After the Great Change, it wasn't even a joke. He'd heard they were selling night pots with his face on the inside of the bowl. Once, the ladies of Adua had scrambled into his bed. Now they queued up to shit on him. He could hardly say he didn't deserve it.

Snow was falling on the park. Just dirty spots and specks against the House of the Maker, silhouetted in the winter haze. The place was almost empty. Lonely figures wobbled on the icy pathways, smoke pluming from their faces. A pair of children, ridiculously underdressed for the season, were chasing each other around leaving spirals of footprints, hands and faces chapped pink, scraping up snow and flinging it. Not so much snowballs as pointless showers of glittering powder. Their giggles rang out as they flopped down together in the white.

"Good to see someone's having fun," muttered Orso. He rather wished he could join them. Especially once his destination became clear. They were calling it the House of Purity now, of course, but its aspect was no more comforting. The same lowering, near-windowless façade. The same guards, prisoners, questions. Even the crimes were mostly the same. Only the direction of the treason had changed.

He had visited several times in the past, for unpleasant interviews with Arch Lector Glokta, but he had never before had cause to go below ground level. He worried that the interviews conducted down here were a great deal more unpleasant yet. It was dim and chill as an ice house. No romance to the place. A cheap, workmanlike feel, and it smelled of damp.

Halder knocked on a heavy door, bound with iron. Orso wondered how he would respond to torture. Badly, he suspected. Who responds well? And what possible preparation could a life of cosseted indulgence be, after all, for expertly and ruthlessly applied pain? He closed his eyes, trying to find that breezy courage that had somehow welled up in him at Stoffenbeck.

"Come in."

The room was a sparse white box, plaster speckled with mould in one corner. There was something that looked like a badly scrubbed bloodstain on one badly whitewashed wall.

There was a battered table with two battered chairs. One was empty. In the other, regarding him coolly with those hard eyes that never gave anything away, was Inquisitor Teufel. Or Chief Inspector Teufel now, he supposed. Everything had a different title than before the Great Change. Well, not quite everything. He had the same title, but it meant the opposite.

Teufel looked up at Halder. "You can go."

"Reckon I'd better stay."

Her forehead showed a beautifully regular set of creases as she frowned. "What's your name?"

Orso only wished he had been able to so easily unsettle the man. "Why d'you want to know that?"

"So I can tell Commissioner Pike who's putting themselves in his way."

Halder swallowed noisily, lump on his throat bobbing. "I'll wait outside." And he shut the door ever so politely behind him.

"Chief Inspector Teufel!" called Orso. "What a lovely surprise, and what a fetching uniform. This has been a delightful outing so far, I must say. Are we touring all the cellars of the Agriont? There must be miles of—"

"I found a letter, Your Majesty. In your bread."

There was a brief and highly uncomfortable silence. Orso struggled to stay upbeat, in spite of the yawning pit of panic that had just opened beneath his chair. "You must be in desperate straits if you're stealing my bread, Inspector, it's positively horrible."

"We're all in desperate straits." Teufel slid out a stained slip of paper, very like the ones Hildi had been bringing him since Tunny's visit to his attic. "Royalist traitors are pressing the People's Army hard, out there in the east of Midderland. And from what I read, it looks like you're in contact with Lord Marshal Forest."

So, there it was. He had been very much looking forward to seeing the murderous smile wiped from Judge's face, preferably by a fall from the Tower of Chains, but he supposed the chances of discovery had always been high. "I've told him to desist but you know how hard it is to stop an admirer once they have the bit between their teeth."

"No doubt. I'm besieged by the bastards." She slowly unfolded the letter, glanced from the writing to Orso's face. Bloody hell, those eyes. When it came to hiding secrets, and to digging them out, he could scarcely have been further out of his league, and well knew it. "Seems Forest and his royalists want to put you back on the throne. Seems they're in touch with your mother and sister, out in Sipani. Seems they've been sending you messages via your servant—"

"I take full responsibility!" he said, far too eagerly, and probably very ill-advisedly, but when Hildi's safety was at stake the time for jokes was over. "My servant knew nothing about...any plot..."

Teufel was holding up a hand to stop him. She glared down, teeth bared, as if working herself up to some distasteful task. Orso did not care to imagine what kind of threats, blackmail or torture might give her pause. She tapped a chewed fingernail on the scarred tabletop, witness to who knew what horrors under the old regime and the new, then finally looked up at him.

When she spoke, her voice had turned oddly soft. "Forest isn't the only one who'd like to see the monarchy restored."

Orso had steeled himself for almost anything but that. "He isn't?"

"No." She considered him a moment longer. "This madness has gone on long enough. Far too long. Judge has to be stopped." She gave a shrug of resignation, shoulders slumping. "And since no one else is doing it..."

Orso felt a wave of relief that came close to loosening his bowels. "You mean...to *help* me?"

"Against my much better judgement. The truth is, far as I can tell... you're the Union's best chance."

"*You*...think *I*..." And Orso felt the smile spread right across his face. A sensation he had not experienced in quite some time.

"Don't get carried away, Your Majesty. I'm saying you're better than carnage, famine and chaos."

"Honestly, that's the closest thing to praise I've heard in months." And not from a source prone to compliments. Orso shuffled eagerly forwards. "What's your plan?" She struck him as a woman who did not get out of bed without three or four strong plans in place. "I mean to say...do you have a plan?"

"Not one I like the odds on. But I can think of a few people who might be brought around to your cause. With the right encouragement. The right threats. The right bribes."

Orso patted his trousers. "I seem to be a little light at the moment. In fact, I've a hell of a debt to my valet, you'd never guess what a shirt costs these days—"

"Four chairs on the Closed Council."

Orso raised his brows. "Do you plan to drape yourself across them?"

"I plan to sell them."

"Four chairs are a high price."

"I'd say it's a pretty low price, given right now you don't have any chairs at all."

He pushed out his lips in a pout. "I have an old box to sit on, actually. Hildi and I call it the throne. When I am feeling beneficent, she gets the corner. I was thinking once I am restored I might have it installed in the actual throne room. To keep me humble."

He wondered if he might have coaxed the hint of a smile from the corner of Teufel's unbendable mouth. "You could do with some help in that regard."

"And, let us be honest, in every other."

"So I have your permission? To make offers?"

"Might I ask to whom?"

"Might be better if you didn't."

"You'll be talking to my enemies?"

"If it works, you'll have fewer enemies and more friends. Isn't that what everyone wants?"

Orso sat there for a moment. He was cold. He was drained. And he suspected it would not be much longer until Judge removed him from his cage in the Court of the People and put him in the dock. He needed to trust someone and, honestly, if Victarine dan Teufel wanted to betray him, there had been golden opportunities when she had far more to gain.

"You have my permission, for this and anything else. You can speak with my full authority, such as it is. And can I say, honestly, for once, that there is no one I would rather have on my side. From the first moment

I met you, I have always felt safe in your hands, Inquisitor Teufel. Or... Inspector Teufel? Or—"

"Vick." She pressed her fist on the tabletop, took a long breath through her nose, and let it sigh away. "If we're going down in flames together, it might as well be on first-name terms."

"Well, Vick. I have no doubt there is a healthy dose of self-interest in this, and an even healthier dose of common good, but on a personal note..." He leaned forwards and put his hand on hers. "I would like to thank you from the bottom of my heart for your loyalty."

Her face gave a strange twitch at that, and she stared down at his hand on hers, jaw muscles clenched almost angrily. For the briefest moment, he had the bizarre feeling that she was about to cry. Or perhaps punch him in the face. Strange reactions, in a way, to the heartfelt thanks of one's monarch. But in the end, all she did was give him a stiff nod and ease her hand from under his, rubbing the back of it with the other as if his touch had burned her. "We're done here!" she yelled at the door.

By the time it swung open and Halder stomped back in, Vick did not look like a woman who had ever shed one tear. She curled her lip at Orso with immaculately acted contempt. He hoped it was acted, anyway. "Fucking idiot doesn't know anything," she said.

# A Matter of Time

"Move over...there." She straddled his good leg, rubbing herself against it, kissing him softly, catching his hand and sliding it up her side while at the same time she slipped her fingers under his nightshirt, started stroking him into life.

"Is this more of your charity?" he asked.

There had been a time, not so very long ago, when she would have slapped him for that. And he would have gasped at the sting of it, and with his eyes he would have asked to be slapped again. When he had been whole, and strong as a lion, and could have flung her across the room with a flick of his wrist, hurting him had felt daring, thrilling, an exhilarating gamble.

Now, so crippled and so vulnerable, the thought of hitting him made her sick. Now, looking in his eyes, she thought she saw a kind of hate for her. A wounded envy. She guessed that he blamed her for how things had turned out almost as much as she blamed herself. And she imagined he would very much have liked to fling her across the room, just to prove he still could.

There had been a time, not so very long ago, when he had been almost too gentle with her. Now his one hand clutched her, gripped her, yanked and crushed and twisted, as if to make a point of how strong it still was. There had been a time, fucking her husband, she had occasionally teetered on the brink of boredom. Now she occasionally teetered on the brink of fear.

It was not like it had been. But what was? You have to make the best of it.

She kept rubbing at him. "What I had in mind...is a fair trade... for both parties."

"Ah, the business arrangement. I can agree to that." And he caught her under the arm and heaved her onto her back. Probably his hope had been to flip her effortlessly, but with only one leg and one arm he had to rock one way then the other and ended up with his stump tangled in the blankets.

One of her hands was busy between her legs, guiding him, the other around the back of his head, pulling him close while at the same time she could prop his shoulder up with her forearm and stop his useless hand flopping into the way.

His teeth were gritted with pain and effort, growling more with anger than pleasure. She wanted to stroke his face, whisper calming noises. Fates help her, the same shushing she would have given her crying children. Could he not have let her ride him? It would have been far more enjoyable for them both. But one works with what one has. She strained up to kiss him—

There was a sharp cry from next door and they both froze.

She dropped back against the pillows. "Fuck."

"Let them cry," he hissed.

"No." She made him grunt as she wriggled out from under him, slid from the bed and into the cold.

"You don't have to be at their mercy."

After all the damage she had done, motherhood was a chance to do one thing right. She pulled her nightgown on. "We're all at someone's mercy, Leo."

Through their dressing room, dimly lit by the glow of the dying fire, and into the nursery. She could tell them apart by their cries. Ardee's howls were thuggish demands. Harod's whines were pleas for mercy. Three months old and already they were so different. Ardee fed with a purpose, and once she was asleep nothing would rouse her. Harod pecked and fussed and shook awake at the slightest sound.

She lifted him from his cot, quivering he was crying so hard. She held him close, shushing and cooing desperately. She pulled the door to and went to sit in one of the chairs beside the fire, the one with the shawl over the back that still smelled like her mother—

She froze with a strangled gasp.

Someone was already sitting there. Someone in the black uniform of the People's Inspectorate, firelight picking out the bones and hollows of a hard frown. Vick dan Teufel.

"Have I been denounced?" asked Savine. Surprising, how cool her voice sounded. Perhaps it was a kind of relief, if it had come, to know she need not worry any more about *when* it would come.

"Not yet," said Teufel. "But we both know it's a matter of time. Judge hates you."

Now Savine had her hammering heart under control she was damned if she would give any hint of being rattled. She sank into the other chair, pulling her nightgown open as though her breast was a hidden weapon she was showing off.

Harod wriggled about, mouth searching desperately for her nipple everywhere but where it was. She finally managed to get him settled and sat back, frowning. "Judge hates everyone."

"Oh, but she has some favourites."

"If all you have is threats you can make them during business hours."

"I've an offer, too. For you and your husband."

"An offer it's better you aren't seen making?"

"I'm not really the front-door type."

"No. Thoroughly underhanded in my experience."

"While the Darling of the Slums never flirted with a falsehood?"

Silence stretched while they carefully considered one another, as they had a long time ago, when they shared a carriage on the way to Valbeck. "I suppose you have me there," Savine admitted. Her trouble with Teufel was not that she was a liar, after all, but that she had proved herself a better liar than Savine. "Do you know where my father is?" she found she had asked.

"No. I wish I did."

"He hasn't even met his grandchildren." A ridiculous, sentimental thing to say to a professional torturer. She half-expected Teufel to burst out laughing, but all she did was thoughtfully narrow her eyes. Savine looked down at Harod. "I daresay I'm the only one who misses him."

"Oh, I don't know. His tenure's starting to look like a golden age. Where's your husband? I need both of you."

"I daresay he'll be along—"

The door crashed open and Leo took a clanking step through on his iron leg, shoulder of his useless arm against the door frame, drawn sword in his other hand, stark naked and still halfway hard.

Teufel glanced over, unmoved by either weapon. "Careful. You might have someone's eye out with that."

He lowered the sword. "If you break into people's houses you can't complain about what you see."

"Oh, I'm delighted someone in the city's still having fun." Teufel watched him limp to the settle, toss his sword down and drop onto the cushions. He winced as he twisted his iron leg off then sat back, his stump thrust forwards. When he'd been a perfect specimen of manhood he'd always been oddly modest. Now he loved to put his many scars on display and see how people reacted. To no one's surprise, the inspector was unmoved.

"I appreciate the visit," said Leo, "but knowing how much you value honesty—I don't like you."

"Good. Mutual suspicion is the best basis for an alliance. Everyone knows where they stand."

Leo frowned. "An alliance?"

"Forgive me for saying so," said Savine, "but the last time you came offering help it turned out rather badly for us."

"You were betraying King Orso then."

"And now?"

"You'd be helping me put him back on the throne."

There was a pause one could only have called pregnant. Savine spent it thinking of the old Union, her old life, her old self, and trying not to let her desperate yearning show. "I somehow doubt... that Judge would simply *give* the power back."

"No." Vick leaned forwards, the firelight bright on one side of her face, the other lost in shadow. "We'd have to take it."

Savine held Harod a little tighter. More blood. More death. She glanced over at Leo. No sign of doubt in his eyes. Quite the reverse.

"What do we get?" he asked.

"Four chairs on the Closed Council, when it's reconvened."

Savine could not help taking a sharp breath. Four chairs would once have been a dazzling prize. In the old days, Arch Lector Sult and High Justice Marovia had ruined lives by the hundred over a single one.

"What if I want more?" asked Leo.

"I'm not here to bargain. Four's what I've got and four's what I'm offering. It's fair."

"Fair might look different from where I sit," said Leo. "With what I've lost."

"You could always ask Judge for more."

"She might listen if I offered her a treacherous chief inspector in return."

Leo's threats moved Teufel no more than his scars or his cock. "Go ahead. But don't be surprised if I say the whole thing was your idea, but you got greedy and wanted more than I could offer. As you both know, I can be quite convincing. I expect we'd all end up in the dock together, probably with a tailor, and an engraver, and a couple of dark-skinned strangers, accused of a conspiracy to make the river freeze."

It all sounded depressingly plausible. "What exactly do you expect us to contribute?" asked Savine. For four chairs, she imagined it would be quite a lot.

"Your friends from Angland, your friends from the Open Council." She paused a moment. "And the People's Army."

"I don't have it," snapped Leo.

"If you stretched, I reckon you could get your fingers around it."

"And what do you deliver?"

"Lord Marshal Forest and his rebels, well-organised royalists inside the city, information from inside the Inspectorate, Styrian contacts and Styrian money. Not to mention the king's blessing. And the king's forgiveness."

"You've spoken to Orso?" asked Savine.

Teufel gazed levelly back. "I have."

She resisted the urge to ask how he was. "And you have his agreement?"

"I do."

"And we're supposed to take your word for it?" sneered Leo. "Forgive me if I—"

Savine cut him off. "Judge has to be stopped." She had dreamed, last night, of falling from a high place, and woken in a cold sweat. "At any price."

Leo gave an unhappy grunt. "Well. On that we can all agree."

"Four chairs on the Closed Council is fair." After everything that had happened, it was far more than they could have hoped for. "We will provide the Anglanders, and the ex-lords of the Open Council, and the People's Army."

Leo took a breath and sighed noisily through flared nostrils. "Great tempests wash up strange companions, Farans said."

"Never had you down for a philosopher," said Teufel.

"I've been catching up on my classics."

The inspector gave a sharp little nod. "Then we all have lots of work to do. I'll see myself out."

The door clicked shut. Harod had stopped feeding, his head rolled back, mouth open, a dribble of milk on his chin. Savine lifted him, carried him to the nursery, softly lowered him into his cot, chewing her lip with concentration as she slid her hands out from under him and left him beside his sister.

She looked down at them, both sleeping. Ardee on her side, one long-lashed eye closed and her mouth wide open. Harod on his back, tiny hands palm-up as if he was surrendering. So small. So perfect. So vulnerable. She remembered something her father once told her. Being a parent means always being afraid. Afraid for your children. Afraid of your children.

When she turned from pulling the nursery door ever-so-gently closed, Leo was watching her.

"So we're in bed with King Orso now, are we?"

Savine winced. Did he really have to use that phrase? "We are taking the best chance to bring this nightmare to an end." And perhaps to repair a fraction of the damage they had done. "We can't trust Judge, Leo, you know that."

"She likes me well enough."

She winced even more at that. He could only be saying it to annoy her. "For now, perhaps. You are a likeable fellow." When he chose to be. "But once she has thrown everyone she hates off the Tower of Chains she will start on the people she likes. That's what she is."

He frowned down at his stump, scratching gently at the scars. "I daresay you're right."

"I usually am."

"It's a gamble, though."

"The way things are going, the bigger gamble would be to do nothing. We are living on borrowed time. Anyone who used to be powerful. Anyone who *is* powerful. All of us."

Leo let his head drop back, looking at her down his nose. "We fought against Orso."

"That was then."

He had that cruel look now. That bitter, jealous look. "Do you still love him?"

Again, the urge to slap him. "I never loved him," she lied.

"Not even as a brother?"

This time she wanted to punch him. She realised her fist was clenched to do it. But she made it open. The satisfaction would not have lasted long. And she could let him be angry. She had all her limbs, after all.

She slipped one knee down beside him. "What can I do...to prove it?" And she worked her other knee onto the settle so she was straddling him.

She pulled her nightgown up with her right hand, down with her left, cool of the night on one bare shoulder, warmth of the fire on the other. She did not look in his eyes. She was not sure she would like what was in them. There had been a time, not so very long ago, when he had claimed to love her and, if she squinted, she had almost been able to convince herself that she loved him. But you have to make the best of it.

She took his hand, guided it, slid it up her chest. She took his face,

226

kissing him, working her hips against his stomach. It was not like it had been. But what was? She reached behind her, found his prick, rubbed herself against it, looking for the right spot—

The cry echoed from the other room. Ardee, this time, hard and insistent. A moment later Harod joined her, higher, faster, weaker. She closed her eyes and sagged.

"Fuck."

# Taking and Keeping

She'd never thought so when it was happening, but Rikke had to admit that she quite liked being bullied. She'd heaps of practice, and it brought out the stubborn best in her. Plucky Rikke. Everyone loved that girl. Sharp thinking, sharp talking, with the odds against her but right on her side.

It was the opposite that landed her in trouble. Folk begging, wheedling, pleading, it made her all weak and nervy. Wriggly Rikke. That bitch was no use to anyone. The problem was, sitting in Skarling's Chair, she was begged a lot more than she was bullied.

"Please!" The farmer went so far as to drop to his knees, the artful bastard, twisting his hat in his hands. "I'm at your mercy."

That was the whole problem. She could've sent him home with a box full of silver. Or she could've sent his head home and kept the rest of him. All within her gift.

She narrowed the one eye that saw anything in the hope it might see through his skin to the truth. That he was a poor honest fool with a sick wife and twelve hungry children to feed. Or that he was a greedy liar with silk hidden under his stained shirt and pots of gold buried in his barn.

But the Long Eye refused to open, and the answer was more'n likely neither one anyway, but somewhere in between, as answers always are. Times were hard, and she could squeeze more out of him, but it'd hurt. It'd hurt him, and it'd hurt her. It'd hurt him more, of course, but he'd only get squeezed once today. There was a whole queue of hat-twisters outside Skarling's Hall ready to fling themselves onto their knees at the least provocation. If she was soft on one, she'd have to be soft on 'em all. And soft might feel good for a day, but it can hurt in the long run. Hurt everyone.

"Hmmm," she grunted. "Hmmm."

All the while, from inside his cage, the watery eyes of that born bully

Stour bloody Nightfall were on her, as if to say, *You wouldn't have caught me showing too much mercy.*

Rikke's father had worn being a leader so lightly no one realised they were being led. Listening far more'n he spoke. Folk nodding at his every word like they never heard such wisdom, even if all he was doing was excusing himself for a piss. Sitting on his bench with the old sheepskin around his shoulders, chin propped on his fist. She tried to sit that way, too, but it didn't work in Skarling's Chair, she ended up squirming around like she didn't belong there. Her father had earned everyone's respect, over years. Rikke didn't have years. And it sometimes seemed folk would indulge a man's mistakes, while they held a woman's against her.

If Isern had been there, she'd have told her to make of her heart a stone. To bury her doubts in a shallow grave. A sprinkle of blood now might save a flood later. Viciousness is a quality much loved o' the moon. But Isern wasn't there. Rikke realised she was fussing at the ring through her nose, and forced her hand away, and ended up picking at the arm of Skarling's Chair with her fingernail instead, which was no better.

"What do you think, Corleth?"

The girl blinked. "Me?"

"Far as I know, you're the only Corleth I've got."

She stared at the farmer, then back at Rikke. "I guess it was a tough harvest. And it's been a tough winter."

"Aye. A tough winter for everyone." Rikke slumped down unhappily. "You can pay half now. But you'll make it up after the next harvest, you hear?"

From her father it would've sounded patient and level-headed. From her it sounded like a thin-beer compromise. She saw it on the faces. Hardbread scratching his wispy pate. The warriors about the hall sighing away like bellows. Now every farmer in the North would be trying every trick to tickle out her mercy.

"You'll be making it up to me!" she screeched as the man hurried out, making herself sound weaker'n ever. There was another fellow shoving in at the same moment. A warrior from Uffrith, used to be one of Red Hat's Carls.

"I've got news!" he called, and from the look on his face it wasn't good. Good news felt like a thing she'd heard about but never actually seen, like dragons or deserts.

"Don't keep it to yourself," she grumbled.

"It's the Nail! He came wi' four hundred Carls. He took Buddlehay, on the river. Killed three men and said the village was his. He said Uffrith'll be his as well."

"That treacherous fucking arsehole!" snarled Rikke, jumping out of Skarling's Chair. "Thinks he can stab us in the back while we're tied up wi' Calder! I'll see the bloody cross cut in him!"

Hardbread looked even more worried than usual. "We send men to fight the Nail, we'll scarcely have enough to keep Carleon, let alone to hold the walls if Calder comes."

Shivers rubbed at his jaw. "Folk here still aren't sure about you—"

"You think they like Black Calder better?" snapped Rikke.

"No one likes Black Calder. They worry what'll happen if he wins."

A silence. "And they think he will," Rikke finished for him.

Hardbread spread his hands. "Isern-i-Phail's gone, the Nail's turned against us..."

Just went to show, people say they want fair rulers but, in the end, they'd rather have a bastard in charge. Case of what they're used to, maybe. She hopped down from the dais so she could talk to the two old Named Men at closer quarters. "So what? We give up Skarling's Chair? After all the work we've put in taking it?"

Hardbread shrugged. "In the end...it's just a chair."

"It bloody isn't!" Rikke snapped, making him turn his wrinkled old face away, as if from a chilly wind. "It's a sign o' who's in charge. I let Black Calder take it back and he'll take back the North, bit by bit, and we'll be stuck where we started, but without Angland to help us. Have we heard aught from Clover?"

"Nothing," said Shivers. "But we know Calder's gathering men."

Hardbread was nodding away. "He's never done things by halves. Might have an army ready to march by now."

"But it's winter still," said Corleth, softly. Everyone turned to look at her, and she went a bit pink in the cheeks, but she kept talking. "Not so cold as it was, but there's snow thick on the roads towards Currahome. No way Calder comes till the weather warms. Should be time for men to make it to the West Valleys and back 'fore spring."

Shivers looked unhappy. Even more than usual. "It's a risk."

Rikke wished she had a chagga pellet to push around her mouth, but Isern wasn't there to roll 'em, so she was going without. "Have to take some risks if you're going to win. Hardbread? Gather every man we can spare."

He gave Shivers a worried glance. "All right."

Rikke drew him close, lowering her voice. "As we discussed, now, Hardbread. You remember what we discussed?"

"I do," he said. "You can rely on me."

Rikke frowned. "Don't like it when folk say they can be relied on. Implies a strong possibility they can't be. My father had three War Chiefs. Red Hat, Oxel and you. I remember 'em fondly. Well, apart from Oxel, he was a cunt. But you're the last of that whole crowd." She reached out and gently adjusted his mail coat. "Wouldn't want you to go the same way."

"They both got murdered in the Circle," said Hardbread.

Rikke gave him a significant look from under her brows. "I know. I'm the one made it happen."

There was a pause. Hardbread swallowed. "I remember what we discussed."

"Get to it, then, y'old bastard! I want to see the Nail strung up by his fucking fruits!"

"Won't they just...I don't know...tear off?"

"I didn't mean it literally." Rikke scratched her head. "But I guess if they did, that'd get the point across." Certainly no one would be complaining that she was too soft afterwards.

Hardbread gave a weary nod, and beckoned the warriors of Uffrith after him, and tramped towards the doors.

"The two o' you had a lot to talk about," muttered Corleth.

"You know how these bloody old men are." Rikke threw an arm around the girl's solid shoulders. "That was some wise counsel you gave."

"Just...what felt right."

"Don't be afraid to speak your mind. I need some good advice, with Isern gone. In fact, I could've used some while she was still here. Heart a stone and beloved o' the moon and blah, blah fucking blah. I want you to stay close to me."

Corleth blinked. "'Course, Chief."

"I know it's a weight, having responsibility dropped on you from a height, all unexpected, believe me I know, but you've got the shoulders for a burden, eh?" And Rikke hugged her tighter, walking her towards the doors. "It's a funny thing, isn't it, how chance throws the right people in your path? But I daresay you want to check in on your grandmother. Make sure her fire stays banked in this weather." Though it wasn't near as cold as it had been, thaw water dripping from the archway above.

"Aye," said Corleth. "Reckon I'll do that."

"Bring me back a bowl o' that soup, eh?" And Rikke watched her pick her way across the yard towards the gate. The snow was mostly gone now, melted down to slushy patches at the corners of the walls. "Best soup in Carleon, I swear!"

Rikke gave a cheery wave. Then as Corleth disappeared she let her hand drop, her smile fading, her shoulders slumping, the worry gnawing at her. "By the dead," she muttered. "It ain't easy, being chief."

Shivers stepped up beside her. "Might be why everyone told you it'd be hard," he said, in that breathy whisper of his.

"Aye, well, I've a habit of not listening to things I don't want to hear."

"You don't say."

"You've got to always look like you know the way." Rikke found she was fussing with her necklace yet again and had to pull her hand away. Bad habit, the fussing and fiddling, it made her look weak. "Like you're always sure, even if you're farting doubts with every step." She glanced about, making certain no one was watching, then looked up at him. "Am I doing the right thing, Shivers? Tell me I'm doing the right thing."

"Take a breath," he said, looking sideways at her. "It's just soup."

"Don't toy with me, you old fucker, you know what I mean. Am I doing the right thing with Isern, with the Nail, with Black bloody Calder." She waved a floppy hand at Skarling's Chair and took the cage with Stour Nightfall in, too. "With all of it."

"You're the one wi' the Long Eye," he said.

"More curse than blessing, that's the truth of it." She pressed her hand against the tattooed side of her face, cold and clammy now, and gave it an impatient rub. "I can pretend I know what's coming, but all it really gives you is more questions."

"Wish I had some answers. Truth is, though..." He leaned close to whisper in her ear. "I spent most o' my life stumbling from one fuck-up to another."

She glanced at his ruined face. "You'd never know to look at you." And she found she was fussing with her necklace and forced her hand away from it with a grunt of frustration. "Just sometimes...I wish I was still someone of no importance."

"You've always been of importance to me." She felt the weight of Shivers' hand on her shoulder and was grateful for it. "There's only one thing I can tell you for sure. Whatever comes, I'll be here."

She put her own hand on top of his, and took a deep breath, and puffed it out in a smoky sigh. They stood together in the entrance of Skarling's Hall, watching the meltwater drip, drip, drip from the archway.

# Thaw

D rip, drip, drip. Cold water, onto Clover's head, his shoulders, his back, working its way through every seam, trickling, tickling against his sore and clammy skin.

"Bloody dripping," he muttered, frowning up at the branches, but rain was just one more of life's buffets he was powerless to prevent.

"Guess we could move out from under the trees," muttered Flick.

"Aye, but then we'd have the mud to deal with." Clover shook his head and scraped a smear of dirt from his trousers with his thumbnail. Wasted effort, since they'd be spattered afresh before you knew it. "Bloody mud. Worst thing about war."

"Worse'n the death?" asked Sholla, who'd been busy for the past hour at least with her endless quest to cut the thinnest slice of cheese imaginable.

"Death is but an occasional hazard. Mud is a constant." And Clover rubbed that bit of dirt thoughtfully between thumb and forefinger. "Strange, isn't it? Soil and water are both good things. Things you can't live without. But mix the two and add an army, you've got a nightmare."

It'd been a cold winter, snow banked up man tall in the High Places. With the weather tilting warmer, seemed the world was melting. Water dripped from the trees. Dripped from the eaves of Currahome's sodden houses. Seeped through the boggy grass and gathered in the streams and swole 'em to dirty rivers. Downside came squelching over, knocking melting snow from the brambles.

"Where have you been?" asked Clover.

"There's two things I enjoy, fucking and killing. I can't do the one, so I've been at the other."

Sholla didn't look up from her cheese-cutting. "And did your hand enjoy it as much as you did?"

Clover chuckled. Flick chuckled. Downside frowned as he worked it through, then he worked it out, and frowned more. Didn't say anything, though. No doubt he could've twisted Sholla's head off in a wrestling match, but he knew that in a battle of wits she was much the better armed.

"By the dead, boy," grunted Clover as Flick nudged him in the ribs, "you've got the sharpest damn elbows in the North—" Then he saw the worry. Black Calder, stalking over with a grim crowd of Named Men, all striving to look mighty while they tiptoed through the winter muck.

"Chief!" Clover jumped up, slapping dirt from the seat of his trousers. He knew he was on thin ice with Calder, so he was being specially accommodating. "Good to see you!"

Calder frowned up from under wrinkled brows. "Don't spoon it on too thick. I've come to tell you we're moving out."

"Moving out where?"

"Carleon."

"High time," grunted Downside with an approving nod, and you know you've a reckless notion on your hands when you win Downside's approval.

"You're marching *now?*" Clover waved at the valleyful of filth, mostly black mud with some sad streaks o' white snow clinging to the hollows, sprinkled with rubbish and the wreckage of tents, crawling with unhappy men like a rotten log with woodlice, the keen wind snatching ash from dead fires and blowing it in folks' faces. "In this?"

"Better weather's on the way."

"Aye, but that'll make things even wetter. Every river'll be swollen, every ford neck high, every road a bloody mire. That's 'fore we even set foot on it. We'll be drowning in mud by the time we get to Carleon!"

Calder narrowed his eyes. "Might be we'll lose a couple of the weak ones, but I'll see the rest there. Aren't you always carping on how a man has to seize his moment? The moment's come, whatever the weather. Rikke's weak. The Nail's swinging his prick down south and she's had to send Hardbread to deal with him." He gave a snort. "When bloody Hardbread's your answer you know you're short on choices." And some of his Named Men dug out a chuckle. "She's hardly got enough warriors to hold on to Carleon, let alone to hold it against us. I mean to get there before she can find any more. And Stand-i'-the-Barrows is growing restless. If we don't find him some folk to kill, he'll find 'em here."

Clover frowned up towards the bone and hide standards planted on the high ground. "You can tell the best allies 'cause they're so fixed on taking men's bones they'll skin friends if they run out of enemies."

"Allies all have their shortcomings."

"Some more'n others."

"Like lazy fucks whose first preference is sitting under a tree and whose second is betraying you? Don't try my patience, Clover, I've none to spare these days. We march today."

Clover took a long breath, then forced the smile onto his face. "Whatever you say, Chief." He made sure he kept grinning as Calder and his men strode off towards the hall, spreading the bad news to each fire they passed.

Flick doused theirs with a hiss and Clover turned about to stare at him. "What are you doing?"

"Well...we're marching, ain't we? Don't want to leave it burning."

"What? You're afraid this fucking morass will catch fire? There's a whole valley to empty and only one road. We'll be lucky if we're off the spot by nightfall. Now we'll be cold into the bargain."

"Hold on," whispered Sholla. "Hold on." She was wincing with the effort as she teased at her knife, a shaving coming off the cheese so fine the light shone through it. "Nobody...*fucking*...move." Like a scrap of paper, it was, as she held up the blade, so pale and perfect, fluttering a little with the breeze. "I've done it."

And a great drip came from the tree above and spattered on the knife, breaking the shaving in bits and scattering 'em across the muddy ground.

"Fucking shit!" she barked, and Downside threw his head back and laughed.

"Just goes to show," said Clover, "how fate can smash all our plans in an instant."

"You've got plans?" asked Flick, looking genuinely surprised.

"I've got plans like I've got boots." Clover frowned down at his waterlogged footwear. "Honestly, I could always do with better ones."

Sholla had stood, cheese in one hand, knife in the other, watching the weary men stirring about their fires, striking their tents, gathering their gear, as Black Calder's orders spread. "What happens when we get to Carleon?"

"That is a question I'm still grappling with." Rikke would be wondering why he'd sent no word back about her offer to Calder and, with good reason, likely thought he'd betrayed her. Calder, meanwhile, knew Clover had betrayed him once already and handed his beloved son over for rough handling by his enemies. Putting it nicely. He might be telling the truth when he said he liked Clover. But Black Calder had killed men he liked more for lesser offences. And that was without considering the outcome if the Great Wolf ever *did* get his freedom.

Clover winced. Something he did whenever he considered the current situation. "Seems we might be trapped 'twixt the mountains and the sea, so to speak."

"You are," said Sholla. "Doubt anyone much cares about the rest of us."

"Oh, you'd be surprised how vengeance, falling from a great height, can spatter the most innocent o' bystanders. And you, my cheese-shaving beauty, by no means qualify."

"Hmmm." She glanced over at Trapper, who was happening past with the remnants of his dozen, and pushed her tangled hair off her dirty face so she could try out a smile. Perhaps unsurprisingly, it won nothing from him. "Running away might be an option," she murmured through her fixed grin.

"By all means take to your heels, but running's for the young. I need to sit down. Somewhere dry. And I reckon my best chance of that is to stay close to the action and try to nudge things my way." Clover scratched gently at his scar. "Close to the action, by the dead. You make every effort to steer clear o' something, and all you do is end up mired to your fucking neck in it."

"We'll all be mired soon enough." Flick stared at the bog in the valley bottom and gave a gloomy sniff.

Sholla leaned close. "D'you reckon there comes a time when you've betrayed folk so often that there's no one left to betray?"

Clover gave a weary sigh. "We may find out."

# Love, Hate, Fear

The palace wasn't at all how he remembered it from his last visit, but King Jezal had still been alive then, and Leo had been a loyal Lord Governor with all his limbs, and the Lords' Round had held a high-minded brotherhood of noblemen rather than a bloodthirsty rabble under the sway of an insane witch.

Times change, he supposed. The winners are those who change with them.

The gilded hallways echoed with strange sounds, something between a demented carnival and a riot. Jagged music came from somewhere. Or maybe someone was smashing a harp. There was an odd smell, like a cheap brothel. Slashed paintings of smug monarchs had been hung upside down. A neatly dressed, dark-skinned man sat in a chair, fussing nervously with his hat and jumping at every sound. Some ambassador, maybe. A pair of women in red dresses scarcely fastened stumbled giggling past, one holding a wine bottle, the other a pot of slopping paint, leaving a snaking trail of red footprints behind them.

"They used to say the heart of the state was rotten," muttered Glaward, with one glance back over his shoulder. "Now look at it."

"It's hell," whispered Jurand. "They've turned it into bloody *hell*."

Snow swirled in through a broken window, bang, bang, banging a shutter against the frame and leaving a chilly puddle in the hallway. Overstoked blazes in every fireplace made it greasy-hot even so, and if that wasn't enough to get the sweat springing from Leo's forehead there were armed Burners everywhere, armour dotted with red paint. Some of them even had their faces smeared with crimson lady's blusher, stuck somewhere between war-daubed savages from beyond the Crinna and murderous clowns.

"Please! He's innocent. I swear!"

A cultured voice, weeping and begging at once, coming from a door ajar, its lock hacked away with an axe.

"They're taking him to the tower today!"

"Maybe I could talk to Judge on your behalf, Lilott…" A man's voice. He sounded like he was enjoying himself.

"Just tell me what I can do!"

"Get your clothes off, for a start."

Glaward faltered, jaw clenched as the strip of light from that slightly open door fell across his face. "Should we do something?" he whispered.

Leo didn't even slow down. "Don't be fucking ridiculous."

Before the Great Change it would've been him asking whether they should do something. Bursting through that door in some self-indulgent, self-defeating puke of gallantry. But then he used to be a reckless, soft-hearted fool. He remembered giving out bread and blankets in the slums with Savine, a thousand years ago. He'd torn his hair at the state of those poor people. Wept that he couldn't do more.

Now he winced at the tiresome interruption of this woman's pain. It felt trivial, beside the pain in his stump. As his mother always used to say, he couldn't allow himself to be swept off by whatever emotion blew his way. He had the big picture to worry about.

"Well?" purred the man's voice. "You want him saved or not?"

"There's nothing we can do." Jurand caught Glaward's elbow and hurried him on, the woman's snivelling soon lost behind them. Leo clenched his jaw and upped the pace, his face twitching with each scrape of his metal foot.

He was finding a way to live with this shit, wasn't he? So could she.

Everywhere the walls were hacked and scored, carvings scarred where the sun of the monarchy had been torn down, chiselled out, scraped away. Slogans had been sloshed in their place in red paint. *Rise up. Equality. Midderland for its People.* And finally, across the tiled floor at the foot of a stairway crusted with gilded leaves, *Fuck yourselves.*

Jurand raised his brows. "I never yet saw the Burners' philosophy so succinctly expressed."

"That gets to the heart of it," muttered Leo as he struggled up the steps. Flat, he could almost manage now without a cane. Stairs were still an embarrassment. He had to take them one at a time, slightly sideways. Cane first, then the false leg, then the good one. There was always a moment, when the weight went through his stump, through the socket, through his iron foot, when he'd feel like he was about to fall. Always a moment when he gritted his teeth against the pain and simply refused to go down.

He realised Glaward was lurking at his elbow, as if to catch him. "Don't hover," he grunted.

"He'd rather you didn't brain yourself," said Jurand, trotting past.

Leo paused at the top of the steps to catch his breath, let the pain in his throbbing stump subside, mop away sweat with the back of his good sleeve, wedge the other more firmly into his jacket. He became aware of a regular creaking of furniture through the closed door beside him. A noisy grunting, groaning, moaning. At least four different voices. One might've been crying.

"They're either fucking or killing each other," muttered Jurand.

"Or both," said Leo, setting himself as proudly as he could for the last few steps to Judge's door.

Her office was a huge domed chamber choked with rubbish. Empty bottles. Full bottles. Bent cutlery. Axes and flatbows. Stained and ripped-up bundles of documents. A half-picked chicken carcass. Antique vases used as ashtrays. An ornate bed the size of a small warship had half its silk curtains hanging in tatters, one of its pillows split and spilling feathers across the floor, dancing in a draft. Jurand was staring at something with a vaguely horrified expression. Leo followed his gaze. He hoped he was mistaken. He very much hoped. But it looked as though someone had done a shit on the floor.

Through an open door, Leo glimpsed limp, bare limbs. Burners sleeping off their revels, maybe, but he wouldn't have been at all surprised to find they were corpses. A woman bound up in bandoliers of little knives squatted against the wall, rolling dice. A pair of scarred men watched the snow fall outside one of the narrow windows. An ill-favoured bastard with a badly broken face sneered at them, arms folded.

Gunnar Broad stood in towering silence, sipping from a bottle as he watched Leo limp in. He'd changed as much as the palace, and in much the same direction. No trace of the careful guardian who'd watched over Leo and Savine that day in the slums. His eyes, tiny behind those thick lenses, had an awful blankness Leo didn't want to meet. As if the only reason he hadn't exploded into violence was that he couldn't decide whose head to crush first.

Judge sprawled beside him on a monstrous couch in front of a monstrous fire. She wore a tattered robe of bright Suljuk silk that showed a slice of pale, knobbly breastbone and an angry dotting of rash all the way up her neck. Her hair hung in a tangled orange curtain over one eye, the other narrowed, red-rimmed, fixed on Leo.

"If it ain't Citizen Brock himself." That black eye darted to Jurand and Glaward. "And the survivors o' the Young Lion's Angland boys' club. Welcome to my parlour."

An ancient mural covered the walls, or its battered remains, at least. Above Judge's head, an old man lay bleeding in a forest, five figures walking away from him on one side, six on the other. Leo hadn't taken much notice of his tutors, so he'd only the vaguest idea what it represented. The death of Juvens, bleeding his last while his apprentices, the magi, marched off to avenge him. He supposed the balding one at the front was Bayaz, but someone had scraped his face off and daubed a red cock in its place.

Probably it had been quite the masterpiece a few months ago, but the Burners had set to work on it like everything else, hacked and hammered at it, daubed bold slogans and crabby treatises and crude horns and tails and childish obscenities over it, adding to Juvens' wounds until he was bleeding a great dripping flood around the fireplace.

Judge grinned. "Fire, death and vengeance. And my favourite wizard." She waved at the wall behind Leo and he twisted to frown over his shoulder. Looming above the door he'd come in by, grim, forbidding and untouched by red paint, was Juvens' brother, and his murderer, the Master Maker Kanedias, spreading his arms wide with a sea of flames behind him. "Now *there's* a bastard who knew how to *set fires.*"

Leo forced a smile over his disgust and limped into the room, feeling like a cockerel strutting into a fox's den. "Citizeness Judge! I believe you sent for me."

"You believe correctly. Why don't you all sit down?" Judge waved to battered chairs. "Just shove that shit on the floor."

"I'd rather stand."

She looked down at his leg and wrinkled her nose in a disbelieving little grin. "That's a funny thing for a one-legged man to rather do. Come on. Take the weight off your foot. Have some fucking tea." She nudged a teapot across the table through a rattling mass of junk, knocking a stack of books flapping to the floor. "Not a fan of Southern habits myself but a little tea can poke the right hole."

Glaward righted a toppled nursing chair and perched nervously on its edge. One of the men at the window bared his teeth and gave a strange hiss. Leo winced as he tried to sit with a measure of dignity. Judge had fished a husk-pipe from the rubbish, was sucking on it hard enough to make her cheeks go hollow.

"You all reckon I'm mad, don't you?" she said, letting smoke spill from her nose in brown plumes like a dragon.

There was a nervous silence. Jurand cleared his throat. "I wouldn't say—"

"Being mad has its uses. Or having people *think* you're mad does. They don't see you coming. King Orso saw you coming at Stoffenbeck, didn't he, Young Lion?"

"He did," said Leo. "From a thousand miles away. A painful lesson. One I'll never need to learn again."

"They're the best kind. Risinau thought I was mad. Still a few bits of him spattered about the moat, I expect. So much for madness. So much for sanity." She offered out the pipe. "Smoke?"

"I should keep a clear head."

"Good idea." She spun the pipe across the floor, leaving a trail of smoking ash. "Very...*sane*."

The dead help him, Leo thought he could still hear those people fucking. Or killing each other. Maybe it was a different set.

Jurand cleared his throat again. "I understand...there has been another defeat. In the east."

"Mmm," grunted Judge. "Forest got the better of the People's Army yet again. General Cutler and a few of his losing officers are being dragged back to Adua to be tried for treason. Seems giving little men big men's shoes doesn't make 'em big. Just makes 'em trip over." She let her head drop to one side. "Now Forest and his traitors are marching for Adua to put our dunce of a king back on the throne, would you believe. *Quite* the military muddle. Seems the Great Change is in need of a hero to save it." Her brows went up as though the idea had only now occurred. "How're you fixed, Young Lion? Keen to get back in the saddle?"

For some months now, in fact, and especially since Vick dan Teufel's recent visit, but Leo tried not to let his desires lead him about by the nose any more. "If I'm called on to defend the Great Change," he said calmly, "I'll do my duty."

"Huh." The corner of Judge's mouth curled up. "D'you know why they call me Judge? It's quite the story. Have some fucking tea, really." And she settled back into her cushions and propped one bare foot up onto the table, staring thoughtfully up at the Master Maker.

And Leo realised with a cold start that her gown had fallen open and given half the room a full view of her ginger quim. He couldn't tell if she'd done it on purpose, but something about the way she stuck it so carelessly in his face faintly terrified him. There was nothing he wanted to see less, but somehow he had to keep steering his eyes away.

"I don't know who my parents were," she mused, wriggling her toes. "Settlers in the Far Country, maybe. But they were killed when I was a child, and I was stolen by the Ghosts. Raised by the Ghosts. In the clan of Great Sangeed, the Emperor of the Plains."

The woman with the knives looked up from her dice and chuckled. Judge frowned over at her. "Do I fucking amuse you?"

She shook her head and went back to her dice.

"They treated me lower'n dirt, the Ghosts. Lower'n a slave. But on account of my being an outsider, they made me judge o' the disputes between their clans. Wasn't about justice, or innocence, or guilt. It was about what had to be done. Keeping the balance between the groups on the plain, so no one got too much power over the others." She rubbed at the patchy stubble on the side of her head. "'Course, the settlers came more and more, in their fellowships, and they picked the Ghosts off one by one, and drove away the hunting and poisoned the water. One day they came to the village and killed everyone I knew and told me I was rescued. And they asked me what my name was, and do you know what I said?"

"Judge."

She snapped her fingers. "You're no fool. Maybe that's why I play judge now. They gave me a passion for keeping the balance."

"That sounds more like an excuse than a reason," murmured Jurand.

Leo frowned sideways at him. "They're the same thing seen from different sides."

"Ha!" Judge jabbed at Leo with a finger. "I was going to say the very same thing! He's not just a pretty face, eh, Broad?"

Broad stared at Leo, jaw muscles squirming, and took a sip from his bottle. Leo wondered whether he was so angry he couldn't speak, or so drunk he'd forgotten how. Maybe both.

"You know the trouble with a pretty face?" Judge was saying. "People get used to its advantages, and when it's took away, they lack the wherewithal to make a success of themselves. Nothing sadder'n a person who used to be beautiful. They have this desperate smile. *Like me*, it says. *Like me*, even though there's nothing left to like."

She sat forwards—putting her groin back in shadow, thank the dead—and slid a hatchet from the table. Glaward stirred nervously as she lifted it, but all she did was hack a leg from the chicken carcass with a couple of echoing bangs that caused a sleepy mew of upset from the room next door. She tossed the axe down, started gnawing hungrily at the bone then paused. "What were we talking about?"

"The leadership of the People's Army," said Leo, as though it was a

242

matter of total indifference. He'd hardly spoken, but he felt as if her eyes were sizing him up and slitting him open and probing at his guts like a physician at a cadaver even so.

"Right!" She stabbed at him with the chicken bone and a piece of meat flew off and stuck to the floor behind him. "A lot's changed this past year or two, but you're still popular. That military business is in your bones and fighting men respect you. Beat Stour Nightfall in a circle of blood and all. I hear you used to be reckless, but I reckon you've been cured o' that. Can't say I trust you, but then I never trust anyone I trust, if you see what I mean? You're a risk, but nothing's safe these days, and nothing safe's worthwhile anyway."

"So..."

"So you're the perfect choice." And she sat and gnawed away at that bone.

"But...?"

"But you're not the only one who wants something." Judge tossed the stripped bone down, licked her fingers, then dried them off by dragging her hair out of her face. "Do you know the person I'd most like to put on trial?"

Leo didn't want to draw this out. A conversation with Judge was a game that could turn fatal at any moment. He wondered who he'd most like to see on trial. "King Orso?"

She wrinkled her nose. "That walking cock? No. Have you ever read one o' Sworbreck's books?"

Leo would rather have drunk Sworbreck's piss. "I'm...not much of a reader."

"You should. They got me through some hard times. The last chapter is the sentimental fairwell. But the climax of the story is a little bit before. The danger. The excitement. The triumph. You see? Putting King Orso on trial," she shrugged her bony shoulders high. "That's the last chapter. It has to be done, but it'll get no one's juices flowing, eh, Broad?"

Broad stayed silent.

"No, the person I'd *most* like to put on trial is Old Sticks himself. Sand dan fucking Glokta. He was the one who set the policies. The one who did the torturing and raised the gibbets and made all the examples. The one who racked up most o' the names we've carved into the Square of Martyrs." Judge curled back her lips in disgust. "But like the cunning old louse he is, he's wriggled away into the woodwork. I need someone in the dock who can help me winkle out the cripple." She raised her red brows expectantly.

"Well, we never wasted much warmth on each other, I promise you. I've no idea where—"

"I want to put your wife on trial."

Judge was smiling, so Leo took it for a joke, and managed a sour grin himself. "You're joking."

"I'm *fucking* not," she hissed, showing her teeth. "I want your word—if I put your wife on trial, you'll do nothing to stop me. She denounces her father, tells us where he can be found, I daresay the court could find its way to clemency. Eh? Eh? *Eh?*"

Leo swallowed. His heart was beating very loud. He glanced up at Broad, but the man's eye-lenses had caught the light from a window and were bright white, so Leo couldn't see his eyes. There was something dead about his thickly stubbled face. Scabs on his tattooed knuckles. A welt of bruises on one side of his neck. He lifted his bottle, and took a sip.

"Leo…" he heard Glaward whisper, and Leo held up a hand to silence him.

It was less than a year ago, if you could believe it, that he had introduced Savine to the people of Angland, cheering on the dockside, full of pride and admiration. He remembered using the word love, even though he wasn't sure now what he'd meant by it. If someone had threatened a hair on his wife's head then, they would've faced his rash and righteous fury. But there had been a Great Change since. A change in so many things. He couldn't afford rashness or righteousness, and fury even less.

"If there is evidence against my wife…" Leo spoke the words slowly and precisely. "The nation must judge her. I agree to your terms."

There was a long, nervous silence. Then Judge started to laugh. "Oh, Young Lion, that's *beautiful.*" She slapped her tattooed thigh. "Love can bring folk together in fair weather, but it won't bind 'em when the chill sets in. Hate's better, in my experience. A common enemy gets folk moving together. But enemies get beaten, and put behind you, like the Breakers beat the king, like the magi beat Kanedias, and then what happens? Folk get used to enemies. They always need more. They turn on each other."

Someone had wandered in from the room next door. A short, heavyset man wearing a vest and nothing else. "Wha' fuck?" he muttered, squinting into the daylight.

"Put some bloody clothes on, you animal." Judge's eyes flickered back to Leo. "Love and hate, they're luxuries. Poets might say they're from the heart, but I say no. They're lies we tell ourselves. They're choices made. But *fear,*" and she lifted her trembling fist, "that's an instinct. Fear and lust and hunger, they're universal. The lowest insects have 'em. Fear is in the gut. It's in the bones. It's in the balls and the arse and the cunt. Fear and lust and hunger are what'll bind us together and keep us on the right path. The people don't need love or hate, Young Lion, but they *always* have to *fear*. Bear that in mind."

Leo thought it over, and nodded. "Sage advice," he said, and he didn't even have to lie. "So..." With an effort he lifted his good foot, used the heel to slide some rubbish out of the way and propped it on the stained table beside Judge's. "Shall I put my riding boot on?"

"At once if not sooner, General Brock! The Young Lion, back in the saddle!" And she threw her arms up, and one of the two men at the window gave a brief round of applause. "Here's the irony! On behalf of the king we've got a commoner who was made a lord marshal, and on behalf of the people we've got a lord governor who made himself a commoner. Life can be horrible," she said, jabbing her thumb at dead Juvens. "But life can be delightful, too," pointing up at Kanedias and his sea of fire. "There's its real beauty, eh? In its *range*. Daresay you've an old uniform lying about somewhere. Might need to take it in around the knee, I suppose."

"The Representatives will agree to it?"

"Well, I haven't noticed anyone disagreeing with me lately. Have you?" Judge jerked her head towards the man with the broken nose. "Sparks? You'll be going along."

He looked as unhappy about it as Leo felt, but he hid it a lot less well. "Me?"

"Are *you* fucking disagreeing?"

Broad shifted, his free fist clenching, and Sparks took a cautious step back. "'Course not, Judge. 'Course not."

"He'll be, what d'you call it? A *conduit*, between you and the Purity Officers. Keep everyone nice and loyal and pointed the same way."

"No doubt he'll be a huge help." Leo gritted his teeth as he rocked his weight back, then shoved himself to his feet, the ache in his stump turning sharp again.

"I'll send him along after. Once we've had a little word. Burners' business, you know."

"I'm sure he can catch me up." Leo tapped his false leg with his cane. "I don't walk too quickly these days."

"I wouldn't want to intrude into the manly business o' war, but one word of advice, General, before you ride to glory." Judge let her head drop back, looking at him down her nose. "Don't lose. Now someone rub my fucking feet! Or start there, at any rate, and work upwards!"

245

The horrible voices seemed to have stopped, at least, as Leo limped back towards the steps. Except for the crying one. That softly went on.

Glaward hurried up beside him, hissing, "She wants to put Savine on trial—"

Leo tossed down his cane and caught the big man by the jacket, lurching into him and pinning him against the wall. "Do you think I fucking *missed that?*"

"I can warn her—"

"You will *not*. You'll gather every man we can rely on and head out with me to join the People's Army at once."

Glaward stared at him. Shocked. As though he'd never quite seen Leo until that moment and didn't like the look of him now he did. "But... your *children*—"

Leo shoved him back again, hissing through gritted teeth. "If Savine runs, Judge will know we broke the deal and it will all be *over*. She has to *trust* me. Trust me enough, anyway. That's the only way this has a chance of working."

"He's right," said Jurand, softly, pushing Leo's cane against his chest and using it to lever him away from Glaward. "There's no choice." He saw it right off, of course. He'd never been sentimental.

"Savine wanted this," snapped Leo. "She should've known where it might lead." He snatched his cane from Jurand's hand and lurched off down the stairway again, the scraping of his iron foot on the marble echoing from the gilded ceiling. "Should I have said no?" He jerked his chin towards the slogan at the bottom of the steps. "Should I have told Judge *fuck yourself*? We'd all have been in the dock together before sundown."

Behind him, Jurand took a long breath. "We all might end up there yet."

# This Half-Arsed Conspiracy

Vick picked her way down the street, a mass of slushy footprints, black-stained snow gathered in the gutters and against the doorsteps. She went against the crowd, as always, and thought about everything that could go wrong.

She'd flung a wide net when she scraped this half-arsed conspiracy together. She'd had to, to give it any chance of working. It had closed around some of the last people she'd have trusted. Savine Brock—as ruthless a schemer as you could hope never to be in business with. Her husband Leo—whose recklessness had already wrecked one attempt at treachery. Corporal Tunny—a legend in the husk-dens and gambling houses for his big mouth and small courage. His sidekick Yolk—who from her brief acquaintance appeared to be one of the stupidest men in creation. Then there was the lynchpin of the whole business, King Orso— born with a silver spoon so far up his arse you could see the end when he yawned. Vick's best hope was that his valet could stop him making a fatal blunder—a fourteen-year-old he'd hired while she was working as a laundry girl in a brothel.

The one person she actually trusted was Tallow, and he was the one person she'd made sure to keep entirely out of it.

All those hard-learned lessons from the camps. All the painstaking risks and calculations. All the lies she'd told to make sure she stayed on the winning side. All pissed away in one moment of folly.

She paused at a corner to tap the dirty snow from her boots, and to take another careful glance back while she was doing it.

That big bastard in the hood was still on the other side of the street, face hidden except for a scraggy grey beard on a heavy jaw. She'd been worried he was following. Now she was sure. There was something in the way he stood that she didn't like at all. Slightly hunched around his left side. As if he was trying to hide a weapon that was too big to conceal.

Tempers were short in the market. Stocks were low and dwindling, prices high and climbing. A beefy labourer was arguing with the fishmonger, feet planted wide and finger stabbing. Vick slipped up through the crowd and, in passing, slid her hand between the labourer's legs from behind and gently cupped his balls. He spun around, but by then she was considering the second-hand cutlery on the next stall.

"What the—"

The labourer grabbed the nearest man, started snarling in his face. Vick dropped and slithered under a wagon, darting through the press bent double, gripping her bad hip tight to stop it aching, folk all straining up on tiptoe to see the blazing row behind. She slipped through the doorway of a pawnshop she knew, which had another door at the far side onto the Middleway. She nodded to the clerk as he frowned at her over his cracked eye-lenses, pulled her collar up against the cold and joined the hunched crowds shuffling south.

It was busy in the tavern. Noisy with idle chatter and hot with wasted breath, the windows misted so the street outside became a sparkling blur. One of those places where rich young men gather to pretend to be poor young men, and vomit up whatever point of view they last heard. One of those places where rich young men once brayed for a Great Change, and now drank hard and hoped desperately it would go away again.

She'd made sure she was early but her contact was there ahead of her. A nondescript fellow with a sprig of holly on his lapel, an empty glass and a plate of unappetising sausages in front of him.

"Inspector Teufel."

"And you are?"

"An employee of Chancellor Sotorius of Sipani." Though he spoke with no accent at all.

She slid into the chair opposite. "Were you followed?"

"No. Were you?"

She glanced about the room without seeming to, but there was no sign of the big man who'd been following her. Just a plump woman in an expensive hat splashed red, reading a poem about the horrors of watching one's children starve. "No."

"Good. You should try these." And he slid his plate across towards her, breathing the words. "A gift from Princess Carlot."

"Looks good," she lied, and drew the plate close so the packet underneath it dropped into her lap. She took a bite from one of the sausages. "And it tastes as good as it looks." That, at least, was no lie. But those eating were the lucky ones. Food that tasted good was a true extravagance these days.

"That concludes our business," said Chancellor Sotorius's nondescript man. "Good luck with your endeavours."

Vick caught his wrist as he got up to leave. "She realises I can't make any promises."

"If there is a chance it will help her brother, she is content." And he nodded briefly, and disappeared into the crowd.

Behind him, a set of young men clashed their tankards together, sent up a spray of froth and dissolved into raucous laughter.

Oh, to be a careless young idiot.

She stopped beside a boy selling matches, so swaddled by his scarf he could barely see.

"First give me some matches," she said, holding out a silver mark so his eyes lit up.

"Then?"

Vick made sure not to turn. "Do you see a big man watching me? With a hood and a grey beard?"

The boy glanced past her. "He's stopped maybe twenty strides back."

She bared her teeth. Bastard had picked up her trail again somehow. "I'm going to take a left here. You hold him up as long as you can."

"For another mark I'll fight him."

"Good lad." She pushed another coin into his hand. "But you can leave that to me."

She ducked past him, darted in front of a skeletal horse dragging a near-empty cart and slipped around the corner, down an alley into one of those blackened scars in the city. Someone had set a fire, burned one of the Southerner's temples down, taken a few streets with it. Now the houses yawned empty—blackened rafters, scorched windows, glimpses of charred wreckage through the broken doorways.

Quiet here. That soft, muffled silence that comes with snow. A few sets of tracks, from people taking refuge in the ruins, or doing dark business of one kind or another, but they'd partly filled up with the most recent fall. She stomped a dozen clear bootprints into the white then backed up quick, planting her feet in the tracks so she made no more. She gathered herself, then sprang sideways into a dripping doorway, pressing her back against the scorched plaster. She made herself silent, made herself small, and waited.

She could've slipped away. But if this bastard had found her twice, he'd find her again, and when he did, it might be him who got the jump on her. She had to know who he was, who'd sent him, in which of the thousand possible ways her rickety plan had shaken apart. There could be a dozen Burners waiting right now at her apartment with a fistful of letters from the king and her name all over them. She had to know.

She slid out her stick, heavy, hard and black. One thing that hadn't changed when the Inquisition became the Inspectorate. A blunt tool for digging out answers, but a shockingly effective one, used the right way. Amazing, the problems you can solve with a piece of wood.

It all reminded her of the camps. The snow, the cold, the dark. The waiting for a man in the shadows with a stick and a clenched jaw. She heard him coming. Heavy footsteps, crunching in the snow. He saw the prints. A muttered curse. Then he strode past the doorway, head down, following the trail. His hand was in his coat, she thought. On the hilt of a weapon, maybe, and she gripped her stick tighter, and slipped from the doorway.

His back was still to her, but he was even bigger than she'd thought. A terribly sturdy look to his shoulders. No way she could risk giving him any chances. Hit first, hard as you can. Chances after.

Her heart was thudding in her ears as she crept up behind him. He'd reached the end of the trail, was casting about, trying to work out what had happened. She took one more careful step towards him, then winced at a twinge in that bloody hip of hers. Snow crunched faintly under her boot as she raised the stick.

His head whipped around, a glimpse of his grey-bearded face, the corner of an eye.

She bared her teeth as she swung for the side of his knee, but at the last moment he lifted his leg and it caught the meat of his calf with a dull smack. He didn't go down. He didn't even cry out. A little grunt, maybe, and a stumble sideways. As he turned, she'd set herself and was already bringing the stick down, overhand, with all the strength she had.

He jerked his head to the side and the stick thudded into his shoulder. He didn't even grunt this time. Just took a half-step back. She swung again but he caught it on one forearm, brushed it off and came at her so fast she barely even saw it, let alone got out of the way.

Vick had been hit plenty. But she'd never been hit so hard.

She folded up like a paper bag, stick tumbling from her numb fingers, and she was on her knees in the snow with her jaw hanging open and a string of spit dangling from her lip, making a kind of helpless wheeze with her arms clutched around her and great jolting waves of pain throbbing from the side of her stomach.

She'd a knife in her boot. But she couldn't move. She couldn't even breathe.

He squatted down in front of her, but she couldn't see anything higher than his knees.

"Inspector Teufel? The king's servant told me to find you."

There was no mistaking that high little voice. It was Bremer dan Gorst.

"There's no one else here?" he asked as she shouldered the door open.

She almost laughed, but even that sent a flash of pain through her side. "No. There's no one else here." Her last guest had been Tallow. When she paid him for betraying his friends. She glanced at Gorst. "Ever feel like you made some bad choices?"

He didn't answer. Somehow, she took that for a yes. She limped down the hall, so narrow he had to turn his great shoulders slightly sideways to fit. Damn, the place was cold. Felt colder inside than out. She eased herself down beside the little table in the little dining room, fumbled out those matches she'd bought and lit the stub of candle. She sat back gripping her side.

Gorst stood in the doorway, faint light chiselling shadows into his slab of a face. "Does it hurt?"

"Only when I breathe." She'd a suspicion he'd cracked a rib or two. "Didn't hurt you, did I?"

He put her stick down carefully on the table and shook his head.

"You could pretend, couldn't you, for the sake of my pride?"

"You're joking?" He said it as an honest question. As if he couldn't really have told the difference.

"I'm trying. Guess we all like to think we're tougher than we are. Having the illusion shattered is never pleasant." She waved a hand towards the empty cupboards, a couple of the doors still broken from when the Breakers first stormed the Agriont. "I'd offer you something, but...I don't have anything."

She looked around the room as if seeing it through new eyes. If the place where you lived was a glimpse into your life, then hers could hardly have been emptier. The dusty squares board that was never played with. The dusty books that were never read. Apart from Sibalt's well-thumbed copy of *The Life of Dab Sweet*, maybe. But looking at one picture over and over while you think about everything you've thrown away hardly counts.

"Not really used to having guests," she muttered.

"Nor I to being one." Gorst pushed back his hood. Vick remembered him with his whole head rigorously shaved. Now he had grey thatch around the sides and a wispy tuft on top. He looked more like an over-sized lawyer than a swordsman. "Corporal Tunny was hiding me in his..."

"Knocking shop?"

"The Burners visited. I was obliged to climb out of the window."

"Must have bigger windows than I'd have expected."

"It was a squeeze." Gorst gave a puzzled frown. "I stand accused of being a royalist."

"Well, you did lead the Knights of the Body for two kings. Don't get much more royalist than that."

"And you?"

"I did dirty work for two Arch Lectors, I suppose. I grew up in the camps..." She sat with her mouth open a moment, wondering where to go with that. "You learn to stand with the winners."

"Then what brings you to the losing side?"

It was a good question. A woman who'd suffered more than most under the old regime. Who'd had her childhood and her youth and her family stolen by it. No one should've rejoiced in its fall more than her. But here she was, risking her life to restore it.

"I've seen enough folk thrown off the Tower of Chains. And I quite like King Orso." A strange thing for her to say. She hardly even knew the man. Just that little bit of appreciation he'd given her, when she came back from Westport. And his hand on hers, in a room under the House of Questions. Was that all it took, to win her devotion? Maybe Glokta had been right. She really was desperate for something to be loyal to. "You can stay here for now. Doubt they'll be looking for you a few hundred strides from the Court of the People. And they've plenty of others to chase. Seems to me they don't care much who they execute as long as there's a queue."

"What were you doing," he asked, "in that tavern?"

"Don't trust me?"

He said nothing. She supposed where the king's safety was concerned, a First Guard trusts no one.

"I was getting these." She winced as she pulled the packet out from behind her belt and slipped it onto the table. "Jewels. From the king's sister, in Sipani. We're going to use them to buy the city gates."

"Greed still works?"

She snorted. "People are still people—"

There was a heavy knock at the door.

Vick met Gorst's eye and put a finger to her lips. A pointless gesture, since he barely spoke anyway. He pressed himself to the wall and silently slid out his short steel, a forearm's length of immaculately polished metal catching the candlelight.

So those dozen Burners she'd been expecting had done the clever thing and waited for her to get home before paying a visit. She grimaced as she bent down and slid the knife from her boot, holding it out of sight behind her arm.

"Coming!" she called breezily as she strolled down the hall, while her heart thudded in her ears. She tried to pull the door open as if she was guilty of nothing and had no broken ribs, then felt a giddy rush of relief, then a giddy rush of pain as she breathed in too hard. "What is it, Tallow? I've got company."

He stood there in the chilly dusk, staring up at her. "Hadn't heard from you in a day or two. I was worried. Then, you know, I heard voices—"

"And the only reason a man would darken my door is to kill me, is it?" She shifted to block the doorway. Not hard to do. It wasn't a big doorway. "We've all got needs, Tallow."

He looked first surprised, then slightly disturbed, by the idea that she might have needs. "Oh. Right."

"I appreciate your concern."

He stood staring at her.

She wafted her fingers off into the night. "You can go." And she shouldered the door shut.

She leaned against the wall for a moment, holding her side and breathing carefully, not too shallow, not too deep. Then she walked back down the hall, slipped around Gorst and over to the window, twitched the shutter back a chink to make sure Tallow was on his way.

"You don't trust him?" muttered Gorst.

"I don't trust anyone."

It was easier to tell herself that, somehow, than to admit she didn't want to put him in danger. She watched him trudge off hunched through the snow, until he was lost around the corner. Damn, he was like her brother.

She glanced at Gorst, a slit of faint light down his lined face, a slice of scraggy beard and a wisp of greasy hair over his forehead.

"So the two of us are the great hope?" She held her side as she lowered herself gingerly back into her chair. "Fates help the Union."

# A Spicy Denunciation

"The state of these," murmured Orso as he was herded past the new statues on what used to be the Kingsway. The freezing weather, and now the soggy thaw, had not been kind to them. The nose of one of the giant nursing mothers had already dropped off, broken lumps of it scattered about her pedestal. There were some troubling cracks in her bust besides. Probably that would drop off next, braining some unfortunate passer-by. Crushed by giant tits. It was the way Tunny had always wanted to go.

"Risinau brought some sculptor over from Styria to remake them," said Hildi, frowning up, "but she was tossed off the Tower of Chains along with him. So they got some masons to do it."

"Oh. Yes." He vaguely remembered that being discussed by the Representatives before court one day. Some young firebrand from the provinces frothing up a fury. "An actual sculptor would have been an aristocratic indulgence. There is no task beyond the skill of a proud working man of the Union!" He puffed out his cheeks. "By the Fates, they can't even destroy things well."

"You're saying you miss the old ones?" asked Hildi.

Orso opened his mouth to answer, then paused. As with so many things these days, he had hopelessly mixed feelings. Lord Hoff had once referred to the statues on the Kingsway as the Union's greatest treasure. A celebration of all that was most noble. A true wonder of the world, if patriotic swagger was your fetish.

Except they had also, of course, been a total pack of lies. A parade of self-serving arrogance in which Orso would one day have taken his place, where rapacious torturers were celebrated for their compassion, vengeful warmongers praised for their forbearance, heedless do-nothings eulogised for their painstaking care. As if to set the tone for this shameless distortion of history, Bayaz, the world's most shameless thief, had been literally raised up on a pedestal at both ends for all that he had given the Union.

"Which do you prefer?" asked Orso, with a shrug. "Grand lies or ugly truths?"

"Reckon we might be better off with neither," muttered Hildi.

Orso had even more mixed feelings about the changes to the Square of Marshals. He tried to keep his chin up and walk with that careless swagger that so annoyed his many guards, but could not seem to prevent his eyes from drifting down. Could not help reading the names carved into the flagstones where a parade in his honour once ended. Here and there, melted mounds of candle stubs, and decaying wreaths, and sodden letters of gratitude had built up, impromptu shrines around the names of the most admired martyrs. So many names. Thousands upon thousands, and each one a person dead so that he could sit on a golden chair and seem to be in power.

Perhaps fortunately, perhaps not, his attention was soon claimed by the jeering. Winter had drastically reduced the size of the crowds before the Court of the People, but the fanatics that remained made up for it by sheer weight of anger, pressing in around the guards, shaking pamphlets and yelling insults.

Orso smiled, waved, blew kisses, as he always did. "Too kind, my subjects! To turn out in the cold, for me? Too kind!" A sneering woman spat on him, and he clutched it to his stained jacket like a bouquet. "I shall treasure it!"

"Long live the king!" came a scream.

"Oh no," said Hildi.

Someone had clambered up on one of the broken pedestals near the steps of the court. A flash of the golden sun of the Union on a piece of cloth, frantically waved. Rage flashed through the mob. "Long live the—" Cut off in a squawk as he was dragged down. A surge as people struggled to get close enough to participate in the beating.

This kind of thing was becoming more and more common. Were these spur-of-the-moment royalists lunatics? Simpletons? Suicidal? Or had the disappointments of the Great Change simply piled on them so heavily it induced a kind of mania? Orso was grateful for any support, but could they not support him silently? Open demonstrations of monarchism did no one any good. Least of all the monarch himself.

In her last message, Teufel had told him that plans were in place. That he should be ready. That it might be a matter of days. He had to smother a surge of nerves at the thought. He leaned close to Hildi to whisper, "I think Judge is going to put me on trial soon."

"You've been saying that for weeks."

"It's getting dangerous."

"You've been saying *that* for weeks."

"And I've been right. Hildi, I mean it, this would be an excellent moment for you to abandon me."

She dropped her voice even further, murmuring through tight lips. "Your friends will come through."

Orso caught a glimpse of his latest supporter dragged past insensible, blood in his hair. One of the guards aimed a lazy kick at him. The crowd had fallen on the old flag like wolves on a carcass and were trampling each other in their eagerness to trample it. Corporal Halder surveyed the scene with an air of bored detachment, hands on hips.

"I still hope they will," muttered Orso, "but, being realistic—"

"When have you ever done that?"

"—the chances of failure are very high." The closer the day came, indeed, the higher the chances of failure seemed. "The *consequences* of failure…" It was hardly worth spelling them out. He spent every waking moment powerlessly turning them over, after all, and every sleeping moment dreaming about them. "If they *don't* come through—"

"You'll know about it when you hear me denouncing you to the Court of the People."

Orso smiled. "That's my girl. Make it a spicy denunciation, though, won't you? None of these droning lists of names we get these days. I want it overflowing with scandal, shocks and low moral character."

"Oh, it'll be a real firecracker," said Hildi. "I'll make 'em shit in the galleries."

"Maybe stop short of that. The place smells bad enough as it is."

"Let's go," grunted Halder, nudging Orso up the steps to the Court of the People. There had been a time when access to the royal person was governed by a book of rules four fingers thick. Now any fool could poke him with impunity.

Judge was getting comfortable in the high chair as Orso was man-handled into the sovereign's cage, but there was a gap on the front benches where Citizen Brock and his Anglanders would usually have been preening themselves. Orso rather hoped they might have been spicily denounced and dragged off to the House of Purity themselves, but that was probably too much luck to hope for. Luck had really not been falling his way the past couple of decades.

"Silence in the court!" And the murmur of voices dropped away as Sworbreck strode forwards. He had acquired a blood-red suit of clothes now, having been appointed Chief Prosecutor for the Great Change. Since the proceedings were less about law than consolatory fantasy and cheap melodrama, no doubt the writer was uniquely qualified.

"After weeks of painstaking investigation," he shrieked, meaning a night spent hauling the latest crop of unfortunates from their beds at random, "the loyal servants of the Great Change," meaning the drunken, drugged and murder-addicted Burners, "have ripped a most sinister conspiracy up by the roots and into the light of justice!"

Always new conspiracies. Always the most sinister. Ever more elaborate, fiendish, impossible to disprove. Intrigues that somehow involved Styrians, Gurkish and Northmen all at once. Schemes that required the enemies of the Great Change to be inscrutable puppet masters and utter idiots simultaneously. Orso wondered what would happen when they had killed everyone. Would Judge try herself last of all in the empty Court of the People, sentence herself to death and fling herself from the Tower of Chains? He gave an entirely inappropriate splutter of laughter at the thought. The shame was he would not live to see it, having been pulped in the dry moat years before. Unless his friend at the House of Purity came through sooner rather than later...

His eyes flickered to the latest wretched group being herded to the dock by Captain Broad, and he sat bolt upright.

Most prisoners strove to appear humble. It was hard not to after a few days with meagre food and no bath, in some chilly corner of the Agriont hastily converted into cells. But the woman at the back of this trio had done the exact opposite, costumed as if for the Summer Contest at the height of the old regime, all piled red wig, dramatic black silk and bosomy flounce.

"Selest dan Heugen," murmured Orso. He knew the woman was nobody's fool. So why had she dressed as the villain of this particular pantomime? She stood proudly in the dock, in defiance of the boos, catcalls and obscene suggestions from the public galleries, but there was a waxy pallor of fear under her over-heavy blush. She glanced at Judge, and the ringleader of this demented circus grinned back as she propped her dirty feet on the High Table and nodded at her prosecutor to get the righteous work underway.

"Henrik Jost!" Sworbreck roared at the first prisoner, a portly man with a double chin and a patched waistcoat. "You stand accused of grand usury and conspiracy! Have you anything to say?"

The man struggled up, looking punch-drunk, a large bruise above his eye. "I admit to serving for a dozen years as a senior lending clerk at the Banking House of Valint and Balk—" Hisses from above. "But it was considered a respectable trade, entirely respectable! I arranged loans for worthy enterprises. Mills and manufactories the breadth of Midderland. Establishments that gave employment to many—"

"Including *businesses* and *establishments*," hissed Sworbreck, as though they were the worst excesses of witchcraft, "owned by *this woman*, Selest Heugen?"

A chorus of boos. Some rotten piece of vegetable matter tumbled from above and sprayed juice across the tiles. The banker stared at Selest. She stared back, breathing hard through flared nostrils. "Well...yes, but in those days, no one thought of it as a crime—"

"Time's no shield from punishment," growled Judge. "Guilty!"

Jost was about to protest, but Sarlby leaned over the dock to cuff him across the head and knock him back into his seat. Sworbreck had already swaggered to the next prisoner, a trembly man with a nimbus of wild hair, his eyes bloodshot behind cracked lenses.

"Piater Norlhorm, you stand accused of disloyal pronouncements, royalist sympathies and conspiracy to incite riot! Have you anything to say?"

"Absolutely!" He sprang up, waving a fistful of flapping papers, scrawled on both sides. "I have established a watertight defence!" Grumbles from the galleries as he perched his lenses on his wispy pate and began rummaging through his mismatched pages. "I fear there was some damage caused by damp during the last search of my cell..."

"I thought it was watertight?" some wag called from the upper gallery. Laughter.

"Ah, yes!" The old man cleared his throat, puffing up his chest to read from notes scrawled on an old shirt, declaiming in an orator's wail, "Was it not Juvens himself who spoke unto the Samnites, 'Justice is more than punishment, more than vengeance?' Er..." He shuffled his papers again, a couple of scraps fluttering to the floor. "And was it Bialoveld, or no, my mistake, one moment, I think it was Verturio who said—"

"We're not here for a fucking history lesson!" sneered Judge, hammering at the table. "He's guilty, too!"

"But I have scarcely commenced my preamble—" Broad tore the sheaf of scrawlings from Norlhorm's hands and shoved him back down. He missed his seat and sprawled on the floor, paper bags, candle-wrappers and scribbled-on sheet music drifting about him.

"Selest *dan* Heugen!" snapped Sworbreck. She rose, an ill-looking blotchiness across her collarbones, but her fists clenched like those of a prizefighter about to enter the ring. "You stand accused of profiteering, speculation, exploitation and conspiracy." Charges vague enough to be impossible to prove or disprove, as they always were. "Have you anything to—"

"I wish to make denunciations!" she blurted, as though desperate to get in before she missed her chance. She did not even bother to protest her innocence. In that, she was probably wise. Innocence was wasted on the court these days.

Judge hungrily licked her lips. "By all means."

Selest spilled names like a broken cask spills wine. Her entire acquaintance came out in a burbling rush. Several Orso knew had already been executed. Tears began to trickle down her face, leaving black powder tracks all the way to her spit-flecked lips. She denounced friends, partners, family members. Boras Heugen, her cousin, shrivelled into his seat with characteristic cowardice. It came as no surprise these days, of course. Orso had seen courage in that dock, and inspiring camaraderie, and towering dignity. He had also seen brothers denounce their sisters, wives denounce their husbands, parents denounce their children.

Judge started to frown. She shifted impatiently in her chair. She curled her lip and reached for her hammer.

"I denounce Savine Brock!" screeched Selest.

Orso felt as if his guts had suddenly fallen out of his arse. And he was not the only one on whom the name fell heavily. There was no cheer. Only a disbelieving mutter. The ex-noblemen looked grim. This was an attack on their leader. An attack on them. And Savine had made herself popular, recently, at the other end of the social scale. She had fed people, clothed people, brought them fuel in the bleak winter when the Burners had brought them nothing but corpses.

Sworbreck glanced worriedly over at Judge, but Judge waved him eagerly on. "Of what do you accuse her?"

"Of profiteering, speculation and usury on the grandest of scales! It is a *fact* that for years she exploited the working men and women of the Union for her own profit! That she conspired with her father, Arch Lector Glokta! That she conspired with bankers, Gurkish agents and Styrian spies!" Selest lifted a trembling finger to point straight at Orso. "It is a *fact* that she conspired with the king!"

He stared back in shocked upset. "Everyone knows she bloody conspired against me!"

"Then why did you spare her and her husband the noose?" shrieked

Selest. It was a good question. One to which Orso had himself struggled to find a satisfactory answer. Selest was less circumspect. "Because it is a *fact* that Savine Brock was for *years* the king's lover!"

Orso sat back frowning on his stool as the whispers fluttered about the public galleries. That one was harder to deny with much conviction. They were memories he still often guiltily caught himself enjoying, after all.

"Not only that! It is a *fact*!" Selest spat the word with a kind of savage triumph. "That Savine Brock is the king's *sister*!"

Orso felt the colour drain from his face. Probably he should have lied his head off. That was what everybody else did in here. But he was taken too much by surprise. Everyone was.

"It is a *fact*!" Selest was screaming now, spit flying, broken voice echoing. "That Savine Brock is the bastard daughter of King Jezal the First!"

There was a breathless silence in the court as people struggled to make sense of what they were hearing. The Representatives sat gawping on their benches. The public galleries gave a collective gasp. Captain Broad stood, flask frozen just short of his mouth. Judge sat bolt upright in her chair, mouth twisted into a delighted grin.

In her last message, Teufel had told him that it might be a matter of days.

It looked as if days might be too long.

"Now *that*," breathed Hildi, "is a spicy denunciation."

# Purity

"Purity Officers of the People's Army!" called Leo.

A hundred of the bastards, their clothes and armour spattered with red. Two from each company. There to make sure every military decision was politically sound and that every soldier stayed loyal to the Great Change. These were the longest serving and most committed Burners. Fanatics who'd stood with Judge when standing with Judge had looked like madness.

"You all know who I am!" he roared. He might not have a hero's legs any more, but he still had a hero's voice, and he meant to use it. "My name's Leo Brock. Some call me the Young Lion." Applause would've been too much to hope for, but he paused for appreciation. There was none of that, either. Only folded arms, impatient grunts, hard frowns on scarred faces. These men weren't easily impressed. They had scant regard for ex-noblemen, ex-Lord Governors or ex-heroes of the Union and had already sent several sets of failed generals back to Adua for the long drop.

Leo took a hard breath through his nose and glanced at Sparks. The man gave a sneering shrug.

"Citizeness Judge has made me General of the People's Army." Leo thought he heard a few disgusted sniffs near the back. "She wants me to lead you to victory against the royalists…" Someone spat noisily on the floor of the barn. "I fought Stour Nightfall in the Circle and won. I fought the king at Stoffenbeck—"

"And fucking lost," someone growled. Murmurs of agreement. Leo felt Glaward shifting unhappily at his shoulder.

"Aye, I lost!" he called. "I was rash. I was reckless. I was vain. It cost me two of my best friends, not to mention an arm and a leg." He tapped at the metal one with his cane. "But I learned my lesson. I learn it fresh every time I try to hold one of my babies, climb the stairs or pull my prick out to piss." Some grudging nods there. Most of them were veterans. They might not respect much, but they respected wounds, and they respected swearing. "I used to be quite the hero! And quite the fucking fool. But I'm not so much of a fool that I'll make the same mistake twice."

He glanced sideways, and Jurand gave the slightest encouraging nod, enough to settle any doubts in a warm rush of confidence. He always knew just what Leo needed. Leaving him in Angland had been the worst mistake of all. One he'd never make again.

Leo puffed out his chest like he used to, when he gave his speeches to the Army of Angland. "With me in charge, there'll be no more compromises. No more half-measures. No more defeats." Some of the arms were coming unfolded. Some of the frowns were fading. "I know you've been short of food and supplies, gone without pay for weeks. I'll put that right first." The grunts had turned appreciative. Even fanatics like being paid. "But I understand why you might not accept me! I was a nobleman. Now I'm a fucking cripple." He grinned and dug out a couple of grim laughs. "I won't force myself on you, whether Judge picked me or not. But I won't fight you over every decision, either. I mean to lead. So I need your consent, now, to be led. I'll give you some time to discuss it, but when I come back I want a straight answer."

A big man with a beard stained red spoke up. "Young Lion, I think I speak for us all when I say—"

Leo held up his hand. "Discuss it! Take a vote if you need to. I don't want to hear later you weren't given the chance." He tapped Sparks's shoulder with the handle of his cane. "Citizen Sparks will make sure you're all heard." And before anyone could disagree, he turned and limped out of the barn into the morning chill, hearing the doors creak as they were swung shut behind him.

He waited, gripping his cane tight. Waited, listening to the birds twitter in the dripping trees, the dewy hedgerows. Waited, watching the mist down in the still valley. He took a cold breath through his nose and smiled. It wasn't hard to do. It felt better than he'd ever expected, to be back in uniform and in charge of soldiers again, even if the uniform scarcely fit him and the soldiers were a pack of scum.

When he left Angland his mother had warned him he was no general. He saw now how right she'd been. Rash and indecisive at once, and so horribly sentimental. Losing everything, and seeing his friends dead before his eyes, and months of pain ever since had cured him of all that. Perhaps he had half the limbs, but he reckoned he was twice the man he used to be. He'd a harder head, a harder heart and, most important of all, a far stronger stomach.

"Generals are forged in the fires of defeat," he murmured to himself. Stolicus, maybe? He wondered what his mother would say now.

"Not having second thoughts, are you?" asked Jurand, stepping up beside him.

"You know me." Leo gave a grunt as he shifted his weight on his iron leg. "I barely even have first thoughts."

"Once, maybe. Not any more." And Jurand grinned at him. By the dead, that smile. Leo could've looked at it all day.

He could hear the raised voices from the barn. The Burners and the Breakers always loved a debate. An argument. A vote. The noisier and more tedious the better. How much of that nonsense had he endured in the ruined Lords' Round?

"Which side do you think they'll come down on?" he asked.

Jurand looked almost puzzled. "What does it matter?"

"Just curious, I suppose. I mean, we all want to be liked." Leo winced as he turned and waved to the dark-uniformed Anglanders gathered about the barn. Quietly, carefully, men slipped forward. They slid a beam into the brackets, barring the doors from outside. Others sloshed oil over the lower timbers of the barn. More came forwards with torches, touched them to the wood and fire bloomed. In a few moments the flames were licking high, all around, right to the eaves of the roof. Leo heard shouting inside, over the crackle and roar. The doors wobbled, clattered.

Leo's men had dropped their torches, now they drew swords and readied flatbows. "Surround the barn!" he called. "Kill anyone who makes it out."

"Yes, Your Grace."

"Glaward, put loyal Anglanders wherever there were Purity Officers before. Jurand, see the People's Army fed and paid with what Savine gave you. When the time comes, I want them loyal. Loyal enough, anyway."

Over the roar of flames, Leo could just hear the wails of horror. Alongside the stink of burning, it reminded him more than a little of Stoffenbeck. He'd been conceived on a battlefield. He'd been reborn on another. He took a wary step back, narrowing his eyes against the heat, and watched the smoke pour up into the dawn sky.

"I guess it had to be done," said Glaward, wide eyes flickering with reflected flames.

"They love the fire," said Leo, tugging his jacket smooth, then turning away. "They can have the fire."

# None of the Cards

"Calder's coming!" roared the messenger, skittering to a halt in the middle of Skarling's Hall and nearly going over on his arse.

"By the dead," someone breathed.

Rikke felt a flutter in her stomach. Fear and doubt, of course, those familiar friends of hers, but excitement, too. So strong she couldn't quite keep the smile off her face. She glanced over at Corleth. "Looks like the weather didn't put him off after all."

The messenger was halfway sick from running and he coughed, spat, then blurted out more in gulping rushes. "He's no more'n...a day or two distant. Strung out on the bad roads, but...lot o' men. Mighty host. Thousands! And a swarm o' bastards from past the Crinna, too. Some fucker rides on a wagon of bones. Stand-i'-the-Barrows, they call him."

There was a murmur in Skarling's Hall. Fear and doubt, of course, but...actually just fear and doubt. From a set of bastards who'd been tigers every man not a few months back, when they dragged Stour Nightfall into the hall on his ruined knees. She remembered her father telling her, *All warriors are brave when they're sure of victory.* Amazing how few stay brave when the numbers are against 'em and the hopes look thin.

"They're burning every farm they find," blathered the messenger, "and skinning the folk there, and taking their bones!"

"Their bones?" someone muttered, face all twisted with sick shock.

"They're the things that keep you standing," growled Rikke. "We could do with a few more in here, I reckon. Shivers, send scouts into the hills, keep a watch on Calder and his men. Make sure we get no more surprises. And spread word in the valleys round about. Don't want this Barrows bastard killing anyone we can save with a warning. Tell any friends Black Calder's on his way, and they should be ready."

"Aye," said Shivers, simply. No hint of fear on his scarred face as he picked a few men out and sent 'em scampering for the doors. He didn't know what fear was. Or if he did, he'd buried his so deep no one would ever catch a glimpse of it. Rikke took courage from that, though her heart was thumping so hard she worried Black Calder might hear it, even a day or two away.

Corleth leaned close to Skarling's Chair. "They're still a ways off. Ain't too late to run—"

"It's way too late." Rikke grinned sideways at her. Had to keep grinning, however her stomach bubbled and her skin prickled and her hands wanted to shake. "I ran from Black Calder once and it was no fun at all. Promised myself I'd never do it again."

"We're staying, then?" grunted one of the warriors, looking like that wouldn't have been his first choice.

Shivers raised his one brow at Rikke.

"We're staying," she said to Shivers.

"We're staying," Shivers pronounced to the room.

"But we got none o' the cards!" someone called. Meaning, Rikke gathered, that she'd thrown 'em all away. "The Nail's gone, and Hardbread's gone, and Isern-i-Phail's gone—"

"Calder's got the numbers," growled a fellow with a gravelly voice but a fearful pallor. "Might have the numbers ten to one."

"He might have the numbers," said Rikke, "but we've got the walls."

"But if those Crinna bastards get inside 'em there'll be no mercy—"

"Hoping for mercy from your enemies is a piss-weak way to start a fight!" She jumped up from Skarling's Chair and sneered at 'em down her nose. "I shouldn't have to explain that to you lot. You're meant to make 'em hope for mercy from you! Look at you, clucking and fussing while the women can't wait to fight!" And she waved a hand at Corleth, who looked, in fact, like she had some sizeable doubts about the whole notion. "Tell you what, Corleth, bring your granny up here to the hall, where it's safe. Safer, anyway!" And she hacked out a laugh. A bit of fearlessness was what they needed to see from her now. Maybe it'd be catching.

Corleth stared. "Reckon she'd be happier in her house—"

"Better sad and alive, though. Shivers'll help you." Rikke was already strolling over to Stour's cage. "And we've still got a card or two left to play." There sat the used-to-be terror of the North, his eyes gleaming in the shadows, one limp leg hanging through the bars so his toes near brushed the stone.

"Your daddy loves you, eh?" she sang. "Ain't a thing he wouldn't give for you. Even Carleon."

That pallid warrior's colour had only got worse. "Maybe Black Calder'll make a deal. But d'you really think he'll stick to it once you give this bastard over?"

Stour put a thin hand on the bars and pulled himself into the light, making the chain creak. First time she'd seen that sharp-toothed, wet-eyed smile in a while and it gave her a most unpleasant feeling to add to her nerves. Folk are rarely made better by suffering, after all. Once he got free of that cage, chances were he'd be a worse terror than ever. "You should run," he whispered. "You should run now, and never stop."

Rikke felt a shiver through her shoulders, but she turned it into a careless shrug. "I'm minded to stay. We're all back to the mud one way or another. Only a question of how. And when. Far as that goes…" And she grinned as she tapped at her cheek, where the runes were. "Maybe I know something you don't."

# Horror on Horror

"**F**inally, you show yourself," Clover grunted at the sun, "you coy bastard."

It was good to feel its warmth on his face, finally. Like an old friend, much missed. Like Wonderful, in that regard. He couldn't help wincing at the thought. She wouldn't be back. His knife had made sure of that. As for the sun, it had turned up too late to help much.

A couple of weeks of marching and Black Calder's carefully stitched-together host was coming apart at the seams. Men sick. Men hungry. Men frozen and frostbitten. Men sleepless and exhausted. Men so filth-caked they looked like devils, white eyes staring haunted from dirt-grey faces. Plenty more chose to turn their backs on this boggy nightmare and run, in spite of the deserters strung from trees by the road and carved with the bloody cross, flyblown guts dangling. Scouts stared into their fires rather than at the far hills. Carls fretted more on warmth than weapons. The only enemy on anyone's mind was the mud, against whom no victory could be won, a great trail of discarded gear, mired wagons, dead horses, not to mention dead men left abandoned across the boot-mashed country behind them.

Not far from the jealously guarded patch of grass on which Clover and his people had got a lick of fire going, a column cursed through the swampy morass in the valley's bottom, spears wobbling at all angles like the prickles of a hedgehog, a filthy standard slumping from a filthy pole. There'd been a road under that slop once, Clover thought, a thing now dimly remembered, a fantastical story once heard, like dry boots, warmth and unchafed fruits.

"I'm starting to think..." murmured Flick as he added a couple of damp sticks to the fire with wincing care, "that war ain't half the fun it's made out to be."

"It's worth all the effort," grunted Downside, "when you get a good battle."

"Good...battle." Sholla held her hands so close to the flames it was only the stubborn damp in their rag-wrappings stopped 'em catching fire. "Not sure those two words belong next to one another."

"A bit like saying it's worth the weeks of slow death to enjoy an hour or two's furious murder." Clover tried to pull his bedraggled wolfskin collar up higher, but there was no hiding from the keen wind knifing down the valley sides, still with the odd patch of melting snow splattered on 'em.

"Talking o' furious murder..." Flick stared wide-eyed the way they'd come, a great wagon grinding towards them, men backing horrified out of its way. "Here comes Stand-i'-the-Barrows."

Clover had expected some raven-haired, brooding giant, like Stranger-Come-Knocking had been. But the new Chief of a Hundred Tribes was a colourless man, with whirls of grey scar cut into his hollow cheeks, thick veins showing in the skull-like rings under his eyes in which you almost thought you could see the blood pulse.

He sat swaying in the wagon's seat as its wheels ground through the rutted mud, calm and easy as a farmer on his turnip cart. Trouble was, his cargo wasn't turnips but bones. Heaps of 'em, boiled bare, white and yellow. The four horses that drew it were covered head to hoof in bones, made devil-steeds, their eyes showing wild through split horse skulls, bones dangling from their tattered manes, woven into their tails. The man himself had tiny bones stitched to his armour in strange designs. Finger bones. Children's finger bones, maybe.

"Bones is the theme, I reckon," muttered Sholla.

"One to which he has committed," said Flick, wider-eyed than ever.

A wretched group were dragged after, chained to the wagon's seat by collars around their necks. Boys and girls, men and women, half-naked and spattered with filth to their hair, beaten and bloody, stumbling and slipping. They sent up a miserable music of moans to which the clunking of the wagon's soiled axles was the percussion.

"Will you look at this fucking pantomime," muttered Clover, as if anyone could've looked away. He was a hard man to disgust, but this spectacle had managed it.

A crowd of spiked and scarred and war-painted savages trotted behind, with their jagged weapons and their strange standards and their pierced faces, eyes rolling in ecstasy at the thought of the blood to be spilled. There were dogs with them, great dogs straining at iron-toothed leads, cruel dogs treated cruelly, big as wolves and far meaner, teeth filed to points, snarling and snapping at whoever was fool enough to stray near.

Carls and Thralls scrambled from the path of this visitation from hell—or beyond the Crinna, which was about the same thing—with various expressions of grim hate, shock, fear, outrage and disgust.

Downside noisily hawked up phlegm and spat roughly in the savages' direction. "It's arseholes like this give the North a bad name."

"For once we agree," said Sholla.

Stand-i'-the-Barrows reined in his bone-covered horses, not moved one bit by the disgust of his supposed allies, and Clover saw Black Calder nudge his own black mount up beside the wagon. You expected a jagged howl to rip from that ghost-pale corpse face. It was almost worse to hear an ordinary sort of voice, saying ordinary sorts of things.

"Black Calder, my friend. Good to see the sun. It may dry things up."

"We can hope," said Calder, voice a little tight. "The scouts are looking down on Carleon, just over those hills." He squinted up at the clouds shifting. "Reckon there'll be a battle tomorrow."

"Lovely." Stand-i'-the-Barrows' colourless eyes were fixed on the horizon. "I still have empty wagons and Bayaz told me you would help me fill them. Should we stop for dinner soon?" He turned around to talk to one of his slaves. "What do we have for dinner?"

Her split lips moved. She whispered something.

Stand-i'-the-Barrows caught her chain from the bunch and dragged her towards him so sharply, the corner of the cart dug into her shoulder and she was knocked down in the mud. He wound the chain around his fist, hauling her bruised face up towards his, her bare toes scraping at the ground. "Did you not hear me? I asked what's for dinner."

She had her fingers squeezed into her collar, skin all white around it from the pressure. "Mutton," she gasped out.

Stand-i'-the-Barrows let her drop and she knelt in the mud, spitting and gasping. "I like mutton. We will have a nice gravy with it, too." He smacked his lips. "I insist always on a good gravy."

"It makes the meat," muttered Calder, watching the girl scramble back to the rest of the slaves.

"Do you like mutton, Black Calder? Will you join me for mutton and gravy later?"

"Other business, sadly. Have to get the men ready."

"You're all work! A man must make time for fun. But still." Stand-i'-the-Barrows laughed a high, good-humoured laugh. "More mutton for me!" And he snapped his reins, and sent his wagon o' nightmares rattling on.

"Y'ever feel," murmured Flick as he watched the slaves dragged after, bouncing off each other, clutching at their collars, sending up a chorus of sobs, "that you're on the wrong side o' the question?"

"Increasingly." Clover scratched gently at his scar. "Whichever side I pick."

"I mean..." Flick was looking down at himself, patting his chest as if picturing a costume like Stand-i'-the-Barrows wore. "Why cover yourself with bones?"

"'Cause being feared is a heady brew," muttered Downside, who was bringing out his whetstone for his favourite hobby of sharpening his axe. "Men get drunk on it."

"First fear's their weapon." Clover remembered winning a few fights before they began, using just a hard stare and the weight of his name. "Then it becomes their shield. Only thing that'll stop their enemies trying to kill 'em. Only thing that'll stop their friends trying to kill 'em. They get scared o' not being feared enough, so they pile horror on horror. Turn 'emselves into monsters. And since memory tends to make the past look bigger, today's bastards are always hunting for ways to out-bastard the bastards o' yesteryear."

"It's sort of... an atrocity contest," mused Sholla, tapping her lip with one finger as she watched Downside grinding at his axe-blade.

"Aye," said Clover, sighing, "and the winner gets the same prize as the losers. An early grave."

"Enough to make you miss the Bloody-Nine. He might've killed more men than winter, but he never made some fucking travelling show out of it."

"The sad truth is, men love to follow a man other men fear," said Clover. "Makes them feel fearsome, too. We tell the odd fond story of the good men. The straight edges. Your Rudd Threetrees, your Dogmen. But it's the butchers men love to sing of. The burners and the blood-spillers. Your Cracknut Whirruns and your Black Dows. Your Bloody-Nines. Men don't dream of doing the right thing, but of ripping what they want from the world with their strength and their will."

"And that's what we'll do tomorrow!" Downside gave his axe one last lick with the stone and held it up to the light to admire its edge. "Something to look forward to, eh?"

Clover watched him, grinning in the sunlight at the idea of mayhem. By the dead, had he once been that way?

"Why hasn't she run?" he muttered, frowning towards the hills. He thought of Rikke, perched in Skarling's Chair with that knowing smile.

That big black eye with the runes around it, the pupil yawning like a pit full of secrets. "What's she seen, with that Long Eye of hers?"

He gave a shiver. A cloud had come across the sun again and cast the muddy valley into shadow.

# The Dragon's Hoard

It was cold, but the lethal sting was off the air. The snow was melting fast, chill water dripping from the eaves, filthy tracks of stomped-up slush down the pavements, dirty slop gurgling in the gutters. The queues were already long outside the bakery and the coal merchant, bundled-up Citizens ready to fight to the death for whatever had leaked into the city overnight. At the street corner a district crier cheerfully called out the names of yesterday's denounced. Most likely he'd be at it a while.

"They found the manager, then?" Tallow gave a long sniff as he looked up at the bank. Before the Great Change, Valint and Balk had towered over every scrap of business done in the Union, an untouchable colossus. Now the marble skin had been stripped from the pillars of its headquarters to show the cheap bricks beneath, the word *Usurers* slopped in red paint a thousand thousand times, all over the ruined façade.

The banking hall had been picked clean. Chill and empty but for broken furniture, torn papers, two or three dozen frowning Constables and dust. Commissioner Pike stood gazing up at the giant vault door, its brass wheel, its two tiny keyholes, no more than a few bright scratches on its black surface for all the efforts of the People's Inspectorate to get inside.

"You found the manager, then?" asked Vick.

Pike glanced over as she strode up. "Thanks to your efforts, in fact. Once that cellar in the Three Farms was shut down there was no one to bring him food. An old woman heard him singing and alerted the authorities."

"Singing?"

"He had bricked himself into a secret space between two slum tenements owned by the bank. He had been hiding there for weeks." Almost as uncomfortable as having Bremer dan Gorst wedged into her tiny apartment, she imagined. "He appears to have gone quite mad."

Vick resisted the urge to ask who hadn't.

"But he did have this." Pike held up a long steel key and offered her another. The one the senior over-clerk for loans had given her the day she broke into the bank with an unloaded cannon. "Perhaps you might help me do the honours?"

She looked up at the towering door, feeling the need for something more momentous than the turning of a little rod of metal. But that's how locks open. She slid the key into one of the keyholes and looked across at Pike as he did the same.

"On three," she said, "I suppose."

"Whyever not? One, two, *three*." They turned the keys together with a gentle click. "Constable?"

The biggest man to hand gripped the wheel, dipped his shoulder and began to turn it. There was a whirring of well-oiled gears, then an answering clatter, faint, from within, and the door began to edge smoothly open.

Vick had never been that interested in money. But even she couldn't help a shiver at the thought of what might be beyond that mighty thickness of steel. Her imagination spun out heaps of gleaming coins, chests of gemstones, jewelled swords, ivory drinking horns. Incense and pearls, silks and resins, too, why not? Sculpted relics of the Old Empire, lost works by Aropella, deeds to whole countries, the Master Maker's private diaries. The plunder of a barbarian army and the profits of a city of merchant princes combined.

Once the gap was wide enough to slip through it became an effort not to start forward. But Pike waited, with epic patience, as the vast weight of steel inched towards them, and past, and the vault of the Adua headquarters of Valint and Balk finally stood open.

It wasn't that big. A room slightly wider than the great door itself, lined floor to ceiling with shelves. And on the shelves, as Vick stepped after Pike, through the vast doorway and into the heavy silence beyond, eyes gradually adjusting to the gloom...

Nothing.

It was entirely bare.

Vick had faced some disappointments, but she wasn't sure she'd ever experienced so intense an anticlimax.

"They moved the money long ago," murmured Pike.

Vick touched a fingertip to one of the shelves and drew it along, leaving a neat trail through a light layer of dust. Sealed up in here, it might've taken years to form. Decades. "If there was ever any here."

"The power of Valint and Balk comes down to an empty vault." Pike sounded almost impressed. "Just promises, just lies, just..."

"Nothing," said Vick.

Pike had started making a sort of gurgling wheeze. At first, she thought he might be choking. She was on the point of calling for help when she realised it was laughter. Of all the unexpected things she had seen since the Great Change, its chief instigator laughing his arse out in Valint and Balk's empty vault might've been the strangest.

He straightened, with a final shiver of mirth, dabbing his running eyes. "Ah, dear me. A vast fortune in gold would certainly have been helpful."

"It usually is," said Vick, her mind on the bribes she'd already arranged with Princess Cathil's jewels, and the ones she still had to engineer.

"But... all this really changes is the timing," Pike was saying. "How is your conspiracy coming along, by the way?"

For a giddy moment, it didn't quite register. Vick stood there with the puzzled frown of someone who sees blood squirting but hasn't yet realised it's their own throat that's slit.

Her first instinct, once she picked back through his words and gathered their meaning, was to run. Her second to fight. A habit from the camps. Her eyes darted to the vault door. Her fingers twitched to her weapons. But the place was crawling with Constables. She wouldn't make it five strides. And with that certainty came an odd calm. She'd always expected to be found out. Every moment she wasn't had been coming as a surprise. She closed her eyes and took a breath.

Would they kill her here, on the spot, her body found floating by the docks as her old master Arch Lector Glokta had been so fond of saying? Would they drag her off to the House of Purity for questioning, then the Court of the People for judgement, then the Tower of Chains for the long drop? Or would Pike make an exception in her case, for irony's sake, and send her back to the camps in Angland?

"Tallow had nothing to do with it," she said. A mistake, of course. Breaking all her own rules yet again. She might as well have torn her shirt open and pointed out the exact position of her heart. But it was a mistake she couldn't help making. As if she wanted, at the end, to have done one thing worth doing.

"You like the boy, don't you?" Pike's face was a mask again. "There's no shame in liking someone. I like you, in fact. Far more than most. To put both Brocks and King Orso together in one scheme? Ambitious, to combine such volatile ingredients. *Reckless*, even. Not at all what I expected. You always struck me as cautious to a fault."

"I always was," said Vick. She thought of Sibalt, then. That sad little smile, in the half-light of the foundry, before the end. "But the time comes…" She supposed she could allow herself a little flourish. "You have to stand up."

"Yes." Pike's burned lips curled back from his teeth. "*There* is the lesson the camps taught *me*." He turned from the empty shelves to consider her, and took a long breath through his nose, and let it sigh away. Then he gave a neat little nod. "Proceed."

There was a heavy silence in the vault. A muffled banging from somewhere behind, where the Constables must have found something still worth smashing. Again, it took a moment for Vick to catch up. Then she gently cleared her throat. "What?"

"The Great Change has done its work."

"Its *work*?"

"A wise man once told me that sometimes…to change the world… we must first burn it down. But Judge is a fire out of control. The time has come to douse the flames and restore order, before everything is reduced to ashes."

"So…" The silence stretched between them. "Proceed?"

"Exactly. I wish I could offer you help beyond turning a blind eye, but I fear, under the present circumstances, there is no one in the Inspectorate that I fully trust. No one but you, of course, Inspector." Pike turned back to consider the empty shelves, clasping his hands behind him. "It really has become almost impossible, these days, to tell where people stand."

Vick stood and stared at him for a long moment. "You don't fucking say," she muttered.

Outside in the chilly street the snow was still melting. The queues still stretching. The crier still busy with his list of doomed names.

"You look pleased," said Tallow, still hugging himself. "Must've been a lot o' money in that vault."

A rare smile was forming on Vick's face. "It was empty."

She wasn't sure how it had happened, but she was starting to think they had a chance. If Pike was with them, or at least not against them. If Lord Marshal Forest and the Young Lion could do their part without killing each other. If Bremer dan Gorst could stay out of sight. If King Orso could keep his mouth shut. If they could avoid disasters for only a few more days, they had a chance.

"And finally!" roared the crier with a parting flourish. "Accused of profiteering and speculation, exploitation and grand usury, betrayal of the Great Change, royalism and incest…Citizeness Savine Brock!"

Vick's smile was gone as quickly as it had come.

"Fuck," she whispered.

# None Saved

"I should caution you," said Citizeness Vallimir, pausing at the front door, "it can be rather...overwhelming." She wore a sober black dress and stained apron. Hardly recognisable as the fussy hostess Savine had dined with in Valbeck. But who had come through the Great Change quite the same?

"Believe me, it could be rather overwhelming when my parents were... still in residence..." Savine trailed off as she crossed the threshold. Jokes did not feel appropriate.

The hallway was full of children. Crowded with them, down both sides. Ragged. Scabbed. Filthy. Five or six haggard nurses stood among them, looking hardly better. Savine's mother had insisted on fresh flowers here, every day. There were no flowers now. Someone had taken away the chandelier, and the place smelled stale. Savine forced a queasy smile onto her face. Nodded a greeting at no one in particular. She heard Zuri take a sharp breath, as unsettling from her as a scream of horror might have been from someone else.

"Children, this is Citizeness Brock! This is her house. It is thanks to her generosity that you have food and shelter—"

"That's all right," said Savine. "Really." She realised the strange carpet of rags the children were standing on were their blankets, wedged in left and right to leave a narrow path of scuffed floor to walk down. "Do they sleep here?" she muttered, flinching away from the great dark eyes of a girl who would not, could not, stop staring. They were like a bird's eyes, unblinking.

"We need the space." Citizeness Vallimir pushed open the door to the room where Savine had once drunk with her mother, laughed with her mother, been sick with horror at the secret her mother had told her. The windows were mostly boarded up, and it took a moment for her eyes to adjust to the gloom.

She had allowed herself to imagine neat files of clean, grateful, pretty orphans. Saved orphans. The sight of those in the hall had shocked her. Now she realised they had been the presentable ones.

The children crowded into the bare room were like some other species. Twisted, stunted, wounded, strange. Shafts of dusty light fell on ugly details. A great bloom of scabs on a hollow ribcage. A hunched shape, endlessly rocking. Mouths gaped and dribbled. Flies buzzed about leaking eyes. Some of them slumped, insensible. Some of them crouched, baring blackened teeth. They were thin as stray cats. They were mad as mean dogs. One girl had puke in her hair. One boy's face was a mass of sores. Another stared at the peeling wallpaper, slapping the side of his own half-bald head over and over. They made strange noises. Not words, exactly. Warbles and wheezes and snarls. Like an abandoned menagerie in which the animals had all gone mad.

When Savine looked into those ranks of hungry faces, it was no sappy desire to hold them and stroke their hair that rose up but a trapped panic. An urge to run, barging children out of her way. The challenge of each of her own two babies was almost more than she could manage. How could anyone satisfy the scale of the need in this room, let alone this house?

"By the Fates," she whispered, unable to stop herself putting a hand over her mouth at the overpowering stink.

"You forget, once you're used to it," said Citizeness Vallimir. "We do our best to keep them clean, to contain the sickness and the lice, but there are too few of us, no soap to be had, no spare fuel to heat water. We keep the younger children downstairs, the older ones upstairs." She glanced towards the great staircase in the hall—down which Savine used to sweep, in the giddy height of fashion—as if she was a general frowning into no man's land. "They are more... malevolent. They form gangs. They prey on each other. At night... well. One must be careful here at night."

"How many do you have?" whispered Savine, staring about her mother's old salon. It made her think of the mill in Valbeck, where children once toiled for her profit.

"Honestly... I couldn't say. We kept records to begin with, where we could. Names, birthplaces, ages, but... once we realised what was happening in the city..." She gave a helpless sigh. "The children band together and huddle anywhere warm. Then they are in terrible danger. They are hunted, rounded up like sheep. They are bought and sold. Traded into slavery in the mills. Pressed into... worse kinds of slavery. They started to come here by themselves. Soon there were dozens of them crowding about the gate every morning. We were less interested in counting them than in getting them out of the cold, feeding them, and then…" She hopelessly raised her hands, hopelessly let them fall, eloquently conveying the size of the challenge.

Savine felt Zuri's reassuring touch on her shoulder. "You have done good here. All the good you could. Never forget that."

It was hard for Savine to imagine, at that moment, that she had done anything more than concentrate the most intense misery into one place. She forced the hand away from her mouth, forced down her panic and tried to think through it, like any other problem. She had been expecting challenges of education, occupation, betterment. Having taken a few steps over the threshold, it was clear no one was looking past survival. "You need money, for food, fuel, clothing." She had given the last of what she had to Leo so he could bribe the People's Army. "If I am to go to the government…" If there was anything left still worthy of the title. "Or find some wealthy benefactor…" Though those who had money were hoarding it to hide behind. "I need at least *some* idea of how many we have."

"I will try to make a count." Zuri slipped her pencil from behind her ear, wagging it at each child as she made a quick circuit of the room, each flick of its point a whole life to be rebuilt, from the ground up. Even counting them was no easy task. There were some wretched bunks, three high, but their blankets were crammed onto every available patch of floor as well, stuffed into every corner.

"It gets worse each day," said Citizeness Vallimir as Zuri slipped from the room to continue the tally. Savine felt faint at the thought of the whole house like this, from cellars to attic. "Those orphaned, abandoned, those who have found their way to the city from hopeless conditions in the country. The stories they tell…things no child should have to hear of, let alone suffer." She lowered her voice to a whisper, eyes darting sideways as though worried she might be overheard. "And with the executions… there are no provisions made for the children of those who fall from the Tower of Chains—"

There was a crash in the hall and Savine jerked around. Another crash, splintering, raised voices.

"Whatever is that?" asked Citizeness Vallimir.

Savine closed her eyes and took a deep breath. She already knew.

Burners were tramping through the shattered front door, their armour spattered with red paint, pushing children out of their way, squeals of fear spreading through the house. They were already stomping up the stairs, getting their pikes hopelessly tangled with the banisters. They were everywhere.

So it seemed Judge would finally have a genuine conspiracy to expose before the Court of the People. Teufel had been caught, or Orso had talked, or Leo had failed. While Savine was thinking that all was lost, she was also thinking that pikes were an absurd weapon for a confined space, and she felt tears in her eyes and almost giggled at once.

Citizeness Vallimir drew herself up. "*What* is the meaning of—"

"It's all right," said Savine, easing her aside. She appreciated the gesture, but it could not do the slightest good. "I expect they are here for me."

"Got it in one," said a sinewy Burner with a red handprint on his breastplate and a broad grin on his face. The grin of a polite tradesman, here with a much-anticipated delivery. "My name's Sarlby."

"I remember. From the barricades in Valbeck."

He gave a disbelieving laugh, then. "You're the girl who lived with the Broads! Well I never. Hey, Bull, it's—"

"I know who it is." The floor creaked as Broad stepped into the hall. He had grown a scruffy beard and there was something crusted at the corners of his mouth. Savine remembered his first visit to this house, with Liddy and May, hunched and overawed. He stood tall now, bridge of his nose creased in permanent rage, the menace that he had once tried to hide, that she had coaxed out to use against her striking workers, put on savage display. The children inside the door frame shrank away into the corners. It was the most Savine could do not to shrink away, too.

Sarlby held up a smudged document. "Citizeness Brock, you've been denounced—quite fucking spectacularly, as it happens—and are summoned to the House o' Purity to await trial."

"Denounced by whom?" asked Savine, though it hardly mattered.

"Some noblewoman. All bosoms. Didn't catch her name—"

"Heugen," grunted Broad.

Selest. Not Teufel, then. Not Orso. Had she simply been caught up in the ordinary, merciless grind of the Court of the People? What a bitter joke it would be, if she was brought down not by a wide-ranging plot to betray the Great Change, but by an old feud with a jealous rival. Savine swallowed, her mind racing. Then Leo might still be free. Their schemes might still be moving forward.

"Citizeness Vallimir," she murmured, "I would be very grateful if you could get a message to my husband—"

"Oh, the Young Lion knows all about it," said Sarlby, pulling out a set of heavy chains, polished bright about the bracelets with use. "Done a deal wi' Judge, I understand. Bull was there, weren't you? What was the phrase he used?"

The light flashed on Broad's eye-lenses. "The nation must judge her."

Savine could only stand, staring, as Sarlby snapped the manacles shut around her limp wrists. As quickly as it had flared up, hope was smothered. Had her own husband turned on her? Or had he done what he had to, to gain control of the People's Army? She hardly recognised him any more. Hardly knew what he might do from one moment to the next.

"Don't worry," said Sarlby, giving her shoulder a reassuring pat. "You won't have to wait long. You've been bumped right up the schedule. Friends in high places, eh?"

Or enemies. The weight of the chains, the coldness of them, had somehow taken Savine's breath away. She wondered how many others had worn this very set. She wondered if any of them were still alive. The reasons for your conviction in the Court of the People made little difference to the sentence, after all. The fall was still the fall.

"Citizeness Vallimir," she managed to say, "might I beg a favour? Bring my children to me at the House of Purity. They are in danger, do you understand?" Her voice was getting higher and higher as she thought of them, helpless in their cots with only a nurse. "They have to stay with me."

"Doubt that'll work," said Sarlby, rattling the bracelets on her wrists to make sure they were locked tight.

"She wants to bring her children." Broad took off his lenses, and breathed on them, and started to polish them with his shirt-cuff. His eyes rolled up to Savine's, red-rimmed and bloodshot. He looked as if he hardly knew her. "She can bring her children."

There was a clattering above, the Burners bundling someone down the stairs. "We've got her!" one shouted in triumph. Savine realised with a lurch of horror that their prisoner was Zuri, wrists and ankles shackled with great black fetters, links a finger thick. She could hardly move for their weight.

"For pity's sake!" called Savine. "Do you need those chains?"

"Can't take chances," said Sarlby as they dragged Zuri roughly to her feet at the bottom of the stairs. "Could be an Eater."

Her hair had come loose, and she gave Savine the briefest look through the black tangle across her face. "Do not worry about me, it—"

"Shut your mouth, you brown bitch." One of the Burners tore the silver watch from around Zuri's neck, the chain catching her ear and making her gasp, gave an approving grunt and slipped it into his pocket. Another pulled her head back and started to strap some contraption of buckles and wire over her face. By the Fates, they were muzzling her.

"Are you *mad*?" shrieked Savine. She regretted it at once. Quite obviously they were all mad. "She's a lady's companion, not a sorceress! You know her, Gunnar."

Broad winced, as if the sound of his first name was painful. "Not up to me," he grunted, and he lifted a flask and took a little sip. "Up to the court."

"How many suspected Eaters have you arrested?" asked Savine as they dragged Zuri towards the door, kicking through the children's bedding.

"Dozens," said Sarlby.

She clasped her hands, her own chain rattling. "And how many have actually *been* Eaters?"

"Once they're chained and muzzled, what difference does it make? She has brothers, does she?"

"But they're... good people," whispered Savine. What a pointless thing to say. She stared at the orphans, cringing against the peeling walls. How foolish she had been, to think she could save anyone. She could not even save herself.

Sarlby took her under the arm and walked her towards the door. "It's a shame, but there's not so many turning up for the executions any more," he was saying, as if they were discussing the weather. "Bored of 'em, I guess. If there's one human ability I've always been amazed by, it's the capacity to get bored. Saw it in Styria. Saw it in Valbeck. Don't matter how mad, strange or outrageous, folk'll get bored of anything. Don't worry, though. Given who your father is... or your fathers were... I'm sure there'll be no shortage of interest." He gave her a wink as he brought her through the door of the house where she had dreamed of being queen and out into the chill air. "And we still get a good turnout for the pretty ones."

# The Same Side

eo had a trick for putting a shirt on. He needed a trick for most things these days. First, he gathered the sleeve and twisted it over his useless hand.

The arm had withered. Thin, soft, pale apart from the scattered pink scars. Sometimes he thought he could feel the metal buried in the meat. Sharp splinters among the dull throb. His left hand looked strange, now. The nails had a purplish tint. Old skin flaking from the numb fingertips. Like the hand of a corpse, and about as useful.

He clenched his jaw, worked the sleeve up his numb arm to his shoulder, then whipped his right hand around behind his head—collar sliding between finger and thumb—and into the other armhole with a snapping of cloth, smooth as a step in a dance.

He had a trick for it. But these days Leo needed a trick for anything more complicated than turning a doorknob.

Jurand ducked through the tent-flap. "They're here. The royalists."

Leo raised his brows as he shoved the tails of his shirt down behind his belt. "Inspector Teufel has made us all royalists."

"They're deploying on the other side of the valley." Jurand pulled the general's jacket from the back of a folding chair and stepped over. He didn't embarrass Leo by asking if he wanted help. He knew what was needed before he was told, just as he always had. "If you can call it deploying."

Leo let himself be handled like a mannequin by a tailor. Or a dead body by an undertaker. Perhaps the most important trick he had learned was swallowing his pride and taking whatever help he could get.

Jurand frowned down as he did up the buttons of Leo's jacket, quick and practised as any valet. "Their men look almost as much of a mess as ours. Almost. There were more desertions in the night."

"Not such a bad thing," murmured Leo. "Weed out anyone with doubts...about the new leadership..."

Jurand was so close Leo could smell him, leather and polish and horse-hair and soap. He could hear his slow breath. Could see each hair of his long eyelashes, a tiny blemish on his cheek, his lips pressed together with concentration, but that little curl at the corner that he always used to have when they were together, before...everything that had happened.

It would've taken no effort at all to lean forwards and kiss him. It was almost more effort *not* to do it. Leo wondered what the roughness of his fresh-shaved jaw would feel like against Leo's cheek. What his hair would feel like between Leo's fingers. What his mouth would taste like—

Jurand looked up and their eyes met, and Leo froze, his breath held, his face tingling. "I...should have been there," murmured Jurand. "At Stoffenbeck. If I'd been there—"

"I'm glad you weren't. Glad you...weren't hurt." Leo thought of Antaup then, and Jin, and Bremer dan Gorst's boots crunching across the ruined square. "I can't afford...to lose you." And he tore his prickling eyes away, lifting his chin so Jurand could fasten his top button. "You'll be there this time," he managed to say, his voice rough.

"I'll always be there." Did Jurand reach gently for Leo's useless hand, as if to help him with that, too? Leo took it first and awkwardly stuffed it into the gap in his jacket, turning to the mirror with a forced smile. "How do I look?"

Jurand picked a speck of fluff from the braid on Leo's chest and flicked it away. "As handsome as ever," he said, softly.

"Lord Marshal Forest!" called Leo as he rode up. He could still ride well, at least, since the horse did most of the work. Gripping to the saddle made the stump of his leg ache, but he was damned if he'd let them strap him onto it. He considered wedging the reins in his teeth, decided that might be a bit informal, and tossed them over his saddle instead so he could hold out his hand, hoping his horse behaved.

The lord marshal, his uniform battle-stained, his scarred face weather-worn, his beard a grey riot, considered that hand with little enthusiasm and finally reached out to take it in a strong grip. "Young Lion."

"It's an honour to meet you. Really. Nothing teaches respect for a man like losing a battle to him. I only saw you from a distance, holding that ridge against Stour Nightfall. You just refused to be shifted. Quite a sight."

"So was that charge of yours," said Forest, grudgingly. "However it ended."

"I'm hoping for a happier outcome this time around," said Leo. "Between you and me, I'm running out of limbs at quite a rate."

One of Forest's frowning aides had a Union battle flag, and Leo was surprised at the bittersweet sting of nostalgia he felt at the sight of it, even dangling limp as a hanged man in the morning's dewy chill. The blazing sun had been torn from the flagpoles of Adua, chiselled from the stonework, burned on cloth and paper a million times over. He wondered how many solar dinner sets had been destroyed since the Great Change.

"Corporal Tunny tells me we're on the same side now," said Forest.

"Thanks to the good graces of Victarine dan Teufel." Or at any rate her low cunning.

"Wasn't long ago you fought against the king," grunted Forest. "Now you're fighting for him?"

Leo puffed out his cheeks as he looked up at that flag. "Honestly, I can hardly remember what the world was like, before." He shifted his left arm in his jacket, tried to work the fingers, winced at the numb aches in his elbow. "I can hardly remember what it felt like not to be in pain. The reasons I fought against you...if there even were any good ones... are burned off like morning mist." He didn't mention the chairs on the Closed Council he'd been offered. He'd got a lot better at judging what to say. And what to leave out. "The Great Change has to be changed back, at least some of the way, before the Union eats itself. That'll have to be good enough."

Forest's shoulders sagged slightly. "Since we're being honest, I'll take all the help I can get. Your men look in pretty poor shape, though."

Leo twisted around to look up the long rise, to where the People's Army were drawn up across the road to Adua. They'd been an ill-disciplined mob when they descended on the capital and freed him from the House of Questions. They were far worse now. It would've been flattery to call their lines ragged. There were scarcely any lines at all.

"*Terrible* shape, poor bastards," said Leo. "Hungry, tired, cold, poor. Above all, they're sick. Sick of fighting, sick of Judge, sick of the whole bloody business." He turned back to Forest, grinning. "All in all, I'd say they're ready for the restoration of the monarchy."

"And they'll follow you?" asked one of Forest's aides.

"They'll follow anyone who feeds them," said Jurand. "Especially if he points them in the direction of home."

"We've weeded out the worst of the Burners," said Leo, "and put loyal men in their place. But the truth is they don't want to fight any more." He nodded towards Forest's tattered companies, drawn up on the rise

284

ahead, no two the same size. "By the look of things, your men feel much the same."

Forest's turn to twist in his saddle and frown towards his crooked lines. When he turned back, he suddenly looked his age, weary and grey. "Reckon they might only have one more fight left in 'em."

"Then let's make it a good one," said Leo, turning his horse. "Glaward, give the order! We're marching for Adua!"

# Break What They Love

The sun shone bright on the gatehouse roof, but Rikke felt an edge on the wind as Black Calder's army spread out around the walls of Carleon. Most likely anyone feels a bit of a chill, though, watching thousands of men get ready to kill you.

"So here they are," she murmured, lowering her eyeglass. "Looks like they've had a muddy old time on the way. State o' these bastards."

Shivers slowly nodded. "But the number of 'em, too." He'd made quite an effort for the battle, with his mail gleaming and his war-horn at his belt, his grey hair bound back neat as a bride's and his shield fresh-painted red with the sign of the Long Eye, the black boss its yawning pupil.

"Aye." Rikke fumbled for a joke but couldn't find one in easy reach. Specially with her stomach trying to climb up out of her mouth and make a run for it. More men and more kept spilling over the hills to the north, through the shadows crawling across the land from the fast-moving clouds above, forming slovenly lines in the fields around the city where the last patches of snow clung pale and dirty in the hollows.

No doubt there were a lot of the bastards. As many as Black Calder had brought to the Battle of Red Hill, maybe. A lot more than Rikke had been hoping for. Her own men looked sparse on the walkways atop Carleon's walls. Nervous and lonely. Carls of Uffrith who'd served her father, far from home and with a leader who looked shakier every day.

Rikke had even less faith in her judgement than they did. She'd seen things, up in the hills, when the witch tattooed the runes around her eye. Splinters and fragments. Enough to take a guess at what was coming. But nowhere near enough to be sure.

"They've got ladders," said Corleth, hair whipping about her clenched jaw, standard of the Long Eye whipping above her.

"Lot o' ladders," said Shivers.

"Lot of everything," said Rikke. "Let's hope they don't have cannons!"

She barked a laugh but nearly puked on it, had to awkwardly swallow an acrid little tickle in her throat. "They don't have cannons, do they? What're those wagons?" She squinted through her eyeglass. "Are those...bones?"

"That'll be Stand-i'-the-Barrows. Those boys from past the Crinna always had some funny notions. Stranger-Come-Knocking was wild for plumbing, as I recall."

"Well, who wants to die at the hands of a man with no hobbies?" Rikke took a hard, cold breath and blew it out. One way or another, it'd get finished today. The scores that began when Scale Ironhand invaded the Protectorate, all those months ago. Scores way older than that, even. When her father told Black Calder he'd cut the bloody cross in him at the Battle of Osrung. When Black Calder killed Forley the Weakest years before. When her father and the Bloody-Nine fought for Bethod, and then against him, all across the North and back and left a trail of corpses both ways. One feud growing from another, blood flowing from blood, all settled today. Or maybe it was folly to think so. Maybe it'd just be new feuds started.

"I'm excited!" called Rikke, stretching up on tiptoes and forcing out a grin, like she knew just what was coming even if she was bubbling over with doubts. She clapped Corleth on the shoulder. She liked doing it. Her shoulders had a meaty, reassuring feel. "You excited?"

Corleth swallowed. "Honestly, I'm shitting myself."

"Two ways of saying the same thing." Rikke rubbed at her belly, tried to kick the aches out of her legs. "By the dead, that's sore."

"You all right?"

"Just the moon pains. Blood came last night."

"Huh. Me, too."

"Fancy that, our wombs have found a rhythm! Same thing happened with Isern." And Rikke gave a wistful sigh. "Reckon it's time to get Stour out of his cage."

"Aye," said Corleth, and she trotted to the steps.

Shivers was frowning out into the fields, sunlight glinting on his metal eye as the clouds shifted. "Doubt that'll be the only blood that comes today," he said.

Calder stood, hands on hips, glaring towards Carleon. The city he'd ruled the North from for twenty years. Had to hurt, having it stolen by a girl with a magic eye. Had to hurt, having to beg for the life of his only son.

But then, you reach a certain age, everything hurts.

"Clover," he grunted, "I want you next to me."

"'Course, Chief. Though battlefields do give me a rash."

"We'll all have to tolerate some discomforts today. Got a horse for you."

"Grand," said Clover, with heavy sarcasm.

He'd owned a horse once, long time ago, but only 'cause it was the type o' thing folk expect a famous warrior to own. Didn't think he'd ever ridden it. Except once, when he bought it, pretending he wasn't scared witless he'd fall off, and only 'cause it was the type o' thing folk expect someone to do when buying a horse. Rest of the time it just stood in a stable, looking sad, eating his hay and costing him money. Strange, how much of his time he'd spent worrying about what people expect. You'd have thought the one upside of being a famous warrior was doing whatever you pleased.

"We should attack," said Stand-i'-the-Barrows, sitting in his bone-covered armour on his bone-covered horse. "Attack, attack, sweep over them, a black wave. Drive them into nothingness. Into hell." That was pretty much the full range of his strategy. "Let's not faff with the talk before. The talk before is always lies and boasting. Waste of your time. Waste of my time. Some day I will die. I wish to gather as many bones as I can first. They say the cities of the South go on for ever, people flooding through them like rivers. And all those people are full of bones. Every one of them." He gave a dreamy smile. "I wish to visit those places."

"They have my son," said Calder, still glaring at the city. "Once I have him, you can have Carleon, and all the bones inside."

Stand-i'-the-Barrows smiled wider. "That is acceptable."

Clover glanced over at Sholla and found her staring back, unable to hide her horror. "You stay here wi' Flick," he muttered.

"Chief, I—"

"Stay here," he said, looking her in the eye.

"Don't worry," said Downside. "I'll look after 'em."

"What a comfort." Clover clambered up onto the horse he was borrowing. He found he liked it even less than he remembered. You forget how bloody high horses are. And it turned all the way around while he was leaning down to grab the reins.

Black Calder was having his own troubles getting mounted. He had to bounce a couple of times before he could haul himself into the saddle. He looked weak when he got there, and grey, and grim. Not much left of the handsome joker who nicked the North from under everyone's noses. A man who'd lasted past his time. A man dragged back for one fight too many.

But then, one is one too many.

Clover had a low feeling as he rode out towards Carleon. As he frowned to the left, towards the great mass of Crinna bastards working themselves up for the bone harvest. As he frowned to the right, watching Calder's Carls bring their many-coloured shield-wall forward across the sun-splashed fields. As he frowned straight ahead, towards the black battlements above the city's gate. A feeling this'd all end badly.

But then, if you leave it long enough, what doesn't end badly?

Rikke took a deep breath. By the dead, she needed to piss. She'd gone not long ago, but now she felt like she was bursting. Wouldn't look too clever, that fearsome witch with the Long Eye, pissing herself on the battlements in full view of her two worst enemies and a hostile army. Still, her da had always said he near pissed himself in every fight. Hadn't stopped him winning most of his.

"Here we go, then." And she twisted her face into that knowing smile and swaggered up to the parapet. The very spot where the Bloody-Nine killed Bethod. Might be the stones she propped her hands on were the ones the first King of the Northmen got his brains smashed out on. She hoped the significance wasn't lost on anyone as she leaned over, grinning down at the two-dozen riders before the gates.

Calder's sign was there, red circle on black, and other famous standards, too. She spotted Jonas Clover loitering near the back. He looked troubled, and Rikke hardly blamed him. He was in some troubling company. No missing the bastards from beyond the Crinna. They were the ones with the paint and the bones. One in particular, grey-haired, grey-faced, grey eyes fixed on her, covered with bones head to toe, his helmet with the skull of some great horned animal on it. And in front of him, on a black horse, a lean man with a sharp face and a fine black fur about his shoulders.

"Black Calder!" she called. "Welcome back to Carleon!"

His mount was restless and he reined it savagely around, keeping his frown fixed on her all the while. "Rikke o' the Long Eye!"

She tapped at her face. "The only one I've got. Who's your clown?"

"Clown?"

"The joker with all the bones."

"I am Stand-i'-the-Barrows, girl! Chieftain of a Hundred Tribes, lord of all the fen country from the Crinna to the sea, master of ten thousand spears! I am here to gather bones for my great barrow. Bones of man and woman, wolf and hawk. Bones of girl and boy, lamb and foal. Perhaps I will see how many bones I can cut from your body while you still live. It is a favoured pastime of mine."

There was a silence, a cold wind blowing up, shaking the budding trees in the distance and sighing across the walls of Carleon. Rikke stuck her little finger in her ear, twisted it, pulled it out, examined the results and flicked them away. "Not very funny, is he?" she said.

"*I'm* funnier," said Shivers.

"You're funny 'cause no one expects laughs from a man with a metal eye, though." She waved down at Stand-i'-the-Barrows. "If you're going to wear the motley you'd better be ready for fun! But let's not drag this out, I've got my monthly bleed on and could do with changing my cloth. If gore's your thing I can toss you down the old one."

Stand-i'-the-Barrows curled back his lips to spit some answer but Calder got in first. "Our mutual friend, Jonas Clover—"

"I'm not sure Jonas Clover's anyone's friend but his own," said Rikke.

The man in question gave a sheepish grin. "Just trying to get through the day is all."

"He tells me you're willing to make a trade," called Calder. "My son for half the North. That true?"

"Could be." Rikke leaned on the parapet, arms crossed, hands flopping, necklace dangling, and cast an eye over all those men spreading out around Carleon. "But you brought an awful lot of friends through an awful lot of mud just so we could strike a bargain."

"My father always said, 'Speak by all means, but the words of an armed man ring that much sweeter.' Thought I'd make my words ring as sweetly as I could."

"They do say you were known for charming the ladies once. Bring the Great Wolf where his da can see him!"

Shivers had Stour under one arm, holding him up and dragging him forwards at once, his hands tied behind him and his bare feet scuffing uselessly. He'd lost half his weight and all his pride, lips cracked, eyes sunken, squinting up at the sun like he'd never seen it before. Hadn't been out of that cage in Skarling's Hall for months, so the sky was coming as quite the shock to him.

"Here he is!" called Rikke as Shivers hauled Stour up to the parapet where the whole valley could get a good look. "The grandson of Bethod! The bane of Scale Ironhand! The King of the Northmen in all his glory! Stour Nightfall!"

And she thrust out an arm towards the ill-smelling cripple who was once the terror of the North. There was a pause while those below took in the state of him and wondered if it could truly be the same man.

Seemed like there might be some damp glinting in Calder's eyes, but maybe it was the wind. "You all right, son?" he croaked out.

"They cut my legs." And there was a tearful whine in Stour's voice that made Rikke think of a child complaining over getting the smallest slice of cake. "They cut my legs." She felt, of all things, a scratch of guilt, and had to remind herself of all the scores she had against him.

"Well, he said he'd see me fucked by pigs," called Rikke. "Break what they love, he said! I reckon he's got off lightly."

Even at this distance she could see Calder grinding his teeth. "Carleon's yours," he growled. "Now cut him free and send him down."

"Well, I've got no more use for him." Rikke snapped her fingers at Shivers. "Daresay you've a knife, don't you?"

"You can never have too many." He pulled one out, the work-polished handle towards her. Not a big one. But a small blade can do the job, more often than not. "Sure you don't want me to do it?" he asked, in that husky whisper.

Rikke had seen this moment. Knew how it'd go. What came after was the question. She gently shook her head. "My father would've said there are some things a leader has to do themselves."

"Just one o' you get on and do it," snarled Stour over his shoulder, jerking his tied hands towards her.

"Patience, Great Wolf." And she plucked the knife from Shivers' hand. She'd seen this come, knew it had to come, but even so, it wasn't easy. Had to make of her heart a stone, like Isern always told her, even if her mouth was dry as dust and there was chill sweat on her back and the knife weighed like an anvil. She reached out, and took one of Stour's wrists, and carefully sawed through the ropes that bound him.

He grinned a twisted grin. "Been waiting for this a while."

She forced herself to grin back. "Oh, me, too." And she stabbed him in the throat. The blade hardly made a sound as it punched into the crosspiece where his neck met his shoulder, and straight out again along with a spurt of blood that soaked her hand. Shocked her, how hot it was.

He flinched, first, with a little gasp, like he'd been bee-stung. He stared at her, wet eyes wide, slack face all red-speckled from the bubbling wound.

"Blith," he said, drooling blood down his dirty shirt.

Rikke looked up at Shivers, and her hand was shaking but her voice was steady. "Send him down, then."

"Right y'are." And Shivers took one step and shoved the Great Wolf over the parapet.

*

Clover had been there, when the Bloody-Nine fought the Feared. Before he won the name Steepfield, even. Long before he lost it. He'd held a shield at the duel. He'd watched Bethod flung from the walls. Now he watched Bethod's grandson flung from about the same place, and crash down in about the same place, crumpled in the wet grass where the Circle had been marked out that day.

Blood spattered Stand-i'-the-Barrows' horse, but it hardly even twitched. Probably good and used to flying gore. Stour lay with his arms spread wide as if greeting his father, but with his head twisted all the way around, his ruined legs buckled under him and his blood spilling black into the green grass. Till a few moments ago he'd been the future of the North. Now he was mud. A stern lesson for anyone harbouring high ambitions.

Calder stared down, mouth hanging open, then up at the gatehouse, where Rikke and Shivers were black figures against the bright sky.

"Kill them!" he screamed, face twisting. "Kill them all!"

If anyone had asked him, Clover would've said there was less than no chance this'd be settled with talk. But you never realise how much hope you're holding till it gets knifed and thrown off a roof.

"See you soon!" Rikke shrieked after them, stabbing at the sky with her bloody dagger. So maybe she wasn't clever, and had seen nothing with her Long Eye at all, but was just the maddest of the whole crowd, and had doomed herself and everyone who followed her. Probably Clover, too, who'd done nothing but try to steer a safe course through a tempest of other men's making.

He'd had trouble controlling his horse at a walk. At a bone-rattling gallop away from the walls in the midst of a couple of dozen other barging, scraping, eye-rolling beasts he was helpless. He barely clung on, gripping with his aching legs, reins flapping everywhere. There were arrows falling around them, flickering down into the grass. His shoulders were itching, sure he was about to get a shaft right in the back. One of Stand-i'-the-Barrows' savages did, long hair tangled around his painted face as he toppled screaming from his horse. There's the big problem with bones as armour. They don't bloody work.

Clover had never been more grateful to reach a treeline in his life, managed to slow his horse by dragging on the reins, then nearly set it trotting back towards the walls, probably would've if Sholla hadn't grabbed the bridle. He slithered from the saddle and stood there with his hands on his trembling knees, just breathing.

"You all right?" Sholla asked him.

"By the dead," he croaked, holding on to her arm as he straightened up. Still felt dizzy. "I think I nearly shit myself."

"What the hell happened?"

"What happened is..." Clover narrowed his eyes towards the walls of Carleon, like a man wincing into a storm. "I was hoping I'd never have to fight in another battle." Black Calder's men had started forwards. Not the most eager of charges, after all the shit they'd waded through to get here. But they'd started forwards even so. Clover gave a sigh, right from his guts. "But there's hopes for you."

# The Little People

Corleth had been sure she had everything tied up neat. She'd known exactly how it'd turn out. Couldn't have known better if she'd seen it with the Long Eye herself.

Then Rikke stabbed Stour in the neck and pushed him off the gate-house. So now there'd be a battle, then there'd be a sack, and who could say how the hell that'd end? Of a sudden, everyone's life was balanced on the brink, including hers. Hard to see how anything could've been less tied up than this.

All around the city, Calder's men were surging towards the walls. Thousands of 'em. Tattered mobs, muddy and messy with metal glinting in the midst, torn standards snatched by the wind, dozens of ladders among 'em, their bloodthirsty cries echoing across the valley. Men on the walls bent their bows, sent arrows flickering out into the oncoming crowd. From where she stood, clinging to the pole of Rikke's standard, Corleth saw a couple fall. Far too few to make any difference.

She'd been sure she had everything tied up neat. Could pick Rikke's every move. Knew she was too soft, too trusting. But there was naught soft about her now, her grin dotted with Stour's blood, that one eye starting from her tattooed face and fixed on Corleth. Staring at her, and smiling, that bloody knife loose in her hand and Caul Shivers huge and craggy beside her. And Corleth got this bad feeling in her stomach, and not the moon pains.

Shafts were flying the other way now, some on fire. Dropping in the town, clattering from the slate roofs. Corleth hunched down, not too keen on being arrow-pricked. She thought she could smell smoke. Shouting everywhere. Panic everywhere. Except here on the gatehouse roof. Except in Rikke's face.

"Your granny gets a lot o' visitors," she said.

"What?"

"Isern-i-Phail's a suspicious sort. Maybe that's what happens when you've a madman for a father and no mother but the moon. She took against you right off. So she set some folk to watch your granny and, phew." Rikke puffed out her cheeks. "They're in and out of her house like it's a brothel."

"Folk come for advice." Corleth tried to keep her voice level, no mean feat in the midst of a battle. "They hold her in high regard—"

"Three brothers in particular. They get *lots* of advice."

"Once a week," said Shivers, frowning down at Corleth. With his hair bound back to show the full scale of his scar he looked a monster, that metal eye flashing as the sun peeped through the clouds. How had she ever got halfway used to it? She couldn't stop her eyes flitting about. Lot of hard faces up on that roof now and, given there was a battle unfolding in the other direction, a lot of 'em pointed at her.

"And they're brewers, you know, these brothers," Rikke was saying, "so they head out on carts all over. There's one place their ale is *very* much appreciated."

"Currahome," grunted Shivers.

"Hold on, though." Rikke frowned. "Who do I know lives in Currahome? It's someone whose son I just killed. Name's on the tip o' my tongue..."

"Black Calder?"

Rikke's tattooed face lit up. "*That* is the bastard."

Corleth's body was tensed to run, but there was nowhere to go. They were setting ladders, outside the walls. She could see a couple swung up against the parapet, men struggling to shove 'em back down.

Rikke was blathering away like there was no danger at all. "Last time one o' those brothers headed up to Currahome, we stopped him 'fore he got there, and the strangest thing...his kegs were all empty."

"Very disappointing," said Shivers. "If you like ale."

"And who doesn't? Must've been some other cargo he was taking up there. He didn't want to say what. But men tell Caul Shivers things they wouldn't tell their own mothers." Rikke clapped him fondly on the arm. "It's that pretty metal eye of his, maybe."

Shivers shrugged. "That or I just won't stop cutting 'em."

"Aye, maybe it's that. Do you know what his cargo was?"

Corleth licked her lips. This wasn't tied up neat at all. This was all coming unravelled. "How would I know?" she whispered.

"'Cause you gave it to him, silly!"

And Corleth felt herself caught from behind. Caught and held, the standard clattering on the stones. She struggled, more of an instinct than any real effort to get free, but one man had her left arm and another her

295

right and a third caught her around the neck and held a dagger to her throat, and the cold brush of steel against her skin made her go slack as rags.

"Secrets," said Rikke, walking closer, the pupil of her Long Eye yawning huge, the other just a blind pinprick. "*That* was the cargo. What we're doing up here. How many men there are. Who's fallen out with who. What I'm saying. What I'm thinking. Or what you think I'm thinking, anyway, which might not be *quite* the same thing. You told granny, and granny told the brothers, and the brothers toddled up to Currahome on their fucking empty ale cart and told Black Calder all about it."

By the dead, not far away down the wall some of Calder's men had made it to the top, blades twinkling as they struggled. Couldn't be long, now, till the city fell. Too long for Corleth, though, maybe.

There was no point clinging to the lie. They'd found her out long before. "Look," she said, voice wobbling, "I can talk to Calder, after the battle's done, make some kind o' deal—"

"After it's done?" Rikke looked at her like she was the one who'd lost her reason. "Why would I need your help then? After it's done, Calder'll be begging to talk to me."

Corleth blinked at her. "You can't win!"

"I've heard that before."

"You're way outnumbered! You chased all your friends away!"

"Did I?" Rikke tapped the tattoo on her cheek. "Or did I see all this coming, and it's just the way I wanted it?"

Corleth had thought she had everything tied up neat. Now it looked like she was the one who'd been tied up all along. "You're mad," she whispered.

"I've heard that before, too! But mad's just a different way of seeing things. Shivers, you reckon it's time for a toot on that horn o' yours?"

Shivers looked out at the fighting like Corleth's granny looking at the soup, judging whether it was the right moment to toss in the carrots. "Aye," he said, one loose strand of grey hair flicking around his frown with the wind, "rude to keep everyone waiting." And he raised his horn to his lips and gave a great blast.

"What's happening?" muttered Hardbread, trying to get a look through the trees. But all he could see was more trees. Distant twinkle of daylight, maybe, between the trunks, through the leaves. But the whole idea was being far enough into the woods they wouldn't be seen. And that meant, pretty much by definition, not seeing much themselves.

"Calder's attacking, I reckon," muttered Brandal, chewing at his thumb-nail.

"Yes, that, I know *that*, I can bloody hear it!" A distant clamour of voices, echoing lazily from far off. Like a fair in the next valley. "But *other* than that, I mean."

Damn, he was nervous. Aside from a couple of Calder's scouts they'd captured and another one they'd shot as he rode away, they'd seen no action. It seemed a mad plan. It had seemed a mad plan all along. No way a man sharp as Black Calder would fall for it. But Rikke had just nodded and tapped her cheek in that knowing way and said, *I've seen it*. It couldn't be denied that she'd seen her way to her father's bench in Uffrith. It couldn't be denied that she'd seen her way to Skarling's Chair in Carleon. That had all seemed mad, too. Who knew what was sane any more? Certainly not Hardbread. And, frankly, it would've taken a braver man than him to tell her no.

But that didn't mean he wasn't nervous. Stomach churning away. He smothered a burp, rubbed at his breastbone where the sore fire seemed to burn up his throat. By the dead, if they waited much longer he'd need to shit again. That'd be just his luck, to get the call while he was squatting in the brush, trousers down.

"What the fuck's—"

And he heard the horn. A long, low, throbbing blast, echoing about the valley. Hardbread had been waiting for it for hours. Thinking of it for days. He'd dreamed of it in his fitful sleep the night before. But somehow when it came it caught him by total surprise.

"By the dead!" He scrambled to his feet, winced at a sharp twinge through his stiff ankle, near fell over and half-swallowed his tongue as he bellowed the order. "That's it!" And he fumbled his sword out and held it high. "Charge!"

There was a great rattle, a great clatter, a great cry as all around him men jumped to their feet and started rushing through the woods.

Hardbread hobbled along for a moment. Bloody hell, his knees, his hips, he was creaking like a wooden man from squatting in the cold damp for hours. He had to stop, hold on to Brandal's shoulder while he tried to shake some life into his legs and men surged past him towards the daylight.

"There we go!" And he set to running again. More of a jog, being honest, it was tough through the trees. Broken ground and fallen branches and tree roots ready to trip you. He was wheezing as he burst from the woods and heard the noise, far louder, far closer, far harsher.

His eyes were weaker than they once were and had tears in 'em from the wind of running, and he had to squint into the brightness, down towards Carleon. Calder's men, crawling in the fields around the city. Swarms of the bastards. They were at the walls already, ladders up, arrows flitting this way and that.

"By the dead," he muttered.

It had seemed a mad plan, but it looked very much as if Calder had fallen for it, and fallen hard. The enemy had their arses stuck right out, trapped between Hardbread's men and the walls.

"Charge!" he roared, though his voice was weak from the effort and the wind soon snatched it away and everyone was charging anyway, men bounding from the trees and into the open, pouring down the hillside. He set off again, Brandal beside him with the standard held high. More of an amble than a run, being honest, it was tough outside the trees. Tough on the knees, the uneven ground on the ploughed field jolting him, making his teeth rattle, the sun flashing and flickering at him as the clouds rushed overhead. Couldn't they have found a nice smooth stretch o' road to charge down?

He tottered to a halt, one hand propped on his thigh and his sword dangling from the other. Damn it, he was blown. There'd been a time he could run for hours. Fastest runner in Uffrith. Used to be sent running over the fells with messages. Thinking on it, though, that had been forty years ago.

"All right, Chief?" asked Brandal, thumping Hardbread's standard into the turf beside him. "You want some water?" And he offered out a flask.

"Aye." Hardbread burped, spat, took the flask and a swig and a swallow. "By the dead, but it's a young man's game, this."

"What is?" asked Brandal.

"War, what d'you think?"

"Running, maybe?"

"Aye, well, the two are not unconnected." Hardbread burped again, and was nearly sick, but managed to swallow it. "The old man's job is to get the young bastards in the right place." He propped his hands on his hips, watched the proud warriors of Uffrith pouring down the long slope ahead of him towards the city. "And from that point of view...it has to be said...I feel rather pleased wi' my old self." He felt the grin spreading across his face. Spent so many years scared of losing he'd forgot how fine it felt to win. "All right, Brandal, hoist that standard up, lad, we can't dawdle. There's a battle to fight!"

*

"Up you go, you fucker!" roared Flatstone, slapping one man on the back and sending him up the ladder. "Get up there, you bastard!" Thumping the next man on the shoulder soon as there were a few rungs free. "Climb, you shit, climb!" Slapping the next man across his arse. They were getting to the walls way too slow, choked up on the broken ground outside the city, arrows flitting down among 'em. Had to push on. Had to throw 'em forward.

"Go, damn you! Go!" And he swung onto the ladder himself and started climbing.

The bastards at the top have all the advantages—fresh, and fed, and dry, and with the height and the parapet—so you've got to swarm 'em, storm 'em, fling men at 'em, care nothing for your losses. But you can't go *too* fast. Then you'll slip, fall, knock off the men below. You'll run out of puff, so you can't fight if you do get to the top. And Flatstone's men were mostly sick and all tired. A bastard of a march down from Currahome, through the thaw. One o' the worst he'd ever seen, and he'd seen some bad ones.

He heard a scream as someone fell from the next ladder down. He took no notice. Nothing to be done. He fixed on the stones in front of his face, kept 'em moving past.

Soon enough he was breathing hard, but it weren't the first time Flatstone climbed a ladder, and he knew his business. Nice and steady, feet on the rungs, one by one, hands on the rails, sliding smoothly, though these ladders hadn't been made too well, and not from the best timber, all a bit rushed, and he was picking up splinters. Still, he'd have worse'n splinters if they didn't get up there in numbers. Once you've pushed the first men onto the walls, you owe it to 'em to fling more up there and smash through.

"Go, damn you!" he roared at no one in particular. The men below, the men above. "Go!"

More cries. Couldn't stop himself glancing sideways. Saw a ladder tipping back. Saw the man at the top clutching at nothing, eyes wide with horror. Saw another dropping, arms flailing, giving a great breathy squeal. Flatstone stuck to the stones in front of his face. Kept climbing. Nice and steady.

And suddenly he was up. Hauled himself over the parapet and dropped down on the other side, Carleon spread out ahead, a hill of crooked streets and grey roofs with Skarling's Hall at the top. He pulled his axe from his belt, swung his shield from his back. Not a moment too soon. Arrows flickered from the windows of a building twenty strides away.

One clattered against his shield. Another bounced from a man's helmet just beside him. Another found its mark and someone fell, screaming, barged into someone else, knocked him from the walkway to topple into the town, wriggling in the air.

Fires were burning. He could smell it. Smoke smudging the sky. Scratch of it in his throat as he struggled to catch his breath. Burning arrows shot overhead. There were men fighting everywhere. Metal clashed as his Carls flooded up the ladders and over the parapet. A grim strain as men struggled to shove back the defenders, shields scraping on shields, boots slipping and sliding in blood, tripping on bodies.

"Yes!" bellowed Flatstone, pointing north with his axe. Above the writhing men he could see the gatehouse Stour had fallen from. The gatehouse where that witch must be. They'd captured a good thirty strides of wall, were pushing the defenders back. "Push on! Drive 'em! Kill 'em!" There was a Thrall sitting against the parapet, dead no doubt, but Flatstone split his head with his axe. No way he could make it through the press to the fighting, not yet, but it helped to get your weapon red, get your face red, get your hands red, set the tone for what would come later. "Kill the—"

"Chief!" someone roared in his ear, plucking at his shoulder. "Chief!"

"Fucking *what?*" Flatstone bellowed, spinning about, and saw straight away what. A great mass of men were pouring down the long slope to the south of town. Towards the walls Flatstone and his men had just climbed. A tide of coloured shields and twinkling mail. Reinforcements! Come to help him storm the city! He felt a rare smile crack his lips.

Then he saw the standards streaming with the wind. Then he recognised 'em. "What the…"

He'd fought some o' those bastards at Red Hill. Seen those signs bobbing on the broken wall of the ruined fort there, where the Dogman made his stand. Now here they were, charging right at his rear.

"Where'd those bastards come from?" he gasped.

"The south, I reckon—"

"I can see that, you fool!"

"They must've had men hanging back."

"You fucking *think?*"

Flatstone stared wildly about, but now there was trouble ahead as well. Carls spilling from buildings in the town, surging up the steps to bolster the men fighting on the walkways.

"Fuck," he whispered.

They had to push north, link up with the rest o' Calder's men, make a fight of it on the walls and in the fields outside the city. They'd been caught off balance, maybe, but they still had the numbers.

He leaned over the parapet. "Get up here!" he bellowed at the men on the ladders, at the men at the foot of the ladders, at the men rushing to join 'em, some of 'em realising what was coming up behind and already scattering. "Push north!" he roared at the men already up, pointing towards the gatehouse. He thought he could see that witch on the roof, the bright red of her cloak, which meant the tall bastard beside her was Caul Shivers, sun glinting an instant on his metal eye. "The man who brings me that witch's head gets its weight in silver!" he roared.

He'd been thinking about gold, but even at a time like this you have to get value for money.

They were fighting, up on the wall. Ignet could see 'em, peeking around the corner of her house. Something was burning. She could smell it. Like burned cakes.

She stared wi' wide eyes, heart thumping. She saw a man kill another, up there on the walkway. Stab him with a spear. He fell, and tumbled onto a roof not far away, and slid down, his leg dangling from the thatched eaves.

"Get inside, Ignet!" screeched her mother, catching her wrist and dragging her in. Her da flung the door shut. Shut it and double-bolted it.

Ignet had always thought how strong those bolts looked, how heavy. Now they seemed spindly little sticks of iron to keep all those furious warriors out o' the house.

She shrank into the corner. She could still hear the fighting. The walls had always looked so huge, but they didn't any more. Would they come over? Would they get into the town? Would they start beating on the door?

She stared at the bolts, her shoulders up around her ears, waiting for them to jump and rattle in the brackets.

"What happens if Rikke wins?" asked her ma.

Her da just stared.

"What happens if she loses?" asked her ma.

Her da numbly shook his head.

"What do we do?" her ma screamed, clutching her da by his wrists.

"What can we do?" he muttered at her.

Ignet crawled under the table and put her hands over her head. Outside, deep and throbbing, she heard that horn blow again.

*

"Come on, come on," muttered the Nail, eyes fixed on the crest of the hill, grass thrashing in the wind. "Come on, come on, come on..."

He was desperate to go. Burning to fight. He could feel the eagerness of the men around him, the men behind him, tensed like drawn bows, straining like dogs at the leash. He could hear the battle joined, the joyous steel and laughter music of it beyond the little rise. He couldn't hold back, and he wriggled up to the crest, up to the waving grass, and peeked over, tongue-tip wedged between his bared teeth, down into the valley.

Over on the left—Crinna bastards, bones-and-hides men, up at the walls of Carleon. Straight ahead—Black Calder's Carls, with ladders to the stones. Over on his right—Hardbread's men had made it down to the city, fighting in the fields, fighting up on the walls, and he couldn't help a little giggle.

So Rikke's plan had worked. Seemed a mad plan, when she whispered it to him, her eyes in the darkness, the one that saw nothing and the one that saw too much, her breath hot on his face and smelling pleasantly of ale. Seemed a mad plan, but such a bold one he couldn't say no. Never even thought of saying no. Didn't know how he'd ever say no to her.

She was honest and wise and beautiful and strange and knew things no one else knew and said things no one else would've dared to and made him laugh when no one else could. He'd never met a woman like her. There weren't any others.

"Come on, come on," he whispered. "*Come* on."

He'd heard of love but never thought it was anything for him to worry about. But maybe this was love, this having of a woman always at the back of your mind. This feeling that any time not with her was time wasted. This aching in him to get back into her bed.

The memory of her kicking her trousers off, sitting in Skarling's Chair with her eyes on him and her legs open, would get him hard at all the wrong times. By the dead, he was getting hard right now, lying on the damp hilltop looking down at a battle.

But this was no day for lovers' thoughts. This was a red day for red thoughts and red deeds. Rikke needed him, and the Great Leveller would pay a red visit to any man who put himself between them.

"Come *on*, come *on*, come *on*, come—"

He was up and sprinting before the echoes of Shivers' second blast even faded, flying down the sedge-patched hillside.

He'd never been one for war cries. Why tell your enemy where you are? They'll learn soon enough.

Surprise, that's the key. Whether you're fighting one man or a thousand or ten thousand. The more you're fighting, the more important it becomes, 'cause shock spreads faster'n plague, faster'n fire, and turns the bravest into cowards.

So he rushed up silent as winter, silent as sickness. He knew the others were with him. His brothers, his cousins, every man he could gather, trekked the long, cold road back from the West Valleys in secret darkness to be here.

The baggage was ahead. Calder's soft underbelly. The dirty horses and the mud-caked wagons that held the supplies. The smiths and the cooks. The women and the children who slogged after the men. Killing the fighters was cutting off the fingers, but hitting the baggage was cutting out the guts. And the Nail felt the fierce smile spread across his face, the fierce fire burning through his limbs, stronger and stronger with every stride.

Might be he loved Rikke, but battle was his oldest love, his first love. That was who he was and who he'd always be.

There were a few guards, but most were already running. He could hear their desperate cries, tugging him on. Women, too, shrieking and wailing. There was a fighter at the front, in bright mail with a bright spear, trying to turn his men, to form a wobbly shield-wall, but they weren't halfway there. Far too late and far too few. The Nail ran right for him, faster'n ever, wind in his face. He always went at the hardest-looking bastard he could find. Bring down their toughest, break the rest.

The Nail was on him. Hit his shield with his axe, staggered him with the force of it, chopped with his sword and it caught the rim, struck a spark, jolted in his hand, a lovely jolt. The breath sawed at his chest, ripped up his throat, hissed through his fixed smile, his clenched teeth. He hacked away, drove the man back into a crouch then caught his leg with his sword and made him howl. Blood spattered.

The Nail dodged his desperate spear-thrust, hooked his wobbling shield down with his axe, stabbed with his sword, stabbed in the open face of his helmet. He fell back, blood pouring from his split mouth. He was trying to say something but all he could say was blood and that was eloquence enough, in its way. The eloquence o' the battlefield.

"Kill 'em all!" screamed the Nail, since there was no need for surprise any longer, just for fury, and he stomped on that warrior's head as he ran on, trampled him into the mud. Others around him, swinging, hacking, shrieking, laughing, dodging between the wagons, springing around the snorting, tramping horses. Flowing through the baggage like a red flood. All drunk on battle. All mad on it.

He slipped past a cart up on blocks to have its wheel changed and a mud-covered man came slithering out from under it, sobbing and whimpering. Must've been hiding there, flushed out by someone else.

"Hello," said the Nail, already swinging as the man twisted about, wet eyes staring. Caught his neck just right and took his head spinning off and it clonked against the side of the cart. Blood sprayed the horse half-harnessed in the traces and it bucked, kicked out and set off at a wild, straining canter, dragging the cart jolting after on one wheel, barrels and boxes bouncing from the back, catching a tent and ripping it up, dragging it after like the train on a bride's dress, torn clothes and dented pots and bent spoons tumbling out and scattered in its wake through the ripped-up grass.

Good plunder here, good takings. A tent went up in flames as it fell in a fire. Stink of smoke and fear. The Nail watched a boy run a few steps, off balance, fall, scramble up and totter a few steps, fall again, get up, fall again. Calder's men had been lazy, foolish, weary from their march and fixed on the city ahead. Now they scattered like a flock of crows and he was the hawk among 'em.

The Nail hacked someone in an apron in the back with his axe, made him scream, knocked him on his face, one of his boots flying off. Someone smiled as he smashed a man's head against the corner of a cart. He slashed another across the backs of the legs and brought him down, rolling over and over. Someone was bashing a wooden chest open with a hammer, joyful splinters flying. He hacked his axe into the back of a man's head and left him staggering around with a big piece of his skull hanging off, and bounded on with a delighted whoop, past some woman sat limp and staring in the grass, shocked tears tracking her blood-streaked face. Someone laughed as they stomped another's face into the mud. He could hear his brothers, his cousins, his men, whooping and hacking and cheering. He dodged a desperate swing of a sword, hacked at the arm that held it, blood flying, hacked again, barged the man out of his way, hacked at him again as he fell, missed and stumbled on, not caring.

The Nail clenched his jaw, fixing his eyes on the city. More men ahead, and not running so easily. Starting to gather into something like a line, facing away from Carleon. Facing him. He took a ripping breath, and blew out blood, and smiled wider than ever. The easy killing was done.

Now came the hard killing.

"Make a line!" roared Trapper.

He'd been heading for the walls, steeling himself for the climb, when he'd seen the men sweep down from the south. Now men were pouring into their rear from the west as well. Black Calder had been caught with his fucking trousers down and no mistake, and they all had their arses out with him.

"Make a fucking line!" he snarled, catching a running man by the shoulder.

"*You* make a line!" A fist caught him on the side of the jaw, knocked him stumbling.

He couldn't even tell who'd thrown it. He had no more'n a score, all of 'em facing different ways, staring numbly at the chaos. He had to drag 'em into place, but he hardly knew which way the line should face. Towards the city, or away?

"What do we do?" someone whimpered.

There were enemies everywhere. Trapper wasn't sure who they were. Where they'd come from. That witch Rikke must've witched 'em up out o' hell. They'd laughed at the Long Eye, back in Currahome. No one was laughing now.

"Shields, you fucks!"

They stared at him with wet, wide, terrified eyes. A horse charged past, dragging the shattered remains of a wagon. A man gave a great squeal, an arrow in his side. Another was on his knees, clutching, clutching, hands clamped to his bloody face. "I can't see, I can't see!"

"Shields!" roared Trapper, not knowing what more he could do than shout. But his men were already running. Even the ones he'd gathered. The little knot flying apart in every direction, tossing down their weapons. Trapper would've run, too, if he could've seen anywhere to run to.

Men were charging at him. Cutting, hacking, driving running figures ahead of them. At the front was a tall, lean bastard with an axe and a sword and a shock of pale hair, his snarling devil's face all dashed with red.

By the dead, the Nail. That mad bastard was supposed to be miles away. Trapper dropped his shield.

There was nowhere to run to.

He ran anyway.

Sholla had thought they'd be far from the fighting on this little hillock in the eaves of the woods. A nice tump with a big flat rock sunk into the lush green on top, a perfect spot to sit and shave some cheese on a happier day. Here they'd be safe, and could get a good view of the carnage, and a sound lesson in why battles are things best avoided.

She'd watched Calder's men and the Crinna bastards move forwards, set their ladders, start to climb. Then everything had fallen apart. First what looked like men of Uffrith had come pouring down from the far hills to the south, then what looked like men of the West Valleys had swept in from the west, ripping through the baggage, splitting Calder's forces in half. Some of 'em were pressing in not too far from where Sholla and Flick were standing.

There's the trouble with avoiding battles. Sometimes they reach out and find you anyway.

Calder's guards had made a ring of shields about the top of the hillock, and on the crest beside the flat stone where Calder's standard was set—the same sign Bethod used to fight under. The great man himself stood in its shadow, arms grimly folded, watching his army and all his hopes crumble.

Clover lurked not far off in that hunched way of his, like he was trying to fade out o' sight. Sholla was glad he was there, though she didn't let it show. She liked Clover. He was a reasonably good chief. He was a reasonably good man. And that was about as good as chiefs and men got, in her experience.

"You all right?" she asked him, her bow in one hand and an arrow in the other so she could at least look like she might be some help.

"Thus far. You?"

"Apart from…all this." And she waved the arrow towards the furious fight not a hundred strides off now. "Where did they come from?"

"The West Valleys, I reckon. The Nail and his boys. Seems he didn't fall out with Rikke after all." Clover rubbed his jaw with something close to admiration. "Reckon she laid a smart trap and we've all blundered into it. *Knew* I should've stuck with her." He put a hand on Sholla's shoulder, leaning close. "Might be a good move for you and Flick to head into the woods." There were a lot of other folk heading into the woods. Heading as fast as their legs'd carry 'em. Most of Clover's boys had already melted away. It was about what their chief would've done, after all.

"What about you?" muttered Sholla.

Clover glanced sideways at Calder. "I've a sense our chief would rather I remained."

"I want to stay," said Flick, weighing his sword in his hand.

"No, you don't," said Clover, simply. "Here's your last lesson. Winning battles is bad enough. Never hang around to see one lost."

Sholla liked Clover. But nowhere near enough to die for him. She gave him a nod, shrugged her bow over her shoulder, then caught Flick by the shirt and dragged him off towards the trees, arrow still clutched in her sweaty hand.

Downside was watching it all with his teeth angrily bared as they passed, turning the haft of his axe around and around in his hand. Plain he couldn't wait to get stuck into the mess, the mad bastard.

Sholla wouldn't miss him.

"When's our moment to be?" grunted Scenn, frowning through the wind-shook greenery towards the battle. Not that you could miss the battle, if you had your eyes open.

'Twas a vast battle. Ten battles put together. Biggest he ever saw by far. Bigger'n any his father saw, in spite of all his bloated boasting, which had been one o' the man's many failings. His father once claimed he killed two hundred men at Yarnvost and Scenn later learned there'd only been a hundred with both sides put together. Thinking of his father made him smile. He'd hated that fat bastard, but he'd been quite the laugh in the right mood. Beloved of the moon, he'd been. Beloved of the moon, and laughing with the moon now, no doubt, as they smiled down fondly on the slaughter.

His sister Isern did not smile fondly. But then she never did. One of *her* many failings. "When the horn next blows," she said, while picking her nose.

"Sure we haven't missed it?"

"Caul Shivers knows what to do with a horn." And she barked out a cackle. "Believe me. Learned it in Styria, he said."

Scenn thought that must be a joke, but he didn't really get it. Which, he had to confess, was one of *his* many failings. "There's good work being done and I itch for my part in it." He held up the hammer and spun it about in his fist, smiling upon the many scars on its heavy head. "Our father's hammer is hungry."

"It's a bloody hammer," said Isern, flicking the results of her nose-picking away among the leaf-rot. "It feels no hunger."

"Well, his axe is hungry, then," said Scofen, holding up the axe, no less battle-weathered.

"Likewise the axe. Might as well say his spear's sleepy." And Isern gave it a shake. "Load o' nonsense. They're wood and metal and have no feelings."

"But I want to get *at* these painted bastards!" snarled Scofen, rubbing impatiently at the tattoos on his face. To start on *his* failings would've kept the lot of them busy all day.

"You'll get your chance," said Isern.

And there was the horn, throbbing through the roots o' the trees and giving Scenn a tickle in his toes.

"There it is!" called Scofen. "It's *time!*"

Scenn grinned wide at his sister. "Da would've fucking *loved* this!"

"Like I care what that bastard loved." She leaped atop a rock, holding high their father's spear, her skirts bound right up and the knotty sinews bulging from her bare legs. "Let's give these Crinna sheepfuckers a fucking they'll not forget!"

With those rousing words still ringing, she sprang away and off they tumbled after, bursting from the trees and down the slope towards the grey city, the good wind rushing about them and their war-songs echoing around the valley.

"For the moon!" someone wailed.

"For the hills!" someone else.

"For Crummock-i-Phail!" roared Scenn.

At his back were any of the hillfolk who'd fancied a battle—which, o' course, was pretty much the full tally, scoured from every cranny in the mountains. They'd been offered a chance to fight, which they loved, and to fight Black Calder, who they hated almost as much as they'd hated Bethod, and also Rikke had offered two rich valleys to those who fought, and though some might think the hillmen lived simple lives, in truth they were as greedy as anyone, if not a little more so.

The Crinna bastards were spread out ahead in a spiked and painted line. Horrible savages, they were, all pierced and puckered and covered in bloody bones. They'd seen what had happened to their friends. Had time to shift away from the city, wheel to face the Nail and his boys as they poured down from the west. But they had no idea Crummock-i-Phail's children were coming on 'em from the north, and the ones at the near end spun about white-eyed, scattered wailing and head-clutching as the hillmen crashed into 'em.

Scenn saw Isern spit one through the face. Saw Scofen hack another's chest open with their father's axe, his red insides popping out. There was a silly bastard with a silly helmet made from jawbones and Scenn dropped his father's hammer on it like a falling boulder and crushed his head into his shoulders in a great fountain of blood.

Smashing left and right, he was, and roaring and spinning the hammer and sending men screaming and reeling and flying. He was a bloody whirlwind, like his father at his best. Or his worst. Beloved o' the moon, he was, and smiled upon by chances. He thought someone might've cut him but it didn't seem to make much difference. He was still swinging the hammer so he reckoned he'd live and if he didn't, well, here was a death the moon would smile upon.

A tall one was pointing, screeching at his men in a jagged tongue, but

Isern bounded up on a wagon in a shower of bones and sprang down on him, spear darting out and taking him in the breastbone and he sprayed blood from his mouth and fell on his knees and Scofen split his head in half with their father's axe.

They might've competed over which of 'em hated their da more, but for better or worse he'd given 'em this, made 'em ready for this, brought 'em to the moon's notice.

A Crinna bastard covered in bones came gibbering at him and Scenn roared, and swung, and the hammer caught him in the side with all its weight, brushed him away like cobwebs, shattered the bones in him and the bones on him and flung him spinning in a shower of red specks and white splinters. A great maddened dog ran past with an arrow in its side. Another came at Scenn but Scofen caught it in the belly with a great sweep of his axe and sent it tumbling away to roll and mewl and wriggle.

There was death smeared all over and the good grass watered with good blood and the moon could not but smile on this day's work. Rikke-o'-the-Long-Eye in particular, who'd looked but a pale and stringy streak when she was carried into the hills but had seen this come, made this come, laid out the good gifts so they could all take their fill.

Scenn laughed as he kicked a limping savage in the back and smashed his arse in with the hammer, smashed his head in as he crawled. Swung for another as he ran and missed, and stumbled around in a circle and was nearly dragged right over.

It was a fearsome weapon, the hammer, but heavy as mountains. He rather wished he'd got the spear, now, then maybe he could've flitted about the battlefield like his sister, darting in and out like a toad's tongue. Mind you, he hadn't the belly for that slippery business, nor honestly the wits, nor honestly the puff.

He set the hammer head-down and leaned on it, catching his breath, watching Scofen hack at the dead and Isern stand on a man's back and stab him through the throat and the rest of the hillmen stream into the back of the Crinna bastards and send them scattering like starlings.

Made him proud to see the hillfolk fighting as one. Hadn't happened in many a long year. Not since the Battle in the High Places, maybe, where the Bloody-Nine had killed his brother Rond. Thanks to his father's endless appetite for wives, though, he had brothers and sisters in plenty, so not too much lost. It's a poor life ploughed that hasn't left a few dead siblings in its furrow. The weak are winnowed out to leave the strong. The chaff is taken by the wind, so the seed beloved of the moon can flourish.

He frowned over at a set of great pots, man high, fires banked underneath 'em, steam pouring from inside.

"What the bloody hell are the pots for?" asked Scenn. "Soup or something?"

"They're for rendering down the corpses, d'you see." Isern frowned at her spear's bloody head. "So they can get at the bones."

Scenn shook his head in disbelief. "What a pack of arseholes."

Rance held his axe tight and tried to work up the anger. They'd come to burn his city, hadn't they? Come to kill his people. Time to be a man.

At a fourth blast from Shivers' horn, ear-splitting from being so close, two big Carls hefted the bar from its brackets, and two others shoved the doors wide, and they sallied from the gates of Carleon and out into the fields in front.

By the dead, the noise. At the last moment, Rance's feet seemed stuck to the cobbles but he was carried along anyway, among the warriors spilling from the city like a cork in a flood.

Calder's men weren't ready. Panicked by the attacks from behind, now panicked by an attack from in front. They wavered, spears wobbling, but Rance didn't fancy running at 'em. Didn't fancy it at all. It came to him, of a sudden, how hard and unforgiving is a spearhead, and how soft and easily torn is a man's belly.

He stumbled from the flow of howling, screaming, charging men. He flinched as someone toppled from the walls a few strides away, a ladder flung down in ruin on top of him. The world smelled of blood and smoke. Bodies everywhere. Wounded crawling, moaning, clutching.

His uncle had warned him it was no business for a boy o' twelve. Now he saw it wasn't only man's work, but madman's work. Someone barged him from behind and he nearly fell, tangled in his uncle's old oversized mail. He nearly tripped over a corpse. A young man, his helmet fallen off to show blond hair matted with blood. One eye open, staring at nothing much.

He saw Caul Shivers cutting his way through the enemy, grey sword going up and whipping down with such terrible speed, with such horrible force, and it came to him how razor-sharp and ruthless is a sword-blade, and how fragile a man's skull. Calder's men were falling back. Falling apart. Hardly seemed like he was needed, really. Most likely there'd be time to be a man later.

He slipped along the wall and back through the gate, into the shadows.

*

"Run!" roared Stand-i'-the-Barrows, and he broke for the trees, and Scunlich loped along after. A great fighter must not only know when to fight, but when not to, and Scunlich was as proud of the few bad fights they'd got away from as the many good ones they'd won. This was a bad one, very bad, the worst.

The hillmen chased after them a way, but fell to picking over the dead for trinkets and were left behind. They sent arrows flitting after, whistling farewells, twittering into the greenwood, clicking into the trunks with their feathers fluttering. Stand-i'-the-Barrows kept up a fast pace on his long shanks and the sound of battle soon faded.

They stopped to catch their breath and listen. Gromma had an arrow in his back and sat down beside a tree, wheezing red, and did not get up.

"We were fools to trust in Black Calder!" shouted Yort. "The cunning of cunning men always runs out, and usually at the worst moment. I said so back in—"

Stand-i'-the-Barrows caught him around the neck and bore him down onto the ground and squatted over him, throttling him, beating his skull against a tree root until the blood flowed, then catching his head and twisting it right around until his neck came apart with a thick crunching.

"That was well done," said Scunlich.

"Aye," he said, standing up. "I wish I could take his bones." And the others grunted their agreement. It was a worthy thought. Then Stand-i'-the-Barrows ran on, his axe in his hand, and Scunlich ran on with him, but it seemed the further they went into the wood and the darker and dimmer and greener it grew, the fewer of them were left.

There was a chill among the trees. A damp chill and a mist clinging to the scrub so the twigs came lashing from nowhere and the brambles clutched out from the grey to snag foot and ankle and bring men down squealing in the undergrowth.

"Whence comes this mist?" hissed Stand-i'-the-Barrows, creeping forwards slowly, and it was true it seemed a thing alive, twisting between the black trunks, sticking to men in tatters.

They blundered into a clearing, Scunlich stumbling forwards with his hands stretched out like a blind man searching. A stunted tree loomed from the murk. Or no, a stump, and on the stump a figure. An old woman, bent, but something gleamed on her forehead as she looked up, and Scunlich tottered back amazed, for he saw that her face was split by a great scar, and the two halves were stitched together with golden wire.

"A devil," he whispered. "A devil!"

The bone-pickers had gathered into a knot, no more than a dozen left where there'd been hundreds, thousands. Now they crowded close about Stand-i'-the-Barrows, back to back, drawing strength from his strength.

"Did you make this mist?" he snarled at the woman.

"I did," she said, "and reckon it a good one." And though she was old her voice was young, as beautiful to listen to as she was dreadful to look upon.

"I do not, witch." Stand-i'-the-Barrows took a step forwards, feet falling heavy in the silence. "Remove it."

"As you wish."

Like water from a broken bowl, the mist drained from the clearing, but Scunlich felt no joy at its passing. He saw figures among the trees at its edge. Ghosts at first, all around, but turning more horribly real with every moment, and Scunlich found he was wishing that the mist would come again.

"Gods," he whispered, his blood turning cold.

They were twisted things. Unholy things. Things of flesh and metal. Of tusks and teeth and rivets. Of rusted plates and criss-crossed scars. Things with flattened heads and bent limbs, cut apart and stitched together. Clutched in their claws they had cruel spears, cruel bows, cruel knives and axes and daggers.

"These I made, too," sang the witch, stroking the hairless head of one of them. They slipped forwards, a tightening ring, dozens of them, hundreds, eyes gleaming in the gloom of the greenwood.

"What do you want?" And Scunlich heard a thing he had never heard before in the voice of Stand-i'-the-Barrows and had never thought to hear. The quaver of fear.

The witch smiled, skin twisting and puckering around the golden stitches.

"Your bones," she said.

# Satisfaction and Regret

"It's all done," said Calder.

He sounded puzzled. But, for a man watching all his dreams dissolve, very calm. Handled defeat a lot better than most great warriors Clover had known. He looked almost amused by the sudden turn towards disaster. "My son's dead. The North's lost. It's all done."

No one was disagreeing, and Clover least of all.

Calder's guards had made a crescent-shaped wall around that little green hill with the one flat rock on top, their shields locked and their weapons ready. Might well have been the only order left in the whole army. The right wing crumbled when the men of Uffrith came pouring down. The centre was shattered when the men of the West Valleys ripped through the baggage into their rear. The hillmen had come howling from the trees and taught those Crinna bastards who the real savages were. Then the gates opened and Caul Shivers caught the last resistance between hammer and anvil. All managed with a few blasts of his horn as neatly as a spring dance. But with a lot more corpses.

Not far off one of those great dogs bounced and rolled and barked, its side somehow on fire, frisking madly across the grass, trying to escape from itself. Something Clover had been trying to do for years, with as little success.

"We've got to run," he muttered, giving the trees a wistful glance. "Run, or give up."

"Run or give up." Calder gave him a withering look. "Ever the counsel of Jonas Clover. I'm surprised you're not advising me to switch sides."

Clover winced. "Fear it's a bit late for that."

"Aye. Just one thing I have to do first. Meant to do it after I won." He breathed in, and sighed out. "But I guess it'll have to be now."

Maybe the years hadn't dulled Clover's instinct as much as he'd always thought, because somehow he felt it coming. He threw himself sideways, the wind of the axe kissing his scalp. He rolled clumsily, scrambled back fast enough that Downside's second swing thudded into the turf right between his legs. He stumbled to his feet, nearly fell again as he tottered backwards up the hill, then dodged behind the big stone at the top, breathing hard.

Not very dignified, but then Clover long ago decided he'd rather have his life than his dignity. The dead help him, he drew his sword. Always the first lesson whenever he taught sword-work—never draw the bastard thing. But he drew it now, and he weighed it, and he saw the gleam run down the polished metal.

"What the fuck are you doing, Downside?" he shouted over the noise of battle.

"Killing you. Ain't that obvious?"

"'Cause Calder paid you to?"

Downside looked confused. "'Course."

"But he's done!" Clover waved with his free hand towards the battle, which was hard not to wave at, since it was all around 'em, pressing in closer on Calder's guards with every breath they took. "Anyone can see he's fucking done! He's saying he's done himself!"

"I'll tell you the truth, Clover." Downside stepped towards him, probing for an opening, his heavy boot working its way into the turf. "I'm not clever enough to keep track of all the twisting and turning. Makes my head hurt. All that cunning, just to end up where you started? No. I say a thing, I follow *through*."

And he sprang forward. He was fast for such a big man. Best Clover could do was dodge back, stumble and near trip over his own feet before he found his balance again. They circled each other, that flat stone between them. At least the rest of Calder's guards weren't posing any danger. They were too busy fighting for their own lives, enemies pressing in tighter with every breath.

Seemed most unfair, after he gave Downside a place when no one wanted the mad bastard. But Clover supposed a man who'd let down as many people as he had couldn't get too upset at being let down himself.

He'd lost count o' those he'd failed. Those he'd turned on. Cairm Ironhead, and Glama Golden, and Stour Nightfall. Magweer with the flatbow bolt in his throat. Wonderful, too, pointing that beautiful raised eyebrow. An accusing crowd of disappointed friends, comrades, leaders, shaking their heads at him from the land of the dead. Clover shook the thought off. Hardly the kind you want weighing on you in a fight. He felt heavy enough already as he backed away, glancing about for anything that might help him and not finding it.

Downside looked big when he was on your side. He looked a lot bigger on the other, with his scarred shield up, heavy mail from neck to knees and a steel cap on. A hard bastard to put down with a sword. Faster than Clover was, and stronger, and better armed. But it's a man's wits that set him apart from the beasts. Or so he told himself. Downside stepped forwards again and Clover slipped sideways, trying to keep the flat rock between them and hoping some opportunity might present itself. The fighting crouch he used to use didn't feel too comfortable. Stiffer joints and a lot more belly than the last time he tried it, maybe.

Calder's standard-bearer stood a few strides off, a young lad with eyes big as cartwheels at all the battle and death, not to mention the duel that had broken out right under his nose.

"You!" shouted Calder. "Kill him."

The standard-bearer numbly drew his sword. He looked at Clover. He looked at Calder. He looked at one of Calder's guards, crawling through the grass with an arrow in his shoulder while the others shuffled to plug the gap. Then he let go of the standard and sprinted for the trees. Calder stared after him. A little wistful, almost, as his standard toppled over and slid down the hill. For twenty years, his authority had been iron-forged. Now it was cobwebs in a storm. All it takes is one lost fight. Clover could've told him that, but he was a little busy.

He gasped as Downside rushed at him, managed to dodge the first whipping axe swing. Clover looked for an opening he could stab at but the big shield came at him fast, the rim crunching into his mouth, snapping his head up. He got his bearings just in time to see the axe flashing at him the other way and staggered clear, heavy blade hissing past and knocking a great chunk from the stone. Clover stumbled away, trying to shake the throbbing from his head, from his jaw, nearly blundered into one of Calder's guards as he ran wild-eyed for the trees. Downside grinned over the bright rim of his shield. Clover stuck his tongue into the sore hole where a tooth used to be and spat blood.

The truth was, a stubborn splinter of Jonas Steepfield was still buried in him. Buried so deep it could never be worked free. Buried so deep that it stung at him whenever he backed down, whenever he ran away, whenever he changed sides. And now it worked its way up to the surface. Worked its way up and came out in a long, low growl.

"All right, fucker," he snarled, fist tightening around the grip of his sword. "Let's have you."

"Have me?" sneered Downside. "Can you even—"

An arrow came looping from the trees and stuck into Downside's shoulder. It didn't stick deep. Just lodged in his mail. Probably didn't even draw blood. But it was enough to make him turn his head, for an instant.

In the end, the only thing a man can really do is pick his moment. Watch for the opening, and recognise it when it comes, and seize it.

Clover feinted left, switched right, heard the grunt of surprise as Downside's axe thudded into the turf where he might've been. Clover was already rolling across the flat stone, came up turning, edge of his sword flicking out and catching the back of Downside's boot, below the hem of his mail coat.

Downside hardly even noticed, growled as he turned, lifting his axe, stepping forwards. Then he lurched sideways with a surprised hoot, clutching the edge of the stone with his shield hand. Clover reckoned that was the tendon snapping at the back of his ankle.

Downside hopped once on his good leg, giving a great spitty roar, swinging wildly. Clover whipped back, let the heavy blade sail past his nose. As Downside spun, he stepped forwards, thrusting under the rim of the shield.

Metal scraped as the point slid through Downside's mail and into his belly. Clover might never draw the thing in anger, but he kept it sharp even so.

Downside's eyes went very wide. He tottered forwards as Clover pulled his sword back, his ruined ankle gave under him and he slumped onto one knee. He took a gasping breath. "I think—"

"No one cares." Clover took his head off with one whipping swing. It bounced once, then rolled down the slope, towards where Calder's last guards were tossing away their weapons. The body dropped sideways, blood spilling out in a great wash that Jonas Steepfield would no doubt have taken great pleasure in.

Calder raised his brows at it. "You can still swing that sword, then."

"I try not to advertise the fact." Clover turned his head and spat blood again. "I find it makes folk want to try to *kill you*."

Rikke stood outside the gates of Carleon, rubbing gently at her red-stained hand and frowning down at Stour Nightfall's broken corpse. No one else was paying it much mind. Nothing on it worth stealing, after all.

She'd often heard it said that there's no sweeter sight than dead enemies. Usually by folk who'd never really had an enemy, let alone killed one. The truth was she felt no satisfaction, seeing the Great Wolf back to the mud.

But she felt no regret, either. It had needed doing. For her father. For her people. For herself. It had been long overdue.

The battle was done with, more or less. A few men still fighting, in little knots against the walls, and a lot running, dotting the valley sides, but mostly Calder's warriors were tossing their weapons down, holding their hands up, kneeling on the wheel-rutted, boot-smashed, arrow-prickled ground. Those that weren't lying down already, of course, never to rise, of which there were many.

She felt no satisfaction at the sight. But no regret, either.

"There's my girl!" Isern came swaggering through the carnage, blood streaking her face from a cut on her forehead but her missing tooth showing in a great smile even so.

"Isern-i-Phail." And Rikke hugged her tight, and kissed her on the cheek, and her sour sweat and chagga smell was a surprising comfort. "Knew you wouldn't let me down."

Isern licked her fingers and rolled a chagga pellet. "Always said you'd come to something, didn't I? Never once doubted it."

"You said how much you doubted it every morning, noon and night," said Rikke, making a grab for the chagga.

With marvellous dexterity, Isern flicked it into her mouth before Rikke's fingers could close on it. "If your faults aren't spread clearly before you, how can you improve on the bastards?"

Men shuffled back as she passed, heads lowered. Men stood out of her way, respectful. Men cleared an open pathway for her, and stomped their boots, and rattled their swords, and tapped their axes against their shields till they sent up a great clatter of approval as she strode by. The same one they might've made for the Bloody-Nine, or Skarling Hoodless, or any of the great War Chiefs of the past. The truth was she could hardly believe the plan had worked. But it wouldn't do to let anyone else know that. So she walked head high, shoulders back, the way she'd seen Savine dan Brock walk, as if she'd never known what doubt was, to the foot of a green tummock under the eaves of the forest where the dead were thickly scattered.

Shivers nodded at her, his shield pecked and scored in the fighting and his hair unbound again and hanging across his face. "All good?"

"All good." No need for more between the two of them.

Black Calder was at the top. Beside a flat rock half-buried in the turf where his standard lay fallen. The man who shaped the North for twenty years, on his knees, with Jonas Clover's sword at his throat. You had to admire his calmness, in defeat. Rikke wondered if she'd have taken it so

317

cool, or if she'd have schemed and blubbed and begged for her life. But then who cares a shit what the losers do? It's the winners that change things.

Clover gave her a nod. "I got him, Chief."

"That a fact?" Rikke nudged a big corpse lying in a slick of blood with her foot. "And did you get him, too?"

"My man Downside. He always did suffer from too much fight and not enough judgement."

"So you've chosen a side, finally?"

"I've always been on the same one," said Clover. "Whichever wins."

All the while, Calder was frowning up at her. "You found my spy."

"Isern-i-Phail had her picked the moment she arrived."

"I can smell a lie," said Isern, spear across her shoulders with her blue hand and her pale dangling over the haft. "And that bitch reeked."

"I thought it all felt too easy," mused Calder, frowning off towards Carleon, across the corpse-scattered fields where even now the last of his army were being driven off or taken prisoner.

"Aye, well," said Rikke, "we're all prone to believe what we want to. It was Shivers handed me the notion, to begin with."

Shivers gave a modest shrug. "No strength like looking weak."

"All I did was…" Rikke fluttered her fingers. "Sprinkle some glitter on it."

"It was well done." Calder narrowed his eyes thoughtfully at her. "Tell me one thing, between us…does it really work? The Long Eye? Did you know how it would turn out all along?"

She looked down at him, thumb inside the chain of emeralds she wore. "I know how it'll turn out now. Years ago, my father swore to kill you if you crossed the Cusk again."

"I remember." Calder nodded slowly, his eyes fixed far off. "It all has to be paid for, in the end."

"Took a while for me to keep his word," said Rikke. "But we got there. Shivers?"

"Aye," he said, and drew his sword.

Calder looked up as its shadow fell across him. "Been a long time."

"Aye," said Shivers.

"I remember when you saved my life. In the Circle at the Heroes."

"Aye."

"Quite the irony. That it should be you who ends it."

"Aye."

"Well. I can hardly say I don't deserve it."

"Seems your father's dream came true after all," said Rikke. "The North united." She put her hands behind her head and stretched up tall. "It just won't be his blood that leads it. Scale's back to the mud. Stour's back to the mud. Bethod's line ends with you."

"Ah." For some reason, Calder had the ghost of a smile at the last. He leaned forwards and spoke so softly only she could hear. "So you don't see everything."

The blade fell. There was a sharp crack, blood sprayed up in dark streaks and Calder flopped face down on the dirty grass.

There was a long silence, after the great noise of the battle. Every eye fixed on the bubbling wound in the back of Black Calder's head. Shivers stood frowning down in the midst of those staring faces, the sword that had been the Bloody-Nine's in his fist, that dull, grey blade with the one silver letter dashed and speckled with blood.

Then Scenn-i-Phail lifted high his hammer, which looked to have some hair stuck to the scarred head. "This was well done!" he roared.

"Truly the girl is beloved o' the moon!" said his brother Scofen, laughing and waving his axe.

"Black Calder ruled the North." Isern slapped a hard hand down on Rikke's shoulder. "She who beat him should do the same. The children of Crummock-i-Phail stand with Black Rikke!"

"And I!" roared the Nail, before Rikke could get a word in, stepping up out of the crowd, so spattered head to toe with blood it looked like he'd gone swimming in it. "I stand with Black Rikke!"

"And I," grunted Hardbread, clambering with some effort onto the little knoll. He gave a burp and thumped at his breastbone, peering down at Calder's corpse. "Your father would've been proud."

Rikke blinked at them. Calder had stolen the name from Black Dow, that day on the Heroes. Seemed now she'd stolen it from him.

"Black Rikke!" men were shouting all around, even some who'd been Calder's men until the sword fell. They had to be someone else's men now, after all. "Black Rikke!" All competing to shout it loudest, as though having a girl with a tattooed face in charge who used to shit herself in the streets of Uffrith was their fondest dream. "Black Rikke!" As though this had been what everyone wanted all along. What they'd expected.

Shivers carefully wiped his sword with a rag, sunlight glinting on his metal eye. "Looks like you win," he said.

Rikke looked from that little hill across the churned-up battlefield, then down at Calder's corpse. She felt no satisfaction in it.

Well, maybe just a bit.

# PART IX

"History repeats itself,

first as tragedy,

second as farce."

Karl Marx

# Ready for a Fight

"Tight enough," gasped Savine, fists clenched on the table, and she heard Freid grunt with effort as she knotted the laces.

Someone had daubed the words *We Will Burn the Past* above the fireplace and taken an axe to the wallpaper, but as prison cells went, she supposed it could have been a great deal worse. A room in the palace where some minor visiting dignitary could have gently aged as they waited on His Majesty's pleasure. One could almost have mistaken it for the dressing chamber of a lady of fashion. Except for the crooked bars bodged into the window frames and the sense of barely contained mortal terror.

They had given her good food and clean linen. They had given her matching cribs in which Harod and Ardee snored, blissfully unaware of the danger they were in. They had supplied her with all the soaps and scents, powders and paints, wigs and dresses the most exacting socialite might need for a grand public appearance. They had even sent for her old maids Freid and Metello to help her prepare. It reminded Savine a little of happier times, before she was a Lady Governor, before she betrayed the king, before the Great Change came. Except that Lisbit was dead and Zuri was in prison.

She winced at that thought. They tortured people suspected of hoarding flour. What might they do to someone accused of being a flesh-eating sorcerer in the service of the Prophet? Haroon and Rabik, too, who had followed her so faithfully. Had their loyalty landed them in fathoms of chain? It was insane. It was laughable. But in the current climate, the insane and laughable could quickly turn fatal.

Savine closed her eyes and took a shuddering breath. She had charges of her own to answer. Some almost as insane and laughable as those against Zuri and her brothers. Others all too horribly true. She had to fight for herself first. If they found her guilty, she could help no one.

"This one?" asked Metello, in her thick Styrian accent.

She had a dress over one arm, a great swag of bright blue Suljuk silk with Osprian lace at the cuffs and embroidered flowers all around the hem. It had been made for an appearance at the theatre, she thought, but never worn. That colour had always seemed to be trying too hard.

Savine waved it away. "By the Fates, no."

Judge hoped to swindle her with good treatment. To put her off guard with familiar luxuries. To coax her into appearing at the trial as her old self. The personification of the ruthless, exploitative, privileged elite that the Great Change had set out to destroy.

She had even furnished Savine with jewels. Some excellent earrings and a very fine ruby necklace, no doubt taken as bribes from some ex-lord's wife in return for a pardon that never came. Judge did not really do pardons, not even for rubies as fine as these. Savine put a finger under them and held them to the light, admiring their bloody sparkle. Then she slid the stand firmly away.

Judge might very well be sending her to the Tower of Chains, but she was a damn fool if she thought Savine would be helping. "Let's keep it very simple, ladies. Very clean and very humble. No jewels and no wig." Metello gave an upset cluck, frowning at Savine's own fuzz of clipped brown hair. "No silk and no—"

There was a crash outside and Savine spun towards the door, took a lurching step for the children, one hand pressed to her churning stomach, the other reaching for the cribs.

From a practical point of view, quite apart from the agony of producing them and the permanent damage they had done to her body, her babies were nothing but an almighty annoyance. Nipple-chewing, dung-leaking, sleep-killing monsters with no conversation at all. But she was even more terrified for them than for herself.

Laughter beyond the door. Another crash, then cheery voices burbling off into silence. Just the Burners, doing what Burners do. Savine forced the panic away. Forced her clutching hand down, then turned in surprise at a great sob. Freid stood with her face screwed up, shoulders shaking.

"Whatever is it?" demanded Savine. If anyone should have been weeping, she rather thought she had the best claim. She had scarcely slept since they arrested her. It felt as if only the savagely laced corsetry was keeping her standing.

"When all this happened...the Great Change, I mean..." Freid's bottom lip trembled, then she blurted it out. "I thought it might be a good thing! It seemed to be, for a while, freedom and all, and folk so happy, but then…" She stared into the corner, eyes brimming. "But then…by the Fates, my lady, forgive me!"

Savine's first impulse was to slap her. She knew she would be lucky to see sunset and did not particularly want to spend the hours she had left soothing a wardrobe maid's regrets. How she missed Zuri. She had never cried. Even when they dragged her away in a muzzle. But we must work with the tools we have, as Savine's father had been so fond of saying. She forced down her anger and put a gentle hand on Freid's shoulder.

"There is nothing to forgive," she said, with an effort. "Perhaps it could have been a good thing. Should have been. And I am not a lady any more. Just plain Citizeness. That is what I need people to see."

Freid sniffed back her tears and picked up the powder. "I'll cover up your scar—"

"No," said Savine, looking at it in the mirror, running pink and crooked up her forehead and into her clipped hair. "Get the blusher. Bring it out a little. Let them see that I know what pain is. We never met Savine dan Glokta, terror of the salons, you understand? Have them put the Darling of the Slums on trial."

"So?" asked Metello, holding up one of her nursing dresses, plain white. "Perfect."

A clonking knock on the door brought another surge of sick terror.

"It's Gunnar Broad," came the rough voice from outside.

"Should I tell him you're dressing?" whispered Freid.

Savine pressed on her stomach again. Smothered the fear, again. One advantage of facing your death was that modesty did not seem so heavy a consideration. She raised her voice so it could be well understood beyond the door. "Gunnar Broad saved my life in Valbeck after I was chased half-naked by a mob, Freid. I doubt the sight of my petticoat will scandalise him. And he's got the key, after all!"

The doorknob turned and the door swung open, leaving Broad framed in the doorway, huge, armoured, red-eyed. He took a heavy step into the room. He frowned towards the children. He frowned towards Freid and she shrank behind the dressing table. He frowned towards Savine.

He looked ill, drunk, furious and sentimental all at once. The definitive Burner, in fact. As if he couldn't decide whether to beg her forgiveness or smash her face in.

"You've got one hour," he said, turning back towards the door.

"I appreciate the reminder. And I have something for you." Savine held the folded paper out to him. "From Liddy."

His slack face twitched at the name. "Liddy can't write."

"I suppose May must have written it. It came with some dispatches from Leo's mother."

Broad's jaw worked, his bloodshot eyes fixed on the letter, his hand halfway towards it. "What does it say?"

"Don't be ridiculous, Gunnar, I don't read letters that aren't addressed to me. Honestly. You'll be telling me Zuri eats people next."

She pressed the letter carelessly into his hand and turned back to her powder, but she studied him in the mirror. He stared down at that paper for a long moment, then walked very slowly to the door, and pulled it very slowly shut. Savine clenched her jaw and made a trembling fist. She might be going off the Tower of Chains—the Fates knew, the odds were against her—but she would not be going without a fight.

Freid was over one of the cribs, cooing gently to Harod. "Do you want me to take the children?" Her eyes were getting moist again. "I mean... when they put you in the dock—"

"I may need you to take them..." Savine lost her voice for a moment, had to clear her throat. "When I am condemned." It was better to say when than if. She did not dare to say if. "Until that moment, in the court, in the dock...they come with me."

This was not a trial. It was a show. And Savine knew how to put on a show. No one better.

Adua was hidden behind a rise, but you could see the great shadow of its smoke from miles around.

"The furnaces are still lit," said Jurand.

"No matter how you try," murmured Leo, "you can't stop progress."

Lord Marshal Forest squinted up at the sun, providing some actual warmth for what felt like the first time in months. "Don't like marching in the open like this."

"If you can call it marching." The drums were beating double time but the demoralised remains of the People's Army and the exhausted remnants of the Crown Prince's Division moved at a trudge, their ranks dissolved into a shambling mass, flags limp and polearms drooping, a trail of mud and rubbish in their wake. A giant military slug, squirming spent across the damp country. "They hardly look ready for a fight."

"They're not," said Glaward. "We've lost more deserters without fighting than we'd ever have lost casualties if we had."

Leo looked to the few well-drilled blocks of dark-uniformed cavalry towards the front. "At least we can rely on the Anglanders."

"They're with you to the death," said Jurand.

Glaward clapped a heavy hand on Leo's shoulder. "And so are we." For a fond moment, it felt almost like old times.

Forest was fretting at his frayed cuffs as he stared towards that smear on the sky. "They must know we're coming."

"They believe we're killing each other miles away," said Leo. "And Inspector Teufel is making sure the People's Inspectorate won't be putting anyone straight on that score."

"You trust her?" asked Forest.

"No," said Leo. "But trust is a poor foundation for an alliance. I've found to my cost the woman's damned effective."

"Even so. You can't keep thousands of soldiers secret for long."

"Who's this?" Glaward spurred in front of Leo, hand on his sword. A couple of Forest's scouts were leading a dishevelled horse by the bridle, a dishevelled prisoner in the saddle with hands tied behind him.

"Caught this article on the road ahead, Lord Marshal!" one of them called out.

"Caught me?" squawked the prisoner. "I was bloody trying to find you! I've a message from Corporal Tunny!"

Forest grinned. "That article's called Yolk, and I'm sorry to say he's on our side. Let him free."

Once he had his hands back the man gave a slovenly salute. "It's Lord Brock I need to speak to. I mean to say...are you lords again, now? It's all—"

"Out with it," snapped Leo.

"It's your wife. She's...well, there's no easy way to say it..."

"Take the hard way, then."

"They've arrested her. Judge is putting her on trial for profiteering and treason and...er..." Yolk swallowed. "Well, incest got a mention."

Silence. Behind them the drums, and the tramping boots, and the clatter of gear went on. Leo wondered how he ought to feel. Would be expected to feel. He bunched his good hand into a fist. "When?"

"Today. The king'll be there. Hell, half the city'll be there, it's set to be the biggest execution since Risinau went off the Tower...that is to say..."

"We'll get there in time," said Jurand. "Don't worry. We'll get there."

"I know," muttered Leo. It was terrible news, of course. His wife was in danger. His children. He made sure everyone could see how deeply he felt it. Terrible news. But he couldn't help seeing an upside. The Burners would be distracted. It might give them an opening.

Forest nudged his mount close. "Listen, Young Lion, I sympathise, but you can't let this get in the way. His Majesty's safety has to come first."

"They'll both be at the Court of the People," said Leo. "Save one, we save the other."

Jurand frowned back towards the sleepwalking soldiers. "We'll save no one limping along like this."

"Agreed," said Forest.

"If I learned one thing at Stoffenbeck," said Leo, "it's that you'll do no good with bad men. Lord Marshal, I suggest you pick out two hundred men you fully trust, the best armed and mounted. Your most loyal. When we make it through Arnault's Wall—"

"If we make it."

"*When* we make it, Glaward and your officers can spread the rest out through Adua. Secure the gates, the docks, the bridges, the squares and crossroads, hold down the city for its own safety. We'll rush my best men and yours straight for the Agriont and take the south gate. Free the king before they know we're coming."

Forest grimly nodded. "And you wife, too."

Leo frowned towards the great pall of smoke on the horizon. Could he see the pinpricks of Adua's tallest towers, peeking over the grassy rise? The House of the Maker? The highest chimneys? Perhaps even the roof of the Tower of Chains..."And my wife, too."

Savine would understand. She used to love a gamble, after all.

"Tight enough," squeaked Gorst, and Vick pulled the strap through the buckle and gave his backplate a thump with her fist. Felt like the right thing to do when helping a man on with his armour. Not that she'd know. Helping men in and out of their clothes was something she'd done less than she'd have liked, down the years.

"Brock and Forest are on their way," she said.

"Will they get here in time?"

Vick could only shrug. No idea how long they'd take to get to the city. No idea what resistance they'd face once they got in. No idea how long the trial might last. Far too many variables, all way outside her control. While Gorst slid his mirror-polished steels into their sheaths, she pushed the squares board aside and spread out the map, staring at it as if some answer might suddenly reveal itself in invisible ink.

"I bought off the guards at the gates in Casamir's Wall, and Arnault's. With any luck our friends can march straight through. The gate of the Agriont is the problem." And she tapped at the citadel's south gate. Always the weakest point in a weak plan. "They blew up some bits of the wall but not enough to make a difference, and Judge has her most loyal men guarding it. Too risky to bribe. The paranoid bastards took all the gates off the hinges, but the portcullises are still mounted. They drop those, our friends will be stuck outside. Might take them days to get in. If they get in at all."

"So...?"

"We have to take the chain room."

"We?"

"You and me. I spin the guards a story about worries over their loyalty, try to get at least a couple out, then...we deal with the rest. We bar the door. We hold it till the Young Lion's cavalry arrives."

Gorst nodded slowly. He didn't say whether he thought it was a good plan or a bad. He didn't have to. Vick already knew it was a terrible plan. She just hadn't been able to think of a better one.

"Timing'll be tight," she murmured, taking the neat row of weapons from the table one by one and sliding them into their various sheaths, pockets, hiding places. "Go too late, they'll be ready, no way we'll capture the room. Go too early, even if we capture the room, we might've lost it by the time Brock gets there." She thought about that a moment. "And we'll probably be dead."

Gorst had shaved his head again, and he ran a hand over the silvery stubble on his scalp with a faint hissing. "How many men?"

"The usual detail..." Vick licked her lips. "Is eight."

Gorst made no comment. She doubted he'd have flinched if she'd said a thousand.

"That seem a lot to you?" she asked.

"It is what it is. Are you willing to kill?"

Hearing it like that, so blunt and brutal, made her wonder. "I understand the stakes," she said, slapping her dagger into her boot-sheath. "I'll do what needs doing. If you can handle the other seven."

She'd meant it as a joke, but he didn't smile. "Fewer would be better."

The fact was, with only the two of them, this wouldn't be easy. She could've asked Tallow along, but she told herself he'd only get in the way. She could've hired men, but there was no one she trusted.

"Story of my life," she muttered, under her breath. Too much trust could kill you in a heartbeat. She'd learned that lesson in the camps. Learned it too well, maybe, because now it seemed too little trust could kill you just as dead. Only it happened slowly, during years spent alone and looking over your shoulder.

Still, if you could only bring one man to a fight with the future of the Union hanging on the outcome, she reckoned Bremer dan Gorst a good pick. He pulled the Constable's greatcoat on with some difficulty. The biggest one she'd been able to find, and still he was close to ripping it at the shoulders, breastplate glinting above the top button, lumps of his many weapons clearly showing.

"I have never been subtle," he said, sheepishly.

"With any luck, folk will be looking elsewhere." Vick shoved the mace through her belt, and she was ready. "I hear Judge means to make a show of this one."

# We Know Who You Are

O rso sat on his stool in his cage in the Court of the People and sweated, and waited, and worried. It had been a while since he'd done much else.

Over the past few weeks, the audiences had thinned out and grown ever more jaded. He had seen trials in which the observers were outnumbered by the accused. He had seen crumbs shower down from people enjoying a quick pastry in the gallery while blood-curdling accusations were made. He had seen elderly Representatives nod off on their benches as young mothers pleaded for their lives.

But today was different. The galleries were crammed, the benches overflowing. For the first time in a long time the sun shone outside, slashing the Court of the People and its squinting occupants with long strips of brightness. An eager babble filled the chamber to the highest point of its slogan-splattered dome with an air of breathless expectation. This was going to be an *event*.

Orso worked his stool over to the corner of his cage. As close as he could get to Hildi, sitting cross-legged on the tiled floor outside with her back against the bars.

"Where the hell's the Young Lion?" he whispered through fixed lips. Not so very long ago, before the battle at Stoffenbeck, he had spent several sleepless nights hoping Brock never arrived. Now he was desperate for the least hint of the bastard.

Hildi glanced towards Corporal Halder, but he and the rest of Orso's guards had long ago given up any pretence of guarding and had slunk into one of the patches of sunlight to bask like lizards, not paying the slightest attention. "They're on their way," she hissed from the corner of her mouth.

"What if they don't get here in time?" He was all too keenly aware how quickly the Court of the People could produce a verdict. "What if Savine's...convicted?"

"Then I've seen it happen to better people."

Orso could hardly deny that, despite for some reason desperately wanting to. "My worry is it'll happen to a worse next," he whispered. "Namely me."

Hildi was showing depressingly little sign of disagreeing when Judge swept into the hall, chains on her breastplate twinkling, hem of her ripped ballgown hissing across the tiles and sending washes of dust motes through the bars of sunlight. Sworbreck, Broad, Sarlby and a few dozen of the most committed Burners stalked up in her wake. The hubbub dropped away into the usual awful quiet as the Union's vengeful nightmare lowered herself into the chair once reserved for Orso, picked up her smith's hammer and gave the already ruined High Table a brutal beating.

"Court is in fucking session!" she snarled.

Orso tried to flap some air into his collar. For months he had hardly been able to remember what warmth felt like. Now the Court of the People was smotheringly hot. Hot with the spring sun flashing and twinkling through the distorting windows. Hot with the excited breath of the crowd. Hot with rumour, gossip, scandal, fear. The only cool thing in the whole place, as the great doors were swung open, was the defendant.

Savine wore a plain nursing dress, pure white. No jewels. No wig. Her dark hair was clipped close to her skull so she looked shorn of all pretence, the scar up her forehead showing red. Orso had never seen her look so beautiful. But then he thought that every time he saw her, with tiresome predictability. He gripped the bars of his cage, face all but pressed to the metal as she passed.

He wanted to call out some encouragement. *Be strong!* or *You'll beat the bastards!* or *I love you!* but she did not meet his eye. She glided across the tiled floor with her hands clasped and her head high, a member of some more virtuous species than the sweaty mass gathered on the benches and in the galleries. Two maids followed, each carrying what looked like a little bundle of blankets.

"Are those her children?" muttered Hildi, sitting up. One of the bundles twisted, made a little mew, and Orso caught a glimpse of its tiny baffled face as it was whisked past.

"Bloody hell," he breathed as a murmur went through the crowd. Were they...his niece and nephew, then? The thought made him feel vaguely nauseous.

Sworbreck, in his blood-red prosecutor's suit, gazed at them with open disdain. "Babies are not permitted in the Court of the People!"

"My innocence may stand in question," Savine's voice rang out with no trace of fear, "but what crime have my children committed that they should be separated from their mother?"

Usually insults would shower on the accused, sometimes bits of food, coins and broken glass, on one memorable occasion a bucket of piss, but the mood was different today. The murmur from above was of approval. Support, even. It seemed there was almost as much admiration for Savine's quiet dignity in the public galleries as there was in Orso's cage. He could not suppress the slightest smile, the slightest shake of his fist. In the Court of the People, one had to celebrate small victories.

But Judge lazily waved it away. "They're Citizens, too, ain't they? All are equal and everyone's welcome." She slumped back in her chair, lifted her legs and let her bare feet drop on the table with a final-sounding thud. "It's not as if it'll change the result."

That was painfully clear to someone who had watched the court send hundreds to their deaths, heedless of proof or process. Savine might bring the cunning of Glustrod, the dignity of Juvens, the will of Euz himself and perch on a mountain of babies in an ocean of sympathy. Orso could not see how it might make the slightest difference. Only the timely arrival of several thousand armed men could do that.

Savine gave her children a final touch then swept into the dock as calmly as she might have her box at the theatre. Orso glanced towards the benches, where Tunny sprawled on the front row, arms spread out and eyes narrowed lazily against the sunlight. His old gambling partner, panderer and occasional standard-bearer did not meet his eye, but he made a subtle turning motion with one finger, around and around.

Time. Teufel's plan was in motion. Forest was on his way with the Young Lion. Orso chewed at his lip, glancing about the court with a new urgency. He had to find some way to buy time.

Judge bashed away for order, then tossed her hammer rattling down. "Bar all the doors!" she shrieked. "I want *no* fucking distractions!"

And a breathless silence closed in.

"Citizeness Brock!" Sworbreck swaggered towards Savine in his absurd scarlet coat, a sheaf of papers flapping in one hand. It appeared the pompous dolt had duped himself with his own play-acting and come to believe he really was the great legal mind of the age.

"You stand accused of epic profiteering, grand usury, consorting with enemies of the Union and conspiracy against the Great Change!" He delivered the charges like the famous final lines of a much-loved play, and with the same expectation of applause. But Savine's old partner Citizen Vallimir must have carried out her instructions to the letter: stuffing the galleries with people who had benefitted from her charity and paying everyone else to act as if they had. Now, as the echoes of Sworbreck's accusations faded into sullen silence, her final investment paid dividends and the faces of the public squashed in at the balconies glared down on the prosecutor with chilly hostility.

She had practised her pose in the mirror. Calibrated it with minute care. Defiant, but not arrogant. Dignified, but not proud. Now that the waiting was over and the battle was joined her fear had vanished. In spite of the feverish heat she felt icy calm. She did not respond to the charges. She implied the charges were beneath a response.

Sworbreck cleared his throat, worked his mouth, then gathered himself for another sally, jabbing at her with an accusing finger. "You look a picture of modesty today, I note! Those of us familiar with your public displays are used to seeing you swathed in silks and dripping diamonds. Your name is synonymous with exhibitions of ostentation! It seems you are a mistress of disguise. A veritable *chameleon*."

"I assure you I am as human as anyone." Her voice echoed from the dome with pleasing confidence. "And with my full share of human failings."

"*More* than your share, some would say! You pretend to be a humble Citizeness of the Union like any other. You hide your infamous history behind your husband's celebrated name." He appealed again to the galleries. "But we know who you are! You are none other than Savine dan *Glokta*, the notorious... the notorious... whatever are you doing?"

She was, in fact, unbuttoning the front of her dress. "Quite obviously, Citizen Sworbreck, I am tending to the needs of my children."

A murmur spread around the court as she undid her nursing corset and worked one breast out. Sworbreck glanced quickly away, colour spreading across his cheeks. Knowing him for a fool and coward, it was no surprise to discover he was also a prude. "I hardly think... *this* is the place—"

"What better place?" She snapped her fingers for Freid to pass Ardee up to her. "The Great Change freed us all!" She settled her daughter on her breast and, heroic little thing, she set to feeding right away. "And yet ever since, I have received many lectures on the proper responsibilities of a Citizeness. Motherhood is always chief among them. Outside these very windows there is a statue several storeys high of Nature nourishing the young of the world. Should I reject her lesson? Should I abandon my responsibilities to my children simply because my life hangs in the balance? Should I reject the tenets of the Great Change, here at its very heart, in the Court of the People? No, Citizen Sworbreck, I refuse! I will nurture them until my dying breath."

There was actual applause. Scattered, but applause. Perhaps she had struck a nerve with some of the mothers in attendance. Judge brought it to a halt with a few blows of her hammer, though, glowering towards the galleries. "Nurture away," she growled. "It's your own guilt that concerns us here today. Fucking proceed!"

"Of course, Citizeness Judge, of course." Sworbreck rifled through his papers, which Savine would not have been surprised to find were blank, trying to recover his lost rhythm. "To the, er... to the specific charges, then! You were a leading light and founding member of that coven of profiteers, the Solar Society!"

"I am proud to say so," said Savine. "A beacon of progress intended to bring prosperity to all."

"Hear, hear," she heard Curnsbick grunt from the benches behind her. Not loud, but loud enough.

"You have conspired with others to claw profits from the common man!" shrieked Sworbreck.

"I have partnered with others to build things where there was nothing before."

"Indeed," she heard Kort say from among the Representatives.

"You have long plotted against the Union with foreign agents!" Sworbreck's voice cracked, went suddenly shrill, and he had to clear his throat. "With savage Northmen and degenerate Styrians! You have harboured Gurkish spies in your own house!"

"I have done business across the Circle of the World and cultivated friendships wherever I could find them. My only plots were alongside men of good conscience, to bring down the Union's callous government."

"True, true," called Isher, always reliable in his own defence.

There was a steady grumble from the galleries now. Sworbreck dabbed a greasy sheen from his forehead. "Workers were exploited in your mills, mutilated in your manufactories, all but enslaved in service of your insatiable greed!"

"Workers were given jobs, fair wages and a chance to better themselves. No one was forced into anything." She eased her breast back into her corset and scooped out the other.

Sworbreck gave an ungainly cough, staring down at his notes as she settled Ardee again. The girl could have fed through an earthquake. "You have participated in usury on a grand scale! Squeezed outrageous rents from the desperate! Lived like an empress while your tenants squatted in filth! You have conspired with the Banking House of Valint and Balk—"

"No!" she barked. "I have *never* taken money from Valint and Balk. Not one mark. Not one *bit*. Accuracy is important in a court of law, don't you think?"

Sworbreck was wrongfooted. He had clearly never had to deal with a defendant who was actually given the chance to defend themselves. He squinted into the sunlight, was obliged to shade his eyes awkwardly with his papers. "Then...well...how would you prove it?"

"I have not your legal expertise, Citizen Sworbreck, but I believe the burden of proof lies with the prosecution." Some light laughter from the public gallery. She shifted Ardee against her breast. "I could easily furnish evidence, however..." She knew she had to stay calm but could not quite keep the edge of contempt off her voice. "Had you not locked up my bookkeeper on charges of being a sorceress."

The laughter was louder this time.

"Bitch is making fucking fools of us," snarled Sarlby. "And with her *tits*. She pay these bastards off or something?"

Broad would've been shocked if she hadn't. He'd warned Judge it was a mistake to give Savine a chance to speak. But she'd been fixed on a big display. On humbling her as well as punishing her. Wasn't quite turning out that way. But all he cared about was the letter. It felt heavy in his sweaty hand. Like a square of hot iron.

He couldn't stop thinking about Liddy and May. All the things he'd done since he last saw them. How they might look at him now. Their disappointment. Their downright horror. He wasn't even drunk. His flask sat untouched in his pocket but his head was still spinning.

Sworbreck was getting booed. Properly booed, like an old show that had started boring its audience. The Burners were looking uneasy. Bannerman stood near the dock, arms folded, frowning worried towards the galleries.

Broad ripped the letter open. He could hardly remember what May's writing looked like. Wasn't as if he was the best reader, even with his lenses. His eyes were swimming. The Court of the People faded. The nervy burble of Sworbreck's questions, the cool snap of Savine's answers, Sarlby's grumbling and the swelling gabble of the public galleries, it all faded.

He heard Liddy's voice when he read it. He heard May's.

*Gunnar. Father.*

*We hear you are in trouble. We hear you have lost yourself. We miss you. Every day we miss you.*

*We know who you are. Our husband. Our father. A good man. You just have to remember.*

*We hope every day that we see you again soon.*

*Your family,*
*Liddy and May.*

A good man. Something pattered on the paper and made the ink run. A drop of sweat off his forehead, surely. He crumpled the letter in his fist, pulled off his lenses and wiped his face on the tattooed back of his hand. It was trembling.

"And now," Sworbreck was screeching, "you would have us believe that you have turned all your undoubted cunning towards *charitable projects*? That the great exploiter has become a great philanthropist!"

"I opened my house to orphans," answered Savine, her voice turning sharper, "and in the slums I try to give bread and coal to the needy. The Fates know there are enough of them."

"Are there indeed?" Sworbreck had a sly smile. He thought he'd hooked her, like an angler with a record-breaking fish, and was pulling her in.

"There are many for whom the Great Change has changed little," said Savine. "People without work, without food, without fuel. The chasm between rich and poor yawns as wide as ever. I simply try my best to bridge the divide."

Sworbreck was triumphant. "Do you presume to say so?"

"No," said Savine. "You do."

"What?"

She reached under her nursing baby to slip something out. Stained, worn, cheap paper tattered at the edges. But the name of its author had been printed in very large type. Large enough for all the court to see.

"*The Darling of the Slums*," said Savine, "by Spillion Sworbreck."

Broad remembered the day that pamphlet was written, out in the Three Farms, and he gave a disbelieving snort. You had to admire the gall of it.

"I...well..." Sworbreck had turned almost as red as his suit. "I'm not...sure I recall—"

"Let me refresh your memory by reading a typical passage." Savine flipped the pamphlet open, and while rocking her baby began to read. "'As Lady Brock moves through those darkened streets, it is as if a beacon shines. Lighting the way to a better life for these neglected unfortunates. As if the sun breaks through the smoke of the manufactories. She gives out bread, yes, she gives out wisdom, surely, she gives out silver with an open hand, but more valuable than all, she gives out *hope*.' You praised my charity and selflessness." She glanced back at the pamphlet. "My apologies. My *remarkable* charity and selflessness." She lifted her brows. "Are you calling yourself a liar?"

There was a cheer from the public gallery. Folk were on their feet up there. Even some of the Representatives clapped. King Orso thumped the bars of his cage in glee and made the door rattle.

"Long live the Darling o' the Slums!" someone roared from the highest balcony.

Broad had never seen Judge look more furious, and fury was what she was all about. Seeing her prosecutor hated was one thing. Seeing him mocked was something else.

"Bitch is making fucking *fools* of us!" snarled Sarlby.

The letter was half-crushed in Broad's fist, a few words of May's writing showing.

*We know who you are.*

Leo couldn't swing a sword like he used to, but a trained warhorse is a hell of a weapon. He spurred through the open gate, face fixed in that mad mixture of smile and snarl he used to wear charging into battle. He caught a glimpse of wide eyes, gripped saddle and reins as a man was trampled under his horse's hooves, another flung against the wall leaving a dash of red on the stones.

Leo wasn't sure whether they'd been armed or not. Only that they'd be wielding the most terrifying weapons you ever saw in the painting he'd have made of this moment.

Other riders were bursting through the archway, surging around him and into the city. Teufel's gold had done most of the job, but there was still work to do with steel. Still some Breakers and Burners fixed on fighting.

"Shoot those bastards!" he roared, pointing up the street towards two running figures. Jurand took aim from the saddle, brought one down at a range of twenty paces.

"Shot!" snapped Leo, wishing he had a hand free so he could clap him on the shoulder. More flatbows rattled. The other man staggered on a few steps then sank moaning to his knees in the street.

"Move!" Forest was bellowing, hooves clattering on cobbles as he waved mounted men through the gate. "Move!" Leo wondered whether there'd be room for him in the painting. A strong leader and an honourable man. Somewhere in the back, maybe. "On to the Agriont!"

Leo leaned from his saddle to shout at Glaward. "Move south towards the docks. Spread out, take charge of the city. Anyone who resists, arrest them."

"If they won't be arrested?"

"We can't afford to let anyone get in the way. Do you understand?"

Glaward swallowed. "I understand." He was a good man, too, in his way, but too soft-hearted to ever really be in the foreground.

A threadbare battle flag was already being hoisted over the gatehouse, the golden sun catching the breeze and flying boldly for the first time since the Great Change. Leo grinned up at it. Certainly there'd be room for that on the canvas.

"What shall we do with these?" Jurand nodded towards a row of men being dragged from the gatehouse and shoved sullen onto their knees.

"Keep them prisoner," said Leo. "We'll deal with them when this is settled."

"Might be safer to hang them now." Jurand had become less sentimental than ever, recently. As though Leo's new ruthlessness had given him permission. "We don't want to send the wrong message."

"Exactly." Leo nodded towards scared faces at the windows. "Folk have seen enough executions. We have to show them we've come to stop all that." He smiled up at a little girl. A glimpse of that Young Lion charm. "We can hang the bastards later. In private."

"Think we'll have trouble at the Agriont?" Forest frowned towards the far end of the square, where the outline of the House of the Maker showed above the rooftops. "If they don't know we're coming already, they soon will."

"We'll have to trust Inspector Teufel to open the gates."

"We bet everything on a woman who lies for a living?"

"It's an upside-down world, all right." And Leo bared his teeth as he spurred across the square. His stump was on fire from the hard riding, but he couldn't stop, not now. The future of the Union would be settled in the next few hours. He'd made himself a promise that he'd never again be on a losing side.

\*

"Ready?" asked Vick.

Gorst's eyes gleamed in the shadows. "Ready."

She fixed her face in the frown of a People's Chief Inspector in a hell of a mood and shoved open the door of the chain room.

It was a cluttered, confusing place. Light shone inwards from slit windows at either end but upwards, too, from slots in the floor that looked onto the entrance passage below. The hanging chains, gears and mechanisms, racks of spears and armour, the wrist-thick gratings of the three raised portcullises, all cast tricking shadows. But it soon became clear there weren't the eight men in there Vick had expected. There were only four.

It seemed there might be such a thing as good luck after all.

"You!" snapped Vick at the most dangerous-looking of them—a big, crop-haired bastard with cauliflower ears and a red smear across his jerkin. "What's your name?"

He glanced at the others, nervously licking his lips, but found no way out. "Corporal Smiler?" he muttered, as if he wasn't completely sure.

"Smiler?" she growled. "Is that a joke?"

"No! They started calling me that in Styria, 'cause I never smiled, and I guess it stuck, and..." He tried a weak smile on her and, indeed, was very bad at it. He cleared his throat and stood to attention. "I'm eager to help, Inspector!"

"Someone had better. Commissioner Pike has concerns about the loyalty of the men stationed here."

"You'll find no one more dedicated!" spluttered one with an oddly lopsided face.

"The Great Change!" shouted another, holding up his fist. As Vick turned to glare at him, he cleared his throat and hid it behind his back.

"Aren't there meant to be eight of you?" she asked, frowning around as if she was looking for weaknesses to put right, rather than ones she could exploit.

Corporal Smiler cleared his throat again, his thick neck shifting. "Well, normally—"

"So where are the rest?"

"I guess...watching the trial..."

Vick gave him a few breaths to stew in his worry. His fellows were easing away from him, like you might from a man infected. One was trying to hide behind a portcullis, failing to realise the essence of a portcullis is that you can see right through it. "Who's in charge here?" Vick snapped at him.

"Sergeant Hambeck!" No doubts now he was naming someone else. If there was one thing everybody knew how to do these days, it was denounce.

"Don't tell me. He's watching the trial."

"They say this one'll likely be a real zinger, so we drew lots and—"

"You two, go and fetch him. *Now.*"

"Right away!" squeaked Smiler, grabbing his friend from behind the portcullis and hurrying for the door, Gorst pressing himself against the wall to let them past.

And as easily as that, the odds were even. Only two guards: the lopsided one and an older one with a beard, frowning at Gorst as if he couldn't quite place him.

"You!" she snapped, bringing his head snapping towards her. "Show me the windlasses."

"The windlasses, Inspector?"

"I need to check they haven't been sabotaged," she said, while wondering what the best way to sabotage them would be.

"Sabotaged, Inspector?"

She took a step towards him. "Is there an echo in here?"

"It's just...that's silly."

"Really? Maybe you want to stand in the dock and tell Judge how silly it is?"

It was plain from his face that he didn't. "The first one's here," he croaked, ducking under a couple of low-hanging chains to lead her over. "Ain't that complicated. This thing with the handles like a ship's wheel, you turn that to raise it, those are gears for the weight, but it still takes three strong men to lift one o' these bastards, believe me..." Vick could hardly hear him over the thudding of her own heart as she slid the mace from her belt. She tried not to look at the scarf he was wearing. A nice patterned one, the kind a wife knits for a husband or a daughter for a father. She focused on his bald spot instead. Few grey hairs there. Didn't want to kill him, but in her experience it was far better to hit a man too hard than not hard enough. "Push this here lever to drop it in an attack—"

The mace made a meaty crunch as Vick smashed him across the back of the head. He crumpled over the windlass, blood squirting from a ragged gash across his scalp, sprinkling across the chains, the gears, the floor.

She heard a muffled cry from the other end of the room. Saw vague shapes shifting in the shadows. Then one dropped and Gorst stood there, short steel gleaming red.

"Oh." The bearded one was pushing himself up from the windlass,

341

blood running down his face in regular spurts and soaking into his scarf. "My head's all—"

She smashed him across the side of the skull, even harder. So hard she knocked him back upright, spinning on one heel, tumbling into the portcullis and crashing down on his back, thrashing like a landed fish, foaming at the mouth in some kind of wild fit. His kicking leg lashed out and knocked a rack of spears clattering across the floor.

She tossed her mace as she dropped on top of him, struggling to pin him down. "Help me hold the bastard—"

There was a sharp crack as Gorst nailed him through the top of his broken head with his short steel. The man flopped down, suddenly still.

Vick rocked back on her haunches. "Shit," she whispered. She should've known limiting the violence would be a forlorn hope. But it looked like their luck had held. They had the chain room, and that was the part that had worried her most. The place was designed to be held even if the walls around it were taken. Now they just had to lock themselves in—

There was a boy standing in the doorway, staring wide-eyed at Gorst and Vick, both of them covered in blood and kneeling over a dead Burner.

She struggled up. "Wait there!"

The boy bolted like a ferret. By the time she'd made it to the corridor, the only sign of him was the fading echoes of his slapping feet.

"Shit!" she hissed again, but a good deal louder. She caught the edge of the door, a good thickness of solid oak, and heaved it shut with a reassuring clunk. She reached for the bar to drop it into the thick brackets and froze.

There was no bar.

There was a hinge against the frame with a couple of dangling screws, but the bar itself was gone. She cast wildly about in the shadows, but there was no sign of it. Might be it got smashed when the Breakers took the Agriont. Or the Burners ripped it off along with the gates downstairs. It hardly mattered why it was gone. That boy would be bringing guards. Lots of guards. And soon.

"There's no bar!" she snarled.

"Huh," said Gorst, without emotion.

If there really was such a thing as good luck, it seemed there was a limited supply.

# The Side of the Saints

"**T**hat's *it*!" screamed Judge, springing up and smashing at the wounded table so savagely she put a great split in it. "*Fucking* stop!"

Savine had not paid enough for all the support that was coming from the galleries. Some of it must have actually been heartfelt. People taking no small risk to show their honest feelings. She had worked all her life to be envied. She had never imagined she might truly be *liked*.

"Broad!" Judge showered spit, tendons starting from her hand as she shook her hammer towards the galleries. "Next bastard makes a sound, get up there and show 'em the quick way down!"

Broad glared up, then towards Judge, then towards Savine. He had a paper crumpled in his fist. The letter she had given him? The hall had fallen quiet as the grave. Being liked was very pleasant. But its limitations as a shield against terror were starkly revealed.

"Any other cunt wants to lend support to our defendant can come down and join her in the dock." Judge's black eyes swept the balconies, the benches. "No? No one?" A silence so complete it was a pressure on the ear. "Didn't *fucking* think so."

Sworbreck wrung his hands. "Citizeness Judge—"

"Sit the *shit* down, you posturing dunce!" she snarled back at him. "'Fore I send you to the Tower ahead!"

Sworbreck sat.

Judge turned her glare on Savine. "Let's stop tickling the rim and come to the point. You've dressed like a nursemaid, and you've smiled at some orphans, and you've handed out a blanket or two, congratulations. But you *are* Savine dan Glokta. You *are* the daughter of not one tyrant, but two, not to mention the sister of a third."

"Should I be punished for my birth?" she asked, but her voice was giving out. It sounded thin.

"I've seen folk convicted for less." Judge nodded towards Orso's cage. "But if you want weightier crimes, I understand you and the king knew each other a little better'n a brother and sister should."

In spite of everything, she could not help looking at him. Could not help meeting his eye. Could not help feeling the same as she always had.

Judge followed the look between them, red brows high. "I mean to say, you'll find no broader minds than mine, but even I get itchy around incest."

Savine felt her face burning and knew she must look guilty as the plague. Knew she *was* guilty as the plague.

"I never knew...he was..." She could not even finish the sentence.

"Spare your blushes." Judge waved a generous hand. "Put the brother-fucking to one side. Put all the rest in the best baby-nurturing, orphan-housing, loaf-giving light you've got. Truth is you *are* a profiteer. You *did* exploit the working man, and woman, and child. You *have* built your palaces from their bones. You're the worst o' the old regime, squeezed into the shape of a woman. You're fucking guilty, girl, guilty as Glustrod, and I know it, and you know it, and we all damn well know it."

Savine did know it. The list of people she had used unrolled pitilessly before her. The desperate supplicants at the Solar Society. The partners she had bullied and blackmailed. The workers she had beaten and tortured. The children slaving in her mill in Valbeck. The soldiers buried in shallow graves at Stoffenbeck. Even her own husband, who she had deftly prodded into serving her ambitions, then left him to pay the bill with his arm and his leg.

One cannot climb high without standing on others, and all she had wanted was to reach the top. What a waste it all seemed now. There is nothing at the summit, in the end, but a long drop.

A different kind of murmur was coming from the galleries, and not nearly so friendly.

"But this court is not without mercy!" called Judge, holding up a hand for silence. "We see you've tried to make amends. We see you've done some good. The same hands that clawed profits from the people have given 'em back to the needy. You've put a toe on righteous earth, even if you left the other foot on evil! So we'll give you a chance. To come down on the side o' the saints, as your Gurkish friends might say."

Judge leaned forwards and pointed with her long forefinger. "Accept your guilt and denounce. Denounce both your fathers. Tell us where we can find Old Sticks. Put him in the dock in your place and live. Refuse?"

She draped herself back into her chair, black eyes fixed on Savine like a wolf's on dinner. "The Tower o' Chains is waiting."

No one called out in Savine's defence now, paid or not, and who could blame them? There was only accusation in the rings of tight-packed faces at the balconies above. She leaned over the dock to lay Ardee in the crook of Freid's arm, next to her brother. The blanket had come loose and she tucked it gently around her again, laid one hand upon her, the other on Harod. He squirmed and snivelled. She wanted to hold him so badly, one last time. But that would only put them in danger. She had to do the brave thing, for once. Put someone else above herself and let them go.

"Try to keep them safe," she whispered.

Freid nodded dumbly, tears on her cheeks. Tears more of fear than sorrow, Savine rather thought, and who could blame her?

She adjusted her dress as she turned back to Judge. Foolishness, of course, but the habit was impossible to break. Her mother had always warned her a man is judged by his best moment, a woman by her worst. One had to make the effort, even for an informal event. Savine forced back her shoulders, raised her chin into that position of eternal slight discomfort her governess always used to call deportment.

"I have no idea where my father is," she said.

Judge narrowed her eyes. "Come, come, Citizeness Brock. That won't save your life."

Short of Arch Lector Glokta throwing off a cloak and revealing himself in the public gallery, Savine did not see that anything could. But she refused to let them beat her. Dignity is not worth much, in the end, but she was determined to keep it even so.

"You picked apt names for yourselves." Savine looked around the ruined hall that was once the Lords' Round. Its scarred marble, smashed furniture, empty slogans, red-daubed thugs. "You are Burners. You build nothing, you make nothing. All you can do is destroy. The old regime was rotten. The people cried for freedom. What have you given them?" She gave a helpless shrug. "Corpses. I do not know where my father is. But even if I did, I would not tell you."

The echoes faded. No sound but the quick breath through her nostrils, and little Harod's faint snivelling.

Her efforts had not even dented Judge's smile. "Then, Citizeness Brock, you give me no choice but to sentence you to death by falling from the Tower of Chains. And may I say that in my long career there's no ruling I've enjoyed pronouncing more." And she raised her hammer.

*

"Wait!" screeched Orso, his sweaty face pressed to the bars of his cage.

Judge turned ever so slowly to regard him through narrowed eyes. "For what, Citizen Orso?"

"If she won't make denouncements, I will!" A swell of whispers went up, in spite of Judge's threats. "I'll denounce anyone! I'll denounce everyone! I'll give you the best damn denouncing you ever heard!"

Judge stared at him for a long, tense moment, while a bead of sweat tickled ever so slowly down his scalp. Then she gave vent to a delighted chuckle. "Oh, this we *have* to hear. Corporal Halder, let His Excuse for a Fucking Majesty address the court."

Halder strode to the cage's door and unlocked it as the eager babble spread around the hall.

"What are you doing?" hissed Hildi as Orso stepped from captivity.

"Buying time." He was no mighty warrior. He was no learned sage. But when it came to talking rubbish he acknowledged no equal.

"Representatives!" he thundered, advancing across the tiled floor where he had once sentenced Lord Wetterlant to death. "Ex-lords and ladies, ex-subjects of myself and my father, good Citizens and Citizenesses of the Union! I, Orso the First, King of Angland, Starikland and Midderland, Protector of Westport and High King of the Union, lately resident in a freezing cellar beneath the palace, come before you now in this sweltering ruin to make denouncements!"

"Do it, then," said Judge.

"I will, Citizeness, I will." Orso cleared his throat, gave the court an apologetic smile, dragged out the expectant silence. "I fear I cannot divulge to you the hiding place of Old Sticks. Not by any means because I refuse to do so! Because I do not know. Honestly, what kind of fool would trust me with important information? Would you trust me? I'm not sure *I* would!" He shook his head as a few chuckles echoed from the galleries. "I'm not sure I would." He was happy to be their clown, if it bought Savine a few moments. "But I'll happily denounce the bastard! He was Arch Lector of the Inquisition, for the Fates' sakes—he more or less denounces himself!" Hearty shouts of agreement. "He was the rotten heart of the Closed Council for thirty years! A hoarder of power. A prolific torturer. An implacable enemy to noblemen and common men alike. Worst of all, he has let his daughter..." He looked over at Savine, who was staring at him from the dock, hands gripping its rail. "His *adopted* daughter, pay for his crimes in his absence. What a withered shit! What a crippled coward! What a two-bit tyrant!"

Cheers and laughter at each insult, and Orso glanced at Tunny, just in passing. The ex-standard-bearer had the ghost of a smile, still turning that one finger around and around. Drag it out. Drag it out. Orso took a huge breath.

"Yes, good Citizens and Citizenesses, His Eminence Arch Lector Glokta was a specimen as morally as he was physically repugnant. But he did not ruin the Union alone! He did not bring us to the dire pass in which we now find ourselves without a willing patsy to warm the throne while he worked. Pray allow me to make an introduction to my noble father, King Jezal the First!"

A few bits of thrown food accompanied the name and some light heckling which Judge was obliged to wave into silence. "Interrupt the defence, people, by all means, but not the fucking denunciations!"

"My thanks, Your Honour." Orso bowed extravagantly, exactly the way his mother had taught him. "I like to think my father had good instincts, buried deep. He would often discuss them, when we fenced together. Projects for the relief of the poor. For the fair distribution of medicine and education. For peace on our borders. But that he had good instincts only makes his total failure to follow them all the worse. You can pardon a man who knows no better. One who ignores the best parts of himself you can only condemn. What a waste of flesh he turned out to be! What a worthless fart! What an empty vessel!"

"Hear, hear!" Judge hammered lazily at the table. "I find the bastard guilty in his absence!"

Far from the worst injustice witnessed in the Court of the People. In spite of his many faults, Orso's father had been a generous sort. He would not have minded being lightly slandered in a good cause. Especially when that good cause was the life of his first-born natural child.

"Thank you, friends, for your patience," bellowed Orso, "but my roll of ignominy is by no means finished. You might suppose the blame would stop at the throne, but you could not be more wrong! There has always been a man *behind* the throne of the Union..." He let the moment stretch, the anticipation build. "I would like next to denounce none other than Bayaz, the First of the Magi, whose statue until recently stood in the Kingsway! *Two* statues of the bastard, in fact, such was his monstrous vanity. The top and tail to centuries of exploitation! *He* was the man who gave my father and Old Sticks their orders. *He* was the painstaking watchmaker who pieced together the corrupt system that ground every Citizen of the Union down. *He* was the one who returned when it suited him, to ensure it was still grinding people down as efficiently as ever. *He* was the one who carelessly laid waste to the Agriont, who killed thousands in the name of his ambitions, then forced the survivors to celebrate him as their saviour! The very personification of ruthlessness, a puppeteer who used kings as his marionettes!"

All eyes were fixed on him as he paraded across the grubby tiles. He caught a glimpse of Savine whispering to her maid and the woman edged away with the children in her arms. Orso redoubled his efforts.

"All this is common—if horrible—knowledge, but do you know how he *profited* from it all? Profited beyond the dreams of avarice? You want usurers? Hoarders? Speculators? Bayaz is the grandfather of them all. A magus more taken with money than magic!" Secrets did not seem so very important now, nor immortal wizards so very frightening. "He is both Valint *and* Balk! The loans that broke the state were all taken from him, the interest all paid to him. *He* was the one who made a Great Change inevitable. Made it necessary, even! *He* is the one who should be standing in that dock, to receive the People's Justice!"

"I'll keep a warrant warm for him," said Judge, her black eyes gleaming, "but sad to say the First o' the Magi's beyond our reach. You done?"

"I beg the court's patience for just one more! The worst of the pack. The lowest of the low. Lastly, and most fiercely, I denounce . . . *myself*." And he spread his arms wide as though inviting the crowd to shoot him full of arrows. There was laughter. There was applause, of a mocking variety. "I have been lazy. I have been vain. I have been as petty as my mother and as indecisive as my father. I could have done good, but I could not be bothered. I could have made peace, but I was too busy making love. I could have made the Union a better place! If only I hadn't been so very, very drunk. I have no doubt that history will judge me to have been not only the last High King of the Union, but the worst, and my brief reign the most disastrous on—"

There was a boom as the doors at the top of the aisle were flung open and a Burner in red-smeared armour staggered breathless to the steps.

Judge leaped up, raising her hammer as if she was about to fling it at him. "I said we weren't to be disturbed!"

"But there's royalists approaching the Agriont!" he squealed, cringing.

"There's *what*?"

"Inside the city! Lord Marshal Forest is leading 'em!"

There was no stopping the noise now. Gasps of "Royalists?" Screams of "Treachery?" Shrieks of "Forest?"

"Where's the fucking Young Lion?" demanded Judge.

"He's with 'em!"

For a moment, even she was lost for words. Everyone was. And as

Orso looked across the staring faces on the Representatives' benches, from Citizens Heugen and Isher to a surprisingly popular beggar elected from the Three Farms, he knew they were all working desperately at this strange new sum, trying to tally up where their best interests lay, and therefore what mixture of emotion to put on display. He suspected loyalties shifted quicker in that moment than at any time since his father was unexpectedly voted to the throne.

Those most loyal to the Great Change shook fists and roared their dismay. Several of the ex-lords did not look surprised, let alone displeased. Most chose, perhaps wisely, to hedge their bets and stay quiet. But up in the public gallery they were more vocal.

"The Young Lion!" someone called, in what sounded very much like full-throated support.

"The Darling o' the Slums!" came a woman's voice. "You saved my—" Cut off in a squeal.

"Freedom! Freedom!" Though for who and from what was not explained.

A kind of fever had broken out. A madness of hope, fear and fury. Like the one on the day the Breakers first took the city, maybe. People scrambled for the doors. Ran for safety, for their families. Others fought their way to the railings of the gallery to bellow their disgust or their encouragement.

"Death to Aristocrats!"

"Enough bloodshed! Enough bloodshed!"

"Down with the Great Change!"

"Hang 'em all!"

"Bastards!"

There was even a plaintive cry of, "Long live the king!" Over-earnest, entirely mad or simply an early bet on a new reality, it was impossible to say.

"I fucking doubt it," snarled Judge. She pointed at Orso with a finger sporting at least four stolen wedding rings. "Since you're so keen to denounce yourself on her behalf, you can take the long drop with her. Corporal Halder, bind this fool!"

Halder looked like he'd much rather have slipped out of a side door, but the habit of obedience was hard to break. He and one of his fellows pulled Orso's arms behind him and the cord painfully tight about his wrists, while Broad brought Savine down from the dock and bound her hands, his heavy jaw fixed, his red eyes staring.

"Burners, to me!" screeched Judge, and they began to converge from every part of the court. From the benches, from the galleries, from their

349

places on guard around the walls. Men and women with red-daubed clothes, red-spattered armour, the fire of fanaticism still hot in their eyes. Men and women who would rather go down in flames than see any hint of the old Union return.

Halder grabbed Orso under the arm and started to march him towards the aisle, a good four-score Burners gathering around them in a grim knot, weapons drawn, with Judge their furious spear-point.

The door shuddered against Vick's shoulder with a sound of splintering wood.

They'd brought an axe, then, and from the feel of it a big one. She wondered how long she and Gorst could hold the door shut. She wondered how many Burners were out there. She wondered what would happen when they got in. She didn't like any of her answers.

The axe blows stopped and there was a sudden shove on the door, harder than ever, so hard it nearly flung Vick to the ground.

She'd wedged pieces of a broken spear into the brackets where the bar would've gone, but they didn't fit, jumping and flexing. She could hear them outside, one voice calling the rhythm. "Shove! Shove! Shove!"

There was a faint squealing, and with a chill horror Vick saw one of the brackets was working loose, rusted nails easing from splintering wood at the pressure outside.

"The frame's rotten!" she hissed through her gritted teeth. The door had eased open a chink, and then wider, the grunts and growls coming louder than ever from beyond.

Gorst's eyes met hers, and she got the feeling they'd come to the same conclusion: they weren't going to be able to hold that door shut much longer.

"On three," he hissed, keeping one shoulder braced against the wood, but sliding out his short steel with the other hand, "we open it."

"We fucking what?" Vick snarled back at him.

"And *fight*."

The door jerked open another finger's breadth. Something slid through, so close to Vick she had to twist her face away, staring at it cross-eyed. The blade of a spear. Someone was using it as a lever, working the door open.

"One," squeaked Gorst.

Vick gave the door a last parting shove then scrambled back, clawing her bloody mace up from the floor.

"Two."

The bracket dropped free of the frame and bounced away, the pieces of broken spear tumbling, Gorst's boots sliding as he was forced back.

"Three!"

And he jumped clear, sweeping out his long steel. Between the half-light and the panic, Vick wasn't sure how many burst through into the chain room. Too many. They were shouting. She'd no idea what, over her own quick breath. Just swearing, maybe. Just mindless shrieking, maybe. She might've been shrieking herself.

One came tottering bent over, almost falling from the pressure behind. Gorst's long steel hacked into the back of his head in a spray of blood. Another got the short steel through his guts and floundered about, screeching, tangled up with his own halberd. Another came with a shield up, barrelled into Gorst and managed to shove him away from the door.

Which is how one could come straight at Vick, screaming at the top of his voice. She caught a glimpse of him as he pounded through a shaft of light, lips curled back, a smear of Burner's red paint across his cheek. Then her mace crunched into his mouth, bits of tooth flying. His head snapped up, his roar turned to a squawk. She tried to swing again but he blundered into her, so the mace missed his head and thumped weakly against his back. She stumbled, caught her heel on a fallen body and went over on her arse. With a kind of wounded bellow, the Burner she'd hit in the mouth flopped towards the nearest windlass, drooling blood.

"Fuck!" Vick scrambled up, rearing over him, swinging the mace with both hands. She smashed in the back of his head, but his hands were already around the lever. Now he sagged onto it, a dead weight.

There was a heavy clunk. Gears whirred as the portcullis began to drop in its frame, its cross-hatched shadow shifting on the wall.

There was a clatter as Gorst dropped his steels and caught the windlass. It dragged him along for a moment, but he twisted, teeth clenched, got his shoulder against one handle and braced himself, trembling, growling, having to strain with all his strength to hold it up. For an instant, everything was oddly still.

Then someone stepped through the door behind him. Corporal Smiler, and by no means smiling. He saw Gorst, he saw all the dead Burners, plus one still screaming, crawling, screaming as he tried to hold his guts in. He heaved up an outsized axe, the one he must've been using on the door, its blade near scraping the ceiling, ready to split Gorst's skull in half.

He gave a surprised *ooof* as Vick charged into him, drove him crashing into the wall, the axe bouncing off her back and onto the floor. She went at him with everything she had. Tried for his balls with a clumsy jab of the mace but only hit his hip, dug her other fist into his stomach but barely got a wheeze from him. She straightened up so she could swing at his throat.

She caught a flash of movement in the darkness, then a sick crunch.

She gave a snorting gurgle. Mouth full of blood. Her face felt weird. Someone was screaming. Choking, horrible screams. Was that her?

There'd been something important she had to do. Couldn't think what. Couldn't think at all.

Something about a tunnel. Ah, portcullis! She groggily shook her head. She could see Gorst, still straining at the windlass, jaw squirming, but he looked a long way off. Everything dim.

There was something tight around her neck. Tried to slap it away but her hands were so weak. It squeezed tighter, and tighter. Couldn't breathe.

Smiler had her around the throat, pressed up against the wall, her feet barely touching the floor. He was snarling in her throbbing face. She tore at his hands with her nails, her mouth blowing breathless, bloody squelches in his face. She wriggled, struggled, but he was too strong. Couldn't breathe.

She managed to work her heel up the wall behind her. He twisted her head up, back, as if he was killing a chicken. Wringing her neck. She wriggled, squirmed, till her fishing hand found the grip of the knife in her boot. Felt like he was going to twist her head off, felt like her skull was going to burst. Couldn't breathe.

He kept holding her with one hand, made a big fist with the other, bringing it back to smash her face again, and she pulled the knife and lashed at him, overhand. Her arm was numb, tangled with his elbow on the way, but the blade still caught something.

He let go and she flopped down on hands and knees. She could just hear his wail over the sudden roaring of blood in her ears. She saw him lurch away, one hand clapped to the side of his head, and he tripped in the darkness and went over backwards.

Fuck, she wanted to lie down. The bastard with the guts was curled up on his side now, sobbing. She wanted to join him. Instead she struggled to her feet, clinging to the corner of a crate full of flatbow bolts, knees bent like a sailor on the slick deck of a storm-tossed ship. She gasped for air, wheezing, braying, wanting to puke with each breath. Her face was one pulsing mass of pain.

Gorst was still straining at the handles of the windlass, veins bulging from his neck, sweat beaded on his forehead, the mechanism grinding. His eyes flickered to his steels, on the floor beside his boot, then to the other side of the room. Over there, in the shadows, Smiler clambered up, growling through gritted teeth. He had a great ragged wound down the side of his head, blood pattering his shoulder and streaking his armour, his ear hanging off by a shred of gristle. A wound bad enough to make him very angry. But not bad enough to put him down.

Vick could certainly have used Gorst's help. But if he let go and that portcullis dropped, all their plans were fucked.

"Thtay!" she snarled at him, her battered throat hardly able to get the air, her battered mouth hardly able to make the words. "I'll handle thith."

She caught the haft of the big axe and dragged it towards her, blade scraping against the stones. Bloody hell, it was a weight, thick haft riveted with strips of steel, she could scarcely even lift it.

Smiler was on his feet, facing her from the other side of the chain room, near the open door, one of his dead comrades' fallen swords in one hand, the other clapped to the gash Vick had dug into the side of his head. His leather jerkin was splattered all over, no way of telling what was red paint, or his blood, or hers. His face twisted into a snarl.

"Come here, bitch!" he roared at her.

Vick charged. Or at any rate she half-stumbled, half-fell. But not straight at him. Sideways at the portcullis. She dropped, which wasn't hard to do, and slid the axe along the floor, ramming the haft straight through the grating until the blade caught against it.

Gorst let go of the windlass. There was a whirr of gears as the portcullis dropped, then a clank as one of the steel bars caught on the axe haft and was held there, loose chains faintly rattling.

Gorst gave a soft growl as he peeled his hands from the handles. He bent down, narrowed eyes fixed on Smiler. He came up with his bloody steels in his fists. He worked his shoulders, then stretched his neck one way, then the other.

"Come here, bitch," he said in that piping voice.

Smiler glanced at Vick. She stayed on her knees and gave a little shrug. He tossed away the sword and bolted through the open doorway. Gorst stepped over one of the corpses, put his shoulder to the door and heaved it shut again, ended up sitting on the floor with his back to the wood. The Burner who'd been stuck in the guts had stopped screaming. Just lay there on his side in a great slick of blood, each breath a shallow squeak.

"You hurt?" asked Gorst.

Vick put her fingers gingerly to her nose. A barely recognisable sticky mass on the front of her throbbing face.

"I've had worth," she mumbled. Would've sounded more dauntless if she could've made the "s" sound, maybe. She thought she could hear something. The blood rushing in her skull, or hooves at a distance? She stumbled on wobbling legs, gripping hard at her aching hip, over to the slit windows facing the dry moat. She squinted into the brightness outside, face pressed to the stone.

She saw the bridge. The slogan-daubed buildings beyond. The wide street that led into the city. And coming up it, at a clattering canter, a great mass of horsemen. Armed and armoured, bristling with steel. Leo dan Brock's lion standard flew at the head, the sun of the Union beside it.

"They're here," she croaked. Would've felt more relief if her neck hurt less, maybe. She tried to sniff and failed, then worked her tongue around her mouth and spat more blood. "So... that's good."

The scarred walls of the Agriont rushed up to meet them.

Leo's eyes were narrowed against the wind, his horse jolting wildly on the cobbled street, riders shouting and jostling all around him, but he saw now that the portcullises were still raised, their iron teeth gleaming in the ceiling of the entrance tunnel.

Teufel had come through. The woman made herself hard to like, but Leo much preferred competence to charm these days. The archway of white light beckoned at the far end. The way into the Agriont was open.

Leo grinned sideways at Jurand, and Jurand smiled back. By the dead, he'd forgotten the feeling of riding at the enemy with good men beside him.

People scattered from the gateway. Shocked faces as they dived aside. Could've been Breakers, Burners, fools come to gawp at Savine's trial or fools running for their lives. All Leo was sure of was that they were in his way.

He gave his horse the spurs, sending a stab of pain through his own leg, knocking a man spinning from his horse's flank to crash into the tunnel wall. His scream was lost in the thundering echoes. Smashing hooves, rattling armour, ringing weapons, roared orders, all the sounds Leo most loved. He was the Young Lion again.

They plunged out into the brightness. There was something like resistance further down the road, where the way narrowed between two white buildings. A few dozen Burners, all daubed with red, trying to throw up a barricade around an upturned cart.

Leo couldn't have stopped even if he'd wanted to, and he didn't. "For the Union!" he roared, aching from the effort of clinging to his horse. "Charge!"

He picked his spot, hunched low as he jumped a few tangled chairs and crashed down among the shrieking Burners on the other side, scattering bodies.

He had to drop his reins to free his sword. You'd think with one arm you could still swing a blade well enough, but without his leg to grip his horse or his other arm to give him balance, he wobbled in the saddle, flailed uselessly, struck someone with the flat and nearly fumbled the grip. His own clumsiness filled him with fury and he clenched his teeth, hacking about him, finally landing a decent blow on the other side, blood spattering yellow hair.

He wasn't the man he used to be, that was plain. He was streaming with sweat under his armour, gasping for breath, useless arm throbbing numbly.

Riders kept smashing into the remnants of the barricade. Jumping over it, blades flashing in the sunlight. Jurand had his teeth bared, swinging away. A couple of horses lay dying, one of Leo's officers was on his knees, coughing blood, but the Burners were shattered, already running.

Some of Forest's men tore after them on horseback, the lord marshal himself close behind, couched over his saddle as his horse jumped the half-built barricade. "Save the king!" he roared over his shoulder and Leo spurred after, clinging to sword and reins at once.

The park opened up before them, a muddy, overgrown mockery of the shimmering greenery he'd swaggered through when he first visited Adua. There were running figures everywhere. Running towards him, running away. Almost as much chaos as the day of the Great Change. Over the roofs ahead he could see the great gilded dome, gleaming dully beneath its streaking of soot, and beyond it the black spike of the Tower of Chains.

The thought suddenly floated up of how much simpler things might be if Savine had already taken the long drop.

Leo pushed it angrily away. She was his wife. The mother of his children. He was duty-bound to do everything he could to save her. The Young Lion might not be swept away by every feeling any more, but he still took his duty very seriously.

"Forward!" he roared over his shoulder. "To the Lords' Round!" He'd be damned if anyone would call it the Court of the People ever again.

# The Sentence

Savine had become something of a connoisseur of mayhem. She had been caught up in the vicious uprising in Valbeck, been a prisoner in the Agriont on the day of the Great Change, borne personal witness to the terror that followed. But the chaos in the Square of Martyrs now was not the purposeful kind that the Breakers, then the Burners, had chosen to impose upon the Union. This reminded her more of the rout after Stoffenbeck. The outright panic of the losing side in a battle. The vicious frenzy of every person for themselves.

Quite a crowd must have gathered for her execution, but now, with news of the approaching royalist army, it was their own imminent deaths that were commanding all their attention. Mobs had formed around the archways leading off the square, people screaming and shoving and trampling one another, tangled with riders and hawkers' carts. Here is how things end: not with some grand drama, but a shameful scuffle in a gate.

Over the slaughterhouse squealing of mortal terror, Savine thought she could hear the faint sounds of fighting. The same distant clamour of men and metal she had heard at Stoffenbeck, and it sparked that same mixture of hope and fear, though with an even more desperate edge now.

Judge glowered back up the rubbish-strewn steps towards the Lords' Round. The Commons' Round. The Court of the People. The heart of the Union, whichever version of the Union you subscribed to, rebuilt even more grandly on the grand ruins of the one Bayaz had laid waste to, its stonework pocked and scarred and daubed with the slogans of the Great Change.

"Burn it," she said.

The way they set to the task it must have been a plan long arranged. Burners trotted off with torches and a few moments later Savine was shocked to see flames flicker up the sides of the building. Wood stacked in readiness, she supposed, and buttresses painted with pitch.

356

Judge took a long breath and blew it out in a sour grunt, like a woman looking back on the dream home from which she has just been evicted. "Court stands in recess," she muttered. "Let's go."

"Let's go," said Broad, steering Savine by the shoulder. There was no violence in it, but there was no resisting it, either.

The Burners pressed in close as they set off across the square. She could see nothing between their bodies but running figures, the odd flash of a terrified face. She could not even tell where Orso was. Somewhere else in this jostling, stinking, red-spattered knot of fanatics. She wished he was beside her. This one last time.

She stumbled, would have fallen if Broad hadn't caught her arm. Candles sent skittering. Set up as a little shrine beside one of the names carved in the flagstones. The names of those killed to keep the old regime in power, half-glimpsed under her shuffling feet, blurred through the wet in her eyes. The names of those her father had beaten, tortured, hanged so that she could be rich.

Broad had tied her hands in front of her rather than behind. They had no fear she would make some mad bid for freedom. She had sometimes watched the arrested taken away, mute and tame, and wondered why they did not fight, however long the odds. But now she let herself be herded to her death without even—

The children! A sudden pang of dread. She cast about wildly, clutching at her dress, straining at the cords around her wrists. Freid had them. She sucked in a shuddering breath. Freid would keep them safe. And if she did not, what could Savine do? Not a thing.

She had been fixed on becoming a better person for them. Better than her parents had been for her. Their best friend, faithful protector, wise teacher, honest confidante. Now they would grow up without ever knowing her. Not even remembering her. Ever since she was arrested she had been telling herself she was doomed. But it was only now that she really started to believe it.

There was a crash as something hit one of the Burners on the helmet. "This is madness," someone was hissing, "fucking *madness*," his nervous eyes darting, clearly less of a true believer than the rest.

"Keep moving," came Judge's snarl.

The sounds of fighting were growing louder. Closer. Leo might be just beyond the edge of the square. Might be cutting his way through to her, even now. A surge went through the Burners and she was shouldered sideways, caught her shoe on something, bit her tongue as she nearly fell. The outstretched arm of a limp body, bloody hair spread across the cracked flagstones.

"Keep moving," Broad growled, nudging her on.

It had been easy to be brave, in the Court of the People. To play the part of the noble martyr. Now the Tower of Chains loomed up ahead, Savine's neck tilting further and further back as she stared towards its roof, and the fear began to grip her. The way it had in Valbeck, when she crawled through her own whirring machinery, when she ran through the ruined streets. Her mouth grew dry. Her knees grew weak. Her breath came faster and faster.

She was so fixed on the tower's top she did not see Curnsbick's lift until they were almost upon it. But then it had few of the flourishes of the inventor's best work. A dizzying column of rickety scaffolding, a wooden platform at the bottom with a rail around the edge and chains at each corner. At the sight of it she could not seem to stop her chest heaving, and yet she could not seem to get a proper breath. Suddenly, stupidly, she desperately wanted her mother.

"It's not too late to talk!" she blurted out.

"It's always been too late." Judge thoughtfully raised one brow at her. "Do you know why they call me Judge?"

Savine stared back dumbly.

"Honestly? Neither do I." She jerked her head towards the lift. "Get her on there."

Broad half-ushered, half-lifted her onto the platform. She felt so weak she thought she might fall as he stepped up himself, his great boot making the whole thing shudder.

"You have the king," said Savine. "You could make a deal."

A few more Burners were finally showing some doubts, but not Judge. "That's your thing, not mine. No one'll be deal-making their way out o' this. You lot, hold the line here! Nobody comes through, you understand? Sarlby, Halder, let's go."

They manhandled Orso onto the lift beside her. He still had that mocking smile at the corner of his mouth. The one everyone thought was contempt for the world, but she knew was really contempt for himself. He was as calm as a man on his way to a card game.

He leaned towards her as more Burners crowded onto the lift around them. "Have you ever been up before?"

"What?" she croaked. It was the first time they had spoken in months. Since she begged him for Leo's life. Since she told him she was his sister.

And he talked as if they were polite acquaintances running across one another in the park.

"The view's astonishing. The perfect spot to watch the Lords' Round burn. You're going to love it."

She stared at him, mouth slightly open. "Are you … *joking?*"

"I rather think it might be my last opportunity."

She found she'd given a disbelieving laugh. Laughed and sobbed at the same time, perhaps.

He nudged her with his shoulder. "It's probably not much comfort, but I'm glad I'm with you."

"So am I." She felt stronger for it. Managed to work up the kind of arch glance she might have given him in Sworbreck's office, long ago. "My mother always told me it's very important who a girl is seen with."

"Aw," said Judge. "This is sweet. Think I might cry, Sarlby."

"Think I am crying," said Sarlby, "but maybe it's the smoke." There was a tickle of it on the air now, as the flames licked ever higher up the Court of the People. Or was it the Lords' Round again, just while it burned?

Broad did not look as if he would cry. He looked like a wooden man, moved by Judge's words like a machine by levers. Another Burner stepped stiffly onto the platform beside them. As if he would much rather have stayed but could not see how to avoid the trip. Savine realised she knew him. One of the men Broad had hired, for labour relations. Bannerman, was it? She had seen him smiling, at the trial. He was not smiling any more. Their eyes met, and he swallowed, the knobble in his throat bobbing.

The sounds of fighting were louder yet. The people trapped in the square even more desperate. The rest of the Burners made a crescent about the base of the tower, weapons pointing outwards.

Judge jerked her thumb towards the heavens. "Take us up!" There was a squeal of gears and the hoist lurched, then began to rattle upwards.

"At least we don't have to climb the damn steps," said Orso, tipping his head back to follow the chains straight up the well of scaffolding to the square of sky at its top. "Thanks to Master Curnsbick's excellent lift."

"There's progress," whispered Savine.

"Save the king!" squealed Gorst, ploughing through the panicking crowds. The badly carved virtues of the Great Change squinted down on havoc, people running, wailing, cringing, blundering into each other. Hard to say what side anyone was on, if there was such a thing as sides any more. Most were just trying to live through it.

"Save the king!" Gorst hacked someone down with his long steel, sent them bouncing from a pedestal, smearing blood across the stained marble. He kicked, shoved, screeched his way through the mob and Vick limped after him, her face one enormous throb, a watchful eye on his steels in case he took her head off with a backswing, wondering what her chances were of finding someone out here who could set a broken nose.

They burst onto the Square of Martyrs and she hobbled to a stop, nearly slipping over backwards, her free hand up to shield her battered face. The Court of the People was on fire. A giant torch, angry flames roaring. One of its great windows shattered, sparks showering, throwing garish light across the chaos.

Something hit Vick on the back of the head and she stumbled. Didn't even know what it was. Where it had come from. Touched fingers to her hair and they came away bloody. But then she was covered in blood already. Her nose was blocked with it, her chin crusted with it, her mouth salty with it.

"Save the king!" Gorst pounded on, people scattering in front of him. Horsemen spilled from the slogan-daubed buildings on the right, clattering across the square, chopping people down, indiscriminate. A horse fell right in front of Vick, rolled, crushed its rider. She nearly fell herself as she staggered around it, barged into a woman clutching an armful of candlesticks.

"Save the king!" shrieked Gorst, pounding on towards the Tower of Chains. Through the tears the smoke had stung from her eyes, Vick thought she could see Curnsbick's lift crawling up the scaffold on its side.

There were Burners there. A curved line of them, weapons ready, sharpened steel gleaming with the colours of fire. A last line of defence around their place of execution.

Horsemen crashed into them. Anglanders maybe, in dark uniforms. Spears darted. Swords rose and fell. The noise was appalling. Tortured metal, tortured beasts, tortured men. Something crunched into Vick's side and sent her rolling over and over, into a fallen wagon with one wheel squeaking around in the air. She squirmed onto her back, clutching at her jacket. Just dirt. She wasn't hurt. No worse than she'd been before, anyway. Mace still flapping around her wrist on its thong and she caught it by the handle and scrambled up.

The Burners' line was coming apart. She shrank back as horsemen thundered past. She saw one catch a spear in the throat, tumble from the saddle. She saw a man drop with his helmet dented right in. She saw Gorst, face locked in a snarl, savagely swinging.

A Burner stared straight at Vick. She stepped up, caught him by the paint-smeared breastplate. Before she could even lift her mace, Gorst's long steel whipped past and took his head off, left Vick staring in shock at the squirting stump. Her hand was tangled with his armour and she was dragged down on top of him, fresh blood in her eyes, in her face.

She twisted free, spitting and coughing. A bearded man sat, very surprised, a shattered spear shaft sticking from his groin. A woman knelt blubbing, great strings of snot hanging from her nose. A rider with a soot-streaked face stared down at his stricken mount, lying on its side, hooves scraping weakly at the bloody flagstones.

"Where is she?" someone roared. "Where is she?"

"Help! Some help here!"

"For the king!"

"My shoulder! Please, my shoulder!"

Vick stood staring, breathing hard through her sore mouth, still gripping the mace so tight her hand ached.

Gorst held his bloody steels in clenched fists, staring up towards that great scaffold, the platform inching its way upwards. "Not again," he growled. "Not again."

The Burners were finished. Most of them dead or wounded, the rest throwing down their weapons. For better or worse, it looked as if the Great Change was done. Or maybe there was a new Great Change, but what it was a change into no one could yet say.

Brock sat above the whole mess on his high horse amid a cluster of dark-uniformed Anglanders, pointing towards the Tower of Chains with his sword.

"How does that bloody lift work? We have to get it down!"

Vick stared up towards the roof. The platform had stopped moving. They were already at the top.

She licked her split lip and spat yet again, then untangled the thong from her wrist with clumsy fingers and tossed the mace on the ground. After a moment's thought, she sat down wearily beside it. Blood had trickled into one of the martyrs' names and picked half the letters out in red.

"We're too late," she mumbled.

Broad stepped onto the roof of the Tower of Chains. It had turned out a fine day. Crisp and sunny, with a cool breeze carrying off the vapours so you could see across the city. That same mad view he'd witnessed a hundred times, but every time it somehow took him by surprise.

He caught Bannerman's eye. The man had lost all his swagger. He looked scared and confused at once. Like he couldn't see how they'd ended up here. Broad knew how. Some men can't help themselves.

He wasn't drunk. Hadn't touched a drop all day. But he felt drunk. Head spinning. He wondered how many people he'd thrown down now. How many he'd seen thrown down. Never someone he knew well, though. Never someone who'd saved his life. His family's lives.

He felt the letter, crushed to a sweaty ball in his fist.

*We hear you are in trouble.*

Didn't think he could hear fighting any more. Just the sounds of the wounded now, thin on the wind. Had the Young Lion won? Was the Great Change done? The thought brought up no real feeling. He was playing dead, maybe. He'd done that in Styria. Told himself he was dead so nothing that was done to him could matter. Nothing that he did could matter.

Peaceful up here, so high above the city. As high as the highest smoking chimneys. He watched Bannerman nudge Savine up the three steps to the platform. He watched Orso shake off Halder's hand and take the three steps himself to stand beside her. Facing the city. Facing the sea.

*We hear you have lost yourself.*

"Don't worry," said Judge, her wild red hair whipped and slashed by the wind, and behind her flames flickered, smoke rolling into the sky from the burning Court of the People. She put a hand on Broad's cheek. "I know this isn't easy. Sarlby?"

"No," said Broad. He tossed the letter over the parapet, watched it drop out of sight. "It should be me."

*We know who you are.*

He stepped forward. Shouldered past Sarlby, and Bannerman, and Halder. Comrades from the battlefields of Styria, the barricades in Valbeck, the midnight beatings of striking workers. Everything took an effort. Like he was wading through a bog.

*Our husband.*

More of the city showed as he stepped up onto the platform. The grimy white towers, the dark mill chimneys, the maze of roofs leading all the way to the sparkling sea. Everything smelled of burning, so strong it was hard to breathe.

*Our father.*

Savine stared towards the long drop, muscles working on the side of her face. Slightly bent over, like she wanted to huddle to the roof. Orso stood with hands tied behind him and the fixed smile of a man attending an event he found insufferably dull.

*A good man.*

"Ready, Your Majesty?" Broad stepped up close, cutting the cord between his wrists with a sharp jerk of his knife, then pressing it into his palm.

Orso looked over his shoulder, brows shooting up. "I'm willing to give it a go."

*You just have to remember.*

Broad nudged his lenses up his nose with a fingertip, took a deep breath, stepped down from the platform and pushed Bannerman off the tower.

He wasn't expecting it. Wasn't braced for it. A firm shove with one hand was all it took. His head snapped sideways, he dropped his sword and he tripped one foot with the other.

He gave a surprised grunt as he tumbled over, like a man who'd sat down only to have his chair whisked away by some joker.

"Wha?" said one of the other Burners. Broad punched him in the face so hard his helmet flew off. He reeled back, hit the parapet, caught it with one wild hand.

Broad bent, grabbed his ankle and yanked it up. He screamed as he went over, flailing at the air.

"No!" shrieked Judge. Half fury, half wounded disbelief.

Orso had stabbed Halder, knife buried under his jaw, blood squirting over the king's clenched fist and soaking his dirty lace cuff. Savine stood beside him, framed by the blue sky, eyes huge in her pale face, a dotting of blood on her white dress.

One of the other Burners was coming at Broad with a mace. Luvonte was his name. A Styrian. Strange, that he'd be a Burner. But then who'd have thought Broad would ever be one, either?

He swung as Broad ducked and the mace caught him a glancing blow, bounced from the top of his head. Broad came up, caught Luvonte by the breastplate, lifted him off his feet and rammed him into the roof head first.

He felt a jolt, a pricking in his back. Hardly any pain. Surprising, to see a dagger sticking out of his shoulder, Sarlby's fist around the grip.

Broad gave a great roar, twisting around. Sarlby punched him. It bounced off his cheek but his knuckle caught Broad's lenses and knocked them skewed, hanging from one ear. Suddenly the world was all fog. A sparkly blur.

Broad tried to catch Sarlby's throat but he was slippery as a fish. He lashed blindly with both fists but Sarlby dodged. Broad tripped over something. Luvonte, groaning as he rolled onto his back, face a red smear. Broad shook his head, squinted, managed to catch his lenses and pull them back on. One was cracked. A crack in the world.

He saw Halder sat against the parapet, hand clutched to his throat, blood squirting between his fingers, black as tar.

Then he saw Sarlby, with Bannerman's sword in his hand and his teeth bared. He swung and Broad dodged back. The blade clanged into the parapet and sent up a puff of stone dust. Sarlby lifted it to swing again but Broad stepped into him, caught the hilt with one hand before it came down, blade waving at the sky between them.

Broad punched at him but Sarlby got his free arm up, fending him off. Broad rammed him back against the parapet and drove his breath out in a wheeze. Sarlby dropped the sword and it fell twinkling, tumbling, spinning towards the bloodstained moat far below. Tiny figures down there, looking up.

Broad could hear Orso swearing at the top of his voice.

He punched again, spitting, snarling, grunting, the strange and beautiful view spread out beyond, snapped Sarlby's head back so it smacked into the parapet, left blood on the stone. How many times had they fought side by side?

He'd been a good man, Sarlby. Better than Broad. Maybe he still was.

Broad did his best to smash his face in even so.

It all happened so fast.

Savine turned from the long drop to see that two Burners had gone off the tower. A third sat staring with his throat slit. A fourth lay groaning, face covered in blood. Broad had Sarlby half-pinned over the parapet, one arm going up and down like a piston as he punched him. Orso spat curses while he struggled with the last.

They staggered to one side, wrestling over an axe, leaving Savine and Judge to stare at each other across the flat roof of the Tower of Chains.

Cold calculation had been the root of Savine's many victories. But there are times only blind fury will do.

She threw herself screaming from the platform. If her hands had been free she'd have flailed away with both fists. Since they were tied she clenched them together to make one.

She didn't think of her children, or the Union, or herself. She didn't think of anything but smashing Judge's head with her hands.

"Die, you mad *cunt*!" she snarled, and clubbed Judge right across the

364

face, sending her stumbling towards the lift. Savine caught her around the rashy throat, rammed her back into the railing and started choking her, making the platform jerk and wobble, chains thrashing, the whole scaffold trembling.

Judge bared bloody teeth, almost a smile, shot out a hand. Nails sank into Savine's neck, ripping at her. She gave a shriek, cut off in a gulp as Judge kneed her in the gut, shoved her staggering off the lift and back across the tower's roof.

Someone careered into her and knocked her flying. Orso, still reeling around in his ungainly dance with one of the Burners. Savine's head hit stone, ears ringing. Her hands were in a pool of blood. She wasn't sure whose.

"*You* fucking die!" growled Judge. A foot thudded into Savine's ribs and rolled her over, the back of her skull cracking on the steps up to the platform. Judge came at her, swinging her bare foot back for another kick.

This time Savine caught it, hugged it to her chest, twisting up, dragging Judge hopping off balance then flinging her back, rusty breastplate scraping as she sprawled across the roof.

The man with the bloody face had caught Broad from behind. Sarlby lifted an axe, ready to chop into the back of Broad's skull. Savine grabbed it below the head and ripped it from his fist.

She spun about, axe held clumsily in her tied hands, just as Judge rammed her into the parapet with a shoulder, driving her breath out in an agonised rasp. They wrestled, tangled, clawed, elbowed. Savine got the axe in the way, snarling as she pressed it into the side of Judge's face, but there wasn't enough force behind it to stop her, only to slowly peel a flap of flesh from her cheek.

Judge punched Savine in the stomach. And again. And again. Punched the breath out of her. Punched the strength out of her. Puke scalded the back of her throat. The axe wrenched from her tied hands, tumbled past her shoulder and was gone off the tower. Savine struggled, twisted, snapped with her teeth but Judge had her, bending her back over the parapet. Blood ran from the ragged wound on her cheek in crooked streaks, dripped from her chin, pit-pattered in Savine's face.

"You're tougher'n you look," she said, showing a red smile. And she caught Savine around the throat, pushing, pushing. "But you're still taking the long drop."

It was true. Savine was slipping. Her toes were off the roof, the parapet grinding into the small of her back. She could feel herself teetering, her balance almost shifted over the void.

She heaved in one last breath and kneed Judge between the legs, loosened her grip just enough to catch her around the back of the neck with both hands, so the cord between her wrists cut into Judge's rash-splattered throat. "So are you."

And she went over backwards.

Time slowed to a crawl.

A blur of clouds and sky. Her eyes full of Judge's red hair.

She hoped her children would have good lives.

A glimpse of the burning Lords' Round, wrong way up, flames stabbing downwards.

The world spun crazily, tiny buildings far below.

She was falling.

Then she gasped as something jerked at her ankle.

A stab of pain through her knee, through her hip.

She saw Judge drop. Just a glimpse of her bloody snarl before she was gone in a mass of clawing limbs and flapping cloth.

Then Savine crashed into something, hard.

But not the ground. Cut stones.

The side of the tower.

She heard Broad growling with effort.

Everything white. Her dress, fallen over her head.

She was upside down, and he had her by one foot.

"Pull her up!" Orso's desperate voice.

She saw Broad's straining face, spotted with blood. Orso behind him, arms around his waist, dragging him back.

She should have told them to let her fall, but all she could do was scream with every snatched breath. She should at least have stayed still and let them pull her up. Instead she tore at her dress, clawed at the soot-streaked stones with her fingernails, whimpering and coughing and choking on her own spit.

The wall scraped at her, scratched at her, cloth ripped, the parapet dug into her stomach.

They collapsed together onto the rooftop. Among the bodies of the Burners. Blood everywhere. Blood on the weapons and dashed against the parapets. Blood soaked into Broad's jacket and streaking his hands. Blood trickling from Savine's scalp, tickling at her eyelid, spattered on her white nursing dress, still turned half inside out.

She could not move. Her face throbbed. Her leg ached. One of her fists had a great hank of Judge's orange hair wedged between the fingers. She could not seem to make them come open. Her breath came in whooping sobs.

It was snowing. Black snow. Ash, from the burning Lords' Round, settling on the rooftop.

Orso held her tight. "I've got you," he whispered, over the wild thudding of her heart. "I've got you."

The lift dropped to the ground with a shudder, and Orso felt a surge of relief so strong he wanted to cry. He actually might have. A sentimental streak or two.

There were lots of soldiers at the bottom. Lots of Anglanders in dark uniforms. There were Burners, too, but on their knees, or having their wrists bound, or lying still, daubed with red, and not just paint. Figures of terror no more.

"Some help here!" he called out.

Broad was propped against the rail, breathing hard through gritted teeth, his sleeve soaked with blood and the knife still stuck deep in his shoulder. Orso had not dared to try to pull it out. Two men in those wonderfully familiar red uniforms of the King's Own rushed to help him.

"He saved our lives," said Orso. "Both our lives."

"We'll see he's well taken care of, Your Majesty."

*Your Majesty.* It was said earnestly, without sneering sarcasm, without being made into a joke or an insult. It had been a very long time since Orso last heard it said that way.

He helped Savine down from the platform, his arm around her. He could not let go of her. As if there was some irresistible force pulling them together. There were faces here he knew. Faces he wanted to cry even more at the sight of. Old friends and loyal comrades. Lord Marshal Forest—battle-worn and reliable. Corporal Tunny—looking as if he'd won big at the gaming table. Hildi—who had stolen a new soldier's cap from somewhere, her face smeared with soot. Victarine dan Teufel—even though her nose was bloated and bloody and surrounded by a spectacular blooming of bruises. Even Bremer dan Gorst—with steels still in his hands and a most unfamiliar grin. Finally, there was one face Orso had to confess he was less than delighted to see—Leo dan Brock, smiling somewhat queasily at Savine.

"Thank the Fates you're safe," he said as she disentangled herself from Orso, bruised and bleeding but very much unbowed.

367

They did not kiss, or fall into each others' arms, but then Savine had never been one for displays of affection. "Where are the children?" she asked.

"They're safe," said Brock. "They're guarded. Everything's taken care of."

Teufel's weary eyes rolled towards the giant torch that had once been the Lords' Round, smoke pouring up from it more thickly than from all the city's chimneys combined. "You sure?"

"We've got men trying to contain the blaze," said Forest. "Say what you like about the Burners, they knew how to set a fire."

The consequences of recent events were only now starting to dawn on Orso. "So...am I king again?"

Hildi watched the last Burners being dragged away. "Looks like it," she said.

"Whoever would have thought?" When Orso denounced himself, he had meant every word of it. Against all the odds, thanks to the loyalty of old friends and the self-interest of more than one old enemy, it looked as if he had been given another chance. He gazed across the corpse-strewn Square of Marshals. More and more people were gathering, staring, blinking in surprise. As if they were emerging into the sunlight after a long time in the dark. Veterans of his Crown Prince's Division, in worn-out uniforms. Men of Angland, in sombre black. Ex-lords of the Open Council, armed with flatbows.

"Things will be different this time, Hildi," he said. "I promise."

"You've never been much at keeping those."

"But things *will* be different this time!" He did not say it only to her. He promised it to himself. He shouted it to everyone in that triumphant gathering at the foot of the Tower of Chains. "We have a *chance* now! For a fresh start. For a *new* Union." One of Forest's men was holding an old battle flag, and Orso felt a surge of pride as the breeze took it and the blazing sun gleamed in the Agriont once again. "A chance...to do things *right*."

He looked across those eager faces. Some of them were even starting to smile. "No more riots," he called, "no more trials, no more executions. No vengeance and no settling of scores. No Court of the People!" He caught Savine's eye, her chin up, her eyes shining. If she believed in him, he knew it could be done. "But there can be no more Closed Council, either. No corruption and injustice. No dead grip of Valint and Balk around the throat of the nation. This time...I mean to govern for the many, not the few. To be a king for *everyone*."

"You really think you can do all that?" asked Vick, and it seemed, behind her customary mask of scorn, she couldn't entirely hide a glimpse of hope.

At that moment, Orso felt as if he could do anything. "I can try. *We* can try. Together. I owe you all my thanks. You especially, Vick." He seized her scabbed hand and pressed it to his lips. "You gambled everything. You didn't have to."

"Seems I've a sentimental streak of loyalty," she grunted, licking her bloody top lip and awkwardly working her hand free.

"I am heartily glad of it." He clapped Corporal Tunny on the shoulder, dragged Forest into a crushing hug. "Where would I have been without you?"

"Just doing my duty," growled Forest, his cheeks colouring above his overgrown beard.

Orso turned to the Young Lion—pale, gaunt and ungainly on his false leg, blond hair darkened with sweat and that sickly smile still on his face. For various reasons, several of them good ones, Orso had grown to dislike the ex-Lord Governor of Angland quite intensely. But his father once said you can measure a man by how he treats those he dislikes. He had said he would be a king for everyone, and he meant it. The lowest as well as the highest, his enemies as well as his friends. And Brock had come through for him today. There was no denying that.

"I owe you, too, Lord Brock," said Orso, since it seemed they were all going back to their old titles. "We have had our differences. We could hardly have had bigger ones. But if men like us can march into the future together, there is hope for anyone." He offered his hand. "There is hope for everyone."

Brock winced down at Orso's open palm, taking a deep breath. As if composing himself for some distasteful task. "Not everyone," he said, then produced a dagger from behind his back and stabbed Forest in the chest.

At the same moment Orso felt himself gripped from behind, a blade pressed into his throat.

Brock's man Jurand. "Still!" he hissed in Orso's ear. "Everybody still!"

Suddenly, there were raised flatbows everywhere, the points of the loaded bolts gleaming. Lord Isher had one, and several of his friends who had once sat on the Open Council, and some of the Anglanders, too. Forest took a wobbling step and dropped to his knees, blood spreading through his jacket in a dark circle.

"What are you *doing?*" Savine nearly shrieked, staring at the drawn swords and levelled spears.

"I am putting an end to the Great Change," said her husband, "and taking back the Agriont in the name of the king." Anglanders were already disarming the stunned members of the King's Own, forcing them onto their knees along with the Burners.

"You fucking bathtard," breathed Vick, but with an air of wounded resignation. Orso could only watch with a familiar sinking feeling. He should have known, the moment things started looking up, that something like this would happen.

"Actually, my wife's the bastard," said Brock. "Which makes my son Harod the oldest child of King Jezal's oldest child. A strong claim to the throne."

"That's not how succession works," snarled Tunny as he was shoved onto his knees.

"Are you sure?" asked Brock. "I have three-score flatbows with a different opinion."

Gorst still had his steels in his hands, bloody metal glinting, eyes narrowed. Now he shifted his weight a fraction.

"No!" shouted Orso, Jurand's knife pressing hard into his neck. Best swordsman in the world or not, he would be dead before he could reach Brock, and the rest of them soon after. "Lay down your weapons. That's a royal decree!" His first in some time and, by the look of things, his last.

Gorst breathed in hard, then gave a bull's snort and tossed his steels clattering down. Two Anglanders stepped forward to bind his wrists. They were already doing the same to Teufel, to Hildi, to anyone who might still have been loyal.

"What have you done?" whispered Savine, back of one hand to her mouth. "Let them go, Leo, please, let them go!"

"You have been through quite the ordeal," droned Brock. "Someone take my wife to our children. They need their mother."

The blood was spreading out around Forest's body. "He was a good man," whispered Orso numbly. "A loyal man."

"Too loyal." Brock snapped his fingers. "Secure the gates of the Agriont."

"Already done," said Isher, smartly. A coward on the battlefield but as proficient a traitor as ever.

"There'll be a price for this!" said Orso as his wrists were tied for the third time that day. He felt the need to register some resistance, however pointless.

Brock regarded him without the slightest trace of guilt or shame. "I've already paid. See all members of the King's Own taken prisoner until we can make sure of each man's obedience. Conduct Citizen Orso and his servants to locked quarters in the House of Questions. Glaward should already have every gate and bridge in the city under guard. I want proclamations printed and pasted at every corner. The Great Change is over."

Isher grinned as he lowered his flatbow. "Long live King Harod the Second," he said.

# Forging the Future

"**R**ight, then," said Rikke, arranging herself in Skarling's Chair in a manner that aimed for carefree and commanding at once and probably missed both by an equal margin. "Time to hand out the rewards."

Isern's jaw worked as she chewed. "And the punishments."

"Aye." Rikke tweaked that fine fur about her shoulders and wriggled her back as straight as she could. "Those, too." Shivers gave the guards a nod, and there was a mighty creaking as the doors of Skarling's Hall were swung wide.

Helps to start on a happy note, so it was the conquering heroes of Uffrith and the West Valleys that were shown in first. Hardbread swaggered at their head like a man a third of his age. The Nail, who really was a third of his age, loped along beside him with that round-shouldered hunch, hand slack on the battered pommel of his sword, a few new scabs and scuffs on him from the battle, but none the worse for that. None the worse at all.

"Well, didn't you boys do me proud?" called Rikke. "I'd offer you gifts but I reckon the dead already did."

"A bauble or two!" And Hardbread whirled a golden chain around on his pointed finger to widespread cheers.

"Hardbread," said Rikke, "you stood by my father through good times and bad. Now you've done the same for me. I'm naming you my Second."

His grey brows shot up. "Y'are?"

"Aye, and I'll need you to start by keeping my chair warm a while."

Those brows rose even higher. "What, Skarling's Chair?"

"He may not have been a hero in quite your league, but I daresay you can lower yourself to his level for a week or two."

"And I can think o' few men indeed," said Isern, "more practised than you at sitting down."

Hardbread eyed the chair as if he had some doubts. "Where will you be?"

"I've a little trip to take before I can sit here secure." Rikke found she was fussing with the emeralds around her neck and let them drop. "I hear tell my old friends the Young Lion and his wife—"

"Fanciest bitch I ever saw," threw in Isern.

"—have seized power in the Union."

"Quite the power seizers, them twain. However you push 'em down they keep floating back to the top, d'you see, like a pair o' goat turds in the well."

Shivers was turning that ring with the red stone around and around his little finger. "I hear little Leo's taken a turn towards the vengeful."

"Something wounded warriors are prone to do," said the Nail, looking thoughtfully towards the corner where Stour's cage used to hang.

"And most warriors end up wounded, one way or another," lamented Hardbread, rubbing at his lip. "Why, I still remember the day Whirrun o' Bligh caught me in the mouth with—"

"I need to go down to Adua," said Rikke. "See if I can patch up the cracks in our friendship."

The Nail gave a snort. "Cracks? You stabbed 'em in the back. More'n once."

"Patch up the knife holes, then, before Leo gets it in his head to put a few in us. The North never does well out of wars with the Union. What we need is peace, and smiles, and trade—"

"And jokes," said Shivers, stony-faced. "I've always liked a laugh."

"Can't think o' many better jokes than me in Skarling's Chair," murmured Hardbread, though it wasn't long ago folk would've reckoned the idea of Rikke in it even funnier. He gave his backside a thoughtful squeeze. "My arse is a fair bit broader'n yours, I reckon."

"So the seat'll be toasty upon my return," said Rikke, to some laughter from the room. "And now the Nail. Wasn't long ago you were an enemy to be feared. I'd thank Stour Nightfall for being fool enough to turn you into a friend, but thanks are wasted on the dead. The West Valleys are yours already. I'd like to add two more to your land on the eastern side."

"You're generous as well as beautiful," said the Nail, with the hint of a grin.

"I'll live with one of two. But I need something from you in return."

"Name it."

"I have heard tell you like a fight."

He grinned wider. "I can stand a scuffle in the right cause."

"Seems folk in Ollensand have come over sour about me taking charge. They've shut up their gates. Say they're doing things their own way from now on."

"Can't have that," whispered Shivers.

"You let one sheep pick its own path," said Isern, "and 'fore you know it the whole herd's got *opinions*."

The Nail slowly nodded. "I'll make 'em aware o' their error."

"Gently, eh? No need to whistle up the dogs to begin with. I'd rather they came willing."

"And if they won't?"

"Bring 'em unwilling."

"Right y'are." The Nail loitered a moment, like he had something more to say. She could guess what was on his mind. What happened between the two of them before he went away. It was on her mind, too. She'd have liked to say stay. Even if it was just for a night. Even if it was just for a quick fumble behind the kitchen. But a leader has to be careful who she lets in. Who she's seen to let in. Specially a she.

The Nail scratched at his pale beard, looking at her sidelong, mouth open like he was about to speak. When he paused, Rikke didn't help him. She couldn't afford to.

"Right y'are," he said again and strode out, waving his men after. No sooner had they quit the place than Isern's brothers were strolling in, a pack of tattooed hillmen and hillwomen at their backs.

"Scofen and Scenn-i-Phail!" called Rikke. "Were two fat bastards ever more beloved of the moon than you twain?"

"My father always said a man should have some meat upon him," said Scofen, laying a great hand on his great belly.

"His worth is his girth," said Scenn, combing his fingers through his riot of red beard.

"There's been bad blood between the clans of the North and the people of the hills for far too long," said Rikke. "Since the time of Crummock-i-Phail and Bethod and since times long before. But that's all washed away. You were there when I needed you, and I'll be there if you need me, that's my promise. But since promises are cheap, you can take the land we discussed as well."

"Truth is, you've already done us a service beyond reckoning by taking our sister off our hands," said Scenn.

"Every moment her tongue is stabbing at you is a moment it's not stabbing at us," said Scofen.

Isern blew some chagga spit which spattered on Scofen's shirt and made him grin. "Mind you don't get stabbed with something sharper," she said.

"I think of her as a sister myself," said Rikke. "An older, tougher, wiser sister, at that. Reckon that makes you my brothers. And family should keep in touch." Rikke sat forward. "I say we open up the ways into the hills. Build better roads and set to trading more than wounds. I've fond memories of that ale I sampled last time I was with you. Coal in the hills, too, I hear, and copper. No doubt we've got things of iron and steel and cloth you might find useful."

"No doubt," said Scenn, reaching out to rub thoughtfully at the sleeve of Hardbread's mail coat between big finger and thumb.

"A couple of you should take the voyage to Adua with me. See the world. Sample the pleasures of civilisation. Take some ideas with you and bring a few back. Show folk down there the North's united. Together we'll make worse enemies, and better friends, and it'll be a thing we can all profit from."

"Ah, enemies and profits." Scofen's eyes lit up. "Things our father loved almost as much as the moon." And there was laughter, and back-slapping, and trading of well-meaning insults and overblown tales of the battle.

But being a leader can't all be grinning at friends. Sooner or later you'll have to frown on your foes. Calder's man Flatstone was marched in next, battered and bandaged. His hands were bound, but he stood as if he meant to die with his pride intact, which was a thing Rikke supposed she could admire.

Lurking at his shoulder, Shivers pulled out that bright little knife. Might be he didn't catch the light on the blade on purpose and flash it in Flatstone's face. But Rikke wouldn't have bet on it.

"You're Brodd Flatstone," she said.

"I am."

"One of Black Calder's War Chiefs."

"I was."

"How many of my folk did you kill in the battle?"

Flatstone gave Shivers' blade a glance, then set his jaw and lifted his chin. "Many as I could."

"Huh. How long did you serve Black Calder?"

"More'n twenty years. Since I won my name at the battle on the Heroes. Joined Calder then. A lot o' folk were doing it." Flatstone took a breath through his broad nose, and let it puff away. "And I'd do the same again. He was a great leader, in his time."

375

"But his time's done."

"No arguing with that." Flatstone lowered his head. "His time's done, and yours has come, and that's the way of things."

"The question on my mind is—could you be as loyal to me as you were to him?"

He looked up sharply and blinked about the room. Then he squared his shoulders. "I believe I could."

"A big man like you could kneel to a little woman like me?"

"I'd say you were over middle height," muttered Isern.

"Aye, but that spoils the balance o' the phrase."

"No shame kneeling to a woman who's proved herself the way you have," said Flatstone.

Rikke raised her brows. "So...?"

"Oh. Right." And with a pained grunt, hands still bound behind him, Flatstone wobbled down to one knee.

"My father always said, why waste what can be used? Reckon that goes for men as much as aught else. More, since so much effort goes into making the bastards." Some mutters of agreement from the warriors about the hall. They didn't mind mercy for a fighter who'd fought his hardest. They knew they might end up kneeling where he was one day, if luck tipped the wrong way. "I want you to gather any of your Carls who lived through the battle and are willing to serve me and take the bones o' these Crinna fucks back the way they came. While you're out there, teach any that've wandered across the water since a hard lesson. You understand?"

Flatstone nodded. "I do."

"I do...?"

"I do, Chief."

Shivers cut the rope on Flatstone's wrists and, as he stood, handed him back the axe he'd given up on the day of the battle, bright gold swirling on the blade. He looked up at Rikke as he took it. "I appreciate the chance. Won't let you down."

"Oh, I know." Rikke turned her Long Eye towards him. "I've seen it."

He swallowed and strode for the door.

"Soft," grunted Isern, sourly.

"It's worth giving your enemies a chance. They know they can't expect one and might be thankful for it." Rikke frowned sideways. "Friends are much harder to please."

And indeed, Isern's scowl got deeper than ever as the next pair were dragged in. Corleth and her granny, dirty from the cells and with their hands bound tight.

376

"Easy," said Rikke. "We won, remember? We can afford to be generous."

"Just 'cause you can afford it," grunted Isern as the young woman and the old were shoved down before the dais and left squinting in the sunlight, "doesn't mean you should buy it. Is Corleth even your name?"

"It is." The girl didn't look much chastened, her jaw jutting. As much fight in her as when she first came to Uffrith.

"Got anything to say for yourself?" asked Rikke.

"I could kneel here and spew excuses but you all know me for a liar. Where'd be the point?"

"We done what was asked of us," croaked out the old woman.

"Shame you didn't do it better," sneered Isern, "you might not be kneeling there."

Rikke held up a hand for silence. "I reckon a lot of folk would like to see you cut with the bloody cross as traitors and spies."

She let the silence stretch, heavy with the weight of lives in the balance.

"But I'm minded to be merciful. We wouldn't have hooked Black Calder without you offering the bait, after all. You wandered into Uffrith so you could tell him what we were about. Now you can wander down to Ostenhorm. Tell me what the Union are up to."

This helping of mercy wasn't at all to the menfolk's taste. They could see past a man trying to kill 'em, but a woman tricking 'em was too much to stand.

"Thought you wanted peace with the Union?" grunted Hardbread. "And trade, and smiles."

"I'll smile easier knowing what they're up to," said Rikke.

"I don't know no one down there," said Corleth.

"Good a liar as you are, I'm sure you'll soon make new friends."

"What about my granny?"

"She really your granny?"

"She is."

"I'm half-tempted to keep her here so she can make me soup." Rikke sat back, considering. "But it seems a shame to split up a winning act. Cut 'em free, Shivers." And he did, showing no sign of whether he thought it a good idea or a bad.

"Thank you, Black Rikke," said Corleth's granny, near kissing the floor. "You won't regret this."

"True." And Rikke tapped her cheek. "I've seen that, too."

"Soft," hissed Isern, shaking her head, and she wasn't alone in her opinion. Lots of grumbling. Some outright scowls. One man spat at Corleth's feet as she walked out. It was a wearying business. Proving yourself once as a leader is never enough. You have to do it fresh with every choice.

A miserable crowd came next, kicked and bundled into Skarling's Hall, forced down on the pitiless stones before her, chains rattling. Stand-i'-the-Barrows' men. Stripped of their armour of bones and with their paint all smeared off, they looked a lot less fearsome. One was trembling. One might've been weeping. Don't matter how savage a face you show the world, few men dare look the Great Leveller in the eye once he comes calling. She felt the old tug towards mercy and sat back frowning in Skarling's Chair.

"You bastards crossed the Crinna," she said.

Their leader shuffled forwards on his knees, his chin near touching the floor and the lank hair hanging around his face. "We was invited, Great Queen," he whined, speaking Northern with an accent which was an offence upon the ear. "We was invited."

"Not by me," she snapped, making him flinch. "Stand-i'-the-Barrows, a man the world will not much miss, planned to see how many of my bones he could cut out while I was still alive."

There was a snivelling and a mewling, like she'd a pack of beaten dogs before her. She took a long, slow breath.

"But I'm not Stand-i'-the-Barrows." She waved a gracious hand. "Suffering doesn't make me smile."

The leader bowed even lower. "You are wise and merciful, Great Queen."

"I like to think so." She nodded to Shivers. "Kill 'em first, *then* boil 'em down to the bones, then get Flatstone to send the bones back across the Crinna. Maybe that'll teach their kind to stay on their side of the water."

She watched 'em dragged out, gibbering and weeping, and had a sense the faces of the warriors in the hall were changed. No scornful glances now. Eyes mostly to the floor, indeed. Her father would've said it's a good thing, to show mercy. Long as you also show, when it's needful, that you can make of your heart a stone.

Isern offered a chagga pellet, and Rikke took it and stuffed it up behind her lip. "You approve?"

"Do you hear me disapprove?" asked Isern.

And so it went. They marched in or were dragged in. Those who'd fought on one side or the other. Those who'd served her, or served Black Calder. She stuck mostly to mercy, but she made some examples, too. Enough, she judged, to keep the North orderly while she was off striking a bargain with the friends she'd turned into enemies. The day wore on and the strips of sunlight from the tall windows crept across the stone floor, from one side of Skarling's Hall to the other, till the room was mostly empty, and the flood became a trickle, and the trickle dried up to naught.

"That everyone?" asked Rikke, sitting back.

"Just one more," said Shivers.

# A Half-Baked Loaf

Clover sat in the yard outside Skarling's Hall and watched the nervous folk called in to receive their deservings. He watched some strut out beaming over their rewards. He watched some dragged out crestfallen over their punishments. He saw a couple noticeably not emerge at all.

Life and death, hanging on the word of Black Rikke. She held more of the North and in a tighter grip now than Black Dow at his most feared, than Black Calder at his most cunning. Who'd have guessed that, when she came tumbling through the wet woods to lie at his feet all those months ago? He gave a disbelieving little snort of laughter. Would've taken the Long Eye to see it coming.

Clover had seen 'em rise and fall. The leaders, the chiefs, the kings. He'd taken a hand in a few of those ups and downs himself, indeed. Bethod, and the Bloody-Nine, and Black Dow, and Scale Ironhand, and Stour Nightfall, an ever-lengthening list o' glory and disaster. Those who served 'em, too, the fortunes of the little men rising and falling with the big men they chose to follow, like boats lifted by the tide, or dropped stranded on the sands. He glanced over at Sholla and Flick. Hoped they wouldn't end up stranded, on account of tethering their fortunes to his.

Maybe, having spent half his life too reckless, he'd ended up playing it too safe. He'd clung to those who'd risen and could only come down, rather than had the courage to seek out those whose tide was surging in. To seek out those he actually *liked*, maybe. But he was still casting a shadow, at least. More'n you could say for Wonderful, or Magweer, or Downside, or all those others he'd put in the mud down the years. Still alive, as the Bloody-Nine was once so fond o' saying. There wasn't much else to take pride in, for a man who carried a sword. Even one who tried never to draw it.

"Clover." Shivers stood there, in the doorway of Skarling's Hall. You never could tell what that man was thinking. No more feeling showed in his living eye than his dead one. No sign of what the judgement would be. But from those coming and going, Black Rikke was proving a tougher judge than folk had guessed. Girl had iron in her, that was plain, and sharpened, too.

"Can I bring my people?" asked Clover.

Shivers looked at Flick and Sholla. "Why not?" And he stood aside to offer them all the way. So he'd be at their backs, o' course. A bad man to have behind you with a sword, Caul Shivers. Just ask Black Dow. But if Clover wasn't used to having bad men with swords about, he never would be.

Rikke sat in Skarling's Chair, an old sheepskin draped over the back and onto the seat, red cloak around her shoulders and green stones around her neck, the tattoos black on her pale face. She looked comfortable, in that uncomfortable-looking chair, one leg crossed over the other with the worn boot gently swinging. There were some big names in the room, but everyone faced a bit towards her, like flowers turning their petals towards the sun. No doubt who had the say in that room.

"Jonas Clover," she said, tapping a thoughtful fingernail against the arm of Skarling's Chair as he traipsed up nervously to stand before her. "Here's a riddle."

"Well." He gave an apologetic little grin. "No one wants to be thought of as simple."

"There are folk who've done me favours and folk who've done me wrongs." She sat forwards, those troubling eyes full upon him as if she could see into his head, see into his heart. "But there's none I can think of that are such a half-baked loaf as you."

Clover scratched at the back of his head. "I'll admit I've been called worse and deserved it."

"You were one of Calder's men. One of Nightfall's. One of those that invaded the Protectorate all those months ago."

"I mostly ambled along at the back, to be fair." He squinted up towards the shadowy rafters, a cobweb fluttering in the breeze through the windows. "In that war, if I recall, I killed more men on my side than on yours."

"That's naught to be proud of," grunted Hardbread.

"No." Clover gave a sorry shrug. "You'll find few men less proud o' themselves than me."

"And once I had Skarling's Chair," said Rikke, "you gave every sign of going back over to Calder's side soon as the chance was offered."

"When you let Stour live, then tossed all your friends away, I started worrying you might not have the bones for the task. In my defence, you did act the part o' someone shitting themselves very nicely."

"Plenty o' practice," grunted Rikke. "And after all, I could only spare Stour 'cause you handed him to me in the first place."

"That was less a service to you, though, and more about settling a score between me and him."

Rikke looked at him baffled. "When I count something against you, you want to disagree. When I count something for you, you want to disagree with that, too."

"In my experience... things are rarely all one way or the other."

"You're right there," said Rikke, sitting back. "And you did let me go, that day in the woods."

"That's one good deed I'll fully confess to," admitted Clover.

"A man who does good, you can predict. A man who does bad, the same. But what do you do with a man who can't make up his mind?"

"I've often wondered."

"I like you. But I can't have you around. Shivers?"

Clover shut his eyes then, expecting the sword in the back of his head. Like Black Dow. Like Black Calder. But when he gathered the courage to squint around, he saw Shivers was offering him a bag. He took it and looked inside. The gleam of silver, and a decent amount, by all appearances.

"That's... more'n generous," he said. "If I was you I wouldn't have me around, either. Hell, I'm me, and I often tire of my company." He put his hand on Sholla's shoulder and drew her forwards. "But if you'll entertain me with a brief hearing, I'd like to recommend this article. Her name's Sholla, and I've never yet had cause to doubt her loyalty. A fine hand with an arrow, the softest footstep I never heard and an undisputed master at the noble art of cheese-shaving. She can get 'em like a sheet of paper. I swear you can see through the bastards."

Rikke raised the brow over her blind eye at Sholla. "If I've one regret it's that my cheese never quite carves thin enough."

"And then there's this, which is called Flick. I have yet to discover any talents but I've no doubt there's one lurking beneath the unpromising exterior, and even if there ain't he has a pleasant manner, which is too rare a thing in the North, I think you'll agree."

Rikke glanced about her closest. Caul Shivers. Isern-i-Phail. She puffed out her cheeks. "Well, I won't disagree."

"Good. Good." Clover gave Flick's shoulder a parting squeeze, then let his hand fall. He gave the room a smile. "Watch yourself, in Adua. I hear folk down there can't all be trusted the way they can up here."

Rikke gave a snort. "Fine advice."

"And if anyone should want to learn sword-work, I am available." And with a gesture caught on awkward ground between a nod and a bow, Clover took his leave.

"Don't we get a say?" muttered Sholla, following him out with Flick. The sun was getting low now, and the yard was half in bright light, half in deep shadow. Rarely all one way or the other, like he'd told Rikke.

"I'm sparing you the pain of it," said Clover. "You're both better off here, and I know it, and you know it, and once you thought about it you'd see you had to tell me so, and it'd be an awkward scene all around. Afford me the dignity o' this one last call as chief on your behalf." He gathered 'em in an awkward hug. Mostly so he didn't have to listen to 'em argue with him. "Thanks for your support through hard times. And thanks especially for that arrow in Downside's shoulder."

"Aye, well," said Sholla, and Clover flattered himself that she might be struggling to hold back a tear or two. "Didn't want to give the bastard the satisfaction o' killing you."

"You're joking! I had that bloody half-head just where I wanted him. Waiting for my moment was all."

"What'll you do?" asked Flick, who wasn't trying to stop himself crying at all and had dirty tear tracks all over his cheeks.

Clover grinned. "Something usually comes up." And he turned and started walking, sword over his shoulder.

# Sunrise

"You don't like the palace," said Leo.

Savine didn't seem to like anything lately, and her husband least of all. "I find it hard to sleep here," she said, with a sullen glance at one of the Anglanders who were guarding every landing and doorway.

He wanted to say she was lucky to be alive but was trying hard to be sympathetic. He'd won, after all. He could afford to be. "After what you've been through it's a wonder you can sleep at all."

"The place is a ruin," said Savine, sweeping past a mural of some grand coronation with all the faces chiselled out. "It still smells." She watched a man in blazing-sun livery teetering on a stepladder so he could scrub at slogans up near the ceiling. "There is evidence of the Burners' tenancy everywhere. Of...Judge's tenancy." She gave an ugly shiver of disgust and held baby Ardee closer. "It feels like a prison."

Leo clenched his jaw. How grateful most people would've been to be kept in a cage like this one. "The children are safest here, in the Agriont." He winced as he shifted Harod's weight in the crook of his arm. "We're already patching up the walls. A king belongs in a palace, and Harod will be king now."

"Harod is a baby."

"That's why he'll need guidance."

Savine looked sideways at him, and hardly with the proper affection a wife should have for her husband. "From you, I suppose?"

"From both of us." But it was only right that a father should have the final word when it came to his son. By the dead, his stump was throbbing, his bad arm tingling, his shoulder aching from the effort of holding the child as he lurched along. "We're together in this."

"Are we? When we discussed bringing back the monarchy we never mentioned changing the monarch."

"Plans have to bend with circumstance," grunted Leo. The sort of thing he'd always hated hearing his mother tell him. "I would've warned you if I could. Of course I would. But how could I? I was scrambling to save your life. To save the bloody Union!"

He had to stop. He'd wanted to sweep into the Hall of Mirrors carrying his son. To be seen as a father, head of the ideal family. The shining example to be copied across the reborn nation. But dropping the tiny king on his head then tripping over him would have won him few admirers. To be a cripple well, you have to accept what you can't do.

"Jurand?" he forced through gritted teeth. "Could you help?" And he dumped the future monarch into his arms and turned away, leaving him blinking with elbows everywhere. No doubt he was handsome and clever and loyal as they come, but he made a poor nursemaid.

Still, the only alternative was Zuri, and Leo trusted her less than ever these days. Even though Savine loved her so much. Because Savine loved her so much, maybe. It was a bad message to send, having brown faces around the royal children.

Savine frowned towards the tall windows as she walked, rocking Ardee gently, criss-cross shadows of the lead between the panes sliding across her face. Her careful powdering couldn't hide the fading bruises from her struggle at the top of the Tower of Chains. Or perhaps—far more likely now he thought about it—she'd chosen to leave them on display, for a hint of the noble martyr. Nothing in Savine's appearance ever happened by accident, after all.

Servants were busy in the unkempt gardens outside, clipping suns of the Union back into the bushes, weeding it back into the flower beds, chiselling it back into the scarred stonework. They must've ripped off those royal liveries when the Great Change made them fatal. Now they rushed to wriggle back into them. People adjust. They adjust more quickly and more completely than you'd ever imagine.

Leo winced as he hurried to catch up. "What can I do?" he asked. "To make things easier?"

"I want no more executions."

An uncomfortable pause. Jurand gave Leo one of those oh-so-expressive glances from under his brows. Leo took his meaning at once, as always, and agreed at once, as always—there would need to be at least one more. King Orso was a problem with only one solution.

"I understand your feelings," he murmured. As if fucking feelings should set policy. "I understand, but—"

"No more, Leo."

385

"Savine, the guilty have to be punished. Quietly, privately, yes, but…
we have to be made *safe*."

"We have to be better than Judge. Otherwise what is the point?"

"The point is that *we* win." That was so obvious he was amazed he had
to explain it, and to her of all people, who had been happy to trample over
her own father, mother and brother if she could use them as a ladder to
her own ambitions. "And some people will always be a threat. Orso's girl
Hildi is too naive, and Bremer dan Gorst is too stubborn, and I wouldn't
trust that bastard Tunny to carry my chamber pot. Honestly, I'm a long
way from trusting Teufel. The woman's proved herself quite the plotter.
I worry she's not loyal—"

"You worry she's *too* loyal, you mean, but not to you."

"What's the difference?"

"She has proved herself effective. My father is gone and Pike was never
apprehended. We must have someone competent in charge of the Inquisition. There are hundreds of Breakers and Burners still at large. Thousands,
maybe. We have to root them *out*." Her grazed cheek tightened as she
clenched her jaw. "We have to make sure nothing like the Great Change
can *ever* happen again."

"It didn't turn out too badly." He caught her staring at him, shocked.
"All right, if it makes you happy, I'll give Teufel a chance to prove herself."

"It will make me less unhappy, at least."

"Anything for you, my love," he said, sulkily. "Don't you trust me?"

"It can be hard to trust men who stab their allies in the back."

"I don't plan to do it once a week!" he snapped. "Or ever again," he
added, hurriedly. He felt bad for Lord Marshal Forest. A good man, a
good soldier. He felt bad, but there'd been no choice. And as a point of
fact, he'd stabbed him in the front. "At Stoffenbeck I bloody dithered, and
we bloody lost, and I swore I'd never let a moment slip past again. So I
saw an opportunity and I grabbed it. For *us*. I thought you'd be pleased!"

The truth was she'd changed, and not for the better. He'd said his vows to
someone who let no scruple get in her way. But then she'd said hers to a man
who could fasten his own belt without help. That's marriage. People change,
and not always in the way you want, and you're chained together anyway.

Leo took a breath as they reached the great doors, fabulously carved
with food and drink and celebration, only slightly spoiled by a burned
patch and a few axe marks. "We have to be united," he said, wondering
who he was trying to convince. "For the sake of the children. For the sake
of the nation. Our marriage made sense. It still makes sense. It makes
more sense than ever."

Applause rang out as Savine swept into the Hall of Mirrors, wearing a radiant smile.

"Lord and Lady Brock!" bellowed Glaward, smashing his big hands together.

There were perhaps two hundred Representatives gathered there, standing up to clap from a mismatched array of seating scavenged from across the Agriont. Battered armchairs spilling stuffing, royal dining chairs and children's schooling chairs, even a milking stool and one great curved bench somehow salvaged from the ruins of the Lords' Round, scorched at one end.

Savine had not set foot in that building during Risinau's reign, but even she could tell the balance of the Representatives had greatly changed since then. Less than half this crowd had been voted for, and those were mostly from the richer towns and districts. Landowners, merchants, men of business. The rest had all once been nobles. Members of the Open Council lucky and unprincipled enough to slip from one body to another. Now Leo had made them nobles again. There were even a few women, taking the places of fathers, brothers, husbands who had met their ends in the Great Change. On the front row, Lords Isher and Heugen gave their own continuing survival a standing ovation, heavy with the furs and chains of aristocracy they had so eagerly cast off.

Thousands of reflections applauded, too, of course. In places a broken mirror split a face into mismatched halves, or a shattered one smashed the world into a thousand distorted fragments. Smears of paint still clung in the corners where the slogans had been hastily scrubbed away. But then the Hall of Mirrors was a vast room. Putting it right would be the work of weeks. The palace? Years. The Agriont? Decades. The city of Adua? The Union as a whole? Could any of it really go back together?

Savine remembered Judge falling. That flash of her sneer as she dropped away. She shed no tears for the evil bitch. The Fates knew, no one had ever deserved the long drop more. And yet she could not stop thinking of it. The hand at her throat. The parapet grinding into her back. The hollow sucking in her stomach as she tumbled over.

She clenched her fist as she sat facing those ranks of false smiles, nails cutting sharp into her palm. She told herself she was safe. The Representatives might well have been outnumbered by Leo's heavily armed Anglanders, standing watchful at every door and window. She could not have been safer. She had to focus on what could be changed, and change it for the better. She glanced down at her infant daughter, nudged the blanket from her sleeping face. She had to turn her back on the past and focus on the future.

"Are you all right?" Zuri murmured in her ear.

Savine forced out a smile. "I should be asking you that."

Zuri looked as composed as ever. She had not breathed a word of whatever tortures she had endured beneath the House of Questions and Savine had not the courage to ask. That way she could almost pretend it had never happened. Except there were some strange marks on the backs of Zuri's hands now. Pinpricks. Dimples. Not exactly scars. But not quite normal, either.

Zuri saw her looking and worked the sleeves of her dress down over them.

"My friends!" called Leo as the clapping faded. "My peers! Noblemen and commoners! Representatives of the people of the Union! The Great Change...is behind us!"

The applause at that was even louder. Few indeed mourned its passing, and Leo had made sure any that did occupied cells in the House of Questions rather than seats in this chamber.

"Thanks to the courage of my wife, Lady Brock—" He was interrupted by cheers, mostly from the commoners' side of the room.

"The Darling of the Slums!" someone shouted.

"The Mother of the Nation!" roared another, smashing his hands together.

Savine had to force out another smile. Kindly meant, she was sure, but their clamour reminded her too much of the crowd at her trial. Of the mobs on the day of the Great Change. She was safe. All those guards. But it was as if her body had not quite realised it. Sweat prickled under her clothes.

Leo, looking slightly put out at the admiration for his wife, held up his hand for silence. "*Thanks* to Lady Brock, Judge has been thrown down. The Burners and the Breakers are routed, their ringleaders dead, captured or even now being hunted down. They'll find there's nowhere to hide! They won't scrub the blood of innocents from their clawing hands. Justice will find them out, whatever hole they wriggle into!"

More applause. Savine had to admit she was impressed. She had always been more comfortable with small rooms, intimate groups, hushed whispers. But Leo knew how to fill a hall. "He speaks well," she murmured.

"Vanity, a loud voice and a loose relationship with the truth," whispered Zuri. "All the qualities of a successful politician."

Leo smiled, relishing his moment of victory, and a hundred reflections in the great mirrors smiled back at him. Was there something horrible in that? Given the price? A hundred reflections of Savine looked on in adoring triumph, but she could see the pale worry hidden in those copies of her own bruised face. She was not sure she had ever really loved him, but there had been plenty to admire, once. He had been generous, honest and brave. She had wanted him to be more ruthless. More ambitious. More calculating. She had moulded him into her image. Now she found she had much preferred him before.

"We must bring back the best of the past!" he was calling. "Families once honoured by a 'dan' in their name will be honoured again. Our restored Open Council will be made up of commoners and noblemen in equal numbers, united in their purpose, with respect given by every member, to every member. A grand declaration has been prepared to that effect. I trust everyone here will sign their names to it and join us in this brave new dawn. This new sunrise!"

Zuri laid the great book open on the table and turned it around to face the Representatives. Neat blocks of her perfect calligraphy on one side. Spaces for two hundred signatures on the other. Savine had brought her lawyer Temple over from the Near Country to help draw it up, the keenest eye she knew for both the art and science of a contract. Leo might like to harp on the past, but this paved the way for a new government, a new monarch, a new Union.

Isher sprang up from his chair. "I will be honoured to be the first to sign!" Though no one had asked him to be.

"And I the second!" shouted Heugen, not to be outdone.

"We must institute a new government!"

"One based on justice and fairness!"

"We must return to our *principles*," said Leo, sternly. "And as the first step, we must elect a new king."

The lords, clearly prepared for this development, applauded again, but Savine saw worried faces on the other side of the room. The Burners might have humiliated the king, after all, but even they had not presumed to replace him. An old man with wispy hair was finally urged to his feet, clasping his hands, more like a supplicant approaching the throne than a proud Representative of the people.

"My Lord Brock, if I may...no one here, I am sure, doubts your motives..." He glanced nervously towards Leo's many loyal soldiers. "Or dreams of denying your contribution, or disagrees with a word of your admirable speech..."

"I sense a *but* coming," said Isher, one white eyebrow raised.

"But when it comes to electing a new king...do we not still have...well...an *old* one to worry about?"

The silence was total. Then Leo shrugged. "I've always been more of a doer than a worrier."

Mocking laughter from the noblemen's benches.

"But, Lord Brock, Orso is the anointed High King of the Union. He wore the crown! He cannot be simply dismissed—"

"Oh, I find he can," said Leo, "like *that*." He snapped his fingers with an echoing crack. "He's put right out of my mind." Some of the lords crowed. Others mockingly snapped their fingers in the old man's face. Others sneered their contempt for the entire commoner's side of the chamber, their scorn reflected in the mirrors over and over, into the far distance. Unity and respect, it seemed, were only for those who did as they were told.

For once, everything was going just the way Leo hoped.

"I'd like a show of hands!" he told the Hall of Mirrors. "Nothing hidden. Nothing suspect. Each man makes his loyalty clear. Now. An open vote for our new king." A vote observed by him, who had all the armed men in the city, not to mention at least a hundred in this room, firmly under his command. Only a fool calls for a vote when he hasn't made sure of the outcome, after all.

Isher stood, precisely on cue. "I propose that the new monarch picks up the bloodline of the old! I propose that our new king should be the natural grandson of our much-missed King Jezal." A man he'd showered with scorn when it suited him. "I propose, as our next ruler, the infant Harod dan Brock!"

Leo watched the Representatives. Reading their expressions. Guessing their intentions. Many weren't happy. But none had the stomach for a fight. They'd have voted for a cart of dung if it meant things went back to some kind of normal, and business could be done, and jokes made, and strolls taken in the sun, without the nagging fear of the long drop from the Tower of Chains.

Leo gave Glaward the nod. "All those Representatives who wish to vote for the infant Harod dan Brock as the next High King of the Union," he roared, "raise your hands!"

On the noblemen's side of the hall, arms shot up so fast it was a wonder they didn't fly off. On the commoners' side they were slower. But they soon saw which way the wind was blowing. With varying expressions of worry, dismay and disgust they raised their hands. Only a few stubborn holdouts sat glaring at the prospective monarch, arms folded, and Leo took careful note of their names. They could be tastefully weeded out later.

He didn't look much like a king, as Leo glanced around. He looked like a white bundle in the arms of his mother, who with her unerring instinct for the centre of attention appeared to have swapped babies while the voting was underway. But King Harod the Second was raised to the throne, as his grandfather King Jezal the First had been, by near-unanimous accord.

The ringing applause jerked the infant monarch from his sleep and caused him to start bleating. But he'd done his work for today. Savine caught Zuri's eye and nodded towards the door, and the cries of the latest High King of the Union faded from the room.

Heugen was already on his feet. "His Majesty is, quite clearly, too young to govern in his own right." He pointed at Leo as though the idea had just occurred. "I propose that his father, Lord Leonault dan Brock, and his mother, Lady Savine dan Brock, govern in his stead as Lord and Lady Regent."

"I second that!" shouted Isher, popping up from his seat again like a toy on a spring.

"I third it!"

The nobles rose as one. The commoners were less happy than ever, but Jurand gave a subtle signal and the guards began thumping the butts of well-sharpened polearms on the tiles to send up a menacing rattle, and it quickly spurred the loiterers to their feet. Judge had taught them well. Nobody wanted to be the last one sitting. They'd let the sluice open a crack and the flood had forced it wide. Now there was no closing it, and they all were swept away into the future.

Leo gritted his teeth, rocked his weight forwards and stood. Ignoring the pain was easy. He'd been through the fire but, seeing his reflection in the many mirrors, it wasn't flattery to say he was still a fine-looking figure.

"My thanks! I humbly accept this great honour, this great responsibility. I'm a soldier first, but now is the time for healing wounds. For reforging what's been broken, stronger than ever. For making us a *Union* again!" He thumped his fist on the table. "We'll have a new age, my friends! Not the corruption of the old regime. Not the folly of the Breakers or the madness of the Burners. The best of both worlds! Justice and good government for all!"

Now there was wholehearted support. The Representatives were already rushing forwards. Queueing up to sign. Noblemen first, as was only right, Isher smiling at their head.

The sun rose on a new age. One that Leo would shape as he saw fit. Savine might not like how he'd done it, but it was done, and all their ambitions realised. How could she not be pleased? How could she not be grateful?

Leo lurched around on his false leg to grin at her.

But she was sitting up tall to look towards the grand declaration, watching intently as the first signatures were scratched beside it.

# We Must Have Enemies

Vick was so tired that when she sat, she nearly missed the chair. She'd been tired for months. For years. She couldn't remember not being tired. And the broken nose by no means helped.

But prisoners won't interrogate themselves.

"So..." she said, the word a slightly painful sigh. "Master Sarlby."

The sight of his face made her feel a bit better about her own. Gunnar Broad had smashed it to barely recognisable mush. You could've said he was lucky to be alive, after the beating he'd taken. But lucky was a tough word to use about a man sitting where he was.

"Not much need to refresh our memories as to your crimes, is there?" she asked. "You've been up to your eyes in the Great Change, right back to Valbeck. You were at Judge's side in the Court of the People. You herded dozens off the Tower of Chains."

"I did," said Sarlby. There was a sloppy sucking to his "d" sounds. The broken jaw, maybe. "And I'd do it again."

Vick pressed gently at the aching bridge of her nose. She was past disgust. Far past outrage. It just made her tired, now.

"Where's the Weaver?" she asked, without much hope of an answer. "Where's Pike?"

"I don't know," he growled. "But if I did, you think I'd tell you?"

She glanced, heavy-lidded, at the box of instruments. "We could try it and see."

"You're a traitor. To your kind. To yourself." He worked his tongue around his broken teeth and spat on the table. "You're a liar and a thief and a traitor to everything."

Vick shrugged. "And?"

"And you'll never beat us! We'll be back! More of us than ever! More'n you can count!"

It wasn't the least bit funny, but Vick couldn't help herself, she snorted out a chuckle, then had to wince at the flash of pain across her face. "Folk can't wait to be rid of you. Breakers and Burners, they're cheering the end of you. You said you'd strike a blow for the common man. All you did was starve them, freeze them and kill them."

She sat forwards with a grunt. Damn, she was aching. "Truth is—and take it from someone who spent a dozen years in prison—in the end, people don't really care much about being free. They want to be warm and well fed and to not have to worry. In particular, they want to not have to worry about being thrown off a tower for wearing the wrong shoes."

Sarlby frowned down at the table. She thought it was a frown, anyway. Hard to tell exactly where the corners of his mouth were. "We were in the right," he muttered, though it sounded like he was trying to convince himself, rather than her. "You'll see."

"I doubt I will. But I know you won't." Vick pressed a thumb into her stiff hip as she worked her way up from the table. "They're hanging you tomorrow."

Tallow was waiting outside in the damp-smelling corridor, a book clutched in his hands and his big, sad eyes on her, as if he still hoped, even now, that she might somehow have the answers. Damn, he was more like her brother than ever. That made her tired, too.

"Another one for the list?" he asked, falling in beside her, their footsteps echoing dully from the damp walls.

She gave a grunt, eyeing the doors as they passed.

Tallow shook his head as he made a little mark in his book. "Feels like the Lord Regent's lists are even longer than Judge's were. At least they're being dealt with quietly. Not splattered across the moat."

"That's better, is it?"

"I guess once these are cleared that'll be it. Back to normal."

"That's what the Breakers said. And the Arch Lector before them, for that matter. A couple of enemies to cross out. Just get to the bottom of the list. Except the list kept getting longer." She ventured a little sniff, a squeak of barely moving air in her swollen face, a hint of salty snot at the back of her throat which she could never quite manage to swallow. "We must have enemies, Tallow. Always."

"You're a ray of sunshine."

"Sunshine's not really appropriate for an executioner. Specially one with a broken nose."

They rounded the corner and Vick stopped dead.

"Oh, bloody hell," squeaked Tallow.

They'd been expecting her, but the sight of Savine dan Brock under the

House of Questions was still as shocking as suddenly spying a diamond in the gutter. She looked a different woman from the one Vick first met in that bouncing carriage on the way to Valbeck, with the glassy perfection of an expensive doll. The same immaculate poise, perhaps, the same assessing eye, but more honest. More human. Fewer jewels, less ornament, lots of virtuous white. The Mother of the Nation, they were calling her. She'd even somehow turned the clipped hair and the scar into advantages. She looked beautiful *and* like she didn't care a shit about anyone else's opinion.

"Lady Regent." Vick gave an awkward bow. "I apologise, but my curtsy's a thing no one of your refined tastes should be forced to see."

"I have braved worse horrors, Inquisitor Teufel. Are you Inquisitors again?"

"I'm not sure anyone really knows at this point."

"We are all finding a course through uncharted waters." Though she looked to Vick as if she knew exactly where she was headed. "Are you well, Master Tallow?"

"Tolerably so..." he managed to gurgle out. "My lady."

"Tolerably well is as well as can be hoped for these days. I understand you swore an oath of loyalty to my son."

Vick raised her brows. Even that felt like an effort. "I spent years working for your father—your adopted father, not the other one—so I learned how to take a hint. I got the strong feeling your husband's offer was to swear the oath and stay in the Inquisitor's chair or refuse and go in the prisoner's one. But then I've always been a traitor and a liar so...wasn't difficult to do." She gave a hopeless shrug. "Far be it from me to stand in the way of the new Union. Or the new new Union, is it?"

The Lady Regent had the good grace to show a touch of guilt about the way it had all turned out. She even managed to make that look good. "Please believe me when I say that things are not the way I wanted them."

You can never let them see your feelings. Never let them think you've got any. Show hurt, you're asking to be hurt. But Vick was so tired, and broken, and aching. All she could think of, for some reason, was Sibalt's last sad smile. Malmer and the rest dangling over the road out of Valbeck. All those names carved into the Square of Martyrs. All those people who fell from the Tower of Chains.

She found she'd stepped close to Savine, found she was looking her right in the eye, found that, for once, she was being honest. "Just...tell me it'll be better." Her throat felt tight, like she still had Corporal Smiler's hands around her bruised neck. "It doesn't have to be some paradise."

She had to force the words through gritted teeth. "But it can't all be for *nothing*, you understand? It *can't*."

It was quiet, in that shabby corridor, for a moment. The Lady Regent blinked at Vick as if she saw her for the first time. Then she gently nodded. "I understand. And I will do my best."

"Good." Vick cleared her throat. "Good." She turned away, trying to swallow that lump in her throat, wiping her eyelids with a knuckle. Tallow stood against the wall, staring at her like he'd seen Euz rise from the grave. "What?" Vick snarled at him.

"Nothing," he squeaked.

She set her jaw and gripped the door-handle. "Let's get on with it, then."

She'd never had much dislike for the prisoners. Even disapproval was an effort these days. But for this one she could make an exception.

"There are still some men it's a pleasure to hang," she said, planting her fists on the scarred tabletop.

Spillion Sworbreck cringed in his chair, stripped naked, cheeks tracked with the tears he'd notably failed to cry on behalf of all those he'd sent to the long drop.

"Inquisitor, please," he babbled, "you are a woman of the *world*. You understand the *position* I was in, the *compromises* that had to be made. I am, I freely admit, a weak man. I have always been so easily led! Swept up by great passions and powerful personalities like a leaf on the wind! I am pleading with you. I am *begging* you—"

"No point asking my forgiveness," said Vick. "I'm not allowed any. You might have more luck with her." She nodded towards the door. "But I wouldn't bet on it."

"Oh," he said, in a very small voice, as the Lady Regent swept in with chill majesty. "Oh dear." She arranged herself on the Inquisitor's chair with a rustling of expensive silk while Sworbreck shrank further and further into his seat, chains faintly clinking. If he could've sucked his head into his shoulders like a turtle, Vick imagined he would've.

"He was caught at the docks," she said. "Trying to get out of the city disguised as a woman. One of the few people in the Circle of the World who can safely say they look worse than me in a dress."

"Lady Savine..." His eyelids fluttered and fresh tears ran down his face. "Lady Regent, I beg of you—"

"*Shut*," hissed Savine furiously through her gritted teeth, "your *fucking* mouth." She closed her eyes, composing herself, took a breath, then opened them, flinty hard. "Understand... the *restraint* it takes on my part not to see you dragged up the Tower of Chains and flung to your death."

"I do understand, Your Highness, I do, I do, please, you must see, I...
I lost *perspective*."

"Perspective? Is *that* what you lost?"

"I got carried away...and not for the first time. When I was in the
Far Country, Fates help me...I am so easily dragged off course! I never
learn! It was the *times*...it was *Judge*...I didn't know what I was *doing*!"

"Please! All you got carried away with, Sworbreck, was your own power,
and cruelty, and self-importance."

"I am a worm," he whispered, head hanging, tears dripping. "An utter
*worm*!"

"Oh, no. Worms do some good." Savine slowly sat back, lip wrinkled
with disgust, the angry flush fading from her cheek. "Cowardly liar you
may be, ridiculous fantasist you may be, disloyal scum you certainly are,
but for reasons I cannot divine...people listen to you."

"They do, Lady Savine!" A sudden hope lit his face. "Your Highness,
Lady Regent, I am *ever so* keen to be of service, in whatever humble and
lowly way—"

"You will write of me again," said Savine.

"I will?"

"Just like you did in *The Darling of the Slums*. Your best work."

The flicker of a smile on Sworbreck's lips. "You think so?"

"The best turd in the sewer," growled Vick, making him cringe again.

"You will *rain* praise upon me," said Savine.

"I will lavish you with compliments, Your Highness! I will burnish
your legend! I will raise you up on a *cushion* of eulogy. The deliverer of
the people! The Mother of the Nation! You and your children," blubbered
Sworbreck. "And your noble husband—"

"My children, yes. My husband can extol his own virtues."

"Sure you don't want to hang this bastard?" asked Vick. Seemed there
was no more justice in the world than there had been when Judge sat
in the Court of the People. But then justice had always been in short
supply. Who'd know better than her, who'd had years of her life stolen
for someone else's crimes?

The Lady Regent considered her carefully. "You spent years working
for my father. You should have learned not to hang what you can use."
She narrowed her eyes at Sworbreck. "I suggest you get to your press and
keep it hot. You live now to make me loved. And you will live precisely
as long as you are useful to me." Savine stood, looking down her nose at
the sobbing ex-prosecutor. "Not an *instant* longer."

# A Sea of Power

"Welcome, one and all, to this exceptional general meeting of Adua's Solar Society!"

Curnsbick, resplendent in a waistcoat embroidered with blazing suns, flung wide his arms and delivered a beaming smile. The applause was positively thunderous. All the pent-up terror and frustration of the last few months released in an outpouring of joy and relief.

"With thanks to our most radiant patron, Her Highness the Lady Regent and Mother of the King, Savine dan Brock!" Curnsbick humbly bowed his head towards Savine's box and she lowered her fan to give a nod and smile of her own. There was a kind of ripple through the audience as every face turned towards her. The ovation grew, if anything, even louder. Her smile grew, if anything, even wider. Joyous screeches, admiring coos. Someone shouted, "The Mother of the Nation!"

Savine liked to think she had changed. She was by no means the same woman who had sat in this box two years ago, jealously hoarding up the adulation. But who dislikes being applauded? She blew Curnsbick a kiss. Sentimental folly, perhaps. But that seemed to be in fashion.

"So much has been wantonly destroyed!" called Curnsbick as the clapping tailed off. "Everyone here has lost friends! Colleagues. Partners. Family." His voice faded to a croak and he had to pause. The crowd murmured encouragement, wiped eyes, urged the Great Machinist on. He made a fist and shook it at no one in particular. "But we who remain *must* not allow ourselves to be buried in the past! We cannot afford to wallow in regrets and recriminations. We must look to the *future*. Our departed friends would not want their seats here to sit empty. Already we have new members, young investors, dynamic inventors boiling over with ideas and enthusiasm, keen to push the great work forward!"

Rowdy cheering. While attention was elsewhere, Savine slipped behind her fan and took the tiniest pinch of pearl dust, eyelashes fluttering at that delicious, invigorating burning in her face. Thank the Fates, trade of all kinds was flowing once again, at least for those with the money. She liked to think she had changed, but the Mother of the King, like any mother, needs a little something from time to time.

"A new age dawns, my friends! A new beginning!" There were tears on Curnsbick's cheeks. "The Great Change is at our backs and before us lies a vista of prosperity such as mankind has never looked upon before!" They were already on their feet. Whooping, clapping, weeping. An almost religious rapture. Curnsbick struggled to scream his final words. "Progress, my friends! Progress!"

Savine stood to clap herself. "Well said!" Zuri was already offering a handkerchief so she could dab a tear from the corner of her eye without compromising her powder. "Well said."

A considerable crowd had gathered beneath the two great chandeliers and the stump where the third had once hung, the air hot with excited chatter, dense with talk of rebuilding and renewal, grand visions and vast opportunities. Knots of brightly dressed gentlemen split and merged, sucked into dizzying currents and whirlpools, the ladies pale dots on the flood.

Her own white nursing dress was everywhere, her own modest lack of jewels, her own wigless, clipped hair and, mercy, did she even see a woman with a scar like hers painted on? Savine had taken pride in being at the forefront of fashion, but this slavish imitation was something new. Something at once gratifying and slightly troubling.

"The Lady Regent!" someone almost screamed.

The talk stopped instantly. Every eye turned to her.

For a moment, Savine felt a sucking of terror. As if they might see through her, to all the secrets, and the guilt, and the things she wished she had not done. As if they might denounce her on the spot and drag her to the Tower of Chains.

Then Curnsbick stepped forwards. "Your Highness," he murmured, lowering himself to one knee. As if it was arranged, every man and woman, several hundred of the richest and most talented in the Union, sank down with him, bowing, curtsying, competing viciously to get closest to the floor.

Savine liked to think she had changed. She had taken a beating in Valbeck. Reeled through the year afterwards, finally put herself back together, then taken another beating at Stoffenbeck. Everyone had taken a beating in the Great Change. Then she had spent six months hiding, giving herself up to her babies, to her husband, to her charity, and finally taken yet another beating in the Court of the People and on the roof of the Tower of Chains. Though there, it had to be said, she had given far worse than she got.

Savine liked to think she had changed. Come through her ordeals a better woman. But perhaps she was like a leaf of steel, bent by great pressure into new shapes but, given the chance, springing all too quickly back. In the warm draft of the foyer the embers of ambition flared up again as hot as ever. There was no denying the satisfaction she felt to see every man and woman not only seeking her money, not only seeking her approval, not only envying her, but kneeling before her.

Savine liked to think she had changed. But who dislikes being knelt to?

She left them kneeling long enough to know she could have left them kneeling all night. Then she smiled her sweetest smile. "Don't be ridiculous, everyone. Please rise."

She swallowed that horrible, lovely pearl dust bitterness and swept down the steps into the foyer. Her foyer. Once she had fought battles here. Now she reigned over the place as the unquestioned victor. The dozen armoured Anglanders who followed her everywhere she went were something of a clattering nuisance, and more had been posted at the theatre's every doorway. She did wonder, in her more suspicious moments, whether Leo sent them to watch her as much as to protect her, but she supposed great figures must have an entourage. There was a wave of bowing heads, a rustle of curtsying skirts, a wake of awestruck respect wherever Savine passed.

"One could get used to this," murmured Zuri, sliding her pencil from behind her ear, and she was right, as always. All Savine had to do was smile to bring them rushing forwards like pigs at feeding time.

"My surveys show there is room for three thousand thoroughly modern houses in the burned areas of the Three Farms *alone*. Thoroughly modern, Your Highness! Running water!"

"New ships, Lady Regent. Towering ships. Cities on the salt, bristling with cannon. Blow anything those Styrian bastards have out of the water. The Union will rule the seas again!"

"Have you had the opportunity to consider my designs, Lady Regent? Better statues on the Kingsway that celebrate the new while harking back to the glory of the old!"

"A new and improved patent office must be the priority, Your Highness, everything is in turmoil, new standards for the new age..."

Zuri was, if anything, more skilful than ever, her pencil moving with almost inhuman dexterity, noting anything worthwhile in the book shorthand, scoring in the appointments, chopping the coming days into slices of opportunity, assigning a worth to every sliver of Savine's attention and not allowing a crumb to be wasted. It was very much like old times, only better. Savine had missed the fan, like a wounded warrior might his sword, and back on the battlefield, she wielded it with twice the savagery.

"Cannons are the thing, now, Lady Regent! With my new casting techniques they fire at twice the speed, thrice the range, ten times the reliability!"

"Rails are the thing! The *potential*, Your Highness, a woman of your vision cannot be blind to the *potential*..."

"Roads *on top* of roads, can you imagine?"

"Just a moment of your time, Your Highness! Just an *instant*!"

One by one, she brought them forwards with their schemes, their dreams, the light of certainty burning bright in their eyes. Her slightest smile lit their faces with delight. The hint of a frown doused them with horror. When she ended each interview with a snap of her fan she thought of cringing through the streets of Valbeck, hiding in the woods after Stoffenbeck, standing helpless in the dock before Judge, and revelled in her power.

"The *one* thing I need is the support of the state!"

"A *word* from you would make all the difference!"

"A *moment* with the Lord Regent!"

"The one thing I need!"

"Curnsbick!" droned Savine, offering her hand.

"Your Highness," said the Great Machinist, leaning down to kiss it. "And Zuri, as radiant as ever. When the hell are you coming to work for me?"

"One minute past never," she said, quickly checking the golden watch that had replaced the silver one around her neck.

"It was a truly moving address," said Savine. "I do believe it might have been your best ever."

"All from the heart, you know, all from the heart." Curnsbick put the gentlest hand on Savine's elbow, drew her to a conspiratorial distance. "We came through all right, didn't we?"

"We did," she said, patting his knuckles. "Even if...the things we had to do might trouble us from time to time."

"We did." The king of inventors had a somewhat nauseous look. Perhaps thinking of his hoist up the Tower of Chains. Or his automatic hanging machine. "But many did not. Sometimes I think...I should have done more. But my old partner Majud always told me a man of business stays neutral." He cleared his throat, shook off the sombre mood, looked to the future. "I am planning to lay a rail route up to Valbeck, you know! With a bridge by your friend Master Kort. I expect excellent returns for my investors."

"You have *never* disappointed your investors, but I have other business to attend to."

"Doubtless. The ground is already broken on your grand new orphanage, I hear." He leaned close to murmur, "And I understand you bought up half the Three Farms for next to nothing. That might yet turn out your best investment of all."

Savine would not have been surprised if it turned out one of the best in history, especially since she'd bought up half the Arches, too. "For the sake of the tenants, you understand. Most of them are paying less than half rent." For the time being, at least...

"I always knew you had a generous heart."

"I remember you saying something of the sort. I may have a gift for you, in fact."

Curnsbick peered at her over his eye-lenses. "Why do I imagine you will want something in return?"

"Because you know my generous heart pumps blood to a calculating brain. It is a chair."

"I am not quite ready for retirement, Your Highness."

"No fear of that. The chair is a decidedly uncomfortable one." Her turn to murmur, shielding her mouth with her fan. "On the Closed Council."

He tried to stay calm, but she noted the eager twitch of his fingers. "Who else have you asked?"

"You are my first choice, of course."

"Then you would want to approach me with some friends already in place."

Savine smiled. "Perhaps you know me *too* well. I have approached Vallimir and Kort."

"And they said yes?"

"Can you imagine either of them refusing me before I was Mother of the King? Now?" She glanced across the foyer stuffed with breathless sycophants desperately trying to catch her eye and laughed. "Please."

Curnsbick glanced towards her heavy-handed bodyguard, lowering his voice. "And...your husband has given his permission?"

Savine did not like the word "permission." It galled her that people might think she had to ask for it. "He will not object."

"Are you sure? I hear the easy manners of the Young Lion are not very much in evidence lately. He is proving to be far from agreeable when it comes to sharing power, and as vengeful as Glustrod at any hint of a slight—"

"Let me worry about my husband."

Curnsbick looked less than convinced. He looked, in fact, rather scared. "Can I refuse?"

"Of course. But I know *you* too well, and you could never pass up the chance to shape the future. I will let you know the terms." And, favouring him with a touch of her fan, she drifted on. Her eye had been caught by someone loitering near the wall.

Selest dan Heugen was, for once, not trying to make an exhibit of herself. In her efforts to fade into the background, indeed, she had done everything short of wear a dress that matched the wallpaper. But Savine was not about to let her slip away so easily.

"Selest!" she called. "I hope you aren't trying to avoid me."

Her curtsy had something of the cornered animal about it as Savine bore down with her phalanx of guards. "Only...because I'm afraid to face you," she said, which was honest, at least. "Your Highness, I have to apologise—"

"It might be a good idea."

"I...always liked to think of myself as fearless." Selest looked down at the floor as though she was blinking back tears. "But the truth is... faced with real danger...I was an utter coward. It is...a hard thing to learn about oneself."

"If the Great Change taught us anything, it is that the vast majority of us are cowards the vast majority of the time."

"Not you."

Savine smiled. Is there anything finer than seeing an enemy humbled? "I have my moments. But we are all offered a new beginning, now. A chance to make ourselves afresh. You may not have covered yourself in glory in the Court of the People, but you emerged alive. You are ruthless, ambitious, clever and persistent. Qualities I could make use of, if you were willing to serve His August Majesty."

Selest swallowed. "I am eager to serve him, of course." She looked up nervously from under her lashes. "Or Your Highness." Which was getting closer to it. "Only...tell me how."

Probably she feared she would be sent as emissary to distant Thond or put into service in the palace as a carpet. Savine was somewhat tempted. But one must work with the tools one has, as her father had once been fond of saying.

She made Selest's distress last just a little longer, then tossed it out as if it was nothing to remark upon. "On the Closed Council."

"But I..." Selest looked as if a fan's waft could have knocked her over. "Women, surely, are not permitted—"

"I was very careful over the language in the Grand Declaration. The gender of the Closed Council's members was nowhere specified. We did not get where we are by having too much respect for tradition, did we? *I* mean to be there, I promise you."

"Lady Savine...I hardly know what to say."

"Say nothing, then." Savine leaned close. "And let your loyalty speak for you."

"Loyalty is so important, isn't it?" Savine frowned around to find that stooge of the First of the Magi, Yoru Sulfur, much closer to her than she would have liked.

"Your Highness," he said, with a stiff little bow. "I have been seeking an audience."

Savine gestured to the eager crowd pressing in around them, though Zuri seemed to have faded into the background. "I see who I wish to, Master Sulfur. For the rest, no amount of seeking will make the slightest difference."

She flicked out her fan to bring the conversation to a close, but Sulfur did not take the hint. "Do you imagine that you have won?" he asked.

She smiled at the foyer full of smiles, queen in all but name. "It looks rather like it."

"Looks can lie."

"Almost as proficiently as magi."

He did not like that at all, different-coloured eyes angrily narrowed. "My master will be satisfied," he said, an edge of menace on his voice. "There is no hiding from him."

"Who's hiding?" asked Savine, lifting her chin. "The Breakers did their worst in Valbeck, and here I am. The cannons did their worst at Stoffenbeck, and here I am. Judge did her worst on the Tower of Chains, and even so, here I am. You tried your very best to destroy me, too, as I recall, blabbing my ugliest secrets around town, and it only made me more powerful."

"Your power is borrowed." He pronounced each word with furious care. "And as any banker will tell you, what is borrowed must be repaid. With *interest*."

As he leaned forwards to hiss the last word, one of Savine's bodyguards stepped smoothly in front of him. "Is this man bothering you, Your Highness?"

"Not really," said Savine. "But throw him out anyway."

Two guards seized Sulfur under the arms and marched him towards the door, his feet scarcely brushing the ground. The constant presence of armed men can be a little harsh on the nerves, but they certainly have their uses.

"You will hear from us!" he called as he was dragged through the crowd. "My master will be satisfied!"

"Your master wants something from me?" Savine turned away with a snort. "He can get in line." And the mocking laughter of the crowd followed the magus to the door.

Savine had not made society a snake pit. She had simply determined to slither to the top of it.

Who could deny that she had?

# Not for the Prizes

The vast banners of Angland and the Union covered the fronts of the warehouses entirely, billowing faintly with the sea breeze. The ranks of dark-uniformed soldiers stood to stiff attention. The buglers blew an awkward fanfare. The threadbare crowd gave scattered cheers as Lady Finree stepped to the quay, a few dozen seasick worthies of Angland in her wake.

Leo limped forward, his one working arm out to embrace her. "Mother!"

You couldn't have said he was used to his wounds. The pain, the shame, the seething frustration. But they'd become familiar. Routine. Seeing the ill-disguised horror on his mother's face was like looking at himself in the mirror, mutilated, for the first time.

"It looks worse than it is," he said. "Curnsbick made the leg for me. So good I'm thinking of having him replace the other one! And I'm getting some movement back in the arm now, too." He waved his left elbow about as much as he could, trying not to let the pain show and hoping his limp hand didn't flop from his jacket.

"Leo." She brushed a speck of fluff from his uniform, and held him tight, very clearly trying to fight back tears. "I thought I might never see you again." And she pressed her head against his chest. Her hair had much more grey in it than the last time he saw her. By the dead, could it really be less than a year ago?

"I'm...glad you were wrong." He could've stayed there all day, holding her. But people were watching. A sentimental attachment to his mother might look well. A desperate need for her support would not. He cleared his throat, and stepped away, and gave her a moment to dab her damp eyes. "Your carriage awaits."

He did his best to walk smoothly, open the door, help his mother up. But his iron foot slid on the step as he followed and the heel got caught.

"Damn it," he snarled, twisting it, pulling it, getting worse tangled in his frustration.

"Leo, let me—"

"No need!" he snapped, finally heaving himself free and twisting back into his seat, teeth gritted against the pain.

He thumped at the door and the carriage lurched off towards the Agriont. He didn't like the dismay in his mother's eyes, so he frowned out of the window at the honour guards riding to either side, harness polished to gleaming mirror-brightness, and wished he was riding with them. He listened to the hooves pounding the cobbles and thought of the charge at Red Hill. The Young Lion, riding to glory.

"I always thought you hated carriages," said his mother.

"I do, but…" But it hurt him to ride, he was in more pain than he could stand and the thought of more made him sick. "Anything for you. Did you bring more soldiers?"

"Another regiment should arrive tomorrow. I swear there's hardly a man under thirty left in Ostenhorm."

"I need every loyal Anglander," said Leo. "To keep the peace. To keep order. To keep the people…safe."

His mother looked even more dismayed at that. "I remember what your father used to say…about the founding principles of the Union." She had always thought Leo's father was a fool, and he was starting to think she had been right. "You can have too much order, Leo. People need liberty."

"Tell that to those splattered to mincemeat at the bottom of the Tower of Chains," he snapped. "Liberty is a luxury we can't afford right now."

"Of course," she said, looking down at the floor. "We have to take things at the right pace. Have to be cautious." She looked up at him again, and she looked pale. "Have you heard from…the First of the Magi?"

Leo frowned. "That old fool? Why would I have?"

"In the past, he held…a *great* deal of influence."

"In the past, maybe."

"It was partly through his patronage that your father became Lord Governor."

"What?"

His mother leaned forwards. A woman who'd fought an army of Northmen to a draw, and she looked positively scared. "*Undertakings* were made to him. He is not a man to simply let a debt *go*."

"Sadly, the banks all burned in the Great Change. I rather think the debts burned with them."

"I very much doubt he will see it that way."

"What do I care how he sees it?"

His mother blinked. "Leo, you don't understand—"

"I have bigger problems than making wizards happy! Have you seen the state of things here?" And he waved towards the window. A burned-out stretch of the city was rolling into view, scorched windows and doorways yawning empty.

"By the Fates," breathed his mother, eyes wide at the sight. Leo had got used to the city's scars, perhaps, the way he had to his own, but now he saw those fresh, too.

"The bastards ruined everything," he said, clenching his fist. "It can't *ever* happen again. We need a strong army. A vigilant Inquisition. The Breakers and Burners are still there, in the provinces. Like bloody maggots in the guts of the nation! We need to ferret them *out*. Teach our enemies to *fear* us. The bloody Styrians, the bloody Gurkish, the bloody Old Empire. We have to get a *grip*."

It seemed obvious good sense to him, but his mother looked more dismayed than ever. "We have to show strength, but...surely we need friends before we look for more enemies—"

"You know I never looked for enemies!" He turned sourly back to the window. "I just beat the ones who looked for me."

He did some watery smiling, some half-hearted waving, but there weren't many people on the Middleway. If the Lady Regent had been in the carriage no doubt they'd have packed in a dozen deep. They pissed themselves for the so-called Mother of the Nation and barely spared a thought for the man who'd actually got the job done. But there it was. Being a hero had always been a thankless task. You did it because it was right, not for the prizes.

"How is Savine?" asked his mother.

"Very popular," he said, grudgingly. "Have you had the bloody pamphlets up in Angland? Savine, bare-breasted in the Court of the People, shielding her babies from the spears of the Burners. Savine, duelling with Judge on the roof of the Tower of Chains and throwing her down like your bloody friend Bayaz threw down the Master Maker. Savine, bringing shelter to the orphans, bread to the starving, hope to the hopeless. The Darling of the Slums! The Mother of the Nation!" He gave a snort. "Anyone would think she ended the Great Change single-handed."

His mother raised one brow. "I seem to remember a few mildly exaggerated songs sung of your victories, up in the North. She has been through a lot."

If that was meant to make him less annoyed, it failed. "We both have," he grunted.

"It can be difficult, when children appear. Your father and I didn't couple for months after you were born."

"Must you?"

"Well, it's true. You cried all the time. You'd only sleep in bed with me. It can change things, in a marriage, that's all I'm saying."

"She blames me," he said, slumping in his seat. He'd never been able to hide anything from his mother for long. "She blames me for everything. For making our son a king. For making her wildest ambitions come true. For bringing order back to the Union. For everything."

His mother raised the other brow. "And is it your fault?"

"Ten breaths off the boat and you're taking her side?"

"It's a marriage, Leo. There shouldn't be sides."

"Feels like there are, though." He frowned out of the window at the lonely well-wishers. "And everyone's on hers."

Savine had wasted no time making herself at home in the palace she so resented Leo for providing. She'd worked her usual magic on a set of rooms even more cavernous than the ones they'd lived in before the Great Change. Rooms on the ground floor, since Leo was scarcely friendlier with stairs these days than Arch Lector Glokta used to be.

"Your grandfather!" said Leo's mother, one hand to her chest as she gazed up at the huge canvas of Lord Marshal Kroy glaring towards victory.

"Where he can stand guard over his family," said Savine, gliding forwards with her best smile. One Leo rarely saw these days.

"Savine! You look breathtaking, as always." They embraced while Leo stood by, grimacing at the ache in his stump. His mother held Savine out at arm's length, taking in her clipped hair, her clothes, her scar. "And thoroughly modern, of course."

"I could say the same of you."

"But you wouldn't dare, because it would be rank flattery." Already they were wandering off, arm-in-arm, leaving Leo to lurch painfully across the acres of floor to a side table so he could pour himself a drink.

"Is that necklace Osprian work?"

"I'd forgotten how good your eye is— Oh!" Leo's mother had frozen on the threshold of the nursery with her hands pressed to her face. "Are these...?"

"Who else would they fucking be?" Leo wanted to snarl at her. He bit

409

his tongue, loitering in the doorway while the ladies advanced on the cribs.

"This is Ardee," Savine was cooing, lifting one of the babies. "She's just been fed, so this is the ten breaths in which she's happy."

"She has your eyes," Leo's mother flung over her shoulder at him.

"I hope not," he muttered. "They're about the only things I have that still work."

All his mother's attention was on the bundle in her arms, that gormless grin on her face women get around babies, as if making a sucking sound is a heroic achievement. "Oh, she's a weight! You forget. Can I ask... have your parents...?"

"No," said Savine. "No sign."

"I'm so sorry." Leo's mother put a hand on Savine's arm. A touch of simple support and sympathy. A touch she never gave him. "I was very much looking forward to seeing your mother again. I always enjoyed our chats."

"It would be nice... to know what became of them." Savine put her hand on top of Leo's mother's. Squeezed it. As if they were parent and child, and Leo was a pushy visitor getting in the way of their reunion. "But there are so many people who lost family in the Great Change. I suppose... one learns to live with the doubts. And I have a new family now." She beamed down at the children. Leo didn't get so much as a glance, of course. That would've been far too much to ask.

"So you do." Leo's mother handed Ardee back and leaned over Harod's cot. "I suppose this must be His Majesty." He gave a panicky clutch at the air as he was picked up. It always annoyed Leo, seeing his softness. Made him want to shake the boy, tell him to be a man. The way his own father had always done.

"You shouldn't coddle him," grunted Leo.

"Surely that's exactly what a grandmother should do," she said, fussing and rocking and squeaking.

Leo had always imagined he'd be a wonderful father. To a boy, of course. A little copy of himself he could give a little sword to. They'd ride and wrestle and fence together. He took a sip of his wine, but it tasted bitter. How could he do any of that now? Holding them was hard enough, with his one good arm, his one good hand. All he could do by way of playing was dangle the useless fingers of the other in their faces.

Leo's mother put her wrinkled nose close to Harod's blankets. "His August Majesty has soiled himself."

"I understand his great-grandfather King Guslav was prone to do the same," said Savine, and she scooped him into her arms and swept from the room.

"I wish your father had lived to see them." Leo's mother dabbed at teary eyes. "He doted on you. Always saying how proud he was of his son."

That was the story they always told, but Leo remembered it differently. His father had never been there, and when he had been he was stiff and distant, and when Leo needed love he'd got empty sayings about being a man, and dry rot about the principles of the Union.

He remembered waking scared in the night, and he couldn't find the pot, so he'd pissed in the cupboard. When his father found out he had refused to speak to him for a week. As soon as he could he'd sent Leo off to Adua, then to Uffrith, where the Dogman had been more of a father to him than his own ever was.

He wanted to say it all. To puke up his resentments. He had his mouth open to do it. But why bother? The past isn't made of facts, not really, just stories people tell to make themselves feel better. To make themselves look better. Everyone was at it. Savine was the bloody queen of it, the Darling of the Slums herself. He wondered what myths that worm Sworbreck was already spinning about the past vile and bloody year. He took another heavy swig from his glass.

"What is it, Leo? You seem... *sulky.*"

It was only then he realised how much he'd wanted her approval. A man who'd made himself one of the most powerful in the Circle of the World, still endlessly trying and failing to impress his mother. The Lord Regent of the Union, jealous of his own babies.

"Isn't this what you were always telling me to do?" he demanded. "To be shrewd? To be prudent? Isn't this what Savine was always telling me to do? To be ruthless? To be ambitious? Then I do it and somehow I've let you all down!"

"Leo, don't be ridiculous—"

"I saved the fucking Union!" he snarled, lifting his glass to fling it against the wall, stopping himself at the last moment so all he managed was to pour wine down his sleeve. "Isn't this what you wanted for me? To be a hero?" He took a step towards her, twisted his iron leg and tottered sideways, gasping with pain.

"Leo, please." She caught him. Held him. Laid her firm hand on his face. "I know I pushed you. I know I lectured you. I know I was too hard. I'm sorry for all of that. Perhaps you'll see now you have children of your own... being a parent... there is no plan. It's just a set of mistakes you hardly notice making. Please believe me..." She winced at his iron leg, as if she felt the pain of it. "All I ever wanted was for you to be happy."

He swallowed, tears burning at the back of his nose. He found his balance again, pulled free of her, tugged his uniform straight. "I wish you'd fucking said so."

Every grate of cutlery, every grind of crockery, every retch of conversation felt like a nail hammered into him.

Leo's stump was on fire. He'd sparred earlier, if you could call it sparring when he lumbered squeakily about the circle while Jurand lied that he was getting better. He'd got frustrated, as usual, then he'd got angry, as usual, then he'd pushed himself far too hard, as usual. Now his back was throbbing, too, sending stings all the way up into his neck. He wasn't getting better, he was getting worse.

He frowned down at the meat on his plate the way he'd once frowned across the Circle at Stour Nightfall. An enemy he wasn't sure he could beat. He picked up his knife, tried to cut, but pressing gently it only slithered around in the widening pool of bloody gravy. He gritted his teeth, pressed harder, but now the whole plate slid about, slopping juice onto the polished tabletop.

"Fuck," he hissed. "Fuck it!" He wanted to snatch his meat up and rip into the thing with his teeth. He could feel Savine's impatience on his right. His mother's concern on his left. He was master of the Union, and the women in his life were having to stop themselves reaching across to cut up his dinner.

"My Lord and Lady Regent..." Solumeo Shudra leaned forwards with an oily smile. "We are *most* honoured by your invitation." He was the leader of the Westport delegation, a big, dark-skinned, shaven-headed man who looked more like a priest of Gurkhul than an honest fellow of the Union. The other five were of every shape and colour. It faintly disgusted Leo that he was obliged to lap up the flattery of mongrels. But Savine said they needed Westport's money. So much to be rebuilt.

He'd always imagined absolute power meant doing whatever you pleased, but it was starting to look like one sordid compromise after another. He wished he was back in Uffrith, among the Northmen, where you could say what you meant and eat any way you fucking pleased and a missing limb or two won you admiration rather than pity.

"And we are most honoured by your attendance," said Savine, touching Leo gently on the shoulder as if they were one person, with one set of feelings. "We are all here to reaffirm our commitment to the Union. To reaffirm our commitment to each other." And she smiled at Leo so warmly, so fondly, she almost had him believing it. As if love was a machine she could turn on with a lever.

"It grieves me that leaders of the same great nation should never before have met," said Leo's mother. "I so look forward to getting to know you all better."

"As do we, Lady Governor Finree," said the greasiest of the Westporters. Filio, his name was, or some such shit.

"Your courage and prowess are spoken of with awe throughout the Circle of the World," added another. Rosimiche, and from his bent nose it looked as if someone had punched him in the face once. Leo wouldn't have minded giving it a go himself.

"They pale compared to my son's." Leo's mother showed every tooth as she smiled across at him. The falseness was strangling.

"It is well that we have a king again," said Filio.

"It is well that we look towards a stable future," said Rosimiche.

"It is well that Angland is once more inseparable from Midderland," said Shudra.

"Anything else would be unthinkable," said Savine.

"But…" And Shudra raised his brows towards the empty chairs on the opposite side of the table. "It is most regrettable that Lord Governor Skald and the other representatives of Starikland have not attended."

"It is," snapped Leo, pressing his fist into the tabletop and smearing it through spilled gravy. "He was given every opportunity, and I take it as a personal affront that he—"

"I am mediating between my son and Lord Governor Skald." Leo's mother laid her fingertips gently on the elbow of his ruined arm. That calming touch she always used to use on him, the one you might use on a peevish horse, though these days he felt little but a numb prickling. "The position is delicate, of course. Lord Skald's wife Cathil is sister to our… former king. But I have no doubt that, given time, he will come around to our way of—"

"If he doesn't he'll regret it," snapped Leo, twisting his elbow away from her. His days of deferring to his mother were well and truly over. His days of deferring to anyone. And the thought of getting back in the saddle, leading men in the field, being the Young Lion again, whoever the enemy, brought on a surge of excitement. He glared across the table at Shudra and his god-bothering stooges. "Anyone who threatens the stability of the Union will regret it. *Anyone*. From outside. Or from inside. Do you take my meaning?"

Shudra bowed his head. "Your Highness makes his meaning most plain."

"I'm a blunt soldier," grunted Leo, shifting his grip on his knife, "and I like blunt dealing."

"As do I." It was the woman who spoke. Mozolia, was she called? Tall and heavy-shouldered, frowning at Leo from under her thick black and grey brows. "Bluntly, then, it seems to us that the greatest threat to the stability of the Union currently comes from its last monarch." Leo stiffened. He felt Savine stiffen beside him. "There are many who still feel loyalty to King Orso. He will always be a focus for discontent."

Leo slowly swallowed, slowly set down his knife, slowly sat forward, looking this brazen bitch right in the eye. "I'm a blunt soldier. I like blunt solutions."

There was an utter silence in the room. For a long moment, it seemed no one even breathed. Shudra winced slightly. Filio peered down at his meal. Out of the corner of his eye, he saw the tendons stand from the back of Savine's hand as she gripped her fork as tightly as a standard-bearer might his flagstaff.

Leo's mother nervously cleared her throat. "Of course...we would not want to do anything that might inflame passions—"

"But sometimes we must," said Leo, cutting her off dead. "A king's just a man, in the end. Meat and bone and blood, like other men, and vulnerable to the same things. The same sharp edges. The same long drops. It's really not so big a problem as you think."

Mozolia gave a satisfied grunt and turned back to her meal. Leo's mother was less impressed. "Leo, really—"

"No, Lady Finree, we must be hard-headed." With all her customary precision, Savine set down her cutlery and gently put her cool hand on Leo's. "I and my husband speak with one voice on this, as on so much. It is *most* regrettable, but, after all we have been through, after all the nation has been through..." Finally, she met Leo's eye. That flinty look she used to have, when trying to convince him to be more ruthless. "I would far rather have another regret than another rebellion."

It was more of a relief than Leo had expected to find the old Savine beside him again. He turned his hand over and gripped hers tight. He needed her guile. He needed her popularity with the masses. The dead knew, he couldn't do bloody everything himself.

"What a woman," he said, treating the delegates from Westport to a beaming smile. "I swear I'm the luckiest man in the world." And he shoved his plate away. "Now could someone bring me something I can fucking eat?"

# Redemption

His Highness Crown Prince Orso would, no doubt, have considered these conditions intolerable. His August Majesty *King* Orso had, however, become something of an authority on cells, a dungeon devotee, and honestly considered this far from the worst he had occupied. It had a bed, a table, a chair. The window was more of a barred slot, but at least it let him feel the sun on his face in the mornings. The food was passable, the temperature comfortable, the odour not oppressive. The guards, clad in the dark uniform of Angland, did not speak to him with scorn. They did not speak to him at all. In most respects, it was very much preferable to the damp cellar in which Judge had kept him. When it came to ways out, however, it was much the same.

There weren't any.

Orso issued a heavy sigh. Sighing was one of his few remaining hobbies and, with all the recent practice, he flattered himself to think he had become quite accomplished. He wasn't in his mother's league, of course, but perhaps one day, if he really stuck at it. If he was given the time. But that was the question. How much time was he likely to get?

Leo dan Brock had stuck his son on the throne. Orso's half-nephew, in fact, by his reading of the tortuous royal family tree. King Harod the Second, not even one year old, which, in practice, left the nation in the hands of his parents. It trampled over all the Union's laws of succession, of course. But laws did not appear at all the rigid pillars they once had. If the Great Change had proved anything, it was that—with enough force, with enough fear—one could bend them into whatever knots one pleased.

Brock had the men and the weapons. He had anyone loyal to Orso locked up along with him. He had the lords firmly on his side, and had no doubt gathered a pliant rump of Representatives around them. Anyone likely to oppose him was weeded out as a traitor, the rest falling over themselves to disinherit Orso and bow down before their new infant king, son of a bastard or no.

Orso served up another sigh. In truth, he could hardly blame them. He was the son of a bastard himself, after all. And people were desperate, exhausted, sick of chaos, sick of fear. He would have happily voted for anything that brought the Great Change to an end himself. It was just a shame for him that this ending almost certainly meant his death.

Leo dan Brock had stuck his son on the throne and that, quite obviously, left nowhere for Orso to sit. The Breakers and Burners had reckoned one king too many, but even he had to admit that two was. As long as he was alive he would be a guilty secret. Not to mention an open enticement to rebellion. He came weighed down with compromises, enmities, disappointments. Baby Harod carried no baggage. He was all rosy cheeks, fresh starts and limitless potential.

Orso shuffled a couple of dead flies across his windowsill with the side of his hand. It would be done discreetly, he imagined. A midnight garotte? A quiet three-man knifing? Poison, perhaps, in his water? When Brock had tightened his grip sufficiently. When he had done the deals, arranged the bribes, won over everyone he could and silenced the rest, and brought some semblance of longed-for peace back to Adua. With Savine to help him it would not take long. No one drove a harder bargain than she, after all.

He heard bolts rattle and turned to face the opening door with as much dignity as he could muster.

And there she was, in the doorway.

She had given up on wigs. Her dark hair was clipped short, the way it had been at the trial, showing the scar on her forehead, the fading marks of her fight with Judge. It made her look both oddly vulnerable and oddly powerful at once. White was her colour now, but today's dress was a very different affair from the one she had worn at her trial, pearls and silver thread glittering as she moved with even more than her usual poise.

She looked like a queen. As much as Orso's mother ever had.

It took him a moment to find his voice. "I am...almost as honoured as I am surprised." He brushed those dead flies onto the floor. "If I had known the Lady Regent was visiting I would have dusted. I fumble for the proper term of address..."

"Your Highness," she said, simply.

"*Most* becoming. I'm not sure how one refers to a deposed king. Am I deposed? Or retired? Or simply...unmentionable?"

"They have been discussing that question. In the Hall of Mirrors."

"I suppose the Lords' Round is a little burned to the ground. But where are my manners?" He pulled out the one chair, rubbed the flaking seat with his cuff. "Might I enquire as to the purpose of your visit? A last word, perhaps, with the condemned?"

"That..." She held his eye. "And to let you go."

It took a moment for Orso to work that one through. "That and to... what now?"

"We haven't much time. My husband means to have you killed."

"The surprise is not so much that he might... as that you might not."

"You came to help me in Valbeck, when I scarcely deserved it. Then you had mercy on me after Stoffenbeck, when I definitely did not. Then, to rub it in, you saved my life on the Tower of Chains. Without you, I would be dead three times over."

Orso waved it away. "I rather wish I had hanged your husband now, but in your case, I have no regrets. I would have felt awful about killing a lover *or* a sister, so killing both at once would have been impossible to live with."

"Selfish decisions, then."

"Ask any of my enemies. I'm the most selfish man in the Circle of the World."

"I suppose we can do good things for bad reasons."

"Or bad things for good ones," he answered.

"Or bad things for good ones." She stepped out of the way of the door and someone slipped around the frame. A ragged man with bright eyes and a moustache.

"Tunny?" breathed Orso. He was followed by a girl in a soldier's cap, a big man at her back, sliding heavy swords into his belt. "Hildi? Gorst, by the Fates!" Orso used to be thoroughly dismayed at the sight of his father's bodyguard. Now he seized his hand and pumped it like an old friend's, much missed.

Vick dan Teufel peered in from the corridor outside, her nose more bent than it used to be and a few multicoloured bruises still lingering around her eyes. "You have to go," she said. "Now."

"A daring escape?" Orso raised his hands at the barren cell and let them fall. "I am packed."

"There's a way ready through the sewers." Teufel tossed a ring of keys to Tunny and he plucked them rattling out of the air. "But the city's crawling with the Lord Regent's men. Won't be easy getting out."

"I wish I had more to offer you than my thanks," said Orso.

"You can thank me by not getting caught."

417

He held Vick's eye for a moment. "Who would have thought a professional turncoat would prove to be one of the last loyal people in the Union?"

Teufel winced. "Maybe we could keep that particular defect in my character between ourselves."

"Your secret is safe." Orso faced Savine, in the doorway. "I hardly know what to say."

"You don't need to say anything. Ask any of my creditors. I pay my debts."

He wanted to take her in his arms. Fates help him, he wanted to kiss her, and not stop there. He knew she was his sister. Half-sister, anyway. He had never doubted it was true. But it did not *feel* true. He was as much in love with her as he had ever been. More, if anything.

But love is not always a solution. In this case, it was very much a problem.

"Goodbye," he said. What else was there to say?

It was Jurand who appeared in the doorway first, staring into the cell with its bed, chair, table and instantly obvious lack of an imprisoned king.

He gave Savine a pained look. "What did you do?"

"What did you do, *Your Highness*," corrected Savine, slipping the little box from her sleeve and taking a pinch of pearl dust up each nostril, feeling that invigorating burn, then that reassuring numbness spreading through her face to the back of her throat.

One generally heard Leo coming before one saw him. The click of his cane, the scrape of his metal foot, the slight squeak of the mechanism at the ankle. He really needed to get Curnsbick to apply a little oil. Jurand faded back to make room, started speaking softly to one of the other Anglanders.

"You let him go." Leo stared into the cell in disbelief. "You let him *go?*"

"He let us go." Savine calmly smoothed the front of her dress. "He let you go."

"He let *you* go!" snarled Leo as he took one lurching step towards her. "He left me to rot with half my limbs in a stinking wagon!" He had lifted his cane as if he might strike her with the handle. She resisted the urge to flinch, instead turned her cheek towards him as if inviting him to do it. The way he used to do to her. It felt like a long time ago.

"He'll be a thorn in our side for ever!" Leo got a grip, lowering his stick. "Where *is* he?"

"Judge couldn't get a thing out of me," said Savine. "Do you really think you will?"

"Don't be so bloody dramatic! You're my *wife*. You're the mother of my *children*. Of the *real* king, in fact! We're on the same side."

"Really? I'm not so sure!"

She had raised her fist to shake it in his face and Leo noticed the rolled-up paper she was gripping. "What's this?"

"Nothing."

"Show me," he said, tossing his cane aside and making a clumsy grab for it.

She hid it behind her back. "No."

"Give it to me, damn it!" He caught her under the arm, making her gasp. He might only have one hand, but its grip was as strong as ever. She tried to twist free, dragging him off balance. He only stayed standing by clinging on to her, his dead weight almost pulling her over. He growled with effort as he took another lurching step, iron ankle squeaking, pressing her against the wall, elbow of his useless arm jabbing into her corset as he made another grab at her hand.

What would people have thought, if they could have seen their new Lord and Lady Regent, the pilots of the nation, staggering about a prison cell, wrestling over a scrap of paper?

She felt a powerful urge to kick his iron leg away, bring him down, pin his good arm and start punching. But that would have solved nothing. She let him twist the document from her fist and leave her standing, flushed and breathing hard. She let him think he had won. That was what he wanted, after all. More than ever.

He pulled the paper open, eyes flickering over the writing. "What the hell's this?"

"A letter of charter," said Jurand, plucking it from his fingers and handing him his cane, every bit the faithful valet. The two of them were always together these days. Hard to believe that Savine had needed to beg Leo to bring him back. "The *Duke Rogont*. A Styrian vessel."

"You'd hand him to the *Styrians*?" Leo looked at her in shocked disappointment. "You'd make a weapon of him, for our enemies to use against us?"

Savine drew herself up again. "I am starting to think your enemies and mine are not at all the same."

"We'll discuss this later," snapped Leo, turning his back on her. "Get men to the docks!" And he limped out, tap, scrape, squeak.

Jurand gave Savine that pained look again. "What have you done, Your Highness?" And he followed Leo.

"That's it!" Glaward reined his horse in hard and swung from the saddle with an ease that made Leo deeply jealous. "The *Duke Rogont!*"

It was an ugly tub, low in the water, a few scraps of gilt still clinging to the unlikely bosom of its figurehead but her face reduced to a pitted mass by years of sea wind. She was about to get underway, men crawling in the rigging, a shabby-looking sailor dragging at the knots of a mooring line.

"This ship is forbidden to leave the harbour!" roared Leo, gritting his teeth as he slithered from his saddle.

The sailor squeaked out a lot of scared-sounding Styrian as Glaward wrestled him down onto his face. More well-armed Anglanders were clattering up, dismounting, pulling out weapons.

Leo limped down the long wharf, iron foot clonking on the boards, waving them past with his cane, Jurand loading his flatbow as he followed. "Get on board! Find Orso! Bring him to me!"

They clattered towards the *Duke Rogont's* gangplank, half-hidden among a mass of boxes and barrels. The leading man looked sideways, took a whooping breath, then flew from the wharf and tumbled flailing into the sea. Leo winced as he skittered to an ungainly halt.

Someone had burst from among the crates and rammed the man with his shoulder. Now he turned towards Leo, blocking the narrow jetty with his body. A very big body, with a noticeable lack of neck.

Bremer dan Gorst.

The king's bodyguard pulled a final buckle tight on his unmarked breastplate and stood, swords at his sides, a bright buckler on his left arm. "I am afraid I cannot allow it," he said in that ridiculous squeak.

Leo's men crowded forward. At least a dozen of them, but there was no way around. Just that narrow path of crooked wood, and the sea on either side. Was there anyone in the Circle of the World you'd want to face less on a wharf than Bremer dan Gorst?

"What do we do?" muttered Glaward, licking his lips.

Leo gave a frustrated growl. "I've nothing but respect for you as a swordsman! But we're boarding that ship. In the name of King Harod, step aside!"

He'd never seen Gorst smile before. He'd seemed a man incapable of expressions. But he smiled now as he raised his steels, metal flashing in the sun. Like a man who feels a wonderful relief. "In the name of King Orso," he piped, his boots grinding into the weathered wood as he lowered himself into a ready crouch, "no."

"So be it," snarled Leo. "Kill—"

Gorst moved before he even said the *him*. One Anglander toppled into the sea with his brains flying from his neatly split skull. Another sank to his knees, dropping his sword, trying to hold his guts in as Gorst ripped the short steel back out of his stomach. The man began to scream. Desperate, whooping screams.

"*Damn* it," muttered Leo.

Gorst was already back in his fighting crouch, eyes shifting calmly between the Anglanders.

One jumped forward, swinging, but Gorst slipped aside and let his sword thud into the wharf. Something gleamed on the back of the man's dark uniform for an instant. The point of Gorst's long steel as it ran him through. A moment later he folded up, keeled forwards like a tent that's suddenly had its guy-ropes cut. Gorst sprang at another Anglander with blinding speed. The man managed to parry the short steel but an instant later the long chopped into his neck, beneath the rim of his helmet, and sent him crashing into a pile of boxes, head flopping.

Glaward swallowed. "Bloody hell."

"Ready your bows!" Leo snarled over his shoulder. "If you see an opening, shoot. You with the spears!" he shouted down the wharf. "Put him in the sea or in the ground!"

Two spearmen rushed forwards, points levelled. Gorst caught one on his buckler and it scraped past. He smashed the face of the man who held it with the pommel of his short steel and knocked him wailing into the water. He growled as the other spear grated against his breastplate, opening a cut up the side of his head, but his heavy long steel was already swinging in a great overhead arc that caught the spearman in the shoulder and split him open down to the chest with a meaty thud.

Blood sprayed over Gorst, speckled his face, flooded across the wharf. Men stepped back in shock, opening a path. Flatbows clicked and rattled. One man cried out as he was nailed in the back by a stray bolt. Another sank into Gorst's meaty shoulder. A third bounced from his breastplate. A fourth caught him in the right arm, dangling from his sleeve. He whipped out of the way, behind some crates, as a fifth buried itself in the wood.

The man who'd been carved almost in half flopped down, legs still kicking weakly at the timbers.

"You're shot, Gorst!" yelled Leo. "You can't stop all of us! And the damn boat's not leaving anyway. Give up now!"

"Tell your mother..." came that high warble. "That I always held her... in high esteem."

Leo ground his teeth. "As if she'd care a shit. Load your bows. You lot, get down there and finish him!"

No one seemed very keen. The wharf looked like a busy day at the slaughterhouse. They edged forwards through the mess of blood and broken bodies.

"Help me," the one with a handful of his own guts was whimpering. "Help me."

"Throw down your arms!" shouted one of the Anglanders.

It seemed Gorst preferred to go down fighting.

He burst from behind the crates in spite of the bolts stuck in him. He slashed one man's throat with his short steel in a spray of blood, left his long steel rammed through another's chest, kicked a third tumbling into the water, shouldered a fourth out of his way and, with a high bellow, came pounding down the wharf, head lowered, arms pumping, short steel held overhand like a dagger.

"By the dead," muttered Leo, dropping his cane and fumbling for his sword.

Planks rattled under Gorst's boots. A flatbow bolt pinged off his breastplate. Another sank into the same shoulder he was already stuck in. He barely noticed, coming on faster and faster, twisted face speckled red, eyes fixed on Leo under his furiously wrinkled brows, short steel going up high.

Leo took one lurching step back, raising his sword, no idea how he'd have met that charge even with all his limbs.

Next to his ear, Jurand's flatbow made a sharp whipping sound.

The bolt punched into Gorst's face, under one eye.

His head snapped up. He lost all momentum.

He took one more wobbly step forward, but with no venom. His eyes had gone soft, slightly crossed.

Another flatbow bolt nailed him through the thigh. As his foot came down, the knee buckled and he toppled sideways, crashed drunkenly into a barrel and came to rest with his bolt-stuck right arm over it, one leg out in front, the other bent underneath him, his bloody short steel wedged harmlessly between two boards of the wharf beside his limp left hand.

Leo let out a long breath and slowly lowered his sword. "Get aboard," he grunted at Glaward. "Find Orso."

There was a red stain across Gorst's eye above the flatbow bolt. But the other one rolled up towards Leo. It seemed, somehow, he still had that smile.

"Do you believe…" His voice sounded much like anyone else's, whispering. "In redemption?"

"I don't fucking care."

"You're young. Give it time."

Leo groped for a cutting reply, but banter had never really been his thing, and certainly it had never been Gorst's. Besides, the old swordsman wasn't moving. His eyes were glassy. Words would've been wasted breath. They usually were.

"Fucking *pointless*," hissed Leo, kicking Gorst's short steel skittering into the sea with a swing of his iron leg. There'd been a time when he'd admired that man more than anyone. When he'd wanted to be just like him. "Goes to show," he grunted, "you have to be your own hero." He limped on towards the gangplank, past the corpses and the sobbing man still trying to hold his guts in.

"Well?" he shouted as Glaward stuck his head over the ship's rail.

"The captain says he's got no passengers and his ship hasn't been chartered. Not by the Lady Regent. Not by anyone. A cargo of cloth and buttons bound for Westport, that's all."

"By the *dead*. Rip this fucking boat apart! Down to the last timber."

Jurand stood with his flatbow resting on his shoulder, hair stirred by the sea breeze about his thoughtful frown. "He was never here." And he offered Leo his cane.

"No." Leo shut his eyes and tried to bring his anger under control. If he'd thought for a moment, he'd have realised it was very unlike Savine to wave so obvious a clue right under his nose. It seemed he could still be reckless, offered the right bait.

"The charter was a fake. This was a distraction." It took Leo an embarrassingly long time to sheathe his sword with only one hand, fishing around with the point for the mouth of the scabbard and near stabbing himself in the hip. "Savine bloody tricked us!" He finally slapped it back and snatched his cane from Jurand's hand, frowning at Gorst's body. "I want every loyal man out on the streets. I want every ship, cart and person in or out of the city searched and—"

"I gave the orders as soon as we found Orso wasn't in his cell," said Jurand. "There's a company at every gate, Arnault's Wall and Casamir's. Others out combing the streets. A rat won't leave Adua without us knowing."

Leo closed his eyes and gave a sigh of relief. He would've hugged Jurand if he'd had the limbs to do it. What madness had made him send away his best friend? "What the bloody hell would I do without you?" he asked.

*

The hooves of the blinkered old boathorse clopped sleepily on the towpath. The water slapped gently against the sides of the barge. A breeze sighed peacefully down the canal, wafting away the worst of the vapours. From time to time, the bargemen would make some growling utterance to labourers, or washerwomen, or ragged children on the banks. Orso could not understand a word. His own subjects, in theory, and it seemed they spoke a different tongue.

Tunny had lit a pipe, shoved it among his unkempt grey whiskers and was calmly puffing away. Hildi had pulled her cap down low and set her mouth hard, glancing inconspicuously about and looking every bit a river rat born at the prow of a barge.

"Can't we go any faster?" murmured Orso. When he'd fantasised about escape it had been thundering from the city among fluttering flatbow bolts on the back of a black charger, hair ripped by the wind of his daring. Not hiding in a greasy coal-heap and floating to safety at a snail's pace. But there was the difference between fantasy and reality, he supposed. A gulf he should have been familiar with by now.

"Slow and steady, Your Majesty" said Tunny around his pipe, very softly.

"You rather assume I am still a king."

"It'll take more than a room full of arseholes dropping a crown on a baby to change my mind on that score."

"Or mine," added Hildi, clambering to the edge of the hold and swinging her legs down.

"What would I do without you?" Orso watched the stained sheds of warehouses and manufactories slide by. "I hope Gorst got away."

"He wasn't planning to," said Tunny.

"What?"

"All he wanted was to hold Brock and his bastards up long enough for you to get away."

"What are you saying?"

"That he hoped to trade his life for yours, and considering his skills with a sword, I expect he'll have succeeded."

Orso stared off at nothing. "I never did a thing to deserve loyalty like that."

"Sometimes loyalty's an excuse for something else," said Tunny, eyes fixed far off. "This is the way he always wanted it, I reckon."

"And it might be you're a better man than you think," said Hildi, hopping down with an oiled tarp in her hands and dragging it over Orso's head to make a foul-smelling hood. "Either way you need to stay out of sight. You can honour his sacrifice by making sure it doesn't go to waste."

"When the hell did you get so profound?" asked Orso.

"I've always been a fount of wisdom." And she hopped back up on the barge's roof, tucking a stray yellow curl out of sight inside her cap. "But you've been too self-absorbed to notice."

"Sounds like me," murmured Orso.

Tunny slipped out a battered flask and took a nip. "So where now?"

Orso had never expected to leave the Agriont again. Not alive, anyway. Now he started to see that escape might be far from the end of his problems. Indeed, it might scarcely be the beginning. He had to find somewhere he could hide, he supposed. Somewhere he could rebuild, gather his forces. Somewhere he could set about a plan to reclaim his throne. That was what deposed kings were supposed to do, wasn't it? Even if they never wanted the damn thing to begin with? Even if it meant they'd bring trouble wherever they went? Trouble for themselves, trouble for their subjects, trouble for anyone who helped them...

Orso retreated into his tarp, working his back against the coal. He could not help wondering about a world in which he simply...let it go. Folded his hand and let the Young Lion have it all. Found some unregarded corner in which to live in harmless obscurity. No more fighting. No more deaths on his account. No more crushing responsibilities.

He was starting to smile. "You know, I think—"

But Tunny was frowning up at Hildi. "What is it?"

She had stood tall to get a better view. "Boats up ahead," she muttered, a warning note in her voice.

"It is a canal."

"But they're not moving."

Orso felt that familiar sinking as he peeked over the prow. He could see Casamir's Wall ahead, through the furnace murk. Boats and barges, backed up in a queue, horses idle on the towpath. Were there men up near the black opening of the tunnel that led out of the city? Dark-uniformed men on both sides of the water and crawling over the frontmost boat?

The handler was already pulling up his horse, one of the boatmen jumping to the bank with a rope and looping it around a strapping post, leaning back hard to bring them to a creaking stop.

"What's to do?" called Tunny at an old coal-smudged fellow in the barge ahead.

"They're searching every boat out o' the city."

"For what?"

"Damned if I know." The man spat over the side into the water. "Bloody Anglanders, they're worse'n the bloody Burners were."

"And a lot more organised." Tunny hopped from the barge onto the towpath, holding out his hand to help Orso across. "Time to go."

"Really? You don't think I could pass for common river folk?"

Tunny and Hildi both stared at him. The boatmen seemed to be looking, too, and men on other barges, and their eyes did not look so friendly as they had. Orso wondered what reward someone might expect, for turning him in.

"No," he conceded, clambering from the boat. "I suppose not."

For once he was grateful for the vapours as they strode away from the canal, footfalls muffled in the murk.

Tunny was shaking his head. "Brock's tightening his grip on the city."

"There were two dozen Anglanders at every gate before you got away," said Hildi, glancing back over her shoulder and upping the pace. "There'll be more now."

Orso pulled that smelly tarp up to make a deeper hood. "I may have started planning my retirement a touch too soon."

# It Was Bad

Sun just up as Broad made his last preparations. Straightened the plates on the rack. Kind of plates Liddy had always admired. Shifted the flowers about in the vase. Only things he knew about flowers were that they show up in spring and May liked 'em. Then he took off his lenses, and wiped them, and put them back on, and stood there, frowning.

After the best part of a year without his family—and a black year, too, drowning in blood a little more every day—you'd think a man would be desperate to see the people he loved, would wait for that knock on the door with the biggest smile his cheeks could hold.

But Broad stood silent as the condemned waiting for the trudge to the scaffold, and smiled about as much, too. There'd been a time when he feared nothing. Now he was scared all the time. He hardly knew what of. Himself, maybe.

Damn, he wanted a drink. Just a nip. Just a mouthful. Something to take the hard edges off the world. To blur the memories of the things done. But he'd promised no trouble. For him, every bottle had trouble at the bottom.

When he looked to the door, dappled sunlight through the trees outside the window shifting across it with the breeze, he had this strange urge to walk out. This strange thought that he didn't belong here any more, in the safe and the warm. Not with what he'd seen. Not with what he'd done. What if no one who stepped in there with him could ever be free of it?

But the path leading out was a coward's path. He took a sharp breath and clenched his aching fists. If there was one good word said over his grave, it'd be that Gunnar Broad was no coward. It'd be a lie, but still.

Took all the courage he had to open that door, when he finally heard the knock. More than it had to man the barricades in Valbeck, or charge into the battle at Stoffenbeck, or fight Judge's Burners on top of the Tower of Chains. But he stepped up to it, straightening his collar, licking his lips, and finally turned the knob.

The door rattled open, and there she stood. She'd changed. Not near as much as he had, but she'd changed. Sturdier, maybe. Softer, maybe. But when she smiled, it still lit the gloomy world, the way it always had.

"Gunnar?" she said.

And he just started crying. A jolting sob first, that came all the way from his stomach. Then there was no stopping it. He fumbled his lenses off and all the tears he hadn't shed the last six months came burning down his crushed-up face.

Liddy stepped forwards and he shrank away, hunched and hurting, arms up as if to fend her off. Like she was made of paper and might crumple in his hands. She caught him even so. Thin arms but a hold he couldn't break, and though she was a head shorter than him, she held his face against her chest, and kissed his head, and whispered, "Shhhh, now. Shhhhh."

After a while, when his sobs started to calm, she put her hands on his cheeks and lifted his head so she was looking straight up at him, calm and serious. She wiped the tears from his face and traced the healing scratches with her thumbtip.

"It was bad, then, was it?" she asked him.

"Aye," he croaked out. "It was bad."

She smiled. That smile that lit up the world. Close enough that even without his lenses he could actually see it. "But I'm home now."

"Aye. You're home now." And he set to crying again.

The thump of May's ledger opening made Broad flinch. Made him think of Judge's hammer as she passed the sentence. He told himself she was dead. Told himself she'd be the last one ever thrown from the Tower of Chains. They were filling the moat again, the water risen higher and the stains in the bottom covered deeper every day. The Court of the People was burned down to charred rubble. He'd seen it. Wasn't sure he really believed it, though. Kept expecting to hear Judge bark at him to drag some fool out, beat some fool down, make some bloody example. Kept expecting to hear her say, *You're mine.*

He tried to hide it under a joke, peered over May's shoulder at the neat columns of numbers he was nowhere near understanding.

"I still say adding up debts is no way to make a living."

She looked up from her book and smiled, and he smiled that he could make her smile, and wondered that someone who'd done all the bad he'd done could've had a hand in making something as good as she was. When he left them in Angland she'd been sharp, gangly, all shoulders and elbows. Her hair had grown now, and her face fleshed out. She looked like a woman, old enough to have children of her own.

"Money's where the money is, Da. Well…that and *labour relations*." She said the words with this knowing twist to her grin that made Broad go cold.

His voice came out a croak. "How d'you mean?"

"Da. I'm not a child any more. Ma might have a blind spot when it comes to you, always wanting to believe the best, but I know where your talents lie." She put her hand over his, sitting limp now, on her shoulder, and patted the tattoo on the back of it. "I know how much Lady Savine's paid you. I can make a guess what you do for it."

He pulled his hand away, worked it up into his cuff as far as he could. Fine cloth, it was made of, but he could still see the stars on his scarred knuckles.

May licked her pencil and turned back to her book, all matter-of-fact, as if beatings, threats and blackmail were just a trade like any other. "And why shouldn't you be paid what you're worth? Everyone else takes what they can get. Someone has to put this family first."

"What are you two talking about?" asked Liddy, coming out of the bedroom.

"Just my parents' quaint notions," murmured May.

"Well, there's no shortage of work to be done. We're servants to the Lady Regent o' the Union, now." Liddy brushed down the front of the fine dress she was wearing, though it was spotless anyway. "Black Rikke's on her way to Adua, and Lady Savine wants us looking after her while she's here."

"Just the circles we move in now," said May.

"Remember when we were living in a cellar?" Liddy smiled around their airy rooms. "It came out all right, Gunnar."

It came out all right. Broad's mouth felt dry. Wanted a drink so bad. He'd been fixed on not saying anything, but now he felt he had to be honest, blurt it all out. Burn it down like the Lords' Round so they could somehow start fresh.

"You might hear…some things. About…what I did." He pulled his lenses off and pressed at the sore bridge of his nose. His hand was shaking. "I was in the Court of the People. And I wasn't on the right side of it." Their faces were blurs. He could hardly see them. "You might hear some things…about Judge. She—"

Liddy gripped his hand. "I don't want to know! Understand? You did what you had to, to get through it. That's all you did. It's in the past. Like Valbeck. Like Styria. We're together now. And all on the right side." A blind spot, like May said. Wanting to believe the best. He owed her that much.

Broad wiped his weak eyes on the back of his hand. "You're right." Hooked his lenses back on. "You're always right." He forced out a teary smile. "It was that letter the two of you wrote made all the difference. That's what saved me. That letter."

Liddy frowned puzzled at May, and May looked back at her, and shrugged. "We didn't write a letter. Wish we could've, but we'd no way to get one to you. And you know Ma, she's not much of a writer." She was already busy in her book again, scratching out the numbers.

A thumping knock at the door made Broad jump. He wanted to tell Liddy not to answer it. To leave them as they were, for a little longer. But she was already on the way.

"Your *High*ness," she said as the door opened and Savine swept in. Zuri was with her, watching Broad carefully with her black eyes, calm as ever, the familiar book under one arm, the familiar watch around her neck, though she had a gold one now, rather than silver. Everyone moving upwards, it seemed. Those who hadn't taken the long drop, anyway.

Savine took Liddy by the hands like an old friend. "Whenever I see your face I am reminded afresh how *very* glad I am that you are here, Liddy. Almost as glad as your husband is. There is no one left in Adua who knows what to do with a hem."

No doubt because most of 'em were paste under the slowly filling moat of the Agriont. Liddy blushed, curtsied clumsily. "We can't wait to serve Your Highness, of course. To be in the palace, it's, well…"

"Not what any of us were expecting. What are you about, May?"

"Some of the accounts for your mines in Angland, Lady Savine."

"I swear you'll own them yourself one day! Might I have a quick word with Gunnar?"

"'Course." May took her ledger and went out. Liddy gave Broad an excited glance in the doorway. Wondering what new reward they were about to get, maybe. Then she was gone, too, pulling the door shut.

"So." Savine raised one brow at him as she lowered herself, gracefully as ever, into one of his new leather-covered chairs. "It must be lovely to have the family back together—"

"The letter you gave me," he said. "Before the trial."

"Yes?"

"The one you said May wrote."

She looked almost impatient. "Yes?"

"She didn't."

Savine frowned over at Zuri, who had her big book open, as though to make notes. Zuri gave the smallest shrug. "Gunnar," said Savine, "if you think I would balk at copying someone's handwriting to save my own life, you really don't know me very well."

Broad had hoped she might say sorry. Had expected her to at least *look* guilty. But she shrugged it off like it was nothing. "Guess I thought you'd changed."

"I like to think so. But I am still me. You needed a nudge in the right direction. I gave you one. Now you are a hero." Her eyes were very hard. "You could just as easily have ended up the villain."

He didn't know what to say to that. Wasn't as if he could deny it.

"How is your shoulder?" she asked.

He winced as he worked his arm in a circle. "Mending, I reckon."

"Good. My husband refuses to move any soldiers out of Adua, whether they throttle the life from the city or not. Especially since the...king's escape." She took a long breath through her nose, and let it sigh away. "But we cannot simply ignore the rest of the country. It grieves me to say that there are still Breakers out there. They are determined to get in the way of the reconstruction. Determined...to cause *trouble*."

Broad blinked at her. "I'm done with trouble," he whispered. "I promised Liddy. I promised May—"

"Must you? Really? I need you to gather some useful men and go to Valbeck."

"To Valbeck?"

"Yes."

"To the Breakers."

"Yes." Savine's eyes grew harder yet. "Break them."

Broad swallowed. "But...Liddy and May, they just got here." A pathetic whine of an excuse. Like saying he couldn't murder anyone today 'cause he had to trim his fingernails.

Zuri checked her watch. "It does not have to be *now*." And she gave Savine the hint of a nod.

Savine stood. "Tomorrow will be fine."

"Tomorrow," croaked Broad.

"Tomorrow early. I am still me, Gunnar. And you are still you. Go to Valbeck and do what you do. If it helps, you can say I made you go. You can pretend you would be happier here." She leaned close to murmur. "But we both know you wouldn't be."

Zuri made a note in her book, then raised her brows, slipped her pencil behind her ear and followed the Lady Regent from the room.

Broad stood a moment longer, skin prickling with horror. Or was it excitement? Judge had the truth of it all along, maybe. Some men can't help themselves.

"What did Her Highness want?" asked Liddy, slipping in.

"To send me to Valbeck," muttered Broad. "She says there's trouble there."

Liddy didn't say anything. Neither did he.

What was there to say?

# So Many Changes

Rikke had to admit to feeling a bit unsteady as she shuffled from the ship to the quay. The Circle Sea had thrown a tantrum on the way and she'd spent the first day or two heaving over the side. Now solid ground was making her queasy. But she kept the smile on her face. That's what being chief's all about, her father would've said. Smiling while you want to puke.

"Jurand!" She ignored his hand and gave him a hug instead. "Still…" She waved a hand at him, trying to find the right words. "Juranding, then?"

He respectfully bowed his head. "I wouldn't know how to do anything else."

"But with more of…" And she flicked at the swags of gold braid festooning his uniform. "All *this*."

"It has pleased the Lord and Lady Regent to appoint me interim Lord Chamberlain."

Isern was giving him an approving look-over. "You can be lord o' my interim whenever you please," she said.

Rikke frowned at her. "I thought I said *good* behaviour? Should it be Lord Jurand, then?"

"Not to an old friend. I'm hardly the only one advanced in the world, after all." Jurand looked towards the strange and varied peoples of the North clambering from the ship to stand gawping at the vast scale, crawling activity and choking smokiness of everything. Quite the entourage. Which was, of course, the idea. Merchants of Uffrith and Carleon, dressed in their best dyed cloth and keen to talk business. Named Men in feast-day cloaks. Chieftains of the High Valleys and the West Valleys and all the valleys in between. Hillmen and hillwomen, too, faces blue with tattoos. "Should it be Queen Rikke?"

"By the dead, no! Black Rikke will do." She glanced at the soldiers on the quay, stiff and polished in big, dark uniforms on big, dark horses under big, dark banners. Must've been a hundred of 'em at the least. "Quite the welcome you've laid on."

"The Lord Regent insisted we take no chances with your safety," said Jurand, leading them across to a set of spare horses.

"Touched," said Rikke. "I never feel so safe as when I'm surrounded by heavily armed strangers." Took her a moment to mount up, as she wasn't much happier on a horse than a ship. "Must confess I was a smidge worried Leo and Savine might not be all that pleased to see me." Rikke nudged her mount close to Jurand and murmured out of the corner of her mouth. "I did betray 'em, after all. Just a bit."

"Lady Savine has always had a cool head."

"She could freeze milk with a whisper, that one."

"And you'll find Leo's not so easily carried away as he used to be."

"So all's forgiven?"

Jurand's smile didn't totally convince. "They both want to look to the future."

It wasn't lost on Rikke that he'd come nowhere near answering the question.

The chimneys still puffed away, leaving a great grey stain across the sky. The streets still thronged with folk of every shape and size, cut and colour. That tower they called the House of the Maker still stuck up into the fog like a giant's finger. The stones still throbbed with that endless unquiet, the snore of some slumbering demon, the rumble of unhappy men and machines.

But not everything was the same. They'd always liked a flag in the Union but since her last visit they'd gone mad with them. Buildings with great banners down the front. Suns painted twenty strides high on the sides of warehouses. Crossed hammers of Angland, too, with Leo's golden lion. There were armed men at every gate and corner. King's Own in red, but always shadowed by dark-clothed Anglanders. Rikke saw barricades down side streets, folk queueing up to be searched, soldiers rooting through wagons, flatbowmen frowning down from roofs.

"Reckon there's more soldiers of Angland here than there were in the army of Angland," murmured Rikke.

Shivers rubbed thoughtfully at his grey stubble. "Feels more like a city fallen to a siege than one delivered."

"Don't trust a one o' these bastards," whispered Isern-i-Phail, in Northern, frowning over her shoulder at their escort.

"Aye, but you hate everyone," said Rikke.

Isern looked shocked to her roots. "Lies! I am all yielding fellowship and good humour! I like Shivers."

"Everyone likes me," droned the most feared man in the North, swaying in his saddle.

"And I'm fond of old Hardbread. And the Nail is a man I could be persuaded to hammer, d'you take my meaning?"

"Despite the many layers of cunning I believe I've dug it out," said Rikke.

"I'm taking to that girl Sholla. She surely can slice cheese fine."

"Like cobwebs."

"Just melts on your tongue. I've been thinking about all the other things she might be able to slice and coming on all aquiver at the prospect."

"High praise."

"Hmmm." Isern stuck out her lips, clearly sorting through the rest of her acquaintance and finding no treasure. "Hardly an army of friends, now I reckon 'em up."

Rikke cleared her throat, pointing a hopeful thumb towards herself.

"Meh." Isern scrunched up her face like she'd taken a sup of old ale and had a fear it was off. "On you I remain to be convinced."

"You said that two bloody years ago!"

"And you're shifting me in the right direction. Love easily given isn't worth a thing, d'you see. Another few years and I might like you as much as my brothers." She twisted in her saddle to look at Scofen and Scenn, gazing about at the great soot-streaked buildings in amazement.

"So . . . you'll ignore me most o' the time, and the rest treat me with open scorn?"

"That's it!" And Isern clapped Rikke on the shoulder hard enough she had to clutch at her saddle to stay in it.

They passed blackened scars through the city. Whole streets in ruins. Burned-out shells being torn down but some carcasses still standing, too, doors and windows gaping like corpse mouths, breeze whipping stinging ash from inside. There were more beggars on the streets even than there used to be. More homeless and helpless, slinking away as their great company clattered past.

"By the dead," breathed Rikke, staring at a great set of marble steps with nothing on top but the stumps of huge pillars, workmen battering away at those with picks and chisels, a great crane towering high over the monstrous building site. "Is this where that bank was?"

"Valint and Balk," said Jurand, with a disapproving frown.

That mighty temple to profits, where the First of the Magi had met his smirking sidekick. Seemed even that could be laid low.

"What're they putting in its place?" asked Rikke.

"I understand there is an urgent need for loans and investment. For new business and construction. The Lady Regent has plans... to build the world's largest bank."

They finally reined in outside a huge house among other huge houses, in a part of the city where the air was cleaner and the sun shone brighter. Rikke had to admit she was a little relieved. Wouldn't have surprised her if they'd been led in state all the way to the House of Questions and straight into a cell.

"Savine's house," she said, looking up at all those windows. "Looks like every leaf in the garden got polished by hand."

"I wouldn't be surprised," said Jurand. "She used to live here. Then it was an orphanage for a while, but it became too full, and the children have been moved to new lodgings. Now it's yours."

"What?"

"As long as you're in the city." He swung down easily from the saddle. "Black Rikke must have rooms fit for her station."

The hall alone was big as a chieftan's audience chamber and a lot finer furnished. Two well-turned-out women were waiting there, one older, one younger, with a dark-skinned fellow wide as a door. They looked a bit shocked at Rikke's face, for which she hardly blamed them; she still jumped herself whenever she passed a mirror. They looked more shocked as Shivers loomed up behind her, then very shocked indeed as the fur- and mail-clad Named Men and the tattooed hillfolk and some great tall woman who ran Yaws these days crowded into the hallway tramping muck across the spotless tiles.

The older woman gave a doubtful curtsy. "Your, er—"

"Just Black Rikke will do," said Rikke.

"I'm Liddy, this is May and this is Haroon."

"An honour," said the dark-skinned man in the deepest voice you ever heard, bowing low.

"Likewise," said Rikke, bowing back. Since half of her people couldn't even speak the language, that set everyone off bowing to everyone else. Quite the sea of bobbing heads.

"The Lady Regent sent us in case there was anything you wanted," said Liddy. "There's a function planned at the Agriont tomorrow evening—"

"Function?" Isern bit at the unfamiliar word. "Isn't that, like, having a shit?"

Shivers rolled the eye he still had. "It's folk drinking and dancing and lying to each other. They pretend it's for fun but really it's for whoever's got the power to show how much power they've got."

Isern slowly narrowed her eyes. "So it *is* having a shit, just on everyone else."

"Mostly on me," said Rikke. "And I'll be thanking them for the turds, frothing with praise over their fine colour and consistency, and asking if I couldn't get a couple more." Rikke raised her brows at Liddy, who was looking more shocked than ever, and switched back to their tongue. "You a seamstress?"

"I've...sewn a few seams..."

"You help make Lady Savine look all..." And Rikke waved her hands around, searching for the word. "Savine-y?"

"I help dress her...sometimes."

"Lovely! Last time I went to the Agriont I looked a fucking dunce." Rikke shrugged the red cloak from her shoulders and ran that fine cloth hissing through her fingers. "Reckon we've got some work ahead of us."

# Good Times

Since the weather was finally warming after the bitter freeze and the bloody thaw, Savine had been keen to throw open the doors of the palace and hold a reception in the budding gardens. Spring, and a new beginning, and a sorely needed opportunity to heal wounds: wounds of the Great Change still far from scarred over, and wounds inflicted since still bleeding.

But the evening was not so balmy as she had hoped, and the gooseflesh on her bare arms made her think of the brutal winter just past. The braying laughter of someone drunk too soon brought back the rioters' clamour in the Square of Marshals. The glint of torches on the armour of the many guards reminded her of the flames towering into the sky above the Court of the People. She wanted to run for her chambers, lock every door and hold her children close, but she had hidden too long. So she squared her shoulders, snapped her fingers at Zuri to pass the box and took another pinch of pearl dust instead.

Savine was far from the only one on edge. Her guests were those lucky, clever or treacherous enough to have lived through the fury of the mobs, the chaos of Risinau, the massacres of Judge. Now, after the briefest period of heady relief, they were starting to wonder if they might end up purged by their new Lord Regent.

Leo was in no mood to heal wounds. He stood grim and aloof, as usual, surrounded by armed Anglanders, as usual, refusing to sit down, as usual. He had taken Adua in a vice-like grip the day Judge fell, but since Orso's escape, and with Jurand to help, he had instigated a crackdown far harsher than any the Burners had dreamed of.

The endless restrictions and searches, curfews and tests of loyalty were bad for morale and terrible for business. The only people prospering were armourers, flag-makers and the painters daubing Union emblems on the homes of Citizens terrified of showing inadequate patriotism. Leo insisted he was infusing Adua with common purpose, oblivious to the fact that nothing proclaims disunity like shrill proclamations of unity on every corner.

"My lords and ladies!" The panicky chatter subsided, every eye turning towards the gateway in the palace wall, flanked by two giant sun banners. The announcer puffed himself up with a mighty breath. "Might I *present*..." He glanced nervously towards Leo then, as if embarrassed by the lack of a suitably magnificent string of titles, deflated. "Black Rikke."

Savine knew how to make an entrance. She had engineered some classics in her time. Starting new trends at the Solar Society. Radiantly happy at her wedding. Proudly defiant at her trial. But she was not sure that she ever made an entrance like Rikke did that day.

"Someone has been to the tailor," murmured Zuri.

The new mistress of the North was a heady concoction of high fashion, black magic and barbaric splendour with a weird twist all her own. Her dress was of fine red Suljuk silk, long and lean like a streak of blood with a cloud of white fur about the shoulders. Her hair was bound up into a ridiculously tall, impossibly shiny black gentleman's hat, cocked right over in the manner of a backstreet pimp. She showed every one of those fine teeth in a knowing smile, the emeralds that Savine once gave her shining at her throat but her eyes shining brighter, one all white, the other all gaping pupil in the centre of those tattooed witch's rings. She raised her sinewy arms and spread them wide, Sipanese lace gloves on her hands but chains, runes and bone bangles dangling from her wrists.

"Greetings from the North!" she screeched, and a strange entourage spilled through the gate and into the heart of the Union. At Rikke's right shoulder came Isern-i-Phail, dressed like a duchess but walking like a docker, necklace of fingerbones around her neck and the toes of her heavy boots peeping under the lace hem of her skirt. Caul Shivers was on her left, oddly at ease in a braid-heavy general's uniform paired with a savage-looking broadsword, metal eye glinting behind his hanging grey hair. There were hillwomen whose faces were stained with swirling tattoos. There were warriors whose faces were criss-crossed with scars. There were craftsmen of Carleon and ships' captains of Uffrith, and all with odd specks and spatters of Union fashion: a crystal-knobbed cane, a machine-patterned shawl, a jewelled pocket watch. One hillman peered suavely through a monocle as though he'd been born wearing one.

"Savine!" And Rikke slipped between her outstretched hands and folded her in a hug. Savine could hardly remember the last time anyone held her that way, and she found herself squeezing Rikke back, as if they truly were old friends, with no jealousies or rivalries or backstabbings behind them.

She found herself both reluctant to let go and relieved when Rikke did, holding her out at arm's length with that unsettling grin. Magic was not a thing one could sensibly invest in, of course. But looking into the black depths of the Long Eye she could not help wondering what Rikke might have seen with it. What she might know that Savine could not guess.

"Rikke. You are . . . a vision."

"Ha! *Vision.* Saying you look good would be like calling snow cold, but I swear you look better'n ever. Motherhood must agree with you. Mother of the Nation, no less!"

"None of us came through the Great Change quite the same." Savine glanced over at Leo, his hard face a pale spot among all those splendid uniforms.

"All both more and less than we were." And Rikke swept a glass of wine from a passing tray, swallowed half at one gulp. "You remember my last visit here?"

"Chiselled into my memory." Savine wondered how many people who had laughed, and drunk, and danced in the Hall of Mirrors that night were dead now. Half? More? A chilly gust swept across the gardens and it was the most she could do not to shiver.

"Not my proudest moment," Rikke was saying. "Played a pigeon at a peacock contest, got caught by the queen in her son's bed, then shat myself at a parade. What's become of Orso?"

Savine tried not to sound strangled but did not entirely succeed. "No one knows."

"Careless, for a country to lose its king. But I hear you found another, so no harm done, eh?"

Apart from that to the stability of the Union, the prospects of Savine's children, her own position and the state of her marriage, all of which she had thrown into jeopardy by setting Orso free against all good judgement. "None that cannot be mended, I hope."

"You were kind to me, that evening. You give the best gifts." Rikke hooked the emeralds around her neck and held them up to the light, then peered down at the runes Savine was wearing. The ones Rikke had given her in return. "And you even kept mine to you."

"Nothing else would have suited the occasion."

"Well, I won't be swapping back, if that's what you're hoping." And Rikke flicked open a fan with a *snap*, started wafting herself as gracefully as any regular at the theatre. "Am I doing it right?" And she peered down her nose, setting a few strands of hair no doubt left loose for the purpose fluttering about her tattooed face.

"I may have to come to you for lessons."

"Ha again! You were kind to me that night and you're being kind now. You're a lot kinder than folk make out."

"I doubt everyone would say so." Savine lowered her voice. "I did betray you to Stour Nightfall, after all."

"I did betray you to King Orso. No doubt we both had our reasons. Doesn't mean we're not friends." And she grinned sideways. A grin with a hint of danger. "I mean, what's the use of stabbing your *enemies* in the back?"

"Those bastards you can stab in the front," murmured Savine, taking a quick pinch of pearl dust. There was a time she would have hidden it, but who would dare disapprove now? She offered the box to Rikke.

"My governess in Ostenhorm once said that, when abroad, one should observe the local customs." Rikke drained her glass, then whipped off one of her gloves to take a hefty pinch, nudged the gold ring through her nose to the side and noisily snorted it up. "By the *dead.*" She stuck her tongue out, blinking back tears. "That burns."

"It grows on you, believe me."

Rikke held on to Savine's arm as she stifled a sneeze, then pulled a little brown pellet from her glove and held it out. "We can swap gifts this time, too."

"Chagga?" Savine took it from Rikke's fingers and tucked it down behind her lip, then could not help a shudder. "That tastes..." She could hardly find the words to describe its earthy bitterness.

Rikke chomped on a pellet of her own and winked. "It grows on you, believe me."

All about the gardens people were swapping gifts and stories, forming strange partnerships and embracing the unknown. Curnsbick was talking in a mixture of broken Northern, shouted common and flamboyant gestures to a set of merchant women swamped in furs. Something about chimneys, Savine thought. Probably they understood the details as well as she ever had.

Selest dan Heugen, meanwhile, giggled as she worked her own brand of magic on the monocled hillman. "There's copper in these mountains of yours?" Her nose twitching as if she could smell the profits, while his gaze strayed so far it was a wonder his eye-lens didn't drop down the front of her dress.

"We have thousands counting on us now." Savine watched Lord Isher and some long-bearded chieftain shake hands with immense dignity. "We must look to the future."

"That's what I'm *all* about. But what could we savages have to offer civilisation?"

"Civilisation just finished a round of slaughter to make the Bloody-Nine blush. The North has some remarkable natural advantages—"

"You said the same about me, when I last came to Adua."

"And time has proved me more right even than I knew. When Leo and I travelled across the North last year—"

"To betray me to Stour."

"Exactly—before you betrayed us both—I saw vast forests ready to be given over to the saw. Great marshes ready to be drained and brought under the plough. Hills rich with coal and iron scarcely mined. River after river surging swiftly to the sea, begging to be channelled, dammed and harnessed by waterwheels."

"You saw opportunities."

"I may have no beautiful runes upon my face, but I can look into the future, too, in my own way."

"Savine o' the Long Eye." Rikke thoughtfully stuck her bottom lip out, glancing towards the wall of the Agriont, beyond which a set of chimneys were still puffing vapours even as the sun set. "So you could help me do to the North what you lot have done to Adua?"

"I could help you do to the North whatever you want."

"For a price."

Savine smiled her sweetest smile. The one she had always used to seal deals. "For our mutual benefit. I *do* give the best gifts." And she slid a gentle fingertip under the emeralds Rikke wore, weighed them a moment, then laid them gently back against her skin. "But not only out of kindness. I freely admit I greatly underestimated you."

"Oh, you didn't come out of it too badly. Stour Nightfall did the same and he's hosting no garden parties, I promise you." From a few strides off one would have taken it all for good-natured blather. But there was an edge on Rikke's every word. A conversation with her was a cake full of razors.

"You proved yourself a cunning and resourceful enemy," said Savine. "When I am lucky enough to find one of those, I do everything I can to turn them into a friend."

"That's nice to hear, from someone as cunning and resourceful as you. Nothing would warm my heart more than your friendship, but...it's not my heart that brought me here." Rikke tipped up her chin, looking down her nose at Savine, then reached behind her head and nudged her hat forwards so the brim cast her eyes into shadow. "My *head* holds a worry…when it comes to looking to the future…" That twinkling left eye slid over to Leo, frowning at the festivities with grim detachment. "I'm talking to the wrong half of the marriage."

When Savine offered a gift, she was used to it being accepted. She never offered one until she was sure it would be. But she kept smiling in spite of her annoyance. "I and my husband have always had an equal partnership," she said.

"Please." And Rikke nudged Savine with a sharp elbow. "When you came to visit me in Uffrith you had him saddled like a pony." She beamed around at the gathering, showing every one of those fine teeth again. "Now everyone admires you. Envies you. Loves you. The Darling of the Slums! When they talk o' you, your girls May and Liddy can't find praise high enough."

"You are all far too kind," said Savine.

"But it's not your soldiers on every street corner, is it?"

And Rikke snapped her fan out between them and glided away, taking the last word with her.

For now, at least.

Leo felt a bit of an outsider at his own party.

It should have been a palace function where he finally felt at home. It *was* his home now, after all. He'd earned it. He'd *won* it. And it was full of Northmen. The feel of the gardens was closer to the Dogman's old hall in Uffrith than the stuffy receptions of King Jezal's reign.

But the blunt Northern accents and the bluff Northern laughter only made him think of how he used to be. That fearless, generous, reckless young fool who could run all day and never tire, who could beat all his friends with their choice of weapons, who stood not far from this spot after he won a duel against Stour Nightfall, loved and admired by all. The Young Lion! A hero with the world at his two good feet! By the dead, he missed that man. He made the one hand that worked into a fist so tight the knuckles clicked. Felt the unpleasant tingling in the other as the fingers twitched in sympathy inside his jacket.

He watched Rikke strut away from Savine, both of them smiling like warmer words were never said. His old lover and his new. Or two old lovers, maybe. Wasn't much affection between him and the Lady Regent these days. Since she helped Orso escape, any warm feelings were strictly for the benefit of observers.

It reminded him of his parents' marriage, towards the end. A lie it suited everyone to pretend was true, even years later. Maybe everyone follows in their parents' footsteps, doomed to blunder into the same mistakes like a blind man into furniture. All our paths set before birth, inevitable, like Curnsbick's useless fucking cart, only running on the rails it's given. The only choice you have is how fast you'll roll to the end of the line. A depressing thought. Leo was having a lot of those, lately.

It wasn't as if he was left alone. The maggots kept coming, to smile, bow, flatter, always with that needy nervousness in their eyes, that oily fear in their voices, always trying to winkle something from him. It made him sick, their petty selfishness, their blinkered greed. He was covered from morning till night in a grease of lies there was no scrubbing off. But that's what you're left with once you've led your real friends to their deaths.

He watched Jurand and Glaward talking to Rikke. The few survivors of those carefree times, laughing together, without him, and he ground his false foot into the lawn until the stump of his leg ached. He'd been thinking about sending Glaward away. Some foreign posting. So Leo wouldn't have to look at his stupid face. So he'd have Jurand to himself. He'd won everything, and still he was endlessly angry, endlessly jealous. But then he'd lost everything, too.

He took a sour slurp of wine, watching Rikke plough through the throng. She didn't work the crowd with Savine's silky subtlety. She did it in a way all her own, with her big smile and her crazy eyes and that easy laughter and those wild gestures, wine sloshing from her glass as she threw up an arm.

He could've limped over. It would've felt good to meet her halfway, to find the honest smile he used to have around her. His face could still make that shape, couldn't it? But she'd betrayed him, so it would've been a kind of surrender. The Young Lion might've suffered defeats, but he'd never surrendered. Never. Whatever it cost him.

So he stood there, patience wearing down, while Rikke chatted to Lord Isher. While she compared necklaces with Selest dan Heugen. While she fanned the hair combed over Dietam dan Kort's head into fly-away wisps. It seemed as if she'd given every guest a compliment before she finally reached him, grinning as if there was no chasm full of broken promises yawning between them.

"If it isn't Black Rikke." The Northern words felt good in his mouth, he had to admit. "The beautiful and mysterious Witch of the North! You look well." She looked better than ever, in her own mad way. No doubt

Antaup would've been nudging and oohing and phwoaring at the sight of her even more eagerly than he used to. Had Leo not got him killed.

"If it isn't little Leo, the biggest man in the Union." Behind the regal bearing and the costume and the tattoos, did he catch a glimpse of that awkward girl he used to know? Used to love, even? The thought seemed to hurt, right in his chest. "We've come a long way, haven't we?" She leaned close, the smell of chagga on her warm breath bringing all those times they'd lain together rushing back. "Since fucking in a stable."

He felt himself blushing, the way his mother always made him blush when a conversation didn't go her way. "Everyone had fun that night," he said, stiff and unconvincing, "and everyone's having fun now," managing to sound bitter, too.

"Not you," said Rikke, watching him over the rim of her glass.

That flash of honesty might've shaken him from his gloom once. Now it pushed him deeper. "Fun is for people with all their limbs," he grunted.

The sun had fully set and the party was turning wild. The pent-up terror of the Great Change released, maybe. Isern-i-Phail had pulled her purple skirts right up to her crotch and was showing a scar on her muscular thigh to Zuri, who considered it with her black brows high. Shivers, general's jacket opened to his grizzled chest, was offering his drawn sword to Glaward, who looked like he might have cut his thumb on the edge as he studied the silver mark near the hilt. By the dead, a hillman had commandeered a violin and was sawing out a barely passable jig to gales of shrill laughter from a tipsy Isold dan Isher.

"I'm sorry," said Rikke softly. She wasn't smiling any more. "Sorry I didn't come to help. Sorry I broke my word. It hurts me, to see you hurt. Can't blame you if you don't believe it. Can't blame you if you don't care. But I'm sorry."

Leo felt the sting of tears in his eyes. He hadn't realised how badly he'd wanted to hear it. He wanted to say he was sorry, too. Take her hand. Kiss her cheek. Be her friend. The dead knew he needed one. The way they had been long ago, sitting up in the rafters of her father's hall.

But those children were long gone. Leo hadn't chosen to make himself fearsome, but that was what the times demanded. For the sake of the country, his family, his wife. Whether they thanked him or not. Softness now was weakness. Weakness now was death. He could see no way back.

A chill breeze whipped the feathers on the ladies' hats, made the torch flames flash and flicker.

"Sorry won't bring my leg back, will it?" he snapped. "It won't bring Jin back, or Antaup, or all the others who died that day."

She glanced at him sharply from under the brim of her hat. "Really? All Tricky Rikke's fault? I didn't make you turn rebel. I didn't talk you into fighting a battle. I didn't put the spur to your horse on the day."

"You sent a bloody letter to Orso, though!" He saw Jurand look over, tried to bring his voice down and failed. "I fought for you, I risked my *life* for you, and you betrayed me!"

He'd been hoping for more guilt. Instead he got an angry snort. "What was I supposed to do, laugh along while you sold Uffrith to Stour? See everything my father worked for—"

"What?" snapped Leo.

Rikke narrowed her eyes, the tattoos on her forehead twisting as she frowned. Somewhere in the distance there was a soft rumble of thunder. "Your wife stabbed me in the back the first chance she got. Bought the Great Wolf's help with my home." Here was a part of the story Savine had conveniently left out. Leo stared over at his wife, standing beside the Great Machinist in her usual dazzling white, and found her looking back. Studying them. Trying to gauge what they might be saying, and how to turn it to her advantage. "You didn't know that?" asked Rikke.

Leo shut his eyes. By the dead, had he learned nothing? Of course he hadn't persuaded Stour to follow him to the Union out of brotherly feeling. Of course Savine struck a deal. And of course she'd done it behind his back. Rain had started spitting down, white streaks frozen in the torchlight. Servants struggled with portable awnings as the wind picked up. A woman chased after a lost hat as it tumbled across the lawns.

"No." He bit off every word. "I did not know *that*." He glowered over at Savine again, but she wasn't even looking now. Laughing gracefully at some joke of Curnsbick's, as if Leo's pain didn't matter a shit to her either way.

So she was as much to blame as anyone for Stoffenbeck. For everything he'd lost there. More. Finding that Rikke had good reasons for turning on him should've been the perfect chance to forgive her. But news of one more wounding betrayal by his wife didn't sweeten Leo's mood. They'd both stabbed him in the back while they stabbed each other in the face, yet somehow they could glide away friends, ruling the gardens, loved by all, while he was left nursing unhealable wounds, hated and feared and alone.

"Why did you come here, Rikke?" he snarled. "Dressed up like the fucking fortune-teller at an overpriced carnival?"

Her jaw worked. "My father always said we should set our feuds aside, if we could. Told me one score settled only plants the seeds of two more.

446

I was hoping to put the past behind us and look to the future. Please, Leo. There's been enough blood shed between the North and the Union."

He gave a joyless snort. "Oh, I could stand more bleeding from the right bodies."

"Your wife seemed minded to forgive, and I always reckoned her the ruthless one."

"So did I. But apparently I've been wrong about a great many things." By the dead, what Leo really wanted was for her to put her arms around him and hold him the way she'd held Savine. But somehow, without meaning to, he'd made himself into a man no one wanted to touch. "It's good to see you again, Rikke. Really it is. I miss what we had. Really I do."

"You miss what you had," she said, softly. "You miss what you were."

"If you like." Another crackle of thunder, louder, nearer. The way the damp banners rustled put Leo in mind of Red Hill, of Stour Nightfall's standard and his own, two young gods facing each other across the bridge. But memories of past glories only made his fury cut deeper. "The truth is I'm a lot less forgiving than I was. The way I see it, you owe me."

"Owe you what? An arm and a leg?"

"Something!" he hissed in her face. Glaward glanced worriedly over. Caul Shivers, too. Leo ignored them. "You owe me *something*, and I'll collect. If I have to march to Carleon and rip it from your hands!"

She didn't back off. Not a step. There was a lot of her father in the stubborn set to her face, glittering specks of rain across the fur on her shoulders. "If you want war, the North'll fight you. Fight you as one, you can count on that."

Anger was safe. He knew where he stood with it. "Oh, Rikke." It might've been the first time he'd smiled that night. A hard smile, half a snarl, lips curled back from his teeth. "You know how much I love a *fight*."

And he turned on his heel and strode back into the palace. Or came as close to striding as he could, metal ankle squeaking with each lurching step.

It was bloody raining now anyway.


"I don't like it," grunted Tunny, nudging back the wet bushes to peer across the Middleway.

"Neither do I," said Hildi, wet shoulders hunched around her wet ears.

"Well, frankly, neither do I," said Orso. "I can't remember the last time I liked anything." He puffed a sigh into the rain. "But what choice do we have?"

Royal servants aren't generally supposed to disagree with kings, of

447

course, but that had never stopped these two before, and he had been faintly hoping they might leap forwards with some unexpected alternative. The only sound they made, though, was the faint chattering of Hildi's teeth.

Brock had the city sealed as tightly as Valint and Balk's famous vault. They were hungry, cold, exhausted and entirely out of friends. A likely reward of thousands of marks for your capture really was a heavy load to place on anyone's loyalty. It was getting to the point where Orso was considering turning himself in if it meant he could afford a decent meal.

They all shrank back at the sound of clattering hooves, a gilded carriage whirring through the wet night beyond the bushes in its own pool of light. Orso was sure he heard a drunken titter echoing from its open window.

"Guests leaving the royal function," he murmured, wistfully.

"Wonder which of the perennial arse-lickers is in there," grunted Hildi, with a sour sniff. "That lying slime Heugen. That treacherous bastard Isher."

"Tongues neatly extracted from my rear and slipped between the Young Lion's scarred buttocks without so much as a blush, no doubt. They used to huddle around me at those bloody events like geese at the trough."

"You miss it?" asked Tunny.

"I don't miss the sycophancy," mused Orso, putting a hand to his growling stomach. "I do miss the food."

"And the clothes," said Tunny.

"And the roofs," said Hildi, squinting up at the steadily pissing heavens.

"And the not being hounded by bitter enemies with unlimited resources who control every gate, wharf and corner." Orso cringed into the shadows again at the sound of tramping feet. Beyond the bushes, wet armour gleamed as yet another patrol came past. "Those were good times," he whispered.

There was a brief pause.

"Admit it," said Tunny, "you miss the sycophancy, too."

"Little bit, but, honestly? I was in a wretched state back then. I actually feel much more cheerful starving out here in the rain." Orso gave a disbelieving chuckle. He was a riddle even to himself. "Once I'm out of the city..." He did not mention the other, more likely possibility. The one involving a halving of the number of living High Kings of the Union. "You should have no trouble getting away yourselves. Tunny, send that standard to my mother and sister in Sipani. They can use it as a tablecloth or something."

"It'll stay on the pole," growled Tunny, "and be ready when you need it."

"Let me come with you." Hildi gripped him by the wrist. "You need... *someone* with you—"

"No. You'd just... get in the way." His voice failed him slightly on the last word, and he had to clear a lump from his throat. He suspected they both guessed the real reason he had to leave them. That their loyalty to him had cost them enough already and it was time for him to repay the favour and take his own risks. He prised her fingers gently free. "What's our tally at now?"

"Two hundred and sixteen marks..." Hildi was pretending her eyes were wet from the rain and fooling no one. "And thirty bits."

"Sounds a touch high."

"I'm never wrong about numbers."

"She's never wrong about numbers," said Tunny.

"No." Orso wrapped his hands gently around her fist. "I am so, so sorry, Hildi, but I think... for now... I'll have to owe you."

"If they hurt you I'll be revenged on the bastards!" she snarled at him, wet eyes suddenly blazing. "I *swear*!"

Orso smiled, then. It was an effort, considering everything, but he managed it. "I appreciate the thought more than you can know, but... *if* anything happens to me... I'd really rather you let it go." He laid a hand gently on Hildi's wet cheek. "Have a life instead. You deserve it."

Rikke stumbled getting down from the carriage and would've gone flat on her face but that nice man Haroon caught her and whisked her up straight again like she weighed nothing at all, which she had to admit she quite enjoyed.

"Thank you *very* much," she said, patting his arm. Quite an arm, far as she could tell. Then she teetered across the slick cobbles towards the steps. Bloody things wouldn't stay still, wobbling about all over the place. Or was that her? She was drunk as shit and making no apologies.

"No forgiveness from little Leo, then?" asked Isern, damp skirts gathered up to her knees so she could clamber to the front door.

"Don't think he's got any," said Rikke. The thought of their little exchange chased the pleasant glow of drink away for a moment. "The boy's turned dark. Dark and vengeful."

"I could've told you that when I saw all the bloody flags. Flags never add to a man, d'you see, just stand in for something he's missing. He always was a bully, and not too clever, but you can forgive a lot for a nice arse and a nice smile." Isern shook herself at the top of the steps like a dog who'd run through a river, raindrops flying from her wet hair. "Now his arse is in ruins and I didn't see him smile all night."

"Might be I was too sharp with him," fretted Rikke. "Come all this way to heal wounds and all I did was rub salt in 'em." Partly it was the pearl dust, which had made her feel quick-tongued, numb-faced and also rather frisky. "Might be I should've grovelled more."

"Shit on that." Isern turned the doorknob and they spilled into the hall together, leaving a crooked trail of wet footprints. "You're the North now, and the North kneels to no one. Besides, a man who's moved by grovelling will never get enough grovelling for his taste. Let him once set his foot on your back and you'll have a fucking bootprint 'twixt your shoulder blades till the day you're buried. What're you doing still up?"

Shivers was leaning against the wall, pipe in his hand, puffing a plume of chagga smoke a manufactory chimney might've been proud to produce. "You've a visitor," he said.

Rikke giggled. "Tell me it's a handsome man!"

Shivers scratched gently at his great scar. "I'm no expert on handsome, but I have heard him described so." And he nudged the door beside him creaking open.

Rikke stepped frowning towards it. "Well, this is a tantalising mystery and no—" She stopped just over the threshold, staring. "Bloody fuck."

He half-sat, half-lay, draped across the cushions on one of those things between a chair and a bed they had down here, a mostly empty glass of wine dangling from one hand. His hair was a damp tangle, his face smudged with dirt, his clothes stained and torn, but his grin was the same as when he'd brought her an egg in bed, and it looked better than ever.

"Bloody fuck, *Your Majesty*," said Orso.

"Everyone's calling 'emselves that these days," muttered Rikke. "I hear even babies are doing it."

"Much to my dismay."

"You look..." She took a step or two into the room. Felt like she couldn't help it. "A touch less prosperous than last time we met."

"I can only apologise for my wretched appearance. I have been slightly on the run the last few days."

"I'd have thought you'd be used to being pursued."

"Of course. Furious creditors, needy ambassadors, jilted lovers, husbands of jilted lovers, families of jilted lovers and so forth, but Leo dan Brock really does represent a new level of damnable persistence. He's like a dog with a bone. Lion with a bone, maybe."

"So you're the bone?" asked Rikke, raising her brows.

450

Orso smiled a little wider. "Poor choice of words, perhaps. You look…"

"Like the fucking fortune-teller at an overpriced carnival?"

His eyes moved over her dress, which was clinging somewhat from the rain, then up to her face. Her blind eye and her Long Eye. The black rings pricked into the skin around it. "I was going to say beautiful and mysterious."

"Oh." Rikke found she was tidying a damp strand of hair behind her ear and made herself stop. "Well. In that case, proceed."

"Don't like this at all," came Isern's voice, in Northern. She was right at Rikke's shoulder, her tattooed arm and her pale tightly folded across her purple ball-dress and her narrowed eyes fixed suspiciously on Orso. "This is dangerous."

"Never mind that!" said Rikke, herding her towards the door. She was keenly aware of how dangerous it was. Maybe that was the appeal. Maybe she was a moth drawn to the flame and would very soon go up in a fireball.

"You need to think about this, Rikke." Isern caught the door frame, leaning close to growl under her breath, "Just don't be thinking with your quim."

"Yes, yes, make of your quim a stone." Rikke managed to bundle her out into the hall, wrestled the door shut and leaned back against it with an over-wide grin.

Orso was looking approvingly around the room, which was almost as big as Skarling's Hall and a damn sight more expensively furnished, with glittering vases and polished wood and candles twinkling in gilded holders. "So…you won."

"I did," said Rikke, enjoying a little swagger about the tiles herself. Nothing had been easily won, after all. Might as well enjoy it.

"I lost," said Orso, but without much rancour.

"So I hear."

He stood, took the stopper from the decanter with a pleasant clinking of glass. "The Queen of the Northmen!"

"Just Black Rikke. If you've got the power you don't need the title."

"I was always the other way around. So many titles. No power at all." And Orso snapped out a little laugh and started pouring two glasses of wine. He looked even more carelessly at ease as the Union's most wanted outlaw than he had as its crown prince. "Your friend Isern isn't wrong. I'm afraid I'm…" And he looked up from under his brows with that smile that seemed to give her a sharper tickle every time. "Trouble."

"And you're happy to tread trouble across my carpet?"

"My old standard-bearer thought it was a bad idea but...no one would expect me to come to you."

"I'll confess I'm fucking astonished." But the truth was Rikke was glad to see him, and not just because of the pearl dust and the drink. Though partly because of the pearl dust and the drink. And partly because he was handsome, and funny, and charming, and the certain knowledge that he was a very excellent lover was kissing constantly at the back of her pearl-dusted mind. She had to keep herself hidden, these days. Behind the tattoos and the knowing smiles and the stony heart. With him, she could let herself show.

"I need someone to get me out of Adua," he said. "Someone powerful. Someone brave. Someone with a large entourage, in which an extra face, suitably obscured, might go unnoticed. And you did write me that letter, after all, so I wondered if you might still have some trifling attachment to my lost cause?"

"Mostly suited my own needs, if I'm honest. But it's true I've always liked lost causes."

"There was...something else." He paused, his grin curling wider, as if he was casting his mind back to a happy memory. "That night we spent together. And that morning after. I've thought about it often."

She couldn't help smiling herself. "So have I." In fact, she was thinking about it right now, and she pulled one of those ridiculous lace gloves off with her teeth. It was all out of shape from the damp anyway.

"I've wondered, now and again, what might have happened...had we been different people."

She licked her finger and thumb and started snuffing out candles, each one dying with a little fizz and a curl of smoke. "So have I." The room gradually grew dimmer, gradually felt hotter, in spite of the clammy fabric clinging to her, till there was only the gleam on the gold thread in the curtains, on the silverware and the glassware, at the corners of Orso's smiling eyes.

"And...well...we're different people now," he said.

"No doubt. We're all of us changed." All the things seen since then. The things done. The people gone back to the mud. He'd lost his throne, she'd gained one. But as she came close and took the glass from his hand, he had that same look in his eyes he'd had that night. That look of unguarded desire. And being looked at that way felt just as good. Better'n ever, maybe.

She knocked the wine off in one throw, then had to stand there wincing, one hand pressed to her chest, fighting the urge to puke it back up. That would've been quite the mood-killer.

"Need a bucket?" he asked.

"No, I think I've got it—" Fighting down an acrid little tickle at the back of her throat with a shudder. "Under control." And she took her wet hat off and started to slide the pins from her hair, toss them on the table beside her so they bounced and clicked and tumbled twinkling on the floor.

She was a leader. She had responsibilities. Hard choices to make.

But they could wait till tomorrow.

"Sometimes feels like life's just a long preparation for something," she said, and she put a finger on his chest and pushed him, so he had no choice but to sit down, hard, wine slopping from his glass. "Hard work getting everything right for a perfect future." And she scrubbed her damp hair with her nails, scrubbed it back into its usual wild tangle then blew a stray strand out of her face. "But nothing's ever finished, is it? Nothing's ever right. Not really."

"Certainly not in my experience," he whispered, slightly throaty, as she reached out and perched the hat slanted on his head.

"And if it is, it turns wrong soon enough." She took two fistfuls of her damp dress and gathered it up. "It rots. It rusts. It dies." Gathered it up all the way to her thighs, goosefleshed from the cold outside and the warm inside. "Life's naught but a set of moments." And she slipped one knee onto the cushions to either side of him, lowered herself gently into his lap. "You've got to live each one."

"I've always thought so," he murmured, eyes fixed on hers.

"All that time spent tending the garden," she whispered. Seemed fine luck now she hadn't bothered with all that mass of underwear they trussed themselves up in down here. "You forget to sit back in the garden and enjoy it." And she pushed her hands into his hair, cool and damp from the rain, and twisted his face up towards hers, and started to kiss him.

# Of Your Heart a Stone

When Orso woke in a comfortable bed for the first time in months he wondered, for a blissful moment, whether it might all have been a dream. The rebellion. The Great Change. The Court of the People. The baying crowds and the prison cells. The figures dropping from the Tower of Chains.

Then he saw the sunlight glimmer from between the heavy drapes, the faint glint on the gilded wallpaper, and it came back in a pleasurable rush whose bed he was in. The smile spread across his face and he stretched, rolled, thinking he might politely offer Rikke the chance to make use of his morning wood, the way she had so enthusiastically made use of the midnight variety—

But the bed was empty.

Someone had left fresh clothes on a chair and he slipped from the covers and pulled the trousers on. He crept to the window, nudged the curtains back with a cautious finger to peer across gardens glistening with last night's rain towards the Middleway.

He caught a glimpse of flags through the budding branches. The crossed hammers of Angland, maybe. He heard the familiar tramp of armoured feet and let the curtains fall. No doubt they were still searching for him. Plainly, he was far from free. But with Rikke on his side he had a chance. In Adua, self-styled zenith of civilisation, they liked to think of anything beyond the Circle Sea as primitive. But they could have learned a lot from the Northmen. About courage, about endurance, about loyalty. About the enthusiastic use of wood, for that matter. He found he was smiling again.

He had no idea what would happen now. But for the first time in a long time, he was eager to find out.

He padded down the stairs into the empty hallway. Far from the first time he had stolen from a lady's bed, but the stakes had rarely been so high. He heard soft voices, talking in Northern, and slipped across to the open door of the dining room.

Rikke sat at the head of a table set for breakfast. Isern-i-Phail had one hand on the back of her chair, leaning down to mutter in her ear. Orso had the impression he had interrupted a difficult conversation, and more than likely he had been its subject. By the frown on Isern's face, his way with the ladies did not extend to hillwomen. But then, since he lost the crown, his way with the ladies probably did not extend very far at all. It was something of a surprise that it still reached Rikke. Looking at her troubled expression now, he wondered whether, in the cold light of morning, it might not fall short of her, too.

But Orso's father had insisted the best way to brighten the mood was to act as if it was already incandescent. An approach he had applied to Orso's mother for thirty years with a total lack of success. So Orso plastered on a smile, strutted into the room and called out, "Morning!" with almost offensive enthusiasm.

"Barely," said Isern as she stalked past him to the door, endlessly chewing. From the short patch of sunlight in front of the windows it could not have been far short of midday.

"My mother would have counted it quite the victory to get me up at this hour." Orso licked his lips as he pulled out a chair. Last night's exertions had left him with an appetite. Well, that and barely eating for a few days. "Do you mind if I . . . ?"

"Dig in," said Rikke.

He started to fork sausages onto a plate, mouth thoroughly watering. "Is there anything better than a good meal after lean times?"

"There's a few in the North who'd swear by a good revenge after a long feud."

He closed his eyes in simple pleasure as he chewed. "Revenge won't fill your belly."

"You sound like my father."

"By all accounts a shrewd man."

"He was all heart," said Rikke, nudging some crumbs about her plate.

Orso felt that need to lift the mood again. "Have an egg," he said, plucking one from a dish and holding it out. Not much of a gift, especially when it had been hers in the first place. But then the whole North was hers now. She was the one with the power, while he had nothing to recommend him but his winning sense of humour. "You don't look . . . entirely happy," he said.

She plucked the egg from his fingers and started tapping it against the edge of the table, gently breaking the shell. "Lots to think about."

"Regrets, eh?"

She looked up sharply. Looking into the gaping pupil of that Long Eye still scared him and excited him at once. As though she might see some secret truth in him that he had never guessed at. "Why d'you say that?"

"I've a few of my own. I recognise a fellow sufferer. It can't be easy. To know what's coming."

"No." She started to pick away the broken shell with her fingernails. "I've often argued with Isern over whether it's a blessing or a curse. I swing back and forth."

"Don't we all? Just flags, tugged wherever the breeze pleases."

"Even when it does open, the Long Eye never gives you all the answers. It's mist and whispers. You have to find your own way to the truth." She looked up at him again, and again he felt that excitement. And that fear. "You want the painful truth? A secret I haven't dared tell anyone?"

"Well...as long as it doesn't hurt *too* much."

She leaned towards him, dropping her voice. "The truth is...I *used* to see things. Before my father died. Before I stole the North. Before I killed Stour and Calder. Before I was Black Rikke and I was...a girl you gave an egg to." She waved a hand at her tattooed face. "But since the runes were written, nothing." She bit into the egg and sat back, speaking around a mouthful. "Reckon my Long Eye's closed for good."

"So...you pretend?"

"I do what my father tried to. Give his people at least a bit of what they want. Folk like the notion of someone who knows what's coming. That way they don't have to worry about it."

Orso puffed out his cheeks. "I'd never know you had doubts. You seem so sure of yourself." He gave a snort of laughter. Perhaps he had a type, after all. "You remind me of Savine, in a way."

She did not take it altogether as a compliment. "I've changed, that's true. I've had to grow...harder."

"As an expert in disappointing their parents...I'm sure your father would be very proud."

He had meant that to be kind, but she winced as if the words hurt. "I wish I thought so. I had a vision. Just a year or two past, though it feels an age ago. It's all come true, one way or another." She looked out of the windows, their bright squares reflected in her eye. "I saw a wolf eat the sun."

Orso pondered that. "Well, I'm no magus, learned in the interpretation of visions... but I'd say that was Stour Nightfall making war on the Union."

"I saw a lion eat the wolf."

He sat back, rather enjoying the game. "The Young Lion, beating the Great Wolf in the Circle."

"I saw a lamb eat the lion."

Orso could not help but grin. "That was me, giving Brock a richly deserved kick up the arse at Stoffenbeck."

"I saw an owl eat the lamb."

Orso's grin faded. "Who's the owl?"

"No idea." Now she looked at him, and with the strangest, saddest expression. "Till now."

He was starting to feel worried. "What is it?"

"I'm the owl," she said.

The doors of the dining room swung open. Caul Shivers was the first in, metal eye glinting. Next came those two Anglanders Orso had often seen on the front benches of the Court of the People, the big one and the lean one, Glaward and Jurand. The final guest was announced before his appearance by the squeaking of the bearings in his artificial leg, accompanied by that familiar sinking sensation of dashed hopes.

"Leo dan Brock." Orso forked up another piece of sausage but it seemed to have lost all its taste. "Do you never tire of *killing* my mood?"

Brock looked even more gaunt, pale and furious than the last time Orso saw him, the day the Lords Round burned and he stabbed Lord Marshal Forest in the chest. All those high qualities everyone had once so envied—the honesty, the bravery, the blunt good nature—seemed to have been crushed out of him like the pulp out of a lemon, leaving just the bitter seeds of pride, anger and an insatiable need to conquer. That and a truly unforgivable lack of any sense of humour.

"You've led me quite a dance the last couple of weeks," he growled, as if Orso's desperate attempts to stay alive were a personal affront.

"Hardly my fault that you have such poor footwork," said Orso.

Leaning back against the doorway, Isern-i-Phail managed a titter. Perhaps unsurprisingly, no one else was in the mood. Orso glanced about the room, wondering if it would have been the done thing to try to make a break for it, but he very much doubted he could fight off Caul Shivers with a fork.

Rikke spoke slowly, softly. As if she was trying to convince herself. "The North has been through the fire, Orso. I put it through the fire. If it was just about me…" She grimaced, then snapped the words angrily. "But I've all those people to think about now! They need peace."

"And I'm the price, I suppose." Orso glanced from Glaward, to Brock, to Jurand, to Isern, to Shivers, and back to Rikke. "You promised to fight with him against me. Then you broke your word. I'm what it costs you to get back in his good graces. If he even has any, these days."

"Constant pain can wear down your patience," said Brock.

"In Adua, we like to think of anything beyond the Circle Sea as primitive." Orso gave a sigh and placed his knife and fork neatly together with a final sounding clink. He was finished. And not just with breakfast. "But it turns out you Northmen can teach us a thing or two about treachery."

Isern might have given the tiniest careless shrug. Shivers did not move even that much. Rikke had, at least, the good grace to wince. "A leader needs to be hard," she said, frowning down at the table, "so others needn't be. She must make of her heart a stone."

"Or get rid of it altogether," said Brock.

"Finally we agree." Isern-i-Phail scratched at the hollow above her collarbone and winked. "Ruthlessness is a quality much loved o' the moon."

Orso was tempted to scream and rage, but it would have ruined an otherwise charming morning. He had acted for so many years, in the full and glaring view of the public, with an utter lack of dignity. Now, in private, he insisted on keeping hold of every shred.

He slid his chair back, stood and gave Rikke his best formal bow. "Please allow me to say that I do not blame you for this in the least. Terrible manners to just drop in. Entirely my own fault. I'm actually…" He gave a disbelieving grin as he realised it was true. "I'm actually rather glad we had this time together."

Rikke winced again, even harder, as Glaward walked over with a set of heavy manacles. "Believe it or not, so am I."

"An unlikely romance, this," sneered Brock, pale lip curled with evident disgust. Or was it jealousy?

Rikke's glance towards him was satisfyingly furious. "We're even," she forced through gritted teeth.

Brock's nostrils flared. The Young Lion might have had fewer limbs than in his glory days, but he yet possessed a full set of heroic nostrils. "Take him somewhere he won't bloody escape from," he snapped at Jurand. "And the Lady Regent won't find out about. Not until it's time." He looked back to Rikke. "We're even. But we'll be keeping our swords well sharpened, just in case."

"The Master Maker forged mine," said Caul Shivers, in that broken whisper of his. "It never gets blunt." He made no effort to be threatening. The one advantage of a giant scar and a metal eye, perhaps, is that being threatening takes no effort whatsoever.

"Huh." And Brock's mechanical leg squeaked faintly as he limped for the door.

The bracelets snapped shut around Orso's wrists. One could almost hear the discomfort in Glaward's voice. "Hope that's not too tight, Your..."

"No, no," said Orso. "Most comfortable fetters I've worn, and I've tried on quite a few lately." He took one last look at Rikke, sitting there in the sunlight, at the head of the table. He would have liked more time with her. But he supposed it had never been very realistic. "Peace between the North and the Union." He gave a little chuckle. "Honestly, it's a far better legacy than anyone expected from me." And he strolled jauntily out into the hall.

Well, as jauntily as you can in chains.

Which isn't very.

# Answers

Vick threw the door shut and it banged from the frame, wobbled back open a crack. She didn't even bother to close it.

Never stay in a place you can't walk straight out of without a backward glance.

She strode down the hall to the dining room, yanked open the narrow cupboard, ripped out the false bottom and pulled up the bag, slung it over her shoulder. She stopped beside the table, looking at the few books stacked on the windowsill.

Never own a thing you can't leave behind.

She dropped the bag, knocking over a couple of pieces from the squares board, grabbed that old copy of *The Life of Dab Sweet* and tossed it inside.

Never make a friend you can't turn your back on. A life that leaves no marks.

She paused a moment, teeth gritted.

"Fuck," she hissed.

Tallow peered around the door, looking shocked to see her. Probably he didn't get many visitors. Certainly not at night. And since the Great Change, who enjoyed a knock at the door they weren't expecting?

"They caught Orso," she said, pushing past him.

"What?"

"He was hiding in the Gloktas' old house, of all places, with bloody Black Rikke." She went to the lamp and blew it out, sinking the room into darkness. "She gave him up."

Tallow looked sadly into a corner. "Guess you can't trust anyone."

"The Lord Regent has him..." She sidled to the window and peered down into the darkened streets. "Somewhere in the city."

"What's that got to do with us?"

460

"It won't be long until they find out I helped him escape."

Tallow stared. "You helped him...*what*? I thought we were supposed to stand with the winners—"

"I'm in danger, Tallow, and that means all my friends are in danger. Luckily, I don't have any friends."

"I'm probably the closest thing."

"Exactly." She flicked the shabby curtains closed. "Which is why you have to come with me."

"I *what*? Where?"

"Still working out the details. The main thing is, not here. Believe me, I'm less than delighted about it myself."

"What about my sister?"

Vick winced. The question she'd always known was coming.

"I can't leave her," he said, voice getting higher and higher, more and more panicked. "I mean, she won't get by on her own, I can't go without her, I—"

"Fine!" snapped Vick. "We'll get her next. But we travel light, you understand?"

"Be gentle," muttered Tallow, stepping up to the door. "She scares easily."

He knocked. Three slow, steady knocks. "It's me," he hissed at the lock. Nothing. He knocked again. Three slow, steady knocks. "It's me!"

"Let's go," hissed Vick. This broke all her rules, and she had a bad feeling. She'd had a bad feeling for years.

Tallow slipped out a key, unlocked the door with a trembling hand, turned the knob and pushed it creaking open. There was a musty-smelling little hall beyond, paper peeling from the mould-speckled plaster.

"Inquisitor Teufel's with me," he said softly, like he was trying to coax a skittish cat down from a windowsill. He stepped into a room where dim light flickered, and Vick followed. "You remember Inquisitor Teufel, don't you?"

"Of course," said Pike.

He was standing in the centre of the floor with his hands clasped behind him. As if he'd been expecting her for hours.

Vick hadn't often been taken by total surprise. But this was the second time he'd managed it. She spun around, but there were Practicals in the hallway. Four of them, black-dressed and black-masked. The way they used to be, before the Great Change.

"I get the feeling you might have been expecting someone else," said

Pike. "I can only apologise for that. Please don't blame Master Tallow. He was only doing his job. Extremely well, I might add."

Vick stared at Tallow. Somehow, he didn't look so much like her brother any more. His eyes weren't sad, they were hard and careful. The way she might've looked at a prisoner before she started asking questions.

"Sorry," he said. But he didn't look sorry at all.

Pike watched, his burned face, as usual, showing no emotion. She wondered, as usual, whether behind the ruined nerves, the ruined muscles, the ruined skin, he was bursting with feeling, or if he really was a void inside. "The Weaver would like a word," he said.

Vick swallowed. "Aren't you the Weaver?"

The corner of Pike's mouth quivered. "A title I borrowed from a better man." He gave a nod.

She was seized from behind and a bag was forced over her head.

She didn't know where they were taking her. She didn't know who was behind this. She hardly knew what the sides were any more, let alone which one she was supposed to be on. She didn't even know what betrayal, what deception, what secret she was paying for. Probably she'd never know. Body found floating by the docks. An unsatisfactory ending to her bitter little story.

Occasionally one of the Practicals would murmur, "Steps up here," or, "Mind your shoulder," in a polite, disinterested tone, often with a steering tug or a gentle nudge. But never rough. No violence whatsoever.

That, no doubt, would come later.

It took a while to get wherever they were going. Lots of time to think. To feel her stiff hip aching. To listen to her quick breath echoing. To mull over all the deceptions, all the betrayals. The ones she'd done and the ones done to her. By the time they stopped, she'd steeled herself. By the time they pulled off the bag, she was ready for anything. Except the one thing she got.

Her own front door.

One of the Practicals carefully flattened the bag, folded it with fussy precision, then slipped it into a pocket while the other untied her hands.

They stood there, in front of her little apartment. Fitting, in a way. All that pain and worry just to get back to where she'd started. They didn't force her in. But they weren't giving her any other choices.

One pointed out the door like an usher showing a valued client to her seat in the theatre. "Just inside, Inquisitor, if you'd be so kind?"

She could've fought, she supposed, but she'd have lost. She could've

462

run, but they'd have caught her. She could've screamed for help, but no help would come. And anyway, now the moment had arrived, she wanted answers. It might be she'd only get more questions. It might be she'd get a final, crushing blow to the back of the skull, and darkness. But she wanted answers.

She pushed the door open with a fingertip. Her face was sweaty from the inside of the bag, the air cool on her skin. A lamp was lit in the dining room. An accusing finger of light stretched out across the boards towards her. She followed it down the hall, her knees a little weak, her mouth a little dry, her heart beating hard.

Vick's guest sat at the dining table in the light of a single lamp, brightness splashed across the sharp bones of his face, darkness gathered in the deep lines. The squares board was set before him, the pieces Vick had knocked over returned to their places, casting long shadows across the chequered wood.

"Inquisitor Teufel. I have been waiting for you."

Now it all made sense. And like every illusion, once Vick knew how it worked, she couldn't understand how she hadn't seen it right away.

"You're the Weaver," she said.

Sand dan Glokta bared his ruined teeth as he sat back in his wheeled chair and considered her calmly. "Yes."

"Not Pike. Not Risinau. You."

"Me."

"You made the Breakers."

"Made? No, no." Glokta let one thin finger trail across the pieces on the squares board, as though considering his next move. "Society is a competition, and one cannot have winners without creating losers. People who lose once tend to lose more, and people who lose too often become discontented. I merely...gathered them into a group. Gave them a name. Pointed them in the right direction."

"You...were the architect of the Great Change?"

"Architect sounds so grand. There was dry straw everywhere, I simply struck the match."

She thought of the bank in flames in Valbeck, the ash fluttering down. She thought of the fires leaving their black scars through Adua. She thought of the Court of the People, burning up like a great torch to leave a blasted shell. "*Why?*"

"Ah, why do I do this? Why?" Glokta gazed down at the squares board. "Because sometimes...to change the world...we must burn it down. Bayaz controlled everything. We all were pieces in his game." He nudged

463

one of the smallest pieces forwards into empty space. "He owned the banks, and the banks owned the merchants, owned the nobles, owned the treasury, even. The king himself danced to Bayaz's music. The Closed Council, too. Even me, though I'm not much of a dancer these days. The Great Change was the only way I could see to cut all the puppet strings at once. The only way I could see to make us..." Glokta shrugged his bony shoulders, wincing as though even that much movement gave him pain. "Free."

"Free?" Vick stared at him. "Is that what we are now?"

"Within reason. People love the idea of freedom but, in my experience, there is only so much they can be trusted with. You saw what Judge did with it. Take it far enough, freedom becomes chaos. The voice of the people...is just *noise*. It is the blather of the lunatics in the madhouse. It is the squeal of the pigs in the slaughterhouse. It is a choir of morons. Most of them don't even know what they want, let alone how to get it. They need someone to tell them what to do."

"Someone like you, I suppose?"

"Or you." He waved towards the bench on the other side of the table. "Have a seat, Inquisitor. Towering over me like that, you're making me nervous."

She dropped down opposite him, numb. "If the Breakers were your tool, why send me to watch them?"

"I needed to know what they were about. You may have noticed that people have a habit of doing stupid, unpredictable things. And *I* could hardly show up to meetings." He gently turned the squares board around, considering the position from the other side. "The Breakers would have been most upset, I imagine, to find they were taking orders from the man they considered their worst enemy."

"Taking orders? A moment ago you were merely pointing them in the right direction."

Lamplight glistened on his empty gums as he grinned. "You always were a sharp interrogator. Sometimes I had to give a little more than guidance, I confess. Otherwise they might all have run off their own way, like woodlice from a lifted log."

"Is that what happened in Valbeck?"

"People are not machines that one can move with a lever. This business is more art than science." Glokta licked unhappily at one of the teeth he still had. "I had planned a dress rehearsal, you might say, but Risinau shit the bed on the timing, just as he shit the bed on everything. I am an inveterate bed-shitter myself, so I recognise the tendency in others. Sadly, as an old colleague of mine was fond of saying, we must work with the tools we have."

"What about Tallow? Is that even his name?"

"Do you know, I forget his original name. I'd be surprised if even he remembers it." Glokta let his forefinger rest on top of one of the smallest pieces, as though considering a move. "I needed to know what *you* were about. You may have noticed that people have a habit of doing stupid, unpredictable things. I placed him with the Breakers so you could take him under your wing and he could make sure you stuck to the script. Which you did, admirably."

"He was your plant from the beginning?" she whispered.

"Don't be upset at him, Vick, it's beneath you. I found him in the camps, like you. I offered him the same deal and he made the same choice. The only choice. To stand with the winners."

So she'd finally found a better liar than herself. Or perhaps she'd just found one she wanted desperately to believe. Strange, that the deaths of thousands left her cold, while the betrayal of one boy made her furious. "How did you know that I'd... how could you *know*—"

"Don't be too hard on yourself. We all have sore spots." He grimaced as he shifted in his chair. "I myself am one enormous one. And finding other people's has been my business for a very long time." He nudged another piece forwards across the board. "I know you like to think there are no chinks in your armour but, really, you're not too deep a mystery to fathom. To me your guilt has always been plain as a sign around your neck. About the Breakers in Valbeck. About Collem Sibalt and his friends. About the rebels in Starikland. About your mother and father. About your sisters and your brother—"

"That was all *you*!" she snarled in his face. "*You* made me do all that! Sibalt, and the Breakers, and the rebels, and all the rest!" She stabbed at her chest with a finger and her voice warbled, cracked. "Why should *I* be guilty? What fucking choice did I have?" It had already become a plaintive whine. Fates help her, almost a tearful one. "*You're* the one... you're the one sent my family to the camps... in the first place..."

"I am aware," said Glokta calmly. He hadn't even flinched. "Where they died, and you survived. I told you to forgive yourself, remember? Your family simply weren't tough enough. You are."

Vick blinked down at the squares board, the anger already drained away to leave her hollow and helpless. Risinau, Judge, Orso, Leo dan Brock, they were all small pieces in the game Glokta had been playing. So small they never even guessed how vast the board truly was. Which made her what? A speck of dust between the squares, at best.

"Where were you rushing off to, anyway?" asked Glokta. "Talins? To work for Shylo Vitari? Please, the woman's a hack. We both know how badly you want a cause worthy of your loyalty." He winced as he twisted to reach into a pocket. "Arch Lector. Commissioner. It doesn't matter what you call it. I believe the time has come for you to go from digging out the answers to posing the questions. To go from being one of the pieces…" And he leaned forwards to place something on the squares board. That ring with the purple stone he used to wear. That Pike had worn after him. "To making the moves. Practical Dole?"

One of the Practicals lumbered in, winced as he manoeuvred Glokta's chair from behind the table. It caught one of the legs on the way and sent a few squares pieces clicking over to roll around in helpless circles on their sides.

"Feel free to refuse. I will understand." Vick's old master leaned to murmur as he was wheeled past. "But we both know that ring will fit you *perfectly*."

She heard the door shut and was left alone in a heavy silence. Just her and all the lies. Some she'd told, some she'd been told, some she'd told herself, until she'd no idea what was true any more. Until she'd no idea if there was such a thing.

Vick picked up the ring, turning it around in her fingers. Who could've dreamed she'd one day wear it? The great stone shone in the lamplight, full of purple sparks. From the prison camps of Angland to the pinnacle of power.

Then she caught sight of something in her bag. The worn gilt on the spine of *The Life of Dab Sweet*. She pulled it out, and it fell open on the table at that favourite page. That favourite picture. The great plains, grass going on for ever. A place where you can make yourself anew. Where you can go as far as your dreams can take you.

Rubbish, most likely. A made-up drawing in a book full of lies. But there comes a time you have to say no to what you're given and reach for what you want.

The truth was Vick had always wanted to be loyal. But not to nations, or ideas, or causes. To people. Orso was gone. Sibalt was dead. Tallow had never even existed. If she'd ever had a debt to Glokta it had only been in her own mind. One she chose to keep because she had nothing else. So she pronounced it long since paid.

She tossed the ring spinning across the squares board, threw the bag over her shoulder and walked out without a backward glance.

She flung the door shut and it banged from the frame, wobbled back open a crack. She didn't even bother to close it.

She thought of a wide sky over a far country.

She smiled as she strode off into the night.

# The Only Crime

"So, short steel in my...left hand?" asked Savine.

"Yes, then your front foot at the mark—"

"This mark?" She worked her shoe into the chalk line on the palace lawn as though she had never seen one before. "How exciting!"

"Isn't it." Jurand was teetering on the edge of impatience as he stepped to his own mark, weighing his steels. "Then when I say *begin*—"

She darted at him with no warning and no mercy, the way her father taught her. Jurand was a skilled swordsman. No doubt he was quicker and far stronger than her, and it was a while since she had held a steel. She could never have beaten him in a fair bout. But who wants to fight those?

His long steel was not even up when she caught it with hers, blade flickering, metal scraping, jerking it from his unready hand. She stepped sharply around him as he stumbled, planting her heel behind his where it could trip him. He made a soft *oof* as her shoulder thudded into his breastbone and sent him crashing onto his back, his short steel bouncing away across the well-tended grass.

His expression of total shock as the blunted point of her long steel tickled him under the chin was positively delightful.

"Would that be a touch to me?" she asked, all innocence.

He slowly lifted his head. "I have a strange sense you've fenced before."

"I never said otherwise." She stabbed her long steel into the turf and offered him her hand. "That was your assumption."

"You could've corrected me," he said as she helped him up.

"I just did. I've been fencing since I was a girl. My father taught me."

He bent to collect his steels. "So...not only have you fenced before, but you were trained by one of the best swordsmen the Union ever produced?"

She gave an artless shrug. "It's fine exercise." The moment he was up she came at him again, but this time he was ready, parried and stepped watchfully back towards the edge of the circle.

"I expected to be giving a lesson," he muttered. "I should have realised I'd be taking one."

"Not at all. I gave up playing with knives, after Valbeck..." The well-worn memory of her sword sliding through that man's back. The faint pressure of the grip in her palm. The look of shock on his face. But she found she could dismiss it much more easily now. She had warned him, after all. If he had not wanted to be stabbed he should have fucking left her alone. "Pregnancy and motherhood are hardly compatible with the fencing circle. I am awfully out of practice."

"That was my first thought just now as I lay on my back with your sword at my throat. How awfully out of practice you seem."

He jabbed warily at her and she flicked it away. Her legs felt heavier than they once had, her breath came harder, but it felt good to be back in the circle. She had spent too long curled up with her babies, growing soft and motherly. It was high time that she exerted some discipline. That she competed. That she *won*. And not just with a sword.

"I confess I was not looking only for a fencing partner," she said.

"An ulterior motive?" Jurand eyed her steels warily as they circled. "You shock me again."

"I wanted to talk to you about the future."

"To me?"

"To you first of all." She danced in, their blades rang together prettily enough but with no real fire, and they broke again. "The new Closed Council must represent the new Union, and you will be its heart. You should be confirmed as Lord Chamberlain."

Jurand looked pleased, flattered and slightly flushed, precisely as she had intended. "I... would be honoured to serve Your Highnesses however you decide."

"Please. I need you at that table every bit as much as Leo does. You are a clever man, Jurand. Subtle and loyal. You have a gift for organisation. I wish you had been at Stoffenbeck with us. I begged Leo to bring you, but... well." She jabbed again, and again, left her wrist limp and let him parry easily. Nowhere near as sharply as she could have done. Nowhere near as sharply as her father once made her, again and again until her whole body was on fire. "Glaward must have a seat, too, of course. As lord marshal, maybe?"

"I think that is what Leo had in mind."

"And perhaps he was thinking of, say, Isher as lord chancellor and Heugen as lord admiral?"

Jurand's forehead wrinkled in surprise. "That's exactly what he was thinking."

"Then it seems sensible to fill the Arch Lector's and High Consul's chairs with seasoned bureaucrats. People who understand the challenges of reform and can bring a weight of experience with them."

"That does seem sensible— Uh!" She made him twist away from a quick cut and trot back into space, shaking his head.

"I am of the firm opinion, however..." Cut, cut, jab. "That it would be a missed opportunity to return to the way things were in King Jezal's reign." Jab, jab, cut. "A regime that ensured its own downfall with its waste, and exploitation, and callous disregard for its subjects." Steel rang with each word. "We need a new kind of person on the Closed Council. Engineers and architects. Investors and inventors." Jurand came back at her and she parried once, twice, thrice. "People who understand the tools of the new age." Jab, jab, jab. "Who can help us build a *better* Union."

"I don't know, Leo can be quite traditional in his—"

"We must move on, Jurand, and we must bring the people with us. After all that was lost in the Great Change. All that was destroyed..." She thought of Vick dan Teufel then, of all people. That oddly moving moment of unexpected honesty, beneath the House of Questions. She lowered her steels and looked Jurand in the eye. "It can't all be for nothing, you understand?"

He blinked, then swallowed, and his own steels slowly drifted down. "I do."

Savine shook herself. "Shall we break?" Jurand was starting to get her measure, and that would never do. "There was a time I could keep fencing for hours, but motherhood changes you in so many ways."

"Oh, of course."

"You are Leo's oldest friend," she said, with a wrong-footing change of subject. "His *best* friend." One should never let an opponent get comfortable in a conversation, after all, any more than in fencing, or business, or politics. "And you are a perceptive man. You must know that he and I...are not entirely getting along." She let him see her pain at that. Her regret. "But we simply *must* remain friends, for the sake of our children, for the sake of the nation. I have always felt one cannot have too many friends." She came closer, looking up shyly from under her lashes. "Are... *we* friends, Jurand?"

He was caught between sympathy and mistrust. "I would like us to be. I mean, I like to think we are."

"I cannot tell you what a comfort that is." She rested a gentle hand on his forearm. A little human contact, carefully administered, can have such a powerful effect. "To know that even if I have made a mess of things with Leo, we will always have a good friend in common."

"I don't want to deceive you, I have to be Leo's friend first."

"Of course! I should have been a better friend to him myself. I know it was a fool's mistake to let Orso go, but I allowed my heart to overcome my head, for once. He is my brother, after all, I have..." She had to swallow, the emotion not entirely feigned. "Complicated feelings about him."

She had thought this might be where Jurand grew suspicious, but for some reason he looked nervous instead. Was there even pity in his eyes? As if he had some secret on the tip of his tongue... but in the end he swallowed it. "Perhaps...you should tell Leo that. I'm sure he'd like to hear it."

Savine would sooner have set herself on fire than apologise for saving Orso's life. She passed it off with an emotional sniff. "I fear Leo will not listen to me any more. For good reasons, I know. But he will listen to you."

"I agree with you about the Closed Council. And about changing the Union for the better. I agree with you about a lot of things. But Leo—"

"Please, Jurand." She did not let her lower lip actually wobble, or her eyes fill with tears. That would have been sugaring the pudding too much. But she let her voice crack, ever so slightly. Jurand was a caretaker. A fixer of problems, happiest when he was needed. So she let herself be needy. "I need your help. We all do." She gave his forearm a gentle squeeze. "For my sake and his." She looked up earnestly into his face. "For the sake of our children." She left herself defenceless. "For the sake of the *nation*. Can I be entirely honest with you? Can I lay myself bare?"

He hardly knew what to say to that. "I, er—"

"I think we are alike, in many ways. I can be quite perceptive, too." She eased even closer, squeezed his arm tighter, made her voice softer so he had to lean down towards her. "I have started to believe that Leo..." She fixed him with her eye and whispered the words. "Is in love with *someone else*. That he always has been. I have often thought about how he reacted...to what happened in Sipani." Jurand's cheek flushed. He tried to pull away but she gripped his arm. "I have come to believe it might not have been disgust at all, but...*jealousy*."

There was a long, tense silence while Jurand stared at her, and the birds twittered pleasantly in the budding trees, and the bees buzzed about a patch of fragrant lavender, and somewhere from a high window in the wall of the palace a maid sang in a fine, high voice as she beat the curtains.

"I doubt he would admit it to anyone," murmured Savine. "I doubt he even admits it to himself, but...if he ever did...I want you to know I would be the *last* person to stand in the way of his happiness." Even softer, so softly it was just breath, she added the last two words. "Or yours."

Jurand's throat made a distinct squelching sound as he swallowed, the knob on his neck bobbing. "I hardly know...what you can mean."

She held his eye a moment longer. Until she was satisfied that neither one of them could have any doubts exactly what she meant. Then, with a final squeeze, she let him go and took up her steels again, all business. "I can only apologise, I have wandered *so* far from the subject. Women! We simply cannot resist discussing affairs of the heart when they come up. We were talking about the composition of the new Closed Council, I think?"

Jurand cleared his throat with some difficulty. "Er...I...yes. Were there...any names in particular you—"

"Curnsbick, Kort, Vallimir and Selest dan Heugen."

He blinked. "You have given this some thought."

"I hate to have my time wasted with ill-considered proposals, don't you? I promise there is excellent sense in every one of those names. Forward-looking people, each with fine qualities. Properly led, with Leo's charisma and your prudent oversight, they will be invaluable servants of the Crown."

"Well..." His mind was clearly elsewhere as he took his mark. "I suppose I can talk to Leo."

"That's all I ask. When do we begin?"

"Whenever you—"

This time she came at him with even less warning, snapping the jabs out in a lethal flurry that would have made even her father applaud. Jurand managed to stumble back from the first, just about parried the second, but the last three thudded into his padded jacket in about the same spot, rocking him back on his heels then sending him stumbling from the circle.

"Oh," said Savine. "I suppose that would be another touch to me?"

Jurand winced as he rubbed at the dent in his jacket. "Is there anything you do badly?"

"Lose." She gave her sweetest smile. "I swear I'm the worst loser in the world."

When Savine walked into the gilded immensity of the Lord and Lady Regents' great chamber, Zuri was sitting in a pool of lamplight, working at the book.

"How was the swordplay, Your Highness?" she asked, setting down her pencil.

472

"You don't need to Highness me, Zuri, not when there's no one else here."

Zuri arched one black brow. "My chicken, then? My pigeon? My dove?"

"How about Savine."

"Then how was the swordplay, Savine?"

She rubbed at the sore patch the long steel's grip had left down the side of her little finger. "I am rather rusty but will soon polish up. And I think I was able to tickle young Lord Jurand where he is most ticklish."

"I never doubted it." She caught Savine's eye, that brow creeping higher. "It only remains to be seen whether he can tickle your husband half so deftly."

"Zuri, you're a devil."

"I daresay my scripture teacher would be deeply disappointed in me."

"You sound rather pleased at the prospect."

"I believe I am. How were the designs?"

Savine crossed tiles already scored with scratches from Leo's mechanical foot and tossed the sheaf of plans on a side table under the ever-disapproving painted eye of Lord Marshal Kroy. "There were some awful ones. We could have a triangular Lords' Round, apparently. Or one that looks like a wedding cake." She slipped the box from her sleeve and took a little pinch of pearl dust. Just to keep things afloat. "But there were some good ideas." She stifled a sneeze. "And they're already clearing the site. Within ten years the Union will have a new heart, bigger and better than ever."

"Progress, then." Zuri permitted herself a little smile. "Whoever would have thought the Union would have a big heart."

"How are the children?" asked Savine, stepping towards the tall door to the nursery, decorated with the sun of the Union in gold leaf.

"They are well, but…" Zuri put a gentle hand on Savine's arm. "You should know they have a visitor." And she eased the door open.

Savine's mother stood beside the cots, rocking her tiny namesake with practised carelessness, pulling faces while the baby gurgled happily.

"Savine!" she said, prancing over. "It's *so* good to see you!" Quite as if they were an ordinary mother and daughter and it had been an ordinary few days since they last spoke, rather than six terrifying months in which Savine had nearly died, given birth, nearly died again, then taken control of a nation.

She leaned forwards to kiss Savine's cheek and gave her a noseful of that familiar, heady mix of perfume and alcohol. The smell of her childhood. The smell of being cared for, in an offhand, slightly lazy way. Savine felt herself caught on uncertain ground between fury at being abandoned and sappy relief that her mother was alive and had danced into her life again.

"You look…well," she managed to say. Sickening banality, considering. But her mother did look very well. As if she had been on a well-earned holiday these past few months, somewhere sunny, while Adua shivered through the bitterest winter on record, in more ways than one.

"All the better for seeing these little *darlings* of yours. By the Fates, Leo's a fine-looking man, but these children are positively beautiful." She leaned over Harod's cot, the monstrous diamond on her wedding band flashing as she waggled a finger at its occupant, speaking in a baby-voice Savine found intensely enraging. "Aren't you, you little beauties, so very *beautiful*."

"Mother?"

"Yes?"

"Are you really going fuss over my children…as if nothing has happened?"

"Honestly, I was rather hoping to."

Savine kept her voice under control with some difficulty. "For six months, while the world was burning down around us, I've had no idea where you were. Not a letter. Not a word. Not a *whisper*."

"I know, I know." She seemed, almost, a little impatient. "And I'm so sorry."

"You don't sound it."

"But you can understand we had to keep our heads down. Savine, please, I'm not the enemy—"

"What are you, exactly?"

She sank into a chair with a rustling of expensive skirts, sitting Harod on her knee so she could look deep into his eyes. "I still feel very much like the same sarcastic drunk I was at seventeen. But now I'm a grandmother, apparently. And to a king, would you believe?"

"Let's not pretend this is the first time you've had a future monarch in your lap."

"Really, that would've been beneath you at twelve. It's certainly beneath you now you're the Lady Regent of the Union."

She was right, of course, but that did not help, of course. "You can't just…*turn up*, Mother."

"Isn't that what grandmothers do? Avoid all the work then whisk in for the glory? It's safe, now, isn't it?"

"Of course, but—"

"It wasn't safe before."

"I am aware. I was thinking very much the same thing while I sat in the midst of at least two different riots, then in prison, then in the *dock*."

"Your father and I sitting there with you would only have made things worse." Harod gave an annoyed burble, and Savine's mother softened her exasperated tone. "I wanted to be there, to help you through it all. When the babies were born, of course I wanted nothing more. But I knew all I could do was to put you in more danger. And I knew you'd make it through. You've always been such a fighter. Such a modern, can-do woman. You really are so like your father. The pair of you simply refuse to be beaten."

"He isn't my father," grumbled Savine, but it sounded churlish. How the hell could she have come out of this as the unreasonable one?

"Whether you like it or not, he's your father in every way that counts."

"Then where was he?"

"It's better...that he explains it himself."

"He's here?"

"I think he wanted me to talk to you first. Break the ice. You know how it is, Savine, married couples tend to specialise, and I've always done the small talk, while he was more interested in—"

"The torture?"

"I was going to say the long-term planning, but no doubt you'll have it your way. You always have."

Savine pronounced every word with angry precision. "Believe me when I say that I have *not*. Where is he?"

Her mother nodded towards an unused door. "Can I stay with them? For a while?"

Savine wanted to say no. But she had never known how to say no to her mother. And Harod was clinging to her finger so tightly, the bloody little traitor. It would only have been punishing the children, and everything was supposed to be about them, now. Having a child limits one's choices. Two at once is an even worse constriction. Make one of them a king and you lose all say in anything.

Savine gave a hopeless shrug. "Since you're here."

She turned the key in the door and stepped through.

She had never found out why they called it the Sighing Room. Perhaps some royal widow had worn her life away in endless mourning there. It had three doors, one to the nursery, one to their great chamber and one out into the hallway. The walls had been scrubbed clean of the Breakers' slogans and freshly whitewashed, but Savine had not got as far as decorating. In any reasonable house it would have been a grand salon. In the palace it was one step above a cupboard. But it had a fine, high vaulted ceiling, and a stone floor polished by the passage of centuries of servants' feet, and a beautiful window. There was excellent light in the mornings, so Leo had requisitioned the place for Carmee Groom to paint his portrait. In the evenings, though, it was quiet, and dim, and full of shadows.

Savine's father—in every way that counted—sat in that wheeled chair Curnsbick had designed for him, knees making two knobbles in the blanket across his withered legs, frowning at the unfinished canvas. The Young Lion bursting through the city gates astride a sable charger to deliver the nation from chaos, sending as yet roughly sketched traitors routing for their cowardly lives.

Savine walked to him, skirts hissing on stone in the heavy silence. All the way her mouth was open to speak, but when she got to the chair she still had not found the words. In the end, she simply put her hand on her father's bony shoulder, the way she might have years ago. He laid his hand on top of hers. They looked up at the half-finished painting of Leo embodying the manly virtues, his iron leg hidden by horseflesh and his ruined arm by gold braid, pointing his sword towards a better tomorrow.

"I think it will be a fine portrait," said her father. "Somewhat over-wrought and sentimental, but so is its subject. It's also an absolute pack of lies." He gave a sigh. "But if people wanted the truth they could look at the real world. In my experience they much prefer paintings."

"Paintings are less likely to kill you."

"There is that. Where is the Lord Regent himself? Delivering the nation from peril once again?"

"Overseeing the organisation of his new army."

"Someone's compensating for something. But I suppose a warrior must have a sword."

"I understand they're calling it the Regent's Own."

"That could apply as much to the Lady Regent as the Lord." Savine's father glanced up at her. "I always thought armour would suit you rather well."

"Difficult to nurse in a breastplate. And toy soldiers were never my playthings, as a girl."

"Neither were dolls. As I recall it was fencing, money and power from the time you could talk, which was precociously early."

"Did it ever occur to you that those things interested me because they interested you?"

"Who cares where they came from? They're fine interests to have." His grin became a grimace as he clawed at one of the wheels of his chair,

476

turning it towards her. "I have to tell you how impressed I am, Savine. You not only plotted a safe path through this madness but made yourself exceedingly popular in the process. Quite the feat, for a woman who once put so much effort into making herself unpopular."

"I can do without your flattery," she lied. Honestly, his approval was still a headier drug than pearl dust to her. No one knew her better than he did. No one understood her so well. Except Orso, perhaps, and he was gone.

He took her hand in both of his, frowning down at it. "You have no idea how hard it has been, to know you were in danger. But with your marriage... and the choices you made afterwards... you put yourself beyond my reach. I hope you can understand that I was always doing my best to help you, in my own way. Someone had to have an eye on the bigger picture. I was working with Superior Pike to bring this madness to an end."

A cold sliver of doubt pierced the warm fuzz of their reunion and began to stab deeper. "Working with Pike? Wasn't he behind all this?"

"No, Savine. The time has come for me... at long last... to *confess*." His eyes slid up to hers, bright in their bruised sockets. There was no remorse in them. If anything, he had a kind of stubborn pride as he said the words. "I was."

Her hand was prickling where he held it. "What do you mean?"

"When I was a young man, and widely admired—there actually was a time, if you can believe it—I always imagined the power was in the Closed Council. But from the moment I first perched my withered arse on a chair there, it was clear we were all puppets. Bayaz pulled the strings, and always had. He controlled the banks, and their roots ate into everything. A web of debts, and secrets, and favours, deeper than you can imagine. Valint and Balk." His eyelid flickered, and he dabbed a streak of wet from his weepy eye with a knuckle. "They were like ivy choking the garden. King Jezal and I... you might not believe it, but we tried to do some good. As long as Bayaz was there... we were helpless." He paused, shadows black in the deep lines of his frowning face. "I had to bring a Great Change."

Savine could only stare at him, while the floor seemed to shift under her feet. Seemed to shift so savagely it was hard, almost, to keep her balance. "*You*... brought the Great Change?"

"I had to burn out the corruption. Rip Bayaz and his bank up by the roots! Dig it all over, so we could plant something new, something good." He sat forward, gripping her hand tight, lips curling back from his ruined teeth. "And now we have that chance!"

"Don't talk to me about *fucking gardening*!" she screamed, tearing her hand from his. "People died! Thousands of them!" She felt dizzy. She felt sick. "*I* nearly died, more than once!"

He gave a frustrated twitch, as if the problem was not his epic ruthlessness but her poor temper. "Progress does not come without sacrifices—you have always seen that more clearly than anyone. The Court of the People was not at all what we had in mind, but once it became clear what a disaster Risinau would be, Judge was the only option. Who could have known Judge would be even worse?"

"Anyone! Anyone who saw what she did in Valbeck! Anyone with eyes *or* ears in their head! The woman was fucking insane!"

"A period of insanity was necessary so that sanity could prevail," grumbled her father, as if she was complaining about footprints on a rug. "I would have liked a more…orderly transition, but Bayaz began to show an interest in you, and I could not risk that. Honestly, Savine, a little gratitude would not kill you."

"Gratitude?" she whispered.

"I did it all for *you*. So you could *truly* rule. All your life, we've been preparing you for this."

"My mother knew what you were planning?"

"It was her idea in the first place. One of her best."

Savine did not often find herself at a loss for words. She slowly stepped back, pointing at her father with a trembling hand. "Because…I was King Jezal's bastard. You knew all along…if Orso could be removed, I could be put in his place!"

"Your parentage was not a choice we made."

"Only something you turned to your advantage!"

"To everyone's advantage!" he barked, wheeling himself towards her. "Put aside your *pique*, Savine, this was war. In war one must make use of every weapon. Restraint is folly. Worse. Restraint is cowardice. You can give us a better Union. A better world! The horrors of the Great Change have left people pliable. Desperate for strong leadership. You are loved as much as I was hated, and the banks are torn up by the roots. We will finally have a free hand!"

"We?" she whispered.

"Your son will be king, but he will need your guidance." He gripped her arm, and there was strength in those thin fingers. A grasping strength. "And *you* will need mine."

Savine stared at him, cold all over. "You freed us from Bayaz…"

"Yes!"

"So you could *become* Bayaz."

He narrowed his eyes. "That is unfair."

"You're right." She twisted her arm free, taking another step back. "He only destroyed half the Agriont for his own ambitions. You destroyed half the Union!"

"You were willing to destroy a sizeable chunk of it for the sake of your ambitions, as I recall. You and your husband's revolt against the crown nearly ruined everything."

She gave a disbelieving gasp. "Was my mistake that I spoiled your efforts to burn down the world? Or that I didn't burn down enough of it?"

"Both," he said.

"I should have denounced you, in the Court of the People," whispered Savine. "I should have denounced you to hell."

"You should have. It might have improved your situation and could not possibly have done me any harm. That is the kind of sentimental mistake I can help you avoid in future. You have a struggle ahead of you, Savine." He gave the painting a significant glance. "Your husband may prove more difficult to control than anyone imagined. We cripples have a habit of surprising people. And freeing Orso was a blunder you may well regret. Then there are the nobles, and the commoners, and the Styrians, and the Imperials, and the Gurkish will not stay down for ever…" Enemies stretching off ahead of her, enough to fill a lifetime. "The time will come, sooner than you think, when you will need my support."

She would have loved to tell him to fuck himself. At that moment, she would have loved to punch him out of his chair. But although her eyes were narrowed, and her fist clenched to do it, she did not indulge herself. Savine had taken many roles over the momentous past year or two, or had them forced upon her. A helpless fugitive, a desperate killer, a disappointed lover, a wife and a partner, a rebel and a traitor, a forger of alliances, a mother to twins, a benefactor to orphans, the wretched accused, the terrified convicted, the Darling of the Slums and the Mother of the Nation. A journey of giddy rises, horrifying falls and wild reverses that could leave no one the same. But, above all, Savine had always been a woman of business. And a woman of business cannot afford to be a slave to her passions. She has to be realistic, and plan for the long term. She must take the world as it is and look for the best deal.

She raised her chin, looking at her father down her nose. "Then I suppose we should talk prices."

He showed those empty gums of his as he smiled. "*That's* my—"

There was a crash. Outside, in the gardens. Savine's father frowned towards the window. An angry cry, cut off in another crash, even louder, as if something heavy had fallen from a height.

"What was that?" For some reason, Savine felt the need to whisper.

Her father held up a hand, eyes still narrowed at the window. "Stay calm."

"Calm? What have you done?"

"Freed us from Bayaz." His eyes flickered sideways towards a muffled yell. "But the First of the Magi was never going to simply let us steal the Union from under his nose."

Savine heard shouting in the corridor, then a long, thin scream. She took an unsteady step away. She had been on a battlefield and knew what genuine agony sounded like. It ended in a sickening metallic crash, and another, closer, then a crunching thud so near and so hard that Savine felt the floor vibrate. The painting rattled on its stand. Dust filtered gently down from the vaults above.

Her father slowly, effortfully swivelled his chair towards the door to the hallway. "Get behind me," he said.

The knob turned and the door swung open. A face appeared around the edge. An unremarkable face, with different-coloured eyes.

"Knock, knock." Yoru Sulfur stepped into the room. He was neatly presented, as he had always been at meetings of the Solar Society. That same polite manner, that same unassuming smile. The only difference that he was spattered from head to toe with blood.

Savine took a quivering step back. These rooms were the best guarded in the Union. He must have come through several well-armed men. She presumed it was their screams she had heard, their gore with which he was showered.

He called himself a magus, but she had thought of it as a hollow title, left over from a distant age of ignorance and superstition. She knew that Bayaz had ruined the Agriont, but that had been before she was born. She had heard people whisper about Eaters, but written it off as small-minded fearmongering. Every day she had seen the dark outline of the House of the Maker, looming over even the city's tallest chimneys, but she had somehow allowed herself to believe that actual magic would never play a role in her thoroughly structured, ruthlessly rational, entirely modern life.

It was with a feeling of chill horror that she discovered her error.

Sulfur smiled at her father. The smile of a disappointed tutor, finally tracking down a wayward pupil. "Sand dan Glokta. You have become a difficult man to find."

"Did you try making an appointment?"

"You know I prefer to arrive unannounced." Sulfur rooted through his curly hair and picked something out between finger and thumb. A piece of bone. Perhaps a tooth. He flicked it away and it bounced clicking across the floor. "I warned my master you could not be trusted."

"What useful people can be?"

Sulfur smiled wider, showing a full set of clean, sharp teeth. "Do you know? Those were his very words." He glanced towards Savine, who was clinging to one of the handles of her father's chair, no idea whether to stand her ground, run for the children or scream for help. "Did you really think you could stuff King Jezal's bastard onto the throne without even a by-your-leave?"

"I did. I have."

"Doing it is one thing. Getting away with it is *quite* another. For a man who complains so much about pain you have been happy to inflict it wholesale." Sulfur gently wagged one finger as he padded across the room towards them. "All this *destruction*, just to end up trapped by your own cleverness."

"No doubt this is a trap." Glokta looked up mildly at Sulfur. "But not for me."

"What will you do, cripple? Wheel your chair over me?"

"You forget, I have some experience with your kind. The best weapon against an Eater...is another."

A latch dropped with a soft scrape and Sulfur froze in the middle of the floor.

Zuri had slipped in through the nursery door. Savine was about to scream at her to get out, to get help, but something stole her voice, so all that came out was a reedy squeak. Zuri's head hung over on one side, her teeth showing very white as she smiled too wide, her eyes gleaming black in the shadows.

"Someone has been a very bad boy," she said.

Sulfur spun towards the door he had come in through, but Haroon had entered from the hallway and now pushed it firmly shut. Rabik dropped from the shadows among the vaults above, spun in the air as neatly as an acrobat and landed silently on all fours. Savine had no idea how she could have failed to notice him, clinging to the ceiling. But she saw him now.

"It has been a long time, Sulfur," he sang, rocking back on his haunches.

"So much to answer for," said Haroon.

The shock on Sulfur's face only lasted for an instant. Then the air above his shoulders shimmered and Rabik was flung across the room as if by a slap from a giant's hand. Savine gasped as he crashed into the window in a spray of glass, bounced from the stone frame leaving a great crack. He should have been dead, every bone shattered. Instead he fell in a ready crouch like a cat dropped from a high place, dust showering from a great dry split in his cheek but his mouth still fixed in a smile.

Sulfur and Haroon were fighting, too fast for Savine's darting eyes to follow, a tangle of flailing limbs, blows landing with thuds and smacks so loud they were painful on the ear. Savine felt an awful sucking in her stomach and Haroon tumbled past like a cannon-stone, missed her by no more than a stride, smashed into the wall with an impact that showered plaster and made the whole room shake.

Savine clung to her father's chair, a great draft nearly dragging her over as Zuri whipped by in a white blur, crossing the room in two impossible strides, springing high into the air. Sulfur was turning, mouth twisted, arm raised, when she dropped on him with a crash like a thunderclap, buckling the polished floor, shattering the polished stones, chips of rock and spots of blood flying, sending out a wash of wind that rocked the painting on its easel.

There was a brilliant flash. Savine squeezed her eyes shut but still saw the bloom of fire through her lids, felt the heat of it stinging her face. She fell on her side, a roar all about her like a great furnace catching light. She coughed, retched, throat full of the acid tang of burning. Haroon was bent over her father's chair, shielding them both with his body, hair on fire, beard on fire, shirt turning black as it burned, hanging off his arms in flaming strips.

Savine tried to shield her face but her sleeve was on fire. She dragged herself up by the arm of her father's chair, saw the blanket across his knees was burning, too, ripped it from his legs, dragging him around a squealing quarter turn, beating at her sleeve with it, trying to smother the flames.

Little fires were scattered across the floor, blurred and sparkling through the tears stung from her eyes. Leo's ruined painting was scorching, canvas curling, the room crazily lit by flickering flames, cast into dancing shadow. Sulfur reeled and thrashed while Rabik clawed at him, bit at him, his hair turned to a burning torch. Sulfur flung him away but Rabik tore a mouthful of meat from his face as he went, ripping one of his ears half off, tumbling across the floor, spinning, sliding, fingernails squealing as they scored long scratches in the stones.

Sulfur crouched, breath coming in hisses, blood coursing from the bite-marks on his face, blood dripping from his fingertips and pattering on the broken flags.

He looked towards the window but Rabik was there, his bloody tongue hanging out. He looked towards the nursery but Haroon was there, giving a rumbling growl as he slapped ash from his body. He looked towards the hallway but Zuri was there. Her charred clothes dangled from her in tatters, and underneath her long limbs were bound in white bandages. She neatly blew out a flame still burning on her shoulder and clicked her tongue in annoyance.

"This was my favourite dress," she said.

Sulfur rounded on Savine and her father. She caught a glimpse of his bared teeth shining, his different-coloured eyes turned black in the dying firelight. The air about his shoulders shimmered once more and Savine took a whooping breath to scream.

Zuri caught him from behind like a trap snapping shut, one arm snaking around his neck, one around his chest, legs locked tight about his hips. He caught her hair but now Haroon was on him, gripping his wrist with one broad hand, his throat with the other. Rabik skittered up, wrapping himself around Sulfur's legs, all three of them pinning him fast.

Savine cowered behind her father's chair, staring between her fingers. Zuri twisted Sulfur's head back, one hand hooking his top jaw, one hooking the bottom. She snarled as she began to drag them apart, his eyes bulging, his mouth gaping wider and wider until with a snapping crunch she ripped his face wide open, blood showering, tearing his bottom jaw from his head until it hung on strings of gristle.

He made a gurgling hiss as he fell, and they swarmed on him with a crunching, ripping, cracking, blood spraying the broken floor, spotting the walls.

The whole impossible fight had only taken a few breaths.

"Out." Savine's father was tugging weakly at her charred sleeve. "Out."

Stupidly, she turned his chair, her shoes slithering on the smooth stones, leaving crooked tracks through the scattered ash and chips of masonry. She whimpered as she wheeled it to the door, got it caught on the frame, snarled as she wrestled it through into the great chamber, skinning her knuckles, the sound of ripping and gnawing echoing behind her.

She dragged the door shut and hung from the knob. Her eyes were swimming. Her legs wobbled. She could scarcely see through the smeared after-images across her vision, scarcely hear for the ringing in her ears. She stumbled, nearly fell, and someone caught her. Her mother. Holding her tight, stroking her head. Savine clung to her, making a little moan with every breath.

"Don't worry. The children are safe."

"Safe?" whispered Savine. Her hand was burned. The sleeve of her dress was scorched. The skin beneath tingled. Faint through the door, she could still hear them, eating. "Zuri is...Zuri is..."

"Yes. Did you think we picked her as your companion by accident?"

"You had to be protected," said Savine's father, baring the teeth he still had as he wheeled his chair towards her. "I made an arrangement with the only ones who could do it."

Savine stared from one parent to another. "You used me as *bait*. Me and my children—"

"We used ourselves as bait," said her mother.

"It had to be done, Savine," said her father.

"God smiles on results, my scripture teacher would have said."

Zuri shut the door behind her. Her dress hung singed and shredded and the bandages beneath were spotted red. Savine had never seen her so much as undo a top button before, had always taken that for fitting modesty, but without even knowing it the Burners had stumbled on the truth.

It was one of those moments—like the uprising in Valbeck, like the battle at Stoffenbeck—when Savine was forced to realise the world was not quite what she had thought it was. When the solid foundations were revealed to be shifting sands, and all her certainties no more than guesses. She wanted to back away. Wanted to run out into the hall and keep running. But she stood her ground. "Who was your scripture teacher?" she croaked.

"The Prophet Khalul," said Zuri, stepping into the room. "As you have no doubt guessed." Her hair had come unpinned on one side, hanging across her bloody face, her bloody chin, her bloody throat in a black curtain. "I wish I could have told you sooner."

"Is your name even Zuri?"

"I have had others, but I am Zuri now. I will be Zuri for as long as you need me."

"You were my friend," whispered Savine. She thought she might be crying. "My one real friend."

The slightest frown wrinkled Zuri's smooth brow as she came closer. "I still am. And you are mine."

"You...*eat* people."

"And you grind them to dust in your mills, and render them to meat on your battlefields, and let them rot when the sickness sweeps through your slums."

"I *trusted* you."

Zuri looked almost hurt by that. "And I have done my best never to let you down."

"Because of some deal with my father—"

"At first." Zuri flitted the last few strides towards her in a flash, a sudden chill breeze making Savine flinch. Zuri already had her hand in hers, so gentle but so strong, the black hair softly settling across her bloody face. "But soon I came to respect you, then to admire you, then... to love you." She reached up and delicately wiped a tear from Savine's cheek with her cool thumbtip.

"I am very old," she said. "I did not think I had anything to learn. But we have learned so much from you. Imagine a South and a Union not opposed but bound together by trade, and industry, and common interest. Not looking always into an ignorant and superstitious past but fixed on *progress*." Her black eyes shone at the thought. "A South and a Union where the people are governed not by the selfish whims of priests or wizards, but by the righteous engineering of the watch and the book."

"What would your scripture teacher think of that?" whispered Savine.

"It has been many years since I cared a *shit* for his opinions." And Zuri gave a little smile. Like a lover, venturing a joke so they could see if they were forgiven for some petty misdemeanour. By the Fates, could Savine still hear the faint cracking of bone from the room next door?

Her father, who had burned half the world so he could control the other half, put a hand on her wrist. "You need our advice."

Her mother, who had helped hatch the colossal scheme, put a hand on her shoulder. "You need our support."

Zuri smiled wider, her teeth still pink with Sulfur's blood. "You need our protection."

They were not wrong. The world might not have been quite what she thought but, above all, Savine had always been a woman of business. And a woman of business must adapt quickly to new circumstances and recognise a bargain when she sees it. She had handled difficult partners before, after all, and come out ahead.

She slid the box from her sleeve and took a healthy pinch of pearl dust up each nostril. Then another. Just to stop her hands from shaking. She wiped her nose carefully, dabbed her eyes on her unburned sleeve, pushed her chin up and her shoulders back, and managed something like a smile.

"Well," she said. "No one ever achieved anything alone."

# Great Men's Footsteps

Wasn't till Rikke was walking up the steep cobbled way from the harbour that she realised how much she'd missed Uffrith. Missed the sea's smell and the gulls' clamour. Missed knowing every street and face. Missed her father. His memory had been getting hazy, in the echoing space of Skarling's Hall, in the grand salons of Adua. Here it rushed back so sharp she wanted to cry.

For the first time in a long time, she felt like she was home.

She wandered beneath the carved rafters where she and Leo had sat together as children. Her fingertip left a snaking trail through the dust on the seat where her father had given his judgements. She stepped from the shadows and into the sunny garden, and dropped down on the time-greyed bench, frowning off towards the sea.

Spring had been busy. The garden was overgrown again, just like it always used to be, the stuff her father planted all erupted in a messy riot, nothing like his plans. A creeper had slipped free from the crumbling wall and spilled white flowers across his grave. He'd have laughed to see it, most likely, and said time makes fools of us all.

She thought of the girl she'd been, when Isern took her up into the hills to prove she had the Long Eye. Foolish and twitchy and soft. Ignorant about so many things. No bones and no brains, maybe, but a good heart. She touched her fingertips to the tattoos on her face. So much changed. She wondered if it was really for the better.

"Your father loved this plot." Shivers stood in the doorway, arms folded.

"Naught he liked more than sitting back and watching things grow," she said.

"It's grown, all right."

"Aye, well, he never had much time for weeding, what with all the wars he got dragged into."

"True enough. But you've made the whole North your garden now."

486

Shivers shook his head like he could hardly believe it. "Reckon he'd be proud."

"Would he? After all I've done? Black Rikke, they call me."

"A proud name."

"A name they hung on a killer 'cause he was the worst man in the North."

"It's just a name. It'll be what you make of it."

"Aye, I guess." And Rikke slumped with her elbows on her knees and her chin propped in her hands. "Did I do the right thing, Shivers?"

"You're asking the wrong man, I reckon."

"I'm asking the only one I trust."

"'Cause I done so much o' the wrong thing?"

"Shows you know the difference, don't it?"

"Not sure there is one." He sank down on the bench beside her. "It's a comfort, telling yourself there's some big right thing out there. That you could seek some wise old bastard in the mountains who's got the answer. Then there'd be no need for doubts and regrets." He looked sideways, sunlight glinting off his metal eye. "But far as I can tell it ain't that simple. Right things, wrong things, well... it's all a matter of where you stand. Every choice is good for some, bad for others. And once you're chief, you can't just do what's good for you, or those you love. You have to find what's best for most. Worst for fewest. Like your father tried to, and with no magic eye to see the outcome." He sat back, one leg stretched out, and looked towards the sea, breeze stirring the grey hair about his craggy face. "Doubts and regrets, they're the cost of casting a shadow. The only folk without 'em are the dead. For what it's worth, I'd say you did the best you could."

Rikke looked towards her father's grave and winced. "Then why does it hurt so much?"

"Said you did your best. Didn't say it wouldn't hurt. One thing I can tell you..." And he frowned down at that ring on his little finger. "Doing your worst feels no better."

"By all the fucking dead, don't tell me you're sitting here pining." Isern strutted into the garden, chagga squelch, squelching as she worked her jaw.

Rikke ground her own teeth. She was tiring of the sound of Isern-i-Phail being right. "Doubts and regrets, Isern. They're the cost of casting a shadow."

"Surely, but you've no time to indulge yours. You've the whole North to lead from the darkness and into the moon's silvery favour. Tell me this—what else could you have done?"

487

"Nothing," grunted Rikke, slumping further into her hands, flicking the ring through her nose with a fingertip so it knocked against her lip. "Nothing at all." Hadn't stopped her turning it over every spare moment since they set off from Adua. Didn't stop her turning it over now.

"Brought him back here?" sang Isern, in a voice leaking mockery. "Put a string on him like a puppy? How d'you keep a king o' the Union secret? He'd have drawn trouble like a ram's arse draws flies, d'you see. And folk here would've blamed you for that trouble and called you a selfish bitch thinking with her quim and said this is what you get when you're fool enough to put a woman in charge, and they'd have been right. Selfishness and folly. All we've worked for would've done like cake in a hailstorm and turned to soggy shit. This way you've got peace. And not just for you. Peace for all."

The same arguments Isern had whispered in her ear that morning, while Orso lay sleeping in her bed, helpless, all his trust put in her. She'd been right then, and she was right now, and Rikke knew it, and it only made her grind her teeth harder.

"I know that," she snapped. "Said there was nothing else I could've done, didn't I?"

"Then why d'you look like you ate a thistle?"

"I know it with my head."

"But what? Your heart hurts? Told you to make a stone of it, didn't I?"

"You might've uttered the phrase a time or two," growled Rikke.

Isern didn't notice her bubbling anger or, more likely, didn't care. "We need to get back to Skarling's Hall." And she planted her hands on her hips and frowned at the garden like it was a midden. "That's where the big choices are made. That's where Skarling turned down a crown and Bethod took one up. Where Black Dow stole the North from the Bloody-Nine. Where you stole it from Stour Nightfall. Every corner of the place, covered in great men's footsteps."

"No."

Rikke was shocked, almost, that she said it. But the moment she made the choice, she was sure of it. "The only place those great men's footsteps lead is round and round in circles of blood," she said. "The only history there is violence and betrayal. Send to Hardbread and the rest. Tell 'em I'm staying here."

"The North is ruled from Skarling's Chair."

"Same thing goes for great men's arses as great men's feet. It's just a chair."

"The North is ruled from Carleon," grumbled Isern, jutting her lip out in a mighty frown.

"It was. Now it'll be ruled from Uffrith. Close to the sea where we can reach out to other lands and I can take a paddle when I'm in the mood."

"Paddle, by the dead. Shivers, tell her."

But all Shivers did was shrug. "Great folk are great 'cause they plant new footsteps. Not 'cause they blunder through the same mistakes some other bastards made."

Isern made a long hiss of disgust. "Folk won't like it. Won't understand it."

"That's their lookout," said Rikke, waving it angrily away.

"It's a mistake."

"It's mine to make."

"You don't know what you—"

"Enough!" snarled Rikke, standing up tall and facing Isern, fists clenched. "I'm Black Rikke and I'm the one with the Long Eye! I'm the one killed Stour Nightfall. I'm the one beat Black Calder. *I* make the choices. Not you. *Me!*" She snarled it in Isern's face and stabbed at her chest with a finger. "If I choose to rule the North from a midden sitting on a piss-bucket, that's how it'll be. If I choose to follow the footsteps my father left in this garden, that's how it'll be. If I choose to make o' my heart a bleeding fucking sponge, then, by all the *dead*, Isern-i-Phail, *that*," and she spat the word like a curse, "is how it *will be!*"

There was a long silence, then. Just the gulls calling, and the sea rolling in, and the faint pulse of angry blood in Rikke's head. The smile started as a crinkle at the corners of Isern's eyes, then it spread to her mouth, to her cheeks, till it was right across her face. "Finally! I'd a worry you'd never get there."

Rikke closed her eyes. "So that was a bloody lesson, too, was it?"

"Aye, a little bit." Isern grinned as she offered out a chagga pellet. "With any luck the last you'll need."

Shivers slapped his thighs and stood with a grunt. "You really going to rule sitting on a piss-bucket?"

"Maybe I will," said Rikke, taking a breath and looking out to sea. "But tell Hardbread to bring Skarling's Chair down here, just in case."

# The Moment

Clover took a deep breath and thumped on the damp green copper with his fist. He waited. He knocked again. He became wetter and wetter in the mist from the river. He raised his arm to knock again. A narrow hatch snapped open, and a pair of rheumy eyes stared at him coldly from between thick bars.

"Who's this now?"

"Jonas Clover's my name."

"Jona-you-what?"

"Clover!" called Clover over the noise of rushing water. "I was sent for."

"Why?"

Clover wondered if he might've somehow come to the wrong place. "To teach sword-work, I was told. That's what I do. Teach sword-work." Well, that and betray employers, but that probably wasn't something a potential employer needed to hear.

"And what was the name again?"

"Jonas Clover!" he bellowed at the slot. Then added, quieter, "Used to be Steepfield."

"Steepfield, is it? You should have said."

Bolts clanked and the door creaked slowly open. An old man, bent under an old-fashioned suit of armour, frowned at him from the other side. He had a long sword far too heavy for him, point wobbling wildly as he strained to keep it level.

Clover held up his hands. "I surrender."

The ancient gatekeeper was not amused as he wrestled the door shut and fumbled with the bolts. "Like I haven't heard that before."

He made quite the performance of sheathing his sword then led Clover past a set of strange houses half-dug into the steep rocks, up a narrow valley and out into a wide yard. Three great, tapering towers were built into the mountainside ahead, joined at their bases but separating higher up, covered in dark ivy. They looked old. So old you might've thought the mountain had been built about them, rather'n the other way around.

"Quite a building to find all the way up here," said Clover.

"It's the Great Northern Library," grunted the gatekeeper. "Never seen a library before?"

"Honestly…no."

Folk were busy with everyday chores in the yard. A thin woman was washing clothes in a tub. A thickset old man was splitting logs with practised swings of an axe. A mass of books were heaped and spread on a table where a girl with a mop of blonde curls flicked at an abacus with quick fingers. No one really looked like they had a pressing need for instruction with the blade.

"Anyone ask for a sword teacher?" called Clover, hopefully.

"I did." The woodcutter neatly split one more log and left his axe buried in the block. He turned towards Clover, slapping dust from his hands. He looked maybe sixty but heavily built, with a strong face, deeply lined, and a close-cropped grey beard.

"By the dead," said Clover, finally placing him. "It's the First o' the Magi."

"None other." The afternoon sun shone brightly off Bayaz's tanned pate as he stepped forwards, took Clover's right hand in both of his and pressed it warmly. "Welcome to the Great Northern Library, Jonas Steepfield. I understand there is no man alive who knows more about sword-work."

Clover raised his brows. "That was a long time ago. Call myself Clover these days."

"Ah. I fear I am out of date in all manner of ways." And Bayaz smiled. A broad, white, beaming smile. His face lit up with friendly creases, but a hardness lingered around his eyes, deep-set and glistening green. Clover grinned back, but the conclusion he'd come to in Currahome—that Bayaz would be a bad enemy to have—was only reinforced. "The world moves along so quickly one can scarcely keep up."

"That why you keep the young folk around?" asked Clover, watching the blonde girl lick a finger and leaf frowning through one of the books.

"What is the point of gathering knowledge if one does not pass it on? What is the point of growing old if one does not try to shape the future?"

"That what you're doing here? Shaping the future?"

"Struggling to do so." The wizard sighed. "I confess it has not been easy lately. People, Master Clover, make wretched building material. People and their restless whims, and their *wilful* intransigence, and their *petty ambitions*." Bayaz bared his teeth, and Clover had to fight a strange desire to back away. "They simply *refuse* to see what is best for them. Imagine bricks that pounce on every opportunity to defy the architect and run off their own way."

"Frustrating," murmured Clover.

"But I never stop trying. Doing better next time, after all, that's what life is."

"I reckon." Honestly, Clover was somewhat troubled by the tone, along with the memory of Black Calder's nervous hand-wringing around the man. But then he'd been serving dangerous bastards all his life. A master no one fears won't take you far, and men who make the worst enemies, after all, can make the best friends. "I...er, have something for you."

"For me?" asked Bayaz.

"Black Rikke didn't want it, and I wouldn't know what to do with it, but I thought..." And Clover drew out the chain that Stour Nightfall once wore, that Scale Ironhand once wore, that Bethod once wore, gold gleaming in the afternoon sun. "Maybe you would."

"Why, Master Clover," breathed Bayaz as he took it, eyes fixed on the dangling jewel. "A gift fit for a king indeed! I know *just* the place for it, in good time."

Clover humbly shrugged. He was out of friends. If this bought him a safe place to sit, he'd consider it well worth the price. "Would've been poor manners to turn up empty-handed."

"Oh, we are of one mind!" said Bayaz, clapping a palm down on his shoulder and leading him across the yard towards the library. "Manners might be out of fashion in the North, but I want you to know that I appreciate them. Aided by people with good manners and good judgement, there is nothing that cannot be achieved. *This* promising young lady, for example, has but recently joined me." Gesturing towards the blonde girl as they passed. "She proves to have a humbling work ethic and a marvellous facility with numbers, so I am teaching her the mysteries of finance."

"What's that? A kind of magic?"

"A very powerful kind. The magic of *money*. Which do you think rings better—Hildi dan Valint or Hildi dan Balk?"

"What?"

"Magic and money are two things I know a little about," Bayaz was saying as he slipped Bethod's chain into a pocket. "Kings, also, are an area of some expertise. But I must confess that when it comes to sword-work, I have always relied on others."

"Lucky for me, I guess. Who's the student?"

Bayaz led him down a set of steps worn almost to a ramp by time, through a low archway and out onto a paved shelf on the mountainside. It had only a crumbling wall for a parapet and a grand valley was spread out beyond it, the lake stretching away like a grey mirror, forest and mountains reflected in its still surface.

A black-haired boy stood at the brink, framed by the view, scarred mouth fixed in a frown, arm up high, sword out straight, sinewy shoulders shining with sweat. He didn't move a hair. Not a quiver. Like a boy carved from wood. Clover got the sense he'd been there, still, for a very long time.

"I know this lad," he murmured, though you might've called him a young man, now. "Black Calder had him around. Who is he?"

"It is not so much who he *is* that interests me," said Bayaz, "as who he might become."

"Shaping the future, eh?"

"Precisely so." There were a few training posts set up about the little yard, and Bayaz rubbed thoughtfully at the deep blade-gnawing on the nearest one. "To my unpractised eye, he seems a more than passing swordsman already."

"I've seen him spar and never saw more promise at the business. The dead know I could use the work, but I'm not sure how much I've got to teach him."

"Oh, I think you know far more than you pretend to. I need him to learn not only *how* to use the sword, but *when*. I want you to teach him the warrior's lessons that his half-brother refused to learn. This is Jonas Clover!"

The lad slowly lowered the sword, and shook out his shoulders, and wiped sweat from his brow, and flicked it away, and finally looked over. "I remember."

"I have brought him here to teach you sword-work."

The lad didn't laugh, at least. Just gave Clover a long look with those pale eyes, like he was the master and Clover the pupil he was thinking of taking on.

"I will leave the two of you to get acquainted." Bayaz leaned close and gave Clover's shoulder a parting pat. "Dinner in an hour."

They stood there, in silence, for a while, and the wind came up from the valley and stirred the grass in the cracks between the stones. Then Clover planted his hands on his hips and grinned out towards the lake. "Quite the view. I could look at that all day."

The lad didn't speak.

Clover wandered to the wall of the library, so ancient and lichen-covered that it looked to be one with the mountainside, put his back to it and slid down till his arse hit the ground. "What should I call you?"

The lad shrugged.

"You've got a scarred lip," said Clover, settling himself back against the old stones, warm from a day in the sun. "I could call you shit-mouth. How about that?"

The lad shrugged again.

"I'm not really going to call you shit-mouth. That was a test."

"Did I pass?"

"You did."

"I didn't do anything."

"That's why."

The lad frowned down at him, sword hanging from his hand.

"You look puzzled," said Clover.

"A warrior hits first," said the lad, like they were words he'd learned by heart. "Hits hardest. A warrior has his sword always in his hand."

Clover slowly nodded. "I can think of plenty of warriors who'd agree. Great fighters. Famous names. Shama Heartless, you ever hear o' him?"

"Aye," said the lad.

"Black Dow, or the Bloody-Nine?"

"'Course," said the lad.

"How about Stour Nightfall?"

The lad narrowed his pale eyes a little.

"Can you tell me what all those fearsome bastards have in common?"

There was a pause, then, and a bird nesting somewhere among the library's roofs tooted gently at the dreamy afternoon.

"Dead," said the lad.

Clover grinned. "I can't tell you what a pleasure it is to have a quick pupil. The swordsman's greatest ambition, if you're asking me, should be not to join those heroes in the mud."

"We all meet the Great Leveller."

"'Course we do." Clover sat forwards to shrug his cloak off, the wolfskin cloak Stour used to wear, a touch bedraggled now from hard use, and started rolling it up. "But I'd favour putting him off as long as possible. How about you? Planning to rush at him, trousers down?"

The lad's black brows drew in slightly as he thought about it.

"In the end . . . the only thing a man can really do . . . is pick his moment. Watch for the opening, and recognise it when it comes, and seize it." And Clover snatched at a handful o' nothing and shook his fist. "Picking your moment. *That's* the secret. You understand?"

494

The boy nodded, solemn as a grave-guest, and it seemed like all the wisdom Stour wouldn't take in a hundred tellings this lad sucked straight up like a sponge. "I think so."

"I think so, too. Now why don't you show me your fearsome skills on one o' them posts?"

Clover shoved the roll he'd made of his cloak behind his head as a pillow, and he crossed one boot over the other. He watched the lad's sword darting. He watched the blade flash and flicker. He watched the evening sun gleam on the lake.

"That's good!" he called. "That's damn good. Pick your moment." And Clover gave a contented sigh, and closed his eyes. Listened to that bird tooting high above. Listened to the wind whispering in the grass. Listened to the click and scrape of steel on wood.

Could've worked out worse, he supposed.

# A Little Private Hanging

I t was a highly exclusive affair.

No carnival atmosphere. No crowds of baying commoners. Certainly no tittering whores in attendance. A small cobbled yard behind the House of Questions, rather than one of the wide public squares in the heart of the city. The tone was sombre, one would have to say. But for Orso to lift the mood seemed a lot to ask.

"I bloody hate hangings," he said, frowning up at the scaffold.

The innovations had all been rolled back. No pulleys, no cranes, no machinery. They were gone the way of Risinau, and Judge, and the Commons' Round, and the People's Inspectorate, and the Great Change as a whole. Just the gallows, and a rope, and a trapdoor, and a lever to open it.

And a prisoner to hang, of course. It would be a hell of a poor occasion without one of those.

A gentle breeze washed through the yard, hardly any smoke on the air, and it tasted sweet. Perhaps your last breaths always do. Orso wasn't afraid. Not even watching the noose gently swing. But then he'd always had a habit of being brave at the least appropriate times. He had blundered blindly from one mistake to another, buffeted by forces he had barely perceived, let alone understood, like a blind man in a prizefight. There was so much he had failed at. So often he had disappointed. This, at least, he was determined to do well.

"No point hanging around, is there?" he said, and he left the guards behind him and trotted jauntily up the steps.

He had tried to do the right thing, he thought, in his own rather ineffectual way, but it was strange how circumstances would rarely let one be the hero, however much one might want to be. However much one might deserve to be. Still, no doubt everyone thinks they are entitled to the prizes. The Young Lion had no doubts about it, that was clear.

He still looked somewhat leonine, if you squinted, but *young* had become a hell of a stretch. There was a premature greying to that golden hair and beard. A leaching out of all his colour. He had an expression of well-earned satisfaction as he watched Orso climb the scaffold. One might have liked to blame it on a total lack of empathy or imagination, but the truth, as everyone knew, was that Leo dan Brock knew exactly how it felt to face the noose.

Some people, Orso supposed, can never forgive being forgiven.

The Lord Regent glanced sideways at his wife, like a winning squares player at their beaten opponent.

But Savine did not meet his eye. Most observers might have thought she was relaxed, a wealthy patron in her box at the theatre. But Orso knew her better than that. Better than anyone, maybe. He saw the muscles of her jaw clenching. Her knuckles white with pressure on the rail. He knew at a glance this was as much of a shock to her as to anyone.

He smiled at her, and she smiled back. A small smile, at the corner of her mouth, but he saw it. He knew what it meant. Perhaps every person is alone, in the end. But in that moment, it seemed they understood each other. Forgave each other. Loved each other still, perhaps, even now. He did not think he had ever let her down. Not in any of the ways that really mattered. That was something. Then she swallowed, and looked to the ground, and the moment was gone.

Orso doubted he would share a profound last glance with any of the other attendees. Lords Isher and Heugen looked smug, but if you let other people's smugness make you angry you'll be angry all the time. Brock's men Jurand and Glaward looked sombre. Decent enough people, probably, if they'd had a different master. You find decent people on every side, after all, as Orso's father had been fond of saying. It was a surprise to see Selest dan Heugen, more soberly dressed than had been her habit, but some people seem always to float to the top. Then there was a bony man Orso only vaguely recognised wearing Arch Lector's white. And there was Curnsbick looking slightly ill, and that fellow with the big jowls, and that fellow with the pointy nose who had once been in the King's Own, what the hell were their names?

It had been impossible to predict even six months ago but these, it seemed, were the winners. Those who would steer the Union into the future. Each with their talents, their rivalries, their ambitions. Probably no worse than his own Closed Council had been. Probably no better than the Closed Councils of his father, of King Guslav, King Casamir, King Arnault, and all the way back to the first Harod, namesake of the new.

"I must admit it's a rather disappointing turnout," called Orso. "Still,

I understand. I've always hated hangings myself. And here's one I'm particularly reluctant to attend!" He barked a laugh. No one joined him. "Dear me. Who would've thought *I'd* be the only one to keep my sense of humour?"

Tricky, with his hands tied, but he managed to nudge the executioner in the ribs with his elbow. "Lovely day for it, at least." He squinted up at the blue sky. The few shreds of cloud, slowly shifting. "Looks like it'll be a fine summer." It made him terribly sad, suddenly, to think he wouldn't see it. He covered it up with a chuckle. "For you, at least."

The executioner, somewhat apologetically, offered him a hood.

"Thank you, but no. I've attended a few of these things. Let's not pretend that's for my benefit." Damn, he wanted to scratch his nose, but his hands were tied behind his back. He wriggled it a little, but that only made it worse. Ridiculous, to die with an itchy nose. He raised his brows significantly. "I don't suppose you could just—"

The executioner squinted through his eyeholes as he gently scratched the rim of Orso's nostril.

"Ah, that's good. A little to the right... perfect."

The man reached up, pulled down the noose, secured it around Orso's neck.

"Nice and tight, there's a good fellow." Orso winked at him. "So hard to find a good valet these days."

The Young Lion looked somewhat nettled. "Have you anything to say?" he snapped.

"Too much, usually," called Orso, "but I'll try to keep it brief, I know you have a country to ruin." The trapdoor creaked under his feet as he stepped forwards.

"Don't grieve for me!" He glanced about the audience, brows high. "No? No one? The truth is, at my best, I've been a barely adequate king. My father's son, I daresay. Though allow me to take just a little pride in my victory against the odds at Stoffenbeck. Unfortunate timing, to take the throne with not one but two bloody revolts on the way, but that's no excuse, really. There's always something horrible on the way, after all. You'll see. Not that I bear any of you ill will, you understand. Ill will is too heavy a thing to carry through life, let alone up onto a scaffold, and it's useless in a fight in any case."

Out of the corner of his eye, he saw the executioner wrap his hands around the lever.

"Well! I think I'm being given the signal to finish up. To my sister, Savine..." He grinned over at her. The way he used to, when they were together, in Sworbreck's office. When he had just thought of the best joke. One he knew she would love. That was how he wanted her to think of him. As he had been. As they had been. "I take some comfort in knowing you'll be a far better ruler than I ever was. We have had our differences, but you remain the woman I most admire. And, let's be honest, the only one I've ever loved." He was gratified to see a tear slide down her cheek. It was not as if it had all been worth it, for one tear, but it was something. He grinned at the Lord Regent. "To her husband, Leo dan Brock, I can only say...how's your leg?"

He gave one last chuckle, and it became a sigh. "Let's get on with it," he said.

There was a clatter as the trap dropped open.

# The Villain

Leo had won.

He'd faced crushing defeats. He'd suffered terrible losses. But he'd won a victory bigger than anyone could've believed. He sat at the head of the Closed Council. The most powerful man in the Union. In the Circle of the World, maybe. Who'd dare deny it?

The Burners had used the White Chamber as a stable. A little fuck yourself from Judge to the old regime which had left the place smelling faintly of horse however thoroughly it was scrubbed. The table and chairs were the same ones King Jezal's Closed Council had used—as battered and scarred as Leo was—but he'd ordered them left in their places. A timely reminder to anyone he let sit in here that they could always be replaced.

The chosen few filed in respectfully. First came Leo's old friends, Lord Chamberlain Jurand and Lord Marshal Glaward. They sat down grinning on his left and right and Leo grinned to see them there. It reminded him for a moment of those high old times. Until he remembered everything he'd sacrificed to win. Everyone he'd sacrificed. He wished Antaup, and Jin, and Barniva, and Ritter were there, too. But wishing does no good.

Lord Admiral Heugen and Lord Chancellor Isher were the next to enter, sporting more gold thread between them than a set of palace curtains, uniforms as splendid as their military records were wretched. The best men on the Open Council. Or at any rate the best runners.

Two bureaucrats followed. Victarine dan Teufel's sudden disappearance—to the bottom of the canal, he hoped—had left the Arch Lector's chair open for Lorsen, Superior of Westport, who seemed a man untroubled by conscience. High Consul Flassenbeck was one of the few officials of the old government lucky and cunning enough to tiptoe alive through the purges. They were hardly the sort of men that Leo admired, but he supposed someone had to take care of the details, and luck, cunning and lack of conscience were certainly qualities his new Union would need.

Finally came the four freshly minted Ministers. People who understood the modern world, supposedly. Jurand had pleaded with Leo to give Savine that much, and pointed out the magic she'd worked on the government of Angland, and in the end he'd grudgingly admitted it made sense. Inventors and industrialists in shiny civilian clothing and, at the back, having toned down the bosom somewhat but still smelling strongly of roses, none other than Selest dan Heugen. A woman in the White Chamber would've caused uproar a few years ago, but *progress* and all that. Leo saw no harm in having something ornamental to look at as long as she remembered her place.

He winced as they grovelled their greetings and slipped into their seats. He'd won. There was no denying it. But the stump of his leg hurt no less. His metal-riddled arm felt no more. There was that same bitter tang in the gap in his teeth. His temper, if anything, was shorter than ever.

He'd won, but it was nothing like his victory over Stour Nightfall in the Circle. No adoration from the crowds, only fear and suspicion. No surge of joy, only a nagging dissatisfaction. No hugs from his friends. He'd led most of them to their deaths.

He was surprised when he heard the door shut and the Lady Regent glided in. She could barely stand to look at him these days, let alone spend time in the same room. The way things were, he'd have been shocked if they ever fucked again, but he didn't miss it. Since he lost his leg it had gone from what felt like work to what felt like humiliation. She could keep her quim to herself, and he'd take everything else, and consider it a fair division of the assets.

"Joining us, Your Highness?" he asked.

"Since there is a seat free." She calmly met his eye as she arranged herself with even more than usually regal bearing in the tall chair at the foot of the table. The one that for centuries had sat empty for the First of the Magi. "Not expecting Bayaz, are we?"

Those might've been the first words they'd exchanged since the hanging. The slightest thaw in the winter of their marriage? Or more likely her ruthless, realistic self was worming its way back to the surface, and she was making the best of what she couldn't change. She'd always been a woman who liked to win. But if she intended to fight him now, she'd better get used to the taste of dirt.

"I think we're all here." Leo sat forwards, setting his clenched fist on the table. "We have a new Closed Council. Young. Hungry. A dozen men—and women—ready to reforge the Union for a new age."

There was polite applause. From everyone except Savine. She sat with that icy dignity she specialised in, glaring down the long table at Leo as though she could taste piss. But he wasn't about to let her wounded fucking feelings spoil his moment.

"It grieves me to say that the nation is *weak*," he growled, grinding his fist into the wood. "The rot was already setting in long before the Great Change. The army is in demoralised tatters. We have to give the men back their pride! Their purpose!"

Glaward clapped his hands. "Well said, Your Highness."

"We could start by returning the Square of Marshals to its former glory. Those names underfoot are…an ugly reminder of things better forgotten. The ruined flagstones must be replaced so we can have drills, parades, manoeuvres, demonstrations of the Union's strength—"

"I feel that would be a mistake," said Savine.

Leo licked sourly at the hole in his teeth. "You shock me."

"It should remain the Square of Martyrs," she said, holding his eye in a challenge he did not at all appreciate. "If we sponge away the evidence of our failures, how are we ever to learn from them? We should leave the names of those who died for the Great Change and add the names of those who died in it. Let us commemorate the horrors of the old regime and the new, in the hope that we shall never repeat them. We must have a *better* Union." Her knuckles were white as she clenched her own fist on the tabletop. "It cannot all be for nothing. It *cannot*."

There was a thoughtful silence, then Curnsbick slowly nodded. "*Very* well said, Your Highness."

Leo frowned sideways at Jurand. He was looking back earnestly, his brow lightly wrinkled, like a puppy begging for a treat. The look he always used to have, when Leo's mother voiced some guff that he agreed with.

"Well." Leo worked his mouth, then with an effort forced his lips into the thinnest of smiles. "Far be it from me to deny the Darling of the Slums a sentimental gesture or two. Call the place whatever you like. The larger point remains. We face threats on every border. Our fortresses are neglected and our navy outdated. The first order of business must be the reinforcement and renewal of the king's military—"

"The Lord Regent makes an excellent point," interrupted Savine, "which is why our *first* order of business must be money. King Jezal's administration made many blunders, but their worst was spending what they did not have."

Everyone turned to look at Leo. "We all know that," he grunted. He needed no lecture on not making the same mistake twice.

"As a solid financial foundation we need a new system of taxation," said Savine. "Minister for Revenue Vallimir?"

"Sweeping reform, root and branch." Vallimir began to hand out neatly bound sheaves of printed paper. Down at that end of the table, it seemed they'd come armed. "You will see various proposals here. Increased levies on land and wealth, abolition of privileged categories and venal offices, tariffs on mercantile and industrial activity, strong measures against corruption."

"We cannot look back," said Curnsbick, peering over his eye-lenses. "We must avoid the ruinous debts which poisoned King Jezal's reign."

"The Great Change freed us from the tyranny of the banks, at least," observed Kort.

Isher leafed through the papers with an ever-deeper frown. "Only to chain us all under the yoke of the tax collector?"

They began to argue, and tediously. Proportions, allowances, exemptions. Leo scarcely understood the issues. It almost made him wish he'd paid closer attention to his mother during those boring meetings of his council back in Angland. But not quite.

He sank into his chair, wishing he'd brought wine. He belonged in the saddle. Or perhaps some kind of open carriage would be less painful? He belonged near other men in the saddle, anyway. His eyes drifted sideways to Jurand. On campaign, with the wind behind them and an enemy in front, calling for the charge with a sword in his hand!

"We need money to rebuild," Kort was saying.

"To modernise," said Curnsbick.

"To mount a summer fencing Contest this year?" offered Selest. "A beloved tradition to give the people inspiration, reassurance and common purpose."

"An excellent idea," and Savine tapped the table approvingly with her fingertips.

Leo smashed it with his fist, jerking the faces back towards him where they belonged.

"We need money for our forces! Cannons. Ships. What use is progress if it can't be made into a weapon? Union arms must be *respected* again. We have to strangle our enemies at sea and crush them on land. We need to be *feared*." Smashing the table had worked once so he did it again, even harder, making a heap of papers slump over in front of Kort. "We should press a claim on the city of Sipani."

There was a nervous silence. The High Consul cleared his throat. "On what basis, Your Highness?"

"You'll think of something."

Loaded glances crossed the table. "But...Sipani has long been considered neutral."

"The Snake of Talins once captured the city," grumbled Lorsen, "but even she did not presume to keep it. We would provoke a furious response from the Styrians—"

"I'm bloody *counting* on it," said Leo.

Glaward and Heugen nodded along, but even Jurand didn't look convinced. He'd gone from the bloody begging look to the bloody pained look. Next he'd be quoting Stolicus on the virtues of patience.

Savine looked evenly at him down the table. "King Jezal fought three wars against the Styrians. All he achieved was to waste millions, kill thousands and pour the Union's prestige down the sewer. We must modernise our military, undoubtedly. We must protect our interests, of course. But we have far more to gain through trade with Styria than war. I suggest we invite King Jappo on a state visit to Adua to discuss areas of mutual interest—"

"What mutual interest could we have with that fucking degenerate?" sneered Leo.

"Styria is a growing market," observed Kort, jowls wobbling.

"Tremendous opportunities," burbled Curnsbick.

"It could be...a pragmatic solution," grated Arch Lector Lorsen.

Savine shrugged. "Sometimes there are better ways to get what you want than through force."

Perhaps there were, but Leo wasn't interested in them, and he certainly wasn't interested in wasting more breath on the subject. "Let's put it to a vote," he snapped. "Those in favour of laying claim to Sipani?"

He threw up a careless hand and arms shot up along with it. Jurand's, Glaward's, Lord Heugen's...but that was all. Further down the table, no one moved. Leo stared at them, unable to believe it. It was like Stoffenbeck all over again, looking out as the sun came up, sure of victory, and finding to his cold dismay the enemy had been reinforced.

As if to rub it in, Savine let the silence stretch a few more awkward moments before she calmly spoke. "Those in favour of a state visit?"

Hands went up more slowly, but no less decisively, and there were a lot more of them. It was no surprise that Savine's four stooges might want to vote her way, but it was a shock they had the guts to do it. It was an even bigger one that Flassenbeck and Lorsen might dare to defy him, but Leo supposed you should never trust bureaucrats, especially those who've survived purges. It was the final betrayal that truly beggared belief, though.

Lord Chancellor Isher, in the seat Leo had just given him, politely raised his braid-heavy arm.

"What do you think you're doing?" whispered Leo.

Isher cleared his throat. "Agreeing with Her Highness the Lady Regent," he droned, careful not to meet Leo's eye. "We have far more to gain through trade with Styria than war."

Meaning *he* had more to gain. Leo wanted to call him a backstabbing coward to his face, then demand to know what Savine had bribed him with, but he was so flabbergasted he couldn't find the breath. He looked across at Jurand, and Jurand stared back, pale with shock. Evidently this was one outflanking that a careful study of Stolicus hadn't prepared him for.

"Eight to four in favour of a state visit," said Savine, making a neat little note. "High Consul Flassenbeck, would you summon the Styrian ambassador so we can advance a formal invitation to King Jappo? Then Lady Selest, could you liaise with my private secretary Zuri on an agenda for the talks—"

"What the *fuck*?" snarled Leo, spraying spit.

Another silence, even more awkward than the last. Savine went on writing for a moment, then looked up from her papers. "Perhaps the Closed Council might give His Highness and I a moment to confer?"

By the speed they scrambled from their seats, they were desperate to do exactly that.

With one nervous backward glance, Selest dan Heugen pulled the door to the White Chamber shut, leaving Savine alone with her husband.

She could not help shifting in that uncomfortable bloody chair at a sudden pang. With impeccable timing, her menses had come for the first time since she fell pregnant and just as painfully as ever, the familiar dull ache through her belly and down the backs of her thighs with an occasional sharp twinge into her arse by way of light relief. As she always used to, she struggled with every muscle to look perfectly relaxed, and forced her grimace into an expression of quiet dignity.

"Do you think I'll let you steal this from me?" whispered Leo, white with fury.

Savine had no doubt that he had become a very dangerous man. She remembered seeing him stab Lord Marshal Forest in the chest without a hint of hesitation. But she had faced dangerous men before. Preparation was the key. That and never backing down.

"Steal this? The Union, you mean?" Savine spoke slowly, precisely, like a schoolteacher explaining arithmetic to a pupil prone to tantrums. Perhaps that would only enrage him further. She rather hoped so. "It is not *yours*, Leo. It belongs to our son, the king. We are merely the caretakers. The *joint* caretakers."

He clawed at the table, catching some papers and crushing them in his trembling fist. He might only have the one that worked, but she knew how strong it still was. "Get out," he snarled through gritted teeth.

Savine set her jaw. "Let me be blunt. You will beat me in a foot race before you remove me from this chamber."

"*I* am in command here—"

"Are you sure? I begin to think you did not read the Open Council's Grand Declaration very carefully. I wrote it carefully, I promise you that. It gives me exactly the same rights, privileges and powers as you. Matters of policy are decided by votes in this council and, as you see, the strong majority are on my side."

"Then I'll remove them."

"Until His Majesty reaches his majority you cannot remove them without my approval, as I could not appoint them without yours."

"Then I'll march a company of soldiers in here!" He had become even paler. The skull-like rings around his eyes reminded her more than was comfortable of her father. But while her father had done awful things, he had stopped short of having heroic paintings made of them. "We'll see which way these bastards vote with drawn swords at their necks."

Savine narrowed her eyes. "You will beat me at left-handed darts before you do *that*. You should know that I have made *comprehensive* arrangements. Try to seize power and the coal will stop coming, and the bread will stop coming, and the money will stop coming. I'll chain you up in strikes and riots. I'll bury you in a blizzard of pamphlets. Have you seen how popular I am these days? Threaten the Mother of the Nation? Depose the Darling of the Slums? You'd have another Great Change on your hands, supposing the army fought for you. But bear in mind, their oath isn't to you, it's to the king. And you are not king, Leo. You're less king than I am."

There was a brooding silence as they glared at one another down the length of that battered table, in the dingy, stuffy, faintly horse-smelling room that was the very pinnacle of power.

"So you've stabbed me in the fucking back." His voice had a wounded whine to it. "My own wife. I should have left you to the Burners."

It was his bad luck that this reinvention of the past coincided with a particularly savage cramp, as if there was a fist clenching around her guts. She jerked forwards, showing him her teeth. "You fucking *did*, you treacherous *shit*! And then you seized the throne against my wishes, and then you killed my brother, and now I'll make you pay the *fucking* bill!"

As she snarled the words his expression changed from fury, to amazement, and ended in a joyless bark of laughter. "Oh, so *I'm* the villain? Funny what we forget, isn't it? Remember *our* rebellion? I wanted to change the Closed Council but leave Orso on the throne! That's what you told me *you* wanted. And the Darling of the Slums wouldn't lie to her own husband, would she?"

Savine swallowed, and said nothing.

Leo stabbed with a finger at Isher's empty chair. "Because the flexible Lord Isher told me a different story. That you agreed with him Orso would be quietly shuffled off, so *you* could be queen. And that wasn't the only deal you made behind my back, was it? I thought it was strange how Stour just…" And he snapped his fingers. "Changed his mind about helping us! No wonder, since you offered him Uffrith!"

Savine had to stop herself grimacing. But her husband had not finished listing her crimes.

"When we hanged your precious brother, I didn't hear you begging for his life. You *knew* it had to be done. You knew, but you wanted someone to blame. Do you believe your own lies, or just pretend to? The *hypocrisy*!" And he clutched at the tabletop, wrenched at it as though he'd rip it off. "How can you sit there with a straight face, talking of the horrors of the old regime? You *were* the old regime! It was your own father who carved those names into the Square of Martyrs! No one profited more than you and no one cared less! Now you *dare* to put on a white dress and preach to me that it can't all be for *nothing*? Play the saint of Adua out there if you please, Savine," he sneered at her, "but in here let's not embarrass ourselves. You can call me treacherous. Call me ruthless. But ask who I learned it from."

Another brooding silence as they glowered at each other from the hard chairs to which their ambitions had swept them. Then, for once, Savine let her shoulders drop.

"You're right," she said, wincing as she tried to press at her aching belly through her corset. He was right, after all. "Maybe…I came to regret the things I had done, and so I hated to see you do the same. The truth is I played my part in it all. The lead role, even. I schemed and lied and betrayed. And you are the one who has paid the price. You, and Orso, and all those I ground to dust in my mills, and turned to meat on my battlefields, and let rot in my slums. I am sorry for that. Sorry for Orso and sorry for you. Sorry for all of it...but...thinking now, if I had the same choices to make...I cannot say I would not do it all again." She met his eyes, and gave a little shrug. "Maybe, after all...I'm the villain."

Leo glared at her from the other end of the table. "So. You'll back down about Sipani?"

"Oh, no. I won't back down about anything."

He stared a moment longer, mouth slightly open. Then he sagged in his chair. "Is this how it always is? You get what you wanted, but somehow it's not what you wanted at all? Every victory turns out to be just another kind of defeat?"

He looked so withered, so ruined, she was caught between disgust and pity. She could not forgive him, but she knew she had helped make him what he was. For better or worse, they were shackled together. She put aside her anger and gave a weary sigh.

"This is not a victory or a defeat, Leo, it is a marriage." Now she slipped the box from her sleeve and took a pinch up one nostril. "I suggested to you, before our wedding, that you should look on it as a business relationship." She smothered a sneeze. "I suggest you continue to do so. Partners need not see eye to eye on every point. They can even, frankly, detest each other on a personal level." She took a pinch up the other nostril. "But sensible ones collaborate, for the good of the business. I suggest we collaborate, for the good of our children. They need their father. For the good of the Union. It needs its champion." She dabbed her nose clean. "We have the chance to do so much good together. It would be a crime to throw it away simply because we cannot agree." And she closed the box with a snap.

"I'll fight you, if I must." Leo shifted his useless left arm in his jacket. "I've never backed down from a fight."

"Please." Savine suppressed a wince at another twinge in her belly. "This is no storybook. You might not be the villain but you're for damn sure not the hero." She forced her shoulders back, and her smile back on. "Selest!"

The door opened a crack to show the well-powdered face of the new Minister for Commerce. "Your Highness?"

"Bring the Closed Council back in. We have work to do."

# Curses and Blessings

In the blackness of the night the Long Eye opened, and she saw it all. She saw a bald weaver, and the work on his loom was all in ruins, a million threads hanging severed. But he was stitching it back together, patience, patience, and smiling as he worked. He put out his hands, and one fell on the head of a black-haired boy, and the other on the head of a blonde-haired girl.

She saw the girl become a laughing woman, flashing lenses on her eyes, a tall hat perched on her golden curls, and the hat belched smoke, spat ash, blotted out the bleeding sun and cast the world into twilight. She blew a kiss, and the kiss became a coin, a thousand coins, a million golden chains. She offered her hand, and the fingers became iron rails, and the rails reached across the sea and made a cage, the cage that Stour had forged, and the whole North was inside.

She saw the black-haired boy became a black-haired man, and he sat on a hill of bones in a circle of fire with a grey sword across his knees, a grey sword never sheathed, a grey sword marked with one silver letter. His scarred mouth spoke, but his words were drops of blood that made a stream, that became a river, that became a sea that broke upon the beaches of the North. A tide of blood. A flood whose red waters would not recede.

She saw the Crinna boil. She saw Uffrith burn again. She saw the graves open and spew up the dead. She saw Skarling's Chair split in two and the broken wood bleeding. She saw a plague of worms writhe in the poisoned fields. She saw a plague of crows shower from the bare trees and blot out the moon, sink the world in darkness.

And in the darkness she saw a bald weaver, and in his eye she saw a burning stone, and in the burning stone she saw a circle of runes, and in the circle of runes she saw a black door, and beyond the door a figure rose from the seething sea, a figure made of blinding light, and his feet left smouldering footsteps in the shingle, and he spoke in thunder.

"I am returned."

Rikke tore free of the furs on her father's bed and crouched in the darkness, trembling, gasping, the sweat of her vision clinging cold to her and her left eye burning hot as a coal in her tattooed face.

She couldn't say whether the Long Eye was a blessing for giving her this warning, or a curse that she would wake every day in terror of what she'd seen.

Maybe the truth was it was both. It had always been both.

"You look like you saw the dead," said Isern-i-Phail, frowning at her as she dropped into Skarling's Chair.

"I did," whispered Rikke. The light from the great new windows she'd had built, with their fine view of the ocean, stabbed at her eyes. The sounds of Uffrith beyond hammered at her ears. Flashes of what she'd seen the night before lurked at the edges of her sight. Seen as if they were already done. She closed her eyes, the one that saw nothing and the one that saw too much, and wiped the greasy sheen from her forehead.

Her father's hall was busy. Folk from every corner of the North, come to pay their respects.

"People," she said, but her voice died in her throat and became a croak. "People!" And they stopped their chatter and looked around, shifting eagerly towards her. "In the night, I had a vision!"

There was a hushed murmur at that. An awestruck murmur, like she spoke with the voice of Euz.

Shivers frowned at her, his metal eye twinkling. "What did you see?"

Rikke hardly knew how to start. Her heart was thumping at the splintered memories of it. She opened her mouth to speak—

Then the doors to Skarling's Hall shuddered open and the Nail stomped in out of the brightness, with a new cut down his cheek which rather suited him and a great smile on his face which suited him even better. "Ollensand surrendered!"

"You beat 'em?" asked Hardbread.

"Didn't have to," said the Nail, slapping him on the shoulder with one big hand and near knocking him down. "They opened their gates to us. And we were gentle with 'em, don't worry! All we took was their promise to kneel and pay their tithes to Black Rikke." He gave a shrug. "Well, that and one other thing freely given..." And he waved towards the door, and a set of Carls came in, each rolling a great cask ahead of him. "A dozen barrels of their best ale so we could toast the new North!"

And they hefted one of the barrels onto the table while folk whooped and cheered and one of 'em banged the peg out with his axe and sent a jet of frothy beer spurting, a couple of folk dancing in the foam till Hardbread had a tap knocked into the spouting hole and started handing out cups.

"Not only that!" growled Flatstone, following the Nail into the hall with grinning men at his back, "but we sent the last o' those savages back across the Crinna, crying for his mummy. Reckon it'll be a good few years 'fore those bones-and-hides bastards dare to stick a toe on our side o' the river."

More cheers, and more ale, and more good news. "The North's ours!" roared the Nail. "Well, yours." And he grinned at Rikke, then it seemed as if he might be blushing, and he scratched his sandy beard, and looked down at the floor. No one much noticed, though, all too busy slapping each other on the back, and marvelling at how everything had come out right.

They all looked so happy. Faces Rikke was used to seeing stamped with fear or sadness. One old bird who'd lost two sons in the last war had tears on her cheeks. Even Caul Shivers was smiling.

"The North's united," he whispered, like it was a puzzle he couldn't solve. "From the Crinna to the Whiteflow. By the dead, your father would be proud."

Rikke thought of her father, then, sitting on his bench, rubbing his grizzled jaw. Making the hard choices so his people wouldn't have the trouble of 'em. Bent under a load of other folk's fears so they wouldn't have to carry their weight.

Isern-i-Phail was showing her missing tooth in a girlish grin. "Always knew we'd get great things from you, Rikke. But I'll confess I never expected half o' this. Not a quarter. Now then." And she offered out a chagga pellet. "What was this vision o' yours?"

Rikke blinked at her, and at the happy room. Then she took the pellet, and stuck it up behind her lip. She forced a queasy smile onto her face.

"Nothing," she said. "All good."

# Acknowledgments

As always, four people without whom:

Bren Abercrombie, whose eyes are sore from reading it.
Nick Abercrombie, whose ears are sore from hearing about it.
Rob Abercrombie, whose fingers are sore from turning the pages.
Lou Abercrombie, whose arms are sore from holding me up.

Then, my heartfelt thanks:

To all the lovely and talented people in British publishing who have helped bring the First Law books to readers down the years, including but by no means limited to Simon Spanton, Jon Weir, Jen McMenemy, Mark Stay, Jon Wood, Malcolm Edwards, David Shelley, Katie Espiner and Sarah Benton. Then, of course, all those who've helped make, publish, publicise, translate and above all *sell* my books wherever they may be around the world.

To the artists responsible for somehow continuing to make me look classy: Didier Graffet, Dave Senior, Laura Brett, Lauren Panepinto, Raymond Swanland, Tomás Almeida, Sam Weber.

To editors across the Pond: Lou Anders, Devi Pillai, Bradley Englert, Bill Schafer.

To champions in the Circle: Tim and Jen Miller.

To the man with a thousand voices: Steven Pacey.

For keeping the wolf on the right side of the door: Robert Kirby.

To all the writers whose paths have crossed mine on the Internet, at the bar or in the writers' room, and who've provided help, support, laughs and plenty of ideas worth the stealing. You know who you are.

And lastly, yet firstly:

The great machinist, Gillian Redfearn. Because every Jezal knows, deep down, he ain't shit without Bayaz.

# The Big People

## Notable Persons of the Union

His August Majesty King Orso the First—unwilling High King of the Union, a notorious wastrel while crown prince but won an unlikely victory over Leo dan Brock.

Hildi—the king's valet and errand-girl, previously a brothel laundress.

Tunny—once Corporal Tunny, pimp and carousing partner to Orso, then his standard-bearer.

Yolk—Corporal Tunny's idiot sidekick.

Bremer dan Gorst—a squeaky-voiced master swordsman, First Guard to King Orso.

Lord Chamberlain Hoff—self-important chief courtier, son of the previous Lord Hoff.

Lord Chancellor Gorodets—long-suffering holder of the Union's purse-strings.

High Consul Matstringer—overwrought supervisor of the Union's foreign policy.

Lord Marshal Forest—a hard-working officer with common origins and impressive scars, promoted to the Closed Council by Orso.

Lord Marshal Rucksted—senior soldier with a penchant for beards and tall tales.

Lord Marshal Brint—senior soldier and one-armed old friend of Orso's father, betrayed Orso and joined the rebels.

Lord Admiral Krepskin—commanding officer of the Union's fleet.

Lord Isher—a smooth and successful magnate of the Open Council, rebelled against Orso but fled from the battle at Stoffenbeck.

Lady Isold dan Isher—an insipid young heiress, married to Lord Isher.

Lord Heugen—a pedantic magnate of the Open Council, rebelled against Orso and was captured.

## From Angland

Leo dan Brock—"The Young Lion," a famous hero and disgraced Lord Governor of Angland, rebelled against King Orso and lost an arm and a leg in battle.

Finree dan Brock—Leo dan Brock's mother and a superb tactician and organiser.

Jurand—Leo dan Brock's estranged best friend, sensitive and calculating.

Glaward—Leo dan Brock's estranged and exceptionally large friend.

Lord Clensher—an old worthy of Angland, with a beard but no moustache.

## In the Circle of Savine dan Brock

Savine dan Brock—wife of Leo dan Brock and disgraced Lady Governor of Angland, once an investor, socialite and celebrated beauty, now imprisoned for high treason.

Zuri—Savine's peerless lady's companion, a Southern refugee.

Freid—one of Savine's many wardrobe maids.

Metello—Savine's hatchet-faced, Styrian wig expert.

Haroon—Zuri's heavily built brother.

Rabik—Zuri's slight and handsome brother.

Sand dan Glokta—"Old Sticks," Savine's father, once the most feared man in the Union, Head of the Closed Council and His Majesty's Inquisition. Now retired.

Ardee dan Glokta—Savine's famously sharp-tongued mother.

Gunnar "Bull" Broad—an ex-Ladderman wrestling with violent tendencies, once a Breaker, then handling "labour relations" for Savine.

Liddy Broad—Gunnar Broad's long-suffering wife, mother to May Broad.

May Broad—Gunnar and Liddy Broad's hard-headed daughter.

Honrig Curnsbick—"The Great Machinist," celebrated inventor and industrialist, and founder of the Solar Society with Savine dan Brock.

Dietam dan Kort—a noted engineer and bridge-builder, partner with Savine in a canal.

Selest dan Heugen—a bitter rival of Savine's.

Colonel Vallimir—ex-partner of Savine in a mill and child-labour scheme.

Lady Vallimir—the colonel's wife, fallen on hard times.

Carmee Groom—a talented artist.

Majir—an associate of Savine's from Adua's criminal fraternity.

## With the Breakers and Burners

Victarine (Vick) dan Teufel—an ex-convict, then an Inquisitor working as a spy for Arch Lector Glokta, changing sides again to stand with the Breakers.

Tallow—a skinny young Breaker, blackmailed into assisting Vick.

Pike—Ex-Arch Lector of the Inquisition, with a hideously burned visage, revealed to be the mastermind behind the Breakers known as the Weaver.

Risinau—once Superior of Valbeck, behind the violent uprising in that city. A self-proclaimed intellectual.

Judge—an unhinged mass-murderer or fearless champion of the common folk, depending on who you ask, the firebrand leader of the Burners.

Spillion Sworbreck—a writer of cheap fantasies and scurrilous pamphlets, turned to pamphleteering and demagoguery.

Sarlby—an old comrade-in-arms of Gunnar Broad, now become a Burner.

Bannerman—a cocky ex-soldier who worked with Broad, then joined the Breakers.

Halder—a taciturn ex-soldier who worked with Broad, then joined the Breakers.

## In the North

Rikke—Leader of Uffrith who has seized Carleon and half the North. Blessed, or cursed, with the Long Eye.

Caul Shivers—Rikke's right hand, a much-feared Named Man and noted humorist with a metal eye.

Isern-i-Phail—Rikke's mentor, a half-mad hillwoman, said to know all the ways.

Scenn-i-Phail—one of Isern's many brothers, scarcely saner than she is.

Scofen-i-Phail—another of Isern's many brothers, still madder than the last.

Hardbread—one of Rikke's War Chiefs, known for his indecision.

Corleth—a girl with stout hips, standard-bearer for Rikke.

Corleth's granny—Corleth's mother's mother. Obviously.

The Nail—a War Chief of the West Valleys, a feared and famous warrior.

Caurib—a witch whose head is stitched together with golden wire, said to have returned from the Land of the Dead.


Jonas Clover—once Jonas Steepfield and reckoned a famous warrior, now thought of as a disloyal do-nothing, betrayed Stour Nightfall to join Rikke.

Downside—one of Clover's warriors, with a bad habit of killing men on his own side.

Sholla—Clover's scout, a woman who can slice cheese very fine.

Flick—an apparently useless lad among Clover's men.


Stour Nightfall—"The Great Wolf," once King of the Northmen, a famed warrior and arsehole, now a hobbled prisoner of Rikke.

Black Calder—once the true power in the North, cunning father of Stour Nightfall.

Flatstone—Calder's most reliable War Chief.

Trapper—a Named Man in the service of Calder.

Stand-i'-the-Barrows—notorious chieftain of a hundred tribes from beyond the Crinna, obsessed with bones.


## In Talins, Sipani and Westport, Cities of Styria

King Jappo mon Rogont Murcatto—King of Styria.

Grand Duchess Monzcarro Murcatto—"The Serpent of Talins," mother of King Jappo, a feared general and ruthless politician, responsible for the unification of Styria.


Princess Carlot—sweet-tempered sister of King Orso, wife of Chancellor Sotorius of Sipani.

Her August Majesty Queen Terez—Queen Dowager and mother of the High King of the Union.

Superior Lorsen—colourless Superior of the Inquisition in Westport.
Filio—a senior Alderman of Westport and fencing enthusiast.
Sanders Rosimiche—a junior Alderman of Westport and strutting loud-mouth.
Dayep Mozolia—a merchant in fabrics, influential in the politics of Westport.

## The Order of Magi

Bayaz—First of the Magi, legendary wizard, saviour of the Union and founding member of the Closed Council.
Yoru Sulfur—former apprentice to Bayaz, nondescript but for his different-coloured eyes.
The Prophet Khalul—former Second of the Magi and arch-enemy of Bayaz. Rumoured to have been killed by a demon, plunging the South into chaos.
Cawneil—Third of the Magi, about her own inscrutable business.
Zacharus—Fourth of the Magi, guiding the affairs of the Old Empire.